30

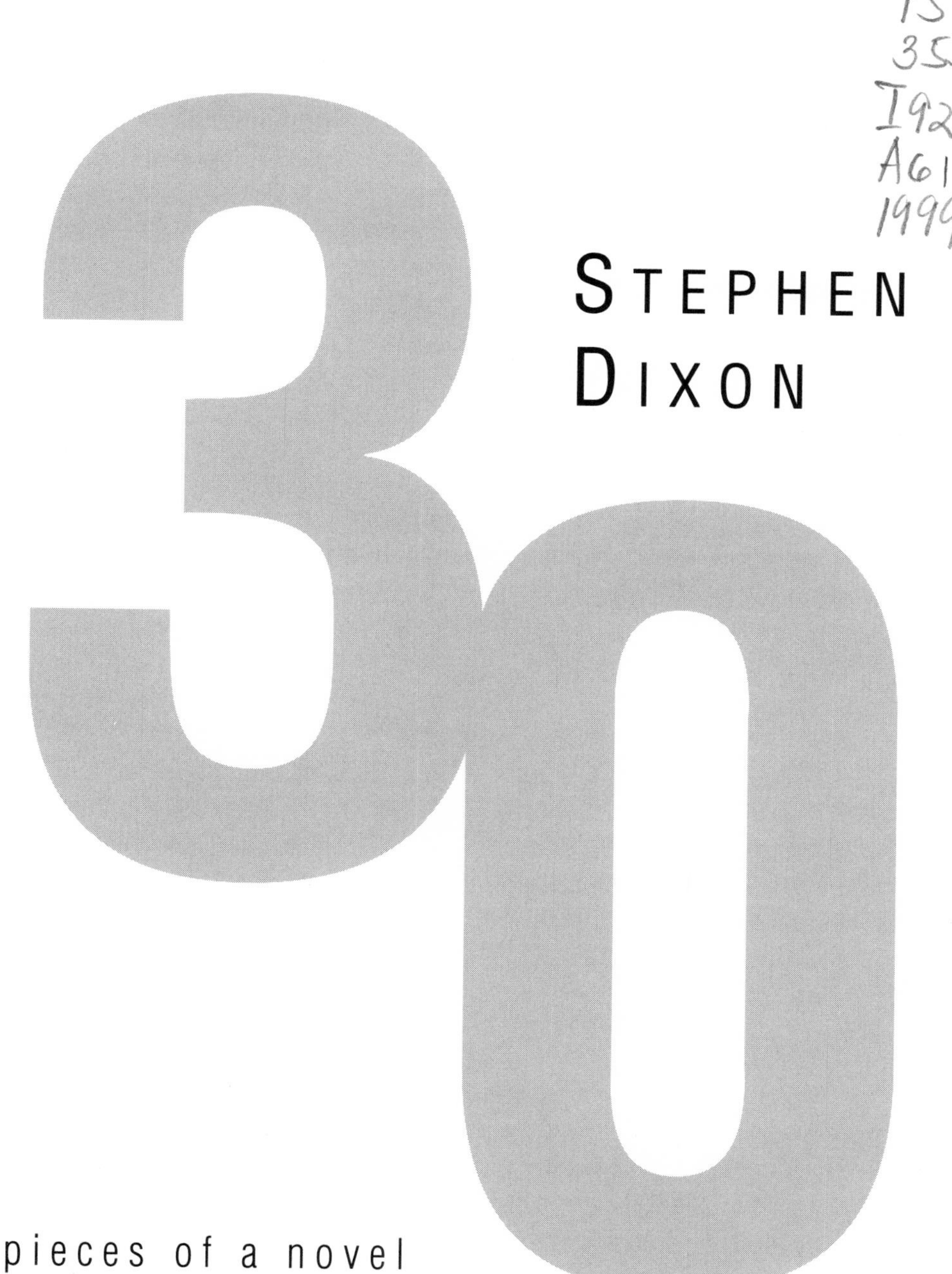

STEPHEN
DIXON

pieces of a novel

HENRY HOLT AND COMPANY NEW YORK

Henry Holt and Company, Inc.
Publishers since 1866
115 West 18th Street
New York, New York 10011

Henry Holt® is a registered trademark of
Henry Holt and Company, Inc.

Portions of *30* have appeared in the following publications:
American Letters & Commentary, American Short Fiction, Antioch Review, Arkansas Review, Boston Book Review, Boston Review, Boulevard, Columbia, Confrontation, Conjunctions, Doubletake, Fence, Fish Stories, Fourteen Hills, Gettysburg Review, Harper's, The Journal, Michigan Quarterly Review, Oxford Review, Pequod, Speak, Spelunker Flophouse, Story Quarterly, Teacup, Thin Air, Threepenny Review, Triquarterly, Virginia Quarterly Review, Western Humanities Review, Witness, World Letter, Zeniada

"The Bellydancer" appeared in the anthology *Anyone Is Possible,* Valentine Publishing; "The Burial" appeared in *Pushcart Prize 23,* Pushcart Press; "The Poet" appeared in *New Stories from the South, 1998,* Algonquin Books of Chapel Hill.

Published in Canada by Fitzhenry & Whiteside Ltd.,
195 Allstate Parkway, Markham, Ontario L3R 4T8.

Library of Congress Cataloging-in-Publication Data
Dixon, Stephen, date.
30 : pieces of a novel / Stephen Dixon.
p. cm.
ISBN 0-8050-5923-7 (hb: alk. paper)
I. Title.
PS3554.I92A615 1999 98-27707
813'.54—dc21 CIP

Henry Holt books are available for special promotions
and premiums. For details contact: Director, Special Markets.

First Edition 1999

Designed by Kelly Soong Too

Printed in the United States of America
All first editions are printed on acid-free paper. ∞

1 3 5 7 9 10 8 6 4 2

To my wife, Anne,
and my daughters, Sophia and Antonia

Contents

Shortcut	3
Popovers	17
The Miracle	33
The Bellydancer	41
100th Street	52
The Pool	63
The Poet	71
Accidents and Mishaps	81
The Motor Cart	101
Fritz	108
His Mother Again	115
The Subway Ride	128
The Paintings	139

School 162
Coney Island 171
The First Woman 184
Home 219
The Dinner Table 236
Conceptions 245
Wishman 252
The Burial 261
Eyes 272
The Suicide 289
Everything Goes 315
Lines 326
His Mother 336
Near the Beginning 351
Seeing His Father 365
A Minor Story 381
Ends 394
The Cake
The Lot
The Phone
The Plane
The Wash
The Barge
The Bed
The Walk
The Friend
The Shame
The Room
The Things
The Son
The Door
The Place

30

Shortcut

THIS IS SOMETHING that comes back at moments that for the most part don't seem to have anything to do with the incident. When he was standing in the bathtub yesterday taking a shower. Well, now that he refers to it he sees where it could sort of be explained why it came back there: the incident happened when he was walking back to the house he was staying at, after swimming in a public pool, and also his nakedness in the shower and no doubt washing his genitals during it. Another time: when he was walking across Central Park on his way to the Whitney Museum. The museum couldn't have had anything to do with it, but the park certainly might have, if he really wants it explained why the incident comes back at certain times: it happened in a state park, and of course he was walking through it when it did. Other times? Plenty, but he forgets, except one when he was making love with his wife in the daytime when the kids were in school. Why it came then is easily explainable, even if he was in almost the exact opposite mating position as the guy in the incident, though who knows if with a little more thinking that couldn't be explained too: for instance, the girl with the guy was in the same mating position that he was in with his wife when the thought of the incident came to him again.

He was walking—this is the incident—taking a shortcut through the state park to the house of the woman he was spending the weekend with. But now he remembers he got there Saturday night after work (so the incident could only have happened on a Sunday, not that this adds anything to why it comes back to him so often), after not seeing her for five days—he was a salesman at the time in the Little Boys Shop in Bloomingdale's and always worked Saturdays, the store's busiest day, till closing around six—and would usually stay at her place till early Monday morning when he'd get a ride back with one of her friends or neighbors in her village: most of the people she knew there worked in Manhattan. He'd been seeing this woman for about a year now. In fact, shortly before the incident, though he doesn't think this has anything to do with the frequency with which he recalls it, he'd lived with her a couple of months and commuted to the store: car ride with one of her friends or neighbors to the city, usually public transportation back, and on Saturdays public transportation both ways—subway to the 175th Street station and the Port Authority bus terminal upstairs, Red & Tan bus to her village, and then the long walk up a steep hill to her house if she didn't meet him in her car at the stop. She was a high school teacher in Nyack, her house a few miles south of Nyack in Piermont, near where the state park and pool were. Her house was once one of the small workers' row houses owned by a huge paper mill on the Hudson in Piermont. Now the mill only made paper bags and all the row houses were privately owned. It was summer, July or August, so the woman was on vacation and her daughter was either at sleep-away camp, if it was July, or with her father in East Hampton for the weekend, if it was August. But the point is he was taking this shortcut on a park service road that connected the pool with a gate about half a mile away in Piermont. He'd swum in the pool, walked on the service road to get to it. If he'd driven the woman's car he would have taken a much longer way to get to the pool, though shorter in time, since no vehicle but a state park one was allowed to use the service road. There were the same two or three park trucks, with nobody in them, parked off the road when he walked to and from the pool, and the car of the incident parked on the road when he walked home. If he'd taken her car he would have parked in the pool lot, swum, showered—*showered;* so that's possibly another reason why it comes back to him while he's showering in a bathtub or stall—then driven back to her house and never seen what he saw that afternoon, and it was the afternoon. After a quick light lunch around two or so she asked what his plans were and he said, Why, what does she have in mind?—nothing suggestive in the remark, as sometimes when he said something like that, with a smile or leer, it meant does that mean she wants to have sex?—and she said she was going to do some errands in Nyack and, if she didn't find what she wanted, then at the Nanuet Mall. Not the greatest thing to do on a hot day, but does he want to come along? and he said it was much too hot—both the temperature and humidity were in the nineties—and he thinks he'd like to go swimming in the park pool. She said she'd drop him off if he wanted to go now, as she was leaving in a few minutes, and he said he didn't mind the walk—what was it, a mile, maybe a mile and a half? and it could be more peaceful—and also he wanted to have another iced coffee before he left and read the paper a little, which he hadn't even opened yet. He knew that as much as he'd cool off at the pool, he'd get heated up and sweaty again walking back to her house, since he'd have to climb that steep hill, most of it in the sun. She said she'd probably be here when he got back, if he wasn't going to leave in the next half hour and just take a quick dip and hustle right home, and she'd see him then, and they'd talk about what they were going to do for dinner, or maybe he wants her to pick up something special on the way home. He said they shouldn't worry about dinner now—too hot and sticky to—and if the weather stays the same, with no breeze or anything, he doubts he'll want anything for dinner but a beer and some celery and carrots and a slice of bread. But he wished she'd change her mind and come to the pool with him. It could be crowded, but they'd find a relatively quiet place in the shade—most of the people who go there like to bake in the sun—and read, relax, chat, even nap, and she said that she never cared for public pools, and the horsing around and all the other things that go on there, and that these errands were essential.

So he swam, then the walk back. But swam several times, read parts of the book review and magazine sections of the paper in between swimming, and once rested on his stomach and closed his eyes for a few minutes and, he thinks, fell asleep. And occasionally just looked at the other people at the pool, especially some of the younger better-built women in swimsuits, and maybe even fantasized about them, but that he forgets. It was mostly shady on the service road, tall trees with overhanging branches above almost the entire area. He was about three-quarters of the way to the gate when he saw from a distance a car parked on the road. There seemed to be plenty of room off the road for it to park, and why they chose there he's never been able to figure out—immediacy of the moment, perhaps? Doesn't make sense. They could have, he's saying—the couple in the car—parked almost anywhere off the road. But maybe they were afraid of possible ruts or mud or something, when there really wasn't that much and nothing a car couldn't drive out of. In fact, the ground was pretty hard, if he remembers. Maybe they thought—or the guy did and the girl went along with it or was persuaded to by him, or the girl did and the guy thought, What the hell, if she thinks so then he's not going to protest, for all he wants is to get to it: the action, the sex—that no other cars would drive by. After all, it was Sunday, they could have reasoned, so wouldn't most of the park's service vehicles be idle for the weekend or just for the day? Actually, probably not, for the weekend could be when they worked the most, Sunday being the park's busiest day by far, but this was a remote area, so how often then would a service vehicle pass by or a police car check it: every two hours, three, even four? And what they wanted to do would take ten to twenty minutes, or for the guy maybe not even that. They might have done all the preliminaries somewhere else—in the parking lot or under a towel or blanket at the pool—and had only come here to finish up because it was so far out of the way. And maybe they didn't know that walkers used the road as a shortcut between Piermont and the pool—they wouldn't if they didn't live in the area—or even that someone from the pool or town might want to take a long walk on it for exercise or because it was so quiet and shady or maybe it was a good spot to watch birds. Or they knew all that or some of it but thought, What, one or two walkers or hikers or bird-watchers every hour or so? Anyway, the car was parked in the middle of the one-lane dirt road, so if a service vehicle or police car was coming from either direction it would have had to go around it off the road. And if one was coming from the pool area it would have gone around the passenger side—or that's the side he would have gone around if he'd been driving a car—and the person in the passing car would have seen the couple doing what they were doing, if they still were, and then what? The couple could have been arrested if it was a police car that passed, and who knows what would have happened if one or two park workers caught them at it? Getting closer—he was about a hundred and fifty feet away now—he thought, Maybe the driver's a bird-watcher and is out with his field glasses somewhere or even looking for birds from the car. Or he could be hunting for wild mushrooms—he'd heard that the Palisades, which this area was part of, had some pretty good edible ones—or went to a nearby spot he knows from previous years where mushrooms are. Or he could be collecting firewood for the winter—lots of spare wood in these woods, and they were woods—but then he'd almost certainly have driven off the road to park out of sight so he could gather the wood secretly, since you're not supposed to take anything out of a state park except maybe berries and mushrooms, if even that. Then he saw a human figure—he was about a hundred feet from the car now, and his eyes were bad from any long distance—a man, and as he got closer he saw him facing the opened front passenger door and looking as if he was peeing. If you are going to pee in the woods along a public road, he thought, better to do it that way, with the door blocking anyone coming from the gate direction from seeing you do it and your body blocking anyone from seeing you peeing who was coming from the pool. And if it was a walker coming, even a jogger, since joggers probably ran on this road too, the man would be able to see that person from hundreds of feet away, if his eyes were good from that distance, and by the time the person got close, unless the jogger was really moving, his peeing would be over, though the man didn't seem to be stopping for him. Now he was maybe twenty feet away and not knowing which side of the car to walk around—the one he'd normally take would be the right, but he didn't want to pass the guy peeing—when he saw legs hanging over the seat, no pants or skirt or shoes or socks on, though the person might have underpants or a swimsuit on, since all he saw was from the knees down. And the man did seem to have his hands on his fly, or one hand on it and the other extended into the car toward the seat, but he couldn't see if his penis was out of his pants. What the hell's going on, he thought, this guy harming or killing someone or dumping a body or what? Gould stopped, didn't know if he should turn around and go back or just walk quickly past the car on the left side and keep going, but wanted to get away from here, a few hundred feet away, at least a hundred, and then look back at it from there, not that he'd see much with his lousy eyes, for he'd left his distance glasses at the woman's home. But then he thought maybe someone was being hurt, though he doesn't hear anything: cries, pleas, things like that. By now he'd walked backwards to the pool about fifteen feet, stopped, and didn't know which way to go now or what to do. Then the legs started moving, it seemed, the feet a little, and the man, who hadn't looked this way once, moved in closer till he was between the legs and up against the seat, with both his arms in the car now looking as if they were pressing down on something, and Gould thought, My God, that's a woman in there and they're fucking; what a schmuck I've been! And right here; who the hell does that? Well, screw them, I just want to get home—and started to walk past their car, since why should he go back and around the long way and all that just because they chose here to do their humping? As he got to the right of the door, walking on the side of the road in some weeds and clumpy dirt, so that he had to look at the ground a couple of times to make sure he wouldn't trip over anything, and ready to say, Excuse me, if the man suddenly turned around and caught him looking, he saw the woman, shirt on but almost up to her breasts and her legs spread apart, lots of black hairs on the side of her vagina that he could see and even a little of that outer lip folded back or some part like that, back flat on the seat and head raised a few inches and staring warily at him and then sort of dopily with her eyes almost closed as she was jammed hard by the man but giving no sign she was in any harm, guy with his tank top on and pants up but belt and pants buttons undone and going in and out of her slowly now and for a moment all the way out by an inch, and then after a few seconds straight in again, hands splayed on the seat on either side of her waist, bracing himself perhaps or just a place to put them, girl with her head on the seat and eyes totally closed now and smiling. Something cool blew through Gould, where—maybe because of the humidity too but probably at just seeing what he'd never seen any two people do in front of him and just the open and eventually oblivious way they were doing it and the point they seemed to be at in the act, or he would be, and the forest air—he had to catch his breath and really felt dizzy for a few seconds and stumbled back onto the road once he was past the car and for a while walked with his hand clutching his neck. He turned around when he was about fifty feet away, thinking that if the guy was looking at him now he'd just quickly turn around and continue on, and only saw the guy's head through the window, still moving back and forth like before and never glancing at him, but nothing of her. It could be, because of all he'd taken in, that he'd stopped for half a minute or so by the car, but he wasn't aware of it. But Jesus, he kept thinking as he walked, never saw anything like it even in the few pornos he'd seen; just two kids, the guy maybe seventeen, eighteen, the girl fifteen or a little more, blank to everything else when she stopped staring at him, for then she looked as if she was doing it out of duty or for money or just for the sake of the guy or maybe she was high. Thought of them the whole way back, her bush, shine on the guy's penis, vagina lip or skin or whatever it was folded over, and her dreamy-to-transported look and smile, sometimes feeling his penis through the pants pocket and pulling it, rubbing the head, knowing if he stuck his hand inside he'd find it wet, wanting to tell his woman friend what he saw but she wasn't back, realizing when he got to her front steps that he hadn't worked up a drop of sweat.

Made himself coffee, sat on the porch in the swing chair and opened the newspaper, unconsciously began playing with himself through his pants, went inside and sat at the kitchen table and unzipped his fly and started jerking himself off to get rid of the tension and stop thinking of them, but then thought, Don't throw it away, save it for when she gets back when maybe he can get her to make love soon or even right away. Story about what he saw won't hurt. Maybe even just coming right out and saying it's made him hot, remembering and then telling it, so would she mind much if they did it now, as a favor or just because he's almost never felt so rutty, and thinking of the couple isn't all there is to it, for of course there's her too, on the couch or floor or bed, though he'd love, even if he knows this is screwy and a silly thought and there's no chance they're going to do it this way, on a car seat in a remote grove with all those forest smells and sounds around, or in a different position than them if she can come up with one, for though he knows it's being done in cars all the time he's never till now known for sure how. Anyway, convincing her that it would be better now or an hour or two later than after her daughter comes home, if it *was* August, when they'd have to be more inhibited and could only do it in bed, with their usual last sex before he left the next day, unless she's just started her period and thinks she's already too messy, as she's sometimes said.

Heard her car drive up, park in back, went out to meet her, kissed her lips as she was getting out of the car, and she said, "Umm, that's nice, good welcome home, thanks mucho," helped her bring the packages and things in—bag of groceries, two six-packs of ale, a planter, plants, bean poles, wire tomato cages or whatever they're called, gardening tools, twenty-five-pound bag of potting soil and fifty-pound bag of cow manure. She said, "Wow, you're being super nice, it's almost as if you missed me," and he said, "Sure, what do you think, and you know Gould, when isn't he, right?" and laughed, and she said, "Okay, I don't want to ruin the mood, so I'll resist answering that. How was swimming?" Touched his head and said, "Your hair's still wet. For shopping, I'll confess, much as I got done, was a dumb idea; you were smart not to go. It felt like it was a hundred both ways outside," and he said, "How do you mean?" and she said, "You know: temperature, humidity." "Swimming was great, water just right: cool, not pee-warm. A bit crowded on the grass but I got a shady spot, and some young women near me, three of them like Graces, even took their tops off to expose themselves and sunbathe. Only kidding," and she said, "But why'd you say it?" and he said, "I have to go into a long psychological explanation? Hey, like everybody else, men especially, stupid thoughts about breasts and sex can suddenly pop into my head. But imagine, I've nothing to complain of since you left—*me,* the arch grumbler from way back when it comes to the country. Even the walk uphill here was nice. But listen to this, you won't believe it," and he told her what he had seen on the service road coming home. "I'm sure they're done by now, but I wouldn't count on it, the way they were going, so sort of lost in the act. Or they probably waited two seconds and began again. In a secluded or semisecluded area in a state park—they ought to call it the pubic area—where walkers, joggers, bird-watchers, service vehicles, even little Piermont kids taking a shortcut to the pool can parade by and watch, and these stupid teenagers didn't even stop," and she said, "Well, from what you said nobody saw it but you, and it was probably over pretty fast, so what's the big deal? They had to do it badly, and I'm sure she was more like seventeen or eighteen. And this could have been their last time for weeks or even months, if he's in the army and going off to basic training or overseas—that could be a possibility—so they chose doing it there because they had no other place. They live with their different families in the city, let's say, or Nyack, in cramped spaces, even, so were dying to be alone. And they're young, impetuous, want to do it ten times a day. I only hope he used a condom or she had her own device in, because it's getting monstrous the number of illegitimate births among teens today, and a lot the men care. I see it in my school all the time: pregnant kids. And where they can't afford it and such, or don't have the interest or time for babies, they palm them off on their parents or grandparents or have these sloppy cheap abortions that kill or maim some of these girls," and he said, "No bag, I saw the whole thing in glimpses. Average-size dick but hard as a rock, it seemed; the opening of her vagina—what is that part called? The labia, lip, vulva, but the flap," and, when she just stared at him, "but you know what I mean. I'm not saying this for any prurient reason. It was really something. I wanted to come back—I'm not kidding now—and just jump on you, or maybe give you a little preparation for the leap, for besides making me somewhat perturbed as to their just doing it in the open there for everyone to see, I have to admit it got me excited too," and she said, "Fine, wonderful; good thing I was still out shopping. Why didn't you do it to yourself when you got back if you felt that excited? It'd seem, if you're going to do it at once like that, that'd be the time," and he said, "Because, if you want to know, I didn't want to lose it for you," and she said, "You mean that when my turn comes around you want there to be something left?" and he said, "In a way," and she said, "Oh, please, how do you know I'd even want to today or tonight?" and he said, "I thought I might be able to convince you if it was immediately apparent you weren't interested. That is, if you were physically up to it: your period or just being too knocked out by the heat or sleepy tonight. Or we'd just do it a last time because I leave tomorrow and won't see you for almost a week. And I didn't want to do it a few hours after or even try doing it an hour after I just came by doing it to myself. It wouldn't be as exciting for me that way, if I could even get it up a second time so soon," and she said, "If I wanted to make love I could suggest it. Or I can get into it when you suggest it, if I want to. But I certainly don't need to be persuaded. I don't even like being persuaded. I definitely don't; I don't like pressure of any kind when it comes to sex. Either we both want to and we do it or one of us wants to and suggests it in an agreeable soft undemanding way and the other says 'no' or 'yes' or 'later' or 'I don't know when,' and that's the way it should be, but you obviously don't agree," and he said, "Why, my face?" and she nodded, and he said, "Well, what I think is maybe sometimes the other should bend over backwards a little—and I don't mean literally, but literally sometimes would be okay too," and laughed, and she didn't, and he said, "Sorry, my silly jokes again, if that one could be called that. Or just my unrestrainable compulsion to make them when we're talking about serious things, but you know what I'm saying," and she said, "No, what?" and he said, "You know, that occasionally one of us might want to do it with the same sort of urgency those two kids had before, if that's what it was with them and not just some lunkhead scoring or a dumb girl trying to trap the guy by getting him to screw her when they had no protection during her most fertile period. 'Fertile period.' That's a good one, since you're least fertile when you have your period. But this doesn't have to happen all the time, when one doesn't and the other most urgently does. Though sometimes the other in this should cooperate that way, that's all I'm saying, or try to—it's part of sort of helping each other out. And believe me, it's easier for the woman than the man, for what's it take?" and she said, "Easier physically perhaps for the woman, under ideal conditions, if you're only talking about male erections here. Because you think all it takes for her is a simple spreading of legs and letting the guy in? That's what you expected of me when I came home?" and he said, "No, I told you, first I thought I'd only suggest we do it—amiably, undemandingly, deferentially—thinking maybe you'd want to, since that's what's happened plenty of times," and she said, "Never on such a hot stifling day—there's no air," and he said, "Then we'd turn the fan on us," and she said, "And get a cold? I hate when that thing's blowing right on me," and he said, "Then we get it to blow around the room. It's got a switch to make it oscillate, doesn't it? I should know, I bought it for you," and she said, "And what am I supposed to say now—" and he said, "You're not, that's not why I said it"—"'Thank you for the oscillating fan, here's my fanny backwards, plug into it from whichever angle you wish'?" and he said, "Of course not; I was only saying—" and she said, "I know what you were only saying. You were saying, 'Listen, first I'll try to ensnare you into sex and if that doesn't work I'll ask you to participate in it as a favor': spread my legs, let you zip it in when I'm in no way ready, couple of pump motions, shoot the works, and out, and heck with me and my feelings and the timing and everything else in the process—I'm to simply be your little dumping ground for semen," and he said, "No, really, but sometimes you wouldn't want it the same way around for you?" and she said, "Absolutely not. Like you, I'd suggest, and if you weren't interested, which'd be surprising—your heightened male ego sometimes I'm practically sure makes you do it when you've no energy or inclination to. Anyway, that'd be it, then: we wouldn't do it and it wouldn't be the end of the relationship but just an example of its honesty and sturdiness and durability," and he said, "Nice words, and I appreciate your putting the situation that way, but I see we have a small disagreement here, nothing major, so it'll be okay," and she said, "If you can't even agree with what I just said then it *is* major or bumping into it. But this entire conversation—finding out what you want and how you want and expect it—has really turned me off, Gould," and he said, "I hope not through the morning too, before I've got to get up for work," and she said, "Yes, it probably has, so don't count on getting laid, all right? Now I want to take a shower and get out of these stinky clothes," and he said, "Get out of the clothes first, I'd suggest," and she said, "What's that supposed to mean?" and he said, "Believe me, nothing sexy or come hither-like; just the order of those two: you'd want to get out of your clothes before you stepped into the shower, wouldn't you?" and she said, "What do you think I am, stupid?" and he said, "I swear, anything but," and she said, "Then what?" and he said, "I'm sorry, my irrepressible joke-making again, maybe. Can't you take a joke, or, rather, can't I fail at making one, if not many? I mean, some guys never make one and some never even try. They're dour, serious, stolid, which I'm by nature not. And it's summer. Though I'm not on vacation, I wish I were, and I should be but the store's not going to give me one, so in a way I am this weekend—I feel relaxed, if maybe a bit witless," and she said, "Oh, get off it, that's bullshit. I don't know, this isn't going to work," and he said, "What isn't?" and she said, "Listen, don't get offended, but why don't you take the bus home now. I want to be alone and do some planting after my shower," and he said, "After you clean up you want to get dirty?" and she said, "Planting isn't getting dirty. And yes, the shower will be to wash up but mostly to cool myself off, and the planting is for some veggies I want to come up in early fall. I still have time: radishes and a variety of late lettuces that can take the cooler weather," so it was probably July that this happened, even early July, though radishes only take, he remembers from when he once planted them when he rented a house in Connecticut ten years ago, about seventeen days to mature, so who knows when it was. And he forgets how long lettuce takes, but the time could vary for different kinds, and he said, "I'll help you and also with the poles for the beans and tomatoes and any holes you want dug, no matter how deep—really, right now I feel energized," and she said, "I don't need help. Planting, to me—any gardening work—is restful, peaceful, a great relaxing activity . . . even spiritual, which you'll undoubtedly laugh at my saying," and he said, "No, do you see me laughing? It probably is what you say; why shouldn't it be? And I can understand it: hands in the ground and so on," and she said, "And also, and I'm a little skeptical about what you just said, but also—the hands thing, and your agreeing so readily—maybe I want a break from you today and I'd think you'd want one by now from me too," and he said, "I don't, everything's fine," and she said, "What I'm saying is that all your previous talk about sex and so forth—not your friendly-enough talk now, which I think you're hiding behind—makes me a bit wary of you. As if you're going to get so keyed up you'll pounce on me and try doing it even when I say I don't want to, though with you believing that eventually, with enough encouragement, pushy kisses, and force, I would," and he said, "You know I wouldn't do that. To be honest and not hiding, as you said I just was, sure, I might think of ravishing you—you know, it'd quickly cross my mind—for I occasionally have these thoughts; what man doesn't? But I never would to you or anyone, that force business, for I also have control—so never, believe me, never," and she said, "Okay, we'll talk tomorrow if you like, but now, what about it?" and he said, "You mean the bus?" and she just looked at him, and he said, "So I'll take it. You ask, and with that glare, I'll do it, for what other choice do I have, walk to New York? Even get you to drive me?" and she said, "You know the bus is easy for you, a half-hour ride and then the subway, and I wasn't glaring," and he said, "You say you weren't, you weren't, and as for the bus, very easy, very, yes, sure," and headed for the stairs, and she said, "Okay, it's a little inconvenient, I'm sorry," and without turning around he said, "Forget it," and went upstairs and packed his bag, got his typewriter and papers, for he always took them to her place weekends, came downstairs, and said, "Should I walk to the stop or will you drive me?" and she said, "I don't want any last-minute scenes and I think we've said enough, so could you get there yourself? You have fifteen minutes to the next bus and it's all downhill," and he said, "I know what it is, I've walked it a few hundred times, up and down, up and down, like sex, right? those ups and downs," and she said, "You're being mean and a bit childish now—yes, like sex, back and forth, to and fro, high and low. . . . So maybe you don't want to come here anymore; well, that's okay with me," and he said, "That's what you think I said? All right, maybe I secretly did, maybe I don't want to come here, maybe you're right—I'll let you know if that's so. 'Bye, honey," and turned around without waiting for a response, if she was going to give one—he knew anyway that right now she thought he was a big pill and she couldn't care less he was going—and left the house. He should have jerked off when he wanted to and had the chance, he thought, as he walked downhill. He wouldn't have been so sexually keyed up when she got home, as she said. Every third word of his wouldn't have been a dumb pun or reference or allusion to sex, and there wouldn't have been that conversation about it either. And then after telling her about what he saw on the road, unless she said or indicated something regarding it or used it to make some point, that would have been it for the time being, and he wouldn't have felt like jumping her, which he actually did think, and then later tonight in bed they could have done it—he still would have had the picture in his head of the way those kids did it and what that lip or flap looked like and the hair around it or could easily have called it up, if he had to—and it would have been all right, exciting, good; it would have been just fine.

At the bus stop he thought, Maybe she'll drive up to it as she did once after a bad argument when he either stormed out of her house with his things because he was livid at her or she was at him and had ordered him to go—one of several times that had happened, his weekend there cut short because one of them wanted it to be or even them both—and say, "Listen, let's talk about this some more"—that's what she said that one time, or something like—"You want to take a drive with me, not to the city but around here, or go for coffee or a drink or come home or something? Let's. But I don't like you leaving like this. It worries me, and your going isn't exactly what I want." But she didn't this time. Bus came and he got on, and as it pulled away he didn't want to look back to the stop or the street her car would be on if she did drive down, since he knew she wouldn't be there, but he looked and she wasn't there and that day was the last he saw her till about fifteen months later at a Columbus Avenue fair in New York on Columbus Day or one of the weekends before when the avenue was closed to traffic from 65th to 86th and she was walking with some guy she obviously liked, and Gould said hello and she smiled and said hi and introduced him to the guy, who stayed silent though continually looked admiringly at her while they talked for about two minutes, how her daughter and father were and had she started another year teaching school? how his mother and a couple of his friends were and was he still working at Bloomingdale's? and then they said goodbye and he sort of saluted the guy instead of shaking his hand, which he didn't want to do, and they went in opposite directions in the middle of the avenue, he looking back at her a few times and only once seeing her looking back at him, though they were now about half a block apart and she could have been looking at something else in his direction and he just happened to be there.

Popovers

A GIRL . . . A young woman . . . a college student or someone of that age—when he was in college they were "coeds," or maybe by then they were no longer called that, but even if they went to an all-girls' school?—comes over to their table and says, "The seater didn't give you menus?" and his older daughter says no, and she says, "I'm sorry, I'll get them in a flash—nobody make a movie," the last in movie tough-guy voice, and laughs. Funny? The movie remark was clever, though she probably heard it somewhere, most likely on TV or in a movie—but sweet, charming, also pretty . . . very pretty . . . beautiful, almost . . . no, he'd consider her quite beautiful, and with a tall attractive figure—she must be five-nine—and sense of humor and spryness and a very nice smile, and, from what he could quickly see, great teeth: white, bright, evenly lined. Oh, boy, if he were only forty years younger, or thirty-eight years younger or -seven . . . let's see, she's about nineteen or twenty, he's fifty-eight, so he was right, he's got thirty-seven to forty years on her—and working in this restaurant. What a place to be for the summer. Northern coastal Maine, in the middle of a national forest, cool nights, great views, the rest of it, and excellent facilities for the staff—he spoke about it with one of the servers last year when they came here for lunch or for popovers at the two-to-five tea. Or two-thirty to five. Looks at the menu. The latter. Seemed all the servers were college students, so he asked how they got the job, just in case one of his advisees during the school year asked if he knew of a good place to work in the summer or he wanted to volunteer the information to one of them he particularly liked. "Jordan Pond House," he'd say—he thinks he even told one but the kid never followed up on it—"in Trenton or Bar Harbor or even Hull's Cove. Just ask Maine phone Information—area code 207—for Acadia National Park and this restaurant there. But good accommodations and food for the staff, I was told, and an unbeatable setting: bubble-shaped mountains, lakes, the forest smells, and the girls"—if it was a male he was saying this to; he thinks it was. "Let me tell you, that's the place I'd go to if I were you. Good-looking, hard-working, and pleasant, and they come from everywhere: France, Canada, South Africa, Japan, and all over the States, and some from what are thought of as the best schools, which probably means intelligent, resourceful, and independent young women paying their own way at college or a good part of it. You know about the schools because each table has a little name card in a holder identifying the server and what school he or she's at." This one's Sage Ottunburg, but it only says PALM BEACH, FLORIDA underneath, so maybe she's out of school or never went to one or the restaurant's stopped listing the schools. He looks at the holder on the next table but can't from here read the name and what's underneath. Maybe the schools aren't listed anymore because some of the non-college kids objected for some reason, or customers, men and women, would later try to locate the server at that school. But would that be any easier—let's say this one goes to a large state school—than finding her in Palm Beach? How many Ottunburgs could be there? If more than one, then probably a relative. So all some guy had to do if he wanted to call her in September, if she leaves here as that server last year told him most of the students do a little before or right after Labor Day, is dial Palm Beach Information, ask for Sage Ottunburg, and if there isn't one listed just ask for any Ottunburg, and if he gets one of her relatives, but not her folks, ask if one of the other Ottunburg numbers is hers. But why's he going on like this? And if some guy did want to meet her, he'd call her here, wouldn't he? Unless he was with his wife or girlfriend or someone; or even if he was: something on the sly. And maybe she goes to school but for one reason or another doesn't want to be categorized by it or doesn't want it listed, or who knows what.

She comes back with the menus. "Take as long as you like," she says, "there's no rush; this place is too pretty to feel rushed, and it smells so wonderful here"—for they're on the outdoor patio—and takes a deep breath, and he says, "Just what I was thinking, and thank you," and opens the menu and when she walks away he discreetly looks at her rear end and legs and when she returns for the order he quickly looks at her breasts a few times and tries to imagine what they look like under her shirt. High and young, and it's funny but when he was in his late teens and early twenties he doesn't think he ever thought how beautiful young breasts are. Older women had lower softer ones; young women, if they weren't top-heavy, had high firm ones, and he doesn't even think he thought of the firmness, but that was about the extent of his observations on breasts then, except if they were flat. Though there was an older woman—thirty-six, at the most thirty-eight, so for sure not "old" to him now; in fact, if he were seeing her today he'd consider her young—whom he went with one summer, about a half year before the Washington reporter's job, when he was just out of college and worked as a soda jerk in an upstate resort and she was the stage designer of the theater there. And another who was fifty or so when he slept with her on and off for a year and he was around thirty, and both seemed to have not lower or high breasts or soft or firm, just very big and full ones. So what does he know? Every time he thinks he's on to something, he quickly refutes himself.

They order; she comes back many times: to bring their food, refill their water glasses, see if everything's "satisfactory," take away his plate, give his wife a free extra popover—she had something called "soup and popovers," which came with two popovers but the kids split one of them. "How do they make those things, the popovers?" his younger daughter asks Sage, and he says, "Yeah, I've been curious about it too. Do you have a brigade of popover makers back there?" and she says, "You mean humans? No, it's all done by machine—two, actually, and a third that mixes the dough and eggs and stuff, and these big popover machines just keep turning them out all day. From breakfast through dinner, *pop pop pop,* they plop out and we just grab them if we have an order and put them in the already prepared basket with a towel around them to keep them warm." "They're the best," his daughter says, and he says, "Well, your mom's made some pretty good ones in that popover pan we always bring up. Did we bring it this year? I haven't seen it," and his wife says, "I don't know, you're the one who packs the car. I know I reminded you," and he says, "Oh, darn, I might've forgot," and his wife says, "No big deal; mine aren't nearly as good as these, and besides, I like them best when we have them here as a treat," and he says, "Yours are wonderful on a cold night or a foggy afternoon with guests when no one wants to go out, and it's something the kids like helping out with," and his older daughter says, "When did we ever do that?" and Sage says, "That's how I like them best too—as a special treat. Here, I think I've overindulged on them, not that we're allowed to have all we want . . . but you know, if a customer doesn't eat one and you're very hungry, because you build up an appetite running around in this job," and he says, "I can't imagine someone not eating his second popover unless one of the diners with him swiped it. But that reminds me—but you're probably too busy, you wouldn't want to hear it," and his older daughter says, "What?" and Sage says, "It's true, I've some orders in the kitchen waiting, and all with popovers, if you can believe it, excuse me," and goes, and his older daughter says, "What were you going to say that reminded you, Daddy?" and he says, "Oh! When I worked as a soda jerk, or fountain man as I was also called, in a resort in New York, I got so sick of eating ice cream, or maybe not so much from eating it as from dealing with it, that's the reason I don't like it today," and his wife says, "Everyone likes ice cream; one has to be scarred by it to develop an aversion to it. For you it was the cigarette butts and other filth in it on the plates coming back to you, but you should finish your own story," and he says, "Your mother's right. You see, I had no customers of my own, just made all the concoctions from the orders the waitresses gave me. And then they handed me their dirty dishes to stick through a window to the dishwasher behind me. And they looked so ugly with all the things the customers had done to their ice cream, the butts and stuff, sometimes stuck standing up on top of the sundae where the decorative cherry had been, that I got sick of it, ice cream melting all over and around this—well, excuse me, but this shit, and that's why I hate it today," and his wife says, "At this place you always help yourself to a spoonful or two of ice cream, so you can't hate it entirely," and he says, "At this place they always have at least one very unusual exotic flavor, which we always get unless it's with peanut butter, and they make the ice cream themselves, so I'm curious," and his daughter says, "Oh, yeah," and he says, "Yeah, I'm curious, as to how, let's say, peppermint raspberry sage might taste. Not 'sage,' that's just because it's our waitress's name, but you know what I mean."

He likes everything about her. He's tried to find a profile or some part of her he could dislike, a bump on the nose, for instance, or not find faultless, but it's all faultless: nose, lips, eyes, hair, teeth, legs, arms, fingers, nails (no crap on them and not choppy or uneven), breasts, hips, stomach from what he can make out, waist, rear . . . the name, though: Sage. Not faultless. Speaks well, big bright smile, pleasant personality, chipper, friendly, though no fake, doesn't give them the bum's rush, as his dad used to say—she has other tables, is obviously busy, yet stops to talk, listen, suggest, answer the kids' questions generously, laughs a lot but not heehaw-like . . . it would be nice, moonlight, cool night, the whole works, just a comfortable unsticky night, the air—smell of it, he means; sounds of the insects—not the biting of insects, though; so you slap on some repellent—even the scent of that on her; especially that scent, perhaps—walking with her, that's what he's saying would be nice: after work, around the grounds, in town for a movie, whatever the town: Southwest or Northeast or Bar Harbor, or for pizza and beers anywhere, back to the rooms they stay at on the property, but now he remembers that server last year saying the staff quarters were a short walk off; sneaking into her room if you have to sneak to do it—the restaurant management might have some proscriptions about this. Doubts it, or not enforced; keep the help happy and wanting to stay past Labor Day. Holding her hand outside, kissing her outside, furtively brushing against her at work: "Need any help filling those water pitchers?" Holding and kissing and with no constraint brushing and touching every part of her inside the room or at some hidden spot in the woods. Falling in love, swimming at Long Pond or Echo Lake or some other warmwater place he doesn't now know of on the island here. Just imagine her in a bathing suit: lying on her stomach on the sand reading, turning to the sun or him with her top off in a cove it seems only they go to, running into the cold water with him at Sand Beach on their day off if they get them on the same day. Forgot to ask the server last year if they get days off, but it's probably a law that a full-time worker has to, once a week at least, and after a while he bets you can switch around your days off to where you and your girlfriend get them together.

"What are you looking at?" his wife says, and he knows she's caught him staring at Sage passing their table and means, Why are you looking at that girl so openly? and he says, "Oh, our waitress? It's just she reminds me of someone and I can't figure out who," and she says, "The girl of your dreams," and he says, "You're that girl, or were when I first saw you, and still are the woman of my dreams, day and night and during catnaps, now that we're married and so on . . . but yes, sure, if I were younger? Oh, boy, you bet. I'm saying if I were working here when I was twenty or so, still in college, feet free and fool loose, hormones up to my ears, and you were working here too . . . that's what I was mainly thinking of before: how come I didn't meet you when I most urgently needed to and not so much when—no, this isn't true, but I'll say it all the same—my companionable and genital exigencies, we'll say, didn't have to be so imperially attended to? No, that didn't come out right," and she says, "If you were twenty, I'd be nine, and I think that sort of behavior's not only prohibited here but may even be frowned upon," and he says, "But you know what I mean," and she says, "I think I do, and I think I appreciate some of your thoughts too, but I also think you are"—and this very low—"a liar," and he says, "Me? Mr. Honesty?" and his older daughter says, "What are you talking of, you two, and why are you calling Daddy a liar?" and he says, "Your mother whispered that, which means even if you heard you're not supposed to give any sign you did and certainly no words," and his daughter says, "But why did she?" and he says, "Youth, youth, *wunderbar* youth, don't lose it, enjoy it, employ it, but don't destroy it—something." "What's that mean?" his daughter says, and he says, "Nothing, everything, some of what's in the in-between . . . I'm in my confusing Confucian period right now"—stroking an imaginary long wisp of chin beard—

"and also don't flaunt it, I should've added," and his wife says to her, "First of all, don't mistake Confucianism with confusion, indirectness, and unintelligibility. Your father was only admiring our waitress, Sage. Or not admiring her as much as trying to recall a young woman he knew many years ago who looked like her," and his daughter says to him, "Do you think she's pretty? I do," and he says, "Very pretty, and she's very nice. One day, you know, you could get a job here . . . in who knows how long, nine years? Eight? Then I could come here and be reminded of another very pretty girl I once knew: you at eleven," and she says, "I wouldn't want to work all day waitressing," and he says, "Why not? You'd earn money for college, travel, and clothes, and you'd make lots of friends and have this entire national park to live in," and she says, "They live here?" and he says, "Yeah, I learned this from one of our waitresses last year: in dorms or their own rooms or ones they might have to share with another girl," and she says, "Then I'd like it. I love it here, so clean and fresh and everything. But I'd hate getting sick of popovers. And if it's the same thing that happened to you with ice cream, then for life," and he says, "Ice cream's different from popovers. And I'm sure, in a place like this, so fresh and clean as you said, customers don't stick cigarette butts in them."

Thinks of Sage on and off the rest of the day: car ride home, shucking corn, taking the clothes off the outside line and folding them as he stood there, little during dinner and then when washing the dishes, and that night, in the dark when he's outside the house peeing, he imagines them standing and him holding her, face looking up at his from a height his wife's would be until he changes it in his head so it's even with his, then on a bed, side by side rubbing the other's body, and then she turns over on her stomach so he can get behind her, then the two of them in the back of a car trying to find a comfortable position to screw in, both completely naked though he thinks they'd only be naked from the waist down, if that, no matter where they parked. He never did anything like that in a car—at the most heavy petting and not for some twenty years, the last time in front of the woman's house in the front seat of her car, just as a joke: "You know," he said, or something like this, and they'd been sleeping together for months, "I haven't made out with a girl in a car for years, and never one behind the wheel, so is it all right if we don't go in just yet and sort of futz around a little out here?" and she said, "Go ahead, I wouldn't mind fooling around like that too; it'd be different." But how does one go about having sex in a car? He knows, to do it half in and half out of a car, she'd sit off the end of the seat with her legs outside and of course the door open and the man would do it standing with her legs up on his shoulders or against his chest or somewhere around there, or leaning over her with her legs around his waist or hanging over the side. He once, in a New York state park years ago, walked past a young couple doing it that way or something like it. But entirely in the car with the door closed? Probably in the backseat with her sitting on his thighs and facing him. Or she could sit with her back to him and in the front seat too, he supposes, depending on the size car. Sage saying when she's on top of him in his head, "I'm in love with you, I don't care about the age difference," with the same smile she had when she spoke of overindulging on popovers. It gets him excited. It's almost black out now, no moon or stars and no other house or light of any kind for half a mile, he's behind the unlit patio, door's closed to it from the kitchen so he's out of view, and he forces his penis back through the fly, zips up or tries to but has to push the penis down again before he can get the zipper up over the bulge, feels the last of the pee dribbling down his thigh, not just drops but a stream. Did it too quickly, should have shook more—why'd he rush as if he were about to be caught with his hard-on out? He might think of her later if he makes love with his wife, but only up to a point. In fact if he thinks anymore of her he'll almost definitely make love to his wife even if she's not at first in the mood to, simply through his persistence and the way he has when he wants to very much and various things he does and her willingness after a while or just resignation to it, feeling it easier to give in than resist if she wants to get to sleep, and she also knows he'll be quick.

Then he thinks of the time—he's sitting at the kitchen table now reading a book, kids asleep, wife somewhere else in the house, little radio on the windowsill next to him tuned to a classical music concert taped in St. Louis—he was a guest waiter in a children's sleepaway camp, still in college but troubled about what he'd do when he graduated—journalism, Garment District, advertising, law, grad school in English or international relations, stay an extra year in college to get his predentistry requirements out of the way or take some education courses the next two terms so he could become a junior high school teacher for a few years, or just quit college now and join the army or odd-job it around Europe and the States till he knew what he wanted to do—and met a girl there, someone very beautiful and intelligent whom he flipped for—marriage, he began thinking, why not marriage and babies early on which'll force him into some profession and give him a draft deferment and all the sex he wants?—and when he tried kissing her the second time one night she said something to him like—it was outside, in the middle of a baseball diamond, and she was trying to get her arm out from under his to point out some constellations she recognized in the sky and which he'd said he was interested in—"Let's be frank about this right away, Gould: I can in no way become involved with you romantically. It's the lack of chemistry or the void of something else and maybe of a dozen things; it's not that there's some other guy I specially like, although this would be the most propitious time for me to start a new relationship, since I'm completely free in every possible way and the surrounding conditions here are so perfect for it. But that's how it is and will always be between us, I'm afraid, so please, I can see you're a very persistent fellow when you want to be, but don't think you can ever change it," and he said, "Hey, fine by me; I can't see any problem with your decision, and not to make you feel small, but there are plenty of little fishies in the sea," and shook her hand good night, and after a few days' sadness and then downright despair for two weeks he got her parents' phone number and called, actually put a hanky over the mouthpiece to disguise his voice, though he'd never talked to them before—he supposes he didn't want any speech mannerisms or defects detected and later relayed to her and she could say "Oh, you mean with a weak *R* and drops his *G*'s; I know the jerk"—and said to her father, because he answered, "Excuse me, you don't know me, but your daughter (he forgets her first and last names now) is sleeping around. All I can say about how I know this is I'm one of the many guys she's doing it with but the only one who resents the others and wants her all to himself, even, if you can believe this after what I said about her activities, eventually to marry her," and hung up. A stupid, awful thing to do, despicable, he knew that then, knew it before he did it but hardly thought twice about doing it, for he was crazy in love and couldn't stand seeing her swimming in the lake or walking around in shorts or escorting her campers into the mess hall and thought maybe her parents would come up and whisk her away and that'd be the end of her in his life, besides being jealous, to the point where his stomach ached and he couldn't sleep because he kept thinking of them, of this drippy, brainy squirt she was going with now and, he knew, would soon be screwing. She later came up to him and said, "Did you call my home the other night and talk to my dad? Don't lie that you didn't," and he said, "Me? How would I even know where you live and what your father's name is and so on to get your phone number?" and she said, "I've mentioned what borough I live in and that his first name is Jackson, a not very common first name, so it'd be a cinch to find him through Information or if the camp office has a Brooklyn phone book, which it has to, since half the campers come from there," and he said, "Maybe you did tell me all that but I don't recall it and I didn't call him, I'm sorry, but also for how it's obviously making you so upset," and she said, "You're a big bull artist if there ever was one and you know it. It could only have been you, as you're the only guy I know stupid and juvenile enough to do it." He didn't believe she was sure it was him, continued to think of her almost constantly, stomachaches, trouble falling asleep, every time he saw her and the brainy squirt; they looked even happier, holding hands, necking in front of everybody, they had to be sleeping with each other now but where would they do it?—each had a bunk with six to seven campers in it—in the woods, maybe, late at night, or they pooled their money for a motel room or did it in someone's car; and a couple of weeks later he called her home again, her mother answered and he said, hanky over the mouthpiece, in what he thought was a thick Middle European accent, that he was the camp director, Rabbi Berman, and he thinks her daughter's pregnant and wants her and her husband, for the sake of Sandy's campers—that was her name, Sandy—to come up and get her off the grounds immediately—"The girl's a disgrace!" he yelled, and hung up. He didn't know what happened after that, if the parents came up or even told Sandy about it or called the director, but she didn't accuse him of making a second call and continued to avoid him the rest of the summer, turning around and hurrying away from him if she saw him heading in her direction, leaving the social hall or one of the local bars alone or with her boyfriend if Gould was there at the same time.

He makes love with his wife that night: first puts his hand on her breast, she puts hers on his—they were lying on their backs, room dark, still no stars or moonlight; he had to trace her face to find her lips—got on their sides to face each other and kissed and more deeply kissed and moved their hands down and now they were really started, he'd thought of Sage a lot before he turned the night-table light off while he was waiting for his wife to come to bed and a little of Sage during the beginning of the lovemaking and then just thought of his wife and now just thinks of a woman in the dark with more appealing—higher, firmer, but not larger—breasts, and legs stronger, harder, longer, slimmer than his wife's, but the same beautiful face as hers—to him almost no woman has a more beautiful face and lovelier hair or skin—and next day Sage is intermittently on his mind: while he's running his daily two miles, swimming in the local lake he likes taking his kids to, reading the newspaper, working on a manuscript, cooking dinner, and washing the dishes after and later listening to another concert on radio, this time an organ one taped in St. Paul. He doesn't know what it is but she's sure as hell captured his imagination, he thinks, which a woman, usually one young as she the last dozen years and up till now always one of his students, does from time to time, but never as intensely or for this long. He thinks of getting her phone number from Florida Information and calling her parents. That is, if they live there, because maybe the college she goes to is in that city or town—which is it?—and she lives in Palm Beach only when she's away from home. Well, he'll find out, won't he? when he calls Information, and that would be the end of it if that's what the situation is. But why call her parents? Not like the last time: to get them to come up and take their daughter away. Just to do something wild, idiotic, and unfuddydud-like, that's all, something he once was or used to do or just didn't feel constricted and tight about being or doing till around twenty years ago, which was a few years before he met his wife. And unfuddydud-like's not the word; it's "uncareful, unheedful, unforethoughtful, untimid, unsmothered, imprudent, unrepressed." In other words, a reason or justification he just thought of but one connected to the memory of what he did with Sandy and her folks. In other words, if he hadn't thought about Sandy in connection to Sage, he wouldn't have thought of doing it. In other words, an excuse to be as stupid and reckless as he can one more time because he suddenly feels compelled to and it feels scary and exciting but damn good. But why be that stupid and reckless? Didn't he just say? Anyway, don't answer, for by questioning it he won't do anything to be like it, for doing what he thought about doing is something you do without giving it those kinds of justifications and reasons and second thoughts, and more so at his age than when he was twenty or thirty or approaching forty. So it's just for him, a release of some sort, last done so long ago it's almost as if he never did it, stupid as it is. And when he gets, if he does, one of her parents on the phone, what will he say? What he has to, what will come out, and, unlike the last time, all unthought-of beforehand and unrehearsed, in any accent or voice he wants, even his real one, since neither they nor Sage know him, and probably the real one is the bravest to do and so in the end will give him the greatest release. If he gets their answering machine he'll leave whatever message he'll leave and call it quits with this wild, idiotic craziness or whatever it is. Or maybe he'll do it as an experiment: once he speaks to one of her folks or their answering machine or the phone just rings and rings till he hangs up, will Sage then leave his mind for good or close to it? Or maybe tomorrow—probably tomorrow—this whole notion of calling will be gone. Is that what he wants? Of course it would be best, along with his not thinking of her so much if at all, for what's he gain by it? But that's not what he's saying and he doesn't want to think of it anymore now or it'll all be spoiled. How's that? Drop it; and he squeezes his eyes closed and stays that way for about a minute, and that seems to do it.

He goes to town next day. "I have some photocopying to do and I'll pick up a good bread," he tells his wife; "anything else you might want?" hoping there isn't, since he doesn't want to make a bunch of stops, especially if what she wants him to get is before the place he wants to make the call from, and she says, "Nothing I can think of," and he starts to leave, then thinks of it and also what a fake he is, considering what's getting him out of here, and goes back to kiss her and then leaves, stomach churning nervously, even youthfully in a way, hasn't felt that feeling in his pit for he doesn't know how long, a feeling like—well, churning, nervousness, and of course he's been thinking of Sage most of the morning, but that could be because he was thinking of making the call and how he would do it, which means he didn't give himself a chance to forget her. Does he really have the guts for this? he thinks in the car: the brains, no, but the guts? Well, he'll find out, and stops at a pay phone against the side wall of the first service station in town, has three dollars in change; if the call's more he'll forget it: he'd have to get change from the guy inside, and besides, it doesn't make sense if it has to be so expensive. Looks in the phone book attached to the phone stand for the Palm Beach area code—it isn't listed but West Palm Beach is—and he dials it plus the Information number and asks for Ottunburg and spells it, "I don't know the exact address but it's there, in the heart of the city, and I think this Ottunburg's the only one." He's told that there are five Ottunburg numbers, all at the same address—Nelson F., pool, cottages two and three, and the children's phone—and he says, "Give me Nelson, not the pool or cottages but the main house," dials, sticks two-seventy-five in when asked for it, and a woman answers and he thinks it could be the maid or cook or someone, what with the spread they must have, and says, "I'd like to speak to Mr. Ottunburg, please"—not sure why he asked for him; if a man had answered he might have asked for Mrs. Ottunburg, probably to give himself a little more time—and she says, "He's not home; who's calling?" and he says, "Is he at work?" and thinks why'd he ask that? since he's not going to make another call and not just because he has no more change, and she says, "He's on a business trip, may I take a message?" and he says, "Is Mrs. Ottunburg in?" and she says, "This is she, who am I speaking to?" and he says, "Then this is for you too, ma'am. Your daughter Sage—who's fine, by the way, best of health, no problems—is having an intense affair with a fifty-eight-year-old man in Bar Harbor, Maine, I'm sorry to have to report to you," and she says, "My, my, not Sage," and he thinks, She kidding him or what? because she doesn't sound serious, which even if he didn't expect her to that much he didn't think she'd be mocking and he says, "Yes, Sage, a waitress, I believe, at the Popover Palace or something there in Acadia National Park—I never get to those places because I can't stand the crowds," and she says, "May I again ask who's calling, since this is quite alarming, sir?" and he says, "I can't divulge my name, I'm sorry, and I have to go now," and she says, "One thing I do know, though, is that you can't be the man she's having this affair with—Sage would never take to someone so gross," and hangs up.

He knew it—didn't he?—that it wouldn't turn out right but was somehow worth the risk, or he didn't know it but somehow sensed it; maybe that's what the stomach pains were about, the nervous churnings: a warning not to make the call because he'd be embarrassed by it after, for it was crazy, really too crazy, and the call could be traced—he hadn't thought of that before—people have the technical means now, the caller's number showing up somewhere on the phone called, he's read about it, remembers seeing in the article a photo of a little box like an electric shaver with numbers in a narrow window, and telephone operators have been using this equipment for years and the very rich would probably be the first home customers to have the device installed, not only because they could afford it, though he doesn't know if it costs that much, but also because they might think that since they've more money to lose than other people they're more likely to be the targets of cranks and criminals and solicitors over the phone and so on, but it was a public phone he called from—he's in his car now, heading for a local produce stand that sells good bread—out of view of almost everyone, including the service station attendant inside, so he's sure nobody saw him by the phone and there must be a dozen cars like his of the same color around the area, and even if someone did see him, just about no one around here knows him—he's a summer renter who comes to town now and then just to buy a few things they can't get at a big supermarket somewhere else and use the library and have his car serviced once a summer at the other station and maybe every other week a pizza and things at a restaurant with his wife and kids—and it was exciting, making that call, more in the expectation than the doing, and gutsy in a way, so he got that out of him . . . got what? Just proving he can do it, stupid as it was, but we all occasionally do stupid things, don't we? or something like it—well, maybe not, and not at his age, but no harm done in the end, he's sure: the mother will speak to Sage, maybe even today, maybe even use his call as an excuse for calling her, if she needs one—they might be very close, talk on the phone several times a week—and Sage could say "What man was he referring to? I know no fifty-eight-year-old man except one of the cooks at the restaurant, and he's gay and I think is even married to his mate—anyway, they both wear the same wedding bands," and her mother will believe her, that's the kind of relationship they have, he could almost tell when she said, and now he's sure it was said cynically, "My, my, not Sage": absolute trust, honesty, et cetera, between them, daughter confiding in Mom and even Dad for years; Sage could then talk of her boyfriend—he's sure she has one, it'd seem that every pretty girl at every summer job away from home like this would—saying she's taking every precaution regarding birth control and disease, but about that silly call: "Don't worry about it, Mom, I've had things like this to deal with before, you know that," and her mother will say, "The price of being so beautiful. Remember what your granddad used to say to me—it doesn't apply to you in this situation, so it isn't a criticism, it just popped into my head—'If you got it, don't flaunt it.' Do you know, I don't think I know what the actual dictionary definition of the word 'flaunt' is—do you, my darling?" and Sage will say, "Why, though, are you telling me this?" and her mother will say, or *could, could*: "As I said, I don't know; it just came to me, and it probably means wave, wouldn't you think?—flutter, flap," and Sage could say, "By the way, Charlie sends his love," meaning her boyfriend, a waiter at the place, and her mother could say, "And give Charlie my very best and tell him to always be exceptionally good and, if the situation ever calls for it, protective of my lovely daughter," and Sage could say, "Mommy, I can very well look after myself, so I don't have to tell Charlie that. Besides, if he isn't good, in all ways, out he goes," and her mother could say, "Still, insist on the best treatment possible—you deserve it—but give as well as you get . . . oh, I am sounding trite today and not truly giving you your due . . . goodbye, my dearest," and Sage could say, "One more thing. Who the heck could that man be who called you, and how would he know how to reach you? He must work here—someone who's made a move on me or something and I told him, or said with a look, 'No chance.' I better find out. A person like that could do a lot of damage before the truth's found out. You said he had a mature voice. Do you mean like an older man's?" and her mother could say, "Yes, I think so, but I seem to forget now," and Sage could say, "No, no older man would do that. It has to be one of the jerky boys here, acting old but doing it convincingly. Two of them are studying to be actors, but they're too nice and sophisticated for that and we like one another, so I know it can't be them. Maybe one of the busboys who has a crush on me—a couple do, or look as if they do—and he spoke to you in a faux older man's voice. Or someone not even from here—why didn't we think of it? Possibly from school, a fellow who has a grudge against me for some reason—a grad student, even—and he knows I'm here and probably having a great time. That's most likely, and I think I've a good idea who it is. Good, I've solved it for myself, so you don't have to be concerned about hiring a personal bodyguard for me," and her mother could say, "The thought never entered my mind. Both your father and I know you can take care of yourself. But you can understand why a parent would get somewhat worried over such a call, though I gave no hint of it to that ugly man."

He buys bread and drives home. His wife asks what he did in town besides photocopying, and he says, "Oh, the copying; I forgot. But why, was I gone so long?" and she says, "Longer, I'd think, than it takes to buy a loaf of bread, if that's what you have in there, not that I'm accusing you of anything," and he says, "Ah, you know me. Thought I'd be back sooner after buying the bread"—pulls the Russian rye out of the bag—"but had a coffee at the Pantry; helped myself to a free second cup—you know, but not because it was free. Read part of today's *Times*. It was just sitting there; a tourist must have left it. The world, for all the recent developments, is still, I can safely report, much the same. Went to the library to do the copying but got distracted at the seven-day shelf. There wasn't anything for me, and I also didn't want to take out another old video there. And then to the bookstore, but there wasn't anything there I wanted either. Maybe one, but it was a hardcover and too expensive," and she asks, "What?" and he says, "A novel; it looked good. Slaslo was his name, or Laslo: his first name, and not with a *Z*. Author I never heard of. But what do you say we go swimming? I still have two hours before I pick up the kids," and she says, "Good idea, I'll get ready," and he says, "Unless you want to do something else, and even then we'd have enough time for a swim," and she says, "You know me, usually willing. But maybe you could give me a rain check on it. I've been housebound for two days and I'm dying to get out."

The Miracle

HE LOOKS AT the postcard she must have written last night before she came to bed; her handwriting's changed from what it used to be a year ago—now it's squiggly like the old often write and most of it in block letters and in places the ink's weak and parts of some of the letters are missing and he can hardly read it—and he thinks, Oh, God, if only I had the power to just say, "May she be well again, *poof*!" and she was well from then on.

There's a thump against their bedroom door, the door swings out into the living room, she struggles out of the bedroom pushing her wheeled walker, one shoulder so much lower than the other that her shirt and bra strap have fallen off it, and says, "Back from taking the kids?" and he nods and is about to tell her what their younger daughter said on the way to the camp bus pickup spot when she starts teetering, one of her stiff legs shaking, and he rushes to her, holds her steady till he's sure she's not going to fall and her leg's stopped shaking, pulls her shirt and bra strap onto her shoulder, and says, "Why don't you use the wheelchair more? it's safer," and she says, "The bathroom door's almost too narrow to get through, sometimes; you don't remember when I got stuck between it?" and he says, "The time when I—?" and she says yes and he says, "Then I've the answer," and waves his hand over her head and says, "Heal, I say let thee be healed," and she says, "What are you doing? This is no joke, my condition, and I have to get to the toilet," and he says, "I know . . . wait, or don't wait, I can do it while you're walking, and it could work, and I'll skip the 'thee' and say 'you.' But you've tried everything else, haven't you? Acupuncture, macrobiotics, chemotherapy, various other drugs the doctors have given you . . . what have I forgot?" and she says, "Don't rub it in," and he says, "Massage, physical therapy, bee-bite therapy for just a few stings, not equine therapy, was it called? for you were afraid of getting on a horse . . . swim therapy you're doing now, and I know there have been a few others over the years. But faith, miracle, an out-and-out act of God or whatever it is but done through the intermediaryship of your husband, Gould, son of Victor who's son of Abe?" and she says, "Listen, you want me to pish right on the floor here and you'll have to clean it up? Let me pass," and he says, mock reverently, "By all that be holy, let this babe not only pass but be healed—at least let her walk again, I mean it, and on her own; this is serious, now, I'm not joking; please make her healed, my wife, Sally, let her be healed," and looks at her, for his eyes were closed while he said the last part, and she snaps her head as if just awakened from something, she seems transformed—her face, the way her body's no longer bent over and slumped to the side and straining but is now standing straight—and she says, "What"—startled—"what happened? I feel different, what did you do?" and lets go of one side of the walker, and he says, "Watch it!" and she says, "Watch what?" and doesn't totter and lets go of the other handle and is standing on her own, something he hasn't seen her do in three to four years and he doesn't know how far back it was when he saw her stand like this for even this long, and pushes the walker away—"Wait, not so fast"—and she says, "I'm telling you, something's happened, what you did worked, I feel totally different: strong, balanced, my legs not stiff but functioning normally again, I'm almost sure of it; I feel they can do everything they once did," and he says, "No, please, don't take any chances, what I did was just kidding around, as you said, but serious kidding, expressing my deepest hopes for you and that sort of thing, but I've no power like that, nobody does, nor am I an intermediary for any powers, all that stuff is malarky, bull crap," and she says, "Watch," and walks. One step, then another, and he says, "Hey, how'd you do that?" and she says, "It was only after what you did, and said, that I could; I had nothing to do with it," and he says, "I can't believe what I'm seeing, goddamn, two steps—by God, let's dance," and grabs her waist, and she says, "Hold it, I'm not used to it yet, I don't think," and he says, "The two-step, we're going to dance it to celebrate those steps, you know how long it's been since I've wanted to do it—not 'want' but *could* do it?" and takes her in his arms, spins her around, she spins with him; he doesn't have to spin her, he finds, and he says, "The tango, that'll be the best proof yet—big steps," and puts his forehead against hers, gets them both into the opening position, and shoots a leg out and she does too, and they keep shooting their legs out together doing the tango till they get to the end of the room, swivel around, and in the same position do the same steps back, and he says, "This is almost I-don't-know-what," and she says, "It's more than that—it's miraculous, but I still have to pee," and walks into the bathroom, door stays open as it always did when she went in with the walker or wheelchair, grabs the toilet-chair arms he installed, then says, "What am I doing? I don't need these," and lets go of them and pees, gets up, wipes herself—"Look at me, wiping while standing, something I never do anymore . . . I want to do all the things I haven't done since I really got hit with the disease," and goes into the bedroom and gets a shirt with buttons and puts it on and buttons it up, puts her sneakers on and ties the laces, goes outside and walks around the house and then into the field and picks lots of wildflowers and brings them back and gets on her knees in the kitchen and pulls out a vase deep in back of the cabinet under the sink and sticks the flowers in and fills the vase with water, then says, "I want to do some gardening, not have you or the kids do it all for me," and goes outside and crouches by the flower bed that lines the front of the house and pulls up weeds, waters the plants, snaps off a flower, and sticks it in her hair; when it falls out she catches it with one hand and sticks it back, says, "See that? When I caught it I didn't smash it with my hands. I want a real workout now," and does warm-up exercises and then runs down their road, probably all the way to the main road and on it; anyway, she comes back in a half hour with the mail—"Got it all myself, even opened one of the envelopes to me without tearing the flap to shreds . . . but I'll read it later. Who cares about mail now? I'm sweating like crazy and want to shower, but without holding on to the grab bars and sitting in the tub with the hand spray," and goes into the house and showers standing up; he watches what little he can see of her where she didn't pull the shower curtain closed and then undresses and steps under the shower with her, and she says, "Please, grateful as I am for what you did before and what you've done the last few years, covering for me with the kids, et cetera, this could be dangerous, two of us in a slippery tub. It'd be ridiculous for it all to end now with a terrific fall. But more than that, I just want to shower the first time like this by myself," and he steps out, she soaps and rinses herself several more times and then shampoos—"Whee, this is fun and I feel so cool"—and gets out, dries herself, and dresses—"Now I want to try reading without glasses, since my awful eyesight was brought on by the disease too"—and opens a book—"I can read as well as I used to, I think"—sits down at her desk and types and says, "It's no strain, fingers feel free and flexible, and I can type with more than one finger at a time, though I'm a little rusty at it. . . . I'm going to get some work done while I can, in two hours do what I couldn't in ten, or even twenty," and works a few hours, takes a break to make them lunch and eat, and after she works at her desk another hour she stands and says, "Oh, brother, my lower back aches but I'm sure this time only from typing so long and hard. This is great. I don't know what you did or how you did it, Gould, but you certainly did," and starts stretching till her fingers touch their opposite toes, and he says, "As a reward, other than for seeing you like this . . . ahem, ahem, excuse me, but just as a reward for all I've done—a single one?" and she looks up and sees his expression and says, "Oh, that," and points to him and says, "You got it, anything you want within reason. I'm as curious as you to see how it goes, besides, of course, which would be nothing new for me, wanting to. But first let me wash the dishes, now that I can reach inside the basin, and clean the house and also see what the kids' room looks like, as I've never been upstairs in the four summers we've rented this place," and does all that and other things and then says, "Okay, I'm ready, and I worked so hard I had to take another shower," and they get on their bed, he doesn't have to pry her knees apart to get her legs open, she moves around agilely, jumps over him, jumps back, gets on top, and then turns them over so she's below, later says, "Did I miss moving around like that and all the exuberance that goes along with it? You betcha. And to think I can do it like that, if all goes well or stays put, again and again and again," and they fall asleep.

"The kids," he says, waking up, and she says, "Time to get them? Won't they be surprised, or who knows. I'll go with you," and he says, "Bus is supposed to arrive at four but usually gets there around three-forty-five and I don't want them waiting in the sun, so I'll have to ask you to hurry," and they dress quickly, get in the van, no wheelchair or walker or motor cart in back—"I think it's safe to, I don't feel any imminent relapse"—they drive to town, bus is pulling in when they get there, she runs to the bus as the girls are getting off, and they say, "Mommy . . . hi," and she hugs them and says, "Both of you have a good time today?" and Fanny says, "We went on a field trip to Fort Knox. The counselors tried to scare us but they couldn't," and she says, "Scare you how?" and Fanny says, "The fort has all these secret tunnels and passageways from olden days, and Chauncy—he's the theater counselor—leaped out on us one time, but we were expecting it," and she says, "Josie, you have fun too?" and Josephine says, "It was all right. Fanny didn't like me being with her; she said she had her own friends to go around the fort with and I should get mine—Mommy, you're walking, you're standing, you ran to us! Fanny, Daddy!" and she says, "Ah, you noticed," and Fanny says, "Yes, I did too. What happened, a new pill? Is it only for today and maybe tonight—another experiment—or in the morning?" and she says, "Nothing like that. Your daddy waved his hand over my head like a wand and said some magic or religious or miracle-making words. We didn't think anything would happen. We both thought he was joking, or he did—I thought he was playing a mean trick on me, fooling around about an illness which all the doctors thought I'd never recover from. . . . I never wanted to tell you that. I always wanted to give you the hope I'd be normal again, but they all said I wouldn't unless some new drug worked, when *bingo!* no drug. It hit, it worked, I started walking, first one step, two, and on and on, doing all the things I once used to; just walking beside your father rather than have him push me in the chair. Sitting in it or riding the cart alongside any of you I was so much shorter that I felt like your kid sister," and Josephine says, "I never saw you walk before without help," and he says, "You sure you want to discuss this in the hot sun?" and she says, "Sure we do, because it's so unusual, my standing and talking to my girls anyplace, hot or not," and he says, "I meant especially you, Sally, for you know how the heat can affect your disease," and she says, "It's not doing anything to me now but making me feel good, so who cares if we get sweaty and a little burned," and Fanny says to Josephine, "You have too seen Mommy walk without help before, you just don't remember it. When you were one; that's when her condition first started," and Josephine says, "So I'm right, it doesn't count if I was too young to remember it, isn't that true, Mommy?" and she says, "I forgot one thing. I should call my doctor in New York and then my parents. Or my parents first; they'll be delirious," and she calls from a pay phone. Then they drive to their favorite town on the peninsula to browse around and go to an expensive restaurant for dinner, champagne, soda for the kids, "Cola, even," he says; "it's a special day and we're celebrating." Home, she shows the girls how she can climb up and down the stairs, plays a board game on the floor with them, wants to give them a bath, and Fanny says she's too old to take one with her sister or be given one by her mother. "But it's something I haven't done for so long, so let me this one time," she says. Bathes them, gets them to bed, reads a book of northern myths from where he left off last night, comes downstairs and washes up and gets in bed with him and says, "I don't feel at all stiff or in pain and no spasticity or anything like that. Just falling asleep with my feet not twisted or freezing and nothing hurting is the most wonderful thing on earth," and he says, "I only hope tomorrow and every day after it'll stay like this, though why shouldn't it?—and oh, what'd the doctor say? I forgot to ask you," and she says, "That he never, through drugs or anything else, read or heard of or saw a remission as quick and total as mine, but that with my kind of disease he'd made a vow never to rule out anything," and he says, "So, a hundred thousand to one, we'll say, or a million to one, maybe, but it can happen. A complete reversal in a single minute, and my waving and incantatory words and everything—if it wasn't a miracle from God, that is—might have set something off. Oh, I don't know, the psychological affecting the physical somehow. Or maybe it was about to happen anyway from one or many of the things you've done the last few years to try to make it happen or at least start it to, and it was just a coincidence it did when I did all those presto-healo things. Or, as I said, it was ready and waiting for that one psychological thrust to lift off—no?" and she says, "You got me, and Dr. Baritz says he doesn't know either. But I'm exhausted from all my activities and the excitement of today, so good night, sweetheart," and kisses him and turns over on her side with her back to him; he snuggles into her, holds her breasts with one hand as he almost always does when they fall asleep, with or without making love, hears her murmuring, and says, "You praying?" and she says, "What do you think? I'm not a praying person but I'm going to open myself to anything and give it all I have so that this good thing continues," and he says, "I'll pray too," and to himself in the dark he says, "Dear God, I haven't prayed to You for years, maybe forty years, even longer, except once when one of the kids was very sick, and I truthfully then felt it was the medicines that brought her around, but please let Sally stay this way, without her illness, thank You, thank You, thank You," and feels himself falling asleep.

He wakes a little before six the next morning, an hour and a half before he's to wake the girls and two hours before Sally usually gets up, does his exercises, sets the table, makes the kids' lunches for camp, gets her breakfast in a pan and makes miso soup for her as he does every morning, goes out for a run, showers, reads, has another coffee, wakes the girls—"Sleep well?" he says, and they both say yes—at around eight he hears her stirring, looks in, says, "How ya doing?" and she says, "Fine," and he brings her a coffee with warm milk, as he also does every morning unless she's already out of bed and heading for the bathroom or kitchen; a little later he hears her shriek, and he runs in and sees she's spilled the coffee on the bed, and he says, "What happened, you hurt?" and she says, "Shit, I felt so good getting up that for a moment I thought I was free of this stinking disease, and look at the goddamn mess I made," and he says, "Don't worry, I'll do a wash and hang everything up and the sun's already so strong it should all be dry by ten," and she says, "You don't have to, I can do it in the machines myself," and he says, "It's okay, you got plenty of other things to take care of; just move your butt so I can get the sheets off," and she says, "You don't have to get angry about it. It wasn't my fault. My hand started shaking and I couldn't hold the mug anymore," and he says, "Who's blaming you? Just lift yourself a little, that's all I'm asking. I don't want it to soak through to the mattress, if it hasn't already done it," and she pushes herself up just enough for him to pull the sheets and mattress cover out from under her; he gets the linen off the bed and sticks it in the washer and starts the machine, goes back to the dining room, girls are reading, their breakfasts eaten, and he says, "Anybody want some toast?" and they shake their heads, and a little later he says, "Okay, everybody, we're going: lunches packed, bathing suits and towels and sunscreen in your bags?" and Fanny says, "Oh, gosh, I forgot my Thermos of water. They never give us enough out there," and he says, "Get one for Josephine too, if that's the case," and she says, "She can do it herself, and I have to get ice out of the tray to put in it," and he says, "Listen, she's your sister and younger, and I'm asking you to help me—with so many things to do, I need your help," and she does it, and he says, "Now let's go if you want to catch the bus," and the girls grab their bags and start for the door; he says, "Say goodbye to Mommy, we still have a few seconds," and Fanny yells, "Goodbye, Mommy!" and Josephine yells, "See you later, Mommy, have a good day!" and he says, "Come on, go in and give her a kiss—she wants to see your faces, not just hear your voices," and they drop their bags and run into the bedroom and probably kiss her and then come out, grab their bags, and he says, "Your caps, everyone has to wear a cap to protect herself from the sun," and they put on their caps and get in the car; he drives to the pickup spot and stays there with them till they're on the bus, on his way home he listens to French language tapes, his big learning project this summer; when he gets back to the house she's pushing her walker to the bathroom, and he says, "Wait a second, the wash is almost finished, I can hear the last of the last spin cycle," and just then the machine clicks off and he goes into the bathroom, sticks the sheets, pillowcases, and mattress cover into the laundry basket, and goes outside and hangs them on the line.

The Bellydancer

HE'S ON A ship four days out of Bremerhaven on its way to Quebec. He'd been in Europe for seven months—was supposed to have returned to New York in late August and it was now November—had delayed college a semester, and didn't know if he'd ever go back to school. Had worked in Köln for three months, learned to speak German, had known lots of women, taken to wearing turtleneck jerseys and a beret after he saw a book cover with Thomas Mann in them, was a predentistry student, got interested in literature and painting and religious history on the trip, and carried two to three books with him everywhere, always one in German or French, though he wasn't good in reading either and now wanted to be a novelist or playwright.

Meets an Austrian woman on the ship who's fifteen years older than he. She saw him on the deck, softly reading Heine to himself, and said she finds it strange seeing a grown man doing that with this poet, as he, Schiller, and Goethe were the three she was forced to read that way in early school. Tall, long black hair, very blue eyes, very white skin, full figure, small waist (or seemed so because of her tight wide belt), embroidered headband, huge hoop earrings, clanky silver bracelets on both arms, peasant skirt that swept the floor, lots of dark lipstick. Her husband's an army officer in Montreal and she was returning from Vienna where she'd visited her family. "I'm not Austrian anymore but full Canadian, with all your North American rights, though always, I insist, Viennese, so please don't call me anything different." He commented on her bracelets and she said she was once a bellydancer, still belly dances at very expensive restaurants and weddings in Canada if her family's short of money that month: "For something like this I am still great in demand." They drank a little in the saloon that night; when he tried touching her fingers, she said, "Don't get so close; people will begin thinking and some can know my husband or his general." Later she took him to the ship's stern to show him silver dollars in the water. He knew what they were, a college girl had shown him on the ship going over, but pretended he was seeing them for the first time so he could be alone with her there. "Fantastic, never saw anything like it, I can see why they're called that." She let him kiss her lightly, said, "That was friendly and sweet, you're a nice boy," then grabbed his face and kissed him hard and made growling sounds and pulled his hair back till he screamed, and she said, "Excuse me, I can get that way, my own very human failing of which I apologize." When he tried to go further, hand on her breast through her sweater, she said, "Behave yourself like that nice boy I said; with someone your age I always must instruct," and he asked what she meant and she said, "What I said; don't be childlike too in not understanding when you're nearly a man. Tonight let us just shake hands, and perhaps that's for all nights and no more little kisses, but that's what we have to do to stay away from trouble."

They walk around the deck the next night; she takes his hand and says, "I like you, you're a nice boy again, so if you're willing I want to show you a very special box in my cabin." "What's in it?" and she says, "Mysteries, beauties, tantalizing priceless objects, nothing shabby or cheap, or perhaps these things only to me and to connoisseurs who know their worth. I don't open it to anyone but my husband, whenever he's in a very dark mood and wants to be released, and to exceptionally special and generous friends, and then for them only rare times." "What time's that?" and she says, "Maybe you'll see, and it could also be you won't. From now to then it's all up to you and what you do and say. But at the last moment, if it strikes me and even if it's from nothing you have done, I can keep it locked or only open it a peek and then, without your seeing anything but dark inside, snap it shut for good. Do you know what I'm saying now?" and he says, "Sure, and I'll do what you say."

She shares the cabin with a Danish woman who's out gambling with the ship's officers, she says, and won't return till late if at all; "I think she's a hired slut." They sit on her bunk, she says, "Turn around and shut your eyes closed and never open them till I command," and he does, thinking she's going to strip for him, since she gets up and he hears clothes rustling; then, after saying several times, "Keep your eyes closed, they must keep closed or I won't open what I have for you," she sits beside him and says, "All right, now!" and she's still dressed and holding a box in her lap. It looks old, is made of carved painted wood, and is shaped like a steamer trunk the size of a shoebox. She leans over and opens it with a miniature trunk key on a chain around her neck, and it's filled with what seems like a lot of cheap costume jewelry. She searches inside and pulls out a yellow and blue translucent necklace that looks like glass and sparkles when she holds it up. "This one King Farouk presented to me by hand after I danced for him. And I want you to know it was only for my dancing, not for my making love. Bellydancers in the Middle East are different from those kind of girls, like the Danish slut in the bed I sleep beside. You know who Farouk is?" and he says, "A great man, of course, maybe three hundred blubbery pounds of greatness," and she says, "You're too sarcastic and, I think, confusing him with the Aga Khan. Farouk was cultured and loved the art of belly dancing—and it *is* an art; only an imbecile could say it isn't without knowing more—and he didn't sit on scales and weigh himself in jewels. That one I never danced for, since it perhaps wasn't anything he was interested in." "Farouk was a fat hideous monster who was also a self-serving pawn of the English till his people dumped him, though for something better I'm not sure," and she says, "This shows you know nothing, a hundred percent proof. He had rare paintings, loved music, and would pay my plane fare back and forth from Austria and reside me in the top Cairo hotel, just to have me dance one evening for him and his court. He said I was the best—to me, to my face, the very best—and ancient men in his court agreed with him, ones who had seen the art of belly dancing before I was born," and he says, "Sure they agreed; how could they not?" and she says, "What does that mean? More sarcasm?" and he says, "No, I'm saying they were very old, so they knew." "I also danced for the great sheikhs and leaders of Arabia and many of the smaller sheikhdoms there. That was when I lived in Alexandria and Greece and learned to perfect my dancing and received most of this"—dropping the necklace into the box and sifting through the jewelry again. "It's all very beautiful and no doubt valuable; you should keep it with the purser," and she says, "They all steal. Here, only you and I know I have it, so if it's stolen we know who did it." "Me? Never. But show me a step or two, if it's possible in this cramped space. I want to learn more about it," and she says, "Maybe I will, but only if you prove you're not just an ignorant immature boy." "How do I prove it?" and she says, "For one, by not asking me how." "That seems like something you picked up in your dancing: clever sayings that put something off," and she says, "You're clever yourself at times and bordering on handsome, a combination I could easily adore," and she kisses her middle finger and puts it to his lips. "This for now," she says, and he moves his face nearer to hers; if she kissed him hard once she'll do it again, he thinks, and it seems he'll have to push the seduction a little and she's making him so goddamn hot, and he puts an arm around her and she says, "What gives now? Watch out, my funny man, and more for the jewels. They are precious, even the box is precious, and some can break," and pushes him off the bunk to the floor. "Haven't you heard? Good things come to those who wait, and even then they may not arrive," and he says, "I've heard that, except the ending, but okay, I won't push—not your way, at least," and she says, "Now you talk in riddles. And come, get off the floor, you look like a dog," and he sits beside her and says, "I meant pushing with the hands. Nor the other way, urging myself on you romantically, though it's certainly what I'd want, the romance—you wouldn't?" and she says, "That kind of talk should only be between lovers, and we aren't that yet and may never be. Time will tell, time will tell," and he says, "You're right. If you're interested you'll tell me, agreed?" and she says, "Now at this point I can see where Europe has sharpened and civilized you, as you told me yesterday, but only in spurts. You need to travel there more. And now that you're in a soft mood, it means I can go past mere love and sex and friends' playfulness and tell your fortune. Would you like me for that?" and he says, "I don't know if I could believe in it," and she says sulkily, "Then I won't; without your faith, I'd only rummage over your palm," and he says, "No, please, do, I'm very interested, and you're probably an expert at it." She closes the box—"I am, but you're a liar, though I like it"—takes his hand, and traces it with her finger, tells him he'll marry early, have a good wife, fine children, then a second good wife, young and beautiful and wealthy like the first. "The first won't die but she will disappear and everyone will wonder why and even accuse you but no one will find out, and the mystery will never be solved. The law will permit you to remarry after two years to let the new wife help you with your babies." He'll do well in his profession. He has a romantic and artistic turn to his nature but also one that will make barrels of money, so much so he won't need his wives'. He'll be well educated, travel around the world twice, marry a third time—"Did I mention that before?"—and he says, "No, just two," and she says, "Perhaps because the first two are real marriages, the second wife running off with someone like your brother—do you have one?" and he says, "Yes, in a way, older," and she says, "Then you have to watch out for him, but it could also be a best friend. And then, soon after, while you're broken down in sorrow—and this is why I must have said you only marry twice—you settle down with a young woman so young she is not even legal for you and you must live elsewhere and out of wedlock. I think it says here," jabbing the center of his palm, "she is first someone you teach like your student and then pretend to take in as an adopted daughter, and have two more children." "How many altogether with the three women?" and she counts on his hand: "Four . . . five . . . six, which is a lot for today," and he says, "And their sex? How are they divided up male and female?" and she says, "It's difficult to distinguish those markings here. But soon after your final child, and while all never leave home from you, it says—" and suddenly she looks alarmed, drops his hand, and says, "No more, I don't want to go on," and he asks why and she says, "Please don't ask," and he says, "What, my lifeline?" and she says, "I won't go into it further . . . please, it's much better you leave the cabin now, I'm sleepy," and he says, "What, did it say something about making love to bellydancers? Is that what scared you?" and she says, "Don't be an idiot. What I saw was very serious. I don't want you to know, and no matter how often you ask I won't tell you. It would only tear at you, and what I saw can't be prevented, so it would be of no use for me to say," and he says, "Is it about someone other than myself? For with two wives and a young lover and six kids and a good profession and art and wealth and lots of travel in my life and, I hope, some wisdom—is there any wisdom?" and she rubs his wrist and examines it and says, "Yes, there's some of that here and another place," and he says, "Then no matter how early I'm cut off—thirty, thirty-five—at least I've lived," and she says, "Then do so without the knowledge I found here. I know from experience that this is what has to be. I shouldn't have played around with your fortune. I should never read palms with people I know and like, for if I find something that's terrible I can't hide it with my face," and shoves him to the door. "Tomorrow, at breakfast, if I'm awake," and kisses his lips—"That's for putting up with me." He tries kissing her some more and touching her breast, and she slaps his hand away and opens the door and laughs—"See, I'm already feeling better"—and with her head motions him to leave.

They take walks together around the ship, kiss on the deck if it's warm enough out there, play Chinese checkers in the saloon; in her cabin, where she takes him to see her wardrobe and jewelry box again, she says, "You once said I was fat; well, see that I'm not," though he doesn't remember ever saying anything about it, and she stands straight and places his hands on her breasts through the blouse and says, "Hard, yes, not fat; no part of me is except what all in my family were born with, my derriere," and when he tries unbuttoning her blouse she grabs his hand and bites it and laughs and says, "You'd get much worse if you had gone farther without my noticing it," and he thinks, What's she going to do, bite me again, slap my face? and says, "Sorry," and takes her hand and kisses it and moves it to his crotch, and she says, "No, not now, and perhaps not later. I'm sure you'll want me to say it's hard like my chest, and I'm not saying the day will never come for this, but only maybe." "When?" and she says, "I'll write down your address in New York and if I go there I'm sure I'll see you. It's not that I don't want to myself sometimes. You're a nice boy. But then I'd have to tell my husband and I don't want to hurt him. You can understand that. But if I do feel a thrashing craving with you the next two days, then we'll do something at the most convenient place feasible, if there is one, okay?" and he thinks she's warming up to him; he really feels there's a good chance she'll do it; she was earnest then and her kisses have become more frequent and passionate and longer, not just mashing her mouth into his and pulling his hair back till it hurts but going "Whew!" after, "That was nice, I was overcome," and she did let him touch her breasts, big full ones, soft; he doesn't know what she's talking about "hard." He'd like to just pounce on her on her bunk and try to force her, pull all her bottom clothes off quickly and start rubbing and kissing, but she'd scream bloody murder and probably punch him and do serious biting and then order him out and avoid him the rest of the trip, though he doesn't think she'd report him. No, go slow, be a little puppy, that's the way she wants it done, at her own pace, and the last night probably—a goodbye gift, she might call it. And then she won't exchange addresses. She'll say something like "We did what overcame us but shouldn't have, but I won't apologize. If we meet again, then we meet—it's all written before as to what happens—and perhaps we can continue then, but only perhaps."

At the captain's dinner the last night everyone can sit where he wants, and he sits beside her at her table and out of desperation whispers into her ear, "Really, I'm in love with you, deep down to the deepest part of me, it's not just sex, but it's about that too. You look beautiful tonight, but you're always beautiful. Please let's make love later, the stars say so," and she says, "Oh, do they? You are tapped into them today? I've had my influence; I feel good about that. Well, we'll see, my young friend, we'll see, because I too think you look handsome tonight," and he whispers, "You mean there's hope? I'm only asking. I won't pout or anything and I'll be totally understanding if you end up by saying no," and she takes his hand out from under the table, brings it to her mouth, and kisses it and says, "Yes, I would be encouraged," and someone at the table says, "Oh, my goodness," and she says, "We are only special shipmate friends, nothing more to us."

There's a passenger variety show after dinner, drinks still compliments of the captain, and people say to her, "Belly dance, please belly dance for us," and she says no and they start chanting, "Belly dance, belly dance, please, please," and she says, "All right, but I'm out of practice, and the air temperature isn't right for it, so perhaps only for a short while," and goes below and returns in costume and makeup and belly dances to a record she also brought up. Her breasts are larger than he thought or remembers feeling that night, legs longer and slim, while he thought they'd be pudgy; she shows a slightly bloated belly, though—it moves, he supposes, the way it's supposed to in such a dance and maybe it's supposed to be that shape, and her buttocks and hips wiggle in what he thinks would be the right ways too, but what does he know? It all looks authentic, but sometimes it seems she's about to fall. Maybe she drank too much, but at dinner she said she'll only have one glass of wine: "Don't let me have a second. Scold me if I even try to; on evenings like this where the sentiment runs so much, one can see oneself getting carried away." Maybe she has a bottle in her cabin. She's less attractive to him dancing. In fact she looks ridiculous, her face sort of stupid and at times grotesque, and too many of her steps are just plain clumsy, and her belly's ugly. She's no bellydancer, she's a fake. She's Austrian, that he can tell by her accent, and maybe married to a Canadian soldier, but that's all. If she belly dances in Canada, it's in cheap bars or at costume parties when everyone's loaded, or something like that. The passengers applaud her loudly, surround her after, want to inspect the jewelry she's wearing, feel the material of her clothes. "This anklet came from a very rich Lebanese I can't tell you how many years ago," she says. "King Farouk, who many people look down upon, and perhaps there's some truth to it, but he would have given me this brooch after I danced, he said, if I didn't already own an exact one. Who would have thought such valuable things could be mass-produced." She looks at him through the crowd and smiles demurely and then closes her eyes and her smile widens and he thinks, So, it's going to happen, whether he wants to or not. Good, he's going to take complete advantage of her after all these dry days and give it to her like she's never got it in her life, and if she thinks he's too rough or just a flop, who cares?—tomorrow they'll be so rushed and busy with packing and customs and getting off the ship, he doubts he'll ever see her. Anyway, it's been weeks and he suddenly can't wait, his last a bad-tempered whore in Hamburg who wouldn't even take her stockings and blouse off.

He put his name on the variety show list as "singer," and when his name's called he gets up on the little stage and says he's going to sing the "never-walk-alone song from *Carousel,* the only one I know the words to." The pianist, who's also a steward, doesn't know the music to it, so he says, "I won't be at my best then, which is never that good, but I'll try to do a semidecent job as an unaccompanied solo. Well, violins and cellos do it—think of Bach—so why not voices? But please, anybody who wants to join in and even drown me out, do." A couple of people laugh. He thought he was a tenor but he can't get above certain notes. So he stops partway through and says, "Excuse me, mind if I start again but as a baritone? I think this song was originally for a contralto—deep—so maybe it's better sung at that range. Anyway, my voice must have changed while I was in Europe—you didn't know I was so young," and the same two or three people laugh. The pianist says, "Sure, if you feel you have to go on, but we do have a big lineup still to follow and it's getting kind of late," and he says, "So, I actually won't. I'm making myself into a first-class ass. Better, if you can't sing, to be voiceless without portholes, right?" and several people say, "Huh?" and nobody laughs, and he says, "Sorry, but I'm not much of a comedian either," and steps down.

They walk on the deck after. He says, "I was really stupid tonight, wasn't I, and you were so great," and she says, "You were quite charming and hilarious; I laughed a great deal. But you liked my dancing? I looked at you once while I was in the middle of a difficult step and you didn't seem pleased. I broke a serious rule of mine tonight and danced for people who aren't special or paying me at expensive celebrations, except for you, my dear," and clutches his hand and nuzzles into his upper arm, and he says, "Thank you, and I can see what you mean about its being an art form." She's still in costume, they kiss and then kiss hard, and she lets him keep his hand on her breast when he puts it there, and he says, "Tonight, right? We'll do something, at least," and she says, "Truly, and without exaggeration, I want to—what better time and setting, and the night's mild for once—but I don't think we should when too many people could be watching. You've a cabin mate, I have one, we should plan for it in a simple but sweet hotel room," and he says, "Where, Quebec? Won't it be expensive and isn't your husband meeting you?" and she says, "I'll pay, if you don't mind, and he'll only meet me at the train terminal in Montreal. But I'm to call him to say the ship got into Quebec, and for that I can be a half day late."

They meet after customs: "To save on the expense," she says, "can we take a tram to the hotel?" They check in as husband and wife—"It's not what I want to do, to fabricate," she says, "but it's the law"—and go to their room. He says, "Would you get peeved very much if we do it right away—at least start? I've been wanting to with you all nine days," and she says, "Let's have a big drink first—I'm nervous. I haven't done this from my husband for many years," and he says, "But drinks will jack up the expenses," and she says, "Just wait," and opens her valise and brings out a bottle of Pernod. They drink, kiss; he feels her breasts, she touches his penis through the pants and then jerks her hand away. "It scares me, it feels so powerful and big," and he says, "Nonsense, nonsense, I'm normal." She says, "Now this is what we'll do, and I insist if we're to go through with it. First I wash up thoroughly and alone. Then you go into the bathroom and take a long shower and clean every part of you, inside and out; every hole there is below the neck, but many times. I want you smelling of so much soap that I would think I'm at a perfume counter in Paris," and he says, "Okay, that's easy enough."

She goes into the bathroom—he hears water running, the toilet flushing several times—then she comes out in her clothes. He undressed while she was in there, is sitting naked on the bed, and she says, "What are you doing? Be a gentleman; put on your clothes," and turns around, and he says, "But I'm going right in there to shower," and she says, "Do what I say," and he puts his pants on and says, "Okay, you can look," and she says, "Did you put everything on? Undershorts, slacks, shirt, socks, shoes? I want it to begin at the beginning and slowly, not just quick without preparations and for your contentment only," and he says, "Oh, God, this is something; funny, but all right," and takes the pants off and then dresses completely, and she turns around and he says, "There, see?" and goes into the bathroom, takes a long shower, washes his anus and penis several times, gets into every hole with a washrag and soap, rubs his ankles down with the washrag, shampoos, makes sure his ears are clean, even the tips of his nostrils are clean, all the cracks and folds and places he wouldn't normally take so much time at. He turns the shower off, dries, and yells out, "Okay, I'm finished. What should I do now, come out nude or just in my briefs or fully or semifully clothed? I'm so clean I think any used clothing I'd wear would soil me," and she doesn't say anything. Bet she's left, he thinks, and says,

"I'm coming out, Lisabeta, no clothes, so let me know," and opens the door, and she and her things are gone. She left a note: *My darling. It would have been exciting but never have worked. Not only would I have had to tell my husband, who I love, but he would have hurt me and I think come to kill you. I decided: All that for one short day's fun? Besides, I checked in my own ways, while you were under the shower, and everything said it was the wrong time. Maybe we will meet another day. I can't say that I hope so. I embrace you.*

He thinks, The hotel bill; she pay it? He calls the front desk and says, "Did my wife pay the hotel bill? I just want to know so I don't have to bother about seeing to it later," and the clerk says, "No, sir. In fact, I saw your wife leave with much luggage." "Yes, she had to go home early, I'm staying the night," and he doesn't know how he's going to get his bag and books out of the hotel without someone seeing him. He calls the desk again and says, "What do we owe you?" and the clerk gives the price in American dollars, and he figures it's about the same or even less than what his things are worth, and he goes downstairs, says to the clerk, "Something just came up, and I have to leave too. Can we get a break on the room because we only used it an hour or two?" and the clerk says, "Sir, what are you saying?" and he pays, decides to take a train because he doesn't have enough money now for a plane, and walks the two miles to the station.

100th Street

"I DIDN'T TELL you this story before?" and she says, "If you did I've entirely forgotten it, so it comes out to be the same thing," and he says, "Well, I was around six, at the most seven. No, because my cousin had to be at least eleven to take me to the movies alone, and he was three years older than me, so I was eight or so; I'll say eight. I'm sure I wasn't nine, for the incident never would have ended up the way it did if I was that old, since by that time I would have been able to get back home on my own. Anyway, very early in my moviegoing life, that's for sure, so no more than eight. I don't think I even saw my first movie till I was seven or eight, so this must have been *one* of the first, though not the first. That one was a Western, while this one took place in a modern city. The Western had this man—the hero, a cowboy—and I could remember only one thing about it. In fact, when I got home from seeing that first movie, a friend of my father's, I remember—it was in the afternoon, probably Saturday—asked me what the movie was about, and all I could tell him was that this man came into a bar and said 'Give me a soda pop' when the bartender asked him what he'd have—" and she says, "I always thought they asked for sarsaparilla," and he says, "Maybe it was, but what I definitely remember telling my father's friend was that the hero ended up destroying the place and knocking out about twenty men and shooting and maybe even killing another dozen of these bad guys, though that was before the gore and shattered-bones-and-brains days, so you really couldn't tell for sure," and she says, "But this movie, the urban one, your story," and he says, "I got into—the show was over and we were standing outside the theater, the Stoddard, I think. No, that one was farther uptown, in the Nineties, and this one was in the mid-Sixties—but I got into an argument with him," and she says, "Who?" and he says, "My cousin. Randolph. He lived near us, and my mother must have given him money to take me to the movies with him, and probably a little extra money for himself. He was with Terry Benjamin, his best friend for as long as he lived near us, and maybe I got into an argument with both of them, feeling they were ignoring me or something; I forget what it was about. But I just turned my back on them and headed uptown, and he's—Randolph is—yelling after me to come back, and I probably said something comparable to 'Screw you' and kept walking, thinking I'd find the street we lived on—the side street that went into the avenue. West Seventy-eighth, I mean, between Amsterdam and Columbus, but I'd find it on Broadway, which was the street the movie theater was on, and walk east to our building," and she says, "That was unnecessarily complicated, to the point where if I didn't know what block you were brought up on I never would have found out by what you just said," and he says, "I always had difficulty giving directions. But I remember I also yelled out something like 'Don't worry'—he was still calling for me to come back or wait up—'I can get home on my own, I don't need you!' and walked to the corner and turned around, and they were still in front of the theater. I was surprised he didn't run after me to say, 'Listen, you're my responsibility, your mother said so, so you have to stay with me,' and grab my arm and force me to. I suppose he and Terry Benjamin just wanted to be together and rid of me, and maybe I had been more of a brat than I'd thought. So I kept walking, looking for the street to turn into," and she says, "Now some of your story's coming back to me. This the one that ends with you sitting on a candy store counter?" and he says, "Drugstore, but one with a soda fountain," and she says, "That's right, but go on; all

I can recall is you sitting on the fountain countertop and possibly someone like a policeman giving you an ice-cream cone," and he says, "No cone. That only happens in movies, or did when I was a boy, and it maybe happened in real life too sometimes, because people weren't afraid to do that then and also because store owners might mimic what they saw in movies, but it didn't happen to me. My experience was a little scarier," and she says, "Then tell it, if you still want to, we've plenty of time"—their kids are on sleep-overs tonight and they're in a restaurant waiting for their main courses to arrive, something they do—go to a restaurant alone—once or twice a year, and he says, "So I continued walking north. And I think I now, just this moment—I'm not kidding—after about fifty years I think I finally figured out how I missed my side street. I bet I was looking for some identifying marker on Amsterdam and Seventy-eighth. Meaning that—" and she says, "That Broadway and Seventy-eighth you weren't as familiar with—the identifying markers—so you missed your turnoff, we'll call it," and he says, "And I think I know why too. At West Seventy-second Street, Amsterdam and Broadway, after running not quite parallel for about a mile, converge. And Amsterdam, which up till that point was west of Broadway, after Seventy-second it's on Broadway's right, meaning east of it, and I probably thought I was walking up Amsterdam when I was actually walking up Broadway," and she looks perplexed and he says, "You know how Broadway, south of Seventy-second, is east of Amsterdam, and that starting—" and she says, "Yes, I know, I know, and you already explained it, but what I'm wondering is why you didn't just look at the street sign for Seventy-eighth Street and then know where to make a right to get home," and he says, "Maybe kids that age, around seven or eight—or this kid, then—don't do that. They look for stores and buildings they're familiar with, and I was familiar with the ones on Amsterdam and Columbus at Seventy-eighth and not the ones a block away—a short one, I'll admit—on Broadway," and she says, "It still doesn't seem right to me. Because if you were so unfamiliar with landmarks and buildings just a short block from your home—but your building was closer to Columbus than to Amsterdam, so we'll say almost an entire block plus a short one from your home—how were you able to know that Amsterdam and Broadway meet at Seventy-second Street and that you were supposed to take

Amsterdam there and not continue on Broadway?" and he says, "My cousin could have yelled it out to me when I walked away from him. I don't remember that, but it could have happened. He looked out for me when he was with me and for sure was never a guy who wanted me to get lost. If I insisted on going home alone, he might have yelled, 'Then get on Amsterdam at Seventy-second where it crosses with Broadway'—something like that. And I either forgot his advice, if he did give it, or thought I was taking it but stayed on Broadway by mistake," and she says, "Okay, that makes a lot more sense, but you should get on with it," and he says, "Or I could have once walked down Amsterdam by myself or with a friend or my mother or Randolph a number of times—maybe even that same day with him to get to the movie theater. My father I don't think at that age I ever walked anywhere with, except to the Broadway subway stop at Seventy-ninth a couple of times. But all the way to Seventy-second and Amsterdam, so I knew that Broadway cut across it there," and she says, "Anyway, you missed your side street, so then what happened, other than your ending up on a drugstore soda fountain counter without a pacifying ice-cream cone in your hand and maybe even without a policeman's cap on your head?" and he said, "Definitely no policeman's cap, since there wasn't any policeman involved in this. I just kept walking north, that's all, and looked back. Didn't see my cousin or Terry Benjamin and after a while forgot about them and got this idea—forgot even about making a right at Seventy-eighth Street, of course, for by this time I was way past it—but this idea that was maybe the most powerful one I'd had in my life till then. And that was to walk all the way to a Hundredth Street, something I'd never done from the mid-Sixties or Seventy-eighth Street and maybe nobody in my family had ever done. My parents weren't walkers. Subways, buses, a rare cab if it was very late and they were at some big affair or my mother was exhausted, but nothing more than a few blocks of walking for her and three to four for my father and usually to and from his subway stop. And my cousin had never spoken of or, should I say, boasted about such a long walk uptown or to anywhere. And then, to make it even more monumental for me, I had it in my head that once I reached a Hundredth Street I'd walk back to Seventy-eighth and go home. Do all this even if it was dark or getting dark by then. And when my parents asked me where I was I'd tell them: on a Hundredth Street; that I had walked about thirty-five blocks to get there and another twenty-two, not counting the side streets, to get home, a total of several miles—three at least—and all done straight with no resting. And if they said they didn't believe me I'd rattle off store names on a Hundredth and Broadway that I had memorized for just that purpose," and she says, "But after you got back downtown from this great journey, how did you expect to get to Amsterdam Avenue, if before you said you weren't familiar with the landmarks on Seventy-eighth and Broadway?" and he says, "Come on, give me a little credit, will ya? I knew . . . in fact I must have known since I was four or so that Amsterdam was one block over from Broadway, and I even knew where Columbus was, if you can believe it. I just happened to miss the side street to Amsterdam because I was looking for those familiar landmarks, or I was oblivious for other reasons—who knows what? Just walking home by myself from the movie theater from so far away when I was so young, maybe. And listen, if I ever really felt lost anywhere on the West Side within a ten-block range of my street, all I had to do was ask someone where Beacon Paint was. I think it's still on Amsterdam between Seventy-seventh and Seventy-eighth, but closer to the Seventy-eighth Street corner—or was till a few years ago—it's big sign a couple of stories tall painted on the side of the building overlooking the school playground there, though when I was a kid that playground was where the old P.S. Eighty-seven was that the new one replaced. Beacon was the largest paint and artist-supply store on the West Side, and maybe in the whole city. I was also somewhat familiar with the Woolworth's on Seventy-ninth and Broadway, so I probably could have got home alone from there too—just walked east on Seventy-ninth a block, then down Amsterdam to Seventy-eighth," and she says, "But it obviously didn't work out that way . . . the drugstore," and he says, "That's right, it didn't, you remember," and she says, "But not how it didn't," and he says, "It was very simple. What I did was look up at the passing street signs as I walked north, or started to look up, probably, at around Eighty-fifth or Ninetieth, getting closer and closer to my Hundredth Street objective and all the excitement that goes with that. Till I saw, or thought I saw—I'm convinced I did but I don't know what the heck happened—100TH STREET on a streetlamp sign, but this is the west side of Broadway I'm talking of, not the east, which could also explain why I missed the Woolworth's on the northeast corner of Seventy-ninth and also missed Amsterdam at Seventy-second," and she says, "I don't follow you," and he says, "You see, if I had been on the east side of Broadway when I left my cousin and his friend—of course I wasn't, since the movie theater was on the west side of the street—but if I had, then I would have come to Seventy-second and Broadway, crossed Seventy-second and been on Amsterdam, and then continued north six blocks and been home. But instead I was on the west side of Broadway, and Broadway sort of stops at that side around Sixty-ninth or Seventieth and only starts up again on Seventy-first, since it's around that point where this whole Amsterdam–Broadway crisscross takes place, Amsterdam veering east and Broadway veering west there—when you're facing north, I'm saying. And next thing across from Broadway at Sixty-ninth or Seventieth, on the west side of the street, is the southern tip of the narrow island for the Seventy-second Street subway station kiosk. To reach that from Sixty-ninth or Seventieth—well, that would have been extremely dangerous for a kid or really for anyone to do then, since there were no traffic lights or pedestrian signals to it and I think, at the time, not even a crosswalk. I don't even think you were permitted to get onto that island then from the southern tip. But lots of people did by racing across the avenue, and then to get to Amsterdam you'd go around the kiosk and cross from the northern end of the island to Verdi Square at Amsterdam and Seventy-second—actually, that narrow park's bound by Broadway and Amsterdam till Seventy-third Street. But the safer way would be to cross to the southeast corner of Broadway and Seventy-second, where I think an Optimo cigar store was—now it's a hotdog and papaya-drink stand. I only know about the Optimo, or remember it so well, because an uncle's brother—not Randolph's father, this uncle; Randolph was actually a second or third cousin—worked there or managed it for a few years. Which now that I think of it could have been who I was with and why I had walked one or more times down Amsterdam from Seventy-eighth to Seventy-second—with my Uncle Bert to see his brother, and who I think always gave me a Hershey bar when I went in . . . Bert's brother did," and she says, "That would have been very complicated for your cousin Randolph to have told you: what and what not to do with that island and even how to get to the east side of Amsterdam and Seventy-second from the west side of Seventy-second and Broadway," and he says, "If he gave me any directions, you're right. Smart and articulate as I remember he was, and also, as I think I said, usually a very nice kid, his directions would have been a lot simpler than that . . . you know, for a seven- to eight-year-old to understand. Probably he told me, if he said anything, and this would have been difficult to yell too if I was a distance from him, to just cross Broadway at the first corner heading uptown, which was Sixty-sixth or Sixty-seventh, or maybe even Sixty-fifth or Sixty-fourth, but a half block from where the theater was. And once I got to the other side of Broadway, to walk up to Seventy-second. 'You might even recognize the Optimo cigar store where your Uncle Bert's brother works,' he could have said, 'so cross Seventy-second to Amsterdam there and go up Amsterdam till you're home,' though I doubt he would have said that since he wasn't related to Bert. He still could have known about him and the Optimo. I might have told him—something a kid my age then would have been proud of or just done—'That's a store my uncle's brother runs,' when we passed it going to the movie, if we went that way, and it *was* the shortest. Or he might have met Bert a couple of times—Bert came over fairly frequently—and even walked to the Optimo with us once. 'In fact,' he might have said, 'if you feel lost or anything at Seventy-second and Broadway, go into the cigar store and ask your Uncle Bert's brother'—Hal or Hank, I think his name was, *Hesch*—'to help you get home.' 'In fact,' he might have said, 'if you're lost anywhere from here to your home, ask someone where that Optimo cigar store is and go in it and get help from your Uncle Bert's brother, and if he's not there then tell somebody in the store that he is your Uncle Bert's brother and you need help getting home.' But all that's lost in the past, what he said and a lot of what I did. He might have just said—this would have been more like him, from what I remember of him then, or any boy his age when faced with a suddenly defiant and furiously independent younger kid, which I don't remember being before that incident, who they probably didn't much like taking care of in the first place. So who knows? Maybe that time was my declaration of independence, so to speak, when I thought I didn't need anybody taking care of me and could do things like walking home alone from so far away. Maybe I didn't even have a real argument with him. Or

I contrived an argument just to get away from him so I could test out my new feeling of independence and taking care of myself. Anyway, he might have just said something about responsibility—his—when I left him. 'Your mother will be mad. And I'm being paid to look after you,' which I think would have made me even more—what?—reluctant to go back to him if I'd already started on my way. Or 'Oh, go the hell off if you want, you little turd, you stupid brat, I'm glad to be rid of you and I hope I am for good,' and went to his house with Terry Benjamin, which was just two blocks from ours, some other route, surely one where they wouldn't have to bump into me. Over to Central Park West, for instance, and then along it—even though that's a dull walk, just apartment buildings on one side and the park wall on the other—till Eightieth, and then down Eightieth to his block. Actually, there's no side street off Central Park West between Seventy-seventh and Eighty-first, because of the Natural History Museum there, so down Seventy-seventh or Eighty-first to Columbus and then north or south to Eightieth, where Terry Benjamin also lived," and she says, "But what happened after? You were saying something about the Hundredth Street that never was," and he says, "Well, I thought I got to a Hundredth and then, I think, because it was dark and I was tired from the walk, I got cold feet about walking back to Seventy-eighth. Or maybe that it was dark only came to me once I reached my goal. But I felt I was lost, all of a sudden became a dependent unself-sufficient kid again, you could say, and needed help getting home. So I went into what I thought was the friendliest kind of store on what I believed to be the corner of a Hundredth Street and Broadway, and I suppose I told them I was lost and about my cousin on Sixty-fifth or Sixty-sixth or someplace down there, and they asked my name and didn't sit me up on the soda fountain counter, or anything with an ice cream, and in fact asked me for a nickel—the cost of a phone call then—so they could call my home from the phone booth in the store," and she says, "Why would they have to call from a booth?" and he says, "Wait. Maybe I wasn't lost or even a little worried about the dark but only exhausted and didn't want to walk home from there because I didn't think I had the strength to and also didn't have the money for bus fare downtown, if I even thought of that, or a trolley; I think they still had trolleys on Broadway. So I went into the drugstore not so much because I was lost, if at all that, but for help getting home, if you can see the difference," and she says, "Okay, that could be so too, but I'm still asking why they would have to call from a booth. It's a drugstore, so there would have to be a private phone to take prescription orders on and so forth," and he says, "I don't know, but it's what I remember. That they asked me for a nickel—*they,* meaning two men there, the druggist and maybe another druggist or a helper or someone—the soda-fountain man, of course! Someone had to be taking care of the counter—and I think they even got mad when I said I didn't have a cent on me. My cousin had paid for everything that day with the money my mother had given him, even for our candy in the theater," and she says, "You remember the candy?" and he says, "I'm just saying *probably,* since I always was able to get a five-cent box of candy then when I went to the movies," and she says, "But out of that money your mother gave him, he didn't give you bus or trolley fare home when you left him? No, he wouldn't have to; he thought you were walking fifteen blocks or so. Still, what these men did doesn't make sense—asking a little kid for a nickel to call his parents, who are probably beside themselves that he might be lost or abducted," and he says, "Maybe that part about the nickel didn't happen. Is that possible? Because I remember vividly it did. Or maybe it did happen and they were only kidding me. That'd be more like it, but it really frightened me. I thought if I didn't come up with the nickel they wouldn't call my home and they'd send me back on the street and I'd have to try another store that might even be less friendly, and—who knew?—I also might have thought, How many stores are going to stay open, now that it was dark? Maybe this is the way people are on a Hundredth Street or just around there or from a Hundredth Street on, I might have thought, but I was scared, I'll tell you. But then one of the men called from a regular phone up front. I was standing beside him and must have given him my phone number or, if I didn't remember it, my last name and address or street I lived on and he got the number that way, from Information or the phone book, and called. But then I hear him say something on the phone that disappointed me I can't tell you how much, and that's that he's Dr. So-and-so, if he was the druggist, with a lost Gould Bookbinder in a drugstore on the southwest corner of Ninety-ninth Street and Broadway," and he stops and smiles, and she says, "So what's the big disappointment?" and he says, "Ninety-ninth—not a Hundredth," and she still looks as if she doesn't understand, and he says, "I didn't make it, don't you see? I thought I'd reached a Hundredth Street and then got a little concerned because it was dark and all that and went into a drugstore on what I thought was the corner of a Hundredth, and this guy—" and she says, "Oh. So you probably, once you reached a Hundredth, walked one block south till you found what you were looking for, a friendly-looking drugstore for someone to call your parents from," and he says, "But that wasn't what happened, even though I could swear I looked up at the last corner street sign and saw 100TH STREET on it, thought I'd reached my goal, and then got worried or something because of the dark and the time and the realization I was very far from home and tired and I'd never make it walking back and had no carfare and probably didn't know how to take the bus or trolley if I did have the fare and also wouldn't know what stop to get off, never thinking I could ask the driver to tell me, and went into a drugstore on that corner to have someone there call home for someone to come get me. So all my walking and defiance and everything was for nothing, I thought, when this man spoke into the phone, because who cared if you walked all the way to Ninety-ninth Street? One Hundredth was like another world, much farther than Ninety-ninth, three numerals to two, and so on," and she says, "No, I'm sure you reached a Hundredth and then went into that drugstore on Ninety-ninth," and he says, "Even if that were true, I couldn't prove it. I knew no landmarks on a Hundredth. The only ones I knew up there because I memorized them before I went into the drugstore were on Ninety-ninth, sort of confirming that I never got to a Hundredth. And I couldn't go a block north to get those Hundredth Street landmarks because I had to wait now in the drugstore till the person from home came. And when I got home? I don't remember what that was like, although I'm sure I got a tongue-lashing from my folks, if not worse: sent to bed without supper and that sort of thing. All I remember after is the ride home in the cab with the person who picked me up—it might even have been Uncle Bert—and him asking me why I ran away, because do I know how much I worried my mother? and I'm trying to explain about a Hundredth Street, and he's saying, 'But I picked you up on Ninety-ninth,' and I just gave up right there, knowing nobody would take me seriously about it, they would only think of all I'd put them through," and she says, "Yes, the story definitely rings a bell now—not the end of it, with your Hundredth Street disappointment, but going into the drugstore and someone picking you up and your feeling bad in the cab, though why you were feeling bad I don't remember your telling me," and he says, "I'm sure I did, because otherwise there wouldn't have been any point in telling the story."

The Pool

AT THE YMCA pool thirty miles from the house they're renting in Maine, only pool within eighty miles from them that has handicapped facilities, wife in the water doing exercises to relieve some of the symptoms of her disease (holding on to the handicapped-stairway rail and kicking her legs in the water, holding on to the pool's edge and stepping up and down), swimming instructor in the far lane across from them teaching some kids on his swim team ("Your head's going too far out of the water, you only need this tiny part of your mouth above it to breathe," and demonstrates without putting his face in), lifeguard jumping off his perch and walking to the pool's deep end (probably to caution some boys who have been horsing around or at least making lots of noise and cannonballing into the water too hard), little girl on the bench at the shallow end where he is (maybe waiting for her brother or sister to get out of the water or for one of her parents to pick her up at the pool; "Don't wait in the lobby," they might have told her, "stay in the swimming area where the lifeguard and other people are"), she must have been in the pool and then dressed for she's now shivering, maybe she's getting chilled because her clothes are wet where she didn't dry herself completely, and her hair too (you can't really dry your hair with a towel, and she probably didn't want to use a hair dryer for about fifteen minutes, if she came with one, or the Y would loan one to her as they do to his wife when she forgets hers), and she's sitting by an open door (it's unusual the door's open but it's hot, sticky, and sunny today and the air-conditioning might not be working or at least up to par), he should say something ("Excuse me, young lady, but why don't you move over to your right a little and out of the draft; then you won't be so cold"), she's drawing and writing on a pad attached to a clipboard, it seems, maybe a story with pictures, which is something his younger daughter loves doing and maybe most kids their age, around eight. She looks up and sees him looking at her and smiles, timidly, and continues to and he smiles back and looks away as he always does when he smiles at a kid he doesn't know; he thinks it'd look peculiar, if not to her then to someone around he didn't know, for an adult not to, for all sorts of reasons. Suddenly, he doesn't specifically know where it comes from, no special look or action of hers, he doesn't think; not the clothes or the way her body's positioned or that her hair isn't brushed or combed or that she's shivering, or yes, of course, the look, her smile, and how someone can do something like this after a child smiles, but it just comes, the thought: How can anyone kill a child anytime but especially out of racial or religious or ethnic reasons or that the state ordered me to or anything like that, a child you don't know or just know from around your area, gun one down, tear her from her parents or him from his and throw him into a pit and shoot him or into a room to gas her or beat her over the head with a gun butt or club till she's dead or slit her throat or throttle her or rape her repeatedly and many men raping her along with you till she's dead or just sniping at her from a quarter mile away with a very powerful scope? What kind of argument—he's thinking about people who aren't insane—could be used to justify such an act? There are no arguments for it. He means the killers or potential ones might be giving them, or think they are, but there isn't an argument for it that holds. He knows this is nothing new, what he's thinking, though when he's thought of it before it was always, How could anyone kill my kid? But it suddenly hits him with this one as it never had, using this shivering girl as an example, he's thinking, and the shivering must have had something to do with it. But let's say someone's told by his commanding officer to shoot all the kids hiding from them in buildings and basements of some town, how could he—anyone—possibly do it, shoot one? All she'd have to do, if this was one of the kids caught, is smile as she smiled at him before, or any kind of smile, a nervous or frightened or pleading one, and how could the shooter shoot? How could the shooter do anything but say—and again, if he wasn't insane or mentally disabled, but he wouldn't be in the army if he was anything like that, or a country's legitimate army and not just a bunch of men thrown together into some military group and given weapons to kill every civilian not of their religion or nationality and so on—This is crazy and wrong, there is absolutely no reason or cause or justification or anything to kill or do anything bad to this girl or to any kid. I shouldn't even yell at her except for something like getting her to duck to avoid a sniper's bullet. She's totally innocent, that's all—or she's not so innocent in some ways; she could be a thief and a conniver and so on—but she's a child and that's enough not to kill her. Whatever I'm involved in, she's not, and whether she smiled or didn't smile, just that she's a kid is reason enough not to shoot her no matter what reason or excuse or whatever some military or political or religious leader or thinker or anyone like that gives me. Nothing like "Well, in eight to ten years she'll begin producing kids who'll grow up to shoot your kids and grandkids or she can grow up to shoot them—male or female, just put a gun in their hands and watch them shoot, and the truth is she can even start shooting your kids at the age she is now." Or "She's scum, her people have always been scum and don't deserve to live. They foul everything they touch, they are beneath anything you can imagine the worst living thing's beneath, they destroy your homes and build their hovels on your land. They do away with your customs and beliefs and impose theirs, their foods stink, their clothes are filth, they have no culture, and there's vermin in their beards and head hair; they are evil incarnate, people of the devil, the scourges and enemies of our ancestors; they keep us powerless and poor and weak, the world will be thankful when every last one of them is wiped out, you will be rewarded generously and praised effusively for helping to do it, and you may even get your own pathway to heaven for having taken part in the slaughter and extermination." After hearing any of that, maybe hearing it for years and maybe all of it and since you were very young and from your parents and teachers and the most revered people you know or in your community and so forth, one's supposed to go out and shoot a kid? Suppose the officer or leader or even your father says, "Do what I say and shoot this girl or we'll shoot you," what do you do? Okay, not your father, but the others, what? You run away. Suppose this person or anyone or group that has this authority over you says, "Do what we say and shoot this girl or we'll not only shoot her but you," what do you do? You run away and try to find your family, or those members of it who don't think that way, and help them run away too if they want to. And if you can't run away or hide? Then you have to die, that's all, or, rather, take the chance to see if they will shoot you, though of course trying in every possible way to convince them not to and also not to kill the girl. But you cannot shoot a little girl or any child, and no threat or inducement or act of persuasion or anything like that can make you do it, though torture might, but how? Torture, if it got beyond anything you could take, could make you do just about anything, it'd seem. And if they grab your wife or daughter or mother or sister and say, "We're going to rape and then shoot her unless you shoot that girl" or "We'll rape and shoot all the women and children in your family no matter how young they are, even if one's only one, unless you do what we say," what do you do? You say you can't and give all sorts of reasons why not and plead and cry and cajole and beg and say, "Shoot me instead, please, shoot, torture, and rape me in place of them, anything you want to do to me do," even though they don't need you to tell them they can do whatever they want with you and there'd be no assurance they wouldn't rape and shoot all of them including that girl after they torture and shoot you, but anyway you wouldn't see any reason to live after they raped and killed all the people they'd said or just your daughter. What about if someone told you, "That boy has a gun, he's about to kill me, shoot him"? All right, if the boy's holding a gun you know is loaded and pointing it close and threatening to shoot and the person you know didn't do anything to warrant being shot, like threaten to kill the boy before he had a gun or his sister or mother, then you might have to shoot him, or even a girl in this case, but in the arm or foot, some place that would stop the kid from shooting but have the least chance of being fatal, and only even that if you quickly gauged you couldn't bring him down any other way. But that's the only reason he can think of to shoot a kid, when his own life, or maybe not even that but the life of someone he knows very well is being threatened like that. Anyway, it was the smile that brought these thoughts up—all the possible killings, he means, and what he'd do and not do regarding shooting a child and so forth—and her shivering too, he's almost sure of that, particularly that she drew her shoulders in when she did, and maybe also because it was such a timid smile, though he's less sure on that score, and perhaps also that she's around his younger daughter's age and his older daughter was once that age so he knows how innocent and un-something, not "unevil" or "uncorrupted" but just, well, unmalevolent or something they are for the most part or ninety-nine out of a hundred parts, and he looks at her and she's busily writing on the pad and she looks up as if sensing he's looking at her, and he smiles and she looks right down without smiling and continues writing. I'm making her self-conscious, he thinks, and swims over to his wife. He's been in the water, dunking himself now and then but mostly just standing.

"Want me to help you with your exercises?" he says, and she says that'd be nice and smiles and backs up to the pool's edge till her shoulders are braced against it. He looks up and sees the girl looking at him and smiles and she smiles and he thinks everyone's smiling, the three of us, smiling, smiling, smiling, and waves with just a flap of his hand at her and she looks back at her pad and resumes writing, though her strokes seem broader now, so she might be drawing. His wife holds on from behind to the lip in the drain—or whatever that part is right at the edge of the pool that acts as a gutter; the gutter, he'll call it, though who knows, that might actually be it—holds the gutter lip from behind and tries to make her legs buoyant but can't raise them to the top of the water. He grabs the left leg, holds it out of the water, and twists the toes around and back and forth as the swim therapist in the Catonsville Y back home told him to, bends the foot and then the calf as he also was told to, presses the leg to her chest at the knee, does the same with the other foot and leg, looks up while doing it and sees the girl staring at them, and he smiles and she looks back at her pad but makes no writing motion on it, just stares at it. He does this with his wife for about ten minutes—it's tedious to him but the therapist says it helps her, loosens up the legs and feet and increases the circulation in them—and then tries walking her in the water; and after a few attempts—she tips left and right and never gets a step forward—she says, "I can't today, the legs are stuck, won't move when I ask them to." "Lean back against this thing again—the wall—and we'll see how strong they are right now," and she gets in the same position as before, shoulders against the end of the pool, and he grabs her calves and sticks her feet against his chest and presses her folded-up legs into her body till her butt's raised almost above the water—and he gets an erection seeing her in that position and thinking of her that way in bed, she on her back with him on his shins above her and watching his penis go in and out as he moves back and forth—and he says "Push" and tries to keep her legs pressed to her chest, and she tries pushing them out but she can't today, she does about half the times he does this with her, when she's really trying, and he says, "Again, push, let's do it," and pretends to exert himself in keeping her legs against her chest but lets them out slowly till she's pushed him all the way back and straightened her legs. "Good, great, way to go; took a while but you did it." She grins—"I didn't feel I had enough oomph in my legs to do it, and boy was it an effort"—and he says, "How about again?" and pushes her legs in the same way, her butt rises a little above the water and he gets another erection though doesn't remember losing the last one, and looks at the girl, who's staring at him and he smiles, checks to see the erection's underwater, and says, "It's exercise for my wife," and thinks, There's no double meaning in that for himself, is there?—no, and the girl continues to look but doesn't smile, and he says, "Exercise for her legs—they're a little weak so we got to strengthen them, make them strong," and his wife turns to see whom he's talking to and says, "Why are you telling her that? You might frighten her," and he says, "Nah, we've established some kind of tacit relationship with our looks and she seemed interested so I thought I'd explain it—no good?" and she says, "Well, you just untacitized it, and maybe I don't like every kid and Harry knowing so much about it if they don't have to or they don't find out for themselves," and he says, "Sorry," and then, "Push, come on, *gibt ihm ein* push," and lets her push her legs out again. "Good, twice in a row; you practically shoved me across the pool. Now walk. I think you have the strength for it now," and she tries, hands on his shoulders, he holding her around the back, but she can't walk a step. "Maybe I'll just swim a little," and she gets on her front and swims out about fifteen feet, her behind for some reason bobbing above the water, and he swims alongside her just in case she suddenly sinks, which she has. Then she turns over and swims back to the shallow area and grabs the pool's edge and says, "I guess it's time to leave; you've had enough, haven't you?" and he says, "I'll stay if you want some more swimming and stuff," and she says, "No, I think I've had it, I'm all in, and not a very successful day—I even got tired with those twenty or so strokes," and pulling herself with her hands along the edge of the pool she gets to the handicapped stairway, sits on the bottom step in the water, and hoists herself up each step till she's on the top. He climbs up the regular stairs, moves her wheelchair to the stairway she's on, and helps her into the chair and pushes her to the women's door, opens it and looks away, so no one will think he's looking inside, though there'd be nothing to see since it's just an entry corridor with a railing and ramp, the door to the dressing room not visible from the pool door, and pushes her inside. "Thanks, see ya later," and she wheels herself down the corridor, and he starts for the men's entrance at the other end of the pool when he thinks, The girl, should have waved goodbye, and turns to her and sees the handicapped stairway and thinks, Oh, God, forgot that too, and removes the landing part of it from the board underneath, disconnects the board from the stairway in the water, puts those two pieces together and drags them to the place against the wall where he always leaves them, then stands at the pool's edge and thinks, Go on, jump or walk down to them but no way you're gonna get the stairs out without getting wet, and jumps into the water and tries lifting the stairway onto the deck. Often, when the lifeguard sees him doing this—maybe every time he sees him doing this—just as when he sees him dragging the various parts to the pool or assembling them or putting the stairway into the water—Gould's never asked for help on this but always welcomed it—he comes over and helps. But the lifeguard's rolling in one of the lane lines at the other end of the pool. The swimming instructor's helped him a couple of times too, but he's in the water demonstrating another underwater breathing technique to his swim team. The stairway seems especially heavy or resistant or something today and he's not getting it out of the water. "Can I help?" the girl says, standing above him, and he says, "Thank you, but I don't want you to hurt yourself," and she says, "If I pull the bar here will it help you?" leaning over and grabbing the railing, and he says, "It's really too heavy; it might fall on you once I get it up, but I'm not kidding when I say it's very nice of you to ask," and she smiles and he does too and she goes back to the bench, looking at him, and picks up her clipboard and pencil and she's shivering again and he says, "Really, sweetheart, don't you want to sit away from the door? That's what's making you cold, and maybe because your hair's still wet," and she says, "I want to be cold; it was so hot today that it feels good," and he says, "Okay," and tries lifting the stairway again, and this time—maybe whatever water pressure or suction that was keeping it down has let up or something—he gets it out of the water and onto its side on the deck. He gets out of the pool, stands the stairway up, and starts dragging it to the wall. She quickly puts her clipboard and pen down, jumps up and runs over, and says, "I can help you do this without getting hurt," and he says, "Why, thanks; you're something, you know, a real helper, but you got to watch your feet," and together they drag the stairway to the wall beside the other parts and he's sure, compared to the times he's done it alone, she made the dragging a little easier for him. Then he asks her name and she says, "Regina," and he says, "I'm Gould, and I know little girls because I have two, one just around your age and both in day camp today, and let me tell you, you're about the nicest and most helpful I've ever met," and she says, "Not more than your own," and he says, "No, the three of you," and says goodbye and walks to the other end of the pool, gets his bag off the hook, looks back—she's still standing and looking at him—and he waves and goes into the men's dressing room.

The Poet

IT'S SNOWING; HE'S in Washington, D.C., carrying his radio news equipment back to the office (heavy tape recorder, mike and mike stands, tapes, extension cords, briefcase of books, newspapers, magazines); gave up on finding a cab; snow slashing his face to where he can barely see two feet in front of him, must be eight to ten inches on the ground already, twenty inches or more are predicted. Snow started this morning when he was taking the trolley to work, let up, his boss told him to go to the Capitol, which was his regular beat, and get a few stories and interviews and about ten choice minutes apiece from some hearings going on, then from the office window of a congressman he was interviewing he saw the snow coming down blizzardlike. "Oh, my God," he said, and the congressman said, "What's up?" and turned around and said, "Holy smokes; well, worse comes to worst, if I can't get to my apartment across town I'll spend the night here on the couch." He called his editor, it's around 3 P.M. now, and Herb said to hustle right back, government's been shut down, "You might as well get here before you can't get here, as we're short of air material and can use whatever you got so far."

Called cabs, waited for cabs he called, went into the street and tried hailing the few passing cabs, for they're allowed to pick up four different fares at four different spots: nothing. So he'll walk, he thought, slowly make his way back till he finds a cab or bus going his way. It's about a mile to the office on K Street from where he is now. Or even farther—two miles—for these streets are so long. No bus, and when he stuck out his thumb several times, no cab or car stopped. Well, who can blame them, nobody wants a sopping-wet fare or stranger in his car with all his sopping-wet gear. Walked about a half hour in the snow, only has rubbers on ("trudged," he means, instead of "walked"), feet are frozen, hands will be next, pants soaked to the knees, doesn't see how he can make it to the office with all this equipment—it must weigh sixty pounds altogether and is cumbersome to carry. He might have to go in someplace, a government office building if one's still open or a museum, and plead with someone there to store his stuff till tomorrow. Should have left it in the House radio/TV gallery while he had the chance, then walked to the office with just the tapes to be edited and aired, and he might have got a hitch without all the gear—when a car pulls up, driver leans over the front seat, rolls down the window, and says, "Need a lift? I'm heading toward Georgetown, I hope I can get there before I have to abandon this car, but you seem stuck." It's the new Poetry Consultant to the Library of Congress, did an interview with him a few months ago, same outfit and tobacco smell: tweed jacket and button-down shirt, bow tie, pipe back in his mouth, smoke coming out of the bowl. "Gosh, you bet, but I'm awfully wet and I've got all this stuff with me," and the poet says, "So what, this rattletrap's seen much worse," and puts his blinkers on, jumps out of the car, and helps him stick the equipment into the backseat; they both get in and the poet says, "Where to?" and he tells him and the poet says, "That on the way to Georgetown? I still haven't got my bearings in this town," and he says, "It's sort of, with a slight diversion, but I wouldn't want you going out of your way—you've been too kind as it is," and the poet says, "Ah, listen, you help a guy in need, you earn a few extra coins to use in the slot machines in heaven, so why not? If it's at all feasible, I'll take you to your door, and if we get stuck in a drift, you'll help push me out. You must have a ton of belongings back there, what do you do? A TV repairman?" and he says, "Radio, a newsman, you don't recognize me, sir?" and the poet says, "Why, you famous? Someone I should be listening to to know who's who in town?" and he says, "Me? Just starting out, but a small news service, so I get to cover just about everything. I interviewed you when you took up your position. Your first news conference. I mean, you gave one, right after you got to Washington, also read a poem for the TV news cameras, and then I asked you for a more personal interview and you granted me one in your office." "No kidding. I did that? Did I say anything intelligent? I must be a nice guy, seems like, but a forgetful one. Maybe it's your hat and your snowy eyebrows," and Gould takes off his hat and rubs his eyebrows, and the poet says, "You want to shake the chapeau over the backseat?" and he does and the poet says, "And the snow on your shoulders and hair—you'll catch a cold," and he says, "Sorry, should've brushed myself off before I got in," and the poet says, "Don't worry, nothing'll hurt this heap and these are intemperate times where just survival is in order," and looks at Gould and says, "You look a little familiar. What'd we talk about? Did I dispense my usual nonsense? I tend to freeze up before you electronic news guys when you jut your paraphernalia in my mug," and he says, "No, you were fine, my boss said. He was afraid, in his terms, I'd get a supercilious literary stiff, since I was the one who suggested my going to your press conference, your building being so close to the Capitol, which I normally work out of. But you know: about your job, what you'll do in it for the year you're here or two years if you feel like staying on. What poetry means in America—there never was a time it commandeered, you said, anything close to center stage in the States. And how you plan to make it more a part of the mainstream—your primary goal," and the poet says, "I propounded the possibility of that? What an idiot! And of course I gave no ways how I'd go about it. Listen, poetry will always be for a small devoted clientele, and nobody in government's interested in it in the slightest. My position's a sham—no one consults me and I can't find anyone to consult—and it took a coupla months to learn that. But I *am* getting plenty of writing done—teaching's much tougher and more time-consuming—and meeting a few nice people, though no one who's read a stitch of my work or knew me from Adam till I arrived here, and I know they think anyone calling himself a poet's a joke, except Sandburg and Frost, because they were homespun and made it pay. Next time disregard any poet who takes on a government sinecure, even with the word 'poetry' in it, or holds a press conference, at least during the first two months of his job." The drive's slow, the poet's funny, garrulous, and lively, slaps his knee, relights his pipe several times, offers him a candy and, when he refuses, a mint and then a stick of gum, drops him off in front of his office building. Gould shakes his hand and says, "I can't thank you enough, sir. I would've frozen out there if you hadn't showed." The poet says, "Drop in on me if you like—when I'm there, door's always open. I can use the company; all the officials and librarians in the building stay away from me as if I've the plague. I won't have anything to say into your machine, but we can have a coffee and chat." He tells his boss what happened: "I meet him in a blizzard and he turns out to be the nicest guy on earth." "Did you get another interview with him? Would have been a good bit; Washington conked out by its worst storm in twenty years, but it doesn't stop the muse." "Oh, come on, the guy helped me out of a terrific spot." "You could have put the recorder on the floor, held the mike up to him while he drove. He would have loved it, maybe composed a sonnet about the storm, on the spot. Poets die for such attention, and like I told you on the phone, with the Hill probably shut down the next two days, we'll need more tape than you ever could have brought in," and for the first time since he got the job he thinks he has to get out of this profession.

Now he hears the poet's in a nursing home and most likely will never come out. He's past ninety, has been sick and so disoriented that he hasn't been able to come to his Maine summer cottage for two years. Gould met him once up here; no, twice. First time at a reception after a poetry reading ten years ago. Was sitting next to him and said, "Excuse me, sir, you no doubt wouldn't remember me, but around twenty-five years ago you did something for me I was always thankful for and could never forget," and the poet said, "I did? We're acquainted? Here, at the colony or at my university?" and he said, "No, this is the first time I've seen you since the incident. You were the Poetry Consultant then—this took place in D.C.—and I was a radio news reporter, and one of the worst blizzards to ever hit the city was going on and I had all this radio equipment to carry back to my office. I couldn't get a cab so I thought I'd shlep the stuff rather than leave it in the Capitol building, which is where I worked from. Nothing was transistorized then, everything was still tubes and complicated circuitry, or at least my tape recorder was. That's right, some radio newsmen had started to use these hand-held ones, but my outfit stayed with the enormous Wollensacks because they said the sound quality was better. I'm just trying to show how heavy my equipment was—metal microphones and mike stands—and so how grateful I was to you for giving me a lift," and the poet said, "How'd I do this again?" and he said, "You stopped on the street in the middle of a blinding blizzard—you were in your car and must have seen me struggling in the snow. I'm not getting this out right, but without knowing who I was and that I'd even interviewed you in your office a few months earlier when you started your position, you offered me a ride back to my office. You even jumped out of the car and helped me with my equipment. It was—I don't mean to embarrass you with this—one of the most magnanimous kindnesses ever done to me, since you were risking your life, almost. Oh, that's going too far, though the streets had to be very slippery and big drifts were piling up fast. I know, for I was trying to wade through them, without too much luck, and I don't even know if you made it back to your Georgetown residence after you dropped me off," and the poet said, "Where'd all this happen again?" and he said, "Washington—when you were the Poetry Consultant, your first year. Winter, during this record-breaking snowstorm, and you were probably driving home from the Library of Congress, told like everyone else to get the heck home while you still had the chance. They closed—the government did—all their offices early because of the storm, Congress included. But who actually does give the order for the government to close up? I just thought of that. Probably no one person or office but each branch, given the separation of branches and such, or even each department gives orders for its own closing, wouldn't that seem right?" and the poet said, "Don't know," and stood up and said, "Lucy, listen to this. This nice young man here. I stopped for him in a blizzard when I was the Consultant in Poetry in Washington and gave him a lift," and Gould said, "Consultant in Poetry? That was the official title? Now it's Poet Laureate," and she said from across the room, "When did all this occur?" and the poet said, "I just told you: in D.C., Washington, the capital, when I was the C.P. to the

Library of Congress, or should I say 'the C.P. to the L.C. in D.C.,' though no one called the Library that. The institution, you remember, that typically came with all the honors and regard money couldn't buy, but scant remuneration. I don't recall the episode myself, not even the blizzard, but this nice young man here seems to recollect it perfectly. I pulled over for him during a raging snowstorm, it seems. Act of kindness, he calls it, because he had a bevy of heavy radio equipment for his news work, and I took pity on him, I suppose, when I saw him trekking through hills of snow. I did that. Do you recall my ever telling you of it?" and she said, people she was sitting with looking at him too, "That was around thirty years ago?" and the poet looked at Gould and he nodded and the poet said, "I believe so," and she said, "No, but it would be like you to do that. That's how you were. But at this moment, for me, though I remember the consultancy well, it's as if this is the first I've heard of the incident, which would also be like you—not so much not to remember but not to tell me of the good deeds you did then. But I could have forgotten," and the poet said, "It was sort of nice of me to do it, wasn't it, something I couldn't afford to do today because of my age? And I don't even drive anymore—you do, or our college-student driver. And a little self-admiration isn't undesirable from time to time if you're feeling especially down on yourself, am I wrong?" and she said, "I think it's fine, anything you wish; you deserve even more," and resumed talking to the people near her. The poet said to Gould, "Thank you for reminding me of it, young man. That was extremely gracious of you. Do you know the quote of Samuel Johnson about the rare friend who will help you celebrate a good review? I like things to be brought back, especially acts like that. What do you do now, still a journalist?" when a woman stopped beside them and said, "Bill, I wanted to say good night," and he said, "Well, good night, and I guess I'll be seeing you at the Academy this year one time," and she said, "The Academy? I've never been to it, so why would you think I'd see you there?" and he said, "You don't go? You never went? I haven't seen you there any number of times? The Academy in New York, the one we've been members of for so many years, of Arts and Letters and things?" and she said, "My goodness, I thought you meant the Maine Maritime Academy training vessel, so I thought, Why on earth does he think I'd step onto that old tub?"

and he said, "Perhaps because we both spend entire summers so close to it, you in the same town and straight up the street from the pier, in fact," and she said, "Yes, but there's still nothing there for me, can't you see that? So why must you insist on winning this misunderstanding instead of simply laughing at it?" and he looked at her, mouth open, stared at the ceiling a few seconds, felt around behind him for the chair arms, grabbed them and made a move to sit, but then sprang up straight, kissed her cheek, and left the room, smiling as if he'd just exchanged some simple but satisfying pleasantries, and the woman said, "Lucy, you have your hands full, I see; I didn't realize how much," and Lucy said, "Don't tell me, dear, let me guess."

The second time Gould met him in Maine was a year later, over drinks at a little dinner party. Gould sat down next to him and said, "So, how are you, sir, you're looking fine," and the poet said, "I know you? What's the name?" and he told him, and the poet said, "Sorry, no bell struck. What do you do, young man?" and he said, "It's nice to still be considered young, but now I'm a teacher though I was once a reporter," and the poet said, "For whom?" and he said, "You mean teaching?" and the poet said, "I mean both: whom, what, where, when, all the journalistic questions," and he said, "Well, many years ago I was a newsman in Washington when you were the Consultant in Poetry," and the poet said, "Lucy, latch onto this; this pleasant young man was a reporter during my Washington consult-the-poet days, can you believe it?" and she said, "I think I knew that," and Gould said, "Not only that, sir—and I think we talked about it before, but at a crowded party in Castine and pretty quickly—but you gave me a lift once," and the poet said, "I did, on one of the roads here—your car broke down, son?" and he said, "I meant in Washington then, during a tremendous snowstorm, and you stopped for me and drove me to my office, something I was always grateful for. I mean, you didn't know me and just appeared when I needed help the most because of all the heavy gear I had on me—I was in radio news, did interviews, so carried my own equipment," and the poet said, "Lucy, did you hear what I did for this young man years ago? Stopped in a snowstorm, didn't even know who he was or what he did, and gave him a ride to his office when he needed one the most," and she said, "It was very nice of you" and, to Gould, "I can tell, after so many years, that you were quite appreciative," and he said, "It was wonderful, one of the most selfless acts anyone's ever done for me, because I'm telling you, this was some snowstorm—a blizzard, knocked out Washington for several days," and the poet said, "Good, I'm glad you survived it and are here today to recount it," and a couple of people in the circle of chairs they're in started laughing and the poet said, "Did I say something that seemed to you unintentionally funny? Well, good, it's summer and we're supposed to be relaxed, so people should laugh."

It's in Maine at the old farmhouse they rent that Gould hears the poet's in a nursing home and his wife died the past year. He asks about him, and the man who told him says, "As far as anyone knows, the old fool's on his way out too." The man's wife says, "Now that's unkind," and the man says, "I only meant he was once a fairly good poet and critic, and two to three of his poems are among the best produced by any American in the last four decades, which is something, but he's been an old fool for more than thirty years, the longest period of addlement I've witnessed in a human being. Besides, with his memory failing for years he's become a menace to our entire cliff colony, forgetting he turned on a gas stove, leaving his suburban van parked on a steep hill with the hand brake disengaged, and things like that." "I'm sorry to learn of it," Gould says, and the man says, "We were too, but worse to observe it. Most of us haven't the kind of fire insurance to cover a completely burnt house. It's punitively expensive because of the local infatuation with arson on our peninsula; nor has anyone devised the type of body armor needed by one of us or our grandkids to withstand a ramming from a megaton van," and Gould says, "Excuse me, but I meant I was sorry to hear about his wife and illness and confinement and so on. What a pity, for what a nice man." "Excuse me, and Dolores will no doubt rebuke my pitilessness to this moribund old fool, whom we both like, mind you, enormously, and, as I said, admire. But to be honest, a greater egotist, braggart, social manipulator, and literary operator never walked so assuredly through the fields of poetry, and I've run across some lulus in my time. An example, and this also of his idiocy, since it didn't start when he first became senile, you know—" and his wife says, "Now that's enough," and he says, "No, let me finish, since I never could make any sense to Bill on this score, simply because he refused to see anything he'd done as wrong, no matter how inappropriate, ill-considered, or just plain dumb it was. Once, an anthologist was putting together a book of poems by poets under forty. When our poet hears this, and he had his ears screwed into anything he thought could help his career, he contacts the anthologist and says, 'Why haven't you asked me for any poems?' 'Because you're over forty,' the anthologist says; 'you're sixty-two.' This was a number of years ago, of course, though he never changed. And Bill's answer? 'So what? If you're compiling an anthology of contemporary American poetry I'd think you'd want my work in it, because who cares what age a poet is when you read his poems?' Does that make any sense to you? Are we talking here of a truly great self-effacing unfinagling realistic guy?" and Gould says, "He's—well, yes, it doesn't make much sense—but still, and maybe this'll seem silly to you, but he once did something so wonderful for me that it's hard to think anything bad of him." He starts to tell the Washington story and the man says, "I know, I was at some party up here when you gushed all over him in recapitulating it, but you must know that everyone has his three to four involuntary selfless acts to his credit, and Bill probably has a few more than that, and not just because he's survived past ninety, but listen to this"—and he reels off a number of stories showing the poet manipulating people and institutions—"and I'm only going back fifty-some years, which is how long I know him," and Gould says, "Still, you can't see what I'm saying? I'm sure there was this other good side to him. Not so much involuntary or momentarily magnanimous but downright selfless and bighearted and generous. Going out of his way for a stranger when most people in the same situation—a blinding snowstorm, which also meant he couldn't have recognized me as the fellow who interviewed him months before—would have driven past. Ten inches on the ground, maybe another fifteen expected, and you're in your warm car with your warm pipe and you want to get to your warm home fast with maybe even a fireplace going? Risking your life, you can almost say—that's not so farfetched. The snow was piling up a couple of inches an hour and the car could skid, when if he didn't stop for me and take all the time it took to load my equipment up and drive me to my office, he might be able to make it home safely . . . anyway, the chances of it would be better. But what did I start out saying? This other good side of him that I caught immediately from that one situation and which I don't hear anything of in what you're saying about him over fifty years. And the interview he granted me when I first met him. That's what I meant by saying he didn't recognize me at first. He didn't have to give it. I was a shrimp of a reporter, and the news service I worked for was small too. And I should've got his press conference on tape when the other radio and TV guys did, if any other radio newsman—I forget—thought there was anything potential there to even attend it, but I asked him for an interview right after. I might even have given him some cock-and-bull story that my tape jammed. I did that then to get solo interviews—lied, finagled, cajoled, et cetera, all the things you said he did," and the man says, "Sure he gave you an interview. For the fame, not because of your cajolery. When Bill saw a newsman's tape recorder and mike, he saw an audience of millions and possible book buyers and poetry-reading invitations and so forth. I bet you even had him read a few of his poems for radio," and Gould says, "I think I did; it's what I normally would have done for an interview like that with someone in his position," and the man says, "That's my point. The regular press conference was what came with the turf of being introduced as the new Poetry Consultant, but your solo with him was gravy that made him giddy. You showed him individual attention that also had a good chance of being on radio for a lot more time than a news report of the pro forma press conference," and Gould says, "But if I remember, he told me to come back anytime for a coffee and chat but not to bring my tape recorder. So if that's the case—" and the man says, "Ah, come on, he was only trying to show he was more interested in you than in what you could do for him. But you probably would have brought your tape recorder and he would have seen it and somehow worked you around to where he ended up gladly giving you another interview," and Gould says, "No, I'm not getting through to you and you really can't change my initial opinion of him, though you have opened me up to him a little, mostly because I didn't know him. Anyway, he did a wonderful thing for me, and I just wish everyone would do things like that for people in similar situations, and I also feel lousy about the condition he's in now," and the man says, "That's not the question; we all do."

Accidents and Mishaps

SHE'S ALMOST TWO years old, on her back on their double bed while he's changing her diaper; as he bends over to unpin the diaper, several coins, three pennies and a dime, drop out of his T-shirt pocket. He pushes them to the edge of the bed, doesn't want her handling them and then putting her hands to her mouth or sucking on one of the coins and maybe swallowing it. He unpins the diaper, lifts her rear, pulls the diaper out and wipes her with it and folds it up and says, "Stay here a minute, Daddy's going to clean this," and presses down on her chest a little, a signal between them she seems to understand that she stay lying on her back where she is while he's gone. He goes into the bathroom—doesn't know why he has to wash the diaper out immediately but he almost always does, something about the smell and that there's feces in it and wanting to get the job over with as soon as possible and not have to think about it later—and empties the diaper into the toilet bowl, flushes the toilet, and after the shit's gone he continues flushing, which he can do with this toilet because it has a flushometer instead of a water tank, while he rinses the diaper out several times. "You okay, dear?" he yells between flushes, and she doesn't answer, and he yells, "Fanny . . . you all right? Say you're okay, Daddy wants to know," and she says, "Yes," and he drops the diaper into the diaper pail, washes his hands, and comes back with a washrag rinsed in warm water, cleans and dries her and is about to poof some cornstarch around her anus when he notices the coins aren't on the bed. "Hey, where'd they go, the coins, the pennies, where?" and she just looks at him, and he says, "Did you knock them off the bed?" and she shakes her head and he quickly looks on the floor and under the bed and lifts her rear up by her ankles and they're not under her or the towel she's on and when he sets her down he sees her eyes bulging out at him and he says, "What's wrong—Fanny—you didn't swallow them, did you—in your mouth?" and she looks scared and coughs but can't expel any air and he says, "Oh, no, what do I do?" and still has his hands around her ankles from when he'd lifted her and jerks her up and holds her upside down in the air and slaps her back and continues slapping it while bobbing her up and down, up and down, and she spits some coins out and starts crying, and he says, "Is that all? You still got something in your mouth or throat? Goddamn, I'm saying are there any more coins inside you?" but can't make out what her expression says because she's crying and is upside down and he looks at the coins on the bed, two pennies and a dime, and then hears a coin hit the floor on the other side of the bed, and he sets her down on her back, jumps onto the bed on his stomach, head hanging off the side so he can see what coin it is, a penny, and he says, "Thank God!" and stands up and sits her up and says, "You all right, coins all gone, no more pennies in you?" and she's crying but breathing normally again, and he grabs the two pennies and dime off the bed and sticks them into his pants pocket and says, "Open your mouth," and nothing else is in it, and he says, "Never stick coins in your mouth, never, nothing but food, you hear?" and she's still crying, and he says, "It was my fault too, Daddy's fault, bad Daddy, leaving them there, but never again will I leave around any pennies or small things like that; you can swallow them and die, just so you know," and she's crying more hysterically now, and he says, "Oh, gee, I'm sorry," and picks her up and holds her to his chest and cheek and pats her back and says, "I'll tell you this another time, when you're old enough to understand."

. . .

IN THE CAR, family heading to D.C. to go to the East Wing of the National Gallery, he's driving, wife beside him, Fanny in her kid's car seat in back, winter, freezing out, but inside it's warm, radio playing what the announcer said was a song cycle by Ravel, something with the word *Exotiques* in it, he thinks, and which he wants to hear to the end to find out exactly what it's called and who's singing it and on what label so he can look into buying it this week, he likes it so much, when the car in front of his on the ramp leading to New York Avenue, or maybe they're already on New York, starts to slow, and he applies his brake a few quick times, the *tap-tap-tap* he knows to do so the brakes won't lock, and his car suddenly spins and he doesn't know what to do, turn the steering wheel into the spin, which he's heard you're supposed to do but it seems unnatural, or away from it, which his instincts tell him to do, so he just grips the wheel tight and yells, "Hold on, I can't control it!" and the car spins all the way around and continues spinning a second round to the ramp railing and his wife's screaming and the baby's shrieking and the car slams into the railing on his side and stops, now facing cars from behind that are now coming toward him, the nearest one in his lane managing to stop two feet away, maybe one. It was ice he didn't see, thought it was a shadow, didn't even see that, just didn't see anything on the pavement, maybe wasn't paying attention because he was absorbed in the music, but later when he gets out to see what caused the spin and how bad the car's damaged he sees that's it, ice, big patch of it, five feet by five or almost, his door smashed so hard he couldn't open it and had to climb over his wife to go out her side, and he thinks, Thank God we're all right and everything was working for us once we started to spin, that the railing was near to stop us, that we didn't spin the other way into oncoming traffic, that I did just hold on to the wheel tight and not try to correct the spin one way or the other, that the cars behind us were far enough away not to crash into us once we started spinning and then, when we were facing them, that they didn't spin out of control when they braked, and so on, and says some of this through the window to calm his wife and daughter, but she's just staring straight ahead, oblivious to everything, it seems, who knows what the hell she's thinking, and Fanny's gone from shrieking to crying.

. . .

HIS WIFE SAYS, "You know, Fanny's standing in her crib and talking kind of funny and doing weird things as if she's high," and he goes in with her to look, and Fanny's laughing but at nothing, it seems, and reaches out to pull his nose, and when he pushes her hand away she laughs giddily again, and he says, "Fanny, everything okay? What's wrong, you feeling all right? I mean, you look all right and seem to be having a good time, much better than you did last night," and his wife yells, "The aspirins!" and he says, "What?" and she yells, "The bottle!" and he looks where she's pointing and sees an opened bottle under the crib and gets it and says, "Oh, my goodness, you think she took some? I must've left it here last night when I—" and she says, "How many were there last?" and he looks at the bottle and says, "I don't know, I think a lot more than this," and she says, "What do we do? She's probably swallowed a whole bunch of them," and he calls the pediatrician and her office says, "Take her to Emergency, but in the minute or two before or in the car try to make her throw up," and gives several ways of doing it, and he tries and his wife tries and Fanny throws up, but nothing like chewed-up or dissolved aspirins comes out, and they get her in the car, in the backseat with his wife, Fanny still crying now because of the throwing up and what they did to make her do it, he driving with the flashers on and horn blaring most of the time so he can go through red lights, and he carries her into the hospital, nurses and aides put her on a gurney and rush her into the emergency room to pump out her stomach, and while they're waiting outside the room he says things like "How could I have left the bottle there like that? I mean, I know why it happened and how. We had no children's aspirins or Tylenol and we both thought it too late for me to drive around looking for a store open to buy some, or I thought so more than you though we both knew she needed something to bring down her fever, so I cut a regular aspirin in half, or even a little less than half, and pulverized it, and gave it to her on a spoon with sugar and water . . . but leaving the bottle there? On her dresser so close to the crib and no safety cap on it? I don't even know if I screwed it closed, for Christ's sake. How could I have been so thoughtless, so stupid, so everything?" and she says, "Shut up, shut up already, it'll be all right, we got here in time. And if she really took too many she would have been sick to her stomach and thrown up long before she got so delirious, I'm sure of that," and he says, "You don't know," and she says, "I know, I don't know where but from someplace," and a doctor comes out of the room and he says to him, "How is it, she'll be all right, right?" and the doctor says, "What I don't understand is why'd you ever leave aspirins around like that, and not even the children's kind," and he says, "I'm sorry, it was my fault, I was the one who suggested she take half an adult aspirin, gave it, and left the bottle there . . . but how's she doing?" and the doctor says, "I don't know if you realize this or not but she can die," and his wife screams, and he says, "What are you talking about—you mean if we didn't get here in time or had her vomit most of it up?" and the doctor says, "No, I'm sorry, but I mean now," and goes back into the room, and he tries to follow and someone in the room stops him and says, "Please, we're busy, this is crucial, you're in the way," and he makes a complete sweep of the room for Fanny but doesn't see her past the three or four people working on her with their backs to him, and he goes outside and his wife's in a chair weeping and he sits beside her and holds her hands and says, "If anything terrible happens I'll die, I'll die." About fifteen minutes later the same doctor comes out and says, "Everything will be fine, parents. We got everything out and in fact there wasn't that much in there that could have done too much damage. Probably the most painful and traumatic thing for her was having the tube stuck down her throat into her belly, but kids bounce back quickly with things like this though her throat will be sore, and you can take her home in an hour"—he looks at his watch—"yes, possibly even less," and he says, "Thank you, thanks, but honestly, why the heck did you scare us like that, saying she could die?" and the doctor says, "At the time, based on the information you gave us, or the lack of accurate information, I thought it was the truth and I was angry, people like you—smart people, supposedly—leaving toxic substances around as if they were simply last night's dried jellied toast," and he says, "But it was an accident, a very stupid one but an accident," and the doctor says, "Still—but all right, perhaps I went overboard in my reaction," and walks away.

THEY BUY HER a sled for Christmas, take it to New York with them just in case it snows; they get about six to eight inches of it that morning and he goes to Riverside Drive and 116th Street with his two daughters to test the sled out and says to Fanny at the top of the fairly steep hill, "I think for the first couple of rides you should go on top of me to see how the steering works and other things," and Josephine, his younger daughter, says, "I want to go too, but just with Daddy," and Fanny says, "But it's mine and I know how to do it—I've been on the same kind on an even bigger hill in Baltimore," and he says, "You went down alone, last winter? Because up till today, perhaps, we haven't had any snow there this year," and she says, "With a friend. And I did it well and all the steering," and he says, demonstrating, "So you know to turn it left if you want to go this way and right to go this way?" and she's nodding, and he says, "It still feels tight, because it's so new, so you'll have to turn the bar hard . . . and there's one big tree at the bottom, so that, of course, isn't the direction you want to go," and she says, "Of course not, Daddy, and I'll never get that far anyway," and he says, "You never know; most of the snow seems flattened down by all the other sleds and disks and cardboard people are using," and she says, "I'm not going to steer to that tree. I'm only going where there are no trees, and straight," and he says, "If you run into any trouble—" and she says, "I know, I know," and he says, "Just listen; if a sled's stopped right in front of you and you can't steer out of the way in time, roll off, just roll off," and she says, "How do you do that?" and he says, "By letting go of the steering bar and rolling off into the snow and making sure the rope's not caught around any part of you and letting the sled go on without you," and she says, "Suppose there's a sled behind coming right at me after I roll off?" and he says, "There shouldn't be; there should be lots of spacing between the sleds going downhill," and she says, "Just suppose," and he says, "Then you're in trouble if you can't jump out of the way," and she says, "What if I jump out of the way in front of another fast sled?" and he says, "The chances of that also happening? Well . . ." and Josephine says, "Can't I go with you?" and Fanny says, "No, first time I want it alone," and he says, "So, have we worked everything out? Staying away, when you're sledding down, from the people walking back up the hill with their sleds?" and she nods and he jiggles the steering bar back and forth to loosen it a little but it seems to stay the same, good enough for steering but not sudden sharp turns, puts the sled down and points the front of it to the clearing at the bottom of the hill; she says, "You still don't have it going far enough away from that tree," and points it even more to the left and gets on the sled on her stomach, says, "Don't push me, I might be not ready and I don't need any help; I can do it with my boots," and he says, "My, you're the professional sledder," and she says, "I told you, I've done it before," and Josephine says, "Have a nice ride," and he says, "Maybe I should go to the bottom of the hill first, just in case," and Fanny says, "Why?" and he says, "You might go faster than you think, past the clearing and into the little sidewalk, or walkway, or whatever it is there, and there's a lamppost by it," and she says, "Nobody so far has gone that far, and if I do go all the way to the lamppost I'll be all slowed down," and he says, "So, you might as well get going, for I want to have a chance too with Josephine. And remember—" and she says, "I know, bring the sled up myself and on the side, out of the way of sleds going down," and he says, "Right," and she says, "Goodbye," and he says, "Wait'll that man goes," and the man to their right on his sled goes, and he says, "Give him about ten seconds . . . in fact, almost till he's at the bottom . . . now it's clear, he'll be nowhere near you, and nobody else is going, so go on," and she pushes herself off with her feet and starts down and picks up speed and is aimed straight for the clearing, nothing in her way, sled going faster than he thought it would with her forty to fifty pounds on it—must be a good sled, runners never used, so like ice sliding down ice—when it starts veering right and he yells, "Turn it slowly to the left, Fanny, turn it left!" but it continues going right and now it's heading for that tree, as if being pulled to it, and he yells, "Fanny, turn the sled left or roll off—roll off, Fanny, roll, roll!" and she goes into the tree—he's sure her head hit it first—and is thrown off, and he screams and runs down the hill and keeps yelling, "Oh, no, oh, my God, no!" and Josephine's somewhere behind him shouting, "Fanny! Daddy!" and he reaches the tree, she's on her back, doesn't seem to be moving, he thinks, Oh, Jesus, her fucking head, her head! and gets on his knees, her eyes are open, looking at the sky, not at him, and he says, "Fanny, my darling, Fanny, it's Daddy," and lifts her head up softly, she's bleeding a little from just above her eye, and he says, "Oh, my poor dear," and her eyes move to him and she says, "I couldn't roll off; I was too afraid to; I didn't know how; I'm sorry," and he says, "We got to get you up the hill; a doctor, a hospital," and she says, "No, I think I'll be okay," and he says, "I'll carry you, or get some people to help me," and puts his arms under her shoulders and knees, and she says, "Are you picking me up? No, don't, Daddy, I just need to rest here; all I feel is dizzy," and he says, "You're really not feeling worse than that? No big headaches, pressure, something hurting terribly? Because I should do something," and she says, "I didn't hit the tree that hard, or didn't feel I did," and he says, "Let me at least do this for you, to keep down the swelling," because a welt's forming around her eye, and wipes the cut with his hanky, no new blood comes out, and puts snow around her eye and on the cut, and she screams and says, "Snow's cold and I'm getting wet, my face!" and he says, "Just stay with it a minute, that's all it'll take," and a few people are around them now, and every so often a sled zips past or stops with a sudden directional shift just a few feet from them, and he says, "This damn tree, I don't know how it happened. It's as if there was a magnet or some other kind of powerful attractor that pulled her right to it from the opposite direction or whatever she was trying to do to get away from it. I feel like chopping it down," and a man says, "She looks okay, talking, lucid, no bleeding from the nose or ears; those are good signs. Want me to help you carry her out of the park?" and she says, "I can walk by myself, but my sled—" and he says, "The back's bashed, I don't know why, you hit it from the front, but we'll get it fixed," and she says, "When?" and tries to get up, and he and the man help her stand and she starts walking and he's holding snow to her eye till she pushes his hand away; has the sled under his other arm and says, "Jesus, what a trooper—I'd sure let someone carry me if I'd just been hurt, but no, not her," and they trudge up the hill where Josephine, near the top, hands over her mouth, seems to be staring at them harriedly. "It's gonna be all right," he yells out, "she's gonna be okay. She's a big brave girl, hurt but in much better shape than your careless lunkhead daddy first thought."

IN THE CAR, heading for kindergarten, Fanny seated beside him with her lunch box and a tiny flexible Disney character on her lap, "Now we're on the peaks of Tunisia, making for the wee seaweed-green beach," and she says, "What do you mean? It's freezing today," and he says, "Imagination, you gotta try using it," and she says, "Are we late for school?" and he says, "We're going down a big hill, that's all, and on time, and after coasting on the crest of it, or cresting on the coast of it—okay, the first one, you like accuracy, one tap for the brake, two taps for a little squeeze," and taps her shoulder twice, a private signal between them, and she smiles and squeezes his arm, and he says, "What a babe," when he realizes the brake tap didn't slow the car any, and he taps it again, thinking maybe the first tap was too light, and it's not slowing but going faster, and he jams his foot down and nothing happens, and he says, "Oh, shit, the brakes, they're not working, what do I do?" and she screams and he yells, "Put your foot down—your voice—shut up!" and thinks, Emergency brake, and puts his foot on it and the car screeches and starts stopping, and he thinks, Curb, and steers the car right and goes over the curb—when he hoped it might stop the front wheels—and into the bushes and through about twenty feet of them, car slowing all the time, before a thin tree stops it. He looks at her. She's crying but all right, no cuts or blood, window's intact, no broken glass, and he says, "You didn't bang your head or any part when we were stopping, did you?" and she shakes her head, and he says, "Oh, God, now I can cry too," and starts crying and continues to for a minute or more, hands over his face, when she taps his shoulder and he doesn't respond and she squeezes his arm twice and he thinks, The signal? and looks up, thinking what a crazy time for her to want to play their game, for when she squeezes him first he's supposed to tap his foot on something twice as many times as she squeezed him—he doesn't know how they came to that ratio, maybe their heights—and she says, "It's over, Daddy, car's stopped. If it won't work now, can you walk me to school? I'll be late," and he says, "The engine," and turns it off and has her come out his door because hers is blocked by bushes.

HIS WIFE'S GIVING her a bath, he takes pictures of the two of them in the tub; then she says, "I'd like to shampoo but not in the tub with her; can you look after her till I come back or, if she wants to, just get her out and dry her?" and he puts down the camera, sits on the tub ledge, and his wife steps out, dries herself, and goes down the hallway to the other bathroom, and he says to Fanny, "Mommy wash you good or are you just in here for playing?" and she says, "Come in to play with me," and he says, "I'd have to take off my clothes and I don't want to. Anyway, I don't like going into dirty water. I like for my water to start out clean and then for me to dirty it. Or if I'm giving you a bath but am in the tub with you from the beginning, then for us to make it dirty and soapy together," when the phone rings, he yells "Sally, you in the shower yet?" and she says, "I'm on the toilet; let it ring," and he thinks how he hates to let a phone ring—who knows who it can be, something about his mother or something important concerning work?—when there's a big splash behind him—he's been facing the door since the phone rang—and he turns around and she's under the water, only her feet above it, and he shoves his hands in, water's murky, he can't see her, and quickly feels around and gets her under the arms and jerks her out and holds her up so he can see her face, and her head's slumped and her face has the look of a drowned person, or what he'd think would be one, water running out of her mouth and nose, the eyes looking lifeless, and he holds her upside down over his shoulder and slaps her back and she coughs and he slaps it again and says, "Cough, cough some more," and she chokes and he holds her right-end-up in front of him again and she spits more water out and he says, "You okay? Speak to me," and the shower in the other bathroom's going and she starts screaming and he says, "Jesus, you gave me a scare, what were you doing? Shh, shh, it's all right, you'll be okay now," and hugs her to his chest till she's only sobbing quietly. "And please, sweetheart, don't tell your mother"—sitting her on the toilet seat cover and drying her body with a towel—"if you do she'll never want to leave you alone with me anymore; you hear me, you hear?" and she nods, and he dries as much of her hair as he can and powders her and puts her bathrobe on her, she sobbing all the time. "What's the matter?" his wife says, standing at the door, hair wrapped in a towel. "And how'd you get your clothes so wet?" and he says, "Splashing . . . Fanny. And boy, that was a speedy shampoo. How'd you do it so fast?" and she says, "Was it faster than usual? Didn't realize. I guess I didn't think you'd want to be left with her so long; it can be boring if you're not in there splashing with her. Why's she crying? What's wrong, dearest?" and he says, "Maybe she was in there too long and the water got cold, or the air was when she got out," and lifts the rubber disk off the tub drain—regular stopper doesn't work—and the water goes. "I fell in," Fanny says to her, and he says, "Oh, just a little, and maybe that's what the crying is, but I always had her hand."

. . .

HE'S WAITING FOR the light to change on Amsterdam, cars roaring north past him, on his way to see his mother, got off the bus on Broadway, unfolded the stroller, and strapped Fanny in; now she's sleeping peacefully, head to one side, hair spilled over her face and both hands holding a shaggy stuffed animal, when a sudden breeze moves the stroller a little and he grabs the right cane-shaped handle with one hand and then a terrific wind and he's about to grab the other handle when the stroller's lifted a few inches off the ground and he lunges at it and misses and it's blown into the avenue and lands on its wheels a few feet away and starts rolling farther into the avenue as he runs after it and he grabs one of the handles and looks around, he's about ten feet into the avenue and no cars are near him and he pulls the stroller back to the sidewalk, cars and trucks going past fast and a couple of them honking at him no doubt, stupid man, taking a kid's life in his hands like that, why doesn't he wait till the light's green before crossing? He clutches the handles with both hands, backs up to a store window, can't believe it, where'd such a wind come from, how could it be so strong to lift a stroller with a kid in it? It means he can't let go of the stroller for a second when he's outside, or not till he's absolutely sure the air's calm and only when she's about ten to fifteen pounds heavier, but never on the street no matter how heavy she is, never. It could have rolled farther and would certainly have been hit by a car or truck and that would have been it, she would have been mangled and crushed, all her bones broken, the worst that he could think of and then some, head split open, limbs torn off and carried a few hundred feet, or maybe the stroller, with her strapped in it, carried or dragged a block before the car stopped *if* it stopped, and then other cars running over it and maybe even dragging the torn-off parts. Light's green but he stands there clutching the handles, shaking; wind's died down to nothing, or nothing he can feel, maybe it's because of where he's standing, up against a building, but maybe he's become numb, maybe that's it, from what just happened, but get off this damn Amsterdam, he thinks, it's a wind tunnel here, calm now, you think you're free of it and can push your stroller where you please, when it can suddenly pick up with even worse force than before, and he starts to cross but an approaching truck gives him the long horn and when he looks across the street at the traffic light he sees he's walking against it, "And with your kid," the driver yells out the window, "you fucking idiot!" He gets back to the sidewalk and waits till the light's green, always holding the handles tight. Then he starts across, eyes on the light and street, freezes when a car enters the avenue from the side street, but it's going to let him pass, he can make out a hand inside waving him on, and he mouths his thanks and runs across to the sidewalk and up the curb cut and looks at her, but she's slept through the whole thing, same position, hair blown over her forehead a different way, but not a peep.

SITTING AT HIS desk and looking out the bedroom window, just really staring into space to help him think how he wants to word something he's writing, when he sees her riding her bike onto the road from their driveway, and he yells, "Fanny! Fanny!"—regular windows and storm ones are closed but he yelled so loud she still might have heard him—and stands, and she keeps riding and now he can't see her because of the bushes and trees, and a car honks and then tires screech and he runs out of the bedroom for the door—it could have been one car honking and another coming the other way or behind it, screeching—and the living room door, not the kitchen one he usually uses because it opens onto the carport and is closest to the driveway—but no bang, he thinks, didn't hear one or a crash or scream so maybe she's okay—and gets out of the house and runs down the few feet of grass and across the little footbridge separating the road from their property and a woman's standing in front of a car in the middle of the far lane of the road, only car there and bike's not, and he yells, "Where is she?" from about thirty feet away, thinking, Was she hit clear into the bushes or the creek? or she could be under the car or back wheels, bike too, though the woman's expression isn't troubled or horrified enough for that, and the woman says, "The poor dear, I nearly hit her. She came out of nowhere—I was lucky to have good brakes—and she got so frightened she ran her bike up that hill"—pointing to his driveway—"didn't even jump back on it. You know her?" and he says, "She's my goddamn accident-prone daughter—she knows never to bike onto Charrenton alone, she knows it . . . so where are you, you damn brat?"—looking around—and the woman says, "Please don't blame her. I'm sure after that scare she'll never do it again," and he says, "Oh, you don't know her—she's always taking chances, thinks she knows better, always getting into near misses. Fanny! Fanny, goddammit, come back here! You've caused this woman and me some great grief, so I want you to apologize," and the woman says, "Really, it isn't necessary for me. And it wouldn't be the right time for it. She's probably cowering in seclusion like a scared rabbit. Just see to her, sir, I'm fine." She left her bike leaning against a carport post; she's not in the house and doesn't come home for two hours. He goes out looking for her in the car a couple of times: nearby market, which he's biked or walked to with her, homes of her best friends in the area. When she walks through the door he says, "Jesus, where the hell you been? And do you know what you did to that lady this afternoon?" and she says, "What lady? The one whose car almost hit me because I biked in front of her? I'm sorry," and he says, "A heart attack you almost gave her—no warning—not to say why you did it, riding alone there, and so dangerously, when you knew you shouldn't. But okay, I don't think I have to say any more about it, you know not to do it again," and she says yes. "Can I be excused now?" and he says, "Sure, go on," and she starts for her room, and he says, "Wait a second, where were you the last two hours?" and she says, "Walking around—at the drugstore for a while—I was safe and dressed warm," and he says, "Anyway, I don't think you should be let off so easily, so I'm going to dock your allowance this week," and she says, "What's that mean: I won't get it?" and he says, "That's right," and she says, "You're not being fair, and I don't care," and storms into her room and slams the door. "Fanny, come back here. I'm not kidding, you either come back and apologize for what you just said and did or it's going to be two weeks you're docked, even three, and no bike riding for that time either," but she doesn't come. "All right, if you hear me, that's it. The bike riding, I don't know about, if you stay off Charrenton, but I'm not changing my mind about the allowance—three weeks." Later he talks it over with his wife, how frightened he was. "Honestly, when I saw her biking onto the road and heard those car honks and tires, I thought she was going to get creamed," and she says, "You were right the way you first approached it—the scare punished her plenty—so don't make any more demands on her for it and without any fuss Saturday give her her regular allowance," and he says, "No way, absolutely not, maybe a two weeks' docking instead of three, but that's as far as I'm giving in or else my word will mean nothing," but on Saturday, when he's driving her to a swimming lesson and she's in the front seat, she says, "Excuse me, but can I have my allowance now?" and he says, "In the car, while I'm driving?" and she says, "Sorry, then when we get there?" and he says, "No, I can get it," and presses the catch to open the compartment under the dashboard, gets three dollars out of it, and gives them to her, though all the time remembering what he swore to her the other day and also later told his wife he absolutely wouldn't do.

POPSICLE STICKS to her tongue; she gags, points to it; he says, "You can't get it off?" and she shakes her head, and he says, "Pull gently, not hard, you don't want to rip something," and she tries but it doesn't come off, and he says, "Wiggle it a little," and she shakes her head and tears are welling and she looks panicky and is gagging again, and he says, "Jesus, what do I do?" and, to the vendor who sold it from a cart in the park, "What do you do in a situation like this?" and the man looks as if he doesn't understand, and Gould points to her and says, "Her tongue, the Popsicle's stuck to her tongue and she can't get it off," and the man says, "Dry ice, the dry ice," and raises his arms as if he doesn't know what to do either; then, after pointing to his own tongue and then inside his mouth, speaks a foreign language Gould's never heard before or can't place, and he says, "Speak English, English, she's gagging . . . choking," and makes choking sounds and points to her, and the man says, "No can, don't know, first time, ice cream, that's all . . . police, maybe police, go to police," and Fanny's gagging and crying and looks at him as if to say, Do something, Daddy, or I'll die, and he thinks she could choke to death if he doesn't get it off her tongue in the next minute, and the only way he can think of is to pull if not rip it off and that'll hurt like hell for her, and puts his fingers on her hand that's holding the stick; she screams in pain, and he says, "Oh, God, what else can I do, sweetheart?" and slides her fingers off the stick, grabs the Popsicle part, and pulls it off her tongue and quickly throws it on the grass. Part of the skin or whatever it is of the tongue came off with it, and she's screaming loud as he's ever heard her, and he gets on his knees and holds her and says, "It's all right now, darling, it's off, it's off," and pats her lips with his hanky where some blood's dribbling out, and a woman passing by says, "What happened to the little darling, she fall?" and he says, "She got a Popsicle stuck to her tongue—the dry ice, it must've been—but was gagging and I had to pull it off and some skin came with it," pointing to where he threw it, and the woman says, "You should have put warm water on the Popsicle, that would have dissolved the ice," and he says, "Where would I get the water? I'd have to walk her out of the park to Columbus, and that's a good ten minutes from here and she could've choked in that time. But now what do I do about the skin and her tongue?" patting her lips again, and the woman says, "There's a refreshment gazebo right down this path; they sell coffee, so they must have warm water. But the best thing for it now—and you'll think me mad but it's what I'd do for one of mine; after all, what you first want to do is get rid of her pain—is have her lick a Popsicle or frozen fruit bar, but one free of dry ice. That'll anesthetize it," and he says, "Which is better?" and she says, "Either, though plain ice, if he has it, would be simpler and, probably for her sake, best," and he asks the man, "You have any regular ice?" and the man shakes his head he doesn't understand, and he says, "Ice, like in a drink," and curls his hand as if he's holding a glass and then makes as if he's drinking from it, "Ice, ice, as in a glass with soda," and the man says, "No that ice, only dry," and he asks him for a fruit bar, and the man says, "What kind?" and he says, "Any," looks at the pictures of the flavors on the stand and says, "Lemon," and pulls out his wallet to pay for it—the man waves no with his hands—wipes the fruit bar on his shirt till all the white icelike part is off, blows on it till the side he's blowing on and wants her to put her tongue to looks wet, and says to her, "Here, touch this to the sore part of your tongue, sweetheart. . . . Fanny, calm down a moment, you have to stop crying—I know how much it hurts but both this woman and I and the man here think it'll make your tongue feel better and take away the pain," and holds it up to her mouth and she knocks it out of his hand and resumes screaming.

HE'S LET INTO his in-laws' apartment (always the same way: one of them looks through the peephole, then unlocks three or four locks and unfastens the bolt and chain), says, "So, how'd it go?" and his father-in-law says, "We had a terrific time together, didn't we? . . .

Fanny? Where is she? She was just behind me, wanted to greet you at the door. Fanny, come, please, your father's here. . . . Well, this is a mystery," and Gould looks around and down the narrow side hall to the kitchen and sees the window's half open and says, "Excuse me, but are all the windows opened high like that? I thought I asked you only to open them on top and out of her reach and close them at the bottom to a few inches," and his father-in-law says, "Oh, well," and looks sheepish about it, "from now on we will; I can understand your concern," and Gould runs around the apartment; his mother-in-law's office window is open a foot, bedroom window's closed, but the dining room windows are open at the bottom a foot and a half. "Fanny, no jokes on me now, will you please come out?" and his father-in-law says, "Don't worry, she didn't fall out; she's a smart girl, I'm sure she's only hiding," and Gould runs to the living room, only room left in the apartment—except for the two bathrooms and there the windows are small, tough to raise, and pretty high, though she could step on the toilet seats to reach them—and sees her behind the sheer floor-length curtain climbing up to a window opened about two feet, one knee on the sill, other foot tangled in the end of the curtain but leaving the floor, and he thinks, I'll never reach her in time, and doesn't know if this'll stop her or scare her where she'll fall forward instead of back but shouts, "Fanny, come down!" and she stops in mid-position and turns her head to him and smiles, and he says, walking to her, "The window's open, my darling, don't you see that? You know what Daddy's said about that. To stay away from open windows, never climb up to them, and if you see one in an apartment or house you're in, to ask an older person to shut it. So come away from it immediately—get down, right now!" and she steps down, seems as if she's about to cry, and he says, "No, don't cry, it isn't your fault and I'm not angry," and takes her hands, kisses them, and presses her face to his belly, and says to his father-in-law, "Jesus, Phil, why do I even bother? Listen, please, and no offense—but you got to, you got to, for you saw what she can do," and Phil says, "I'm truly sorry, it got hot; I thought it was too early in the spring to use the air conditioners and we hadn't had them serviced yet this year. . . . I didn't think what I was doing, that's all—never again," and she looks up at Gould and says, "Are you mad at Grandpa?" and he says, "No, why would I be? You don't get mad at people older than you—no, that's not true—but your grandpa's the nicest guy in the world, much nicer than me, so I'd never get mad at him," and squeezes Phil's shoulder.

SWIVELS AROUND, SHE's not there, looks around and there are hundreds of people, kids and adults, woman carrying two small dogs, walking all around him, but he doesn't see her, scans the area again; where the hell could she be? "Dammit," he says, "doesn't she know better?" Dashes into the store they just came out of and quickly looks around—"Anything I can do for you, sir?"—and he says, "My girl, this high," and puts out his hand to show how tall, "blondish hair . . . well, blond, almost bright blond, and I was just in here with her and thought she came out with me," and the man says, "Oh, they can get away from you very fast, can't they," and he says, "Yes, but did you see her, long hair hanging past her shoulders—combed down, kind of wavy—and about that high"—his hand out again—"and very pretty?" and the man says, "I don't remember you from before, did I take care of you?" and he says, "No, we were just browsing; in fact, she dragged me in," and looks around the store again, man's saying something to him, but he runs out and stands about twenty feet in front of the store and starting from the last store to his left before the escalators makes a complete sweep of the area and then, a little faster, sweeps back again, then turns around and does the same kind of sweep of all the stores there and the little public rest section, thinking, What the fuck, where is she? Goddamn kid, why's she always running off like this? Man, when I find her I'll really let her have it! and goes inside the first store to the left of the one he was just in, a pipe and cigar shop, though he doesn't think she'd ever go there—the tobacco smells, but he's being thorough—looks quickly around and then goes into the next three stores to the left and then the stores to the right of the one they were in, five of them—in a large one, with lots of aisles, dresses, and displays concealing most of the place, he says loudly, "Fanny, are you there? Fanny?"—and then outside in the public walking area he thinks, How far could she have wandered off? Maybe some guy grabbed or enticed her and is putting her into his car now, or just now taking her out of one of the ground-floor doors and walking with her to his car in the lot, or just approaching one of those doors and walking her somewhere, maybe to some out-of-the-way spot like where the garbage trucks pick up most of the refuse here, when he remembers the large square pool they passed in the center of the mall under the glass rotunda at the end of the long corridor they came in; she wanted to stop there and look at the fish in it, and he said, "Later, I came in for something, first we do the shopping; then if we have time we do the snacking and fun," and runs to it, about three hundred feet away, keeping an eye out for her as he runs, and she's sitting on a little wall around the pool and looking at the water, probably the fish inside, and walks the rest of the way to her. Jesus, does she ever get to me sometimes, he thinks, and says, "Fanny," and she continues looking at the pool, hands folded on top of her purse on her lap—he forgot the purse, which he also would have mentioned to the man in his description of her—and he says, "Fanny, listen," and she turns her head to him and says, "The fishies are so big here, can we take one of them home?" "From here? To home?" He sits beside her; what's he going to do, teach her another lesson? He can talk about it in the car. "Don't wander off. You wander off and it scares me. You don't understand what can happen to you. You can be stolen. I hate telling you that, but you can. You're beautiful, and little girls and boys are sometimes stolen by horrible men, and the more beautiful ones the most." He said that to her once and she said, "By women too. At school I learned that," and he said, "Your teacher told you?" and she said, "A policeman at assembly came in," and he said, "So, he's right," and she said, "The policeman was a woman with a gun," and he said, "Then she's a policewoman, and she was right, but kids are stolen mostly by men." So he sits with her and says, "Not that we can take one—the mall owns them all and we'd get stopped by a guard and maybe fined lots of money and perhaps even barred for life; the last thing I said's an exaggeration—but which fish do you like best and would take home if you could?" and she says, "A big orange and black one with stripes; it was here before but now it's gone."

SITTING IN THE enclosed patio of a restaurant in New York having lunch with a friend. Fanny's in her stroller beside him, was sleeping while he and the friend ordered, but now stretches her arms up to him, wants to be unstrapped, maybe changed or just held, but taken out. Hears a noise from the street, something rumbling, getting louder, sounding as if it's rolling around loose inside the container of a truck. His friend's sipping a beer, eyes closed dreamily. "What's that?" and his friend opens his eyes and says, "Wha'? Talking to me?" and he says, "That noise, don't you hear it?" and his friend shuts his eyes and makes a pretense of listening a couple of seconds and says, "Noise?" People on the sidewalk by the patio are now looking up Columbus where the noise and traffic are coming from. Then one of them points and shouts, and they all run in different directions on the sidewalk; one man makes a move to bolt into the street and then jumps behind a car, and Gould stands and sees in the street about a hundred feet away a wooden cable spool, must be six to seven feet high, rolling down the street at an angle straight for the cars parked adjacent to the patio. Must have fallen off the back of a truck and landed upright and started rolling and picked up momentum, and now it's heading for the one free parking space, between two cars, and their window table. He glances at Fanny—she's still sitting up with her arms out, looking as though she's hearing the noise and is wondering what it is—and he yells to his friend, who's back to sipping his beer with his eyes closed, "Watch out—duck!" and throws himself on Fanny, knocking her stroller over but covering her, and listens for glass to smash but is later told by his friend—who said, "I never moved, didn't budge, figured if I'm about to die, I'll die, so no use fighting it, though I did keep my eyes open to see my own death, if that's what happened"—that the spool jumped the curb and hit dead center a thin parking signpost on the sidewalk and somehow didn't knock it down or roll over it and keep coming but dropped flat on its side and wobbled, the way an ordinary thread spool would, before stopping. How come nothing like this ever happened to Josephine? Why always Fanny? There was also the time she was in her car seat in back of their car and his wife didn't engage the emergency brake far enough when she parked, and the car started rolling backward after his wife got out of the driver's seat, and she screamed and he looked out the living room window of the house they were living in at the time and the car started down the steep hill and could have gone maybe all the way down till it crashed but was stopped about twenty feet away by the front bumper of the one car parked anywhere near their home on that side of the street. Josephine's fallen on thin ice she was skating on but didn't crack it, ran into a door or a wall a few times and bumped her head and saw stars but never cut it, fell off a chair arm she was sitting on and sprained her hand, if it was even that; he took her to Emergency (didn't want to, since didn't think it serious enough, and only did it because his wife and a doctor friend over the phone thought it the safest thing to do), and they waited for four hours and her hand was x-rayed and he was told it wasn't broken and probably not even sprained and she was given a sling to wear a day or two but, because she liked the attention she was getting, wore it for more than a week; when she was around five and had only till then swum by herself a few feet at a time she suddenly started swimming to the deep end of the pool, and he yelled, "Josie, stop right there!" but she kept swimming and he thought, Maybe she can do it, and swam beside her and she did the doggy paddle all the way and when she reached the other end and held on to the edge of the pool and was panting he said, "Fantastic, who knew you were such a great swimmer, the entire length of a long pool, congratulations, but from now on—" and she started to swim back to the shallow end, and he said, "Stop, that's enough, both lengths are too much, you're exhausted from the first one; I was just going to say that from now on you wait for Mommy or me before you try another swim like that," but she kept swimming and he swam beside her and she made it without any help from him. But that's about as close as it got to a real accident or mishap with her in her first eight years, and nothing he or his wife did ever put her in danger. He doesn't understand it.

The Motor Cart

WAS IT ONLY last week when some guy called and said, "Hi, you Mr. Booksomething?" and he said, "Yeah, Bookbinder, what can I do for you?" and the man said, "Good, I got you. You don't know me but your wife gave me your number and a quarter and said to say she's at Broadway and a Hundred-eleventh, north corner of the street on the east side of the avenue; that's what directions she told me to give," and he said, "What's wrong, she hurt, spill over?" and the man said, "No, but she told me to say her motor cart stopped dead while she was riding it and she can't get it started. I was passing by and she asked would I push her to a phone booth a few feet away, so me and another guy did, but the phone was broken, the whole change part where the coins come down ripped open. And because we couldn't push her to the next nearest booth a block away, or she didn't want us to—the cart weighs a ton and she said it was too hot for us to do it, and much as I hate to admit it, she was right: we would have died—she told me to say you should come with the wheelchair so she can get off this hot street and home. So I called you and you know where she's at and you're coming, right?" and he said, "One-eleventh, northeast corner," and the man said, "I guess it's the northeast—right by the Love drugstore or a few stores away, but downtown from it and that side of Broadway," and he said, "Got it. But you're sure she isn't hurt, just the cart that won't operate?" and the man said, "Altogether stalled. This guy and me gave it a hefty push to see if we could turn over its engine like a car's after she started it, but it wouldn't because it only runs on batteries, she said, and she tried every other which way and she needs the wheelchair. And if you could hurry, she said, that'd be great, and if I didn't get you would I come back to tell her. But I got you, right?—you're her husband," and he said, "Yes, and thanks very much, sir, very kind, for everything," and the man hung up.

Now they're in the country, five hundred miles away, it's sunny and cool, city's still hot, they hear on the radio every day, and he was glad to get out of it for another reason, because every time she left the apartment something awful seemed to happen to her. He thought, after he spoke to the man, What's he going to do now? He can't leave the cart on the sidewalk while he pushes her home in the chair, and she can't get home in the chair on her own. The cart he can dismantle, as he's done a couple of times when its lift didn't work and he had to get it into the rear of the van by hand, batteries disconnected and removed, seat taken off, and back and pole separated from it, and so on, and he can get the five or six parts into a taxi and carry them to the apartment from the cab and get someone to fix the cart there. But the cart cost more than two thousand and is still in pretty good shape and not insured, so he doesn't want to leave it on the street to be stolen. He can wheel her into an air-conditioned store, he thought, then break down the cart, get it to the apartment and come back for her, unless she has to get home immediately for some reason. But some way, he thought; he hasn't figured it all out yet. Maybe he can drag the cart into a store and say it's worth five bucks to him if they just keep it there for a half hour or so while he wheels his wife home, though he doesn't think any store person would accept money for something like that. Then he went downstairs, wanted to run the four blocks and one long street to where she was, but it was very hot and sticky out and he ran about two blocks, stopped because he was breathing so hard, and suddenly sweat burst out of what seemed every part of him and he said, "Dummy, what're you doing running in the sun?" and walked quickly in the shade, mopping his head and neck and arms with a handkerchief and, when that was soaked, with his T-shirt.

He wants to call his mother today but it's so cool up here (and he knows how hot it is in New York) that he doesn't want to hear how bad it is for her. The room she stays in in her apartment is air-conditioned and he hopes the air conditioner's working, but she can't get out, she's stuck in that room because of the heat and what it does to her breathing, and she knows she'll probably be stuck like that for the next few days, which is how long the radio and newspaper say the heat wave's going to continue there.

When he got to her she was sitting in the cart with her back to him, holding a quarter between her fingertips and looking at the people on the sidewalk coming toward her. "Sally," he said, and she turned to him and grinned and said, "Oh, wonderful, it's you; I was just looking for someone to phone you. I was beginning to think the man I asked hadn't done it," and he said, "No, he got me, was very nice and precise: a good choice, followed your orders to a T-shirt—I only say that because mine's soaked and I want you to know I know it—and repeated your message just the way you gave it, it seemed. Jesus, it's hot. What the hell is it with this weather? Why would anyone ever want to live here, and for the old Dutch, even settle here?" and she said, "But he wouldn't even wait till I wrote your name and phone number on a paper. Just said he'd remember and would call you from the next street where he knows another public phone is, and, if that one's broken, then the street after that, and took my quarter and flew off." "Well, he did his job; I'd ask him anytime. Now, what's the problem, other than the thing not moving?" and got on his knees and checked to see that all the wires were connected, and she said, "We went through that twice, some men here and I. In fact, one of them who said he's an auto technician, but not of battery-operated vehicles, traced every one of those lines," and he said, "It doesn't need new batteries; we got these two last winter and they're supposed to be good for at least two years, and I only recharged them yesterday," and she said, "The day before, but I haven't used it much since, so that can't be it." He pulled out one of the battery containers, unplugged and opened it, and she said, "Wait, where's the wheelchair?" and he looked around and said, "Oh my gosh, I didn't bring it. I was in such a rush to get here. . . . I'll run back for it," and she said, "But what am I going to do in the meantime? I have to pee," and he said, "Wait wait wait," and looked inside the container, everything seemed to be in order, closed it and went around to the other side of the cart and unfastened and unplugged and pulled out that container, opened it and saw a nut was loose, the end of some inside wire barely around the battery rod or whatever it's called; and he wrapped the wire tightly around the rod, tightened the nut with his fingers, closed both containers and slid them back onto their platforms and fastened them in and replugged the outside wires and said, "You might be moving, don't get startled," set the speed dial to the lowest number, pushed the starter key all the way in, pressed the right side of the driving lever and the cart moved forward a few feet, pressed the left side and it went into reverse, and pulled the key halfway out of the starter so the cart wouldn't move. "You did it," she said, "it's working," and he said, "Really, I hardly knew what I was doing. Just figured it was maybe like a lamp that isn't working because of a loose wire, or one that isn't insulated right—the wire, I mean—and is causing some kind of short," and she was beaming and said, "It's amazing. Not even the professional auto mechanic could figure it out or even consider that that's what it could be," and he said, "He didn't have a vested interest to look deeper. . . . I bet he didn't even have a vest. Believe me, if it was his own wife—" when a young man said to her, "So, you got him," and she said, "And he got it working," and put the key all the way in and pressed the lever and the cart moved backward a foot, and the man said, "Fantastic, you didn't need your wheelchair," and she said to Gould, "This is the gentleman who called you," and the man said, "Hiya," and then, to them both, "Well, see ya," and Gould said, "Thanks for calling me; again, that was very kind," and walked beside her as she drove on the sidewalk toward home, thinking, She's got to feel good about what he did, not so much in him coming but in figuring out what was wrong and fixing it, when someone tapped his shoulder; it was the young man, who said, "Listen, buddy, long as things are working now, I was thinking my call to you's worth a few bucks, don't you think that?" and he said, "Jeez, I don't know . . . I mean, you only made a phone call," and she said, "I do, give it to him; he went out of his way," and he said, "But he was heading that way—weren't you?" to the man, and the man said, "Sure, but I had to stop, wait for some guy to finish his call; that took me out of the way: in time," and he said, "Well, you should be feeling good just that you did something good like that. Why does it always have to be money?" and she said, "Please, Gould, stop arguing and do it. He also helped push me to the broken phone with another man, and in this weather, and he would have pushed me to the next corner if I hadn't told him not to," and the man said, "The lady's right, I forgot I wanted to do that," and he said, "Still, who wouldn't do it for anybody? I'm just saying—" and the man said, "Hey, what am I asking for? I go out of my way, work up a fat sweat for her, then ask for a few dollars after, and you're holding back when your lady says to give?" and she got her wallet out of her belt bag, and Gould put his hand over it and said, "No, I'll do it, don't worry; but I just can't see why people don't stop and do these things all the time for people who are in trouble, and never with any thoughts of money in mind," and the man said, "I didn't for money. It's something I only thought of asking for now. And it's fine if you don't need the cash and do these things, but I'm tight now and a little extra would help," and he said, "Rich, medium income, or poor, even: everyone, if he or she has the strength, should stop. And when you don't do it for any kind of remuneration—money and stuff; a payback, as my dad liked to say—then you know you're really doing something good," and the man said, "Oh, screw it, man," and to Sally, "This here what you were about to give?"—she was holding a five—and Gould said, "Not five bucks, that's way too much," and she said, "It would have cost us that much to get the cart home in a cab," and he said, "Yes, but a cabby's got to charge; a Good Samaritan, though . . . well, one can't be called that if one's going to ask for money and take it," and the man said, "I was what you said then, a Good what you said—I know what it is. But now, seeing how it all worked out so nice for you, I thought I could use the money and you'd feel good in giving it because of the way it went," and Gould said, "Boy, does he have a line. Anyway, I give up," and walked away and stopped, his back to them, and thought, She's probably giving the guy the five; or maybe he's now saying "Actually, if you have a ten that'd be even better," and she'd give that too. She gives and gives. Whatever charity or institution or organization sends her an envelope through the mail asking for a donation, for this or that cause except for some blatantly crazy or politically antipathetic one, she writes out a check. "What's three dollars?" she's said, or "four," or "five," and he's said, "Not worth the time to write out the check and for them to cash it. But they put you on their sucker list, and other charities and do-gooding and -badding organizations buy those lists and every other month send you requests for dough, and you give three to five bucks to them without checking if they're legit or if ninety percent of the money they collect goes to soliciting that dough. And you also get on those groups' lists, and they're sold, and so on and so on, till we end up getting six to seven solicitations a day through the mail or over the phone and some so preposterously unethical in the way they ask for money—URGENT it'll say on what looks like an authentic express letter when it's actually been sent bulk rate—that they ought to be reported to the attorney general of the state," and she's said, "Now you're exaggerating," and he's said, "Maybe, but only by a little," or "Hardly—I've barely touched the tip of the icepick." She pulled up to him right after the incident with the man and said, "Now that was unnecessary," and he said, "I'll clue you in as to what was unnecessary," and she said, "Listen, sweetie, he helped me when I needed help the most, and that counts for something," and he said, "He weaseled five to ten bucks out of you for what should have been . . . well, I already said too much about what it should have been for: the good feeling he was supposed to get," and she said, "It could be he not only feels good now that he helped me but also feels a few measly dollars richer. So what's wrong with that if you're hard up for cash?" and he said, "Ah, you schmuck, you know nothing," and she said "What!" and he said, "Sorry," and she said, "No you're not; screw you too, you bastard," and rode off, and he walked after her, and when she turned the corner at their street he thought, Oh, the hell with her, and ducked into the bookstore there to look through the literary magazines, and he wasn't in there a minute, holding a new magazine he hadn't known of but which looked good because of the artwork on its cover, when he thought, Will she make it all right into the elevator? She can do it by herself most times, but sometimes the cart gets stuck, especially when she backs out of the elevator into the lobby or hallway, and if she has to pee badly she can get flustered opening the apartment door and working the cart into the foyer; and he put the magazine back and left the store and ran down the block and caught up with her at the elevator, and the moment he stopped, sweat burst out of him again, even from his legs this time, it seemed, and he stood beside her, wiping his face with his wet handkerchief and then with the bottom of his wet shirt, till the elevator came and she drove the cart inside it while he kept his hand over the slot the door comes out of; then he got in and pressed their floor button and they rode up silently, she staring at the wall she faced.

Fritz

MAN LOOKS AT him and Gould thinks, Oh, no, is he going to do it again? and the man looks at his face even harder with the look I-know-you-from-someplace, and Gould says, “Hi,” and the man says, “Fritz?” and he says, “You know, you did the same thing last summer when we first saw each other, and I was almost going to head you off this time when you looked at me as if you knew me from a long time ago.” “I did it before? I thought you were Fritz?” and he says, “Yeah, at the market in town . . . really, maybe the first week after I got up here, just like now. And I asked you who you meant and you told me and I said what a coincidence because he was my music teacher at City College in New York. Not so much my music teacher but the head of the chorus, and I had tried out for it when I heard they were doing the *German Requiem*. And though—this is what I told you then—I had wanted to be a tenor in the chorus, he—” and the man says, “Have people done this to you before? Not just me but do others mistake you for him?” and he says, “No. I mean, why would they? Excuse me, it could be you haven’t seen him for years, but he’s got to be thirty years younger than me—I mean, of course, older." "Not thirty, I don't think. And I saw him recently, or maybe not recently, but certainly in the last five to ten years, and closer to five, and he can't be thirty years older than you," and he says, "You're the violist for the quartet at the Hall," and the man says, "One of two of them—we alternate on the programs—and for trios, quartets, duos, anything we do, and I'm part of the faculty in the summer program there too. So, nice to see you, sir," and he says, "Not at all," and the man—who's been holding a tray with two fried clam rolls on it and a can of soda and what's probably an iced coffee, since the drink is dark and there are two half-and-halfs and some sugar packets and a stirrer next to the cup—goes to an outside picnic table where a woman's sitting. Gould recognizes the woman from some of the Sunday afternoon concerts he went to last summer with his wife and a couple of times with his kids.

"Why'd you say, 'Not at all,' when the man said, 'Nice to see you'?" his older daughter says, and he says, "Did I? I'm sure he knows I meant, Yes, it has been—you know: 'Thank you very much. . . . Not at all,' meaning—well, 'You don't have to thank me,'" and she says, "That's different; then you're answering him. I'm sure he felt insulted, that you were saying it wasn't at all nice to meet him," and he says, "And I'm sure he didn't feel that and that he didn't even hear my response to his 'So nice to see you, sir.' He's probably now telling his wife, 'I can't believe it. For the second summer in a row I thought that man—you see him standing there with the girl, waiting for his order to be called?—was Fritz Sepulska. You remember, the pianist who has a summer home around here or, for all I know, now lives here full time. Fritz looks just like him, or did till a few years ago, when I last saw him. The resemblance is remarkable: same hairline, long face, the nose, height, slender build, narrow eyes. You'd think he'd be mistaken daily by people who know Fritz up here—he's very well known, particularly because of all the musicians around—and that if Fritz ever saw him he'd think he was seeing his long-lost never-known twin brother, or his brother a couple of years younger than him. But this guy says he's thirty years younger, or at least twenty-five. He can't be. Maybe he doesn't take care of himself and Fritz does; I know Fritz used to work out rigorously and was pretty much a teetotaler. And somehow because of that—well, other than for disease and drugs, nothing ruins you faster than heavy drinking, right?—and though there might be a vast age difference, they're physical look-alikes. Now you can see him; he's picking up his order. But actually, with a child that age . . . no, she's probably his granddaughter, not his own kid. In fact, maybe it *is* Fritz and he doesn't want to talk to me for some reason, or to anyone. But he said I made the same mistake last year, and I remember it, though not as well as he; he says it was in the market in town. But he could still be Fritz, and last year when he told me that it was also because he didn't want to speak to me or anyone. I haven't heard anything about this, but maybe Fritz has become a recluse of sorts, or simply gone nuts or lost his memory through some disease, so he doesn't even remember who he is. But then why wouldn't the girl have said something? "Excuse me, sir, but Grandpa Fritz has had some trouble the last few years. . . ." Anyway, if he isn't Fritz—and really, he can't be; Fritz would have to be seventy-five by now, possibly eighty; he's been retired from teaching for ten to fifteen years, if my memory's right—then what do you think this man does, something in music or a related field? Certainly not a violist or violinist—no permanent abrasion under his chin from years of pressure of the instrument's body. He has the slumped posture and slight pot of a pianist, and I didn't look at his fingers and hands, but they could be as long and strong as a pianist's too. He also has the face of a musician—the unhealthy complexion and head lost in sounds. And, like most of us, not a very deep intellectual look, since I have to admit we don't read much but music scores and occasional escapist literature when we have the time, or have much interest in any other art or interpretive form or theory or even news but music. In other words, we're typically not big thinkers. We feel and express—that's us—and without that and the hours of practice we have to put in a day, what would we be? I bet that he's a high school music teacher who was trained as a serious pianist for a number of years but loves jazz and hated practice and rehearsals and in college where he got his education degree to teach music he played in an extemporaneous ragtime band and might even have been a disc jockey on the college radio station. And that those two kids—you see the second one who just joined him? Even younger than the first—are from a second marriage. And that he also has two from his first marriage, but they're grown up and maybe in college or past it and are interested in becoming, just as these two will be, anything but musicians or music teachers because of their father's meager income and displeasure with the profession. And his wife, the present one. Well, I don't know what she does; usually they're opera singers or musicians, or have been trained to be, or music teachers too. But for some reason I think she's very much like the first—in looks, build, hair color, and the way the hair's combed—and that both of them resemble his mother. But I see her reading a lot of serious books—women musicians are different that way from men—that she checks out of the library in town, every so often firing a piece she's made in some pottery class and cooking gourmet meals from recipes she's cut out of the *New York Times*. What he must be thinking of me, though? "Is that guy clear out of his head? Does he forget notes and whole musical passages when he plays as much as he forgets faces and potentially embarrassing mistakes from year to year?" Well, I can tell him I didn't forget his face; that I actually remembered it but put the wrong name to it, not that if he told me his a dozen times I'd remember it. I'm saying, I bump into him by mistake once a summer, so why should I be expected to remember his name or not to mix it up with someone else's every now and then? While he must see my name and photo in the program notes if he goes to the Hall's concerts, and I'm almost certain he does: a Sunday-goer with the wife—kids left with friends—rather than the Friday night concerts, since they don't want to leave their children with friends too late or at home alone. Or he's saying, "You see that gentleman over there?" Saying this now to his kids. "He's one of the two violists for the Hall's artist-faculty concerts and also a viola teacher of young student artists who come up to the Hall's chamber music school for seven weeks. He's pretty much a hotshot in his field, having helped found the Razumovsky Quartet, which was one of the best in America for many years. And from what I read in the local newspaper last year and in the area's arts free weekly just last week, he's made a couple of recordings and been a soloist over the last thirty years with some of the leading orchestras and chamber ensembles in this country and abroad, as well as being the principal violist for the Metropolitan Opera. Now why he thinks I'm Fritz Sepulska is a mystery to me. But you kids like to read mysteries—Nancy Drew and such—so maybe you can solve this one for me. Because do I look so old? Sepulska's got to be approaching eighty. So let's say this violist's eyesight isn't too good . . . so because of that we'll add ten years to the Fritz he sees. In other words, and not to get too confusing, though he thinks of me as eighty, he sees me as seventy but feels that's what a healthy eighty-year-old man looks like . . . but do I look that? Even sixty? I thought I looked pretty good for my age—fifty, maybe; possibly forty-five. I haven't lost all my hair and my jaw hasn't begun to slack, and my neck, in only the last year, I think, is beginning to get wrinkled and also a little hollow in front the way the necks of most older people do. And that pot that people past fifty-five seem to have no matter how thin they are and how much they purge themselves and exercise—well, that's starting to show despite every countermeasure I take, including sucking in my stomach while holding my breath. And the gray, if not even the white hair in places, like the sideburns and on my chest; and those webbed feet, I think they're called, off the ends of my eyes, and that deep quarter-moon gash running around both sides of my mouth . . . you know," and, as would seem with this guy, because of the inarticulate way he spoke to me, he shows with his fingers what he means, since he doesn't have the words to explain it. "But my posture's pretty good—sturdy, straight, I'm not bent over at all—and my ankles are still strong and not turned in and my legs don't wobble and shake. And my arms because of the stretch band and ten-pound dumbbells I work out with are as solid if not solider than they were when I was twenty or thirty and never exercised. How old do you two think I look? Be honest," and his younger daughter says, "When will they be ready with our order?" and he says, "Everything's freshly made here, though maybe a little preprepared, so if it had come out in a minute or two I'd have wondered how far in advance the dishes had been cooked," and the older one says, "Shouldn't we have ordered the large portion of potato skins? It's only fifty cents more and you get twice as many pieces," and he says, "Listen, last time we did, you left half of it here," and she says, "We had what was left wrapped and took it home with us," and he says, "And threw it out several days later. This time, you finish the small order, you can get another small order, and the second one will come out hot like the first one, just the way you like it, and with a new container of sour cream. But my biceps," he says to them, "my forearms and arms—I mean, they're not, they couldn't be—the arms of a seventy-five- to eighty-year-old man. No man that age could have arms as solid and thick as mine, and if he did—well, it'd be highly unusual. And I just don't see a musician—and a pianist, no less, who has to take such delicate care of his hands and arms, and one still playing as I'm sure Sepulska does. Those guys never stop practicing and performing, with some of them in their nineties, and one of them—Mishaslavski or something—a hundred, but still banging away onstage when they're long past remembering their own names, even, or at least the names of their children. Anyway, I don't see any musician my age, except maybe a bass player or tympanist, and both of them mostly from dragging their instruments around, having the arms I do," and his younger daughter says, "Show us your arm muscles. You always say you will someday but never do," and he says, "It's too silly. I did it as a young boy and later as a joke to girlfriends, but I couldn't do it anymore and for sure not here," and she says, "You can say we're now your girlfriends. Just show them once and we'll never ask again, agreed?" she says to her sister, and the older girl says, "Okay, agreed," and he says, "When we're in the car maybe, or sitting down here, if no one's around or looking, and very quickly," and the younger girl says, "Good," ' " when a woman in the enclosed stand where they take the orders and make the food yells over the loudspeaker, "Ninety-two!" and Gould says, "That's us, or maybe she's saying how old she thinks I am . . . anyone want to bet?" and Fanny says, "Don't be funny, Daddy," and goes to the pickup window in the stand, their tray's waiting, and she carries it to a picnic table—the man's at the next table and looks at them and smiles and turns back to his wife—and Gould says to his daughters, "Ready?" and Josephine says, "Ready what?" and he says, "The muscle thing," and Fanny says, "But people are around, and that man who called you Fritz is looking," and he says, "Shh, don't rub it in by repeating it so he hears; I don't want him thinking something's wrong with his memory—older people get very sensitive about that, think maybe their mind's going or something," and raises his arms and flexes his biceps, and Fanny touches one and Josephine the other, and Fanny says, "Oh, they're big, like the poster I saw of a big hockey star without his shirt," and Josephine says, "Where'd you see that, in one of your teen magazines?" and he glances at the next table, and the man and his wife are looking at him and the man shakes his head, not disapprovingly, really no expression whatsoever that says anything, and looks away, and the woman nods while she smiles and seems to mouth something to him like, "Very pretty girls."

"I don't know why I did that with my muscles before," he tells the girls a minute later. "I'll have to think about it," and Fanny says, "You wanted to get it over with because we've bothered you about it for so long, that's all," and he says, "No. Anyway, enjoy your food," and Josephine says, "Why don't you ever have something but black coffee? You never eat anything when we come here or go out anywhere for snacks," and he says, "I have a good time just watching you two eat it all up." When he looks over again, the couple's gone. "I know why," he says to the kids. "So the man won't call me Fritz again, not that I didn't like it—I'd love it as my name," and Fanny says, "But what about?" and he says, "These," crossing his arms at the wrists to point to his biceps.

His Mother Again

HE CALLS UP his mother. He's in the country; she's in the city. Said he'd call the day he got here, and it's been three days and it's the first time he's called. Her helper answers, and he says, "Hi, it's Gould," and she says, "How are you, sir?" and he says, "Fine, thanks, how's Bea?" and she says, "Who?" and he says, "Bea, this is her son," and she says, "I know that, sir, she's told me about you, but I didn't know she went by that name. I thought 'Beatrice.' She's well as can be expected," and he says, "Why, anything wrong? I tried calling a couple of times yesterday but nobody answered, so I suppose you were out," and she says, "No, yesterday we didn't leave the house. It was too hot; she only wanted to rest inside," and he says, "Is it still hot? It was quite warm up here the last two days—humid, even, which we don't get much—but cooled off today, strong winds and a cloud cover, so no hot sun," and she says, "Very hot: steaming, the TV said." "Oh, I'm sorry, I know how miserable it can get there," and she says, "It's New York, the summer, so you live with it. Your mother—what an attitude!—she keeps saying it can't last forever. Here, I'll get her," and she says, away from the receiver, "It's your son, Beatrice," and his mother says, "Who?" and the helper says, "Your son, unless you have two alive ones, and you told me he's your only one," and his mother says, "What?" and the helper says, "Beatrice, listen carefully. He's on the phone waiting, and long distance—your son, Gould; speak to him," and his mother gets on and says hello, this slow hello, not sickly, just weak, and he says, "Mom, hi, how are you?" and she says, "I could be better . . . who is this?" and he says, "Don't you recognize me? Gould. I'm sorry to hear you're not feeling well; what's wrong?" and she says, "What?" and he says, "I said what is it that's bothering you?" and she says, "What?" and he says, much louder, "Do you have your hearing aid in?" and she says, "I heard that. Yes, I think so. Is my hearing aid in?"—away from the phone—and the helper says, "I put it in before and checked the battery; it's all working," and his mother says to him, "This nice girl—I don't know what I'd do without her, she's a real doll—she says my hearing aid's in," and he says, "Good. Now, is it anything in particular that's bothering you—any ailment?" and she says, "Yes, I can hear you normally now. I don't know why; we didn't do anything new to it," and he says, "Maybe you're concentrating better, because after a minute or so you're more used to the phone. So tell me, why aren't you feeling well?" and she says, "No, not particularly. I just feel weak, which I should expect, I guess, when you get this old," and he says, "Why do you say that? You have lots of good days, when you're out and around and your voice is strong and peppy. But today, what is it specifically that's ailing you?" and she says, "What?" and he says, "Ailing, bothering you," and she says, "I heard that too. I have no energy. I just want to rest in bed; that's not so bad," and he says, "But unless you're really sick, which you don't seem to be, you should try to be up, exercise, walk around some, and in regular clothes. Are you still in your bedclothes?" and she says, "Yes, I know, maybe you're right, I'm not sure. But how are you and the kids?" and he says, "We're fine, thanks, and Sally too," and she says, "Yes, how's Sally? She's all right? And where are you, in the city where you live?" and he says, "No, nor in New York. I left you, said goodbye, me and the kids, two days ago, or three. But we got here in Maine two days ago," and she says, "How was your trip?" and he says, "Without incident," and she says, "What happened?" and he says, "The trip to Maine was fine, easy, fast, no problems," and she says, a little alarmed, "You're not holding anything back from me? Something in your voice says you are," and he says, "No, really, the trip was . . . it was easy, smoother than usual," and she says, "You didn't drive too fast?" and he says, "I never do. I listen to you. You tell me not to, that it could be dangerous, so I don't," and she says, "I feel better, thanks for asking. Just hearing your voice does that. But I still think something must be wrong with this hearing aid. No matter how many times the company fixes it for me, they can never get it right. Here . . . miss," she says, away from the phone, "could you see if this thing's in right?" and the helper says, "It's in fine, I saw to it. And I turned it on, checked everything, the little battery screeched, so unless you switched it off since then . . ." and his mother says, "I don't think I did. Is that what you said? But could you check it?" and the helper says, after about a half minute, "It's fine, look, it's on, my finger just felt it," and his mother says to him, "I don't know what's wrong. I know it's not working properly. Usually my hearing's much better. But everything in this house is falling apart, including me. At my age, the eyes, the ears go; sometimes I don't know what the hell the use is in living. But it's nice hearing your voice. That for me always makes everything okay. But I haven't seen you and your family for a long time; is anything the matter?" and he says, "I saw you just three days ago. I came with the kids; we took you out to lunch," and she says, "We had lunch? Seeing you I sort of remember, but not the lunch," and he says, "At Ruppert's. You pushed your wheelchair almost the entire way, but not back. And you had your usual, eggs and bacon, the eggs turned over, and a Jack Daniels with a lemon twist and water—before the meal or during it—but you finished everything," and she says, "If I finished the drink then I must have been feeling good, because they make a strong one there. But then I always feel good with you and the girls. How's Sally—did I ask about her?" and he says, "She's okay, preparing her course for next semester, or starting to, since we only just got here . . . she sends her love to you," and she says, "I know, I'm not my regular self today, but I'll get better. And the girls . . . they back in school? Did it start yet?" and he says, "It just ended for them, Mom. It's the beginning of summer. Don't even mention school to them; they've two months off from it," and she says, "I didn't know; what month we in?" and he says, "July second; in two days it'll be the Fourth," and she says, "July? God, where have I been? Well, I was never sharp with dates. And Sally?" and he says, "She's fine, really, working hard, feeling okay," and she says, "That's all that matters," and he says, "What about you? Is there anything you can do to feel better?" and she says, "What can you do? It's just a case of no get-up-and-go. Mostly, I just feel weak," and he says, "You mean most of your waking time you do?" and she says, "But I'm not so bad off compared to most people my age. When I go in the park with the girl and see them sleeping in their wheelchairs where we stop, they look more dead than alive. But maybe I do to them too, though I tell the girl if my mouth opens and doesn't shut when I'm asleep outside, to close it for me. It's no good to be vain, it's no good to have once been considered pretty, but that's the way I was. Everybody told me and boyfriends entered my photo in beauty shows, and now I look at myself in the mirror and I'm such an old hag I don't want to be seen on the street. I can see how everybody stares at me," and he says, "Not true. You're still very pretty and elegant. Listen, maybe you're only feeling weak because you just got up from a nap. Is that what you did?—though you are speaking more clearly than before," and she says, "No, it's all right, thank you, dearest. I hate to complain and I don't like complainers. And anyway, it's not that," and he says, "What isn't, the nap?" and she says, "I forget. What were we talking about before? I think it was leading to something," and he says, "What about your eating? It's okay?" and she says, "I was never an eater. Even as a girl, food never meant anything to me. But don't worry, I've enough of an appetite for the little I do all day," and he wants to say, Mom, I wish there was some way we could get you up here for a couple of weeks, but I don't see any way to do it, and says instead, "Mom, I wish I was in New York to come by every day, take you out to lunch, things like that," and she says, "That's all right, I could feel better, but you have a good time," and he says, "Did you hear what I said?" and she says, "Sure, why do you think I didn't? I'm not stone deaf. But the air conditioner here. Maybe you can use it," and he says, "No, I bought it for you, and why would we need it in Maine, if that's what you're saying?" and she says, "Then take it with you when you come back," and he says, "Come on, you'll need it for September and next year. Is it on now?" and she says, "I think so. Just a minute," and says, "Miss—I'm sorry, I don't know your name, what is it?" and the helper says something and his mother says, "Angela. Thank you. Is the air conditioner on?" and the helper says yes and his mother says to him, "She says it's on. It does feel cool, so I should have been able to tell. But it's not that. I don't know what it is. I just don't feel like getting up," and he says, "But you should. For a walk or in the wheelchair, if it's not too hot, or to sit in front of the building awhile," and she says, "I don't think so, but I'm not sure," and away from the phone, "Have I been out today?" and the helper says, "You said you didn't want to, didn't have the energy, but if you want to go I can get you dressed and outside," and she says to him, "No, I haven't been out today, this nice woman says. But I'll get there yet; I've time," and he says, "Do it now before it gets too hot. Take a shower first. Tell Angela you'd like a shower and to get dressed and go outside. It'll be okay out there if you get right to the shade or the park," and she says, "The park can be so nice, very beautiful. We go to the spot you always take me to, with plenty of shade and long benches," and he says, "Good, just so you do something different. You need that variety; you can't just stay inside. Or have lunch out with Angela—at Ruppert's. I won't mind if you go there with someone else. Or go out just for an ice-cream bar at the corner. But you can't stay in your bed or your room all day, it isn't healthy for you. You can get bedsores, if anything. The fresh air outside, even if it's a bit humid—" and she says, "You're right, you always make good common sense for me. I'll try, dear, but I don't know if I'll be successful at it. Excuse me, is it all right if I get off the phone now? I'll call you later. I have your number? Wait, the girl will take it down for me," and he says, "You have it, in the address book on the side table by your bed," and she says, "What's the best time to reach you?" and he says, "Anytime, we're in Maine, I'm not going anyplace," and she says, "Mornings or evenings better?" and he says "Really, Mom, anytime you want. If I'm not in, one of the kids or Sally could be and they'll give me your message and I'll call you right back, but I'm never out for that long," and she says, "No, you call all the time; I've gotten lazy at it, so I'll call you," and he says, "Okay, fine; evenings, after six, is probably better and you get a better rate too," and she says, "I have your number?" and he says, "In your address book by your bed. Do you see it? It's pretty big, has an Impressionist painting on the cover—Renoir, I think; we gave it to you last Christmas, it's from the Met," and she says, "Is my address book here with my son's phone number in it?" and he yells, "An address and daily calendar book, actually. And it's a Pissarro on the cover—Camille, Camille Pissarro—last year's was the Renoir, I think," and the helper says to her, "Is this it?" and his mother says, "It must be; was it on my side table?" and the helper says, "Your regular helper said all your important phone numbers are in it: doctors, ambulance service, everything. And your son's, wherever he is; so if he's in Maine, it's in there, by alphabet, his last name," and his mother says to him, "You in Maine?" and he says yes, and she says, "When did you leave?" and he says, "Three days ago. I came over with the girls the day before; Sally had a last-minute doctor's appointment, but she saw you the day before that," and she says, "Tell me, how's the family?" and he says, "We're all okay, Sally too; nothing's changed with her," and she says, "With me, seems as though everything's going wrong," and he says, "What particularly? That's what I want to know," and she says, "I can't even point it out. A time comes for everyone; I think that's what they say," and he says, "Don't think like that, Mom. You're just tired, or a little weak today—maybe from the heat—but the next time I call I'm sure your voice will be bouncy and chipper again and you'll feel—" and she says, "I remember now you going. You came over with the girls. You see, I can remember when I want to. But I have to go now, sweetheart. Give my love to everyone," and he says, "I will, and much love from us to you, and I'll call tomorrow," and she says, "Oh, one more thing. Usually before they go I give them each some money for their birthdays," and he says, "Their birthdays aren't till November, same month as yours," and she says, "Did I this year?" and he says, "Yes, in November, you were very generous. We came in especially for your birthday and you gave them each ten dollars," and she says, "Only ten? Usually I'm a much bigger sport. Why'd I give so little?" and he says, "Because that's all I wanted you to give. You're trying to cut down your expenses, and besides, I don't want them getting too much money at one time. They'll just spend it," and she says, "So, they're girls, what's wrong with that? They like to buy pretty things," and he laughs and says, "I'm glad your sense of humor's back," and she says, "Why, did I lose it? I'm losing everything these days," and he laughs and says, "Good, you're feeling better. And you're right—next time give the girls what you want; from now on that'll be just between you and them," and she says, "But did I before you left?" and he says, "Mom, their birthdays are in November; November, same as yours. You have more than four months to think about giving them a birthday gift, just as we do for you," and she says, "I don't want anything; what could I need? But November. What month are we in now?" and he says, "What month do you think?" and she says, "I think I know; I'm just not sure. You tell me and we'll see if I'm right," and he says, "The beginning of July," and she says, "July? Don't fool me," and he says, "You mean you don't think so?" and she says, "No, I mean how could it be?" and he says, "Look, maybe your apartment's so cool you think it's also cold outside or something, late fall weather—is that it?" and she says, "But it just doesn't look anything like July," and he says, "What do you mean? The sun, when the sun's out; just the brightness, which you never get any other time," and she says, "Not to me," and he says, "Mom, stop, think; how could it not look like it? All right, so your eyes aren't what they used to be. But when you go outside, then: the heat, the humidity, the intense sun, the kids off from school and that you go to the park in light clothing, but also that I'm calling from Maine. So more than just looking and feeling like summer, you know we never come up here except around the first of July. And you've been here maybe ten times, so you know we only come to Maine during the summers. And I said goodbye to you day before we left, came over with the kids, and Sally saw you the day before that," and she says, "So what are you saying, that I'm crazy?" and he says, "Of course not; I meant nothing like that. I was only saying that it's got to be July. The summer, the park and trees and weather. The kids off from school and my being on vacation and the light clothing everyone wears and so on. These are all things to help you remember what month, or season, at least, we're in," and she says, "Well, they're not doing such a good job. And don't talk to me as if my mind's gone. It's not perfect, but it's far from finished. I remember most of it; it isn't that I don't. It's summer, and July. You said so, so it has to be, and not only that, it is, and not just because the newspaper I read every day says so too. And that's right, I remember now too. How sorry I was to see you go, for my sake, but glad for yours—that you'd all be away from the heat. But I have to get off the phone now," and he says, "Look, I'm very sorry; I don't want to leave it like this," and she says, "Like what?" and he says, "That you, you know . . . I don't want you to feel bad over anything I said," and she says, "Why do you think I do? I don't, I just feel tired, suddenly; I have to rest. Goodbye, dear," and he says, "Me too, goodbye, and my love to you, and I'll call again soon," and she hangs up.

Maybe he should call right back and explain more that he didn't mean some of the things she thinks he did, but she already might be being helped to the bed, if she wasn't sitting on it when she was talking to him, or now laid back on the bed, head on the pillows, legs straightened, shoes or slippers removed, and could be too tired to talk to him. Later, tonight, better. But why'd he say all those things? Why'd he do anything to make things worse for her? Confuse her with some of the things he said, scare her, even? Why'd he say anything about her mind other than reassuring things: she's sounding bright, chipper, lively, full of energy, she's really on the ball today, not that she isn't every day but today even more than most? He doesn't know, he only wants her to feel better; those things just came out. And why'd he lie about having called her several times yesterday and they didn't answer? Shame, that he hadn't called sooner—same day he got here as he told her he would—and that he's up here and she's down there and summer's only started and the weather can only get worse there while staying pretty much the same here: a little warm some days, maybe even a few days with the temperature and humidity in the 90s, but cool every evening and, because their rented house is on top of a hill with a big clearing around it, windy, even if a warm wind, most afternoons. How could he get her up here for a week if he wanted to? He wants to, that's not the problem, and she stayed with them here for a week for ten summers straight and always had a good time and they with her, but hasn't come since she broke her hip three years ago. This time he could buy round-trip plane tickets for her and her main helper, but the doctor says she's too frail to travel that distance anymore, plane or car, so that's out. Then what's in? Nothing. It's all out for all time. So she stays there doing nothing all day, and that's why he feels so lousy for her. She goes out, in, wheelchair down the block if the weather's not too hot, up to the park where she sits in the shade, looking, yawning, maybe falling asleep in her chair there, napping at home in the cushioned chair by her bed or in the bed if she asks to, napping after breakfast sometimes, often after lunch, another nap late afternoon, eating little, napping in the wheelchair lots of times while the helper pushes it outside. Little comments to the helper through the day, same ones she's made to him the last couple of years: "This is no life. . . . This isn't living. . . . I'm vegetating, not even just existing, so why can't God order my body to call it quits? . . . Believe me, if I was plugged in now I'd ask you to take me out, and if you didn't want to, and I could hardly blame you, then I'd somehow manage to myself. . . . People are lucky when they go before their health does or before they get too feeble and old to enjoy or do anything." He and his family were in the city for three weeks before they drove to Maine, staying at their old apartment, which most of the time they sublet, and he came to see her every day but one, sometimes with the kids, took her out to lunch most of those days, later wheeled her to the park and sat with her there or stopped in with her at a coffee bar, took her out to dinner a couple of times, and once wheeled her across the park to the Frick to show her his favorite Rembrandt and El Greco portraits and the two or three Vermeers, but she wanted to leave after ten minutes because she said people were staring more at her than the pictures. She perked up when he was with her, though, more so when he brought the kids; it even seemed she looked forward to his visits, but some days she was still in bed when he got there and he'd ask the helper if his mother wasn't feeling well or didn't get much sleep last night, and if the helper said no he'd say to his mother, "Mom, why aren't you up? We're going out," and she'd say, "Why, where're you taking me?" and he said, "For a good time, lunch, the works, wherever you want to go," and she'd say, "I'm too tired to go out, I only want to rest," and he'd say, "Mom, you're not sick, you got about twelve hours sleep last night, maybe sixteen for the entire day, so come on, you got to get up, showered, dressed, refreshed, I don't mean to be a tyrant but getting out will be good for you, and better now before the real heat comes, and I'm hungry," and, if the kids were with him, "and so are they," and she usually got up when he told her to, in fact did it every time because he was very persistent, wouldn't take a no, and she always enjoyed the lunch and park and stroll and drink and coffee and cake or whatever they'd do, and then that last time when he got her home she wanted to get right into bed without even first stopping at the bathroom, and he said, "You know, today's the last day we'll be seeing you for two months . . . well, less than that, barely seven weeks, though we'll be seeing you again for a few days on our return. We're off to Maine early tomorrow, so I can't even drive by before that because I know you won't be up, you're so tired now," and she said, "You're going? So soon? It seems you only just got here," and he said, "Do you mean about today or our entire stay in New York?" and she said, "Both. But they say if things go so quickly like that it must have been fun," and he said, "I'm glad you think that, it's certainly been fun for us with you," and she said, "I'll miss you all . . . I've grown so used to seeing you and my little sweethearts. I just feel much better when you're around, but I'll live with it; I have before," and he wanted to say, Mom, I wish you could come with us or fly up later, but thought saying it would be worse than not saying it. He used to look forward to her visits in Maine, pick her up at the airport, show her around, invite people over for drinks or dinner whom she might like. Her younger sister would usually call him a few days after she got back and say, "Bea looks great, trip did her wonders, highlight of the year for her, she said; you're such a dear for having her every summer; I know for myself that having old people around can be very hard," and he would say, "No, she's very easy, a big help." When he took her back to the airport those summers he could always say, "So, see you in a few weeks—month at the most" and she'd usually say something like "This trip was just the lift I needed, so it ought to hold me for the next few weeks without all of you." The last day he saw her he said, "Kids, come on, we're going, kiss Grandma goodbye, you won't see her for a while," and they kissed her and he kissed her and said, "So, see you on the twenty-third of August—a Thursday, I think—and I'll call every day without fail, I promise," and she said, "August? That seems so far away. What month are we in now?" and he said, "Last day of June, so you can say beginning of July," and she said, "Then August and the twenty-third day of it is very far away. Why so long?" and he said, "Because that's how long we'll be away. As I said, it's about seven weeks total," and she said, "It still seems long to me. What month are we in now?" and he said, "Mom, I told you, and you have to start remembering: it's just about July. So August is next month almost—all right, we get back near the end of it—but I'll speak to you on the phone every day, and if you need me just say the word and I'll fly in," and she said, "No, I want you to go; it's the best thing for everybody, being away. And you work hard and have a lot at home to do and can use the long vacation, so I wouldn't interrupt it for anything," and he said, "Really, if you need me," and she said, "But I won't." He broke down the last two years after he left her apartment the day before they were to drive to Maine and thought, This the last time I'll ever see her? This time, while he was still in her room—she was lying on the bed, eyes closed, near sleep or asleep; he'd helped put her there, took her shoes off, straightened her legs on the covers, made sure her head was comfortably centered on the pillows, then kissed her forehead and ran his hand along her hair and said goodbye and she didn't give any reaction like a word or nod or smile—he started to cry—kids were waiting for him outside—and thought, Why am I crying? Because I don't think I'll ever see her again? That's what I thought the last two years, and she's not much worse off now than she was then. So it's partly that and just leaving her here for two months. Later, walking with the kids down the block to the bus stop, he wondered if she'd thought something like that about them just before. Like "Will I ever see them again? I don't know. Not the way I feel now, that's for sure. But that's what I thought the last two years, and I made it through the summer and saw them again, so why not this time too? Because I'm more tired more often and for longer periods; because some days I just don't think I can get up." Her look when they were talking about not seeing each other for two months suggested, "There's no way you can see to taking me along or sending for me midway through the summer? I suppose not because I'm supposed to be too frail to travel, but as my dad used to say, 'If it's packed well, any bottle of wine can be shipped safely.' And I'm not sick; I'm just old and tired and bored silly and I can use a little vacation too from this place, just a last one if it has to be that. Wouldn't it be better for me, no matter how hard it is to get me there, to sleep for a week where it's mostly cool and dry and the air's real and healthy and clear and everything smells fresh and where I can see other things than this city block and the noisy avenues and the park, pretty as it is but made ugly by all the old people like me in it, and just to be with all of you for a while as I did so many summers in a row? I can come up with the weekday girl, even if I wouldn't mind a short break from my helpers too. And if there's no room for her or you don't want a stranger in the house, though she's very honest and sweet and would be more help than bother, then alone—a little extra work and inconvenience for you, since with my bad hip and brittle bones and weak bladder I'd now have to sleep downstairs on the pullout and near your one bathroom. Though for the more personal things, I can still take care of myself, and for bathing all I need is to be alone by the sink with a washrag and sponge. The food would be much better with you too. Here it's only so-so, the wrong bread, none of the exotic cheeses I used to love to eat, and I'm not particularly fond of Caribbean cooking, which is the only kind these girls do well. Or takeout Chinese or barbecued chicken from the barbecue shop or eggs, eggs, eggs, cooked the way I like them, sunny-side down, but with too much grease; and there's also not much conversation or mutual interests with my helpers, and the TV always on; and that pounding music, which you could hear through twenty doors and walls no matter how deaf you are, would drive a sane man nuts. And you'd give me a drink every day, maybe also a glass of wine or beer at dinner. Here I have to beg for one—they're looking out for my health and want me to have soda or juice—and when the bottle runs dry it takes a couple of weeks for them to buy another one. But it's tough, I know—you have your kids, and your wife now needs some taking care of, and the house has a lot of trouble accommodating more than four, if I remember it correctly, especially now that the girls are bigger, and whatever else is preventing me from going." Now, still seated by the phone, he feels terrible about her, knows he'll feel this way after every phone talk with her the next two months, wonders what she thought soon after she hung up and why she didn't, as she usually did, say the final goodbye right after his (because she was too tired, depressed, a combination of the two, and what she thought?)—that she wishes she was up there with them or could look forward to going in a month or so, but he made no offer, though he must know what it'd mean to her, and she can't plead with him, it wouldn't be right, he'll have to come around on his own and that doesn't seem promising, so this is her lot. And then maybe what it was like when she was here: the sights, smells, quietness, sleep-inducing sounds of bugs at night, moderate temperatures, mostly low humidity, those beautiful blue Maine days, their dinners together, watching the kids play, reading the *Times* outside in the sun if it wasn't too hot—"A little direct sun is good for me," she's said, "vitamin E, or whichever one it is, D," and other things. And then maybe she'd feel sleepy and want to nap again and ask the helper to get her to bed, and she'd lie on top of the covers, shoes off or, if kept on because the helper would only have to put them on again in an hour, then her feet placed on a newspaper section or paper shopping bag at the end of the bed, and close her eyes and soon be asleep, the helper sitting across from her for a while and then getting up and leaving the room and closing the door till it was almost shut.

The Subway Ride

TRAIN'S CROWDED WHEN he gets on, he says, "Excuse me, excuse me, just want to get to the aisle, please," bumps into someone from behind, a woman, who turns to him and says, "What the hell you think you're doing?" and he says, "Excuse me, I was just going to say excuse me," and the train starts and she says, "But you intentionally shoved your cock against my behind, you bastard," and he says, "Did not, I swear, the train's crowded; I was just moving to the aisle where there's more room," and she says, "You did too, you stuck your fucking dick up against my behind; who the fuck you think you are?" and he loses his balance a little because of the ride, doesn't want to bump into her again, that's all he needs; she's holding onto the pole by the door, other people are looking at him, some men and a woman smirking, sort of, and he says to the woman, "Honestly," and the train lurches and he grabs the pole she's holding, his hand touches hers, and he pulls it away and says, "Excuse me, and honestly, I didn't push you intentionally. I was moving to the aisle, past you, and someone must have pushed me from behind or just jostled me—I forget—or the car's so crowded that I got closer to you than I wanted, believe me, and, well—" and she says, "Don't tell me. This isn't the first time it's happened with one of you guys. You think you can get your kicks shoving your fucking dicks around where women are going to think it's a mistake or be too scared to say anything, because who knows what kind of nut this creep can be, and so on. But I'm not one of them. My mouth is big. I don't take shit from a man. Is there a cop in this car?" she yells; "because some goddamn guy tried sticking his pelvic region into me and I want a cop to grab him," and someone from a few people away says, "Who did what?" and someone else yells, "I saw a policeman in the next car—the one further up—when I was getting into this one, but how you are going to get him, lady, is a problem." A woman says to her, "Good, you're doing it, that's what every woman should do," and a man says, "Maybe he didn't mean it, accidents can happen, the train can push you," and Gould says, "That's what happened, I swear, an accident—I was moving into the aisle where there's more room to stand, and someone from behind me must have pushed me into her and I tried pulling back, but when you start falling . . ." and the train slows down for the next stop and she says to him, "If you think you're getting off"—for he made a move to the door—"I'm getting off with you, because I'm not letting you get away with this crap, thinking you can shove up against whoever you please," and he says, "I wasn't getting off, this isn't my stop; I just got on. I was only trying to move a step to grab the bar above my head instead of the pole. I feel I'll be able to hold on to it better and I also didn't want to be too near you to accidentally bump against you again when the train pulls in and maybe lurches," and she says, "Some accident, you bullshitter, you lying worm," and everyone around them is now looking at them, and the train stops, people get off, on—no cops, she's looking—and he says, "Honestly, miss—or missus—I didn't mean it; why would I? I'm married. I've kids. I'd never do anything like that to a woman. That's not how I get my kicks, and I'm sorry for bumping into you and I wish we could just forget it. I mean, who in this city hasn't by accident bumped into the back and front and every part of some person's body on one of these trains?" and she says, "You specifically did it. I felt your tube and you aimed straight for between the buttocks and you're a slob for having tried it. If a cop was in the car now I'd have you arrested and prosecuted and accused and everything; you're just lucky one isn't." He shuts his eyes. It's going away. She's becoming less threatening. The words, how she says them, not as much cursing and stridence; she's backing off. She got out what she felt she had to and now she's had her fill of it and it'll soon be over with. If he got off at the next stop he doesn't think she'd pursue him, though she might yell something at him as he left the car. She for sure would yell something. So what? He'd be gone. Some eyes might be on him on the platform and then fewer eyes as he went up the stairs, and once on the street that'd just about be the end of it. Maybe one person who had come upstairs with him from the platform might still be looking at him on the street and thinking of him in relation to what the woman had said, maybe two, and maybe both from the car he was in, but then that'd be the end of it, or it absolutely would once he was a block away from the station, walking in whatever opposite direction it was from the person who came up the stairs with him. If it had been more than one who'd come up with him from the same platform or car and maybe even out of the same door of that car—well, then he doesn't know what he'd do: probably just stay by the station entrance till they were gone and then go down it to take the train. Or else—and this is what he'd do no matter what, since the woman might actually get off the train and then give up on following him and be standing on the platform—he'd take his time walking south to the next station on this line and get the train there. But the thing is, she might not have imagined what she said he did to her. He thinks he might have lost control for a few seconds and intentionally moved into her, something he never did to anyone in this kind of situation before. He was up close to her and was aware how close and also that if he didn't want to cause a commotion by touching her he should stand still and not move past her, but he continued to move toward her and thinks when he got very close he suddenly thought of his wife, or was thinking of his wife all the time he was moving toward the woman or even when he first saw her, of the times when he wanted sex and to give her some indication he did he'd jam his penis into her backside in bed or bend it back a little and spring it against one of her buttocks or legs or, if they were standing someplace, then put his arms around her from behind and press his penis against her, and around that moment jabbed his front into the woman's rear end. He was semierect or even erect when he did it—he forgets, but one of them, most likely from having just thought of his wife in one of the ways he mentioned—which the woman didn't bring up, thank God. Maybe she didn't feel his penis particularly but just his pelvic area moving into her backside, since it doesn't seem like something she'd hold back in her accusations against him. Though it could be that's where she draws the line in describing what happened in something like that and also feels that anyone listening to her could figure out or imagine for themselves what state his penis was in. Train doors open, people get off, others are waiting to get on; one man slips around some people getting off and grabs the one free seat near Gould. He thinks, while gripping the overhead bar so nobody getting off or on shoves him into her: Make a dash for it now; so many people left the train to go upstairs that he'll quickly get lost in the crowd, when a man in the car shouts "Officer . . . say, Officer there . . . over here, you're wanted, something important," and the woman says to Gould, "Finally, now you're in for it," and he says, "For what? You still onto that? I did nothing," and sees a tall policeman making his way through the car from the direction the man before said he saw one. "Step aside," the policeman's saying, "please, folks, move, move, I gotta get through." He could still make a dash for it, policeman might not be able to get to the door in time to stop him, and if he was caught on the platform or stairs or even on the street by this policeman or another one—for this one could radio to another transit cop or even to a regular city one about a bald white guy in green corduroy jacket and chinos and button-down blue shirt getting away—he'd stop and say . . . he certainly wouldn't put up any resistance if one of them approached or ran after him or ordered him to stop, but he'd say . . . well, he could give several excuses why he was trying to get away: the woman was bothering him, cursing at him, harassing him, even—the train would have left by then, he thinks, so there'd be little chance, if she got off it with the policeman, that she'd have any witnesses—"I just wanted to be rid of her. Believe me, I wasn't six inches from her"—not six inches—"I wasn't anywhere as near to her as she says, but she jumped on me like I was the worst masher there was; something must be wrong with her and what I think it is I won't go into, but I swear to you, Officer, I swear. . . ." Train goes, he's still clutching the overhead bar with one hand, book's tucked under his other arm, woman's telling the policeman what happened, policeman interrupts her and says, "Too bad I didn't know beforehand what it was, I would've asked you both to leave the train and all the witnesses to the issue, pro or con, to join us. But this is not something to discuss in a crowded car while we're still going," and Gould says, "I agree. Besides that, what she told you is absolutely the biggest crock of—" and the policeman holds up his hand for him to stop and says, "Save it; don't make things worse for yourself, that's my advice. You've something to say? Later. Now, you and the lady and me will get off at the next station with any witnesses to the incident, if one occurred," and looks around and nobody volunteers, and he says to the people standing and sitting near them, "Excuse me, folks, I don't want to take you out of your way. But are there any witnesses to what this woman's claiming? You heard what the charges are if you were around then, and it's not within my jurisdiction to repeat them. So did anyone, I'll only say, see anything for or against what she claims about this man?" and some people shake their heads or quietly say no, others just stare back blankly or turn away or look at their newspapers, and the woman says to a woman standing beside her, "You were here when it happened; you had to see him do with his front what I said he did," and the other woman says, "I was here, all right, but I didn't see anything. I only heard you saying it. I'm sorry, I wish I could help," and the policeman says, "So just the three of us will get off and we'll settle it there, or if there's any rough talk, then in the transit police station on Thirty-fourth," and Gould says, "No rough talk from me. My argument is simply that I didn't do it. I was moving to the aisle for more room and to read when I accidentally must have brushed up against her when either someone pushed me from behind or the train suddenly shifted or did something, but where I lost my balance, causing me—" and the woman says, "You bullshitter," and the policeman says, "Please, the two of you, we'll talk off the train. And *you*"—to Gould—"I thought I told you to save it for later."

They get off at the next stop; the policeman says, "Let's go where we can hear better," and leads them upstairs to the area near the turnstiles, and he has the woman go through it again and then says to Gould, "Now's your time, sir, how do you answer her charges?" and Gould says, "What I started telling you before but said completely to her on the train before: it's ridiculous, I'd never do it. I didn't, period.

I can appreciate why she'd protest, though, if she thought something like that happened, for it's awful when men do that to women on trains—anyplace. I can also understand, if it's happened to her before or even if it hasn't, why she might think I did it on purpose—that it just felt to her as if I did. But I swear, if my body did touch hers, and I'm not even sure it did, it was purely by accident and nothing else. As I told her, it's just not what I do. I'm married, with young children and a good job—I know those aren't valid excuses; the most deeply married man and best father and worker and religious person and everything could be a psycho on the side—but I'm not, and more than that I can't say," and the policeman says to her, "Ma'am, I don't take sides. You say this, he says that, and it's up to me to listen. Now I heard you both and I'm going to say what I'm going to say. You really don't have any witnesses to it, so it ends up being your word against his, and I don't think you'll get anywhere with it," and she says, "I know he put his body intentionally to mine and so does he. He's a good liar. He had plenty of space to go around me, but no, he turned to me, not with his back but his front, something I caught out of the corner of my eye but didn't have the time to stop it. And next he squeezed into me as if I was his little doll or something—his girlfriend or wife that he says he has—and I'd like it. Well, I didn't like it and I want to make charges against him, big charges. I want to stop all these creepy bastards like him from riding back and forth on the subways and trying to stick themselves against women and smaller girls and every kind of female and the rest of it." She's almost screaming now, and the policeman says, "Lady, calm down please. Okay, you want to make charges, we can do that, but you'll have to come to court once his case comes up, you know. You don't, for no good reason, then the charges are dropped and can't be renewed. Even if you don't come to court for a good reason—sickness, or your kid's sick—" and she says, "I have no kid, and I'm not married; I'm on my own, which is another—" and he says, "I was giving examples. Then the case is postponed for two months or so, even more if there's a big court overload," and she says, "Don't you worry, I'll be there the first time," and the policeman says, "Okay, so I guess we got to go to step two, and I want everybody to remain peaceful, calm and nice," and starts to fill out a report, asks Gould for identification, says he'll get a court notice in the mail when to appear. "Same with you, miss, and

I'll see you both there. Okay, now we're all free to go," and Gould says, "I'm going downstairs to continue my ride, I hope that's all right," and the policeman says, "Sure, it's what I said," and the woman says, "So am I. I'm not staying here waiting for him to get the next train first and my missing even more of my time," and the policeman says, "So how about us all going downstairs together, since that's my direction too," and they walk downstairs and stand on the platform waiting for the train. Gould says to the policeman, "I'm not trying to show anything by this, but if you don't mind I'd like to move a ways down the platform so I can save the embarrassment for this woman and me, or just uneasiness, of being in the same car," and the woman says, "It makes no difference to me if we're in the same car so long as this officer's there with us," and the policeman says, "I'll get in the same car with you two—I did plan that—but I'll have to start circulating my presence throughout the train and, after a stop or two, the train system in general, if you know what I mean. So why don't you," he says to Gould, "just to make life easier for us, get in with me, and if Miss Pizeman wants, she can get into another car. I think that's the best solution," and she says, "Why?" and he says, "Because I think so. Because I know what I'm doing. Because if I'm with him you know nothing can go wrong between you, from whichever end it comes," and Gould says, "Nothing could go wrong again from my end. I didn't do anything before and I wouldn't do anything now," and she says, "That's what you say, but you lie on one and we're supposed to believe the other?" and the policeman says, "I already assumed nothing would go wrong now. I was only trying to come up with a compromise that'd make this woman feel a bit easier. But if you think"—to her—"you want me in your car and him to be in another car and he agrees to it, though he's not by law obligated to and I can't insist he do it since he's not acting in any way as if he's about to get out of hand—" and she says, "One or the other, I guess; I don't care. Just so long as you're with one of us. But what happens if when you start circulating he comes to the car I'm in, after you're out of mine or when you're off the train entirely?" and Gould says, "I won't go into your car. You don't seem to understand that you're the last person I ever want to be in the same car with. So whatever car I get into, I'll stay there, but we have to make sure from the start we're in different ones." Platform's crowding up, some people have moved closer to listen to them, and the policeman says, "Please, folks, what you see's not anybody else's business, so move it," and Gould thinks, This is awful; besides that, it's embarrassing. You got to get yourself away from here before she says something that makes you say something and then she's sure to come back harder and you'll give even more in return, to where you're in big trouble again and with everyone watching, and looks at the wall with the station's name on it and says, "Jesus, I can't believe it, but I don't even have to get on the train. This is my stop, and in all the confusion before I didn't know it," and the woman says, "Sure it is," and the policeman says, "So why don't you leave then, sir," and she says, "You just want to separate us, don't tell me; well, good," and Gould says to them, "But it's the truth; I don't know how I can prove it, but it is," and the policeman says, "Don't prove, just go where you have to and if I'm not on some other thing that day and the woman here doesn't drop the charges before then, I'll see you," and Gould says, "Thank you," and, to the woman, "Believe me, miss, I'm sorry for the misunderstanding between us, for that's what it was. And I hope, in the next few weeks, you can see to dropping the charges, because they're—" and she says "Bullshit," and he says, "No, really, I was going to say—" and she says, "And I said bullshit, bullshit, do you hear? Bullshit!" and the policeman says, "Please, lady, don't make it more," and Gould says, "Thanks again," and touches him on the arm and goes upstairs, thinking, I've never touched a cop before.

He gets the summons a month later, saying he has to appear in court on a day a month from now, and his wife says he should get a lawyer, and he says, "No, I thought it over and I think it's better I go without one and declare my innocence and take the consequences. Since it's only my word against hers, unless she comes up with a witness who's prepared to lie, and I don't see how she could get one, I'm sure nothing will happen to me. Besides, I don't want to pay for a lawyer, and I feel confident about it because I'm a good defendant. I don't come across as guilty and I do as penitent for even the minor crimes or misdemeanors or whatever that other people are guilty of," and she says, "I don't understand," and he says, "I meant—what was I talking about before?—what are you referring to, I mean?" and she says, "What did you mean by 'penitent for other people's crimes and misdemeanors'?" and he says, "Just that I make a good case for taking on the burdens of the world, so to speak, the mini to major minor ones; is that any clearer?" and she says no, and he says, "Let me see. That these crimes and things exist—preying on women and girls in subways, for instance, as she accused me of—and I can't believe she went through with it and didn't do what I'm sure the policeman that day was suggesting and that's to drop the charge—but anyway, is wrong, though don't look at me as someone who does them," and she says, "If you think that makes it clearer, you're mistaken," and he says, "Don't worry, I'll get it right by the time I have to appear," and she says, "I don't know; I'm worried," and he says, "Don't be; I'll look well, speak well, dress well, and they'll know right away I couldn't have done it, besides there being no witnesses." He's wanted to tell her, a few times, that he thought of her rear end a second or so before he pushed into the woman, but that'd make him out a liar and then she'd insist he get a lawyer. And he doesn't know if he really did it intentionally because he thought of his wife; he only might have or he might have seen the woman's curvy body from behind and some impulse took over—of course some impulse, but that's something he'd also never admit to her, except maybe after this was long over with—and he brought up the image of pressing into her simply to have a greater impetus to push into the woman. Oh, it's getting too confusing and it happened so fast that day and he forgets so much of it and maybe he should forget it for now. That wise? Why not? Because one day of ignoring it won't hurt and some good idea or strategy about it might even come out of his unconscious in that time. One thing he wants, though, is his wife to come to the courtroom with him; she'll make a dignified impression and it'll be in his favor, he thinks, for the court to know she's behind him. He'll ask her tonight or tomorrow when they get up, and he's sure she'll agree.

They go to the courtroom that day and the woman doesn't show, nor did she notify the court she wouldn't be there, and the court clerk says he'll send them both a second notice to appear in a month or so, and if she doesn't appear and gives no reason beforehand why not then the case will be dropped, and Gould says, "The transit policeman who took down the report from her and me said it'd be dropped the first time if she didn't show up and gave no reason why she didn't," and the clerk says, "That's not how it's done and the police officer couldn't have told you that. They handle these cases every day, so they know better," and his wife says, "Excuse me, sir, but I believe the policeman did tell my husband that. Anyway, it's exactly what Gould told me the day this all took place and he came home after the incident. Or called from downtown, rather, his voice quivering, he was so distressed at what that woman had accused him of; and I could tell by his voice and what he said, besides knowing him so many years, that he didn't do," and the clerk says, "I'll put it to you this way, Mrs. Bookbinder. If the police officer informed your husband that, he was wrong," and she says, "All right, that's good enough, I'm no one to tell you your business and the law; thank you."

He doesn't get another summons to appear or any notification why. He wants to write the court about it—to find out if the whole thing's been dropped, for one thing—but his wife says, "Best to let it disappear by itself entirely. By writing them you may encourage them to think they dropped something they shouldn't have, and next thing you know the second summons will arrive in the mail, and this time she'll come to the proceedings, and who knows what could happen then?" That night she says, "There's something I never asked you but several times wanted to," and he says, "No, absolutely, I didn't intend to stick my damn thing against the woman's rear end; it just happened. You know trains," and she says, "Boy, you really know you've been married a long time when your spouse starts answering your questions before you ask them," and he says, "I'm sorry, finish; what was it?" and she says, "I don't have to; you said it. But if you had, you know, done what she said you did, it does happen, and though it would have been wrong it wouldn't have been the worst thing that ever took place. It's not as if you pulled it out and waved it and then mashed it into her. People get crazy urgencies sometimes. We're not all made perfectly forever, so occasionally we follow, no matter how good and sensible and moral we are, our most immediate fancies and urges," and he says, "You mean impulses," and she says, "Yes, but the rest too. You're a horny guy a lot—lascivious, might be a better word, sexy—you don't try to be; it's the way you're made. I know that because of how you behave with me and also the way you look at other women sometimes, eyeing the pretty or shapely ones when they pass, staring at their breasts and butts, and at the time who knows what you're thinking?" and he says, "When? When do I do that?" and she looks at him, and he says, "All right, I do it sometimes," and she says, "So I'm saying if you had done what that woman asserted you did, once in ten to fifteen years on a subway or bus, I don't think it would have been that terrible a thing to do, since I'm sure these urgencies or impulses have been in you to do it lots of times, not that that excuses it," and he says, "But I didn't do it; I've never done it. The idea may have popped into my head a few times, but it's not the way I act to women—taking advantage of the uncomfortable conditions of a crowded subway car to get a quick feel or rise," and she says, "Anyhow, that's good to know, that you have that kind of restraint while still being a very horny and lustful guy sometimes," and he says, "But you knew that, didn't you, about the restraint?" and she says, "No, I told you, I wouldn't have been surprised or even angered if you had done that to a woman on a train once or twice in the last twenty years, but not to a girl."

The Paintings

HE'S COME TO like Bolling's painting so much that he wants to get another one. Lots of people have also told him how much they like it. They'd walk into the living room for the first time and see it on the far wall above the piano and say, "My God, that's fantastic!" "Exciting" is another word they've used; "Takes my breath away" a typical expression. "The colors, those lines, the strength. The whole thing looks as if it's about to soar through the ceiling." "Saw? To cut? I don't understand." "To rise or fly through it. It has that kind of winged quality, in addition to some mystical or spiritual one where it can go through something without breaking it. I don't know what the painting means or is supposed to be of, but I love it. Is it as good up close?" and whoever was appreciating it this way would approach it and always say it was. "Who did it? Where'd you get it?" "It's a long story." He didn't like to go into it. "It looks very expensive." "Maybe it's the way it's framed." "Do you mind my asking what something like this would go for?" someone once said, not a friend of theirs but someone who came with one. "It was given to me by the artist." "You're so lucky. You didn't even have to pay for it? I can see why you did such a nice job framing it." "That was Sally's—my wife's—idea. If it had been up to me I would have done the cheapest job possible, which means the simplest. Four wood strips and that's it, or not even that but just getting it stretched." "If I was interested in buying one this size, or a little larger, where would I go, to the artist or his gallery or agent?" and he said, "I'm sure the painter's wife would be happy to sell you one, since I don't think the painter had a single sale—you see, he died—but she's in New York. I can get you her phone number, even call her for you to set up a meeting. She's right in the city," and this person said, "Nah, I hardly ever get up there, and when I do it's always rush rush."

It had been nailed to his New York apartment wall for about a year after Bolling had given him it: "For all you've done for me, I want you to have any painting of mine you want." Gould said, "Come on, let me give you something for it. An artist should be paid. But a little painting, one I can afford," and Bolling said, "Not a cent, and take the biggest if that's the one you pick. I've come this far in not selling one, don't spoil my legacy for the future. Who knows? Maybe being tagged with that—like Van Gogh, minus one, since Theo sold one of his and could have sold others if brother Vincent had been more cooperative or sent him more. . . . I forget what the circumstances were, or if I meant 'minus' or 'plus one' then. I'm losing my memory and figuring-out head, as you can tell. I used to know that art history junk backwards and forwards. But what I think I was saying was that maybe being tagged as a never-ever-seller will help the sale of my paintings after I'm dead." Gould said, "What're you talking about, you're not dying," and Bolling said, "Who said I was? I said 'after I'm dead.' You can say that about anybody alive." "So you have plenty of time to sell your paintings," and Bolling said, "Okay, joking's over, we all got a big laugh out of it. Now choose a painting and then give me my pain shot so I can get back to my nap," and Gould and Bolling's wife unrolled about twenty oil canvases on the furniture and floor—"Don't be afraid to step on them," Bolling said, "the paint's so thick, nothing could hurt them"—and Gould pointed to the one he liked most. "You sure that's the one? You're not choosing it because it's the second smallest? If you got to know, it's among my three top favorites of those, but I didn't want to say anything to influence your decision against it. Before you change your mind, give me your pen. I'm going to do something usually only reserved for book authors, which you should appreciate," and with his wife guiding his hand, Bolling wrote an inscription in the right bottom corner.

Gould nailed it to his wall that day. Bolling died a week or two later, and a year after that the painting fell off Gould's wall and he tried nailing it back up and it fell again with even more plaster coming off, and he tried to stick it up with duct tape but the painting was too heavy and he didn't want to put more tape on because the painting's paint came off with it, so he rolled it up and stuck it in a closet. When Sally and he got married and moved to Baltimore four years later, she said she wanted to get the painting framed. He said maybe they could just nail it to the wall—his New York apartment walls weren't made out of the right kind of plaster for that and there were already nail holes in the painting's corners—but she said, "You'll see. It'll look better stretched and with a relatively simple wood frame. It'll also be good for the painting: fewer creases and cracks, things like that."

The painting's of the sea, sky, mountains, and a huge waterfall, or that's what the plunging blue and white looks like, of one of the Balearic Islands. Or one of the Canaries. He'd have to look at an atlas. But how could he find which group of islands it is if he also doesn't know the island's name or the name of the town the scene was painted from? It starts with an *N,* the town, or a *D,* and he thinks it ends with an *A*. It's the one Robert Graves lived on for many years. So he supposes he could get the names of the island and the town from a book about Graves. Anyway, Bolling lived there with his wife for two years, same time Graves did but he didn't know him, he said, small as the town was, or know him enough to say more than a passing hello when he saw him out walking or in a store or café, "and by then the man may have been demented, or that's what some people said, though he was living with, and no doubt screwing—because you could see by his swagger and look what a lusty guy he was—some young attractive American gal. So of course all the expatriate male writers on the island, no matter what nationality or how they felt towards him, wanted to screw her too because she'd done it with Graves. And if he won a Nobel, which some literary chiefs were predicting, an even greater feather in your cap and maybe more luck in your writing. . . .

"One story, though, I can tell you firsthand," Bolling said, a few weeks before he died, when Gould was wheeling him across Central Park to the Met. "It's a good example of the moronic, worshipful following Graves had attracted to the town and which ruined it for us, to tell you the truth, even if most of them had got there before us. We came for artistic stimulation and intelligent communality (besides cheap living), but these louts just hung around, drinking and soaking up the sun and waiting for some new sign from the great man or duty to do for him, like accompanying him to the local bar. They never produced art or letters the way Graves had and which he was still doing in abundance. I know from the island's telegrapher that he was sending out reviews and articles once a week, so how demented could he have been? Now it's too late, but why didn't I think that then and say something to those loafers and spongers who claimed he was addled? But this neighbor of ours came running into our little cottage, waving a pair of men's Jockey briefs. You guessed it: 'They belong to Graves,' he said. 'I was walking past his house, peered through his bedroom window, hoping to catch him humping his newest concubine, and saw these lying on his bed. I climbed through the window and swiped them. One day they'll be worth a bundle. They even have *R.R.G.* written on the label in laundry marker. You'll see, a collector will buy this from me and frame it behind glass and hang it on his most visible library wall. Bob had probably taken them off,' this guy goes on, 'tossed them on the bed, and put on a fresh pair before he left the house, or maybe he took them off to put on swimming trunks. I'm thinking if I should wash them, since they have a shit stain on them'—toilet paper was a precious commodity on the island, I want you to know—'or keep them as is,' he continued, 'because they'd be more of-the-person and so more valuable that way.' I told him to get them back to the bedroom without Graves knowing they'd been stolen, but he wouldn't hear of it. Of course this idiot probably forgot whose underpants they were a week later and either put them on himself without washing them or his wife, after wondering where they had come from, used them to swab the kitchen floor."

Fifteen years after Gould was given the painting, he says to his wife, "This thing's really grown on me since you got it framed. And Bolling had a lot of them, and I'm sure his wife—" and she says, "You want to buy one?" and he says, "If it's all right with you, since you'll have to live with it too," and she says, "I like the idea, so long as it doesn't cost a fortune." "No chance. They were very fair and modest-living and ungreedy people. It's even possible she'll want me to have it for nothing because of what I did for them then, but which I won't let her do. Anyway, good, settled, I'm about to purchase a painting for the first time in my life; before, they were always given to me by the artist, and that lobsterman drawing from you," and she says, "Won't it be odd, though, phoning her after so many years, but to buy something rather than to ask about her and her son and maybe even, after so long, to invite her out for lunch?" and he says, "How do you think I know she's still in the city in her old apartment? When I've gone up to see my mother—same neighborhood—so I bumped into her on the street a number of times." "You never told me," and he says, "I'm sure I have. Or else I forgot by the time I got back or didn't think it worth mentioning, since you never met her," and she says, "Of course I have. In a restaurant once, when we were with your mother, or right outside it on the street, and then at the memorial for Bolling a year after he died," and he says, "Six months," and she says, "Six months, not that she'd remember me from that, she was so distraught," and he says, "Funny, but I can't remember her as ever being even a little emotionally upset," and she says, "Crying her eyes out. Just crying them out. Though you were pretty shaken up too," and he says, "That I think I recall, which I guess is why I don't remember how she was at that particular event."

He calls and says, "Grace, hi, it's Gould Bookbinder, how you doing?" and she says, "Hello, Gould Bookbinder," and they talk about her and her son and his family and mother and then he says, "Listen, another reason I'm calling is because of Bolling's paintings. I have one, you might remember, and I'd like to get another, but to buy it this time," and she says, "I'd be delighted. But what was the arrangement before—he gave it to you?" and he says, "And inscribed it. It's almost as if you both did, since you held his writing hand." "Your memory's too good," and he says, "I'm sorry," and she says, "No, no, but I haven't sold one since he died and I've tried like the dickens, believe me, and I could use the extra money. How's the one you have doing?" and he says, "I got it framed. Looks great. People are always marveling at it. It's above our upright piano at the far end of this long living room, the perfect place for it, as you can see it from about twenty feet away when you enter the connecting dining room." "Which one did you get again?" and he says, "It's hard to describe. If it has a title, I don't know it," and she says, "All of them did," and he says, "Then if you told me, I either forgot it or never heard it. But it's kind of small, first of all—one of the smallest of the I-don't-know-how-many you spread out for me there—maybe three feet by two, but three feet across. It's of the mountains—you know, the Spanish island—and lots of dramatic sky and sea, very bright colors—the blues and yellows, anyway—and I think a waterfall in it," and she says, "Couldn't be. None on the island, and I don't think Bolling ever saw one in his life. He lived there, and here in different boroughs, and two years in the army on an ice cap, and before that at an army base in New Jersey not far from here." "He must have traveled around Europe or just Spain before he got to the island," and she says, "Both times he went it was by ship from New York to a large Spanish port and from there a ferry or small craft of some kind to the island, and the same when he returned to the States. That island was everything to him—in imagery, inspiration, ties to a particular spot on earth, you name it—which he knew before he got there, and he didn't want any other setting interfering in his memory of it. He used to say—actually, he said he thought along these lines way before he went to the island. It was a movie theater travelogue of the island when he was a young man that first prompted him to think this and eventually bore him to the island—that he only needed this one landscape and he'd paint it and dream of it and be reminded of and recharged by it for the rest of his life." "Then I don't know. Because how do you explain this plunging blue-and-white thing and what looks like raging water foam at the bottom of it?" and she says, "More crashing sea, probably, or a stormy sky. You sure you hung the painting right side up?" and he says, "Yeah, the mountains. It wouldn't look like anything recognizable upside down, and I never thought of him as a pure abstractionist." "Now the painting's coming back to me. Does it have two large pointy mounds that are unmistakably mountains as you said but could also be mistaken for a woman's enormous breasts?" and he says, "Right, two, of equal size just about, but I never saw them as anything but mountains," and she says, "That's what they are, but breastlike mountains, and what he called the painting, in a way: *New Peaks.* He was fascinated with the idea of taking old mountains and turning them into young breasts. He loved breasts more than any other part of the woman's body, just as he loved mountains more than any other part of the land, so it all fits, and naturally the younger the developed breasts the better," and he says, "By the way, what was the name of that Spanish island town where he did all those paintings?" and she gives it, and he says, "And the name of the group of islands it was part of?" and she says, "What group? It was just an island, Majorca, and near it were a couple of smaller islands, but no big group and certainly not a chain," and he says, "That's what I meant, and I actually knew but just wanted to make sure. But the town I always forget the name of, though knew it started with a *D*, and I bet I forget it again next time someone asks what place the painting's of or where the painter lived on Majorca and so on. My mind . . . I don't know: drink, age, something scarier? But I once wanted to—let me see: thirty-five, almost forty years ago?—wanted to live there too when I fashioned myself a would-be painter and writer. I heard it was dirt cheap, lots of wonderful free-thinking and -living women of various European nationalities, and it just seemed like the best thing to do for a while right out of college . . . sun, beaches, jug wine, all of which I stay away from today," and she says, "You should have gone. That was the time. Now the island's expensive, overcrowded, with rich tourists, grand hotels, and topless beaches—though I hear Deja hasn't been touched as much—so the natives probably aren't as hospitable and pleasant to you in a genuine way as they were then, but imagine what Bolling would have done in his work with the nudie scene. He was there with his first wife around the time you said you wanted to be, and it was such a small English-speaking community you almost certainly would have known them and become fast friends. She was supposed to be very nice." "Wait a second. I thought you were the wife he was with there," and she says, "I only went for a month about ten years after, a sort of rekindling-the-memory trip for him. But I can remember Bolling telling you of his years there with her and even, I think, you saying how you had once wanted to go there to paint or write, and he saying how you then would have met him and Sally there," and he says, "Sally? That's my wife's name," and she says, "I know. In fact you came over for coffee with her once—this was another time, much later—and Bolling pointed out the coincidence of the names. He also said he hoped that your Sally—you were talking of getting married and I'm not sure if he said this more for my benefit than yours, since he had eight good years with her before he deserted her when he somehow got hooked on me—anyhow, that your Sally would be your first and only wife. He really liked her and it had nothing to do with her large breasts, since by that time, with all the painkillers and pain and the tumor behind his eyes fouling up his vision, none of that meant anything to him." "I don't remember taking Sally to your place. On the street, yes, you and she met, but after Bolling's death, and she also came to the memorial, though which of those was the first time you saw her I don't know." "Gould, believe me, I can even remember where we all sat: you two on the love seat, I was in the rocker across from it, at an angle, and Bolling was directly across from you in his wheelchair, to my left. You ended up switching from coffee to wine and Sally stuck with her herb tea, and after a while I not only had cookies out but crackers and cheese. But I'll tell you, if you had gone to Deja it's possible you would have written or painted something but more likely have become a terrific young wino, café habitué, and wife swapper—or girlfriend swapper, in your case—as that's what almost all of them did. Bolling said that most of them were big fools, or became ones there, when before they had been responsible family men and executives or staff writers or chief graphic artists on magazines like *Time* and *Business Week* or some oil company newsletter, et cetera. There to paint the great Mediterranean painting or the literary equivalent with the three-act domestic drama or thousand-page novel or epic poem. But in a year or two, once their funds had run out, they were back in their old high-rolling jobs and cushy living. Bolling was the anomaly, eschewing most of the fun and games to get some real work in while he had the chance and which he had depleted his savings for, and only sleeping with his wife. Did he tell you the story of Robert Graves's underwear?" and he says, "That someone stole a pair and he told this guy to put it back?" "One person stealing one pair? Please, it became the principal recreation of the expatriate community there; even friends visiting for a week tried to land a pair. For years people were sneaking into Graves's home for one or ripping one off his washline or out of the maid's laundry washtub while she was siesta-ing, and one jerk even got a week of dirty underwear out of his bathroom hamper.

Word was that Graves was unamused by all this but had boxer shorts shipped in by the dozens to keep the thieves supplied so they wouldn't steal more valuable things like letters and manuscripts and books and works in progress." "It's funny but I never took the story quite seriously, and I also had heard it was a pair of Jockey briefs that were stolen," and she says, "Boxer shorts. Bolling was there and he told me. And in all his time on the island he never found the activity anything but deplorable, and anonymously he returned by mail a pair to Graves that had been given to him as a birthday gift."

He tells her he'll be in the city in a month to see his mother and if it's all right he'd like to come by to choose a painting. She says to call her a week before so they can make a definite appointment. "I don't want to pretend I'm a busy person or that dealers are batting my door down to get his works, but occasionally I do see a friend for lunch." Three months later she calls him. "I got your number from the woman taking care of your mother. She said you were in New York last month. If you were, it's possible you called and I missed you," and he says, "I've actually been there twice since I spoke to you, but only for a day—in and out, by train. I'm sorry, I forgot. But we're all coming in for two weeks in June. I'll call before we drive in, or just get me at this number in New York," and gives it and the day they'll be there. She says, "Incidentally, you never said what you were interested in of Bolling's: the drawings, pastels, satirical pen and inks—they're of Lyndon Johnson and his cronies; I don't think he was ever better, satirically, than with those—or his Majorca watercolors: the sunrise series, the sleeping cat sequence, another one of just beach stones—there were these enormous boulders along the shore, some like the Easter Island ones, though not carved—and of course the oils." "The oil paintings. Something like what he gave me, since the last time we spoke you said you hadn't sold any for a long time," and she says, "What I said then was 'never.' Not one. Not in his lifetime or mine. Not even a single drawing. Whatever he did that's not here has either been given away or donated to a school's art sale, but I think even those came back." "So," he says, "one of those, the oils. I hate to sound dumb about it—because, you know, I really admire most of them—but one to sort of complement, for another wall in the same room, the one I already have of the sun and sky and such of that island and town . . . I can never remember the damn name. I know it starts with a *D*—the island, of course, is Majorca—but the town. I know I also said the same thing one of the last times we spoke—that it starts with a *D* and I can never remember its name. But my mind can't be that bad off if I'm able to remember almost verbatim, and maybe even verbatim, what I said about not remembering the town's name and that business about the initial that last time, some—well, I don't know how many months ago, but several," and she says, "Deja, De-ja, D-E-J-A, though the Spanish spelling of it is different and not just with a little diacritic," and he says, "Don't tell me it; one's enough, and I wouldn't want to confuse things even more. I should write it down, but I know I'll lose the paper I write it down on. That has less to do with memory loss than absentmindedness. In my address book, under your name and number, I'll put it, and then I'll just hope I remember it's there when I want to recall the name, if I don't from now on recall it automatically. As for the address book, somehow it just turns up whenever I look for it. Anyway, I'll call you the day after we get in."

She calls him in New York. "Damn, how'd I forget?" he says. "I won't even say I was going to call you. I mean, I intended to but we've been so busy: my mother, whom I see every day, and taking the kids around—movies, museums, shopping sprees, you name it. When they're out of school and too old for day camp—they think—it's 'What're we gonna do today, Daddy?'" and his older daughter, who's beside him, says, "I don't talk that way, Daddy. And you don't let us shop." "If you're no longer interested in buying one of Bolling's paintings," Grace says, "that's all right too, Gould. People are allowed to—" and he says, "No, I want one, very much so," and to his daughter, with his hand over the mouthpiece: "Only kidding, sweetie. Just making talk. . . . When shall we meet? Tomorrow at one, maybe? I think I can be free then," and she says, "No good. I'm a dog walker now—a professional one; I have no animals of my own—and I've four dogs to walk between one and three." After that, she's busy too. "Thursday?" and she says, "I've dog-walking jobs from eight to twelve, and the last one, for an hour, is five at a time, so would two o'clock be okay? I need some rest, and also a shower, after a long spate of walks—picking up all that doodie, and they can slobber over you when they get playful. And it's hard sweaty work, getting pulled forward, holding them back, really straining at the reins when some outside dog barks or jumps at them. But I've got to make money somehow; I'm really short." "Two, then," and gets her building number—the street he knows, since he had once lived around the block from them and it was how he'd met them more than twenty years ago: in the stationery store at their corner on Columbus where Bolling bought most of his art supplies and he bought things like typewriter ribbon and reams of paper, and he said, when they were on line to pay, "You must be an artist," and Bolling said, "And you? It's obvious what you do too, unless you have an unusually extensive correspondence going and you mail all your letters in those manila envelopes," or something like that.

He's at his mother's when the phone rings. It's Grace: "Your wife told me you were there—I'm not following you, I want you to understand. You don't remember we had an appointment at two?" "Oh, my God"—and looks at the wall clock—"it's twenty to three and someone's picking me up here at three-thirty. How can I be such a dunce. I'll be right over, should take me no more than ten minutes if I run," and she says, "You won't have time to look at the paintings." "I'll have time, don't worry; I know what I want and it won't take long," and she says, "Really, we can make it another day," and he says, "No. I don't know what the hell our schedule is the next few days before we leave, and I want a painting and won't let my being a forgetful blockhead stop me. Are you free now?" "Yes. I set aside two hours for you to look at his artwork," and he says, "Good, then we have enough time; just tell me your building number again." He finishes making his mother coffee, puts it in front of her with some cookies he brought over, apologizes that he has to leave early but he'll see her tomorrow when he'll take her out for lunch, gives Grace's name and address to the woman who looks after his mother, and says, "Tell him to ring the vestibule bell for me there—it's only six blocks away—and I'll come right down, or in a few minutes, and he can stay in the car," and she says, "I can't remember all that, can you write it?" and he says, "Just tell him to ring the bell and ask for me," and runs and walks fast to Grace's building, rings her bell downstairs, and she says, "Gould?" and he says, "Yes, at last, I'm sorry," and she buzzes him in.

She has cheese and crackers out, grapes, two wine glasses on a tray, and in the center of it an unopened bottle of Burgundy. There are stacks of sketchbooks of different sizes on the same table. When she opened the door he kissed her cheek, apologized again. She says, "You know, for a while there I thought you were only saying you were interested because you wanted me to think someone still wanted Bolling's work." "No, I am, very. You have sketchbooks out. For me, or you just keep them here?" and she says, "You said you liked the mountains and seacoast of Deja. Some of his best watercolors of those scenes are in these. And some have words he wrote on the bottom of them—reflections, some of it real poetry, I feel, but his own, the only time he ever wrote it—and sometimes all around the edges like a frame, so are sort of mixed media. I thought because he used words in a literary way on them that you'd be especially interested. They could be expensive, though, compared to his other watercolors, since I think they're his most innovative work in any medium, or at least unique for him, which should count for something in an artist's body of work," and he says, "Probably, but I only came for the oils; is that all right?" "Oh, those. I don't think I've had them out since you chose one. It means burrowing into the long closet, pulling out a whole bunch of things first to locate them, and then untying and unrolling them and they're no doubt dusty . . . who cleans the back of a closet like that one? I know I should have looked after them better, wrapped them in a way that would have best preserved them, making sure nothing hard or jagged was against them so the paint wouldn't flake or the paintings themselves get punctured . . ." and he thinks, What'd he get himself into? This could take an hour and he doesn't have the time. She has crackers and cheese out. They're for him, unless they're for someone coming later. But then the cheese wouldn't be here now. If she just wanted it at room temperature she would have left it in the kitchen. Putting it here she'd have to think he'd think it was for him, and then the wine with it. Two glasses. Of course it's all for him. But what'd he expect, all the oils would be spread out and waiting for him on the floor and furniture and taped to the walls and he'd just look at them quickly and hit on one and say, "That's it," and pay up and carefully roll it up and put some twine or a few rubber bands around it and help her get the rest of the paintings rolled up and back into the closet and then kiss her goodbye right after his friend rings and leave? And there must be fifteen of them, twenty, because she hasn't sold any and that's about the number there were before, though she might have given some away since then . . . he hopes so. He says, "I'll get them. I'm not afraid of work and dirt, and I swear I have good quick taste and judgment and I know there are—know from the last time . . . my memory's perfect on that, with maybe the most minuscule of lapses—but what was I saying? Oh, yeah: that there are a few oils of his from that period that I truly loved, but all, of course, of the ones shown me from the closet and the two from the Deja period you still have on the walls—I'm just guessing they're the same ones," and she says they are and he says, "But that I liked." All this is a lie. He forgets what he felt that last time. No, he remembers: a few were awful—half of them, maybe; amateurish, almost; paint slashes here, there, drips, drops, lots of splashed-together flashy colors meaning and representing or just plain doing nothing to him, or maybe a few hints of mountains and sea. What he remembers most is that he didn't want one too big. What he remembers before *that* is he didn't want one at all, from what he'd seen of Bolling's works on the walls from all his periods, but he knew he couldn't say so once Bolling said he wanted him to choose one for himself. And now he remembers there weren't just Deja scenes in the closet but portraits, self-portraits, nudes, a few cityscapes. Bolling and Grace thought he'd like the cityscapes best because he'd lived in the city most of his life and they'd never heard him have a good thing to say about the country or beach, and he said something like, "I've had plenty of it, thank you; last thing I want to be reminded of when I'm in my apartment is the city outside." So they brought all the oils out and unrolled them on the furniture and floor, and there were so many, and there was so little space—some of them were so big and all of them were large—that there were usually two or three lying on top of each other, and he'd peel one off without saying anything but inwardly rejecting it and underneath was usually another big splashy nude or Deja scene or self-portrait or very dark cityscape, so dark he almost couldn't make anything out in it but a few lit windows. Till he saw a Deja painting he liked, and that it was the next to smallest of all the paintings must have helped his decision. The light colors were bright but not flashy, the dark colors weren't that dark, and he could recognize mountains and sea and what he thought was a waterfall without absolutely recognizing them as such, so it was both realistic and abstract and he liked that, or impressionistic or expressionistic and abstract—anyway, not absolutely one thing or the other, or he at least thinks that's what he thought then. And Bolling's face lit up when Gould looked at the painting longer than the others and he said—after Gould said, "It's all right if I pick this one, right?"—"It's one of my favorites. Did things in that I never did anywhere else. So why isn't it on the wall? I forgot, and now who cares? But I'll let it go without a grimace because of how kind you've been to me and helpful to Grace, and I know it'll be going to an appreciative and aesthetic home," and then, "On second thought," hoped Gould wasn't just taking it because it was one of the smallest. "No, size meant nothing. You said to choose one and I took that to mean any one except maybe the very largest, which I'd also have a problem with since I wouldn't want to seem like a hog," and then Bolling asked for Gould's pen—"I know you always have one, so hand it over, brother, though spare the paper"—so he could inscribe it to him.

Gould removes from the closet filled suitcases, boxes of clothing, old lamps, an easel with two legs missing, a crib mattress, and other things before he reaches the paintings. They're rolled up like a carpet and he tries to lift the roll, but it's too heavy so he pulls it out to the living room—"This a good place?"—and she says, "The light will be better for viewing over here. When Bolling was alive we had terrific light everywhere—he couldn't live with a lot of dark spots, not even in the closets. But each time a lamp goes I don't get it fixed or replaced and the ceiling fixtures, other than the kitchen one where I stand on a counter, I can't reach." He starts pulling the roll along the floor, and she says, "You can't lift it? Dragging it like that won't do the outer one any good and it might be the best of them all." He hoists it to his shoulder and gets it to where she tells him to and gets on his knees to set it down: between the love seat and the rocker and chair. Cocktail table that was there is against the wall, a little scatter rug on top of it. This is going to be hard, he thinks, untying the roll, and they never talked price. He can't afford much; was figuring on a hundred bucks. Thought she'd be glad to take it—as an incentive he'd wanted to give it in cash, and she can't be doing well—and rid of a painting. But she's put out for wine, cheese, and grapes and spiffed up the apartment for him. The setting's a selling one and he doesn't want to hurt her feelings or have her think he's wasted her time by saying the one he chose is just too expensive for his tastes, and there might not be another he likes or would want to pay even a hundred for. Hell with the hundred. He's here, he's led her on, she's put herself out for him, and he's going to have to buy one. He flattens the paintings out best he can—there must be thirty or forty—and starts going through them. Top one he's already dismissed: a small ugly nude, with a good arm and a withered arm and breasts that seem in the wrong place, though it's a realistic studio portrait, and a belly-button hole wide enough to fit a nickel in, and some of the paint's cracked and peeling. Looks as if it's from Bolling's art-school days, if he went to one; he doesn't know, or forgets, how Bolling got his early training. Pulls it back to the next: a candlestick and Chianti bottle standing on a wrinkled red cloth, velvet or something shiny. This one probably means something, with a candle in the bottle but not the candlestick, and just barely lit, or maybe that's an attempt at flickering. Then a still life of oranges and apples and an unidentifiable fruit, a lemon or kiwi or even a big walnut. It could be considered a good painting, light seems all right, oranges and apples look real, but he hates paintings of this sort—all still lifes except drawings—even by Cézanne. Or he doesn't hate Cézannes but doesn't admire them and by now just walks right past them in museums. Bolling would have said, "Your loss," and they may have even talked about it, but unfortunately they never went to a museum together, except when he pushed him to the Met once, but it was quick because Bolling was incontinent by then and, he thinks, silent through the entire visit. Next are three self-portraits. He doesn't remember putting them back this way fifteen years ago, by category. Maybe there'll be a few straight Dejas. They aren't good paintings or likenesses and he wouldn't take one for sentimental reasons, even if she gave him it for nothing. Bolling was a nice guy, smart, generous, amiable, maybe a bit grouchy sometimes, and they had good conversations about politics and art and such, at the most saw each other twice a year for drinks and peanuts at this apartment but bumped into each other a lot in the neighborhood. He only became close to him—seeing him daily for weeks—when Bolling's sickness got much worse and Grace had become exhausted from taking care of him and couldn't push him in the wheelchair anymore or get him off the floor when he fell or slid off a chair or take him to the doctor or hospital alone and was never able to give him his painkiller shots, so he volunteered to do these things, since he was just around the corner and had given insulin to his father years before, but they were never friends. "I like these, some better than others; the self-portraits are especially—I don't know what—strong," and she says, "Aren't they? People used to think me frivolous when I compared them in honesty—the whole exposed man—to some of the late Rembrandt ones and all of Van Gogh's. But I couldn't hang one here, for obvious reasons. I'd rather have the LBJs, much as I loathed the man—so shrewd and coarse and what he did to prolong the war. You knew him, didn't you?" and he says, "I didn't actually know him. But when he—this is what you must mean—put his arm around my shoulder—the news service I worked for then covered regional stuff for a few Texas radio stations, otherwise he wouldn't have said boo to me—it was like a bear's, which I think was how Bolling said he depicted him in his caricatures there. Or maybe that's where I got my bear analogy from . . . I forget, it was so far back, reporting. But that's how big Johnson was and maybe how thin I might have been then." "Oh, my goodness, you just reminded me. Why'd I have them out if I wasn't going to offer you? Glass of wine? You'll have to uncork the bottle; I always bungle it," and he says, "No, thanks, too early. And no cheese either; I'm stuffed. A grape I'll take," and she holds out the bowl and he pinches off a cluster and goes through fifteen to twenty more paintings while sucking and chewing grapes one at a time. "So, you haven't seen the paintings you liked? There was a Deja landscape among the ones you looked at—one of the mountains, but from a different perspective, and no sea," and he says, "There was? I didn't catch it or recognize it. Was it very abstract?" and she says, "No, relatively realistic; about three back," and he says, "I must be going too fast. Or else you sold the ones I remember or gave them away." "I told you: no one's looked at the oils since you. I would have shown them to art dealers, or anybody for the asking, but no one asked or responded positively to my hints or inquiries." "That was in 'seventy-nine, when I did that," he says, and she says, "Bolling died on May sixteenth, so you saw them about a week before. You went through them exactly as you're doing now," and he says, "I thought they were all spread out on the furniture and floor, and after it you and I got them together and stacked them the way they are now," and she says, "No, sir, they were in a big pile from the start. We got them out and unrolled them and you selected the one you liked and Bolling inscribed it to you. He even borrowed your pen for it, and when he saw it was a real fountain pen—a Sheaffer—he said this might ruin the nib and you said you didn't care," and he says, "I remember that. In the bottom right corner, and it didn't ruin the point. I don't have that pen anymore—I misplace, or they slip out of my pockets, about one a year; it kills me, they're so damn expensive—but I remember it worked after. The inscription's covered by the frame now, the canvas edges tucked under and probably stapled to those—what are they?—the stretching boards." "The stretcher." "Right. I didn't want it to be and I specifically asked my wife—she brought it to this hotsy-totsy framer—to keep the inscription visible, it was very important to me, but that's how it came back from the shop and, you know, I wanted to return it for them to do it right this time or just correct it, but never did, or it was too much bother and we wanted it on the wall more. I know the inscription said something personal," and she says, "It said, *To my dear friend Gould, who came to our rescue in this time of crisis and deep need, always our love and thanks, Bolling Sneeson.*" She starts crying. Seeing her, or something else—what she said Bolling wrote—he does too. She goes on longer than he and he thinks, Should he hold her, pat her shoulder? but doesn't want to. He says, wiping his eyes, "Listen, I'm sorry, but someone's picking me up at three-thirty. Here. He's going to ring downstairs. He was supposed to at my mother's but I told the woman taking care of her—" "How is she?" and he says, "Fine, considering. No, she's okay, no real health problems, ailments: just her memory—like us all, right?—though a little worse. But you see, this was before I knew or realized—seeing you, seeing her—because like a dope I forgot our appointment, and what I should have done was call this guy from my mother's but I was in too much of a rush to get here," and she says, "Then it's impossible for you to choose a painting today. I know all about your taste and judgment, but something like this takes time. It's like choosing a dog. You want to observe it first—it could be too vicious or frisky for you, and I'm not talking about puppies—or a cat or even a parakeet. To see if you want to live with it, and live with it you must. You don't want to put all that money into framing a painting and then stick it in a closet because you now don't like it," and he says, "I made my decision that way the last time and I can do it now. Sometimes quick decisions—well, you know, and I love the painting he gave me as much today as I did then." "You were wonderful to him, and to me too—I've told you. But to him you were a lifesaver those last months and he wanted to give you two paintings but you said—your characteristic modesty then, and I'm sure now too—'One's more than generous,'" and he says, "Two? I don't recall that. Though it was true: one was more than enough. Not that I wouldn't have appreciated two and known what to do with them, but as I told you on the phone—or did I say it here?—I didn't want to be a hog. I also wanted you to sell the rest; that's what I remember from then. That you didn't? So, other people don't know what they're doing, only zeroing in on the latest young hotshot who's made by . . . I don't know, art entrepreneurs who have a stake in him and important friends. Anyway, I know in this pile is the one I would have taken if I had taken two. Of course, this time around I'm going to pay. And we never talked price, I'm afraid." "Oh, that's another matter. How much an artist deserves to be paid for his work. Does it involve how much time went into the labor, how much thought went into the conception, all the expenses that went into making the painting and keeping up a studio to work in and so forth. Bolling only used the alcove here, which had our son's loft bed and dresser and no window and explains why his work became sort of somber, and because the room was so crowded and small he rarely did any paintings in it but tiny oils. But also how many prizes the artist's garnered and critical praise he's received and shows he's had and who's his current gallery and agent and how he does abroad and where and what museums and private institutions his works are in and the amount paid for them, though don't make me laugh. If all these, or only some, are the criteria to price one of his works, I should be paying you to cart it off my hands. But there's even more to it. Forget friendship and past good deeds and how much the potential buyer wants and loves the work—that's just between you and me and which I know to Bolling meant a lot too. But how long the work's been sitting around unsold and how many canvases the painter's done overall, and is the one the buyer wants considered among his best in period and style and is the medium the work's in supposed to be the best the artist has ever done?"—Then she goes on about Giacometti: His portraits or artist studio paintings? And if the portraits, then which should be considered more valuable, the ones of his mother or brother or wife or favorite non-family model—"Some adorable little girl the artist had an old man's crush on late in life?" And should his sculptures be worth more than his paintings, if there's a way of fixing a price on them competitively, because they cost more to make and have had a greater influence on other artists and have interesting anecdotes about some of them, like the matchbox figures, though those couldn't have been too costly to make even if they were whittled down from much larger blocks? But then most of his sculptures are bronze, particularly the famous stick figures and that mangy dog, which means a number of the same ones came from one mold. So why shouldn't the clay model be more valuable than its cast bronze? True, it's clay rather than the more durable and expensive bronze, but it's the original and singular. . . . All this while he's going through the rest of Bolling's oils. Then he sees one, third from the last—he quickly flips through the final two and doesn't like them—that's a lot like the one Bolling gave him. He doesn't remember it from before, but he sort of likes it. Not as much as the one he has but he doesn't remember liking that one immediately either, just being drawn to it. Not even that; it was the best of a lot he didn't much like any of and it was only after Sally got it framed that he started liking it and increasingly over the years till he liked it so much he wanted another of Bolling's oils of a similar scene or something close. It's worth a hundred. It's larger than the one he has, though that's not why, with more sky, less sea, same mountains but not as pointy. In fact they look more like a woman's breasts than the ones in the other painting, but a mature woman's rather than a mature girl's, and there's nothing in it that can be mistaken for a waterfall. It also has a large blue egg-shaped object on its side in a lighter blue sky to the right of the mountains. It doesn't seem to belong there, looks unfinished as an idea and cheap, and what's it supposed to mean: a sun with the color of a darkened sky? Maybe it'll blend in better later on, but for now he can live with it because of the rest of the painting. No, this one's the best of the bunch here, in his opinion, and since he feels he has to buy one, this one's it. He looks up. She's saying, "For instance, this work over here." He looks at the wall she's looking at. "That's Bolling's? I wouldn't have thought so. Nothing in this group or on the walls even remotely—"

and she says, "It's by a cousin, on my mother's side. He didn't buy one in return, which kind of disappointed me," and he says, "You bought it? Or Bolling did, years ago? I don't remember it from then," and she says, "That's what I've been saying. I got it last year, the most extravagant present to myself ever. But that's another matter, my cousin not buying one of Bolling's works for even a quarter of what I paid for his—we won't talk about true worth. There's very little tit-for-tatism among painters. They mostly exchange works of comparable value, and what better time than when they're both not selling anything? But when their art starts selling, then you have to buy and if you're lucky they let you have it for half of what their gallery would charge. Since my cousin only started painting five years ago, there was no chance for Bolling to exchange anything with him. He only paints now and has begun to become one of your young hotshots. Being a professional and successful go hand in hand. Otherwise what goes hand in hand is elementary school art teacher and weekend artist, bartender, and intermittent painter. No, bartenders usually aren't painters, nor are dentists. Plastic surgeons often are, in their spare time. But you get my point. And I paid sixteen hundred for it. I didn't have the money and am paying in small monthly installments. I wanted to help support him because by doing so I was supporting all art in general, I felt, and I like the work immensely." He doesn't. Looks like some turn-of-the-century work. That's not accurate. There were plenty of great artists then, though mostly French. But like an Audrey—Aubrey?—Beardsley drawing or poster of a beautiful young woman with wavy locks and sensuous lips and tiny waist and perfect bosom and long body in a long diaphanous gown looking as if it's being blown by a wind machine. Pre-Raphaelite, that's it—Dante Rossetti and others—but maybe he has the time wrong. The woman in the painting's somewhat modern, see-through blouse and dreadlocks on a Caucasian and smoking a pipe, but she's even barefoot and behind her is a thicket of curlicued trees. He says, "Sixteen hundred. That's nowhere near to what I was thinking of paying—I mean, on the downside. I didn't even think of it, how much. I should have because I should have assumed his works would be worth something by now," and she says, "Didn't I tell you? I don't want to make things worse for myself here, but I had slides made of some of these to get them exhibited and sold, but no luck. So, selling one now at a more affordable price—remember, I said I would have taken a quarter of what I gave my cousin if he had shown any interest in one of Bolling's—would be all right and might renew my energy to try and sell more." "Shit, I feel like such a vulgarian, rushing through these and bargaining even before I tell you the one I like. Maybe, to give myself more time with all this, I should look at them again in September when we're on our way back from Maine. But where you don't go out of your way again with wine and cheese, and I promise I'll keep the appointment and get here on time," and she says, "You selected one? Then let's see if we can settle on it now," and he holds open the pile of paintings and says, "This one okay?" and she says, "You like that? I do too. So take it," and he says, "It's much larger than the last one I got, so a hundred dollars wouldn't be right for it, would it?—just say so," and she says, "Not from anyone else. Just as I wouldn't have sold, if you hadn't been given it, that last one for a hundred dollars to anyone but you . . . though a hundred then is worth about two hundred today, no? and maybe more. They say in the last twenty years the dollar has lost half its value every decade. But it's going to a good home and a good person, and Bolling would love that you have it for a hundred. This very minute he's probably even scorning me for selling it rather than giving it to you, but he'd also have to know I can use the money." "So, deal then, great; I'm so happy, and thanks," and takes it out and says, "Can I roll up the others for you?" and she says, "Better let me, there's a special way," and rolls them up and ties them and the buzzer from downstairs rings. She goes to the intercom while he carries the paintings into the closet. They seem lighter, which is ridiculous. "Yes?" and his friend says, "I'm here for Gould Bookbinder. My car's double-parked, so can you tell him I'm waiting?" She turns to him, and he motions he heard. "Want me to . . . ?" pointing to the other stuff, and she says, "No, I may want to throw some of it out. And it's raining now so you'll need to protect your painting," and goes into the kitchen. He rolls up the painting and she comes out with newspapers and two shopping bags and says, "Oh, let me see it one more time, I feel I never will again," and he holds it up and she says, "He did mountains and trees like almost no one. A real nature boy for a city kid," and he says, "Trees?" and she says, "Here and here and behind these two a whole grove of them. They're not brown or green and no little olives or white flowers on them, but that means nothing." "Listen, I know the guy's in a rush but can I put some ceiling lightbulbs in for you? I'm a half foot taller and have a long reach," and she says, "I've nothing but sixty-watters for table lamps, so don't bother." He writes out a check, says, "Remember, cash it," and she says, "Why wouldn't I?" and he says, "If you're anything like me you'll keep it in your wallet till it's ragged and unre- . . . in- . . . just not negotiable." She rolls up his painting, wraps it in newspaper, sticks the bags at either end, and says, "There's still some space in the middle where it can get soaked, so keep your arm around it there." Intercom rings and she says into it, "He's coming down now; give him a minute." They say goodbye, kiss, she says, "If you and your wife have the time when you drive back—" and he says, "I don't see how. Got to see my mom, Sally's got to see hers, we'll only have two days, but if we can we will." Walking downstairs he thinks, Look at me: T-shirt and shorts and old sneakers, while she was smartly dressed. She's probably thinking now, "The slob, Philistine. If I hadn't caught him at his mother's he never would have come here before he left for Maine. So insincere. And thinks he can choose in two minutes and offer me a hundred for it and that I'll take the money because I need it and what he did for Bolling years ago. Oh, it's sold, what's the point of complaining? and his wife is nice and might like it and putting it in a frame will preserve it." Or she isn't thinking much of anything; just putting the wine and cheese away and clearing up the closet mess.

His friend's in the building vestibule and says, "What's that?" and he says, "Painting by some guy I knew and sort of helped out. I bought it from his wife." "Very good, you're buying paintings now, and it's a big one and in oil, I can smell, so it must mean you've money," and he says, "Not really. And you smell the oil? It is, but I don't smell it," and puts his nose to the newspaper, tears out a piece, and presses his nose against the canvas, but still doesn't. "Your back door unlocked?" and his friend says, "In this city?" and he says, "Do me a favor and open the back door on this side, and I'll run with the painting and put it inside? I don't want to get it wet," and his friend says, "But it's all right for me to get drenched," and he says, "Then give me the key and I'll open the door and you run with the painting to it, but you know your car so I'm sure you'll be able to get it unlocked faster than me," and his friend says, "Only kidding. And for art, anything," and gets the key ready and runs outside.

During the drive Gould says, "I feel like such a vulgarian. How I bought the painting, the little money I offered, how much she values his work—he's dead, fifteen years ago, brain cancer, awful—and just that she was a friend too," and his friend says, "Why worry over it? You got what you liked; you do like it?"—and he says yes—"and at a good price. And now others will see it on your wall—this artist have more?" and he says, "Plenty." "So they'll possibly want one of their own, and you don't have to say how little you paid for it—for her sake, you could even inflate it—and she could wind up making lots of dough," and he says, "I had the same thought, but it hasn't happened so far." "It could start. Word could get around, and buyers will trickle to her place and then flock to it in even greater numbers, and she'll appreciate you in a way she never has before. And because of all this the value of the one you own will go sky-high," and he says, "I hope so and am going to try and make it happen—not the last part; that I've no interest in. But I bet the next person to buy one, and this time I'm going to offer her much more for it . . . well, of course, will be me."

School

AT THE INTERVIEW the assistant principal looks him over and says, "Yeah, you're the right height, age, and musculature for the job, so whataya say you're hired?" and he says, "Great, you don't know how much this means to me—I finally get to teach my own classes. I'm telling you, I'm going to do a terrific job, going to whip those kids into shape and they're really going to learn. I'll go to their homes if I have to, because they're being especially unruly and screwing up the atmosphere for learning in class, and speak to their parents. Keep the kids after school, even—anything. But I swear they're going to leave my classes at the end of the school year a heck of a lot smarter and more knowledgeable in English and grammar and writing and things than when they came in." "That's what their three previous teachers this term said, but who knows, maybe you got something different going for you. But I do like your spirit. I didn't see that in them—they threw in the towel too fast—so it's what I like to hear. As for keeping the students after school, no can do. Some of these kids have jobs to help out their families, and we don't have the Board of Ed's clearance for keeping students after school, or the facilities or staff for it.

Besides that, the people looking after these kids might not like it. As for going to their homes and such, nice idea but I wouldn't do it if I were you. You say 'parents.' Don't we wish all our kids had them and that they were interested in how their children do. But some have no parents, or none to speak of, and are living with a grandmother or uncle or married sister or sister who's not married but has three tots of her own to look after, or this unruly student's helping her to take care of them with babysitting or a paying after-school job. And most of the time they live on a block you don't want to walk down and in a building you don't want to go into. Though do what you think best. Sometimes in teaching like this you have to be adventurous and innovative, I'm aware of that. But I'd think you'd be at a much better advantage sending home letters to the parents or guardians and calling them on the phone after school or whenever you can get them and seeing the ones of the most obstreperous if not dangerous students in the much safer and more academic environment here when we open the school to parent-teacher conferences." "But if I go to the kids' homes they and the people looking after them will know I mean business. And I want to give my students as much time and attention and help as I can, get their families involved in the learning process—everything like that—or try to, at least." "All to the good," the assistant principal says, "all to the good. Now, since you never taught before except as a substitute, I doubt you ever made up a lesson plan, correct?" and he says, "Other than in that Education One-oh-one or One-oh-two course at City—I took both, a few years ago, but only did, you know, practical classroom teaching, where you observe for a month and then take over the class for a period—only did the lesson plans under the regular teacher's supervision." "It went well, though, I hope," and he says, "Very well. She liked my class. And if the kids were grading me, she said, they would have given me—" and the A.P. says, "That's good to hear. So, go home and write up five of them for next week, and come to this office ten minutes before the first bell and we'll go over them and see if you're prepared," and he checks with friends who have taught junior high school, and one gives him a whole term of lesson plans for eighth grade Language Arts that he'd received from someone years before. He brings in five of the plans that Monday. The A.P. looks at them quickly and says, "Who'd you get these from?" and he says, "No one. I read through the grammar book and reader you gave me, figured out around where the classes had left off from what you told me the last teacher did, added those dictionary definitions for the fast class, and wrote them up." The A.P. makes a couple of corrections and shows him the rooms he'll be teaching in and the stairway he'll be expected to be at every morning between the first and late bells. "You never leave this post even if you have to take a leak, so make sure you go beforehand," and he says, "And if some kid falls down the stairs and breaks or twists his leg?" and the A.P. says, "None should, so none will. You're at this spot to maintain order and keep the decibel level down and have them walk upstairs slowly, and at this hour nobody should be coming down. You see one doing it, you about-face him upstairs," and he says, "Suppose this kid says his homeroom's on the floor below?" and the A.P. says, "You tell him he's full of shit, but never in those words. You say, 'Then whataya doing one floor above it, mister? Get moving upstairs!' Don't worry, he'll find another stairway to come down, but not yours because as you say they gotta know you're tough, you mean business and carry through, and don't flip-flop because of inept simpleminded excuses." "Excuse me, sir, but I'm kind of an overcautious meticulous guy and like to be apprised as to what to do in these kinds of situations before they happen, so what if a kid actually does get hurt? Falls, slips—let's say there's water on the stairs because it's pouring outside and the kids are still dripping," and the A.P. says, "Listen, this is time-wasting, going over the most unlikely eventualities. But you say it's important for you to know and I'm here to answer all your questions, so if a kid slips and breaks his head on the stairs, this is what you do. If no other adult's around, choose whoever you feel's the most trustworthy-looking student within a ten-foot radius of you, take down his name and homeroom or at least pretend to jot them down so he thinks you'll go after him later if he doesn't do what you ask of him, and write out a quick note as to what's happened—always have a pen on you, always, and, of course, paper—since just the opposite will usually come out of this kid if he tries putting it in his own words. Then send him to the main office to give the note to whatever adult's working there, though don't forget to include on it what stairway you're on—they're all numbered—and what floor. But the point is, and I can't make this any more emphatic to you, that if you abandon your post—especially if the stairwell's wet—all hell there will break loose. Anything else?" and he says, "Teaching tips?" and the A.P. says, "Discipline's the key, which I assumed you learned something about when you were a sub. For this school and your grade I'd say to just go in there and start teaching as if it were second nature to you. That means to keep talking, never smile, don't even smirk at any of their jokes and stunts, don't try to kid around with them, never show you're warming up to them the first month or they'll walk all over you from then on. Keep them working constantly, maybe let up the last three minutes so they can empty the trash out of their desks and clean up the area around them and get their belongings together and be ready to leave the moment the bell rings, and keep writing their names down for detention for even the slightest infraction, though resist as much as possible sending any of them to their respective deans. Those offices are already too full as it is."

His first period's free and he goes to the teachers' lounge, introduces himself to a couple of teachers, one says, "Welcome aboard when we're all about to jump ship," and he says, "Jesus, it can't be that bad, is it? Well, I'll live," and sits on the sofa, puts his legs across a chair in front of him, and thinks, Now this is the way to start off Mondays, and reads the newspaper and has an instant coffee from the hot-water urn and then goes over his notes and in his head how he'll conduct his first class. During the change of periods he stands, as he was told to by the A.P., outside his classroom, smiling and saying good morning to the students coming in, peeks into the room every fifteen seconds or so to make sure nothing wrong's going on there, gets a few funny looks from his students walking in and some good-lucks from teachers passing in the hallway or standing outside their rooms. When the second bell rings he goes inside, writes his name on the blackboard while facing the class, something he was warned to do by the former-teacher friend who gave him the lesson plans—"Rule number one: never turn your back on them"—and says, "Hello. My name . . . please, everyone sit down and let's have some order. Hello. My . . . please, everyone *please* pay attention. My name, as you can see, is Gould Bookbinder—*Mr.* Bookbinder—and I'm your new permanent Language Arts teacher," and a boy raises his hand, and he says, "Yes? And your name, please, so I can begin cross-checking it with all your names on my roll book here and begin knowing who each of you is?" and the boy stands and looks around at the other kids and then straight at him as if trying to stare him down and says, "I'm not taking no orders from no white man," and the class laughs, and he says, "Are you saying—and you can stop with that staring look; I'm not affected by it—that you don't want to give me your name?" and the boy says, "I told you; you don't have to be dumb, so I don't have to repeat," and he says, "Wait, I don't understand that, honestly. And I bet that most of you, even though you went with the *whew-whew* as if he just sliced me apart, don't understand what he said either. And about that white-man business—really, that's unfair. I don't know what your Language Arts teachers were like before I got here, but stuff like that's the exact opposite of what I feel. But let me just say how odd it is that what you said's the first words spoken to me by a student since I got to this school—not even a hello or good morning or 'Where'd you get the snazzy tie, teacher?' . . . nothing. And I'm kidding about the tie, of course; it's a piece of junk," and no one in the class laughs and the boy continues to stare at him, and he says, "Oh, just be seated," and another boy raises his hand, and he says, "I'd call on you, young man, but I'm waiting for your classmate to be seated. Though I'd also like an apology from him for his rudeness, or I swear the whole class will suffer," and the second boy stands, and he says, "I didn't tell you to stand," and the boy says, "I only got to say I'm not taking any orders from no white man either." "What's your name, sir?" and the boy says, "'Sir'?" and cracks up and the class starts laughing and howling, but the first boy's still just staring at him, and he yells, "Now that's enough . . . both of you . . . all of you! But you two, be seated now, I've taken all I'm going to take from you, so I said to be seated, *be seated*!" and the A.P. comes into the room and the boys quickly sit and the class gets quiet, and the A.P. says, "Everything all right, Mr. Gould? I heard a bit of commotion from outside," and he says, "Bookbinder; I'm sorry but Gould's my first name. And no, everything isn't all right, I'm sorry to say. I've already had two unfortunate incidents of insolence, but I'll be able to handle it," and the A.P. says, "Insolence from whom?" and he says, "Really, it's all right, I'm sure it won't happen again. They were testing me out and they know now I'm the wrong guy to be doing that to, and also because they know you're around will help things too," and the A.P. says, "I want to know who was being disrespectful and insolent to a teacher on his first day, or any day, so I can have a brief chat with him or her," and the first boy's shaking his head at Gould not to say anything but he says, "This one, who started the disruptions and refused to identify himself, though I asked him several times—*and* to be seated—and that one, another troublemaker with no name," and the A.P. says, "Up front, Daryl; you too, Gregory," and they come up front, and the first boy says to the A.P., "I didn't do anything," and the A.P. says, "We'll see about that, and if the charges prove false you'll be exonerated and returned to your class," and grabs them by the back of their necks so hard, or maybe the boys are exaggerating, that their faces stiffen and walks them out of the room that way. Ten seconds after they're gone the class starts howling and laughing, a couple of them saying to him, "You shouldn't have told, Teach; now they're in trouble and their mothers can be called," and he says, "Class, please be quiet. No one should be out of his seat or speaking till I give him permission. Now I want everyone to be quiet, please. That's an order or else I'm calling in the assistant principal again and telling him who's continuing to cause trouble even though what he did to those other two boys should have been a lesson to all of you," but they continue talking, sitting at one another's desks, horsing around, ignoring him till about forty minutes later when he says, "Okay, everyone collect their things, bell's about to ring. And remember, boys and girls, this is the first and last time you're ever going to be allowed to behave like this in my class."

It's six years later; he's been calling in sick a lot and the school he's teaching at now has started to complain about it till finally the principal summons him to his office and says, "Anything bothering you, Mr. Bookbinder? Or wrong with your health that I should know of—something serious? You've missed, on average, a day a week the last seven weeks, and sometimes two days in a row, and you know how difficult it is getting subs for you this far out in Brooklyn. Also, your colleagues are saying they've filled in for you enough, and if they go to your union about it and the assistant principal is unable to take over your class, I'm at a loss what to do. Do you need to take a leave and for us to hire a permanent sub?" and he says, "It's the kids, to be honest. They're driving me crazy. I shouldn't be admitting this, or maybe that's a sign of just how unsteady or something I've become, but either my teaching's down or never was too good or the kids are getting more brazen and uncontrollable, though I know some teachers don't have that trouble. But then when they yell, their students shut up. While when I do it—" and the principal says, "I can well sympathize, since it can happen to all of us." "I don't instill fear in them, that's my problem," and the principal says, "That can be good too, if the opposite approach works, and probably better—less strain on the vocal cords, and so forth. But you can't let it get to you too much. Worst thing for you is when it does, and you leave us in the lurch too," and he says, "I'll try, and I appreciate your warning me about it—the consequences. I don't want to lose the job and I can't afford to take an unpaid leave and I'm not sick in a way where I can take a health one. Or maybe the leave system, the . . . the . . . what are they? Not the constitution, but like it . . . the guidelines—but I don't think it has," and the principal says, "What hasn't?" and he says, "The guidelines of the health-leave policy," and the principal says, "Normally it has to be accident related. You get bopped on the head or fall accidentally and split your skull open or some kid on school grounds—and he doesn't have to be a student—pulls a razor on you and just the trauma of that experience, even if the kid doesn't *use* the razor, is enough to do it—so I wouldn't count on getting a paid leave that way. But if you like, and I don't see how I can be any fairer about this, speak to your union rep here about it. Maybe she'll come up with a loophole for you, much as I'd hate to go hunting for a permanent sub more than halfway through the school year," and three weeks later, shortly before the Easter vacation and right after a day when he didn't want to come in but felt he had to and then didn't think he'd make it through the day, his classes were so unmanageable, he's walking his second-period class through the halls to an assembly in the auditorium, a break from regular teaching since it means a class and maybe a class and a half, if the assembly goes on that long, is suspended and all he has to do in the part of the auditorium he's assigned to patrol is keep the kids quiet, when one of his students breaks from the double line and runs to a phone booth near the school's entrance, and he yells, "Patricia, get back here, I didn't give you permission," and she pushes in the booth door and shouts at the boy inside, "You're speaking to her, you liar. You're love-talking and you said you wouldn't never," and kicks and beats the booth glass, and the boy says, "Hey, hey! Stop. I'm talking to my mother, and what you're doing's not looking good to her," and she says, "Your fucker, you mean, you liar," and keeps kicking the bottom glass panel till it shatters, and the class screams, "Kill him, Trisha, kill him!" and the boy jumps out of the booth and puts his fists up and says, "Come on, you wanna duke it out, I'm not afraid to hit pussy," and she lunges at him and he swings and grazes the top of her head or just her high hair and she pushes him down and leaps on him and starts punching his face and pulling his ear and he punches her face from the ground, and Gould's yelling, "Stop, stop, get off him, get up!" and other kids in the class and from other classes surround the boy and Patricia, and a girl in this crowd screams and turns around and says to Gould, who's trying to pull some kids away to get through, "Morris grabbed my tit, Mr. Book; I'm just standing here and he did it; say something," and Morris says, "No, I didn't; I can't; she has none," and he says, "Both of you, out of my way, let me get to them," and other teachers are pulling kids off one another and Gould grabs Patricia off of the boy and says, "You stinking bastard—you had to do that? Look what you caused," and she says, "Don't be calling me names," and he says, "I meant because of what you did. Like a savage, you acted, like a savage. Look at that glass; you're lucky you didn't cut yourself," and she says, "I told you, don't be calling me names; I'm reporting you," and he says, "Ah, Jesus, what the hell's going on? All of you, just get away from me, enough of this goddamn shit," and goes to the main office while some kids are yelling, "Teacher cursed, teacher cursed!" and the school secretary, standing at her desk behind the counter, says, "What's happening out there? I never heard anything like it. Should we call the police?" and he says, "Is Mr. Vandenburg in?" and she says, "If he was, don't you think he'd be attending to that racket? No, he's at a meeting in another school," and he says, "Well, tell him I punched out, I was sick, I couldn't take another minute of it," and grabs his time card out of its holder and punches out, and she says, "You can't just go like that. You need authorization. I'll get your A.P. Which one is it?" and he says, "Then forget I punched out, but I'm leaving. It's that or lose my mind. . . . I spoke to Mr. Vandenburg about it," and she says, "If you desert your classes before the school day's over and fail to get someone to cover them, you can be docked an entire day's pay, and I won't even tell you what the principal's reaction will be," and he says, "Didn't you hear me? Take my day's pay, take two; take the whole week's and the month's and I-don't-care how long," and goes to his homeroom, gets his coat from his closet and some things out of his desk. There are all sorts of supplies in the cabinets and closets that he bought with his own money to use in his classes because the school couldn't pay for them, but forget it—he'll never need them again—and leaves the school.

Coney Island

HE USED TO go out there to see his uncle and aunt and cousin and sometimes stay overnight with them. More than thirty years later the cousin was killed there when he got into an argument with a hustler. The hustler was selling drugs; his cousin told him there were kids around so peddle his stuff somewhere else. The hustler told him to mind his business if he knows what's good for him. His cousin said, "Why'd you come to Coney Island to sell your crap? This used to be a good place; my folks and I used to come here to an apartment every summer and you could walk along the boardwalk even late at night without guys like you screwing it up for people." "Get lost, will you?" the hustler said. There were witnesses; they listened from a few feet off, didn't butt in. "In Coney Island," one witness said, "you don't stick your nose into anything today. That's the mistake this fellow made and that's why he got killed. What used to be the old days hasn't been those days for decades, you could say, so why'd he think that drug pusher would listen to him?" His cousin persisted: "Look, I want you to get off the boardwalk and stop selling your poison or I'm calling a cop." "And I told you to walk backwards," the hustler said. "Now get moving, stay out of my business, or you're going to get very hurt." "So you're not leaving?" his cousin said, and the hustler looked around, said to the small group of people watching them, "Do you hear this chump? Can you believe anyone would be so stupid? Where's he think he's telling someone this? Okay, because he drew a crowd and I can't deal with him in private, and also because his breath stinks, I'll go, but you tell this dope he's finished, finished." His cousin followed him till he was off the boardwalk, the hustler turning around every few seconds to stare back and point at him and say things like "You're dead, mister. You might think you're alive because you're breathing, but you're as dead as they come. So take the last of your deep breaths because there aren't going to be any later. If you didn't hear me I'll repeat it. You want me to repeat it? Then believe it. I bullshit nobody." Some people came over to his cousin and patted his back and said, "I can't believe it, you stood up to that bastard. But you better get going the opposite way from him; that guy's a killer if I ever saw one." "A blowhard, that's what he is," his cousin said. "Drugs he has to sell to little kids or to big stupid ones who then turn on and screw up little kids? I caught on to him right away. I'm walking by, just taking in a day at the beach before the real season begins, and hear him with his nickel-bags line to these kids passing. 'Nickel bags, nickel bags, joints,' and some other crap that kills you but only goes by its letters, TNT or something. You know, when I was a kid I used to stay here summers with my folks," and someone said, "Yeah, we heard." "Then you know what I'm talking about: it was nice, lively, safe then. You could sleep on the beach on very hot days, send your kids into the ocean for a midnight swim, even, if there were no jellyfish in the water, and nobody would touch you. Girls could go in alone too, if they maybe only got a few whistles, the older ones." "Those days," someone said. "You can't bring them back and, much as I admire you for what you did, you shouldn't risk your life trying to." "Who was risking?" his cousin said. "If there was going to be any trouble, it would've been then. But I could see he wasn't that kind of hustler. When they don't talk or only say very little and just look at you like they want to slice you in half, then you could be in trouble and then I'd walk the opposite way, or till I saw a cop." Next morning someone found his cousin's body under the boardwalk about a half mile from where the incident with the dealer happened, his throat slit and pockets torn and necktie pulled around his neck and hanging over his back, but when he was a young man he used to put Gould on his shoulders and walk him at night along the boardwalk for a mile or so, give him money to play skeeball, treat him to the bumping cars and merry-go-round lots of times, buy him soft ice cream and saltwater taffy and a big salty pretzel and always a souvenir to take back to the city, a miniature metal Parachute Jump or a pennant with CONEY ISLAND and a picture of a Ferris wheel or the Steeplechase ride on it. Gould went to see his cousin and uncle and aunt a couple of times a summer, usually late June before he left for camp for two months and during the Labor Day weekend. The ocean wasn't clean then. Sometimes shit floated past, human shit, and condoms. But when there was nothing like that around, though he always kept his eye out for it when he was in the water, it seemed okay to swim in. What he liked best was getting in front of a breaker and being knocked off his feet and tossed around. Once, he really was tossed around, couldn't get his footing when he tried to, swallowed lots of water, and thought he'd drown, when his cousin grabbed his hand and jerked him out of the water and ran with him to the beach and set him down on his stomach and pumped the water out of him, and then, when Gould was sitting up and breathing normally again, held him in his arms and said, "Oh, boy, what a scare. I never should've let you go out that far. But you wanted to take chances and I thought, He's not my kid, and taking chances is good for a boy, so let him, but never again like that when I'm in charge." Gould got sick one time there, violent stomach pains, vomiting, high temperature; it was around eleven at night and his aunt said, "You want to take the subway back home? I'll call your parents and tell them you're coming," and he said yes, had been screaming he wanted to go home, feeling he didn't want to be this sick in someone else's apartment, thought he'd die if he stayed, that only his mother could take care of him when he was like this. He was practically delirious, it turned out, going in and out of it, he means. He doesn't know the details of what happened after that; he knows he spent the night there, eventually fell asleep, and went home by himself the next day. His aunt must have called his home and his mother must have said something like, "Are you crazy, send him home so late when he's this sick? Put him in a tub of cool water, or rub him with rubbing alcohol, but get the temperature down. Then, if his stomach can take it, give him an aspirin." His aunt, who usually looked after him well, sort of panicked then; he could tell from her eyes and voice: she just wanted him out of the house. His cousin wasn't home at the time, so maybe he got back later after a date or movie or meeting some friends—though Gould's folks used to talk about how he never had many friends and the only women he saw were whores—and his uncle had stayed in their apartment in Brooklyn closer to the city—same place on Avenue J his cousin had lived alone in for about fifteen years till he was killed—as he had to be at work early the next morning.

Now Gould takes his own kids to Coney Island. Did it the last two Junes too, and late in the month, since there was a better chance then, before they left for Maine on the first, the water would be warm enough to swim in. He always brings the kids' bathing suits but not his own—he just wants to read on the beach, in the shade if he can, while watching them. They haven't gone in to swim yet, but the last two times they *did* put their suits on in the decrepit toilet-and-changing building on the beach and wade in up to their ankles. "The water's filthy," his older daughter said the last time, and he said, "Why, anything floating in it?" and she said, "No, because it's brown, not like the Maine ocean," and he said, "That's the sand stirred up, your feet in it, all the activity in the water or something, or the surf's just rougher here and that's doing it, but it's okay to swim in. In fact, there's much less pollution emptied into the ocean around here than there was when I was a kid and used to come to Coney Island, so the water's probably cleaner now than it was then and maybe, because New York might be stricter with its pollution laws, cleaner than the Maine water. You can't imagine what they used to empty into the ocean then," and she said, "What?" and he said, "Things, terrible things," and she continued to look at him that she wanted an answer, and he said, "Toilet paper. Human feces, even," and she said, "What's that?" and he said, "Body waste from people. All right: shit, but not anymore."

After they get off the subway the kids tell him they want to go straight to the rides, which is the main reason they like coming out here, and they walk on the boardwalk—some of the cheaper rides are right off it—and he wonders, just as he thinks he must have wondered the last two times, what spot under it his cousin was killed. "Should we go on that big turning wheel?" his younger daughter says, and his older daughter says, "Yes, please, Daddy," and he says, "Okay by me, if you're game, but it's going to count as two of your permitted six rides, it's so expensive," and they walk to it while he's thinking, Or did the killer, who was probably the drug dealer, kill his cousin somewhere else? Or a friend of the dealer, or two friends, or just two thugs working for him, on the beach at night, his cousin somehow lured there, or maybe his cousin walked out there on his own—to see the stars better, he was somebody who'd do that, or because he liked solitude and he'd find it there more than any other place here at night—and they followed him, or even on the boardwalk when nobody was around, and dragged him under the boardwalk to get him out of sight and go through his pockets and slice apart anything that might contain money or credit cards. Why the tie over the back? Maybe in the scuffle, if there was one. Or else as a symbol of something then or only in this particular part of Brooklyn: "This is what we do to someone who pokes his nose into our business." Lots of cops around, he notices. He read in the paper a week or two back about a Russian woman being raped under the boardwalk by three boys, so maybe that's it. Kids, she said they were: fourteen, fifteen at the most. They slashed her face and chest with knives and razors, then raped her. They used condoms. Why, they were afraid of getting AIDS? This respectable Russian émigré mother of two small children, jogging on the boardwalk, would have AIDS? And they'd think like that? Or it could be they thought it cool, using condoms. "Hey, let's all use bags when we rape her, that's something new." Or else they didn't want—this is probably it, and learned from some older guys—to leave any semen in or on her. You can be identified as the rapist by your DNA. And they must have taken the condoms with them, the newspaper article said, since the police canvased the rape area and the three or four condoms they did find were so old they could have been from the previous summer. He didn't tell his wife about the woman because he didn't want her to use it to keep them from coming out here. She knew about his cousin, but that happened years ago and, as she said, "Deplorable as his murder was, in some ways you could almost say he was begging for trouble. Because what would you have done? Confronted the dealer if you saw him trying to sell drugs to kids—even to our kids?" and he said, "Maybe," and she said, "Don't ever, *ever.* You get a cop. Otherwise, you put not only yourself in danger but also our kids."

Lots of garbage, he notices, while his girls are in one of the cars high up on the Ferris wheel; plenty of screaming from up there and he listens carefully but can't tell if any of it's from them. The area around here always had lots of garbage, but he doesn't remember this much. "Why are you going out there?" his wife said this morning, and he said, "Because the kids like it, they can let off some steam, it's a day at the beach after a couple of weeks in the hot city, and some old memories for me are brought back when I'm there. Looking up through the boardwalk slats at people walking. My Aunt Essie and her family. Nathan's. At the time it was—before it was a chain—*the* place to go just before you took the subway home; it's right across from the station. With the best hot dogs, best fries, and certainly the best hot buttered corn anywhere, or that's what we thought. And as a kid, you go out there thinking that, you usually end up confirming it, even if the food really isn't that great. Or maybe it was. Maybe the hot dogs were kosher then and fresh and grilled perfectly and the corn was the best any joint could buy and picked that morning and they boiled or steamed it the absolutely right number of minutes, but not anymore. Last year and the year before—I gave them a try twice and that's enough—the food was crap and the place was seedy and dirty."

The kids come off the Ferris wheel hungry, and he says, "Okay, let's get some grub," and they chant, "Nathan's, Nathan's," and he says, "You don't remember last time? One of you got sick, even, I think, but I forget on what." They go to a fast-food chicken place on the boardwalk. He has coffee; they get a plate of fried chicken and fries and cole slaw. The slaw's sour and the chicken tastes funny, the kids say. "Taste it," and he says, "I take your word. After we drink up, we can get something somewhere else," and his older daughter says, "But we don't want you to think we're wasting good food. See for yourself," and he pulls a piece of meat off; it looks okay but it tastes as if it's been cooked in the same oil they fry fish in. He thinks, Should I? Ah, go on, no harm here, and they give me one bit of lip I'll say, "Okay, just saying," and goes up to the counter with the plate and says to the woman behind it, "Excuse me, but was the chicken and maybe even the fries—I didn't have one—fried in the same oil the fish is? It sure tastes it," and she says, "This is a chicken place, we don't cook fish here, just chicken and things that go with it," and he says, "Then I don't know, then," and goes back, and his older daughter says, "No luck?" and he says, "Well, I didn't really try." A dog walks in off the boardwalk, sniffs around, the kids offer it a chicken leg and just as he's about to say, Don't, people eat here, the woman says, "Please, there, nothing for the mutt or he'll never stop coming back. Give him a kick outside, but watch it he doesn't bite. I know him from before: a stray," and he whispers to the kids, "Let her do the honors," and dumps their plate and cups into the trash can, yells "Thank you," and they leave.

Few more rides. The last, the Water Flume, is the only one he ever goes on, because the spray, whenever the boat makes a sharp turn or slides down the tubing and hits the water, cools him off. "Okay"—wiping his arms and face with a handkerchief, he had the lead seat—"now time for the beach, and I'd like to read," and they both say they don't want to go, and his younger says, "I can't stand that horrible smelly house to change in," and he says, "Listen, we came this far to the ocean—more than an hour's subway ride; the walk from the station to here—we have to spend some time in the water or along the shore. Half hour max, then, I promise," and they go down to the sand, kids take off their sandals and roll up their shorts and look for shells by the water. He puts his sun cap on, lies on a towel facing the water, and reads. It's windier here, sand gets in his eyes and on the pages, sky gets darker—is it going to rain? Wasn't forecast and there's still plenty of sun behind him and are those rain clouds or just—well, another kind of cloud?—when some lifeguards at the station nearest him are blowing whistles and shouting and waving and people on the beach are pointing out to the water and some are running down to it and the lifeguards throw off their caps and shirts and race to the water with ropes and a small surfboard or float, and he squints in that direction and sees someone in the water about two hundred feet out, maybe more, can't tell if it's a man or woman but it's an older person, he's sure, and now it seems a bald one, so a man, or maybe that's a racing cap, waving his arms to be saved, it seems. He listens but can't hear the man, if he's screaming, maybe because of all the yelling around him to the lifeguards in the water: "He's over there . . .

there . . . to the right . . . to the left . . . get him before he drowns." Lifeguards are halfway to him by now, then reach him and seem to stretch him out on his stomach on this board or float and start bringing him in, two on either side, one in front pulling a rope, when a woman, it's clear by her voice, about fifty feet out and thirty feet to the left of the lifeguards and the man, yells, "Help, help, stuck, help!" her arms flailing, and then her head disappears and bobs up again and two of the guards swim hard to her, grab her from behind and hold her out of the water by her waist and she seems to calm down—Gould even thinks he sees her smiling—and swims in with one of the guards, the other swimming back to the third lifeguard and the man on the board. Gould's standing now, kids beside him, his younger clutching his hand. More lifeguards drive up to the shore in a Jeep, two of them jump out to help the three lifeguards walk the woman and the man out of the water, another lifeguard stands on the front seat and says over a bullhorn, "All swimmers out of the water now. . . . Attention, attention. All swimmers must leave the water now. This is your lifeguard speaking, this is a city lifeguard speaking: everyone out of the water till further notice. No swimming in this area till further notice. Serious undertow, there is a serious undertow, so nobody in the water till the all-clear signal's given. I repeat: no going into the water till the all-clear signal's given," and a man asks her, "And what's that?" and she says, "When the time comes, we'll let you know."

"I guess that's it," Gould says, and they start collecting their things. A man goes over to the man who spoke to the lifeguard and says, "What do they mean no swimming?" and the first man says, "That's what the lady ordered," and the second man goes over to her in the Jeep and says, "What do you mean no go in the water? It's a public beach, I can do what I want so long as I don't hurt no one or cause a mess," and she looks at him, and he says, "Yeah, that's right," and she yells to the other lifeguards, "Buzz, Jake," and waves them over, and Gould says to his daughters, "Why's the guy acting like that? They're the bosses here; they know what they're doing," and his older daughter says, "Daddy, come on, we got to go, and I don't want to see a fight," and he says, "Surely there won't be . . . just talk," and she says, "*Please,* Daddy," and they head for the boardwalk, Gould looking back every so often to see what's doing between the lifeguards and the man—for now, the biggest guard has his chest close to the man's face, but the man isn't backing off; he's staring right up to the guard and making some point with his finger stabbing the air—when it starts raining. They run for the boardwalk with a lot of other people from the beach—the lifeguards and the man stay where they are, still arguing, and the two people saved don't seem to be anywhere around—get under it, and put their sandals on. "Okay," he says, when the rain dies down, "safe to leave, just a few sprinkles left," and they walk to the subway, Gould setting the fast pace, when it suddenly starts to pour, then lightning, and he says, "Holy shit—excuse me—but out of this electric storm," and grabs their hands and they duck into the nearest shelter, a game and gambling area without walls—just a big tent, almost like a circus one, he sees—and dry themselves on one of their towels and just stand there, though his older girl circulates a little, watching people play the various games and machines.

"I've been robbed!" a woman shouts. "Over there—that boy and two girls," and Gould says, "What? Where's Fanny?" She's right behind him, and he throws his arms around his kids and brings them in to him and watches the two girls and the boy running through the rain, ten or eleven years old or so, the boy holding a woman's bag, one of its shoulder straps cut. "You kids . . . hey, you kids!" some people yell, but nobody goes after them and the kids never look back before they dart into an alley and are gone. People crowd around the woman—"What the little punks do? You didn't see them at it? They get your arm?"—and his younger daughter says, "Was she hurt?" and he says, "I only got a quick look, but I think just her bag was stolen, which is bad enough, plenty," and she says, "I'm scared here, I don't like the people," and he says, "Shh, they're all right, it's those kids who stole from her who aren't nice. But don't worry, nothing to be frightened about. And lightning's not supposed to strike a place twice," and she says, "What do you mean?" and he says, "Lightning, they say—I'm not too sure how true it is . . . in fact I'm sure it isn't; I can't see any scientific basis for it being true, though I'm no scientist. Anyway, that it's not supposed to strike the same place twice, meaning in this case that no one will get robbed here again today. People will be more careful now. And it'll be all right for us too, once the rain and real lightning stop," and she says, "And the thunder," and he says, "That too," but he doesn't know, maybe it won't be, maybe someone or a gang of kids will try to rob them when they go through that dilapidated dark subway station, or on the stairs there, or the platform. Though usually—no, always, it seems, and for no doubt good reasons—cops are in the station and more than enough people are on the elevated platform and a train's waiting there with its doors open, since it's the last stop for a couple of lines, and if they just miss a train then another's usually pulling in. But they could also be robbed on the train once it goes, since he doesn't recall the last two times seeing many people in the car. Why did he come out here? They were here the last two Junes, so why again? It's not as if the place had added new things to it lately. He forgot to tell his wife that the kids also loved the freak show on the boardwalk and a few days ago had asked him to take them to it—he'd planned to do what he did last year: get a coffee and sit on a boardwalk bench while they were inside—but they found out when they got there that it had been closed down. But this place has become too damn threatening, even dangerous. His cousin and uncle and aunt stayed for three months in an apartment on the third or fourth floor of a building only for summer rentals. Two bedrooms, living room, kitchen, all very modest, even shabby. Where'd he sleep? On the living room couch; he was small enough to be comfortable on it. Little balcony where you could talk to your neighbors, or hear them at least, on the balconies on either side of you. They were screened, he remembers, and the bathtub was in the kitchen and the toilet was in the public hall. There were two toilets to a floor, so you never really had to wait long if you had to go badly. The shower was in the courtyard downstairs. Anyone in the building and in the other buildings facing this courtyard could see you go in and out of the shower from their balconies. Now that he thinks of it, the shower had to be for just getting the sand out of your hair and off your feet, because one wouldn't have been enough for all those buildings if its purpose was for people to take a real soap shower. You hung your towel over the wooden shower door, or maybe there was a hook there, he forgets. Hook, over the door, what's the difference? Your feet could be seen while you were in the stall and if you were tall enough—he wasn't—your head. You stood on wooden slats and the water was usually cool to cold. In fact, he doesn't even know if the spigot went to HOT. He'd take the subway from Manhattan by himself—down to 42nd and Times Square on the Broadway line, then switch to the Coney Island line, or that's what he called it—it had a more complicated name, one that was told to him often but he could never remember at the time, and now, well, it's gone. To make the transfer, he walked through the hub of the Times Square station, with shops and always lots of fast-walking people around, and then down a long ramp to get to the platform, and for some reason he sees it as a terminal stop too, a train waiting with its doors open, or one train pulling in as the other pulls out, but he could be wrong. When he got to the Coney Island stop, he took a long trolley ride to their building. A man came around the building several times a day selling snow cones from a cart he pushed. A trailer with kiddie rides would park near the building, recorded calliope music would play over a scratchy loudspeaker, and kids in the surrounding buildings and on the street would run to it. A photographer would take your picture on a pony in front of the building or in the courtyard, but he doesn't remember having one taken and there are no photos of him on a pony in his mother's albums and photograph drawer. Passing street bands, knife sharpeners in a truck or on foot, icemen, people selling produce from horse-drawn wagons, others selling cleaning supplies and pots and pans. His cousin took him on the Parachute Jump once. It was night; they sat in the same seat, strapped and barred in. His cousin seemed to laugh all the way up; well, he was usually laughing or smiling broadly, telling jokes, bantering, making fun. "Don't be scared," he said, as they ascended slowly, "they only lost ten people in twenty years on this ride, and just five of them were kids your age. Only kidding." When the pole above their seat hit something at the top, there was a loud pop of their parachute opening and they were supposed to quickly float down. But the seat got stuck up there for about half an hour. He must have been afraid because his cousin kept saying things like, "Take it easy, nothing to get worried about, and this time I'm not kidding you. It has to be something to do with the electricity or some snag in the release hook on top that they'll soon fix. But there was never even someone hurt on this thing in all its years here, and I've kept track. Believe me, if I thought it was something really bad and Uncle Victor's kid was in danger, I'd do everything I could to save you, even get off this seat and risk my life holding on in the open air out there if it was because the two of us on it were too heavy. Or grab you up if there was any immediate danger and carry you across to a seat that worked, even if it meant climbing a little down the wires with you to get there. But you see how calm I am, and normally I can be a mess," and lit up a cigarette, took a few drags, and then did his swallow-the-cigarette trick he'd done lots of times, sometimes when Gould had asked him to—cigarette on his extended tongue, pulls the tongue in, mouth closes over it, he swallows, opens his mouth, no cigarette, then closes and opens it again and cigarette's there and still lit and just with his tongue he switches it to his lips and takes a puff and grins—pointed to the ocean and talked about what a great view, does he see the ship out there? must be a tanker, and look around while you can because you'll never again have so much time to sightsee from up here, but forget the pickle we're in, it's really only a tiny gherkin and we'll be out of it soon enough. A man in overalls rode up on another seat, stepped onto a platform, climbed a few rungs up a ladder to a big metal cabinet, unlocked it, and with his tools started working inside it, and Gould's cousin yelled up to him, "So how we doing, Mr. Mechanic?" and the man said, "It's gonna be fine; just stay buckled in, and I'll have you down in a few minutes." Then: "Okay, kids, grab hold of your testicles, you're ready to sail," and there was a loud snap from above their seat pole, their parachute opened, and they started to drop and Gould doesn't remember this but his cousin must have held on to him and he must have screamed.

Rain stops and they go to the subway station. Car they sit in is empty so Gould says, "Let's go to the next car, I don't like this one." That one's empty too and he says, "I'm sorry, kids, but for some reason I don't like this one either, you mind if we go to the next?" and his older daughter says, "Why? They're all the same," and he says, "Just follow me." The next one has two young women and their little children in strollers. They sit across and a few feet down from them. Doors close, train goes, stops after a few feet, doors open, he hopes more people get on, doors close, train starts moving again, and his younger daughter says, "Look, Daddy, that baby," and he says, "What? Shh, don't point," and she says, "But look what she's drinking," and he sees that one of the girls in a double stroller of two girls, the other about a year younger, is drinking out of a Pepsi can. "She must be two years old. She's going to ruin her teeth," and he says, "You've got to let people do what they want." "But she's too young to, she doesn't know better," and he says, "I'm talking of the mother, but let's forget it, they might hear." The connecting car door's thrown open and three boys skulk through it and head down the aisle. They're all dressed alike: long shorts about six inches past their knees, top part of their boxer shorts showing above their belts, baseball caps, shirts unbuttoned most of the way down their chests, looking rough, ready for a rumble. One looks at him as they pass and he looks away. They go through the car to the next one, then two stops later that door's thrown open and they're coming back. Several more people are in the car now. Same boy looks angrily at him as they approach, as if saying—well, whatever his look's saying, but something like: Look at me crossly and you're a dead mother. They go through the door they came out of a few minutes before. "You know something?" Gould says to his daughters. "I don't think we should come back to Coney Island next year. Never again, in fact, till they clean it up, but really clean, and it's a bit less dangerous and threatening." "That's all right with me," his older daughter says, "but where will we go for our once-a-year trip to the rides?" and he says, "We'll find a place. Rye Playland, maybe. It's in Westchester—north of us, along Long Island Sound, I think, so maybe it has a little beach or swimming pool, and I bet it takes about the same time to get there. I saw an ad for it on the subway the other day. The amusement park there's supposed to be one of the best. And I'm sure they've lots of private guards around and such and it can't be any more expensive than the rides at Coney Island, but we'll see. I'll have to find out how it is first. We can take the car or a train—not a subway but a real train from Penn Station or Grand Central, whichever one the train leaves from, though of course a subway down to the train station." "The train, not the car," his younger says. "It's more fun." His older daughter falls asleep against his shoulder and the younger reads the entire trip back to Manhattan. They get off at Columbus Circle, transfer to the uptown Broadway local, and his older daughter sits against him and says she got a bad burn at the beach—she's read that sometimes the worst burns come when the sun goes through the clouds at you—and she doesn't feel well and is very tired and after they leave the station would he carry her to their building? He says, "You're too big, and I'm a little tired myself. The ocean always does that to me, which I don't think Rye Playland will. I don't know what it is. The salt, the ozone, the air."

The First Woman

AFTER HIS WIFE left him, what? First woman he had anything to do with was much younger than he. Thirty-five years younger, more. Didn't intend to. Sure, saw her numerous times walking on the street and entering or leaving what he assumed was her apartment building and admired her looks; body and face, intelligent expression, way she walked, her bounce, height, hair. Sometimes would turn around to look at her walking the opposite way and once slowed down so she could catch up and get ahead of him and he could look at her from behind. But she was so young, around the age of his older daughter: young body, young face, rest of it, her clothes. So he would never think of stopping her, saying something, doing anything to initiate a conversation and see where it would lead: even saw her in the market a block from their buildings and could have started something there. "We must live pretty near each other; seen you so often in the neighborhood and on my block and a couple of times here." (Wouldn't want to give away that he knew what building she lived in; that might seem a bit peculiar to her: Knows what building I'm in? Does he also know what apartment? Does he look through his window into mine? What else has he seen?) Wouldn't think of doing that to any woman stranger on the street or in a market, and probably not in an elevator or waiting for one, even if he knew they lived in the same building or he was in hers visiting a friend. Dinner parties perhaps, but he's only been to two the last six months and both had people mostly his age to around ten years younger. At work at a lunch table might be all right if he happened to sit next to a woman and then found himself attracted to her or walked into the lunchroom and saw a woman he'd been attracted to and sat at her table with the intention of starting a conversation—"Excuse me, but pass the pepper, please? The chicken salad good? I've never had it here, if that is chicken salad"—which might lead to meeting her for a coffee or drink sometime. Possibly in the same lunchroom—"So, nice talking, and see you again, maybe: tomorrow, here at one?"—or to going out with her, even: movie, play, museum, or just for a long walk. But *she* stopped *him*. That's how it happened. He was walking up the hill on his side of the street, she was walking down—her building's almost directly across the street from his—when she smiled at him, he smiled back, they were about ten feet from each other, and he immediately turned away, thinking, That was a nice smile, if he didn't know better he'd say she was interested in him a little; no, that's going too far. But this is the street and New York and even if he were thirty years younger he wouldn't try to capitalize on a smile to make a pass. Should he look around to see if she's looking back at him? If she is it'd embarrass him that she caught him looking and would make her uncomfortable and then when he saw her next he'd have to make a point of not looking at her when she passed or she'd think he was some kind of street lech and after that would avoid looking at him every time she came within a certain distance of him: thirty or forty feet, let's say. It could be she's just beginning to recognize him, having seen him so much; figures he lives on this block or around it on Riverside Drive so she's just being friendly. She could even be from out of town—so many residents around here seem to be—and still has that out-of-town hi-neighbor behavior, and that's all it is. It's true he's fantasized about her, but he's living alone now and hasn't been close to a woman since his wife, so he fantasizes about lots of women, ten a day maybe, especially good-looking ones he sees on the street, and because of all the colleges in the area, and one just for women, there are loads of them to fantasize about—when she said, "Excuse me. Excuse me there, sir, you up the hill," and he turned around and she was about forty feet away and he pointed to himself and she nodded and started up the street to him and he walked down and said, "Yes?" and she said, "I'm sorry, I didn't mean to stop you and then take you out of your way like this, and I should have thought of it sooner," and he said, "No harm done, a few feet, and I'm not really in a rush to anything, what is it?" and she said, "You see . . . oh, this sounds silly—will sound, saying it . . . I'm embarrassed, almost, and really will be if it isn't so, but I believe we're acquainted. It's why I did that smiley greeting before. You're a friend of my father's, knew him a few years ago—as colleagues—and came over to our house with your wife once or twice, or once or twice when I was there. I recognize you, in other words—wow, I don't know why that took so long and was so arduous to get out. I forget your name, but your face is the same. You both taught together, Dad and you," and gave the name of the school. "Well, that's right, I did. I no longer teach there, but you are . . . or your father is . . . ?" She told him, and he said, "Oh, how is he?" She told him, and he said, "And how's your mother?—excuse me, I forget her name." Told him and asked about his wife and children. "Two daughters? I don't think I ever met them but I remember my father waxing ecstatic about them . . . wanted me to meet them, even be like them, I think. No, why wouldn't they have come to the house with you if I was there, unless they had sleep-overs that night, or I did," and he said, "I don't recall that ever happening, double sleep-overs. Maybe my wife and I only came by for drinks," and she said, "Could be, so it was just the adults and a quick introduction to me. But they were supposed to be very smart, artistic and literary—reading, writing, way beyond their years—acting too, I think," and he said, "Your memory, whew!" "I always had—I still do—an extensive memory for insignificant details—not insignificant to you, naturally, but to my own life," and he said, "That can't be true," and she said, "Why do you say that?" and he said, "I don't know. But I'm like that myself in ways, but with significant details—forgetting to take my pajamas off and put my shoes on before I go out—only kidding," and she smiled, obviously didn't think it funny, said, "Wait a second. Are your daughters even my age? That could be why they didn't come over," and he said,

"One's twenty-three, other's twenty," and she said, "So I was right. Your eldest and I are the same," and he said, "Really? And as for my wife—you asked about her—well, she left me. It all happened pretty quickly. I'm sure your folks know. You can say I'm still shuddering from the shock of it and moving back here permanently, or maybe I'm melodramatizing it a bit. Anyway, it's very nice that you stopped me. You probably have someplace to go now too." Then he just looked at her, had nothing to say, she didn't seem to either, or he couldn't think of anything to say—wanted to but nothing came and he'd save the regards-to-your-folks for when they said goodbye—she smiled, then almost laughed into her hand, he said, "What's wrong?" and she said, "Why?" and he said, "So where do you live, around here? I've seen you on this street a couple of times, on Broadway too, and I think once in the market up the block. Of course you understand why I didn't recognize you," and she said, "Of course." "So. Regards home, and I'll be seeing you," and was about to put out his hand to shake, and she said, "You didn't ask where I live. I mean, you didn't wait for an answer. In that corner building. Moved in a few months ago," and he said, "It's a Columbia-owned building. So I assume, and I should have asked this before, grad student, same field as your father's? Or maybe your mother's—I forget what she did. Anyway, we're neighbors and both newcomers, though I'm an old newcomer, meaning I used to live here years ago but have recently come back. And that's a funny thing to say, at least to my ears, 'neighbors,'" and she said, "No, it's all right, and we are. And I know you have to go now—you have your right foot pointed up the hill already, but"—and he said, "Do I? It was unconscious, believe me," and straightened his feet so they were both facing her—"but maybe one afternoon, if you're free, you'd like to get together for coffee . . . you're probably always busy," and he said, "No, that'd be nice," and asked her first name and said he'd pass by her building on his way back and get the number of it and would call Information for her phone number, if it's in, and she said, "It's in," though he doesn't get the point. He's certainly attracted to her, what man his age wouldn't be?—any age, if he likes women; she's practically a beauty—so he's flattered, but why would she want to have coffee with him? Entering her intellectual phase or something? No, that's condescending. And he should have found out what field she's in in grad school; it may be the same as his. Wants to talk to an older man, an academic, have her mind stimulated? Well, he'll stimulate her, all right, but fat chance, and why's he thinking like that? She's a kid, has a sweet smile, she must be a lovely girl, parents were very nice people, intelligent, decent, so she must be, and he's got all those years on her, so he doesn't know. Doesn't know what? Doesn't know. "But maybe it's a good idea I take your name and phone number down now—the old mind ain't what it used to be and never was much, when it comes to remembering," and wrote them down in his memo book. "Or I can call you, you know," she said. "That's what I originally intended with this open invitation. But to be honest, I forget your name," and he gave it and his phone number and said, "You don't want to write the number down?" and she said, "I can remember, it's an easy one. So"—smiling—"see ya," and he said, "See ya," and they parted, and he thought, he meant to shake her hand but was glad he didn't. Kids don't appreciate it, may even wonder about it, mostly because they're not used to it, or maybe he's wrong. Anyway, looking back—picturing it—it would have seemed funny to do.

She didn't call, and he thought about calling her for a week. Then always thought no, why should he? She can't be too interesting. Or let's say she is, in a little way, but what would they talk about? Well, he'd have to know what she's interested in. But after a while he'd make as big a fool of himself as he's ever done in his life. That an exaggeration? No, because what could be more foolish than an old guy making a pass at what's really a girl? Being rejected, maybe, or accepted—he doesn't know which. For that's what it'd probably lead to if it went on, since if they did have coffee he'd say at the end of it, "Why not let's do this again? That is, if you want to and have the time; it's been enjoyable"—politics, they could have talked about, literature, writers, painting, teaching, learning, living in the city—and if she agreed, fine, and if not, well, that'd be okay too, but if they did meet again for coffee, or a couple of times after that—"We got a regular coffee-klatsch going," he could call it—he'd say, "What about we go out to dinner one time, for a change of pace, or just lunch? My treat, someplace fairly simple around here—actually, I'm not much for lunch; if I eat a carrot it's a lot—but I'll go and have something," and suppose she said yes or "If you don't eat lunch, then let's have dinner." He'd pick her up at her door? Probably lives with a roommate. University housing off-campus can be very expensive. All this is to say if she doesn't have a lover or serious boyfriend, and with them is there a difference? And then what? When you have dinner or even lunch, you talk about things you don't when you're just having coffee—he thinks that's right, at least about dinner. And different too from when you're just having a drink. A drink—a bar—picturing it: all those college kids in the bars around here; it'd look absurd. And what would they drink: beer, wine, and the first time clink glasses and make a toast? What would they even talk about that second time for coffee, and the third? Her father, mother. Siblings, if she has any. Growing up in an academic household. What she's taking in school. They probably would have gone over that already. Well, what she learned that day or week in classes or read for them. A paper she might be writing; maybe he could help. But would he be interested in any of it? How does he know? And he hated writing papers in school. Movies, that's what young people like most today, and music, but not his kind of movies and music, he's almost sure. And no going to her apartment building if it's only occupied by young college students and no married couples and some with kids, nor going there either if she has a roommate, female or non-lover male. Maybe they could skip lunch or dinner and just go to a movie—he could meet her at a corner or in front of her building or the theater—and discuss it over coffee after, no matter how bad it is. Actually, the worse it is the more he could pinpoint what he thinks is good in a movie from old ones he saw. And while they were talking he would probably look covertly at her body and no doubt fantasize having sex with her, which would be wrong—sex with her would. She's too young. Besides, she'd be put off by the suggestion. How would he even make it? He wouldn't have the words, and if he found them, he'd feel too silly saying them. But say she was open and relaxed about it and said something like, "Your look; what is it, Mr. Bookbinder?" and he'd say, "Gould, please call me Gould; what is it with you?" and she could say, "It's still hard for me to, but okay, Gould, even though my folks"—Oh, your folks, he'd think; just at the right time—"my folks weren't the type, when I was small, to insist I call all adults by mister and missus and their last names," and he could say, "But you were saying?" and she could say, "About what was on your mind. The look you had. I'd never seen it on you but recognized it from other men," and he'd say, "Then I guess I'm caught and will have to come clean," and would apologize while saying it: "I know it's wrong, stupid, our respective ages, all of that . . ." and she could say, "I don't know. It's true I haven't done it with a man more than five years older than me, maybe because there was never one who interested me. But it's not like I have anything terrible against it. And isn't it every young woman's fantasy—" and he'd say, "Don't talk about girls and their fathers," and she wouldn't have; she could just say, "I don't mind the idea," or, "The suggestion's not the worst one, so what do we do next?" or not even that: none of it. He'd just come out with it, find the words—"I've been thinking"—say them clearly, wouldn't give any kind of look, and she'd go along with it and they'd go to his apartment—well, where else? unless she was living alone in a building which didn't only have other young students in it and wanted to go there, and they'd do it—have a drink, sit down and kiss, whatever they'd do first—and it wouldn't work. Sure, it'd be pleasurable for him, though you never know what can happen when you get too excited, and maybe in a way for her too: the pleasure, as he knows what to do and still has plenty of energy for it and would just hope that he could go slow, because once is usually it for him till the next morning. But she'd see his body and even if it's in pretty good shape for a sixty-four-year-old, it's nothing like the bodies of the boys she's used to and she might be turned off by it, even repulsed. The gray pubic hair, or most of it gray; chest hair that's totally gray and in fact mostly white; wrinkles everywhere; way the body sags in places no matter what strenuous exercises and long running and swimming he does; this, that, from top to bottom—the elbows; especially around the eyes—it's a ridiculous notion, sex with her, so what's he even thinking of it for? It won't happen. He shouldn't call. It's probably why she didn't call; she somehow saw it in his face that time they spoke: that this is what he was interested in, not talk. And even if they had sex once—her experiment with a much older man, let's say—that'd be it, because she wouldn't want to do it again. Why would she? He's an old fart, far as she's concerned, and if she doesn't see it at first, or blocks it out for some reason, she'll see it after: older than her own father by more than ten years, he figures, as he had his children late. So: nice to talk to, perhaps, but not to make love with, and then they'd see each other on the street once every other week, which is about how often he saw her before, and what then? What would he say? She? And suppose she let on to her folks about it? "I met this old colleague of yours—you'll probably remember him too, Mom—or former colleague, rather, though he's quite old also but still in some ways considerably attractive for his age"—not intending to tell them what happened, but her father's a smart guy and was a very good college teacher so knows how to ask questions and extract answers from students, and kids can't hide things well the way adults can, and maybe it's also not how they act today: the compulsion to tell the truth, lay it all out, no matter how much it hurts or shocks someone else, as if that's a virtue, or is he thinking of a time ten or more years ago?—and then her father could call or write him and say something like, "How could you? Not just that you knew she was my daughter. You're forty years older than her. What are you, some sort of predator, ravener, plunderer, vulture, hyena, monster, perverse addled dirty old dotty fool? Women twenty years older than she, which a man your age of any decency and brains would still think far too young for him, aren't good enough as pickings? Why are you trying to mess up her life? What's in it for you but a slap on the back you give yourself for fucking a child? If it weren't that I didn't want to embarrass her and that she's five years past the legal age of consent, I'd report you and probably try to prosecute you, and if there were some academic court of law I'd work to get you fired from your teaching post." Or he wouldn't write or call but he'd think it, or it could be he'd think, Lucky stiff. Shacking up with a girl so beautiful and young. Wish it could be me, though naturally not with my daughter.

So he didn't call but she did. "Hello, is this Mr. Bookbinder?" and after he knew for sure who it was, he said, "Damn, I had a premonition you'd use that if you called—the 'mister' or 'professor' or 'doctor'—which I'm not: I barely got through elementary college—instead of just my name Gould," and she said, "I didn't want to, honestly, nor thought beforehand how to address you. It simply came out, whatever that latency means. My subconscious should probably keep that a secret," and he quickly tried to think what she'd just meant but said, "Okay by me. So, what's doing with you?" and she said, "My goodness, plenty of things, but we'd mentioned something about meeting for coffee one day—do you still want to?" and they met. She was interesting: wide range of interests, knowledgeable about a lot, quick mind, some wit, articulate delivery, funny at times, charming, her parents send him their regards—the "life of the mind" came up twice in her conversation, and she seemed earnest about it—and she seemed to find him interesting: laughed at his jokes, said several times, "What you say makes a lot of sense," looked into his eyes as if he were her equal; someone she could be interested in, or even involved with, is what he wants to say. He wanted to say to her right away, "Listen"—or after they got a coffee refill and second pine-nut macaroon horn they shared between them—"listen, what are you doing tonight?" He gave advice, after he asked about her graduate-school work, on some courses she was thinking of taking and some eventual career moves. "But the truth is, if I had to take those same courses I'd no doubt fail and be mustered out of the program, especially the long novels of Melville and that one you mentioned on Puritan literature," and she said, "Oh, please," and he said, "No, I haven't the mind for that stuff. *Bartleby* and maybe *Billy Budd*, though I can't stand the grandiloquent language of the latter, if I remember the book correctly and have the word right, but those two are about it. I don't know: the brain; who knows where the hell it goes or, with me, ever was, but I couldn't keep up in your class. And write papers on the long ones? Forget it. It's a fluke that I'm teaching. But if you notice, I only do short things and very clear and modern and interpretable . . . so it's a good thing I'm retiring in two years. My younger daughter will be out of college then, and that'll be it for half-tuition remission from my university, and I bring down the entire profession. Now your father: I don't know how many years he's been professing or has left in it, but *there's* a teacher, a scholar, a learned man, with eclectic interests and the ability to compress and express them, just like you. I used to feel a little stupid sometimes talking to him, not that he was ever high-hat or pooh-pooh or self-important. He just knew what the hell he was talking about and had good ideas. Me, I'm a fake," and she said, "No you're not," and he said, "Oy-oy-oy, now you'll think I brought it up to get sympathy or lower my level or show I'm vulnerable or some other ulterior reason, but just ask him. I'm talking about teaching and understanding the subtleties and particulars of literature and making the connections and seeing its big reach. He'll tell you. But let's change the subject; it's too much about me." Politics: some things about the coming presidential election they both read in the *Times* and a couple of liberal weeklies. Then they analyzed the mind of the lit professor turned U.S. senator who killed his wife and her lover a month ago: ran over them when he saw them walking hand in hand across a street. What could have induced him, so much to live for and all that, and they had three young kids? The story goes he was having an affair of his own with a young staff worker and had had several before with all kinds of women and wasn't living with his wife—they were getting a divorce, had amicably worked out a settlement and this was her first man since they broke up—so why? She said, "Male honor—that another penis had superseded his?" and he said, "Are you speaking metaphorically . . . hey, how about that word?" and she didn't smile and said, "Both," and he said, "Anyway, no, I don't think so, or just a little, and what do I care about that vile jerk? I'm only interested in what happened to his wife and kids and, to a smaller extent, the poor schmo he killed. I'm sorry, I don't always mean to direct us, but the conversation's gotten too morbid, so can we change the subject again?" "Do you like movies?" and he said, "Sure, some, who doesn't? though I prefer the older foreign ones in black and white—late fifties, early sixties, long before you were born—but I bet you like the new ones a lot," and she said, "Only if they're good." Has he seen . . . ? and he said no, but does she think it's worth going to? If she does he'll make a point of it, and she said if he's serious about that she'll go with him, since she wouldn't mind seeing it again: it was probably among the best five or six movies she's seen in her life, and he said, "Oh, it was that good?" and she said, "Are you playing with me, because I don't like it," and he said, "No, why, something I said, or the way I said it? Oh, I won't lie; I was playing—patronizing—and I'll try not to do it again. It could be I just don't know how to express myself well in social matters also, or have degenerated the last few years, no fault of anyone's but my own, so please excuse me," and she said, "And stop flattering yourself too," and he said, "What? Okay, if you say so, I won't. So what's our next topic?" and she said, "That's not how I engage in conversation," and he said, "Of course not, I was only saying," and she said, "And the truth now: you weren't being a touch sardonic to me then?" and he said, "No, why would I, I wasn't, but if you don't mind I think that should be my last apology for the time being. All right, that said, when do you want to meet for that movie, if you still do? And it'll be dutch treat, okay? since I know you'd object to my paying," and she said, "I wouldn't—I'm only a grad student without a major stipend—but fine with me," and after he left her he thought they almost blew it then but that could be because they're both a bit unsure and maybe even nervous about meeting again because they think it's the wrong thing. Is it? No, it's simple, it's nothing.

They went to the movie two nights later. Met her at it, got there fifteen minutes early to buy the tickets and have the excuse, "Got here early so thought I'd save some time in line by buying the tickets beforehand—not to save time so much but more to make sure we got seats—I hope you don't mind," and she said, "No, I told you, if you mean about buying both tickets. Do you want to be reimbursed?" and he said, "It's not necessary," and she said, "Excuse me, I shouldn't have put it like that," and took out her wallet, and he said, "Please, put that away. So, where do you want to sit?"—as they entered the seating area—and she said, "Anyplace you do but not too near," and he said, "Should we have stopped off at the candy counter?" and she said, "I don't eat in theaters—distracts from what I'm seeing, besides making too much noise," and he said, "Same here: the snacky stuff and not sitting too near. In fact, because of my eyes I like to be pretty far back. So maybe, if that's not what you want, we should sit separately and meet after," and she said, "The back's good." They sat, movie started, she took his hand a few minutes into it. He couldn't believe it. He'd already decided—when he walked to the theater—that this would be the last time he'd see her except for chance meetings. He'd gotten too anxious about this movie date; it would lead to nothing and he could see himself falling for her a little, but not making a fool of himself—keeping it a secret from everyone—and it would be upsetting. He'd think of her a lot, want to call her, but wouldn't. He'd planned to say nothing about it after the movie and when he accompanied her back to her building or however they'd leave each other, and if she said anything like, "Want to meet again?" he'd say, "It's probably not a good idea and I'd rather not go into why, though believe me it has nothing to do with you. Meaning nothing you did or said, since for you I've nothing but admiration and respect," or not go quite that far, as it might come out sounding like a line to inveigle her into a relationship, and he was sure she'd say, "Okay, if that's what you want," and shake his hand good night and that'd be the end of it. So they were watching the movie, right at the start after the opening credits, his hands on his lap, when suddenly she was holding one. He didn't see or feel her hand crawl to it or anything. His right, her left, she just took it and squeezed, about thirty seconds after she started holding it, and he thought, still facing the screen, She's squeezing my hand, what does that mean? and then she squeezed it harder and he thought it's probably a signal for him to look at her, the second one harder because he didn't look at her after the first, and he looked at her and she was smiling at him and looking as if she wanted to be kissed, and he thought, I can't do that, it's enough she's holding his hand and squeezing it. It was a dark scene on the screen so the theater was fairly dark, and her head turned just so toward him and lips parted a bit and that smile that said, Kiss me, we could do it now, just once if that's all you want, but come on while we've time and the theater's dark and people around us can't see, and if you do kiss me I'll kiss you back if you don't pull away right after, and he thought, Not here, probably not anywhere, there are some things you don't understand; at least they have to be talked about, and how would it look?—people will see and think, Look at the old fart and the young beauty, first I thought she was his daughter or even his granddaughter, then they're kissing on the lips, maybe doing worse things below, how could he and, even uglier to think of, how could she? He smiled at her, faced front, didn't squeeze her hand but continued to let her hold his. Occasionally glanced at her and she was always watching the movie. She gently squeezed his hand a few times and then so hard his knuckles hurt, and it wasn't during an especially tense movie scene as the other squeezes since the first one had been so seemed she wanted him to look at her again and he did, and her head was like it was an hour before: turned and with the mouth open and smile just so, and he mouthed, What? and she squeezed his hand and tugged it a little toward her and he pulled it back but left it in hers and said, "What? What?" and she said, "Oh, what?" and someone behind them said, "Shh," and he mouthed Something wrong? and her expression said, With this look and smile and my neck arched and head turned so and mouth parted in a preparation-for-kiss position, you say you don't know what it is and that something could be wrong? What's wrong with you? What was wrong with you before? Or maybe I should ask, What do you see or sense wrong in me? You embarrassed? What don't you like? Our ages? Me? My looks, mind? People all around? That I made a move on you? That I'm stopping you from watching the movie? Listen, it's going to happen, mister, you better believe it, here or somewhere else, now or later, this kissing. And probably tonight or another night this week—unless you confess beforehand to being gay, impotent, perverted, or having a sexually transmittable disease—we'll be in bed also, so you better get ready for that too, and she turned to the screen, and he thought, Suppose she was thinking some of that, he hasn't yet told her about his wife and why they separated. And there's her father, mother, all the other things. What else is she expecting him to do besides kiss her here, kiss her later on the street, at a bar, a big long one in an elevator? Dance with her at some preppy club? Double-date with her friends? Hold hands with her the entire way while they walk to wherever they walk to after the movie? Last time his older daughter was in she took his hand on the street and held it at her side and they walked that way for about a minute till he raised their hands to his mouth, kissed hers, and took his out of it, and said, "This'll sound awful to you. But as much as I loved holding hands with you when you were a girl, probably as much as I loved anything, some people will get the wrong idea now. They don't know you're my daughter so they'll think what they think, and half of it won't be nice things, and I don't want them to," and she said, "What of it? We know how we're related and that there's never been anything like that, so why let the petty small minds run you?" and he said, "You could be right. Ideally, you are. But there's a certain public decorum I have to hold to. I get uncomfortable easily, for both you and me, even if I know I'll never see these people again, or if we do there's very little chance we'll recognize each other, so what else can I say except that I hate it to be this way. Maybe if we wore signs—HIS DAUGHTER, HER FATHER—and arrows on the signs pointing to the other person, which'd mean we'd always have to walk in the same position to each other. No, that's silly and nothing will work. Anyway, you're all grown up, and I've been wanting to say something about this since you were around thirteen, so walk with me normally from now on and save the hand-holding for when you're with one of your beaus," and she said, "Beaus. Oh, boy, that's a word," and he said, "You mad over this?" and she said, "It's a bit sudden, but no."

In the movie now he looked front, she pulled her hand away from his—a sign she was angry or disappointed, maybe—and he whispered close to her ear, "Really, did I do something wrong? Anything I said I should be thinking about apologizing for?" and she whispered, looking serious, "Why, because I removed my hand from your sweaty palm? It was getting physically unpleasant, just as mine must have been getting to yours, and I thought I might be annoying you with it and distracting you from the movie." "Shh," the person behind them said, or another one; "please, the movie. You want to talk, do it outside." He mouthed, Later, and smiled, and she nodded but didn't smile, and he thought, Jesus, I'm such a creep, I can't believe it, and they watched the movie and discussed it on the way to a pub, she called it, she knew around here and wanted to go to for a drink before heading home, and standing at the bar in it he felt funny, all the young people standing around them, just as he thought he would a week ago. He'd suggested when they came in they get a table—his main reason: not to stand at the bar with all the young people, though what he told her was, "We can relax and talk better"—but she said, "A table's too formal for just a piddly beer. And I've been sitting all day at my desk at home, and then at the movie, so I'd like to stretch my legs." Some men around her age at the bar or walking past them seemed to want to make a pass at her. Anyway, were definitely interested. Kept looking over, tried to catch her eye directly or through the long bar mirror above the liquor bottles. One handsome young man sitting at the bar stared at her through the mirror now. When they came in she looked around briefly, seemed to nod hello to someone in a standing group but he didn't see who, and then only looked at him—"Chins," she said, clicking her beer stein against his glass of wine, and drank from it and said, "We done discussing the movie?" and he said, "Unless you want to talk some more as to why they make these things so noisy, jumpy, and uncomplex," and she said, "I don't. Now tell me what happened in the theater. And don't say 'What do you mean?' I won't allow you to give yourself extra time to think up an evasive answer, though of course my going on about it now has given you that time. How come, to put it bluntly—oh, I hate phrases like that when it's obvious I'm being blunt—you didn't kiss me? Was I—and I don't like babbling people either but feel I have to finish this, so forgive me—asking for so much? Or you simply didn't want to, or thought it the wrong place, or the shusher behind us stifled you, or what? There, you've had lots of time to think up a clever evasion, and meanwhile I've exposed myself as an unattractive babbler, but say something," and he said, "I have to talk here? How do you know we're not being monitored? This looks like the kind of joint that might do that—state-of-the-art slick and insipid singles bar with its newest gimmick being to entertain its masses through hidden recorders. One of the drinkers nearby could have one under his shirt or up her armpit and then management lowers the deafening music a few dozen decibels and plays our conversation back over the same sound system and everyone laughs himself silly," and she said, "You're not talking, then," and he said, "Okay, I talk. 'Didn't want to kiss'? You said that, lady? Well, let me think about it, not with any excuse-making goal but to see my reluctance then as clearly as I can," and he looked at his glass and thought. This is the approach. He can have it both ways and also appear thoughtful. He can protest his unresponsiveness yet give all the arguments for not getting involved further: the age difference, her family, he has a daughter also twenty-three and maybe even a few months older than her, she's just a student, she should be going out with much younger men, same frame—frames?—of reference, and "just a student" meaning he's a teacher, she's a grad student, it wouldn't look right or seem good. Other things he'll come up with: what could it lead to? That it'd embarrass him being affectionate to her in front of people, and kissing? Out of the question. Meaning in front of people, not that he wouldn't like to. Mention the hand-holding incident with his daughter. That he'd think himself a hypocrite he could only be kissy-poo alone with her? No "kissy-poo" reference. Besides sounding awful, he doesn't want to ridicule the act of kissing her, because then he'd be ridiculing her; she was the one who practically put her lips to his. Anyway, something like that, and if she accepts his reasons and respects his reactions but says it still doesn't make any difference to her—she'll go along with however he wants to conduct himself in public, within reason (she's not going to be passed off as his daughter, for instance)—then what? Then—well, he doesn't know. Does he want to see her again? Yes, he thinks so. Yes or no? Yes. Sleep with her eventually? Yes, surely. Sleep with her tonight if she lets on that's what she wants and actually does all the asking or prompting? All depends: his place or hers, roommate, type of building she lives in.

But his building. People in it have begun to know him. If one's waiting for the elevator with them or the next morning is already in the car when they get on it to ride down? They could walk down—it's only the seventh floor and he could say it's good exercise and how he almost always goes downstairs; that's the truth—but someone could see them going through the lobby to the street, and what if a neighbor's waiting for the elevator when they leave his apartment? So? Means nothing in the morning: student of his who dropped by early to deliver a late paper and they just happen to be leaving at the same time. Doorman? Why would he care? He'd see them come in at night and think, Hey, what a doll, lucky old fuck, or maybe that's another one of his daughters. But he's way off track: first the negative arguments. "I've thought about it," he said, "even if the music's hardly conducive to thinking—that bang bang screech bong," and she said, "It's not anything like that and don't digress; tell me what you thought," and he said, "For one thing, I'm still married," and she said, "This is what you sunk into deep contemplation for? Because I thought you were separated, the two of you marching lockstep to an amiable divorce," and he said, "Where'd you hear that? I never told you. Maybe your folks did, but I never told them either, though it's true," and she said, "I've only spoken to them briefly since we met, and not about you—I forgot to," and he said, "Ah, best you not, right now: what would they think? Anyway, you're right about the divorce—you must have just assumed it, or something I said—but you don't know the reasons for the amiability. My wife's quite sick. She wanted to divorce because of that. Sort of sacrificing herself. Thought she was being a drain on me. I took care of her as much as I could but couldn't anymore. She was that sick—still is—but even worse—she's eleven years younger than me—moved back with her elderly parents and they're taking care of her now with a nurse, the kids coming around often but not to help, and she doesn't want to see me anymore when she's so sick, because—" and she said, "I didn't know; that's terrible," and he said, "It's awful, yes, except it isn't true," and she said, "What isn't?" and he said, "What I said, all of it, except the separation and amiable divorce procedure. I don't know what came over me to do that—I'm sorry," and she said, "Wait, what you just—" and he said, "Yeah, made up. As I said, I don't know what—" and she said, "But why? Something wrong with you, a screw loose, to play with my emotions like that?" and he said, "Listen, I can understand why you'd be mad, but maybe we should tone it down here," and she said, "Okay, but answer," and he said, "No screw loose. Oh, I'm normal, so like everyone else who is, minimum of a little. But I'm nervous with you, so maybe my nervousness makes me feel a tiny bit extra screw-loose, giddy, say dumb things, even turned me into a liar," and she said, "Okay, okay. Not entirely satisfactory and I'm not sure what to say, but okay, okay. What's the real situation between you and your wife?" and he said, "Separation and eventually a divorce, all quite amiable and compatible. Twenty-eight years, which includes the four we lived together before marriage, and she got tired of it, felt we had little to say to each other, et cetera. No common interests left, now that the kids were grown, though the younger is still in college, so we should separate for a while and if it's what we continue to want . . . I'm sorry about that bizarre story. As I said, where it comes from, who knows, since she's healthy as all hell, and that excuse about my nervousness around you can't be all of it. I think, maybe, and this is just speculation, and I don't want to go into another long solitary thought session to try and figure it out"—and she said, "What were you saying?" and he said, "I didn't want to talk about a separation, one we're trying out, because then you might think Sally and I could go back together," and she said, "So, fine, if you did, but what's it got to do with our silly kissing?" and he said, "I suppose little, that what you're saying?" and she said, "Well, does it? Just for curiosity's sake, where's the separation stand now?" and he said, "Oh, that's another thing. She met a man, is very happy with him, lots in common, so we'll probably end up getting divorced and she remarried. I don't know what could stop the divorce—certainly I wouldn't, if it's what she wants—thus the amiability," and she said, "Fine, and you don't seem too torn up by it," and he said, "I'm not, but you know . . ." and she said, "Which means what, the long stretch with her is enough to stop you from stepping out some too?" and he said, "You mean with you?" and she said, "Not only, but for argument's sake, yes," and he said, "No, but our respective ages, you bet. Every time I think I knew your parents twenty years ago—" and she said, "Fifteen, probably less," and he said, "And now you're all grown but still forty years younger—forty-one; that's a chunk," and she said, "I'm not looking for anything long-term. I'm just interested in you, would like to see where it goes. We stop when we want to, even at this pub's door. We for certain don't have to get serious. We have fun, talk a lot, do what comes naturally if that's what develops, see movies, read, stay away from my parents, go to the beach if you like beaches—" and he said, "I don't. I like mountains. Beaches are too bare and hot." "Then I could never go out with you." "Good, you shouldn't. And I look ludicrous in a bathing suit with my shirt off." "What are you saying? You've a nice build." "How would you know?" "I can see through your shirt, the way you fill it out, and your big arms." "Maybe the arms are the last to go. But I'm gray. I've gray hair on my chest and, if you want to get personal and frank—can I say it?" and she said, "Say anything you want," and he said, "Around my pubes, on them, but there, and in some spots, white." "What of it? Maybe I do too." "You couldn't." "I could be prematurely gray, coloring the gray away in my head hair, maybe everywhere else too, or the places where I don't shave it off. You never know." "Listen, let's walk and talk and, if it rains, run for cover." "It's not supposed to rain, but were you speaking metaphorically?" and he said, "No, I thought I read it in a weather report."

They walked and talked. She took his hand, he let her for a minute and then pulled it away, patted the hand that had held his, and said, "I might meet someone—this is home territory, the whole Upper West Side is—or you might. They won't know what to think. That concerns me; what can I tell you? They'll maybe think you're with your grandfather. And if they see us crossing the street, that you're helping him across, and if they do think that, we'll be lucky," and she said, "Don't be maudlin. And how can anyone think I'm helping you across if I'm not holding on to you?" "I see you, I see my daughter, what can I tell you?" and she said, "And I see you and I don't see my father." "You have to." "Don't tell me what I have to see. And you don't see your daughter in me either. Besides, you need as much help getting across the street, and look it, as I do. Please, don't be such a schmuck. You're too old for it; it's unbecoming and to me unattractive," and he said, "Listen, I can't take a girl forty-plus years younger than I, a young woman—a woman, all right, a woman—calling me a schmuck. 'Unattractive,' fine. When I was your age or ten years older that might have hit me, but not now." "I meant in an ugly way, that 'unattractive,'" and he said, "Still, I don't care. But you don't know what that 'schmuck' does to me." "Then what should I call you, 'my darling'?" "Of course not; it wouldn't be true." "I know. That's why I said it," and he said, "Good, then you also know now I'm slow." "Really, Gould, we should talk some more about this and your perspective on it, but not while we're walking. Would you care to go in someplace quieter and less crowded this time for another wine and beer?" "Coffee," and she said, "I could make us coffee at my place." "Oh, jeez, I don't know. Haven't I turned you off sufficiently where you'd rather have seen the last of me?" "You're doing your darnedest but it hasn't reached the point where I see anything too difficult to overcome." "Nicely and graciously put, but I don't deserve it. Okay, your place, so long as you know there'll be no commitment from me to go further. 'Urgency . . . push.' I'm not saying it right—I'm doddering—but you must know what I'm getting at." "Just coffee. If it only comes to that. Because I don't like any prearranged restriction if there really seems no call for one." "Listen. Suppose it went further—I'm definitely not saying for today—and you hated it, were even repulsed by it because you suddenly saw how old and doddery I was, and then we'd have to walk around each other on the street after that when we met, not wanting to say anything to the other or even approach him—" and she said, "So? First of all, we wouldn't stalk around, or what you said. What does it mean anyway? You make it look like two snarling panthers—lions, cheetahs, one of the feral cat families—because one's in the other's territory, by gosh—or maybe cheetahs and panthers only go roaming—but the other doesn't want him there." "That's not what I meant. I was talking about potential embarrassment, uncomfortableness." "So I got it wrong. My turn to be incoherent. Sorry. But we'd just—and my 'sorry' was for insinuating you were being incoherent; you weren't, or not much. But if I now have it right, we'd just say hello, talk politely a little, ask after the other's family—I feel I know enough about yours to do that, or would by then, and I also know how much you love talking about them—and then go our two ways, something that shouldn't be new in relationships to either of us. We all come across people we don't particularly want to meet, but we deal with them civilly, don't we?—no inclination to hurt or get revenge? But tell me why we're talking like this. It's ridiculously premature. For now, let's just have coffee. Or if you want—I feel I'm pushing you too much on this, as you said, or did I get that wrong too?—maybe we should go home, you to yours, me to mine, so long till the next time, if we meet on the street or in the market or one of us wants to call and the other doesn't object to receiving." "No, coffee and dessert, on me and at a coffee bar, please." "You paid for the movie tickets and drinks." "I like to pay; I do it without argument or for reward," and she said, "If we've settled on coffee and dessert, I have some Mondel's chocolate lace cookies in a tin, just a few days old . . . well, I've given myself away: but at my apartment? I also have a new espresso machine never used: cappuccino, espresso, the works. And brandy, which I use for cooking, but it's good stuff, if you want to cap the night," and he said, "Do you have a roommate? Only because I don't want to converse with anyone else tonight under forty," and she shook her head. "I live alone. I thought I told you that," and he said, "Not that I remember, but we're both pretty aware by now of my deficiency that way," and she said, "Well I do, my big luxury; the espresso machine was a housewarming gift from my folks, along with a Bokhara rug."

They cabbed to her place. He looked at his building as he went into hers. He forgot to ask if it's a student building, lots of young students around, and if there's a Columbia University security guard at the door, but there wasn't, and nobody in the lobby or at the elevator, and what would he have done if there was? He'd have gone in with her. She was the one who wanted to cab. "But it's only ten blocks," he'd said, "and I like walking and it's a nice night," and she said, "I'm tired: my feet. I haven't been on them all day, but they hurt. I'm older than you think, physically; I also have a waitress job three days a week," and he said, "Oh, you didn't say," and wondered where it was and what would happen if he went into it by accident in the next few days and saw her there, or let's say if they said, later tonight, It isn't a good idea to see each other again, and then sometime in the next few days he went into the restaurant, sat at a table alone or at the counter—he prefers counters to tables when he eats alone: it's quicker and also easier to read a book on them—and she turned out to be his server. In the cab she'd asked if he had any siblings and he said, "One, a few years younger, but he died when I was a boy," and she said, "So did mine, an older sister by two years, but she was killed by a hit-and-run when she was nineteen," and he said, "I didn't know; I'm very sorry. I only remember one girl from my dinner at your house, and I'm almost sure it was only once, so maybe it wasn't even you I saw then," and she said, "You forget it was I who first recognized you. It could be that Sue was sick that night and had to stay in her room or was on a sleep-over. Anyway, we've something very deep in common," and he said, "But my loss was almost sixty years ago. It was in Central Park. We were standing by the bridle path. I was supposed to be looking after him, and a horse went nuts, tossed its rider, and kicked my brother in the head, and he suffered for a long time with a blood clot and seemed to recover, and then, like an old man shooting an embolism or whatever they shoot, died doing his rudimentary schoolwork at home. I think he was drawing the cover of his book report." He thought, riding up the elevator and staring at the gash in the ceiling panel and cable moving above it, Why'd he lie about his brother, and what's going to happen now with her? He's not prepared for it. What does he do with a young woman? Not prepared with a bag either, but she probably has a packet of them in her night table or another kind of protection. If it comes to that, as she said, if that's what she meant. It's been so long with any woman. But a young one with such a young body, everything flat and firm, it seems. And he hasn't made love with anyone but his wife since he met her—has kissed a few but hasn't even touched one on the breast, and he thinks every kiss he did was when he was a little high and standing in someone's kitchen. All his hand and finger movements will be the ones he did with his wife thousands of times. He knew what she liked, how she wanted it done, and if he didn't, she told him, so he thinks he'll probably do things to this girl's body as if it were his wife's. If he ends up inside her, he'll come in a minute. No, he knows how to hold it back if he wants to, or for a few minutes after it seems he's going to come soon, but that was with his wife and after many years with her. It's going to happen though, sex, if not tonight then soon with her. If there's a chance for it tonight, will he do it? Yes, because when she decides to do it—his age and looks again—that might be the only time she does. She'll give him the smile, he'll kiss her this time, it could even start right after they close the door and hang up their jackets: she'll start rubbing his back, he'll rub hers, they'll be standing and embracing at the time—best it starts up after their jackets are off and maybe even their sweaters: more maneuverability, fewer layers to tug up and go under—then the legs, sides, behinds, they'll feel around and this piece of clothing will be off and that one and soon all of them, and it'll be many kisses later and he'll be worrying if his breath stinks to her, if she's imagining it stinks because he's old, if she isn't already turned off by him, his skin, wrinkles, and flab. But she'll still be kissing—lips and tongue don't change, he doesn't think—and maybe thinking she'll do it with him this once, what's the harm? a different kind of experience, et cetera, and she's already a little excited, see him on the street after that, say it just wasn't going to work, that's why she didn't call or answer his answering-machine messages, but no regrets—and they'll go to the bedroom and so on and then he'll have done it, first time with someone since his wife, if it, please God, comes to that.

So they went to her apartment. She asked for his jacket, hung it in the closet alongside hers, and went into the kitchen to make coffee; he stayed in the living room, flipping through some of the books on her end tables, cocktail and dining tables, and a few on the couch. "Would you like some of that brandy in your coffee?" she yelled out. "I see it's Spanish," and he said, "On the side, why not, sure, thanks, if you'll join me, but even if you don't," and she said, "Yeah, I could." They both had brandy in a small glass that looked like half a shot glass with a stem. They had another. "Two of these is just one," she said, "so don't think you're going to get sick by the morning." She sipped from her espresso coffee—she wasn't able to figure out how to operate the steamed milk part of the machine and didn't want to disturb him to try and help her; he didn't touch his coffee, and she never referred to it till it was cold. "Want me to heat it up? Or better yet, make a fresh one for you?" and he said, "The brandy's all I need," and then, "May I?" and poured himself another. They talked about a lot of things quickly. Does her waitressing job cover her rent and other expenses? No, not in this city, so her parents contribute about half. Does she get in some reading at work? A little, during customer lulls or when she escapes to the toilet, but there's this dismal recorded restaurant music that never stops and the readings she has to do are often unnecessarily complex or unpardonably impenetrable, so it's hard to concentrate. Next year she's supposed to be a teaching assistant, which will mean full tuition waiver and a stipend, so she can give up the waitressing job. "You're a teacher, so give me advice as to what to do when you know a student isn't doing the assignment. I've always wanted to know, and I think now I'll have to." "You whip him or her," and she said, "Be serious, this is important." He told her his tricks how to make sure the students read everything he assigns them. She said, "I should get this down on paper, but I'll remember," and he said, "Or you can ask me at the time, if you run into the problem," and she said, "You may be too busy with your own work then," and he said, "No, I'm always accessible, and to my friends even more so." She asked if he liked teaching; he said, "Not especially." She said, "Maybe because you've been doing it so long." He said, "No, I've never liked it, and if your next question is why do I do it"—"It would've been"—"Well, to support myself and the things I like doing." She asked what they were and he said, "Too few to enumerate," and she said, "Come on, don't get highbrow and fussy; it's the one thing I've disliked most about academics," and he said, "You're right. Reading, long-walking, my daughters, of course; my typewriter diddling most times, and for more than twenty years of our marriage, my marriage and my wife, who is still quite nice." "What made you break up?" and he said, "I thought we talked about that. If we did, I shouldn't have, as I don't like discussing it, I'm sorry," and she said, "Please, no excuses or apologies required. Have you seen any women since you separated?" and he said, "Dated?" and she said, "I guess you could use that term," and he said, "No, what about you? When was the last time you were involved, or maybe you are even now with someone special," and she said, "That's a funny question, and if you don't mind I'd rather not answer it, and not to get even with you, you understand." "Why, did I say something inappropriate again? If so, I'm sorry, but I've been out of circulation for many years, and in ways I'm like a rustic," and she said, "You were married, though," and he said, "Yeah, but my wife acted as my social intermediary. I, for the most part, reclused myself except in school, though I'd flee from there the minute my work was finished, and could barely endure answering the phone at home. I've come out of that somewhat since I've been living alone; I mean, you gotta if you have a phone but no answering machine," and she said, "Good, I'm glad, it's better for you not to be that way. As for me, let me explain that I don't like talking about someone I was involved with, at least not to someone I only recently met," and he said, "You mean me?" and she said, "Who else? I don't even have a pet here," and he said, "I see, and that was dumb of me to say, 'You mean me?' Of course me. As you said, who else?" Then they were silent. Something about her face: he was saying the wrong things and she was looking away. It wasn't going well. It had become strained. She wanted him out of here, he was sure of it, and well she should. It's not that it's late. What time is it? He'd look at his watch but that might annoy her even more: He's that bored with me? she could think. Well, who the hell does he think he is? Or give her the impetus to say, "It's getting a little late, isn't it? and I'm also feeling tired, so perhaps we should call it a night." He looked at his empty glass, wanted to pour another, but thought she might think he drank too much or had to drink to be with her and have things to say. "Would you mind if I have just one more of this?" tapping the brandy bottle. "It's very good stuff. I always thought Spain, brandy, it'd be harsh, but it's not. I was once there but I don't remember having brandy. I only drank beer then—lots of it; I had a terrible pot—and some wine: white, which wasn't produced much in Spain, while I now mainly drink red and hardly touch beer. So, I missed my big chance, with the brandy and red wine. Port I remember in Portugal—I was even in Oporto, where they made it; you took a tour of the porteries—what would they be called?" and she said, "I wouldn't know." "Maybe just distilleries. And these glasses are pretty small, as you said, and I'm not used to drinking this much, so I'm curious—you're curious, I'm curious—the effect it'll have on me. What an awful thought, you taking care of me—awful for you—if I got really pissed. Only kidding about all that except the beer, red, and pot," and she said, "Please, I'll join you in one more." She seemed back in the mood from before and asked when was he in Spain. He said, "Several years before I met my wife. I went with a woman and her kid—I'd been living with them—and we mostly hitchhiked. The boy had blond hair, so it was easy," and she said, "You know, the truth is—as you'll see, all this time you've been talking, I've been listening some but mostly thinking—why not talk about that subject from before?" and he said, "What do you mean?" and she said, "Why am I reluctant to talk about it: my last two involvements? And I couple them up like that because they were practically back to back—a mistake; I don't think I had a week's break between them—and equally intense and both men seemed so young for their age and they even looked alike. Very tall, gaunt, lots of shocks of dark head hair; even the bony noses and enormous feet and hands and same-shaped eyes. I know it wasn't unintentional on my part, choosing the second with the looks of the first. I mean, with the second one—but you know what I mean. And the hair matter—that's no reflection on you, you understand. Younger men just have more hair. You must have had it too," and he said, "I actually began going bald when I was thirteen, I think, or started worrying about it. That I still have some hair on top and so high on the sides surprises me; I thought I'd be a billiard ball. But these two young men: you liked them both, equally, what?" and she said, "I loved them, one no more than the other and both a lot, but knew it wouldn't last with either for more than a few months, if that. Still, I fell for them because they were so attractive and congenial, and it quickly worked out well. The conversation wasn't that good, though did it have to be, right at the beginning? But the sex was, and that's something. So there," and he said, "How long ago, the last?" and she said, "Not long, but maybe I've spoken enough about it, not so much confessed but gone on almost nonstop," and he said, "And sex, now there's a subject," and she said, "Why, do you have something to say regarding what I told you? It could be you found my quick activities with successive men repugnant, or something less severe, or my cavalier attitude to the whole thing," and he said, "Not in the least, we're just talking. I only meant *sex,* the universal subject for adults, the Esperanto in body language of a different kind, we could say, or not only for adults. Kids are good at picking up languages easily, right? So whenever it starts. So much to talk about there, in so many aspects," and she said, "I'm not sure I understand what you're saying," and he said, "I wasn't being clear?" and she said, "Not really. What is it you're sort of circulating around, something again about those two men I mentioned?" and he said, "Well, if you've no objection to talking about it, yes, you and these two guys, back to back, front to front, but instead we can start at the start, since I assume the first wasn't the first and so the second not the second, were they?" and she said, "Oh, you're funny; of course not. I'm twenty-three," and he said, "So how old were you when you had your first involvement?" and she said, "Do you mean sex or just liking a guy?" and he said, "I guess so: sex, involvement, one and the same, I suppose, today or for about the last twenty years—I'm not sure. But let me know if this is the wrong question—out of line—if I'm being that, and I'll immediately change the subject or shut up," and she said, "Real sex? Being penetrated? Losing the locket? Fifteen. You?" and he said, "Closer to fifteen or to sixteen?" and she said, "I forget; what's the difference?" and he said, "For me, things were a lot different when I was a kid," and she said, "So you were much older when you first did it?" and he said, "No, fourteen. I remember it was December, right after Christmas—I was on school vacation—but with a whore. Most girls I went out with didn't do anything but kiss and, if you were lucky, on the fourth or fifth date would let you touch a breast through the blouse and, after a dozen dates, through the brassiere. For more, you had to go steady with them for half a year to a year—and I'm not saying too much more—or go out with a particularly wild usually homely girl you didn't want to be seen on the street with, and with her on the first date you could sometimes get bare tit, as we called it—it really sounds stupid now, and the way we regarded these girls, repulsive," and she said, "But a professional whore. What a depressing introduction, though I suppose how most adolescent boys lost their virginity then," and he said, "That's right. Most of my friends first went to prostitutes. I don't like the idea of it now but didn't think it depressing then. In fact, I have to admit I found it very exciting—the prospect of going to one and seeing a woman for the first time totally naked. I was practically heady at the thought of it, though it wasn't a great experience when I actually did it: she was crude and smelly and smoked a cigarette during a little of it, and her apartment was ugly. And it isn't, as I said, that I didn't want it to be with one of the girls I liked and dated," and she said, "And you continued going to prostitutes after that?" and he said, "With my friends, when I was a teenager, yes, sometimes five or six of us to the same one in the afternoon. She'd take us one at a time and the others would wait on the street telling infantile dirty jokes to one another or in a small waiting room she had, all of us crammed onto one couch. But not for almost forty years, I want you to know. which means as a man—twenty, twenty-one—a very young man, my first two times in Europe? . . . Yes, there more than anywhere else. The women in the Amsterdam windows, a London prostitute or two right out on a quiet side street, against a car fender—that's where and how you did it, standing up. I've never seen anything like it in New

York, and it was much cheaper there too. And Paris, *rue du* or *de* something or other—it was famous as a hooker street, but all gone now, I hear—near Les Halles, which has been torn down too. But I didn't do much whoring here, and usually when a friend set something up and maybe—this is, I'm still in my early twenties, you realize—because he had the dough and didn't want to go alone, was afraid he'd get beaten up and robbed. I was a big guy; most of my friends then were rich little guys . . . anyway, where he paid for me."

"As far as my first, it wasn't that great either. I didn't want to but wasn't forced. I did it mostly because all the other girls my age did, or said they were doing it—wouldn't that be something if they were all lying? But why are we talking of this, or focusing on it rather, after all the other subjects we started to discuss?" and he said, "We just got into it; who knows why?" and she said, "No, I bet there's a more deliberate reason," and he said, "What?"—thinking he knew what she was going to say, and she said, "Simply to get ourselves worked up. What do you think?" and he didn't want to say, I knew you'd say something like that, but said, "What do I think? Truth is, I am a little excited, genitally—so you think I started the conversation for that reason, both for you and me, or intentionally turned it around to it at a time when we really didn't know each other or much about the other?" and she said, "I'm not accusing you. I feel I'm just as much responsible for the conversation's sudden turn and focus and am a little excited by it myself and enjoying the feeling. Because what's wrong in it? Is there any danger, do you think?" and he said, "Why should there be? Or maybe I'm missing your meaning," and she said, "I'll put it this way: what do we do next? What about that? What do you think we should pursue next?" and he said, "You mean, do something?" and she said, "Only if you want to; it has to be consensual; I'm not about to spring on you," and he said, "Of course, I know, and I'm delighted, but where?" and she said, "Let's go to the bedroom. We don't have to do, unless you insist on it, the preliminaries out here, do we? We've done most of it with chatter, so we can skip the couch stuff and save the rest for inside after we've taken off our clothes," and he said, "You don't like being undressed?" and she said, "Not especially; I can undress myself," and he said, "My wife did, even long into our marriage, and rebuked me for not doing it more often with her, undressing," and she said, "If you're asking me to undress you, I'll do it if you want, but in the bedroom. I think this room we should keep as is," and he said, "Nah, it'd be silly; I can undress myself too," and she said, "Fine," and stood up, put her glass down, and said, "One more thing before we go in. I'd prefer you not mentioning your wife again tonight or till much later, and only if it's necessary or involuntary, like if you're talking in your sleep about her. It can be disconcerting," and he said, "Sure, though you can talk about your gaunt hairy men all you want," and she said, "Why would I want to? That's so stupid," and he said, "Hey, maybe it was—no, I'll concede it was and that I don't know where it came from—but I wish you wouldn't tell me that something I say is stupid, at least not till much later," and she said, "Okay, I can see that's important to you, and I was wrong. So we won't talk about anything like that: your age, your wife, my youth, or any of my former boyfriends or lovers and nothing about either of our intellectual and social deficiencies," and he stood up, finished his drink, and said, "Can we at least, while we're here, and without messing up the room and because I think the moment can use it and that it's also important we do, kiss?" and she said, "I want us to," and they moved to each other. He said, "My mouth has brandy on it but so will yours, but if mine's stinkier with it it's probably because I drank more, so excuse me," and she said, "Really, it's not an offensive smell. I even kind of like it: that and cognac and a French pear brandy, have you ever had it? I forget what it's called in French," and he said, "I don't think so, what's it look like?" and she said, "Clear, like vodka," and he said no, and they kissed.

They went into the bedroom. They'd kissed a few times standing up in the living room and he felt woozy from it, light-headed; at one moment he thought his legs might give way, but that's all he needed. Screwy old guy, she could think, next thing I know I'll have to hold him up, sit him in a chair. Such soft lips, he thought. His, in comparison, he was sure were a bit cracked and stiff. She knew how to kiss, hand on his neck and squeezing it a little and then fingers climbing up the back of his head almost in a spiderlike way, but only in the way the spider moves, nothing about being trapped or any of the other bad spider associations. Doing it almost as if she was thinking this is how she's supposed to hold a man and move her hand when she kissed, but he liked it. Her hand was warm and soft, and it made him shiver a few times. The brandy was a good idea; it had relaxed him, maybe made him say a couple of things he shouldn't have, but because both of them drank it it sort of neutralized any smell he might have on his breath. He didn't sense brandy on hers; it just smelled fresh. Kept his tongue in place because she didn't use hers, but he was thinking as he kissed her that if she started to use it he would too. She undressed, unbuttoning her blouse and taking it off, sitting on the bed and removing her jeans, unhooking her bra, but her breasts didn't plop out as he expected when the bra came off; they just stayed there, sticking straight out and almost pointing up. Maybe only the breasts of girls fourteen or eighteen or so did that. He's only seen them in photos, never even saw his daughters' once they started to develop, and when he was young and felt girls up and once got a shirt and bra off one—or maybe just the bra; the shirt she kept on but open in front—it was always in the dark. She slipped off her panties and then her socks—he tried not to watch, or just made quick looks, and she sometimes caught him but didn't say anything with her expression—and threw them under the bed. Light hair down there, he thought he saw, while her head and underarm hair were almost black. She color it to make it lighter? Wouldn't think so—doesn't see the purpose; shaving, yes, or whatever depilatory process if you're self-conscious of having what you think's a lot of hair—but he won't bring it up. "Aren't you going to disrobe?" she said, and took off her watch and shoved aside two little heart-shaped wooden boxes at the edge of the night table to put it down. That's probably the side she'll sleep on, he thought, since there's a night table on the other side. What could be in the boxes? Maybe one day, if they're still there and the relationship goes on that long and when she's not in the room, he'll look inside. "I'm sorry," he said, "but I've been dillying. I have to admit I became a bit fascinated, almost like a voyeur, or voyeur minus one, watching you undress. Excuse me," and she said, "Why? It's got to be natural. Which might seem as if I'm admitting to the unnatural in that the peeper instinct has never been in me," and he said, "That's hardly unnatural; neither is, wouldn't you say?" and she said, "I suppose," and he took off his shirt and watch, put the watch in his pants pocket, and undid his belt. His penis was erect and a little curved to the left and sticking through the fly of his boxer shorts as he pulled the pants down. She looked at it, made no expression, and looked away; but it had to look comical sticking out and curved that way, maybe even obscene, and he pushed it back in, folded his clothes up, and put them on a chair. She shut her eyes, twisted her arm around her back to scratch the middle of it, gritted her teeth as if the scratching or something else back there hurt, yawned, and said without opening her eyes, "Sorry if you heard that," and he had but said, "Heard what?" and she said, "I yawned, but nothing to do with you. Just I'm tired . . . long day," and got up to get something from the top dresser drawer. We're like an old couple already, he thought; ah, maybe that's good: we'll be relaxed, no poses. And a diaphragm, probably, from the drawer, but he can hardly believe the whole thing. Stepped out of his shorts; he was still erect but so what? Just that he was going to make love with her, this beautiful body and face, that's what he found so unbelievable. Because she was so young, maybe she was more beautiful to him than she actually was, but again, so what? Firm, lean, strong, no fat or bumps, impressions, or pocks in her thighs and buttocks, ass so high, nice-sized breasts and the shape they're in—she's in perfect shape all around. Slim legs, body like one in a bathing suit or Caribbean beach ad. No tan, divisions of dark and light on her skin, whatever they're called. She's evenly white as if she's intentionally stayed out of the sun and in fact had rarely been in it or never without covering or chair or beach umbrella or wide-brimmed hat. But the light pubic hair, dark head and underarm hair; something there he didn't understand. Important? No, but why was she letting him go through with it? Look at the differences, lady, compare; for one thing, his neck. He saw it as john-whore, but only because she had a body and face a guy his age usually had to pay for. And smart, too, going for a degree he'd never have the brains to get. Any advanced degree: never wanted one, but that's another thing. Not that he would pay to lay her. What's he saying? Sure he would, once: a hundred, maybe even two hundred, once, but if it was in a normal apartment, not a whorehouse, and she said something like, "I don't ever do this but I suddenly need the money," and she was absolutely clean. Clean? Hadn't thought of it but sure she's clean, and she must know he is after no woman but his wife for almost thirty years. But he's not going to tell her what he thought. Unless, let's say, they were lying around on the bed after lovemaking one night or any other time, tonight, for instance, tomorrow morning, but lying around casually, maybe her head on his chest, his arm around her shoulder, and that hand resting on or holding her breast, and he said, "For curiosity purposes only, and you don't have to say if you don't want, but what did you think when you first saw my body with no clothes on, and I'm not talking about my penis, but you want, even that—the testicles, the works. And don't worry about offending me about this. I know what I look like—the neck, for instance. I don't want to call any more attention to it than would seem necessary or normal, because then it'll seem like self-pity's motivating me, but there it is, the neck, getting a little scrawny just like everyone's eventually does. So believe me, say what you thought about my body at that time, even what you think of it now, even the neck, what it does to you, if it in any way repels you—that's not a good way of putting it—but I'd really like to hear."

She turned around, had what looked like a miniature athletic bag in her hand, bright red with electric-blue straps and some words inside a circle on it—a basketball, he now saw—and said, "I'm going to wash up," and he said, "I should too," and she said, "Why, what do you have to do—you mean the toilet; you want to go first?" and he said, "No, my body—you know, wash my penis; I mean, it's okay, but just to wash it anew—and also all around the anus and inside, sort of like that, if you want me to be honest," and she said, "With what? Not with one of my washrags, I hope," and he said, "Why? You just throw it in the wash after. But if it bothers you . . . anyhow, I wasn't thinking of using a washrag, actually. My hands—lathered up—one hand, and if you have tissues in there, or toilet paper will do, which I'd dry myself with. And I won't throw the tissues into the toilet bowl, so I'd need a wastebasket too," and she said, "Good, my bathroom's fully set up for all of that," and he said, "Then good, we're set. Now, before you go, and you should go first—my activity isn't crucial—may I also hold you a little and maybe a kiss before? I suddenly want to," and she said, "That'd be nice, I'd like it," and smiled, stepped toward him, they kissed, he pressed his body into hers, ran his hand up and down her side, rubbed her back, on her rear end, clutched it, leaned over and stretched his arm down till he got his hand under her buttocks and between her legs, and she said, "Please, Gould, not so fast," and he said, "Oh, my name," and she said, "What about it?"—his hand was away by now—and he said, "Nothing; that you used it: a second, I think. It sounded nice, and I'm sorry, but I didn't think I was going so fast," and she said, "It was, for me, and I also want to wash up, as I said, and do some other things in there"—her head nodding to the bathroom—and he said, "Okay, all right, but so many rules here; whew. Don't do this, do that; or not so many do's, just don't do this or that," and she said, "I'm only telling you what I have to do first and what I don't like done too fast—that's so bad? Standing up and fooling around here, for instance. It's nice for a minute, but maybe you even had in mind doing it right here," and he said, "I didn't," and she said, "I'm glad, because we don't have to, isn't that true? The bed's a much better place. And I'm tired; I already told you. So standing up and feeling each other after a while can be an effort when I'm this way," and he said, "Come on, will you? Stop telling me—please, I mean—how to make love and how not to. I've done it before, I do have some experience. Okay, you do too, but understand that everything I'm doing here with you—if there's any action that isn't, I'd be surprised—is coming from some need or urgency of mine or something to touch and feel and paw you and the rest of it, now and later, so what the hell's so goddamn wrong with that? Tell me," and she said, "You don't have to get vulgar and I think angry there, all of a sudden. And the truth is, too much talk too, okay?" and he said, "Listen, don't now tell me not to talk or how to and then when to talk and more of the not-to-do-this stuff unless something I'm doing is physically hurting you—that I can respect," and she said, "Right now your talking is hurting me, is that coming through?" and broke them apart and pushed him away a few inches. He said, "Hey, maybe this isn't a good idea—this whole thing—how about that?" and she said, "I think you're right," and he said, "So maybe then I should get dressed," and she said, "I think that would be the best thing to do, yes," and he said, "Boy, that was one fast coming together and breakup," and she said, "It was, though I wouldn't exactly use either of those terms for it. Let's just say something is definitely wrong, or had become that, and whatever was materializing between us tonight isn't such a good idea now," and he said, "Okay, everything's wrong, even the goddamn terms and words," and she said, "Please, don't get angrier and make it into a big clamorous embroilment. And I'm really not trying to escape from this conversation—I just have to go badly, excuse me," and went into the bathroom and shut the door.

He started putting his clothes on. Should I? he thought when he had his shorts on. Or should I stay naked and, when she comes out, say, "I thought maybe you had a change of mind? I know I have, but if you don't, fine, I'll get dressed," but then thought no, just go, they're never going to end up in bed, and if she sees him sitting here naked . . . well, he could say something quickly why he is, that business about her possibly changing her mind and he didn't want to get dressed when he'd only have to undress again—he'd say it jokingly—but she could get annoyed that he hadn't started dressing and say something like "It's no laughing matter, and your delirium about my changing my mind is in fact a bit depressing," and he got his shirt and pants on and was sweating heavily and his stomach hurt and chest felt empty because he had so much wanted to do it with her and had even seen something good and happy and long-term from it for a while and he knows he's going to kick himself to kingdom come once he leaves her place—a chance like this will never happen again, never—and was putting on a sock, thinking maybe he can come up with something to say to change things around, an artful apology, blaming it on his newness to this kind of male-female situation and which he swears—"I'm a quick learner"—will never be repeated, when she came out wearing a bathrobe tied tight at the waist. "As you can see, I'm almost dressed and would have been completely but I couldn't find the mate to this"—pulling at the sock on his foot. "No, that's not true; I just didn't want to be entirely dressed and out of here by the time you came out, don't ask me why," and she said, "I see; it's all right, take your time. And look, I want you to know—I don't want you to think I was being a tease before. I meant to do what we were both heading for, but it was something you said, and the bad feelings I felt coming from you . . . a certain crossness—" and he said, "All right, all right, can it. Jesus!" and she said, "You don't have to become insulting," and he said, "How was I?" and she said, "Just now, in what you said: another example of what I meant about the bad feelings coming from you," and he said, "I'm sorry, then. I'm feeling particularly lousy and frustrated about this evening—mortified too, in a way . . . morbid, even. I feel just terrible, to tell you the truth, but I'll get over it, though the whole thing should have been avoided because it was stupid from the start," and she said, "No, it wasn't," and he said, "No?" and she said, "I never would have asked you up or even wanted to see you a second time if I had thought it was," and he said, "Well, you don't feel any different about it now, do you? because I think I do," and she said, "I'm sorry, no," and he said, "Then it was stupid, and now even stupider than when I said it was. It's got to be our vast age difference"—putting a shoe on—and she said, "You certainly do struggle with that theme, and so sedulously," and he thought, Sedulously, what's it mean?—oh, yes, and said, "Listen, I'm trying to be nice about this, polite, civil, because I feel so goddamn rotten about everything and I don't want to feel even worse, but will you stop telling me about myself—will you just please stop?" and she said, "You're angry again; I'm sorry," and he said, "Angry? You're sorry? Oh, I don't know," and had his other shoe tied now and said, "So long," and left.

Saw her a week later. It was late afternoon and they were going opposite ways again on the same sidewalk and he said, "Hi," and she smiled and said, "Hi, how are you?" and he said, "Fine, thanks, and you?" and she said, "I'm in a rush to something very important now so I really can't stop, excuse me," and he said, "Don't worry, I understand," and walked on. He turned around a few seconds later and looked at her hurrying up the hill. God, what a shape, and so goddamn beautiful! If only he had gone along with what she was saying that night, stopped talking or only spoke softly, not got angry or vulgar, touched her where and when she wanted to, pretended to have more dignity, just held back, let her make the moves, call the shots, the rest of it, because it should have been obvious that was what she wanted, something he only realized after he left her place, then it would have happened. She was a little scared, or wary, had reservations, that much he knew when he was there—meaning she had to; it would only be natural; you don't want to just jump in with an old guy, no matter how forward and out front she was in the apartment, bar, movie theater, et cetera, but he didn't deal with it intelligently. And again, with someone so young and lovely. Ah, you've gone over it plenty, too much already, so don't start killing yourself some more over it. That it didn't happen, wasn't successful, but got so close: no clothes, their bodies pressed together, kissing, his hand on her ass . . . forget it, and you don't ever want to try it again with someone her age, not, as he's also told himself too many times, that he'll ever have another chance. They really don't want to be doing it with you, that's what it comes down to. They think they have the body and face and youth and spirit and who knows what else—the time; they got just about everything, far as they're concerned, and instant oblivion also—and can dictate the terms because of that, if they do, for whatever fluky reasons they have, want to go through with it, and that can take care of the scariness and wariness and so on. So what's he saying? He's saying nothing. Or he's saying little. But he just should have shut up. But also done what he did in the theater, and that's pull his hand away from hers—in other words, something like that—or is that what he did? No, he just didn't, when she wanted him to, kiss, but anyway, done what she wanted but with some reservations and reluctance or wariness himself till he got her in a position where she couldn't call things anymore, where he had her pinned or locked but was inside her and nothing was going to stop it till he was done, and after that told her to screw off with her demands if she made any from then on or made them excessively. Because just to have done it once with her. To be walking down this street, after having just stared after her from behind, and thinking, I laid that gorgeous girl, and then to be able to go over it all in his head. But he didn't think of that then.

Saw her a few more times after that, and they waved or smiled at each other or both or said hi or hello and went on. Then he saw her when he was with his younger daughter. They were going the same way, she was at the corner waiting for the light to say WALK and he was a little behind her and got alongside her and said, "Hi," and she said, "Oh, hi, hello"—and smiled—"how are things going?" and he said, "Couldn't be better, and you?" and she said, "Same here, thanks. Well, I'll see you," when the light said WALK and she crossed the street, and he and his daughter crossed it a little more slowly. Then he yelled out, "Lorna, by the way . . ." and she turned around, and he said, "This is one of my daughters, Josephine," and she waved and said, "Hi, Josephine, nice to meet you," and continued on, and Josephine said, "Who's that? One of your students?" and he said, "No, just someone I know from the block," and she said, "I didn't know you were so popular," and he said, "I'm not."

Home

WHERE'S HIS MOTHER? Didn't expect his father to be here, he's always too busy for things like this, but did his mother. Other kids are picked up. They run to their parents or just their parent or grandparent or older brother or sister. Lots of shouting of names, hugging, squealing, kissing, just what he expected to do with his mother, though no squealing; that's for girls. He looks around and around. Half the kids were picked up the second they were brought to stand under the big Kodak sign. Most of the others were picked up in the next few minutes. "Mommy! Daddy! Nana!" and so on. Now he and a kid he didn't like all summer are the only ones left from their division. Of all people to get stuck with, this one: Arthur. Not Art or Artie but Arthur, he had them all call him. "My mother said that's the name on my birth certificate and the only name I should be called and not to answer to any other name," or something. Good thing he also wasn't in his bunk or on his team in color war. July first, camp started; now it's August twenty-fifth. In a little more than a week, the day after Labor Day, he'll be back in school. The thought of it makes him sick. Really, he has this sudden sick feeling in his gut at the thought of going back to school. It won't be so bad the first day. There shouldn't be too much to learn, the teacher will try to be nice, and he'll see which kids he's with, though they were told on their report cards last June which class they were promoted to, but he forgets who'll be in his of the ones he likes. His best friend, Willy, won't be in his class for the first time since second grade. His mother said it was just a fluke they stayed together this long in the same class. That it defied, she said, the law of averages—always big talk like that and with words he has to ask her the meaning of. She's the reader in the family, the brain, and the one people say he takes after that way. But he gets his sense of humor and gabbiness from his father, they also say, besides his looks. Which, someone said in joking, he got shortchanged on or the worst of the bargain, his mother being thought of by most people as some kind of beauty when she was young and still a little today. Anyway, he forgets what he was thinking. School. In about eight days. No Willy in his class, but he'll see him every day and walk to and from school with him unless Willy gets another best friend. But they'd still walk together, he's sure, because he's the only other boy on the block from their grade who goes to that public school. But his mother: where can she be? Maybe the subway got stuck or she took a taxi and the driver drove her to the other train station by mistake. What would he do if she stayed there waiting for him and all the campers here had gone, and the counselors and Uncle Sol, the camp director, wanted to go and she didn't know where he was, maybe thought she got the pickup day wrong and went home to check because she'd left the camp schedule there—or didn't have to go home at first, phoned and his dad wasn't there; he was working, even though it was Saturday—so then she had to go home and the schedule said today and Grand Central Station and she was already two hours late and Uncle Sol by this time had got tired of waiting for her and left him there alone with his duffel bag—his trunk had already been sent home from camp by truck. But the camp would never do that. They'd stay with him till someone picked him up or they'd deliver him to the person his parents had told them beforehand about if his mother couldn't come and get him or just didn't show up. In other words, an emergency name and phone number. His father's office, even. So, nothing to worry about, really.

"Where do you think your parents are?" Arthur says, and he says,

"It's probably just my mom who's coming, and I don't know. She's usually never late—she's a stickler about time—so something must have gone wrong with the city: a detour by cab because of a parade or something, or a car crash in front of hers. And your mom?" and Arthur says, "My parents, and they're always late, so I'm used to it. They'll be here, though, that I'm sure. They never fail. Look," and points to the ceiling; it's as high as any ceiling Gould's seen. Higher up than the one in the Great Hall at the Natural History Museum, even, which he's seen hundreds of times, since he lives so close to it. "Yeah, that's a pretty high ceiling, all right, but near where I live? The Natural History Museum?" and Arthur says, "The what museum?" and he says, "The American Museum of Natural History," and Arthur says, "Oh, that one; I didn't know which museum you were talking of," and he says, "Why, there aren't two like it in the city," and Arthur says, "There's one in Washington, D.C., and another in San Francisco and in Philadelphia, I think, and probably lots of other places in America. That's why you have to distinguish them or identify them correctly, because there's only one called the American Museum of Natural History, and that one's in New York," and he says, "But I did say 'near where I live,' right? and that couldn't be Philadelphia or San Francisco, right?" and Arthur says, "Sure it could, for Philadelphia. It's only an hour away by train from Pennsylvania Station. For you never told me what city you specifically live in. Or if you did, this summer or last, I forgot," and he says, "Oh, what's the sense in talking to you? You always say this and that instead of talking about what we're talking about," and Arthur says, "If you remember, Gould, I was the one who was pointing something out when this conversation started, and it wasn't the height or breadth of this train station either. I mean, both those we know, correct? I'm saying, both of us left from here two months ago, didn't we? and we both left and came back from here last year too." "All right, so what's your point?" and Arthur says, "My point, sir, is pigeons," and he says, " 'Sir'?" and Arthur says, "I was only joshing with that. But look up. Did you ever see so many pigeons inside a building like this, if at any time any bird flying in one? It's so mysterious and eerie," and Gould sees way up, right at the top—it must be a thousand feet away—with big long sunbeams slanting through the whole station from the big windows, making the place look like it has prison bars: anyway, a whole flock of pigeons flying around up there, or just birds. Because they are so far away, who can tell for sure what kind of birds they are? "Why do you say they're pigeons?" and Arthur says, "What else can they be, in a city so filled with them? Besides, they flap and flutter like pigeons, and I think I heard one before, even from way down here, go *coo, coo, coo*. And they also have to be them because look at those two there," and points, and about a hundred feet away, walking between some people and their luggage on the floor, are two pigeons, a mother and father it was pointed out to him once, the father with a green shiny neck and much bigger and more beautiful—or handsomer, you can say—than the mother, who had no colors like that on her neck and not as many feathers there and no puffy chest either or not as much so and her head sort of shaped like a woman's. More graceful, a softer look; something like that. "Well, I guess that clinches it in a way," Gould says, "though if all those by the ceiling are also pigeons, how come these two aren't up there?" and Arthur says, "Boy, you're a hard one to convince. Because they're resting from flying, what do you think?"

"Arthur," a woman says, and they look and it's his mother. Gould recognizes her from a visit during Parents Day, even if she's wearing city clothes now while this summer she had on shorts and a camp T-shirt. She must have not come with the right country clothes then, so borrowed the shirt from Arthur or bought it at the camp store and maybe the shorts from someone else. He forgets what she had on her feet; here it's high heels. But what he remembers most about her is her ugliness. She's maybe the ugliest woman her age he's ever seen in real life—"Ugly as sin," as his dad's said about some people, men and women and even a couple of kids, though he isn't completely sure what that expression means—with big everything on her face: nose, eyes, chin, even her lips, plus holes in her cheeks and yellow pimples and bushy hair, but a normal unfat body and legs. Arthur runs to her and Gould stays there and they hug and she stares at Arthur's face and for a moment almost looks as if she's going to cry but then grins, kisses the top of his head and one of his hands, and starts talking, and Arthur covers his eyes in embarrassment, it seems, so it must be how tall he's grown the last month and how older he looks and more mature and so healthy with his tan and things like that and how his hair's grown so long and it's going to have to get cut for school.

Though who knows? They might be weirdos, as his dad also likes to say about some people, so they'll let him go to school with hair halfway down his neck and over his eyes. "Where's Father?" and she says, "We couldn't find a parking spot so he's sitting in the car. He can't wait to see you. Think you're strong enough to carry your duffel bag alone? You look it," and he says, "I don't know, I'll try," and with some struggle gets it onto his shoulder; then he begins to sag under it, says, "Help," and she grabs a handle at one end and he the other and he says, "Give me another year," and they laugh. As they're starting out she looks at Gould and says something, and Arthur shrugs and they come over, put down the bag, and Arthur says, "Mother, this is a friend from camp, Gould Bookbinder," and he thinks, Friend? I talked more to him here than I did all summer, but he wants to lie that he has lots of friends, that's okay. She says, "How do you do, Gould, did you have a good summer?" and he says, "Yes, thanks. I just hate the end of it because it means going back to school," and she says, "I don't think Arthur will have that problem. You're looking forward to school, aren't you, dear?" and Arthur says, "Sort of. It can be stimulating and fun," and she says to Gould, "Did I meet you this summer when I came up?" and he says, "I don't think so; Arthur and I were in different cabins." "You're waiting for your parents, though, yes?" and Arthur says, "Just for his mother; she's unusually late," and she says, "I'm sure she'll come, and if not, Mr. Birmbaum will look after him, so don't worry." Mr. Birmbaum—Uncle Sol to the campers—has just run over and says, "Glad I caught you whisking Arthur away before you got past me. But I guess Gould would have let me know who swiped him, right, there, kid? So, so long, Arthur, my boy, and hope to see you at the camp reunion. It'll be at the President Hotel, February, same as last year," and Arthur says, "Will we be notified of the exact date a little longer beforehand than last time?" and Uncle Sol says, "I'll see to it personally that you have plenty of time to get it into your engagement calendar. Goodbye, Mrs. Singer," and she nudges Arthur, and he says, "Goodbye, sir, and have a good winter, Gould," and he says, "You too, see ya," and they go.

Now, out of the whole camp it's just him and this very young boy who's left, and then the boy's picked up and he says to Uncle Sol, "Where do you think my mother is? She's always on time, even a little before. Should we call her?" and Uncle Sol says, "Good idea, kid," and gives him a dime and points to a booth nearby and he goes to it, puts the dime in and thinks, What's my number again? It's been so long, I forgot, and knows he can dial Information for it but then he might lose the dime and he's not sure he'd know what to say to the phone company to get it back and also what to say to the Information lady to get his number and then to Uncle Sol if he really lost the dime, so he goes back to him and says, "You don't have my phone number on your clipboard there, do you?" and Uncle Sol says, "It's been a long time, hasn't it?" and he says yes, thinking Uncle Sol either means long time away from New York or since he's used his phone number or called home or maybe since he's asked anyone for it. Anyway, he gets the number, says, "That's it; now I won't probably forget it till the end of next summer," and calls and nobody answers. He offers to give back the dime but Uncle Sol says, "Nah, hold it; better than asking me for it again," and he says, "What'll happen if no one comes?" and Uncle Sol says, "Then I take you to my house and throw you into the basement pit with all the other campers from previous years whose parents didn't pick them up and work you twelve hours a day only on bread and water and at less than slave wages, digging a tunnel to China so I can open up a fast new lucrative rice route. Only kidding; don't look so scared," and he says, "I wasn't; I could tell you were fooling," though he did think while Uncle Sol was saying all that that he might do something mean to him—raise his voice, pull him by the arm to the phone to call again or something—not by the story, which was silly, but by his sharp voice and face, which seem a bit angry. "And listen, don't even say your mother might not come. It's never happened in ten years where a camper's been stranded, knock wood," and looks around, then taps Gould's head. "It'd be the worst thing in the world for me, hunting down a parent. After two months of camp without a day off and another six weeks straight preparing to open it, not to mention going to everyone and his uncle's home for three months to show them pictures of the camp and stuff to come there and in between that hiring a staff and setting up the camp reunion, you don't think I need a few hours to myself with no campers around before I go back tomorrow to help close the place? You've any idea what that closing entails?" and he says no, though he didn't understand all of what that last part meant since he doesn't know what "entails" means, and Uncle Sol says, "You don't want to know, believe me, but if you're smart never become head counselor of a camp you're also part owner of. I thought it'd be easier than school-teaching, but like every time I plan my life for something better, I was wrong. But if your folks aren't here in half an hour—and God help me I hope it doesn't take that long, my feet won't stand it—then I contact one of your relatives or someone like that close. I have a sheet with the names of three people to reach in case of emergency for all my campers," and Gould says, "What kind of emergency could it be?" and Uncle Sol says, "I said, in case of, *in case of*. You gotta listen better, Gould, it'll help you later in life and possibly even a little today. But there won't be an emergency, so relax and enjoy the station and don't make me even more nervous than I am." Now I'm worried, Gould thinks. Did his mother take a cab and it crashed? Maybe she forgot about today and was at home when he called and for some reason didn't pick up the phone, but then why wouldn't his dad have reminded her he was coming back from camp today? Something really bad happen to her at home? He should have called his father at work after nobody answered at home, but Uncle Sol only gave him the dime to call home and he didn't think of it then besides, and if he got Dad at work he might get mad Gould took him away from important business or customers. Maybe there was some catastrophe at home: a fire, something in the electricity or with the stove. It could be happening right now and the phone when he called kept ringing through all of it. That could be why the camp wasn't told why his folks couldn't pick him up. He's sure something bad's happened, though maybe not as bad as he just imagined. He's going to ask Uncle Sol if he can use the dime to call his father at work, and if he gets him he thinks his father won't be too upset with him when he learns how worried he is about his mother and that he's the last camper here and Uncle Sol's ready to bust a gut over it.

Just then a woman says, "Excuse me, but Gould?" She's holding a photo and looks back and forth at him and it. "Gould Bookbinder, this is you"—showing him a photo of him last summer—"Bea's son, right?" and he says, "Yeah, who are you?" "Can I help you, miss? I'm the head counselor at Gould's camp," and she says, "Mr. Birmbaum. I was supposed to look for you too. I'm a friend of Gould's mother and I've a letter from her giving me permission to collect her son and deliver him home," and Uncle Sol says, "May I see it?" and takes the letter and reads it. "Gould, this your mom's writing?" and he looks at it, and it starts off with, after the *To Sol Birmbaum or Whomever Else It May Concern: I hereby give permission to Lynn Jacobo, a trusted co-worker of mine at Lord & Taylor's and a friend . . .*" and he says, "I think so; it looks it, the way she makes circles over the *i*'s and the nice handwriting," and Uncle Sol says, "But you didn't seem to recognize the lady," and she says, "He couldn't have. We knew there'd be this problem, because you should be extra cautious with your charges, so that's why this letter. I only met his mother this summer at the store we work at," and Gould says, "That's another thing that sounds a bit fishy to me, Uncle Sol. My mother never worked at a store," and she says, "Excuse me, he's right, though she works at one now forty-four hours a week. And two days ago she gave me this note, in case she couldn't pick him up, much as she wanted to, and then called late last night for me to do her this favor and fetch him. She said she'd call you before your buses left for the train station, but she didn't?" and Uncle Sol says no and she says, "Well, what can I say? But I still got the arrival time wrong by an hour, it seems, if all the kids are gone, because if you can believe it I thought I was getting here ten minutes early, just to have a doughnut and coffee and a quick peep around. I really apologize for coming late, Gould; you must've been worried," and Uncle Sol says, "I'm sorry, Miss Jacobi—" and she says, "Jacobo, and missus, and we didn't properly say hello, did we?" and shakes his hand and then shakes Gould's and says, "It's so nice meeting you after hearing such wonderful things about you from your mother. My, does she talk of you!" and he says, "Thanks." "Still, Mrs. Jacobo, you're not one of the names on the list of people allowed to get him. I have Louise and Max Rand down here, her sister and brother-in-law it says, and a Florence Hoff," and she says, "The last is her neighbor—I've met her, and Gould certainly knows her—and she's at a psychotherapists' convention. That's what she does, psychotherapy, out of her apartment," and Uncle Sol says, "That so, Gould?" and he says, "I know Flo; I don't know what that psychosomething is, but she does work in a big room that she has." "As for the Rands," she says, "all I know is what I heard from Bea, and that's that they're at a resort in New Hampshire till Labor Day, so that left little me," and Uncle Sol says, "You do know a lot about the family. But you'll still have to give more proof, because I can't release a child to just some family knowledge and a letter. And when we called his home before, no one answered, so is Mrs. Bookbinder at work?" and she says, "She's home—didn't I say?—waiting for me to bring him. I'm on my lunch hour, which is really just forty-five minutes to the dot, so I have to be quick. Even if I cab back and forth I won't make it; so what are they going to do, dock me for fifteen minutes? And she's okay, Gould, nothing to worry about; your mom must've simply not heard the phone ring, because otherwise I'm sure she would've answered. But may I speak to you, Sol, out of earshot, if we can?" and Uncle Sol looks at her peculiarly. She gives an expression, the way her forehead's folded and eyes are half closed, that seems to mean what she has to say is very important and will explain what she can't explain here, and Uncle Sol says, "Sure. Don't go away, Gould, we'll be back in a flash," and they go off about twenty feet and talk. Uncle Sol nods that he understands. She takes some papers out of her pocketbook and shows him them. He nods some more, then looks over to Gould and back to her with the expression Think-he-knows-what-we're-talking-about? and she shakes her head no. They come back. "Gould, this Mrs. Jacobo's legit. She'll take you home to your mother," and he says, "How come she's taking me and not my mom?" and she says, "I'll tell you everything in the cab," and she and Uncle Sol look at each other and she nods, and Gould says, "How come you can't tell me now?" and she says, "Because in the cab we'll be on our way and I gotta get back to work soon. These your bags?" and he says, "Just two," and she says, "Gosh, I didn't know what I was getting myself into. They look heavy. You'll help me with them?" and he says, "I grew four inches this summer; I can carry them both," and puts the big bag on his shoulder and the smaller one under his arm. "We can stop at a stand here for a hot dog and you can eat it on the way," and he says, "No, I want to get home, and my mom always has something good waiting for me." "See you at the camp reunion," Uncle Sol says, "and I hope everything at home turns out okay," and he says, "Why wouldn't it? She tell you something?" and Uncle Sol says, "Nothing; what'd I say? Just an expression, kid, like 'good luck' and 'stay well' and all that. So, you had a great summer, Gould, hope to see you as a camper next year, and now I'll also be on my way," and salutes them and goes.

In the cab she stares out the window at the city and he says, "You said you'd tell me why my mother didn't pick me up," and she says, "Did I? I forget. Well, on second thought, better she tell you when you see her," and he says, "Is she all right? My father? Either one sick with something? That what happened? Because that's what I'm starting to think," and she says, "She's fine, in the pink, and as far as I know about your father, he's healthy too, or at least she didn't say anything that he wasn't," and he says, "You're holding back something; I can tell by your voice," and she says, "Okay. She told me if you were really smart and persistent and getting more worried by not knowing than knowing, and I was an absolute moron in being cagey and sly, that I could tell you this, so don't think I'm overstepping my boundaries," and he says, "What's that you mean?" and she says, "What I mean is I'm not saying anything here your mother told me I couldn't." "And my father?" and she says, "He I never once spoke to. Maybe because he's not been around lately, which is my point, so do you get what I'm saying or do I gotta spell it out further?" and he thinks, Oh, no, they've split up, his worst fear, maybe even got divorced, because they wouldn't need him there with them for that—had a fight, lots of fights, they used to yell a lot at each other, but this time they used their fists and hit one another hard, so hard his mother got knocked out cold and had to call the doctors and cops, or someone had to for her, and when she woke up in the hospital she told him to leave, because by then he was sorry for what he did and wanted to apologize and take care of her, but she screamed at him to go and he left, and with another wife he might already somewhere be starting another child by this time with no thought in the world for him and his mother, even if by now she could be willing to take him back. "You don't look good, Gould, did what I say disturb you? I told you I didn't want to say anything," and he says, "No, you can tell me; I always knew something was wrong," and she says, "Good, you're mature, just like this Sol guy was intimating, and you're a good little fella too, because you're making it easier for me than I thought. Okay: your father's moved out and your mom's terribly distressed over it. I don't see why she should be, if you'll take my two cents. From what I know, they've been fighting like cats for years, so this could be a good thing," and he says, "No, they didn't. They just argued sometimes, but I've seen them in plenty of happy moods together. Did he get married again?" and she says, "It's too soon, how could he? It's only been a month, and it's not some other woman with her claws in him who's making him do it, so don't think that," and he says, "Then I want him to move back. The place is better with him in it—funnier—no matter how much they fight. They can make up and only argue now and then and not so loudly," and she says, "Maybe you're right. You're a smart kid, as I said, so maybe you know what you're talking about. Anyway, that's all I'm permitted to tell you—what I just did. To prepare you, if I thought I had to, for having no daddy at home right now but that he'll probably call you tonight or in a day or so. And that your mother's depressed over it, not so much because of him but that it finally came to this and the family's broken up, so mostly depressed by the effect it'll have on you. It could be, between you and me, she's thinking she held on to your father this long just for your sake—I don't know, I'm only speculating." "What's that?" and she says, "Raising the possibility of, I think. But my authority stops where I said, as I don't have the go-ahead from your mom to go any further than I did, and as it is I think I went too far." She looks out her window. "Catch the traffic," and he says, "Why? There hardly is any," and she says, "That's what I mean. New York, in this area, is like a—well, maybe almost all over except in front of Bloomingdale's and down on Times Square and the square where Macy's and Gimbel's are: Herald. I'm talking of summer weekends, but like a little town, quiet and empty like one, when all the people are in church." "We don't go to church; not even to a synagogue except maybe the very holy days in September," and she says, "I didn't mean literally. I meant it's as if New York's just a small town today, it's so deserted around here, though where everybody is I don't know. Vacationing, probably, the last big week before Labor Day, and the ones working on Saturday, instead of walking around on their lunch hours, are inside their buildings because of the sun and heat. You all right, Gould, not too upset from what I said? If you want I can still stop a block from your building and buy you a hot dog or ice cream. I don't mind getting back to work late, if it'll help you. So they dock me. So sue me too," and he says, "No, I just want to get home. I'm kind of tired."

She unlocks the front door with the keys his mother must have loaned her, leaves them on top of the breakfront by the door, and says, "Cool in here; you're lucky. That's because your mother keeps the blinds down. Anyway, gotta get going, so I'll see ya. Say hi to her from me and that I had to dash," and she goes. He yells, "Mom, I'm back, I'm back, you around?" and she says from the bedroom, "I'll be out shortly, darling; welcome home. Take something in the refrigerator. I bought lots of things you like," and he says, "I'm not hungry but I'll look," and goes into the kitchen, opens the deli wax paper of several packages, takes a slice of liverwurst from one and a slice of Swiss cheese from another and stuffs them together into his mouth. Drinks a glass of milk, nice and cold. The apartment looks different. So clean and everything neat and put away and counters and floors shining as if washed and mopped and waxed. That's how he always remembers it when he comes home from camp, and the coolness of the place compared to the outside, but then forgets it till the next year. Also no lights on, to keep the heat of the rooms down too, his mother said. So it looks strange, a cross between day and night, when it's just the middle of the afternoon and the outside's maybe its brightest and hottest. The place also seems smaller, but not as much smaller as it did last year, and he wonders if his room's the same way and goes into it and it is. So what does that mean, that next year everything will seem the same here as when he left, or close to it? He looks for things he missed: a board game, a sponge ball, a book, feels his bed to see if it's still as comfortable—he got used to the hard cot at camp but what he never got used to was how narrow it was, and when he was sleeping he fell off it at least three times and once, even, during the rest period they make you take after lunch. Opens his middle dresser drawer for no reason but to look at the folded stacks of clothes. In a week it'll be messy and in a few weeks his mother will ask him to fold his clothes in his dresser if he wants to find anything in it, and if he says he doesn't want to she'll say then he won't be allowed to play outside after dinner. Smell of mothballs comes out of the drawer. That's what he always remembers, and he fingers around and finds a couple of the balls she missed, for his mother must have taken the rest out when she cleaned his room for his coming home. He gets out the mothballs she missed in the other drawers—they're all in the back corners. He doesn't mind the smell much, but it can get embarrassing when people start sniffing hard in front of him and then point out the smell on his clothes. Sits on the radiator cover, holds open some middle blind slats, and looks out his second-story window at two rows of backyards going all the way to the end of the block, a lot of the close ones overgrown with bushes and vines and trees whose branches hang down to the ground. In one yard a woman's sunbathing in a skimpy swimsuit. He doesn't know how she can just lie there in the sun, her arms turned up so the forearms show and her legs spread wide, and get burned and hot and sweat so much. He stares at the tall apartment building at the end of his block, at a small propeller plane passing over it till it flies out of sight, then looks at the woman—she's drinking right from a glass pitcher—and goes to the bathroom because he has to pee and after it taps on his mother's door. "What is it, Gould?" and he says, "I thought you'd be out by now, anything wrong?" "No, it's okay, don't worry," and he says, "I also forgot to tell you: Mrs. Jacobo, your friend, said to say goodbye to you, that she had to get back to work," and she says, "Did you like her?" and he says, "She was all right, but she talked too much," and she says, "She's nice; helped me out a lot by picking you up, and she had to come from work to do it," and he says, "I know. She also told me you work there together and all about you and Dad," and she says, "That's why I'm in here, Gould. The shock of it keeps coming back and back, and today it really got to me, probably because you were coming home, know what I mean? Okay, okay," and opens the door; she's in her bathrobe, hair a mess, face looking as if she just got up, hugs him, kisses the top of his head, and says, "Good, I've made my grand appearance, so you won't think me entirely strange. But I'm going back in to rest some more, if you don't mind and can understand. Play with Willy, if he's home," and he says, "Good idea. Can I take the keys Mrs. Jacobo left or should I leave the door unlocked?" and she says, "The keys," and goes into her room and shuts the door and he calls Willy down the block and gets the keys, though he doesn't know which one fits which lock. If you don't fix the button, door locks automatically, but he'll be able to get back in and if he can't he'll ring till his mother comes to the door. It might even be a good excuse to get her out of her room again. But when he gets back he's going to ask for his own keys and he bets she gives him a set now that there's only the two of them.

Plays, and when he lets himself in a couple of hours later the table's set for one, with a note on the plate: *Gould, dear. It was so wonderful seeing you again. You look great (I neglected to say then), grown a few inches, even filled out some, but in a husky way: you're getting so tall and strong. I've made what used to be your favorite sandwich. If you want something else, leave it and make a sandwich of your own choosing from the assorted deli I also have in the refrigerator. In the bread bin are a fresh loaf of rye bread and a package loaf of white and several fresh Vienna rolls (without seeds). For a special treat, but only today, take the bottle of White Rock ginger ale in the refrigerator too.* The sandwich is liverwurst and Swiss and lettuce, tomato, and mayonnaise on white bread, which he still likes but it's not his favorite anymore: ham and Swiss on white with mustard but no lettuce and tomato is—but he doesn't feel hungry for anything now. He wonders when his dad will call. He should have asked her. Should he ask through the door for his dad's new phone number? It's almost too late to call him at work, if he went there today, and asking for his home phone number might make her mad and maybe even sad too, and he drinks the soda and reads a book and listens to a radio show and answers the phone and writes down the message from a woman whose name he never heard before, and at eight raps on her door and says, "Mom? Mom?" and tries the knob, but the door's locked and she says from what sounds like across the room, maybe from her bed, "I'm so sorry for acting like this, Gould. Did you have your supper?" and he says, "I'm not hungry," and she says, "You have to be hungry; maybe you noshed a lot, then," and he says, "Only a piece of liverwurst and cheese before," and she says, "I'm sorry, I know it's all my fault you're not eating, but I can't seem to be able to make even another grand appearance. I feel repulsive and look a wreck, but it won't go on past tonight, I promise. Maybe things will improve with your father where he'll come home, and maybe they'll even get worse, where we have to set up two permanent separate households, but the worst thing about it is the effect on you," and he says, "I'll be all right, and now that we talked about it, I'll be fine. Can I come in now?" and she says, "This will sound terrible, but it's probably better if we next see each other at breakfast. Then I'll be all rested and feeling and looking better and we can do something together, like go to the park if it's not too hot. Now I'm still so tired I only want to go back to sleep. I've taken my phone cord out of the wall, so if it rings, answer it, but I'm not able to come to the phone for the rest of the night." "A Mrs. Corn called and said for you to call her. She didn't say about what but that you'd know and you have her number, so I didn't take it; was that all right?" and she says, "Of course, and I'll do it tomorrow. She's my boss and very sweet and probably wants to know if I'm coming in Monday. You know I had to go back to work because we needed the money," and he says, "I guessed so, but doesn't Dad give you any?" and she says, "Not enough because his business hasn't been doing too well and now he has his own rent and expenses. Somebody will be looking after you on Monday, so don't worry," and he says, "Who?" and she says, "A very nice woman. To take you to the movies and things. And later next week you'll go to your aunt's in Coney Island for two days, and I'll have a day off to be with you, and your father will be around, and we'll all work something out for when you go back to school," and he says, "Can I have his number so I can call him?" and she says, "I don't have it, or don't know where it is right this minute," and he says, "Can you get it for me?" and she says, "I wouldn't know where to look," and he says, "Do you know where he lives so I can dial four-one-one for it?" and she says, "It's such a new number they won't have it," and he says, "They give you new numbers; I've heard you and Dad on the phone with them. You say the number's new and give the name and address and they find it," and she says, "I don't even know where he lives. I'm afraid that's where your father and I stand now, Gould," and he says, "Come on, Mom, you have to have it," and she says, "Are you saying I'm lying?" and he says, "No. Could you tell me what you do at work?" and tries the door and it's still locked, which he figured it'd be. "That Mrs. Jacobo and the woman on the phone before didn't say anything about it," and she says, "Sales. Mrs. Corn is the head saleslady in our department: Girls' Clothes. Lynn—Mrs. Jacobo—has a much better position as a buyer, and if I stay at it long enough and get good reports I can eventually move up to that. They can do very well. But I'll tell you it all tomorrow morning. Now get a good night's sleep, which means not staying up too late reading. Your bed's freshly made, and also don't open your window too high. There's a floor fan in your room if you want—I bought it just last week but haven't plugged it in yet," and he says, "I saw but didn't know it was mine. Thanks. And good night," and she says good night and he thinks usually he likes to get a kiss but he's not going to ask for it.

He takes the sandwich out of the refrigerator, scrapes off as much of the mayonnaise as he can from it, smears on mustard, and eats it, has some milk, cookies, a plum, washes up and gets in his short-sleeves-and-shorts pajamas, and lies on the bed with a book and opens it and thinks, The fan! and plugs it in and turns it on to SLOW and gets back on the bed and thinks, When I grow older I'm never getting married. It'll end like this if I do—things are passed down from father to son more than they are from the mother, not just looks but I bet the kind of woman you choose for a wife—with my son's mother locked in her room and me some other place cheap and dirty because I have so little money or have given most of it to her for my son and not calling him also because I'm too upset and am afraid of getting my wife on the phone who I now hate more than anything but both of us believing the worst thing possible has happened to our son when it hasn't, he's actually glad they've split up because now he doesn't have to hear them arguing back and forth almost every dinner and Sunday mornings and sometimes from the second his father comes home from work and from time to time telling each other they're going to kill the other—not so much that but that they'd be better off dead than living with the other—and the only way to stop that from happening is never to marry and have a child, never, because you don't ever want to put him through that and make your own life horrible and crazy and mean besides; and he grabs the pillow from under his head and throws it across the room and then jumps out of bed and knocks all the treasures off his desk and picks up some and throws them against the wall and yells, "Shut up!"—to the fan—"just shut the hell up!" and pulls its plug out by the cord and pushes the fan over and would kick it if it wasn't that he had bare feet, and pounds the closet door with his fists and screams, "You bitches, you louses, you rotten bastards, I hate you, I hate your guts!" His mother comes in and says, "What is it with you; why are you acting like this?" and he says, "Nothing, go away," and runs to the night table and turns the light off and gets back in bed and under the covers and faces away from her and wishes he had his pillow to lie on but isn't going to get it till she's out of the room, and she says, "That wasn't a nice thing to say," and the room's still a little lit from the hallway light and he closes his eyes tight and she says, "And especially not after all you know I've recently gone through with your father, besides the things I've tried to do to make your homecoming as nice as it can possibly be for you," and he says, "Leave me alone; I can't stand either of you," and she says, "*Gould,*" and he doesn't say anything, and she says, "Gould, that was awful, apologize," and he holds his breath till he can't hold it any longer and lets it out slowly so she won't hear. She turns the ceiling light on, picks up the stuff he threw around, puts some of it in his wastebasket and the rest on his desk, brushes off his pillow and drops it at the foot of his bed, then turns the light off and leaves the room, and he thinks, I wish I could fall asleep right now, but so what, because even if I do I'll have to wake up in the morning.

The Dinner Table

THEY NEVER HIT each other. Oh, he raised his fist plenty of times, and threatened to clip her in the jaw or give her a nose job free, or his hands, sometimes, as if he wanted to strangle her. And she raised her hand also, saying how she'd like to slap his ugly face, and he'd say if she did he'd really crack her in the mouth, hit her so hard, he once said, that he'd knock her out cold and then he would just step over her and not give a plug damn whether she was alive or dead. To that she said, "Try it, you just try hitting me, and I'll get the police in here so fast you won't even see them coming through the door and have you manacled and carted off to jail." And he said, "And who'd take care of you then?" and she said, "I'd manage; I for sure don't need you," and they'd bicker like that, shouting across the dinner table, and that'd be when Gould would usually throw down his napkin and run to his room and slam the door, but he'd still hear them shouting for several minutes after, sometimes on and off for another hour or two, and even when he was asleep their shouting would wake him sometimes, and some of what they were shouting was about him: "How could you threaten me like that in front of Gould?" and his father would say, "Who threatened who? You're the one that said you'd slap my puss," and she'd say, "But only after you started it," and his father would say, "Started it how? If you mean I initiated it this time, that's because you both initiated, continued, and finished it the last time, so it wasn't over for me yet, though you for sure got your licks in. Believe me, this was started a long time ago, years, maybe a few weeks after we met. I never should have hooked up with you, certainly never married you. My brother was right a hundred percent about you, a thousand," and she'd say, "Just as my dad had the goods on you, and same figures," and it'd go on; Gould would often clamp his pillow to his ears, and later, even if he was asleep, one of them would usually come into his room—they must have decided who would go in to him or the other would send the more guilty-feeling of the two—and if it was his father, he'd say something like "Gould, you up? Your light's not on so I thought maybe you were asleep by now," or if his light was on and his eyes open his father would say, "Gould, everything all right?" and he would think, How could everything be all right? but he'd say, "Yeah, I guess so," and his father would say, "But you don't know, is that it?" and he'd say, "No, I'm okay, I'm okay, what?" and his father would say, "Good. Listen, I'm sorry—we both are—about the argument before. We do go at each other every now and then, don't we? and I'm not trying to pass it off here as if it's nothing. But we're all made up now, everything hunky-dory again, and we're sorry it ever happened, especially when you were there, but it's not going to happen again, I promise," and he'd think, Yeah, tell me more, as if I haven't heard it all before. "If there ever is another argument between your mother and I—and people who live together have their differences, you understand—it's going to be done in a reasonable way, not with such loud voices or anything," and Gould would say, "I'm glad," and his father would come closer, maybe sit on the bed if Gould was lying on it and wasn't drawing or doing homework at his desk, and say, "But I still haven't got from you if you realize how disturbed we are as to how the argument might have affected you," and he'd say, "It's okay, I understand, it's over; I'm much better now," and his father would say, "Fine, that's good, what I wanted to hear, thank you," and pat Gould's cheek or rub his hair and Gould would think, Sure, it's what you wanted to hear, and sure, it won't happen again till the next time when they shout and scream and raise their fists and hands and curse at each other like they hate one another and forget he's sitting there or anything or is alive and it doesn't touch him. One day one of them's going to kill the other: his mother is going to get so angry she'll grab a kitchen knife and stick it in his father's chest when he has his fist up ready to hit her, or his father will slam his mother so hard the first time she'll bang her head against the wall and break it so her brain becomes dead, or he'll strangle her or shake her so hard he breaks her neck and she dies on the floor. Then the one who killed the other will go to prison and he'll be sent to live with his uncle, who he doesn't like and who will beat him every night because he's so mean, just as he's heard his father say his uncle's beat his own wife and kids; or he'll be sent to a home with rough boys and get beaten every day and night by them and also by the people who run the home till he runs away and is caught and beaten and then runs away again and escapes because he knows how, this time, and he'll get on a railway car and get halfway across America on his own before a hobo climbs into the car and steals his shoes and beats him to ribbons and tries to stick his penis in his behind and threatens to slice his penis off if he doesn't do what he says and throw him off the car when the train's moving at fifty miles an hour; or he, rather, jumps off the car to keep the hobo from sticking his penis in him and rolls down some steep rocky hill, his head bumping on every stone along the way till his eyes fall out and his face is torn to shreds and his brains are bashed to mush and start spilling out of his ears and he's dead.

Or his mother would come into the room and say, "Gould, sweetheart"—if the light was off and he was in bed—"are you sleeping soundly, dear?" and if the light was on and he was in bed or at his desk or playing with something on the floor, she'd say, "My darling, could you give me a few minutes? I want to say some things to you, clear up what happened between your dad and me. We both can be hotheaded people unfortunately, your father perhaps more than I, but that's still no excuse for yelling at each other in front of you the way we did, or arguing anytime like that. I apologize for it, we both do, and though I know your dad and I have both said this before, and know that you know it too, I promise we'll both try hard as we can for it never to happen again. You have to believe me, dear. You're everything to us, the light of our lives, and we love you more than we've ever loved anyone or anything. We're heartsick over tonight—I can speak for your father because I know how he feels. We hate it when you get so upset because of something terrible we do, so we want to say nothing like that will happen at the dinner table again. And we also hope never anywhere in front of you either and maybe not even again between your father and me," and he'd think, Don't I wish, and I won't even say you said the same thing the last time, because I said that a few times already and you both always promise that the argument you just had, where you almost started to fight each other with your fists, was the last you'll have like that, or at least the last I'll ever have to sit through and see. "Gould, do you hear me?" and he'd say yes, and she'd say, "So come on, what do you have to say to it?" and he'd say, "That I heard you, what else?" and she'd say, "Could you maybe say you feel a little bit better now that I've made that promise from us?" and he'd say, "All right," and she'd say, "And what's that mean?" and he'd say, "What you said: that it's all right," and she'd say, "Honestly? because I don't see it on your face," and he'd say, "Honestly," and she'd smile and kiss his forehead and sit on the bed and hold his hand if he was on it or sit on it even if he was in the desk chair or on the floor and say something like "*Calmly,* that's how Dad and I are going to work out our differences and bigger problems from now on, or at least not so furiously . . . *judiciously,* that's the word and how we'll do it," and he'd think, What's that? and she'd say, "And I can only hope and pray you believe what I say is true," and he'd say, "I already said I do," and sometimes she'd look sad and sniffle a little and cover her eyes and motion him to her, if he was on the floor or in the desk chair—if he was on the bed she'd just reach over or down and hug him—and he knew he'd have to come to her or she'd say something like "Why aren't you coming over when I'm waving for you to, it's important for me," and he'd come and she'd sit him down beside her and put her arms around him and cry into the top of his head, and he'd say, "Don't, Mom, don't; it's all right," and she'd say, "It's just the relief the whole thing is over and won't happen again and I'm sitting here with you like this. A sentimental person, usually, I'm not."

So they'd fight, never once hitting each other when he was around, almost always at the dinner table; sometimes his father would throw money across it at her and say, "There, take the lousy dough"—or "filthy *gelt*" or "stinking green stuff"—"that's all you're interested in: what I can bring in," and once she tore some of this money up and threw it back at him, though it flew all around the table—when his father flung it at her he'd bunched up the bills till they were one chunk—and said, "This is what I think of your money," and Gould said, "Why'd you do that? That's good money; now you'll have to Scotch-tape it and some stores might not even take it," and his father said, "She's crazy, your mother, that's why she did it," and he said, "No, she's not. She's angry at you for what you did; it wasn't nice," and his father laughed and said, "What'd I do? I always get the blame. And who asked you? Mind your business, like a good kid," and a few minutes later Gould thought that was the first time he ever talked back to him about his actions at the table—the yelling, cursing, throwing—and his father said, "Besides, you don't like it, take a walk," and Gould said, "Good, I will, you gave me permission," and got up, and his mother said, "No, it's our fault, not his, he should stay; don't leave, dearest," and his father said, "Our fault? You mean yours; me, I'm clean," and she said, "No, both ours, admit it; both!" and he didn't hear what his father said next as he was already in his room, door slammed and, he thinks, his hands over his ears.

When he got to his teens—sixteen, seventeen—he stopped running away from the table when they argued and would say things like, "Why can't you two work it out somewhere else? Why does it always have to be at the dinner table when we're eating? Who do you expect can eat anything when you're snapping at each other like a pair of hyenas? I don't want to get ulcers every night. You get them, if that's what you want, but don't bring them on me. Christ, on and on and on it goes, year after year—it's ridiculous," and his father would say, "What do you know? Shut your mouth or you'll get it from me," and he'd say, "Get what? Your fist? You always threatened Mom—a thousand times at this table—but you never once delivered, thank God. That's the best I can say about your arguments here—both of you—the best," and he'd finish his food, or would eat a little more of it, just so they wouldn't think they were chasing him away from the table, and would get up and say, "Excuse me, I'm done," and leave, but usually go out these times, for a long walk or to a movie or a bar for a beer when he reached eighteen—or with a fake draft card when he was seventeen—and come home, and his parents would be in their room by now, and his mother always left a note on his bed or by the kitchen phone, saying something like *We were both worried about you. You stayed out so late that we didn't know what to think. It can be unsafe on the street, especially when you're alone. Please don't do that again. And even if our room's dark, knock on the door to tell me you're home,* and he'd knock and say, "Mom?" and she'd say, "You're home? Now I can fall asleep. You get some too—it's late," and he'd say good night and she'd say it. His father was probably asleep—he liked to boast that nothing stopped him from getting his eight hours every night—or who knows what.

Later his father got sick and his mother looked after him and they both mellowed, no more arguments at the dinner table, or just minor disagreements but no shouting or cursing the other. His mother would say, "Do you want some of this?" or, "I can make you some more of that," and his father would say, "Yes, that looks good, thank you," or "No, thank you." The TV news would usually be on during dinner the two or three nights a week Gould ate home, and once he said—he was in his early twenties now—"Do we always have to sit down with the news at dinner?" and his father said, "We don't always. It just happens to be on the same time we sat down tonight, and lots of other nights. What's so wrong with that? It really bother you, or you just want to have something new to complain about?" and he said, "It does bother me. It eliminates all possibility of conversation between us, and I don't like that unctuous TV commentator guy sitting down with us as if he lives here," and his father said, "He isn't all bad. He has a nice voice and personality, seems bright, and doesn't run at the mouth too long, and they give you lots of interesting newsreels. And the sound's not too high, and we can hold our conversations till after the news. It's only fifteen minutes, thirty minutes total with the local news. And it gives us something more to talk about when it's over," and he said, "It's repetitive and banal and almost nothing I'm interested in, the local stuff worse than the national and foreign reports, and only touches on a few facts and usually the worst things happening in the city and world, or most sensational, and nothing in depth. And art and culture? Well, out the window with you, little fellas, the public doesn't go for it, so you don't exist. And I hate commercials, smiling actor fakes always trying to sell you something you've no interest in buying or you thought you had no use for till they ran the dumb ads," and his father said, "Without commercials the economy wouldn't be what it is. It's a capitalistic society, the country's founded on it, the whole making and selling and buying and using things and then throwing them away when they break down or get old and buying some more. You should know that from the economics course you took. But all that means you got to have advertisements—it's imperative if you want to sell and be part of the competition—and what better place than on TV with half the country watching one show or the other at this time? And besides, they're only for a few minutes of the thirty and the news is the rest of the time," and he said, "But I don't want to know about another bombing or killing or mutilation or massacre or congressional hearing or trial or sports score or tomorrow's weather when I'm eating. I want my stomach to be relaxed. If anything electronic has to be on other than the lights, then good serious soothing music from the record player or radio," and his mother said, "If your father wants to listen to the news during dinner, it's his privilege. He worked hard long enough in life to warrant at least getting that when he retired," and Gould said, "But there are other people and other stomachs to be considered also," and his father said, "Your mother's right. If you don't like it, move out, you're old enough, you don't need our permission," and he said, "I will and I had planned to, just as soon as I finish school and turn in the poor-paying part-time job I have now for a good full-time one," and his father said, "Oh, boy, oh, yeah. You were always too sensitive as a kid. And now as an adult I thought you'd've stopped, but you're still the same, and no letup either on being a big complainer," and he said, "Sensitive to what when I was a kid? And are we supposed to argue with the television going? Okay, let's just eat and watch it," and his father said, "No, go on, big shot, get it out, you can do it over the TV sound. What were you saying—you were sensitive to what when you were a kid?" and he said, "Your yelling, I was saying; your cursing and throwing money at Mom, as if 'Here, here's your weekly allowance, though you don't deserve it,' and threatening her too with your fists and sometimes worse for most of my life at this miserable stupid table," and his father said, "Huh? What left field is that out of? Tell me, where?" and his mother said, "Gould, stop. This isn't nice or right, and you should apologize," and he said, "Apologize, just like both of you did a thousand times to me for upsetting a thousand of my dinners here plus hundreds of Sunday breakfasts, when they could have been nice dinners, good breakfasts," and his father said, "When? A few times? So what are you making a big stink for? And don't start blaming your mother all of a sudden just because she stuck up for me, not that I need any protection from you, when before it was only me, your target, and you know it's still me you only want to blame. You're a little meshugge, that's how I see it, always shooting your mouth off before you know what you're talking about. Well, get lost, will ya, because it's my house and my TV and I'm the boss in it, or made the dough to pay all the bills since you were born, and if I want to watch the news while I eat, I will. That's all I got to say to you," and Gould said, "Then watch it yourself or together but never again with me at dinner," and his father said, "You already made that threat, if I heard right before. Now we'll find out how serious a one it is, if it means no eating for you, since you were always a guy who liked his food. But fine, any way you want it," and took a bite of food and looked at the television set, and his mother said, "All I'll say on the matter, because of course I want Gould to sit with us at dinner for as long as he wants, even when he's peeved at us, is that his behavior has been totally uncalled-for," and Gould said, "Oh, you two, you're really something. But I'm glad about it: at least things are quieter between you now," and his father said to him, "Believe me, if I had the strength I'd send you and your luggage packing, and tonight, not tomorrow, so are you going to apologize as your mother asked you to? If not to me, then just her, because you *were* insulting," and he said, "I don't see why I should," and left the table, and his father yelled, "That's not enough, what you said," and he went to his room, shut the door, and lay on his bed, and said, "What a joke, what a joke they are: so lovey-dovey kissy-horseshit. It's bullshit!" he yelled. "That's what this shit is, goddamn bullshit, do you hear?" and his mother knocked on his door and he said nothing and she came in and said, "Gould, please, I hate to see you like this, so put a stop to it. Your father isn't well and you're making me feel awful," and he said, "Just think what I had to put up with you both over the years. Ready to kill each other a few hundred times, and all that screaming," and she said, "You already told us. And as Dad said, it was only a few times over more than twenty years—something no other married couple's done? And not kill each other, just very angry sometimes, but what's that got to do with your behavior at the table tonight?" and he said, "Nothing, I guess, right?" and she said, "I'll put it this way: much less than you think. Now come in and apologize and finish your dinner," and he said, "I told you, Mom—" and she said, "For the peace of the house, please, and for my sake too. And if you don't feel like eating, then just apologize, and make your excuses for not sitting down with us, and leave," and he said, "Oh, what's the difference," and went to the table—she stood behind him; his father was chewing some food and watching the news—and he said, "Dad," and his father didn't seem to hear him, and he said, "Dad, I want to say something," and his father still stared at the news, and he went to the set and turned the sound low and his father said, "What the hell you doing?" and he said, "I'm turning it low for a few seconds so I can apologize to you for my behavior before. I was wrong and I'm sorry," and his father said, "Okay"—didn't smile—"now turn the sound up; that was an important story they were doing, something on China," and Gould turned it up and his father said, "You said you were sorry to your mother too?" and he said, "Yes. Or maybe I didn't, not formally. But she knows the apology's for her too," and his father said, "Good, okay, I accept it also," and went back to watching the news, which was already on another subject.

Conceptions

IT'S EARLY AFTERNOON, he's lying down, kids in camp, when his wife comes in from the kitchen and says, "You look so nice there, mind if I join you, or will that be ruining things?" He shakes his head, shuts his eyes again. He was near sleep but he'd lain down to think about things, particularly what work he was going to do next, so is trying to stay awake. Then, when he'd thought of something, he'd let himself fall asleep for his unconscious to work on the thought. He'd finished a project two days ago, yesterday he just did errands and read and walked a lot, and today he wants to start something new, or at least tomorrow morning. Thought if he lay on his back an idea might come. Has, lots of times before. She's in her wheelchair. He could say, "Need any help?" Often says that when she wants to get from one place to another and it's obviously difficult for her or has been in the past. She has trouble getting off of things into the wheelchair and out of that chair onto things. He's on the daybed in the living room. Kids sleep in the one bedroom. She'd say, "No, I'm okay, I can do it." She doesn't say it; he didn't ask her or even give a look that said does she need help, but he thinks she'd say it if that's what he'd said or had given that look. Come again? Forget it, too lethargic to work that one out. Just wants to lie on his back, think about what he'd intended to think in the few minutes he has before she gets on the bed, and it will take her a few minutes, two to three at least. She's across the room by the couch, wheels her chair to the bed, the middle part of the long side of it. (Knows there's a simpler way to say that.) Looks at her out of the right corners of his eyes. She's hoisting herself up, hands gripping the armrests. Hoisting's the tough part, and then suddenly shifting her weight when she sort of flings her rear end onto the object she wants to sit on. If she misses she can fall, and if she doesn't get far enough onto the bed she can slide down the side of it. He should sit up, stand up, put his arm at the crook of the elbow under her arm at the armpit, and, holding his arm stiff, help her onto the bed. He doesn't. Lying there, he feels immobile. And she doesn't fall all the time. One out of ten, maybe, and she's smiling, so it seems—or one out of fifteen or twenty, even—she's confident she's going to make it, and a bed is an easier target to land on than a chair or toilet seat. More space, not as slippery. And if she fell she wouldn't hurt herself, or chances would be less, as the side of the bed's soft while the side of a chair or seat's hard and even sharp. The chairs of their apartment, anyway; they're all dining chairs. A toilet seat's always sharp and hard, except for the padded ones, which are more like novelties and neither of them thinks they feel good to sit on, and they probably don't clean as well, and a bathroom's the worst place to fall, of course. He shuts his eyes. He just got an idea. Seems like a good one. Starts with lovemaking—a man's parents—and ends with the man making love with his wife and the conception that comes from it and which produces their first child. "Oh, gosh," she says. She's on the floor. He didn't see her fall. She must have done it slowly, certainly softly. He looks to his right, with his head still flat on the bed—the bed pillows are all behind the bed's bigger couch pillows leaning up against the wall—and can only see the top of her head. "You all right?" "Yes." "Your voice didn't express any alarm, that's why I didn't jump." "I went down easy." "Need any help?" "Thanks, I don't think so." "I'll help, you know." "No, rest, you're tired, and I'll manage. It's good practice." Moves on his back closer to the edge of the bed and watches her. She's on her knees, holding on to the wheelchair while she unlocks the brakes, steadies herself with one hand on the floor, and with the other shoves the chair to the couch about eight feet away. Then she crawls to the couch and tries lifting herself onto it. He's seen her do it before. The first part she almost always does successfully: hoisting herself up to a seating position on the couch. From the couch, which is a couple of inches lower than the daybed, to the chair is more difficult. That part he'll probably have to help her with, because the chair, even when locked, tends to slide away when she tries to get on it. If the chair's braced against something unmovable, she usually can do it, but here it's in the middle of the floor. His idea again! Doesn't want to lose it. Conceptions, two of them. His parents—not *his,* just "parents" mating and conceiving a boy, and ending with the boy now a man and, with his wife, conceiving their first daughter. What happens in between? He'll find out when he does it. So, two conceptions, as bookends, so to speak. Is there something there to work on? Thinks so. But these days he likes to have some idea—conception, if you will—to work with before he begins. Didn't used to do it like that; would just sit down and jump in without a thought in his head and most times one would suddenly come. . . . She's on the couch. Didn't see her get there. "Need any help now?" he says, still on his back. "I'm all right, I think." She starts laughing. "All this because I wanted to join you. Am I disturbing you a lot? You looked so nice there—I told you that—but so deep in thought, but calm thoughts, restful, that you made me want to join you. Or join up with you, or something." "Be my guest, really. We'll see what happens. And nothing much on my mind now. And if you need any help, tell me." "I don't." "But if you do." "I will." He closes his eyes. Then opens them in a way where to her they'll still look closed, or he thinks they will, and watches her. She's locked the wheelchair, tests how locked it is by pushing it—it doesn't move—then, seat facing her at an angle, she grabs the armrests to maneuver herself into the chair. She doesn't move. She doesn't feel confident yet. She stares at the chair seat, grabs the armrests again, and makes a move with her upper torso as if she's going to swing her whole body onto the seat, gets about three inches off the couch, holds herself up there a few seconds, and then plops down. Damn, she mouths, looks disappointed. She wiggles all her fingers, to loosen them up probably; cracks the knuckles of her right hand, notices him, says, "Sorry," slides herself off the couch onto the floor, and tries lifting herself backward into the chair. She knows she's not going to be able to; she won't have the strength, and the chair could slide away. It does. She almost falls on her side, rights herself, turns around on the floor till her back's up against the couch, leans forward, and pulls the chair closer to her. "Listen"—his eyes wide open now—"let me help you. If I could I'd pick you up and just carry you to the bed and drop you down. Set you down, I mean—you know—but I can't anymore. I've lost strength with age, my big confession." "Please, you're as strong as you ever were. It's me. I've put on too much weight in the tummy and ass, being confined to this freaking chair. And when could you ever pick me up in your arms like that, if that's what you're speaking of?" "It's true, I never used to. Oh, maybe once or twice, but with great effort." "So much effort that I don't think you ever tried again. Not that I was ever overweight. What I have now is just the same weight that sort of redistributed and settled in those two spots, and so close together. But I was always big-boned and rather tall, though you can't see the tallness anymore. But it's a nice thought, your lifting me effortlessly, and a pleasant image too. I wish you were that strong. It'd make things a lot easier for us. Meanwhile, let me try to get there on my own. I have to learn how. There's got to be a better procedure than what I'm doing. Let me think about it. You rest, and maybe I'll see you there eventually." "But if you need me . . ." "I know, thanks." He shuts his eyes. He has his idea, doesn't need to develop it here—that'll come while he's working on it—and now he's sleepy. It's muggy in the apartment. One exposure; probably a lot cooler outside. "It's muggy. Maybe that's why you're having such trouble. If there was only some better way to get the outside air in to cool this joint. An air conditioner, of course, but you can't stand them." "Maybe." She's back on the couch. Pulls the wheelchair near. Tests it. Tries to lift herself into it. Maybe what? he thinks: that it *is* muggy, or that mugginess is what's affecting her, or she's changed her mind on air conditioners? She can't get off the couch. Shakes her head. She's very frustrated now. He should get up, help her. They'll make love when she's on the daybed. That's what she meant by what she said, right? Doesn't know if he wants to or even has the energy for it, or both those plus it's so muggy, but he can usually get started. Hand here, there, close your eyes, kiss. They should turn the fan to high. Thinks it's on medium now. He'll do it later, once she's on the bed.

Should do it now, also get her on the chair, over here, on the bed. But he just wants to lie where he is, hasn't the stamina or whatever it is for anything else. "I can't make it," she says. "The chair's too high. It's the strength thing too. I'm getting weaker and weaker—I can feel it and my flesh shows it. I'll try crawling over, though." "No, you shouldn't crawl." "Why not? I started with crawling, I'll end with it, if I'm lucky." "What do you mean: as a kid—started then? For as a kid you didn't start with crawling. Just turning over on your back was probably your first big locomotion. Am I using the word right? Here I come, though," and he opens his eyes and turns to her on his side. "Don't help me. I didn't want to disturb you. I shouldn't have even started this whole move. But now I'm determined. Not so much to lie beside you anymore, but to get there and show myself I can. You won't mind if I come over, will you; steal some of your bed space?" "No, of course not, come on." He's lying, she probably knows it—way he said it, or more the way he didn't—but it'll be fine once she's on the bed. He'd really right now just like to nap for an hour or so. An hour, that'd be about right. Then take a shower and get some work in before he has to pick up the kids. She's crawling. Her hand reaches above the bed just where his face is and clutches the bedspread. Pulling her hand up won't help her. Might even hurt her wrist, twist it, pull it out of the socket—whatever goes on inside there—and she also might slip. Should get up and help her up. She's on her knees, head above the bed now, smiling. "Hi," she says. "So you made it." "I did, but not by a long shot." Long shot? Long shot? No, he has no remark to that. "Nor has the last round been fired yet." "Oh," he says. "But we're getting close. Now it's all huff, puff, and wait and see," she says. She gets her arms on the bed, tries pushing herself up onto it. She's not doing it. Face is strained, she's sweating. Then she starts crying. Just bursts out. "Oh, come on," he says, "it's okay." He could put his hand out, touch her cheek, slide his hand back and forth across it, but he sits up, stands behind her, gets his arms under her armpits, and helps her sit on the bed. "You okay now?" "Fine, but what a struggle." "I'm going to lie back on the bed, then, if you're all right," and gets around her and lies down on the other side of her, close to the pillows against the wall. It's true, it's crowded, but if it gets too much, throw the couch pillows, if he can lift them from this position, over her to the floor and the bed pillows—this he's sure he can do—to the couch. If he misses, big deal; floor's not dirty, swept it yesterday, washed it down with a little ammonia solution the day before. "Oh, God," she says, for she's sliding off. He quickly sits up but she's already on the floor, not much of a thump. "Damn," he says angrily. Immediately knows he shouldn't have. "You okay, Sal?" "Yes, goddammit." "I'm sorry for what I said." "Why?" "Or the way I said it; I'm sorry." "I still don't know what you're saying. Anyway, let's forget my getting there, or staying. I'll rest on the couch if I still feel like resting. Do I? Yeah, this has totally exhausted me, totally." "No," he says, "you got me started." "Well, then, you have to help me. From where I am, and after what I went through, I admit defeat." He gets up, helps her to sit on the bed, swings her legs around so they're parallel to the bed, and rests them, and she lies back. "There, we made it, and I think I centered you enough where you won't fall off. You feel secure?" She rolls right and left a little and nods. He climbs over her and, lying on his side, throws all the couch pillows to the floor and then the bed pillows to the couch. "Save one for me," she says, and he puts the last one under her head, runs his hand across her breasts, and kisses her. They kiss a few times, and she says, "Maybe we should think about getting a bed closer to the floor. Something like the Japanese have, but with a platform, so not where we have to roll it up every morning. I don't want it to be even more work for you, and I want it to always be there for us for naps and brief interludes like this." "Those things can be expensive, and if it's too close to the ground it'll get dirty from all the dust in the place. I'd be sweeping the floor daily to keep this new bed clean, but sweeping very carefully so not to raise the dust, and washing down the floor too." "But it's so difficult for me to get on the bed now." "Think what it'll be like getting from that low bed to your wheelchair. Same difference. So then you'll need a wheelchair that's lower, which will then make you too low to sit at a table right, unless there are wheelchairs that can adjust up and down like a bicycle seat, but even simpler. Imagine what the new wheelchair would cost, if there was one like it." "Okay. I didn't think of the chair problem. So we'll keep things status quo till things become practically impossible for me, if they ever do." "No, we'll look around; we'll explore; we'll see. How about that?" and she says, "If you're serious, fine." "Serious. Serious," and he starts to remove her blouse and shorts. She pulls his shirt over his head and his shorts with his boxer shorts in them down past his knees, and he kicks them off. "Can you unhook my bra? I can't, just as I can barely hook it sometimes." "Get one that hooks in front and from underneath," and she says, "You're suddenly the big inventor, though I don't know if that one would do it." He unhooks it, pulls her underpants off, pushes down on her thighs and knees till her legs are straight, thinks, When she's lying like this, legs stretched out, it's much like it used to be. They're almost the same length in bed, and though there are certain things she can no longer do with him here, or almost can't, she's compensated for that by doing other things. So? Well, just thinking. He should suggest she come to bed when he's on it, do it more often, he means, even when she shows no inclination to. He should say things like "Want to take a break with me, a quick one if that's all you feel like or have time for?" and if she doesn't—well, then, she doesn't. But he's saying he likes it so much lying here with her like this. He lies on his side to kiss her. Her right leg's off the bed. "Your legs," he says, and she looks and says, "I didn't even feel it move, but they do that sometimes." She tries lifting the leg up to the bed and starts sliding off. "Help me, I'm falling," and he grabs her thigh and neck and pulls her to him and keeps pulling her while edging nearer to the wall himself till he's got her past the middle of the bed. "That was close," she says. "I thought I was lying right before but I obviously wasn't. This is where I should maybe always get to on the bed before I think I'm really safe. But you still want to continue after all this? I'd think you would have lost interest by now or been put off. If you want we can just stay here awhile, take a nap, but with you holding me so I don't somehow slide backwards." "No, it's all right," and puts his hand between her legs and she shuts her eyes and smiles and feels around for his penis and he inches himself up higher on the bed till she can reach him and starts kissing her breast.

Wishman

IN THE PARK with his mother, sitting at a refreshment-stand table, she in her wheelchair, when a man with a bowl and a bell in the middle of it, and dollar bills and change around the bell, stops two young women walking and says, "Ring the bell and make a wish and don't tell Momma. You can make it in any language. Whatever you put in you'll get back a hundred times." The women laugh and he says, "Say, this is serious business I'm talking here, proven facts. Make a wish after you stick a little donation in the kitty, and it gets me a good meal tonight, and I like to eat." One of the women puts a coin in and holds up the bell. "Ring it," the man says. "Concentrate on the clapper. Ignore the neighborhood and chirping trees and there's entirely too much green. Close your eyes, ring-a-ting gently, be relaxed." She shuts her eyes, rings, puts the bell back in the bowl. He says, "Nice ring, one of the most refulgent I've heard. Is that a word?" One raises her shoulders, the other indicates with her face she doesn't know. "Don't ask me, or even if it was used right. Knowing the accuracy of my vocabulary, probably not. But my command is now your wish, and my digestive tract salutes you," and he goes over to an older couple who've been watching them from the next table and says, "Ring the bell and make a wish, half price for seniors with IDs. Be relaxed, don't gloat. Close your eyes and stick some money in, and whatever your wish is don't tell Mommy. Never tell Mommy. And it gets me a good meal tonight, and do I love to eat? Even though I'm a skinny-marink, you're allowed to say I do." The man of the couple puts a coin in and rings the bell. Gould knows the man with the bowl's eventually going to come to them. Hopes not, as he doesn't want to deal with the guy—wish, do anything like that—and is afraid what his mother might say. The man stops a woman holding a dog in her arm and says, "Make a wish and ring the bell. Half price for seniors with IDs, ten percent off that for women walking dogs, and a hundred percent off for anyone out here today on ice skates. You can make this wish in any language you choose, but don't tell Momma. Whatever you put in the pot—" and the woman says, "Catch me tomorrow," and the man says, "That will do. I mean, that I will do, thank you," and eyes Gould and holds the bowl out to him. "Ring the bell and make a wish. Whatever you put in the kitty you'll get back a hundredfold, and don't tell Mommy." "This is my mommy, and there's nothing I want. So I don't see how getting back a hundred times of nothing I want will help me in any way." "Your mommy then, maybe she wants to make a wish?" and Gould says, "No, why should she?" and looks at her and she's smiling at the man, and he says, "All right, maybe she does. Do you, Mom?" and she says, "What do I got to lose?" "Good," for even that—the response and her smile—is something, and he puts a quarter in the bowl, the man looks at it as if he's used to getting more—though the last man gave only a quarter, and the young woman dropped a single coin in and by the sound of it he thought it was a quarter—and the man hands her the bell. "Close your eyes and wish, but don't forget to ring it," and she shuts her eyes, opens them in a few seconds, and says, "What do I do?" "You ring the bell after you make a wish, and everything you wish for will come back to you a hundred-tenfold. But don't tell your momma, and you can make the wish in any language. French, Spanish, Pakistani—do you know Pakistani?" and she says, "What? Me? What?" and the man says, "Even if you don't, for who does?—and we don't even know if it is a language, so you're off the hook, Mommy—make a wish and you'll get back a hundred-ten times what you put in or, just to be even, a hundred times," and she says, "I know what I'd wish for, and a hundred times that would be gratifying. It isn't money," and the man says, "Don't snitch what it is or isn't. For it to come true, tell no one, not even your money—I mean your mommy." "My mother's been dead a long time," and the man says, "I'm sorry to hear the news, but I won't say it's surprising. Blessed be your mother and blessed be you, my dear lady, kaddish aforethought, though I'm no priest or certified clergy of any sort. I used to train alligators in Florida, I want you to know. But this is what I have to do to stay off welfare. A wishman. I would even change my last name to Wishman to make it official—to make it my first name, that would be eccentric—but people might mistake it for Wiseman, and that I'm not. Now close your eyes, hold the bell upright, concentrate on it, ignore your neighborhood, be relaxed, be gentle, and gently tinkle." She shuts her eyes, opens them. "Did we put anything in your bowl?" and Gould says, "I took care of it," and the man says, "Sparingly, though, so if either of you cares to contribute a mite more to secure your wish a hundredfold, it'll be received generously. When I was a trainer in Florida, there were three female alligators to each male. I don't think that's the rule throughout the world Loricata population. When the lady alligator was in heat, we'd open the hatch to her quarters to let the gentleman alligator in. That's all I'll say on the matter. Then I went into the alligator glove business and was doing well till accessories of any sort made with that skin were outlawed. It's still legal in Paraguay, but it gets too steamy there and the natives are restless. But make a wish and you'll get it back a hundred times, and don't tell Sonny. Tell nobody. This is a private wish," and Gould says, "Make it already, Mom," and she shuts her eyes, man says, "Don't forget to ring the bell after and put something in the pot if you can; it'll help me get a good meal tonight, and do I like to eat? Don't ask." "I told you, I already put something in," and the man says, "So you did, thanks. Then this one's on the house; if it's her first and only wish, then it isn't." She moves her lips, rings the bell, opens her eyes, and raises them, as if thinking of something. "Now put the bell back—that seemed like a very good wish—and don't tell Junior," and, to Gould, "You know anyone else here?—got an in, we'll say, at that third table?—because I can really use the business and my tummy the activity, not to mention my underemployed digestive system. I make a big killing from it, I'll cut you in ten percent," and he says, "Sorry." "Have a kind day, nice lady," and goes to some people at the refreshment counter and does the routine for them. His mother's staring at the paths in front of them with lots of people walking, cycling, roller-blading, smiles when she sees a small child or a wheeled or carried baby. Wishes, he thinks, what bunk. But if he were making one—forced: "A wish or your life"—what? Nothing, or maybe for a little more money to live on, but how would that come? so forget it. But these are wishes, magically granted or you've passed some tests to earn them, so, more money, but that's not what he wants. That he not get tired so early in the day so he could have the energy to do more than he does? Come on. Good health he's got, along with good teeth, just that all the daily chores and work wear him down. So maybe that there wouldn't be so many chores, but then who'd do them? And besides, he wouldn't want anybody else but his family around or in his way. More hair on top and to be six-three, his goal as a teen? Maybe a young beauty to go along with it risk-free for a day? No, just kidding. Then why'd he think it? Because he was kidding. Example of his lack of imagination. So, for more imagination for things to wish for. But there's really nothing he wants for himself; he wasn't just brushing the guy off before. Now, for others: peace and prosperity and such for the whole world, of course, but that's so dull, general, and insincere. Then: all the land mines of the world dug up, the guns and bombs and stuff chucked. Get smaller: his wife being well, able to walk, his kids well too: no big sicknesses, horrors, dangers, et cetera. His mother to be well. But she's lived a long life and her health's been pretty good, considering, so what should one expect? as that guy with that no-surprise line sort of said. Just no debilitating illness and pain and long-drawn-out death. And for now that she could get around on her own more, see better—because she can hardly read print an inch high and she loved newspapers and books—and her disposition much better, and that they had more to say to each other. He takes her to the park and they just sit there, each staring at the people passing, into space, off with their own thoughts, like this one. That they had long conversations about lots of things, that her hearing was better too so she wouldn't have to say back so much, "What? What?" or, more often, pretend she heard him. But to have something to say. Wishes he did and she responded to it and he responded to that and the two to three hours they spent together nearly every day went quickly and enjoyably for both and they'd look forward to seeing each other the next day. Well, maybe they still do—he knows he likes getting her out and a good lunch in her—but also to the liveliness of it. But they don't talk much: she usually with the same questions and answers that have little to do with anything. "Where are the children, in school?" and he'll say, "Camp." "Camp?" and he'll say, "Day camp, I pick them up after I leave you at home." "When does school begin for them?" and he'll say, "It just finished. It's June. It doesn't start again till the first week in September, almost three months away." "They're done with it? You must be very proud. How's your wife?"—it must be she can't remember Sally's name, as she never uses it when she asks a question like this—and he'll say, "Fine, good as can be expected." "Glad to hear it. But you leave her home alone?" and he'll say, "It's all right, she can get around, and I call her every other hour or so, just in case." "Good," and often right after that, "Where is home for you these days?" and he'll say, "We're in our apartment here now. But usually we're in Baltimore, where I work, and in July we're going to Maine, but we'll see you on the way back for a week." "You're lucky, all that traveling," or, "It must be nice in Maine, not hot like this city, though I've never been there so I can't say," and he'll say, "You've been there—just not recently; it's become too difficult for you. I've explained all this to you before," and she'll say, "Have I been there? How come I can't remember? You must be kidding with me," and he'll say, "I'm not. You'd stay for a week to ten days, come in and out by plane. I'm sorry," and sometimes she'll say, "What for? You should live it up while you can," and he'll say, "Having you there wasn't a problem. We liked it, and it gave you a good rest," and she'll say, "Why, what did I say?" Then later she'll ask again about the children, where are they today, how come he didn't bring them with him, he knows she loves to see them too. "Are they all right? You're not holding anything back from me?" and he'll say, "They're in day camp now, I told you that, Mom, and I brought them over to see you a few days ago," and she'll say, "Did you? It must have been longer than that, else I would have remembered. My memory has lapses, but it's not so bad as you think. Has school started for them yet?" and so on. Then, somewhere in all this, that she knows his girls have birthdays the same month and she always gives them presents and she forgot to this year and wants to write out two checks and doesn't want him saying no. "How much do you think I should give? Be honest, I don't want you to think I'm cheap, but would twenty dollars each be enough?" and he'll say, "You're right. They're two weeks apart and in the same month, November, and you gave them checks for their birthdays last year." "What month is it now?" and he'll say, "June," and she'll say, "June, so soon? I thought it was that other month." "What other month?" because her doctor once told him that when she gets things wrong like this to ask her what she thinks it is, like if she says, "I want to go home now," when she is home, he should say, "Why, where do you think you are now?" and she'll say, "Just one of the months: November. How can it be June?" and he'll say something like, "Time goes, you know," or, "How can it be November? Really, Mom, it's so warm and all the trees are full of leaves and it doesn't look or smell anything like November. November has a decomposing smell in the park around that time of the year, leaves rotting and turning and blowing down around you and so forth. And the trees are already half bare and it's usually much colder than it is now; we could never be sitting here like we are, or not for as long," and she'll say, "So it isn't November. You're right, how could it be? A real dumb mistake, so shoot the old dog," and he'll say, "No, it's nothing. Not one everybody would make, but my memory or sense of where I am occasionally plays tricks on me too." So he wishes they had more to say, she wouldn't repeat herself so much, was more in touch with things. But for him, what? He's losing it too and he wishes he wasn't. What he's said to her about his memory and sense of things—some truth to it. Can't remember lots of things. Can't find his memo book he puts things down in to help his memory. Loses his pen, watch, keys, wallet, glasses all the time. Finds them in the most unlikely spots—refrigerator once, kitchen cabinets a couple of times. Loses his ability to speak coherently sometimes, but in a way where when he tries correcting himself he forgets what he started out to say and then bumbles all over himself trying to correct that. So, wish? For a younger, better brain, twice the capacity and memory it has now, but that can't be what the man meant. That he was livelier. Usually physically energetic, but never an especially interesting guy to anyone, he's become even duller and more boring lately, barely says anything anymore, so why's he think if her mind and hearing were in better shape, he'd be able to have a good conversation with her? He's interested in his kids and what they do and a few books and some items in the paper day to day and his work, but nothing that he likes to talk about, and other than for some things his wife does, that's about it. Wine, but after the first two sips, he just drinks it, so that's the list. And wine and food and stuff, unless he really got involved in cooking, shouldn't be on it. Music, but just to listen to at home and in the car, so probably a few other things. He feels sorry—*sleepy,* so why'd he think "sorry"?; nothing, a slip or something more, but what of it?—he could fall asleep right here, and says, "Mom, when you're finished we'll go, okay?" "If you like," and she finishes her ginger ale, and he says, "What about the Danish?" and she says, "You have it, I've had all I want," and he says, "No, thanks," and she says, "You never eat anything when we're out. Coffee, that's the extent of it, and always black. And in restaurants a house salad, maybe the crust of a slice of bread, so nothing. You starve yourself. You look thinner than you ever were," and he says, "I like crust, it's the best part," and she says, "You got to be kidding me—that's an answer?" and he says, "Believe me, I'm not thin. I don't like to eat as much as I used to—and usually nothing for lunch—but I do okay." "And you look tired. You sleep well at night?" and he says, "Sure," and she says, "How's your wife?" and he says, "Fine." "Good. That's what I like to hear. Good news for a change. Though you look tired. Maybe you're only sleepy, though you're not yawning." "Why should I be sleepy? I'm on vacation. It's three in the afternoon or so. I sleep seven to eight hours a night now. I still got to get the kids up for camp, but they don't have to be there till nine, and it's right up the block from us." "I don't know, but that's what you look like: beat. I hope you're not coming down with anything," and he says, "What could I be coming down with? If I look a little bushed, it's probably from the humidity and heat the last few days. We only have a fan, and the apartment really gets hot, so maybe I don't sleep as much or as well as I said." "Has it been hot? I don't get outside." "Of course you do. Every day for a couple of hours. After I take you to the restaurant for lunch, and it's not raining, we go to the park. Or just to the park sometimes, like this place, where I get you a snack." "I don't remember, isn't that terrible? What's happened to me? I can't believe it. I mean, I know I'm outside today—I'm not dreaming this, and where else could I be?—but those other times you said. With that bowl and bell before—that strange man—I should have wished for a long period where my mind's really functioning. Something in addition to what I wished for, I'm saying, which was—" "Don't tell your mommy or your sonny," he says, wagging his finger at her. "Oh, I didn't take him seriously. Who can take a clown seriously? You see how old he was? And his costume—thick flannel shirt on this hot day and that yellow tie and those socks, and acting so stupid. There's no dope like an old dope—I've told you that. Someone used to repeat that slogan to me," and he says, "Your mother." "She said it, that's right, and it isn't a slogan. But what I wished for was for you . . . the best things both for you and your family. That's all I want in life." "Come on, there must be other things. Be honest, what?" "Truthfully?" and she looks at the sky as if thinking about her answer. "Oh, that I hadn't lost my first boy so young. That really hit me and Dad. And that I could have had another one after you, if not a brother for you, then a sister. You should have had someone at home to play with, because Dad and I didn't do that well. That your father had been healthier and not suffered so much at the end and lived longer. It hasn't been easy for me being alone so long, even if he and I fought a lot. You're with me, but you know what I mean, and then you go home. And lots of grandchildren, though the two I have are nice; they're dolls. What else? Your wife: that she was well, running around, but in the good sense—doing healthy things. But that goes in the 'best things for you and your family' category. Myself? That I'd be comfortably retired from a profession I wanted to enter, chemistry or law. I loved school and studying, but your father wouldn't have let me go back to it for so long after I had you. And that feebleness didn't always have to go along with getting so old. I hate my face now—you can't even tell anymore how good-looking I might have been ages ago—and I wish I had the stamina I had even when I was seventy. And I hate forgetting. I might not look it, but I usually know how incapable I'm being or bad I'm behaving. That's when I want to go to sleep the most, no matter what time of day. Even pretending to be tired sometimes so I can be helped to bed, close my eyes, and shut out the world, though once there I sleep like a baby. So I wish I felt better in lots of ways and could enjoy life more. I could if I had better eyes. All those books I read and wanted to reread and now with my ears I can't even listen to them well. Why can't they do something with my eyes? I know, my general physician says my heart couldn't take it. So maybe we should get another doctor who says it can or call that strange man back so I can have another shot at it, what do you say?" "Nah, I had my fill of him. His spiel got to be annoying," and she says, "You're probably right. One couldn't just look at things when he was here. Because I love being here with you and seeing real life around: kids, their parents. You're the one I rely on and who means the most. The girls are nice who take care of me. Sometimes a bit rough. They don't mean it, I'm sure, or if they do it's quick and I tell them off and they stop." "I didn't know," and she says, "Oh, yeah, but don't say anything to them. I can handle it in my own way. So I'd like for it not to have turned out this way, but what can I do? To have died earlier and peacefully in my sleep would be more like I wanted than just vegetating like I am." "I'm sorry," he says, "and please don't talk like that." "Why not? We're talking over things, discussing, so don't be silly." The man's back at their table, sticks the bowl out, and says, "Make a wish, ring the bell and put a contribution in the potty, and whatever you put in you'll get back a hundred times, half price for seniors with IDs." "You already hit us," Gould says, and the man says, "Did I? I ask so many people, I forget their faces. I can't be expected to remember each one. Did you get your wish?" and he says, "My mother was the one who made it, and it was just before." "She didn't tell you what it was, did she?" and he says no. The man says to her, "That's a good girl. Did any part of your wish come true, or maybe we haven't had time yet. I only want to know to see how good and even fast my system's working," and she says, "What's that?" "Your wish, lady. Did any part of it come true? . . . the one you made with my bell before. Or maybe you'd like to try another, put some more money in and ring the bell again?" and she says, "What are you talking about?" and the man says, "Oh, boy, the two of us with our memories. We should get together," and he goes.

The Burial

HIS MOTHER DIES and he makes plans for the funeral. Days before, in the hospital, when she was still lucid, she said she didn't want any funeral-home service. "Too expensive. They charge a fortune to rent a chapel and a little side room and for all their employees to act as ushers and doormen, and it's also so unnecessary. Why should people, if they want to see the whole thing through, have to come to the chapel and cemetery both? And in addition some even to the funeral home the night before, just to view my cheap coffin and pay their respects to you, and I want it to be the cheapest so you don't go broke for a stupid box, and I also don't want you opening it once I'm inside. Have it at the cemetery only. Open air and light, even if it's raining, is better than the solemn nonsense and awful recorded organ music of a chapel. A few people I knew saying brief things about me if they want or just praying to themselves or together from some little prayer book the cemetery could loan you, or even staring at their feet or into space if they like, and then drop me in the ground between your father and brother, and you go home. If the whole thing takes more than half an hour, starting from the time you get there till you leave, then it's taken too long. People's time shouldn't be wasted for things like that. It's already enough they had to get there." "That's why a funeral home might not be a bad idea, in spite of the expense, if we have to talk about it now," and she said, "We do. If you're not going to be the practical one, then I have to, so what were you saying?" "I was saying I could find a home in the city. People wouldn't even have to drive their cars to it, if they lived there and weren't planning on going to the cemetery. They can come by cab or subway or bus, and for some who live on the Upper West Side, where I think the best place is, they can even walk. Then the ones that also want to go to the cemetery can go in my car or someone else's if someone else who comes has one, or even a limo I'll hire if there are that many people coming. I mean, how much can one cost? The cemetery's not *that* far away, if I remember. The rest will feel they've paid their respects and did their duty and so on by coming to the service or to the funeral home the night before, if they also did that, and they can go back to work or home. But please let's drop the subject," and she said, "Who are all these people you're expecting? If you get six, tops, it'll be a lot, or seven, right? but don't look for a crowd. That's also why the funeral-home service makes no sense. You'll have to get someone to conduct it—a rabbi or some expert in Jewish religious services the home gets for you—and you want him speaking to a practically empty audience? The cemetery: have it all there. And don't let them do anything to my body for it. Put me in the pine box straight from the hospital, store me for the night someplace—if it's got to be at the funeral home, let it be—then ship me to the gravesite the next day in the cheapest conveyance allowable, and that'll be it. All this is almost a favor I'm asking of you. Since I won't be in any position to argue, do what you want except to cremate me. Even though I'll be gone at the time—*dead,* why not just say it, what else do I expect will happen to me by the end of the week?—the thought of all that fire scares me. If you don't promise you won't cremate me, I swear it will kill me sooner. Worms and bugs and whatever else is underground don't make me feel that much easier, but I just think if there is a soul in your body and it doesn't get completely out of it once you die, it won't survive those terrific temperatures. Besides, I'm leaving you almost no money. I don't have much, that's why, since whatever I had or Dad left me was mostly used up to keep me alive the last few years and for someone to look after me. So why waste what's left plus some of your own on even a simple chapel service when you also have to go through one at the cemetery? I know the burial will also have to cost something. But so would anything you do—cremation; hiring a boat to drop me in the ocean, which by law you can't do—so we know there's a minimum you have to spend on this. You can't, unfortunately, I'm saying, just make me disappear. I wouldn't even have a rabbi or any kind of burial professional at the grave, since they can set you back a bundle too. Just ask the cemetery to get one of those little old religious guys who hang around the cemetery, and who know the right prayers for the dead, and slip him a twenty to read some passages over me and maybe to point something out for you to read. Or conduct it any way you want on your own, with you, or whoever has come there, reading or speaking whatever you want. In the end, what's the difference? And I don't say that to you that way to make a joke. Let's face it, dead is dead, and I know that whatever you say and read and however you say it, even if it comes out fumblingly, is meant well."

He decides to have the body sent to that West Side funeral home, put in the cheapest pine coffin they have there, and with nothing done to the body, not even washed or reclothed, since once she's in the coffin and it's closed nobody's going to see her again, and next morning sent by simple van to the cemetery for a short burial ceremony, though he doesn't know what he's going to do there yet. His wife's cousin and her husband will meet him there, same with his mother's best friend from her street, whose son will drive her and the woman who took care of his mother the last two years. Later that day, someone from the funeral home calls him and asks if he wants her marriage bands removed from her finger—she added his father's band to her own when his father died—before she's put in the casket, and he says, "Oh, God, she never told me what to do about that, and I don't know. She should probably be buried with them, right?" and looks at his wife and points to his own band and she points to her chest and shakes her head, she doesn't want them, and the man says, "Look, yes or no, because we won't be able to get them off later without, if you'll excuse me, chopping off her finger. And that, unless it was absolutely necessary for some other reason, I'm not allowing any of my workers to do," and he says, "Then okay, leave them on.

They're hers, whatever that means, and eventually I'd just lose them."

The next day, on the way to the cemetery with his wife and two girls, he blurts out, "Damn, just thought of something. I mean I've been thinking and thinking what I'll say at the ceremony after someone reads a couple of prayers, and simply decided to say what comes naturally but to keep it brief. But there's a poem she loved, and though she didn't mention it when she talked the other day about everything she wanted and didn't want after she died, except for the wedding bands—do you think I made the right decision on that?" and his wife says, "Too late, don't even think of it." "But the kids might have wanted them for when they're older," and his younger daughter says, "What?" and his wife says, "Nothing, we're not going to talk about it. It'd be totally futile and it wouldn't seem right. What'd you start out to say?" and he says, "I remember a couple of years ago when she was very sick and I was called to New York and we thought she was dying . . . we're talking about Grandma, of course"—to his girls—"and she said if there's one thing she wanted read at her funeral—but not by a rabbi, she added—it was an Emily Dickinson poem about dying. She gave me the title but I can't remember it, though I probably wrote it down then," and his wife says, "I don't think hers had official titles. They were all the first lines of her poems, weren't they? Either she decided on titling them that way or someone did it for her after she died and the poems were found. Wasn't that her?" and his older daughter says, "Who, Grandma again?" and he says, "Emily Dickinson, a poet of the last century. And it was her, I'm sure." "Oh, I know her. We read her in the advanced humanities class I took, but I can't remember any of them now or anything about them except they were all short." "There's one very beautiful one I recall," his wife says, "that starts, 'Because I could not stop for death,' and then goes on, 'so death stopped for me,' or something," and he says, "That's it, her favorite, or one of them. She used to read me them when I was a boy. And for years she kept a copy of all the poems on her night table—there weren't many, or, as Fanny said, they were all short. The collected works in one volume, plus the letters, I think, or some of them. I haven't seen the book around in a long time, and before that one day in the hospital she hadn't brought up Dickinson in years. It's probably still in her apartment somewhere, or someone borrowed it and never gave it back—it could even have been me—or she just read it till it fell apart. No, I could never have taken it from her; it had been by her bedside for maybe ten years and you don't borrow a book like that, nor loan it out. Did she say then that it was at home and I should get it from there? I don't remember. But I have to read that poem at the burial. It might be all I'll read or say, in fact, except that this was one of her favorite poems, maybe her favorite, and that Dickinson was her favorite poet, or certainly among her favorites, and the only one whose book she had by her bedside so long, if I'm remembering right. And that she used to read them to me and I thought this one appropriate to read today, because of all I've said about it and its contents—the poem's—and so on. Do you remember the rest of the poem?" he says to his wife. "It's short, right? You can write it down for me, or one of the girls can; you can just recite it," and his younger daughter says, "I'll write it down—I've a pad and pen with me," and Fanny says, "No, I will; I know her works, or read her, and those first two lines Mommy said I especially remember and won't need her to repeat," and he says, "Either of you, so long as it's written clearly," and his wife says, "I only know those two, I'm afraid; the second's 'He kindly stopped for me.' " "That's right, that's right," he says. "Think, come on, remember; Josephine, get your pen and pad out," and his wife says, "I can't; that's it, a blank: 'Because I could not stop for death,' and 'He kindly stopped for me.' " "Then I'll stop in a town on the way—we've time—and buy it at a bookstore if there's one, or an anthology of some sort with that poem in it. It's one of her most popular, so it'd be in one. And every bookstore must have an anthology like that or a collection of her poems, or at a bookstore at a nearby mall where most of them seem to be now," and his wife says, "But there could be people waiting for us already. I think even the receptionist in your mother's doctor's office said she was coming. And the funeral-home people with the coffin in their van. They all expect you to be the first one there, and for the funeral people, probably for some paperwork to fill out or sign." "Then this is what. I'll drop you all off. Anything to sign, you do it; you're my wife. If anyone's there or they come, tell them to wait, I'll be back soon. As far as the funeral-van people: well, they can just put the box over the grave; the rest is up to the cemetery. Good thing no rabbi, though. If we had one and he was there he wouldn't let me go because he'd probably have a wedding to run in an hour or another funeral somewhere and he couldn't give us even five minutes more than what we hired him for. I'll go to the nearest store and buy the book. I won't be more than half an hour. If it takes more, I'll drop it. A half hour from the time I leave you might just be when I told everyone the service would start anyway. And tell them I'll keep the ceremony shorter even than I had planned to. *Ceremony, service,* whatever you want to call it: fifteen minutes, if that." "Please don't look for any book," she says. "Why not just talk about the poem? Read the first two lines . . . read them twice, three times; they're that good and right for a funeral service. After that, say you don't know the other lines, but tell what Dickinson's poetry meant to your mother: the night table, reading them to you, all that. And how you wanted to read all of this poem, how you almost even started out from the cemetery to get the book at the last minute—" and he says, "No, that's all circling around to avoid it, and dishonest—on my part—and lazy, because this is what she wanted. She told me that first time two years ago and then again about a year later, I just remembered; I think we were in the waiting room of a doctor's office. Didn't say anything about it this last time in the hospital, but she was on drugs and not clear-headed—" and she says, "What do you mean? You said she was about as lucid and articulate and well-informed as you've seen her recently, using the big words she loved and with you having a long and absorbing personal conversation with her as you haven't had in years," and he says, "She was still on medication, and I think a painkiller, and being fed intravenously, and anyway, not clear all the time . . . dozing off, sleeping a lot. Besides—" and she says, "I don't know how much to believe you," and he says, "Yes, believe me. Besides, maybe she thought I already knew about her poem wish and didn't want to repeat herself. That she didn't want me feeling she thought I had a lousy memory and that she had to say things over and over again for them to sink in. After all, she told me at least twice before. Listen, you have to see how important this is to me. I don't want to put you and the kids in a bind, but this'll be my last good thing to her, or last chance to do it, rather, besides how much it'll help me get through the day. If I can't find the Dickinson collection or that particular poem in an anthology, or one close to it on death or immortality or the ending of life and transmigration of the soul or something, I swear I'll give up after the first store and rush right back."

He drops them off at the burial site. Nobody's there yet, not even the van or the prayer reader he called the cemetery for late yesterday. A secretary in the cemetery office tells him how to get to town and says there are two bookstores there—"Lots of people must read around here, and perhaps there are two stores because the nearest mall is fifteen miles away"—and he drives there in five minutes. Both stores are on the main street. The first is really just a used paperback shop, with mostly romances, spy fiction, mass paperbacks of every sort, and the only poetry is religious; St. Augustine is in this section, plus several of the same editions of a book of poetry by the pope. The second store has an anthology of twentieth-century American poetry and books of poems by poets like Hardy, Whitman, and Blake but no Dickinson. "I know we had one," the salesman says. "The Everyman edition: hardback, complete works, and only eleven dollars—a steal. Ah, it was sold, it says here," looking at the inventory record on the computer screen by the cash register. "Last week, May third. I could order a copy today," and he says, "No time; I need it right away." "Try the library; they should have it if Miss Dickinson hasn't been assigned as a class project at one of the local schools," and he says, "Great idea, why didn't I think of that?" and at the library down the street he locates a volume of Dickinson poems with the one he wants in it and goes up to the main desk and says, "Excuse me, I don't live in this area; I'm not even a resident of New Jersey. But I'd like to borrow this book just for an hour or so," and the librarian says, "If you want to sit here and read it, that's fine, but we can't loan a book to a non-New Jersey resident." "Let me explain why I need it," and he does, points out the poem, and she says, "I'm sorry, I appreciate your reason and offer my condolences, but it's a bylaw of our town's library system I'd be breaking if I loaned you the book. In the past we've had every excuse imaginable for loaning books to non-residents, and if we see a fifth of them returned we call ourselves lucky. Try to imagine what that figure would be if—" and he says, "Believe me, I'll return it. I'll drive back here right after the burial. You can even call the cemetery—I have the number here—to see if my mother's being buried today," and she says, "Whether you're telling the truth or not—" and he says, "I *am,*" and she says, "Then even though you are telling the truth, which is what I meant to say, it's strictly prohibited to give loaning privileges to people without valid library cards of this town. If they have cards from other New Jersey localities, then that town's library has to request the book for them and it's sent to that library through the state's interlibrary loan system." "Look, I have people waiting at the cemetery for me; the burial service was supposed to start five minutes ago. Not a lot of people—I don't want to lie to you—but my wife and daughters and my wife's cousin and her family from Brooklyn—they drove all the way from there to come—and other people; cemetery personnel, et cetera. Again, it was among my mother's favorite poems and to have it read at her funeral was really one of her last wishes. But because I was so upset over her death yesterday—confused, everything—I forgot, and we didn't—I didn't; I'm the only surviving child—have a regular funeral; this is the only ceremony we're having. And when I was driving to the cemetery I suddenly realized—" and she says, "I wish I could. What if I photocopied the poem for you?" and he says, "I thought of that as a solution. But I want to hold a book—not a Bible, not a prayer book, since she didn't go for that stuff at funerals or really anywhere, but a book of poems—and read from that. Look, I'll leave a deposit. Ten dollars, twenty, and when I return the book I'll donate the money to the library," and she says, "This book"—turning to the copyright page—"is more than forty years old. In excellent condition for a book that's been circulating that long. Maybe it's the delicacy of the poetry that makes readers handle the book delicately, though I don't want to engage in that kind of glib speculation here. I don't know what it originally cost, nor do I know what this copy's worth now. Fifty dollars, perhaps, though more likely five, but around twenty to replace. I'm not a rare book collector, so that's not my point. We simply can't be loaning works to out-of-state residents because they're willing to give money to the library. That policy would mean only the more privileged among you can borrow from us, which wouldn't be the right perception for a library to give." "Okay, okay, I'll try and get the book somewhere else," and starts back to the poetry shelves with it, and she says, "You can leave it here, sir; I'll reshelve it," and he says, "Nah, I've put you through enough already," and she says, "Thank you then, but please make sure it's in the right classificatory order," and once there he thinks,

Take the photocopy; better than nothing. Have her copy two or three different Dickinson poems; they're all there in that last Resurrection-and-something section he just saw. . . . No, you want what you said you did and that's a book to read from and not some flimsy photocopy sheet, and this edition particularly because it has a real old-book look, and he looks around, doesn't seem to be anyone else here but her, and sticks the book inside his pants under the belt. Feels it, it feels secure; he'll take it for the day, return it by mail tomorrow with a donation and his apologies, won't give his name or a return address, of course. Though she can probably find out who he is, if she wants, from the cemetery, for how many burials can there be there at this hour in one day? and he gave her enough information to give himself away. But what is she going to do, get the police to arrest him in Baltimore or New York for stealing a book for a day after he sent it back carefully wrapped and in the same condition and with a ten- or twenty-dollar bill?

Alarm goes off as he's leaving. She's looking at him from behind the main desk. "Oh, Christ," he says, "who the hell thought you'd have these books electronically coded in such a small library. Here, take it, will ya?" and sets it on a chair by the door, and she says, "Oh, no, mister, you're not getting off as lightly as that. I don't believe your mother-burial story one iota now. And don't think of bolting or I'll follow you outside and take down your license number," and dials her phone and says, "Officer Sonder? . . . Anyone, then, though he's the one I've dealt with so far for this particular problem. Amy LeClair at the library. I have a man here whom I caught stealing one of our items. . . . A book, but a potentially valuable one, and I believe he knew it. . . . Thank you," and turns to him and says, "He says for you to wait; a police car will be right over," and he says, "Call back and tell him I can't; to catch me at the cemetery on Springlake," and she says, "Leave now and you'll be in even deeper water. We've lost too many books and documents as it is, and this is the only way to stop this kind of petty crime that tallies up for us to grand larceny." What to do? Take the book, read the poem at the burial, and then tell everyone what he did and wait for the cops there, or leave it and go and just hope they don't come after him, or wait for the cops here? Surely they're not going to arrest him. "Do you mind, while I wait, if I call the cemetery to hold up the burial?" and she says, "If that is whom you'll call," and he says, "Then you dial for me—I have the number right here, or get it out of the phone book," and she says, "I'd rather not waste anymore of the library's money by using the phone, even for a local call. We have restrictions regarding that too. We're barely surviving, you know. People aren't exactly putting this institution in their wills." "Then will a dollar cover the phone cost?" and she says, "I'd also rather not take money from you. Who knows what that'd imply." Just then a policeman comes in. Gould explains quickly. She says, "Nothing for me to add; whatever his reasons for the theft were, he just admitted he was caught walking out with one of our books," and the policeman says to him, "Looks like I'll have to write out a summons or even arrest you if Miss LeClair insists I do," and she says, "I don't think we have to go that far, but certainly a summons." The policeman starts writing one out. "This means you'll have to appear in county court in a number of weeks. Unless you check the 'no contest' box on the court notification you get and request to be fined through the mail and the judge accepts it," and he says, "Okay, but please hurry it up. I don't mean to sound disrespectful, but there are all those people waiting at the cemetery for me, and I still have my mother to bury," and the policeman says, "No disrespect meant either, sir, but I can do it much faster with machines at the station house if that's what you want."

Only his wife and children are at the cemetery when he gets there, sitting on a bench several plots away; casket's on a few planks above the open grave. "By the time your message got to us," his wife says, "Rebecca and everyone else had left. They all had to be somewhere later this afternoon and didn't know when you'd get back. They were concerned about you, paid their respects to you through me, and said a few words of their own to your mother. You'll tell me everything later, all right? Now we should get the cemetery people to help us get the coffin in the ground." "Did you get the poem, Daddy?" his younger daughter says, and he says, "Oh, the poem; Jesus, I even forgot to get it photocopied. I could have before but this librarian, you can't believe it, she gave me the option to, but I wanted to hold the whole book, this beautiful old hardbound copy of Dickinson, as if it were a religious book, rather than read from this skimpy transient sheet—" and his wife says, "What are you talking about?" and he says, "The poem. 'Because I could not stop for Death.' There's a capital *D* in Death. The prayer guy ever show up?" and she says, "He waited awhile, then said he had to go to another gravesite, and made some prayers over her coffin and left." "So let's do it ourselves, though we'll have to get the cemetery workers to lower the box once we're done. Maybe that's all it should be anyway, since we're the only ones left of her family who are still semisound."

He drives to the office, returns with a cemetery official and two gravediggers in a truck behind him, and standing in front of the grave says, "Please, now let the funeral and burial and service and everything else begin. Sally, do you have anything to say?" and she says, "Just that we all loved you, Beatrice, very much. You were always wonderful to be around, wise in your ways, delightful to the girls, and, because you're Gould's mother, special to me, and we're profoundly sorry to see you go. Kids?" and the older shakes her head and starts crying and the younger says no and then, "Yes, I have something. Goodbye, Grandma. I wish I knew you longer and when you were younger, and I feel extra bad for Daddy. And I love you too and am sorry to have you die and be buried." "Thank you, dears," he says. "As for me, if I mention the word love and how I feel I'll blubber all over the place and won't be able to continue. So to end the service, because I've kept everyone here way too long, I'd like to read something—I mean, recite—and very little because it's all I know. I tried to get more but that's another story, Mom, so just two lines of an Emily Dickinson poem you like so much. 'Because I could not stop for Death' . . . what is it, Sally?" and she says, "'He kindly stopped for me.'" "Right. 'Because I could not stop for Death, he kindly stopped for me. Because I could not stop for Death, he kindly stopped for me. Because I could not stop for Death, he kindly stopped for me.' Amen. Now if you gentlemen will lower the coffin, we'll go home."

Eyes

HE'S WITH HIS mother in the park. He's on a bench; she's facing him from her wheelchair, drinking ginger ale through a straw. "Cold enough?" and she says, "It hits the spot." She looks around, then at him. "Excuse me, but you *were* talking of my soda?" "The ginger ale; yeah." "Hits the spot. It's my favorite drink on a warm day and always has been, even when I was a girl. That's so far back, nobody but me could remember. Ancient times." She looks at the trees behind her. "They look like shadows." "The trees?" he says. "Like shadows, but not scary ones. Those I wouldn't like. Even at my age, I get afraid." They do; he can see what she means. Silhouettes, at least. "Why do you think they paint them black?" she says, pointing to the trees. "What do you mean black? The tar they sometimes put on them, or whatever that substance is, so when the tree's slashed or something—a limb sawed off—the sap won't run?" "Aren't all the trees there painted black?" "No, they're just dark: the bark is. Elms or some others. I used to know trees. I can't tell what these are by their leaves, though I know they're not maple or oak." "My eyes, I suppose, playing tricks on me again. One eye I can't see with almost at all. The other eye lets me see things but very darkly. Together they're practically of no use. And even worse than that, ugly, because I'm sure people, especially children, who look straight at them, cringe. The soda's good," she says, sipping. "I'm glad you like it. Better than the orange flavor, I thought." "Oh, the orange would have been good too." "So, the next time." "If I'm lucky and live that long, though sometimes I wonder." "What? That you'll live till the next time I take you to the park? I take you almost every day. This isn't a one-time thing." "No. I meant 'ancient times.' You can't expect me to live forever, you know." "Yes, I do. Now let's stop talking about it."

A woman walks past, young, maybe around twenty-five. Tank top, shorts cut high, flapping a Frisbee against her thigh. The kind of body he loves: thick strong thighs, compact high butt, small waist, flat stomach, large breasts. Blond hair but seems dyed, and a pretty face and not dumb-looking. Looks at him as she passes, and he looks back and she looks away. She's alone, and she sits on the grass in the shade about thirty feet from them, shakes her head hard so her hair falls in front of her face, parts it away from her eyes, and looks at him. He smiles at her, she just stares and then looks away; he turns to his mother, who's looking at the tree covering above them as if she's studying it, then back at the woman. She's stretched out now, leaning back on her forearms, facing front, one knee up, other leg extended out, hair now in a ponytail. How'd she tie it so fast? Must be one motion—ah, he's seen it done by his wife and his older daughter, so he knows: pull the tail back with one hand, other already has an elastic band stretched wide for it to go in, and, for women with straight hair like his wife and this one, done in a matter of seconds. But what was with that shaking-her-head motion, then, after the hair fell over her face, parting it and looking what seemed coquettishly at him? On the last he might be wrong, but doesn't see the sense of the head shake. He looks at her long enough, without her once turning to him, to imagine her with no clothes on, on a bed, legs like that: one knee up, other leg straight out though turned a little toward him so part of her inner thigh's exposed, breasts hanging over the sides of her chest as the outline of them (or just the one he can see) against the tank top makes them appear to be doing now. She grabs the Frisbee off the grass and turns it around clockwise between her fingers while looking at him, then looks at it and continues turning it, but faster, till it's practically spinning. A good show, but for him? and why's she looking at him so much? Maybe because he's looking at her and she's using the spinning motion as some sort of thinking trick while she wonders why he's looking at her; and why is he? Wife's in the apartment, he'll be picking up the kids from day camp in two hours, he's with his mother, and he'll have to wheel her to her home and maybe wait with her and make her comfortable till the woman who looks after her gets back from a movie, so it's not as if he's going to make a move on the woman. If his mother sees him eyeing her, what'll she think? That he's a bit of a fool, eyeing someone so much younger and who's dressed in a way to provoke those kind of looks, or that something's wrong in his marriage, or some connection between the two, or simply that it isn't right, staring at a woman that way, no matter how she's dressed or what the disparity is between their ages—she knows because she was a beauty and must have got plenty of stares—and she'd be right, but it's hard to stop: the woman attracts him, he's sitting rather than really doing anything, it's also that she reminds him of someone he went with twenty years ago (her breasts, though, were small, but everything else including her height was pretty much the same); wanted to marry her, even. Looks at his mother; she's resting with her eyes closed, may be napping. "Mom," he says, almost so softly that she wouldn't hear; she doesn't respond. He also raises his hand to touch hers, but doesn't want to disturb or wake her; right now he'd rather look at and fantasize about the woman. She looking at him now? Take a guess: she is. Looks: she is but quickly turns away, looks straight up at the sky, shuts her eyes, and smiles the way people do when they face the sun contentedly: the pleasure of the warm rays, especially on your closed eyelids. But she's in the shade. So she's just feeling content, maybe from the coolness of the shade. But why would she close her eyes while smiling like that? A breeze she's getting and he isn't, or something she thought of that made her smile, and she only looked at the sky to look away from him: didn't want him disturbing her thought? Fun she had last night? Sex she had this morning? A guy she likes, just met, something somebody recently said? Or just that he's looking at her, this much older not very attractive man, and that he in fact looks sort of funny with his unruly wiry hair made more unruly by the humidity, and is probably going through some big sex fantasy about her, and she finds that amusing though also a bit pathetic. Then she gets up—Well, see ya, honey, he says to himself—and sits on the grass in the sun about ten feet farther away from him, which could still be thirty feet; he's not too good at gauging distances. So maybe she had been thinking of the sun before when she had her eyes closed in the shade, but forget it, forget her, will ya? He can if he wants; it's just that before he didn't want to.

Looks at his mother—sleeping, definitely: the breathing. If she weren't he'd initiate a conversation about something: that they're much better off in the shade than the sun, don't you agree? How can people, like the ones on the grass there, lie in the sun, not just the heat and humidity but the sweating and harmful rays? And what do you get from it? Brown, red, possibly a bad burn. Her soda! and he looks but she placed it on the ground by the wheel. The Frisbee? Lying by the woman; she's flat on her back now, no towel or anything like that beneath her that he can see, arms and legs stretched out, sandals off, and eyes closed. So, out to get a tan—maybe the main reason for coming to the park and explanation for the brief clothes—but why the Frisbee? Looking for someone to play with? A come-on or you-come-to-me or whatever the term. A ploy. Guy sees the Frisbee, says, "Wanna toss it around?" and she likes athletic, forward young guys. So they throw, start talking. First: "Good catch," or "Sorry," if that one misses it. "No, it was my fault. I threw it too far over your head," or "I didn't keep it up long enough for you to get under it." Then: "You throw and catch well, where'd you learn?" "Frisbee school." "Yeah, funny, me too, classes right here in the park." "Really, I just picked it up; it's not very hard." Suppose it's a woman who sees the Frisbee lying beside her and says, "Wanna toss it around?" "No, thanks, I came out here mainly to rest; maybe later." Suppose the woman then says, "Mind if I borrow it and me and somebody else toss it around?" "I'd just like to keep it beside me, if you don't mind." And she has no sunglasses on; she looks the kind that would. Anyway, after they toss it around he invites her to the kiosk nearby for a soda or iced coffee or tea, or she invites him, or they both say they're hot, at the same time say, "Let's get something cold to drink," and the thing's started: tonight, or an hour or two from now, in one or the other's bed, or not so fast. Gould's energetic enough to toss a Frisbee around, knows how to, doesn't think he'd get winded from it if he didn't do it too long or hard, but would he do it if he weren't married or with his mother and so on? What "so on"? Well, overcoming his natural shyness and anxiety about being rejected and other things to go over to her and say something like, "Excuse me, miss, but I see you have a Frisbee; would you like to toss it around?" He doesn't know. Would depend on how long he hasn't been with a woman, what he thought he looked like at the time. Also if there were other people near her; now there aren't. Other things. You think about them at the time, you never do it. But he loves her body. He has to admit that. It's the body for him. So many bodies for him. So many in the park. So many in tight tank tops and shorts cut high and with full breasts and rears and small waists and long solid legs or just solid legs of normal length like hers. So many people exercising and in shape today. He's in shape too. Exercises, runs—not much but enough to stay in shape or look as if he's in good shape for a guy his age. Doesn't want to get a pot, likes the feel of his hard muscles, especially the arms, after he exercises with stretch bands or does pushups. But the point is she's the only young woman in a long time who's looked at him in a curious if not even a flirtatious way.

Looks at her. She's leaning up on her elbows again, turns to him maybe two seconds after he looks at her, then looks the opposite way. In the distance, direction she's facing, some kids playing badminton without a net. He imagines going over to her with her back turned, saying, "Excuse me, I don't mean to startle you"—and she turns to him—"but you have a Frisbee and I could use the exercise, so I was wondering if you'd like to toss it around for a few minutes. No problem if you don't, and I'm sorry if I disturbed you." She says, "Sure, why not, I could use the exercise too." She gets up—does he help her? Only if she extends her hand for him to. He has a book with him, so he says, "Mind if I move my book to where your things are? Just for safekeeping; we can keep an eye on them both at the same time." "Sure, it's okay," she says. They find a more open area but not near the kids playing badminton. They toss, back and forth, little encouraging things said between them like the ones he thought of for her and some other guy before, and after about fifteen minutes he says, "I'm thirsty and hot, and to tell you the truth, a bit tired; like something cold to drink?" She says, "Sure, that'd be nice." They go to that kiosk nearby. First they pick up their things. He pays, they talk. She's an actress, she's a dancer, she's a singer or violinist or pianist; she's a grade school teacher of language arts or a high school teacher in a private school teaching one of those things: music, theater, dance, maybe art. She's intelligent, well read, good sense of humor, smiles a lot at him, seems to like his company. She looks at her watch—does she have one? Can't see from here. Could be in her bag. Does she have a shoulder bag, little knapsack, something like that? Doesn't seem to, and he doesn't remember one. Just the Frisbee. Maybe what she needed to go to the park with—tissues, keys, money, wallet, watch—are all in her pockets. She have pockets in those shorts? Probably. But where was he with her? She takes a watch out of her pocket and says, "Oops, getting late; thanks for the drink but I have to leave now." He says, "I better be going too." She says, "I'm going out this way." He says, "My direction too, which can't be much of a coincidence, since we were both on this side of the park in the first place." "Sixty-fifth Street exit?" she says. "Seventy-second, but I can go out Sixty-fifth too, then walk up Columbus. Lots of things to look at, though on the west side of it, not as interesting or aesthetic." They walk, talk, bump into each other, laugh. He accompanies her to her building. First he says, "I can walk with you right to your door, if you don't mind. It's on the way to Columbus," or, "It's on the way to Broadway, and I just remembered I have some things to get there." She can say, "Where?" he can say, "Fairway," she can say, "I love that store, but gee does it get crowded. Maybe that's another reason I like it: so many characters." When they reach her building, what? He has her name by now; maybe asks for her address—no, he has her address; he's standing in front of her building—so her phone number. Or she says, "Listen, like to come up for coffee? I still have a little time." "Sure, I'd like that, thanks," he says. They go up. Once inside, or a short time after she shows him her apartment, or in the kitchen, where she's putting on the teakettle, he kisses her. She kisses back. They kiss, fondle, start to undress each other. She says, "Whew, wow, a little fast, I don't know if this is such a good idea, but what the heck, you seem all right, and it's probably too late now. You have a condom? If you don't, I do." He hasn't. She gets one out of a night table drawer, takes off the rest of her clothes, lies on the bed, one knee up, other leg straight out, stares at the ceiling. He says, "That's how you were lying in the park, though substitute ceiling with tree covering first, then sky. Where do you think we get all our body positions from, the ones we repeat over and over and naturally fall into, the womb?" "What?" she says. "Nothing, just talking." He takes off the rest of his clothes, gets on the bed, kisses her, feels her breasts. She says, "Let's just get right to it. I feel like it, but the truth is I have to be somewhere in an hour, though I also don't want you to rush." He puts the condom on, or she does for him, or they do it together.

Looks at her. On her back again, hands under her head this time, eyes closed. He looks at his mother. She's looking at the trees behind her, then turns to him. "Oh, there you are; I didn't want to disturb you. You seemed very deep in thought, almost troubled. Are you?" "No. And you were napping before and I didn't want to disturb *you*. Feel okay?" "Of course, why shouldn't I? Just because I'm an old lady who's gone to pot and who should probably put an end to herself before she gets worse? But tell me; I was looking at those trees there. Why do you think they're all painted black? It's very unusual, isn't it? Not just for the park but anywhere." "They're not painted. You asked me that same question before, Mom." "And what did you say?" "You tell me." "Please, dear, don't make fun of me; it isn't right." "I'm not; this will help you concentrate better the next time you want to ask that question. What did I say before, after you asked me why do I think the trees are painted black?" "I don't know and I won't pretend I do. What did I say? That I was getting daffy and should be put in a home?" "I said they weren't painted." "They're not? This one right behind me, for instance, isn't painted black or some other dark color?" "No; it's the natural bark color, and it's nowhere near being black." "Well, that's odd. It has to be my eyes, then. One I can hardly see out of; the other one, everything I see through it is dark and dim." "So that's obviously the reason," he says. "And we both know there's an operation to correct it but that Dr. Brenken—your personal physician, not your eye one—doesn't want you going through it: too many risks." "I know," she says, "because you already told me, right? It's what I want to do, but you don't want me taking chances." "Both Brenken and I, yes." "Who's that?" "Your doctor, Brenken, the one you see for checkups and stuff. The eye surgeon's leaving the decision up to him." "But if I have a heart attack and die on the operating table, what of it? Living without seeing, and with everything else about to go on me too, what's the point in life?" "Come on, for a woman your age you're in remarkable health. And you can see, just not well." She waves dismissively, looks away.

He looks at the woman. She's sitting up, has sunglasses on, and seems to be staring at the ground between her legs. Sunglasses must have been in her pocket or in a case clipped to some part of her clothing he couldn't see. Continues looking at her, wondering what she'll do if she looks his way and catches him. Continue to look at him? Look at him angrily, if he can see that through the sunglasses, and then look away? Smile? Probably what she did before: give off no emotion, just look away. Stares at her legs. When they're in that caret position, he'll call it, they always look better than when they're on the ground straight out or standing up. Women that age have the best-looking bodies. The ones in good shape, that is. Better than girls in their end teens or very early twenties, though for all he knows she could be twenty, twenty-one. So what's he mean then? That usually women around twenty-five or so, which by her face and the very thing he's talking of he thinks this one is, have the same flat stomachs and firm busts and so on of the teenagers and early twenty-year-olds but a roundness to their shapes the others don't have, and that maybe mid-twenties is when a woman's body peaks. Ah, he's really not too informed on the subject, so best he keep that speculation to himself. He imagines making a pass again. She has sunglasses on this time. What would he say? Frisbee again. "Excuse me, miss, but I saw the Frisbee—*noticed*—and wondered if you'd like to toss it around a little. I haven't played in a while, but my mind suddenly started going back when I saw it lying there—" She's taken off her glasses and cuts him off with "I want to lie on the grass in peace; I got to be bothered every time by some guy?" "I'm sorry, I didn't mean to, but to be honest it's partly because when I saw you looking at me before, I thought—" "Saw me looking where? Were you sitting someplace around here? Because if I was looking in your direction it was probably at the scenery behind or around you. That's why I come to the park and to this particular part. Not only because it's quieter and cooler but to see the trees, the birds, and to relax with none of the typical hassles." "Well, you had a Frisbee—" "The Frisbee's my business why I have it." "Sure, of course, I misinterpreted it somehow, and I really did want to toss one back and forth—" She's looking at him with the expression Will-you-please-get-lost-or-do-I-have-to-call-a-cop? and he goes. When he walks away he looks around to see if anyone nearby heard or saw him getting brushed off. Nobody on the benches closest to her is looking at either of them, so either they didn't hear or are being discreet.

"Look, that's called a dog walker," his mother says, pointing to a young woman walking a dog. "I never knew such people existed till someone told me of them. They get paid." "Why do you think she's a professional dog walker and not just a woman walking her dog? I always thought real dog walkers walked four or five dogs at a time, seven or eight, even, I've seen." "No, she's a dog walker who gets paid." "But how can you be sure? I'm not saying you're wrong. I'm just curious what you think distinguishes her from a regular person walking her dog." "I'm sure, I'm sure," she says, "but you don't think she is? Maybe I am losing my mind if I can't remember who told me or even now if anyone did. No, I'm sure someone did. I don't make these things up." "Listen, maybe you're right. I'm in fact positive you are. I've heard of dog walkers but didn't know that some walk only one dog. Now that you mentioned it, though, it makes perfect sense they would. Some people have so much money today, especially around here—Central Park West—that they can afford anything. A walker for each of their dogs if they have more than one?—you got it, whatever the fee." "A dog for every walker?" she says. "I don't get it. What are you saying?" "Listen closely, Mom. I'm saying that some people, if they have two dogs, will then get two dog walkers to walk those dogs individually, or the same dog walker to walk the dogs separately." "Now I see," she says, but it doesn't seem she does by the down-in-the-dumps look she gives him, so he says, "You're all right, right? My talk about dogs didn't bother you?" "No, why would it? But what specifically were you saying? Oh, better we don't talk about it. You'll think I forget everything, when I don't," and she leans back in the wheelchair and slowly closes her eyes.

Looks at the woman. She's lying mostly on her side and looking at him through the sunglasses. Or is looking his way, since all he sees are the dark lenses, no eyes. He imagines her coming over to him. He's been sitting alone where he is now. She's thinking, I see a guy who looks interesting, he seems by all his looking at me that he's interested, then I can make a pass at him as well as him doing one to me. If I see right away once I talk to him or even when I get near him that he's gay or a nut or not interested and that I've misinterpreted his glances and even the direction his looks went or find out he's been playing some sort of flirty game with me and has nothing else in mind but fooling me into thinking he's interested, I say, "Sorry, I thought you were someone I know; it must be my dark glasses," or say nothing but just walk away. So she comes over. He sees her coming and doesn't know what to make of it. She seems to be looking at him and heading his way, flicking the Frisbee against her leg, but maybe she's going to go right past him. She stops beside his bench and says, "Excuse me, but bad as this introductory remark must sound, about as unartful and unimaginative as one could be, I just can't think of a way of putting it different: don't we know each other from someplace? And don't crack up at what I said either, or I'm really going to be mad at you." He says, "I won't, and not to my recollection, our knowing each other. Because where do you think it was?" "Funny, but I thought someone introduced us in the park last week. At this Frisbee game over there where the kids are screaming, or you just came in on it and after we were playing awhile we got to talking. I think we were even on the same side." "I know that's not it. I like to play Frisbee a little, or did—last time must've been ten years ago. But would you like to have a catch now? Is that what they say, 'catch'?" " 'Throw it' rather than 'catch.' Or 'toss' as the next best thing, if you get tired of saying 'throw.' " "I meant as the noun, when you're practicing or playing around with the Frisbee," and she says, "That's what I meant too. But yeah, I brought it out here hoping maybe I'd get some exercise with it. So, you want to?" He asks if she knows a good spot to throw it and she says, "Follow me," and he gets up, takes his book, and she leads him to an open area about fifty feet away from the nearest group playing or person sitting on the grass. "Okay," he says, "what do we do, just throw? I think I remember how it's done." "Sure you do. No one forgets once they get the knack. Flick it like this," and she demonstrates without releasing the Frisbee. "Now let's step back about fifteen feet." "Each?" "Each. We'll start off nice and easy, and if we start clicking we'll move back even farther. Now I'm not saying I'm great at it, I want you to know"—both stepping backward—"but I can throw it without a wobble most times and snatch most anything within reasonable reach, behind or front." "So it's all in the wrists, that it?" he yells, making the throwing motion with his hand, and she says, "No, I don't think so," and laughs. What's funny? he thinks, nodding and opening his mouth as if he's laughing. Sex? She's out here primarily for that? Meets a guy through the phony line about knowing him from someplace but not having a better way of putting it at the moment, and the Frisbee's to see if he's athletic enough for her, isn't too clumsy or something, and doesn't drop after a few throws. "Ready?" she says, when they're about thirty feet apart, or forty or so, and he says, "Let her rip." She throws. It's for him what would be a perfect toss, gliding smoothly and straight toward him but goes over his head by about two feet and lands some ten feet past him. "Sorry," he says. "You should have leaped for it, or at least run back and got under it. I kept it up long enough." "Thanks, but I'm no pro basketball center or cheetah." He wants to get it right, practices flicking it a few times; she yells, "Come on, get rid of it!" and he lets it go. It wobbles from the start and flops about fifteen feet in front of her and rolls to the side on its end and down a hill a little so she has to chase after it. "Sorry." She says, "Hey, who told you you can play? No throw or snatch. You're getting old, man, old." "Thanks," and, under his breath, "Up yours, ballbreaker." "Only kidding," she says. "You're okay, just a bit rusty. One's coming to you; mind your head," and throws another perfect one but right to his chest. He reaches out for it, and it bounces off his fingers—"Sorry again"—and picks it up angrily and sends it flying without concentrating on throwing it right. It spins well but too far to her left to give her any chance of reaching it. "Big improvement in the aerodynamics, but you're not there yet," she says, and flips it to him gently and he catches it. "Now we're hot," she says. Again he just lets it fly without thinking of how to throw it and it's a graceful one a few feet over her head. She backs up, waits for it to drop, and turns her back to it and grabs it from behind. "Great, two in a row," he says, "and fantastic catch." "And good basic throw also. You had it hanging up there long enough for me to get creative." They throw it around like that for about twenty minutes. Then, tired, he says, "Okay, I give up, you win," and makes a calling-it-quits motion with his hands. She says, "A few more, but from much farther out. Let's really strut our stuff." She signals him to step back, which he does, till they're about thirty to forty feet apart again, since they'd moved closer and closer to each other once they'd started. She flips it to him; he wants to let it sail past and fall to the ground but grabs it on the run and almost in the same motion whips it back to her; she makes another fancy catch, this one with her arm behind her neck. Back and forth a couple of dozen times or so and then she says, "Now I'm bushed and drenched; let's get a cool drink and wipe ourselves off. You did good, my man, really good," when he comes up to her. "What's your name?"

"Did it suddenly get cloudy?" his mother says. "No. Same blue sky, no clouds, pretty high humidity, temperature around eighty-five." "Not going to rain? It looks like it, everything darker, as if a real storm." "I told you, Mom, it's only your eyes. The day's clear and sunny." "That hot?" "It could be worse, believe me. Eighty-five degrees is nothing," and she says, "What I've become, I can't believe it. What did I do wrong in life for my body to get so fouled up as this?" "All you have is an ophthalmological problem—you know, your eyes. Otherwise, you're in relatively good shape." "I know. And as for ophthalmology, remember: I once wanted to be a doctor. I should consider myself lucky. No cancer or major brain disconnections, and I still got an appetite and my hearing hasn't gone completely kaput. But I don't really care about my health, much as I talk of it. It's you and your wife that—what's her name again? I suddenly forgot." "Sally." "Sally, excuse me. What a doll. And your dear children. How are they?" "Fanny and Josephine. They're fine. You saw them yesterday." "I did? I forget. And your wife? There's nothing to help her?" "The scientists are working on it." "They'll come up with something. When I was still able to read the papers, I read about it. A breakthrough any moment, they say, right? How'd she get what she's got?" "Nobody knows." "No signs when you first met her? It just came? They say if you work hard enough you get what you work for, but it's not always true." "What do you mean?" "I mean your wife, your children, your life. That she's such a good person. That God isn't always looking after us, and how can He? Not that I believe in Him after all I've seen." She picks up the ginger ale can. "What should I do with this?" "You done with it?" "For now I am, but I don't want it anymore. Are you permitted to just throw them away? You can't get fined?" "The scavengers canvass through the trash cans here and get a nickel apiece for them, so I think it's okay. By the time a cop comes over to arrest us, the evidence will be gone." "What?" "Nothing. I'll get rid of it." He takes it to a trash can near the woman, though there's one much closer to his bench, and drops it in and looks at her sitting on the grass, sunglasses off and somewhere, head arched back, eyes closed, facing the sun.

"Henrietta, Henrietta!" a man yells from the path and waves to her. "Gosh, where the heck were you?" she says. "I was getting set to leave." The man sits beside her, fanning himself with his hand. He puts her sunglasses on, looks at her as if to say, How do I look?, takes them off, grabs her Frisbee, and throws it up a few feet and catches it. "Where's Jackson?" she says, and he says, "I decided to leave him home. I wanted to really get a workout this time. Whenever he's with us he ruins it by leaping at the Frisbee and, if he gets it, hogging it, and you know he's only going to tear it to pieces one day." "I love it when he goes after it." "Well, then get a dog."

He goes back to the bench. "I'm feeling tired," his mother says, "think we should go home?" "Anything you want." "I don't want to spoil it if you're enjoying yourself here, but let's leave. I hate falling asleep in public, with my mouth open and people staring inside." "Don't worry, nobody's doing that. Looking and staring's just one of the things—two of the things?—people do in the park, but I don't think they do it too deeply and I've a feeling they forget what they see in seconds, because it's always on to the next." "What?" "It's always on to the next thing they look and stare at not too deeply. Do you understand?" "I didn't hear it." "I'll tell you at home." He unlocks the wheelchair, looks over, and sees the woman and man talking animatedly, the man slapping his knee and finding something very funny. As he's wheeling his mother, she says, "Those trees over there—" He leans over her and says, "Mom, why do you keep insisting the trees are painted black when I've told you a dozen times already—" "That isn't what I was about to say." "I'm sorry, what was it then?" and she says, "When do you go back?" "First week in September." "September? That's right around the corner. Before you know it, it's over." "Mom, it's mid-June, two days or a day or three—whenever the first day is—before summer even begins. We have to go through more than two months till September. Till that time I have another two weeks here and then go to Maine. Then we come back to New York and see you for another five days or so, and then I head south back to my job." "It's not September? I can't believe it. Why do I always think it is?"—shaking her head. "I got to get my head examined, but I know you'll tell me I don't have to." A minute later, while he's pushing her, she says, "Those trees over there. It's so mysterious." "Why? Because you think they're painted black and you don't know why?" "They're not? I didn't see how they could be, because what would be the reason? But that's how they all look to me, as if someone came with a brush. It's terrible getting so old and losing everything at once." "But you haven't, which is what I told you before. Listen"—bending over her from behind—"I want you to listen to me. Are you listening?" "Yes, but you're not saying anything yet." "I'm saying, which, as I said, I've said before, that regarding your health you at least haven't got some horrible and painful and disabling illness, disease, or affliction. One not just where your walking's affected, like now, but where you can't walk at all. You were never really sick in your whole life, which is something for someone in her early nineties who smoked a lot and probably drank too much too. You're going to be in reasonably good health till you're past a hundred, I'm sure. Good genes, it must be, though they seem to have skipped over your siblings and folks. And just luck and I don't know what else contributing to it. A certain vanity, a feeling of things due you, and so on: positive outlook, though you don't have too much of that now, but you'll bounce back. And just that: when things went truly bad for you, you didn't dwell on them too long but quickly worked them out and bounced back. Though I can understand—I don't want you to think I'm not sympathetic—what you mean about the little infirmities and things—your hearing, that you don't have the energy you once had, and of course your eyes—that can make you feel much worse." "Is that what you were saying before? I don't believe it," and she turns around and looks at him and laughs. "So you think what I said's funny and maybe even everything I say is funny too? Well, that's good and no doubt healthy for you too. And for the most part I agree with you," and he laughs too.

He's pushing his mother to the park entrance when he thinks of the young woman again. Jesus, what a body! He imagines lying beside her in bed, all their clothes off, and reaching out to touch her, but shakes the thought away. But she had to be somewhat interested in him to look over so often, isn't he right? No, and for all the reasons he gave. Or she was a little interested, and just maybe, but after a while, no matter how many times she looked over, he should have stopped sneaking looks at her. Oh, well, gone now, and next time he takes his mother to the same spot—it's her favorite because it's so shaded, where they sit, and quieter and cooler than just about any other place in the park nearby, while still being safe and having a steady flow of people walking past to distract her—and if the woman's there he'll make a point of not looking at her once he first sees her. He'll in fact sit on one of the opposing benches with his back to her and his mother facing her this time in her wheelchair.

As he's leaving the park he imagines the woman rushing up to him. First he hears from behind, "Mister, say, mister!" and turns around and sees her coming. He stops and points to himself, and she says, "Yeah, you, could you hold it there a second?" "Yes?" he says when she reaches him. He doesn't know what to expect, though it doesn't look good; she seems solemn, a bit angry, and she says, "I want to ask you something. Before, when I was sitting on the grass back there, didn't you have anything more interesting to look at than me? Because if you want to know, and I don't care if you don't, since I'm going to tell you anyway, your constant looks at me made me nervous and uneasy and, frankly, just plain pissed off. I mean, where do you come off doing that crap?" "What do you mean?" he says, and his mother turns around and says, "What is it, Gould? Do you know this young lady?" "No, and I don't know what the heck she's talking about, either." "You damn well know what I'm talking about, so don't try to worm your way out of it with that bullshit. It took all the courage I had in me to chase after you, for even my friend I was sitting with told me to forget it. But I had to tell you what I thought. And now I'm not going to be put off or made to feel confused or crazy or anything like that by your saying you know nothing about it and some other lame excuses you might be thinking up. I also don't care if this woman's your mother or the person you look after or whatever she might be to you. If she is someone like that, it's about time she saw what you're up to when you're supposed to be taking care of her, if she already doesn't know." "What is she saying?" his mother says. "I didn't quite get it." "She's saying nothing, believe me," he says, and the woman says, "I'm saying something to you, all right, and that's that from now on go ogle-eye the trees or rocks or people passing by or anything like that, but leave women like myself alone. We're tired of having your eyes poring over us without stop and intentionally, really, trying to make us uneasy, when all we want to do here is relax and get away from that stuff like anybody else. So, I said what I had to and have always wanted to tell guys like you. Maybe, but I doubt it, it'll keep you from repeating your behavior with other women in the future. If it doesn't, you can be sure some other woman my age will say the same thing to you I did till you finally let the message sink in." "Excuse me," he says, "I can see how upsetting the whole thing is to you, and I understand why also, but you got the wrong guy, believe me, the wrong guy." "Yeah, sure, you bet." She starts walking back, every few seconds turning around and looking sharply at him, and then he faces forward and resumes pushing the wheelchair. "I still don't know what that was all about," his mother says, "but she seemed annoyed at you for something. Was she?" "It was a big mix-up. She had to have me totally confused with another man. Or else she caught me looking at her when I was sitting on the bench before. You know, I was looking around as people tend to do when they're sitting in a place awhile and the conversation, for instance, suddenly stops or the person you're with drops off into a nap. And my eyes in their wandering happened to land on her for a few seconds and maybe stayed a few seconds more because she was fairly good-looking, and she got it in her head I'd been gawking at her since I sat down. So like a lot of women today, and some not as young, she used it as an excuse to nail a man for looking lecherously at a woman, when it was nothing like that with me, nothing, but what could I do? When someone screams at you loud enough, you just shut up and hope they go away soon." "For some reason I still don't get what you're saying now. Come in front and tell it to my face," and he says, "It's not worth stopping the chair and coming around and saying it to you or even repeating it from behind, so let's forget it," and pushes her out of the park.

He wheels her along Central Park West on the park side for two blocks. "I think we should cross here," she says, when they reach the side street before hers. "The next block doesn't have a curb cut on this side to get the chair down." He says, "I can get it down without the curb cut, but okay, why not make it easier on myself and less bumpy for you?" He waits for the light to change, starts pushing her across the street. "Look both ways," she says. "Even though there's a crosswalk, the cars making a left out of that side street never seem to stop for pedestrians. I can't see them well, so if one is coming I'm dependent on you to get me safely across."

The Suicide

SOMEONE'S BANGING ON Gould's door. Time, what, who could it be? "Hey, what's going on?" he yells from his bed. Banging continues, harder thumps, and someone screams, then gags. He jumps out of bed—his shorts, where'd he put them? Fumbles for the light switch on the night table, turns it on, light blinding him, squeezes his eyes shut to adjust, opens them, can see now, and runs to the door. "Yes, who is it?" Nothing, and hasn't been anything last half minute. "Who's there? The banging and screaming. Who was it? Anybody still there?" "Help," a voice says, man's, weak, "help me, help." "What's wrong?" Nothing. "Just a second; I got to get my pants on." The man bangs on the door. "I said I got to get my pants on; hold your horses." "Help me, help me." What am I doing? Gould thinks. Opening the door before I see who's there? Looks through the peephole. No one. Door's banged from below the hole. "Listen, I'm sorry, this is New York and not the best of neighborhoods. You'll have to stand up, show yourself. I got to see who it is first before I open up." Door's banged from even lower than before. Guy must be sitting there, lying, crouching, something, maybe ready to pounce on him.

And where are my neighbors? Certainly by now, even at 2 A.M., a few of them must be looking through their peepholes. "Who is it out there? Your name? Someone I know from this floor?" "Help, I'm dying." "Excuse me, but dying how? From what? Literally?" "Please." Sounded too real. "Just a second, I'm getting my pants on." Banging, lighter, the guy saying, "Hurry, dying, help me." Gets his pants on. No undershorts or shirt but doesn't matter. With his hand on the door lock he thinks, Should I? But has to be someone hurt. Make sure not to lock yourself out—and takes his keys off the hook on the doorjamb and puts them in his pocket—am I ready to look if it's something real bad? Suppose it's from a knife, razor, in the face, neck, and the guy looks awful, bleeding everywhere, what do I do? Just shout for your neighbors if they're not out, that's all. Unlocks the door and man sort of falls over the threshold on his face. "Jesus, what happened?" Terrible smell, doesn't know what it is, chemical, not shit or vomit or anything like it. "I said what's happened to you?"—standing over him—"I can't help if I don't know." "Poison," the man mumbles into the floor, and Gould says, "What, poison? You took some? Stuff that can kill you?" "I'm dying. Wanted to when I took it. Get me help now." Still nobody else around. "If anyone's in their apartment looking," he shouts, "please help me with this guy. He took poison, says he's dying." Gets on one knee, steels himself, and turns him over by his shoulder: Roland, fellow from down the hall and someone he went to college with. Eyes clenched in pain, mouth open, that terrible stink; black inside and his tongue, for a moment making motions to speak, also black, and some foamlike dark stuff coming up and making him choke. Gould quickly puts him on his side and holds him there so he can throw up. "What can I do for you, what can I do?" Gould says, holding his breath. "Help me," Roland says, opening his eyes to slits. "I don't want to die." Couple of doors open; maybe they saw it was Roland and Gould on the floor beside him and thought it safe. Someone yells up the stairway, "Hello, you with the noise up there. This is Aaron Wallenstien from 6-H: what's happening, need any help?" "Call the police," Gould yells. "An ambulance, emergency! Guy here—Roland from seven something, end apartment—took poison and he's in very bad shape." Woman in a trench coat leaning over Gould at Roland says, "I'll call them, I'm closer," and runs into her apartment and slams the door.

"Ask him what he took," a man says from a few feet away; doesn't recognize him but could be a tenant on the floor. "What'd you take, Roland, my friend?" the man says. "We should know that if we're to help. Pills?" "Arsenic. In soda." "A sweet soda?" Gould says. "Baking soda? What kind? Club soda?" and the man says, "Why you asking, what's the difference what with?" and Roland says, "Coke." "Then you got to throw it all up, my friend," the man says, and Roland says, "I did, did, *still.* Help me. Doctor. Someone for the pain. Hospital on Amsterdam," and Gould says, "Of course, that's the one that lady should have called. Ring her bell, Mrs. D," to a woman he's spoken to from the eighth floor, "and tell her—that one, that one, 7-K—to get the emergency from St. Luke's," and Mrs. D rings the woman's bell. "And you should drink water and throw up some more"—to Roland—"with salt in it or whatever you're supposed to take to make you heave. Isn't that what they say to do, salt?" to the man, and the man says, "Any fluid should do. Stick a finger down his throat would be faster," and Gould says, "I couldn't, could you?" "Roland, my friend," the man says, still from a few feet away, "why would you want to kill yourself with arsenic? Of all poisons, the worst and most painful. Oh, my poor boy, what a mistake." Lots of other people are at their doors, by the elevator and the stairs, hands over their mouths, in clothes they must have quickly put on, zippers unzipped, buttons and belts undone, one with a suspender hanging off his shoulder, most in coats and bathrobes, and one pretty young woman in leotards under a man's boxer shorts. "Listen," Gould says, letting Roland go when he starts screaming and shaking violently and makes throwing-up sounds but nothing comes out, "doesn't anyone know what to do to help this guy? He took arsenic. And the woman who phoned. What'd she say?" to Mrs. D, and she says, "She said she knew herself to call St. Luke's." "Bread," someone says. "Get him to swallow bread, doughier the better. Absorbs it and then it regurgitates out." "Then get some soft bread and salt water," he says to him. "Others of you. Hurry. Bread and glasses of water mixed with salt. And someone go downstairs and wait out front in case the hospital people and cops go to the wrong building." Roland's screaming, stands, bangs his fists against the wall, doubles up clutching his stomach, and yells, "My insides . . . on fire! Don't let me. . . . Get me there yourself." Woman comes out of her apartment. "They're on the way.

Ambulance from the one right up here, and police. The dispatchers for both said minutes, a few, and that was more than two minutes ago—I had something very important to do." "Did they say what to do about the poison?" Gould says. "I didn't ask; you didn't say to." "Call the hospital back and say we just found out it was arsenic and what should we do in the meantime?" She runs into her apartment and locks the door. A man's standing beside Gould with a glass of water. "I mixed in plenty of salt and made it not too cold. I'm sorry but all my bread was grainy or stale." Gould holds the glass out to Roland. "Drink this. You have to keep throwing up to get rid of that crap." "No more," Roland says, reaching for the glass, then falls back to the wall as if thrown there—people clear away from him—and flops to the floor and holds his stomach and screams. "Please, drink the water," Gould says, holding it to his mouth. "I don't want to force it down you." Roland's just screaming now, tongue out, eyes bulging, grabbing his stomach, then his throat, gags and coughs and spits but nothing comes up. "That's why we want you to take the water. So there'll be something to mix with the poison." He gets the glass near Roland's lips but his teeth are chomping at nothing, and Gould thinks he'll bite the rim off and pulls it away. "What do we do?" he says, looking around. Nobody's near them. The man who called Roland his friend is by the stairs, one foot starting down. "Come on, you, you got to help me think of something," Gould says. The man throws up his hands. Then someone yells, "They're here!" just as the woman comes out of her apartment and says, "Detergent and water, they said. Or bicarbonate and water, or soda water, but really any liquid and lots of it to wash it out of his system," and two policemen rush out of the elevator and say, "Where is he? Which one is it?" because Roland's lying on the floor, quiet except for some dry vomiting, and people standing around are blocking the police from seeing him. Several of them point, and the policemen get on the floor next to Roland and one says, "What happened, kid, some bad dope?" and a couple of people say, "Arsenic." "Holy shit, by accident?" and one says, "On purpose, suicide." "That's hospital emergency business; I never had one that took arsenic. You, Mark?" and the other policeman says, "I guess we do like we do with all poison swallowings till Emergency comes—an emetic. God, I never smelled such a smell from anyone; it's like paint remover. He's gotta throw up bad," and Gould says, "He's been doing it all the time; there's nothing in him to throw up anymore. I've been trying to get this salt water down." "Good, that's one of them," Mark says, and takes the glass and holds it out to Roland and says, "Wake up, kid, drink. It's good for you; it'll save your life. Come on, do what I say; this drink's all you need," and Roland's shaking his head with his eyes shut tight, trying to speak, it seems, but no sounds coming out, then grabs his stomach and screams, "Help me, the pain!" "Where is it, can you point to it?" Mark says, and Roland's just screaming and beating his stomach, and Mark says to Gould, "You on this floor?" and Gould says yes and Mark says, "We can't do anything but hold him down. Let me use your phone to get the ambulance guys here sooner," and Gould says, "I don't have one; she does—several of the others must," when someone shouts, "The hospital people!" and the elevator door opens and the policemen clear a circle around Roland and the emergency team immediately gets busy on him, giving him something to swallow; when he won't take it one forces his mouth open by pressing the back of his jaw, keeps it open with a rubber tool while the other pours some stuff into it. Roland vomits real liquid in a few seconds and keeps vomiting till nothing comes up, and then they stick needles into his arms and a tube down his throat and work on him for about fifteen minutes; more emergency people have come with machines they carry and wheel in, and then they strap him to a stretcher and stand him up in it in the elevator and take him downstairs.

"He looked dead just now," Gould says, after the elevator door closes, and a man says, "Couldn't be. I saw his heart going, *pump-pump, pump-pump;* he'll pull through and will be back here in a week as if nothing happened," and Gould says, "I hope so, but he looked dead to me, I swear: his body limp, head just hanging. I bet that's why they took him out of here. There just wasn't any sense working on him any longer," and someone else says, "If he was dead they would have kept him here to write up a report because there wouldn't have been any hurry to get him out. They must have thought they could do better on him in the ambulance to the hospital and of course even better than that in the hospital and that they got enough of the arsenic out of him now to get him to start surviving again. Believe me, though I didn't get a look at him the last few minutes, no hospital's about to waste the time and cost of one of its emergency units on a dead man," and Gould says, "As I told this fellow, I certainly hope you're right. Where can you buy that stuff anyway? You'd think it'd be outlawed, it's so lethal." "Chemistry labs," someone says, "and he was going for his Ph.D. in the area, wasn't he?" and someone says, "By area do you mean Columbia?" and the woman says, "Columbia, I knew he was a student there, in chemistry." "I thought it was history or political science," Gould says, "since that's all he seemed to talk about, politics and spheres of influence and such. And he knew everything about the subjects no matter what the era." "And I thought ladykilling," a man says, "because Jesus, if there ever was a guy in this building who scored well with the ladies, he was it. In fact, he had so many of them and at all hours that it'd be difficult to think he had time for anything else." "So taking that into consideration," another man says, "and his good looks, which is part of it, and the impressive way he spoke, and his intelligence and obvious charm, you have to think, Who had more to live for than Ronald?" and a woman says, "*Roland.* And always the last one to leave the elevator, always there to help you with your packages or say a nice word: things like that. A lovely person, an absolutely lovely person, with no sign of the slightest sadness or distress. That's why it's such a shock, what they say he did, and why I'd have to think he swallowed it accidentally." "No, I'm sorry," Gould says, "and really, shouldn't we all pitch in, or at least the ones who live on this floor, and clean up the mess he and the hospital people left? Anyway, Roland happened to bang on my door for help when he was in the worst throes of it and told me he took the arsenic because he at first wanted to die but that he now didn't want to, maybe because he found how painful it was or just getting so close to death he realized his mistake." "He probably didn't think it'd be that slow, either," a woman says. "But you have to admit that if he was a chemistry doctoral student—" "He was," a man says. "I know his dissertation adviser, and Roland and I talked about her." "Then he knew what he was getting into and how long it'd take, and at the time, as this man here stated, he must have meant it but then had a sudden about-face. Now I guess all we can do is pray for his poor soul, for I'm sure he took enough to kill several men."

A tenant on this floor tells the police that Roland's door is still open and should she shut and lock it? "We know about his door and apartment and everything," a policeman tells her, "and we're about to attend to it, thanks. Just tell us if you know if he has any animals in there," and she says, "No, I remember he once said he thought it unkind and a nuisance keeping pets." A few police officers go into Roland's apartment with the super and find the arsenic with the container capped, the super later tells some people, the empty can of soda he took it with, the glass he mixed the solution in, with a note pasted to it saying something like *Don't drink from this! It might contain poisonous residue! Throw out but break first, if I can't because I'm suddenly incapacitated by the drink* and a suicide note. It's addressed to *Apt 7J, a man whose name I once knew but I apologetically say I can't recall now:* his next-door neighbor and someone he vaguely said boo to, the man tells Gould a week later while they're waiting for the elevator on the seventh floor. "He might have seemed friendly to others, from everything people here are saying of him since he died, but he acted to me like I cooked the worst-smelling fish in the cheapest corn oil every day and never dumped my garbage, cleaned my room, or took a bath." The note, which the police held for a few days before giving him—"Let's say that was stretching a bit their constitutional privilege of holding evidence," the man tells Gould, "but since he meant relatively little to me and I was dumbfounded he chose me out of anyone to write the note to, I let it slide and didn't make a legal case out of it, as I could have and conceivably got compensatory damages from the city and made it a test case against these kinds of questionable practices of the cops"—said he wants to die by his own hand because of a number of convincing articles and books he's read the last year on how life's not worth living in spite of the many little exciting if not fleetingly thrilling short-term things that can happen to adults. "You have to assume he meant orgasms, both of the masturbatory and copulative sort," the neighbor says, "and good hash, a few brief poems and paintings over the centuries, several smashing sunsets and maybe a sunrise or two, and seeing the aurora borealis the first time." Also because of a love he had for a certain woman who'll go nameless because she's blameless—"You wonder, at a time like that when he's writing his death scrawl, and from such a bright and I suppose well-read guy, why he'd resort to such trite rhyming," the neighbor says—but who didn't return his love for her one iota, or perhaps, for half an afternoon at the most, just a trifle more than an iota—"You can imagine what happened during those few glorious hours," the neighbor says, "since I'm sure he's underestimating the iotaness of them." The neighbor must have seen him with her once or twice, Roland wrote, but he tells Gould, "I saw him with, in my two months here, over a dozen different girls—I'm in and out of here ten times a day, so I miss practically nothing in this building—and of a wide variety of races, colors, shades, nationalities, and languages. And all lookers, and once three in a single day, so why'd he think, unless he described her for me, I could distinguish this one from the others because of maybe a particular glitter in his eye or bigger bulge in his pants that day?" Also because he's going nowhere fast: he can't stand historical research, writing bibliographies and papers, or other scholars and academics; the last thing he wants to spend two years on is a dull derivative dissertation, and the last thing he wants to become, he's found, is a teacher or father, besides knowing he'll never be even half fulfilled in any profession or capacity or with any woman over a long time or in any city or climate in the world. Life has been relatively to deeply depressing for most of his life, especially when he was a boy, so it seems the most sensible thing is just to end it. Could the neighbor personally tell his grandmother how much Roland appreciated her for bringing him up (here he gave her Bronx phone number, which turned out to be a disconnected one, the neighbor says, and with no listing of such a name in any of the city phone directories), when his parents died—both from cancer and just months apart, which had to influence his dark outlook and attraction to literature holding such a view—and how sorry he is for the sadness his death will cause her. He didn't have the courage to write her directly and thought it best that what he would have said to her come secondhand in abbreviated form from a stranger. Please be patient with her; if she wants the neighbor to come to her apartment for tea to talk about it, please do, though he only has to go once. He also wishes he had a lot of dough to leave her so she could live comfortably in her last ailing years, but he dies, as she well knows and the bank- and checkbooks on his dresser will confirm, just about penniless. The young woman he loved, if anyone does discover her name, is not to be blamed one bit for his suicide, as he said, and the writers of those articles and books he read, some of which the neighbor will find in Roland's bookcases and by his bedside (a few should go back to the library), are only to be commended—the ones still alive (most died natural deaths twenty to a few hundred years ago)—for having told the truth about what life is: endless tasks, meaningless efforts, illusions, repetitions, titillations, the occasional high, and tons of horseshit, this letter and statement about what life is included. "When I first read the last part," the neighbor says, "I thought, Well, we've all heard that before and never thought much of it, but in the final line he sort of covers himself." Gould says, "I'm surprised at that last part too, if you're being accurate in your paraphrase of it, since I always thought of him as one of the deepest and most knowledgeable and clear-thinking guys I've known, and I'm not saying that now just because he's dead."

Roland started City College two years after Gould but they graduated together. He got out in three years while two of Gould's five years were in night school, though they were around the same age, as Gould finished high school at sixteen. He was a tall handsome guy, lanky or wiry—you never saw him with his shirt off or in any garment that sort of stuck to his chest—sought after by lots of college girls, it seemed, praised and encouraged by his teachers to go on to graduate school but thought of by most guys Gould knew at City as a smart aleck, stuffed shirt, and pretentious bastard. He paraded his intelligence, was intolerant of anyone's point of view if it differed with his, was bitingly witty and sarcastic, had no time for small talk, joking around, or even smiling, won every intellectual argument because he was such a good speaker, knew his subject so well, and never got emotional when he spoke, and also something about the attentive way he listened and focused on you without ever interrupting no matter how long you rambled on, and maybe the longer the better, for you to lose what you were thinking; cold-shouldered just about every male student unless he stopped you to ask your opinion about a particular topic that had been engaging or perplexing him lately, as he put it, waited till you were done or fed you some questions or lines to keep you stumbling and then decimated everything you said in the order you said it, often enumerating your points. He hadn't changed much in any way a few years later when Gould moved into the apartment building. Jesus, not on the same floor too, he thought, since there were few people he liked less and no one he had felt more threatened by every time they had met. (Later he thought, What if I had lived next door to him? I doubt he would have written me the suicide note. But he would have knocked on my door sooner and I might have been able to save him by doing the same things I did. Then would he have moved back? How would he have reacted to me after that?) Usually Roland ignored Gould's automatic greeting and smile, when they passed each other on the street or in a store or at the mailboxes downstairs, or would just grunt a morose, "Yeah, hi," if they were waiting at the elevator, and then remain silent during the ride, lost in what seemed like a profound thought—eyes closed and head raised or head face down and hand covering his eyes—or reading a book he was obviously deep into and didn't want to be taken from. Though occasionally Roland would ask a question in the elevator or the lobby—start it off with something like, "I was mulling over something and considered you the perfect person to discuss it with, if you have a minute"—about a subject (politics, religion, history, philosophy, literature, metaphysics) Gould knew nothing or little about, and if he knew more than that or even a lot and allowed himself to talk about it—usually he'd say, the five or six times this happened, "Really, I'd like to discuss it but I just can't think straight now" or "I'm honestly in a rush"—Roland would still always end up ridiculing him, or not "ridiculing" so much as challenging Gould to prove what he said wasn't shallow or softheaded, sentimental, commonplace, uninformed, "pilfered from a recent *Times* editorial," just plain wrong, backing the challenge with quotes and facts and aphorisms and lines of poetry and Latin and French maxims, making Gould wonder about his own intelligence compared to Roland's (not about himself personally compared to him, since he knew he was a nicer and more likable and maybe even more compassionate guy and would never treat someone's opinions like that or inveigle anyone into a discussion simply to show off his mental prowess and range or to humiliate or discomfit that person), and how it's unlikely he'll ever think profoundly and speak that articulately and succinctly and formulate his thoughts so methodically or even be able to justify and defend well his simpler notions and arguments, and that as far as the so-called life of the mind's concerned he'll never be more than a half-baked intellectual with minimal perceptiveness, limited erudition, and few original ideas. All this was especially disturbing, since there was nothing he wanted more and worked harder at than to be a deep thinker.

What also annoyed him about Roland was that if he saw you with a pretty woman—riding up the elevator with her, for instance—he'd shoot her a look that said, Listen, drop that jerk and step out with me. In other words, Give me a signal you're interested, and I'll take it from there. So: a come-on—and once one of the women Gould was seeing and liked did drop him, saying it's impossible for things to ever really work out between them since she knows she can never feel strongly toward him, and about a month later he saw her walking out of a neighborhood movie theater with Roland, his arm around her, her face close to his and looking as if she was going to close her eyes for a kiss. He didn't want to interrupt her, wrong time to, but said, "Hello, Beca," and she said, "Oh, Gould, hi, did you just see this picture too?" and took Roland's arm off her waist. "I know you two live in the same building and I think you're even on the same floor, but this is New York so I feel it necessary to ask, do you know Roland Meese?" and he said, "Do I know him? No, only since college," and Roland said, "That's right, we were in the same graduating class, or yours was the one before mine. How are you doing? Like a cigarette?" and Gould said no and Roland lit one and looked away, admiring the sky or something in it while he blew smoke straight up. "Well, nice to see you both," Gould said, and walked ahead of them, not knowing how they first got together or when, but it was obvious she was stuck on Roland, though he couldn't tell by Roland's expression or anything how he felt about her. One day if he ever sees her again he'll tell her, if she doesn't know already, since they lasted only a few weeks or so together—once, when he saw Roland getting off the elevator, this popped out, "How's Rebecca?" and Roland said, "Beca Kahn? Beats me; haven't seen her for months. I didn't know you knew her"—what happened to him: "Killed himself, I'm not kidding; arsenic, though soon after he took it he wanted to live, banged on my door for help; it was so strange: mine, which just shows how desperate he was, since the only thing I was good for before to him was dating girls, which means bringing them into the building, that he later went out with. But what a sight: his mouth foaming, gums and nostrils and tongue coated black. And a hellish stench coming out whenever he tried to speak and then suddenly no stench to my sensory apparatus when from about twenty feet away people on the floor were complaining about it," and then say, "By the way, how did you two ever first get together? I'd just like to know. What'd he do, secretly get your number when my back was turned or you were leaving the building without me, or did you, without his even asking, slip it to him?" No, he won't. Couldn't hurt someone intentionally like that. He'd just say, "Did you hear about Roland?" and if she said no, he'd say, "Sorry I have to be the one to tell you. He committed suicide: poison, what a pity, guy so young and bright."

The name of the woman who didn't reciprocate Roland's feelings for her is Naomi. He finds this out from a tenant on the ninth floor. "Learned anything new about our poor Roland?" she asks in front of the building, when they're both going in. "Because I heard you were good friends," and he says, "We knew each other, not well, paths crossed, that sort of thing, and no, nothing about him for a while other than what everybody else knows; the same things get repeated endlessly," and she says, "What I heard the other day, and no one else seems to know it except the person who told me, so it must be new, was that the great love of his short life—you remember, there was something about this mysterious no-name woman in his suicide note to 7-J—and one of the main reasons he killed himself was Naomi somebody—last name starts with an *S*—that gorgeous tall dancer on the third floor . . . or she used to be there; someone said she moved a few days after to somewhere else around here, just too upset. But you couldn't have missed her if you ever saw her, she was so striking. Actually, she probably escaped a lot of people's notice because of her odd working hours and that she walked up rather than wait for the elevator that never comes. She could do that, only on the third floor. In fact, with her physical condition and youth she could probably run up fourteen flights twice a day without a sweat." He says, "I'm trying to place her . . . the third floor?" and she says, "Don't tell me. Long black shiny straight hair combed down to her waist when it wasn't in a bun or braid, and maybe six feet, and legs about half that length? An absolute standout by anybody's standards, and gifted too—in the corps de ballet of the New York City Center ballet company, if that's what it's called, and with a promising career going—this I knew before the recent chatter about her part in Roland's death. Once—someone here said he saw her in it and she was terrific—a solo role or maybe only part of a pas de deux or trois: a Todd Bolender ballet, this person said, a protégé of Balanchine? He I know of, but this Todd choreographer I don't, do you?" and Gould says, "Yeah, I've seen something he did with an American western or Shaker theme, I think. He's very modern, very good, lots of crazy hand and leg and neck movements." Gould had seen Naomi a few times. Her looks were ordinary—not gorgeous for sure, as this woman said; he even thought her a little homely—and she seemed private, always alone, gangly in a way and guarded and usually in a hurry to get into the building and up the stairs or to Broadway, and with that toes-bent-in walk he's always associated with dance students rather than professionals, so he figured she was a dancer but only studying it, but a dancer also because of her hair and cheekbones and big forehead that was always showing and her posture and makeup and dance shoulder bag she carried. But she didn't seem someone Roland would go nuts over—take his life, he means, or even fall in love with. Roland seemed to have his choice of women he went after, and most were a lot better-looking than her and some were true beauties and with more voluptuous—so to Gould more attractive—bodies, since she was small-chested and slim and much too bony, though of course she probably had the perfect body for dance and must have had beautiful legs—from what he saw of them below a skirt and could make out through her slacks, they were. "So what do you think?" the woman says, and he looks at her and she says, "Where've you been? I'm saying you think this Naomi Sugarman, I now remember the *S* was for, is the mysterious Miss No-name of Roland's suicide note?" and he says, "I wouldn't know. Based on your description of her, I never saw them together or her alone on my floor, though an image does come up that she lived in the building . . . I seem to see her"—closing his eyes—"going in or out. What's the difference anyway?" and she says, "Oh, good time to tell me, after I spent the last few minutes telling you everything. I think you know more than you're saying—what is it?" and he says, "Nothing, honestly. He came, he went—I'm talking about to and from the building and our few words to each other over more than a year, though we had gone to college together but I knew him there mostly from reputation and sight. He was a ladies' man and considered one of the academic comers. But if you want to know, from what I could make of him he wasn't a guy I ever especially admired for his character. He could be caustic and contemptuous, and his was a screw-you-I'm-for-me attitude—'you got a girl I've eyes for, I want her; you're enjoying a book I didn't like, pardon me while I dump on it'—though otherwise he was fine and admirable and with enviable brains. And outside of that one time, which was perfectly excusable—I'm not complaining, I'm saying, and I also probably never should have said the lousy things I just did about him, but you asked for honesty so that's what I decided to give—he never caused any commotion or scene on our floor." "Maybe that should have been in the *New York Times* obit of him if there had been one—you know, the ones with photos, not just put in by the close survivors," and he said, "I no doubt said it wrong, excuse me. He's gone and they're right, what they say (or those Latin maxims do) about the dead—to forgive the deceased and no bad words about him and so on, if the guy didn't do something really despicable like rape his little sister or murder someone other than himself."

So there are a couple of things he doesn't understand about Roland's suicide. Oh, no doubt lots of them, but the one that stands above them all is why in hell did he do it? For here's this guy, who except for his personality, which counts for a lot, okay, even if he couldn't care less what other people who "didn't matter" thought of him, though who knows?—but anyway, who had just about everything going for him in life. He didn't have money, came from a poor background, but so what?—since having it easy and lots of money from the start can often be as much of a hindrance to you as good, and if anyone was going to make it in whatever field he finally decided to get serious about, it was him. He had looks, intelligence, erudition, gift of gab, was clever, et cetera, nicely built, tall, and dressed well even if he didn't have many clothes at the time. He was very presentable, in other words, and had the brains to back it and could be charming if he wanted to—certainly with the people that mattered to him: professors, women he wanted to sleep with, maybe bosses—Gould doesn't know who else but he's sure Roland could be like that to anyone. Why? Because he also was smart enough to know what worked for him. It was probably people like Gould who he knew could do nothing for him, at least for the time being, that he showed his worst side to. So how could he make such a drastic decision, because of some things he read, and one woman he might have found gorgeous and alluring and immensely likable and so forth, and the tragedy of his parents some twenty years ago, and question marks about the future, and carry it out in so horrible and final a way? If he'd jumped off a building thirty stories up or into the Hudson from the George Washington Bridge, Gould would be asking the same thing—Why the hell do it?—but with arsenic he also had to know the pain it'd bring, though he might have thought it'd be quicker than it was. But wouldn't he have read up on it? And had he tried killing himself before? If he had, that could explain the drasticness of taking arsenic—he wanted it to work this time—but not why he did it. Did he have an illness no one knew of, one that he'd been told would eventually kill him or permanently damage his mind or nervous system or something? Nothing like that came out from what the police found in his room—notebooks, checkbook stubs for medicine or drugs—and not in the suicide note, and he never mentioned it to anybody in the building, so far as anyone knows, and no doctor was located who'd been treating him for anything, and the grandmother the police finally turned up on Long Island and whom 7J and another tenant spoke to knew nothing about anything like that either—no disorders whatsoever; he was in terrific all-around health, she said, although she hadn't seen him for almost a year. Was it chemical then, an imbalance of some sort, or whatever it's called, that even Roland didn't know about or just avoided dealing with and so hadn't been treated? Again, no one knew of it and Roland never spoke to anyone about having any up-and-down feelings or mood swings or depression of any kind. He was as stable and confident as they come, was the general summation of him: never an inkling he was feeling blue and only his disillusionment with his academic studies and a couple of his professors and the future possibility of getting a junior-level appointment was the one thing along those lines that he talked even a little about with a few people in the building. Someone even called up Naomi and told her about Roland, and she was shocked as anyone and saddened and all that but also said he hadn't hinted to her anything was wrong with him other than his studies—he didn't see how he'd be able to write the expected two-hundred-page dissertation, since his topic wasn't worth more than a hundred-twenty and he doubted he could squeeze out more than that from what his research had given him—and how he felt about her breaking off with him. But even there, this person tells Gould when he bumps into her in the market up the block and says he heard she spoke to the dancer, Roland told her he was dejected but he understood why she thought they'd never be able to make a go of it and he'd soon get over the breakup. Gould says, "What did she say was the reason they split up? And how could it be she didn't know about the suicide before?" and the woman says, "You think I'd ask either? What's wrong with you? It's enough that I called and had to give her the news, and now I'm not sure why I told you even this much. It's her business, what went on between them. If she'd wanted to say, she would've volunteered. The point is she was surprised he alluded to the breakup in his suicide note. Or so prominently, since he seemed reconciled to it the last time they spoke—maybe a few days before he took the arsenic; though they both still lived in the building then, it was over the phone—and even a little relieved to be completely unattached and on the loose again. But I think you're right about what I understand from others you felt about Roland—he didn't have the sweetest or most politic disposition in the world—but whatever any of us thought of him in that regard should be dropped because of what he did to himself."

His own brushes with suicide? They were nothing much—short-lived, not very serious, or maybe more romantic than serious and he was pretty young so maybe still immature—but it's a subject he's been thinking a lot about lately because of what happened to Roland, and it might help him understand better why Roland went through with it while so many others who think about doing it don't, or not as thoroughly. The first time was when he was just eighteen. He'd finished a year of college, hadn't liked what he'd studied, and was now taking two boring courses in summer school. He wanted to be doing anything but working eight hours a day at a tedious job in what seemed like the steamiest part of the city, midtown, and going to school four nights a week and then coming home to study for an hour or more. He also wanted to be living away from his folks and have a girlfriend or someone to date and a close friend or two, which he didn't then. So a couple of times, maybe more, but while he was on a subway platform—going downtown to work or after work heading uptown to school, probably the latter, as that'd be the worst possible time for him and also the hottest in the subway station: between job and school when he was most tired and perhaps susceptible to thoughts of suicide—he thought about jumping in front of a train speeding into the station. He remembers thinking, Go on, end it now, what the hell's life going to do for you anyway? In the long run it's just going to go from bad to worse: studies, more loneliness, crappy jobs, girls who bust your balls, sickness, old age, death—and other things, maybe a little of it like what Roland was thinking at the end. He even got close to the platform's edge once but backed away behind a pole when the train got to about twenty feet of him and was whistling. He was depressed most of the summer; his parents noticed it and wanted to know what was bothering him and if there was anything they could do to help—"You don't want to continue summer school, quit it and concentrate on your job," his father said, "and if that work's too hard and you'd rather be a waiter in the Catskills or a counselor in camp, there still could be time to get something"—but he always said, "That's not it. And the courses are important to finish if I'm to take a lighter night-school load next year so I can get a good full-time job. I'm just going through something; it'll pass," and it seemed to pass by the start of the fall term, when he got a better-paying day job and night school was easier and the weather was better and he had made a couple of close friends.

The other time, or only other time he remembers, was over a girl. They'd been sleeping together and he wanted to marry her: she had her own apartment and was studying to be a stage director; he was twenty-two and just out of college and didn't know if he wanted to go to grad school for something—law, journalism, art history, international relations—or try to get into some profession; and she said yes but not to tell anyone yet, she doesn't want people getting excited and making plans for a wedding before she's had time to adjust to it, and then a few weeks later she said marriage was the worst idea imaginable for her, what could she have been thinking of? good thing they kept it to themselves, they'll of course continue going out with each other, but she'll see about marriage with him in three to four years, if they last that long and no reason they shouldn't; it's not that they don't love each other as much, is she right? and he said sure, what does she think? there's no one else in the world but her—though for the time being she still doesn't want him to move in with her, she has too many things to do first and wants to continue being totally on her own for at least another year, but since he spends almost every night at her place anyway and seems to buy most of the food and wine it's just a formality that one half of the bedroom closet isn't designated his and his name isn't on the mailbox—but grew cool to him almost immediately after that and soon broke off with him, saying something's happened the last two weeks, she can't explain it but she doesn't feel the same to him, it wasn't anything he did and it isn't another man, but she thinks it'd be best—no, she's sure of it—that they stop seeing each other completely; is that going to make him very upset? And he said no, if that's what she wants, it's not what he wants at all but he knows from experience not to push somebody when he knows they don't want it and he thinks he can get used to it, and they didn't see each other for a month, then got back together; he called—well, he'd been calling every other day or so, just to see how she was, what she was up to, and so on, though really just to hear her voice and with the hope she'd say she wanted to see him—but this time asked her out to dinner, made up an anniversary: "It's almost fifty weeks to the day we met and to me fifty weeks constitutes a year—I prefer round numbers—so what do you say?" and she said one dinner can't hurt them unless they get food poisoning, and they saw each other almost every day for a month, then she broke it off again—it got too close, she said, when she thought they could keep it casual—though after this breakup they went out to dinner about once every three weeks and slept together that night—she said this was good for her and the way she wanted it, seeing him just as a friend and in addition getting rid of some of her pent-up sexual tensions and same for him, right?—and he said, "You won't get me to disagree on that; it's fine as is, and if it gets better, that's okay too, though you're telling me you haven't slept with anyone else since our last big break?" and she said she can't say that, and he said, "Well, that's okay too; I wouldn't expect you to only hold out for our once-a-monthlies. Do what you want; you're a free bird," and she said she doesn't need him telling her that, and he said, "I know; I'm sorry," till she said one morning, "Really, this is getting ridiculous and even a little humiliating and pathetic and painful and everything," and he said, "What is?" and she said, "Don't play the fool with me. Seeing each other and occasionally sleeping together when I don't want to, especially the last part. I don't want to sleep with anyone. Forget what I said about pent-up sexual energy and tension getting released. I have to be on my own completely—do you remember that old tune? I've school, I've assistant directing work to get after school, I've lots of things to do and no time for you. Besides, we're not working out. We'll never work out. We have to cut it off for good because it's too obvious that continuing as just friends and sporadic bedmates isn't working, and I don't need or want it to," and he said, "Okay, message coming in loud and clear. What's that you said, darling? No, only kidding. So if that's what you don't want or need—all of what you said you didn't—then it's over once and for all and for good, forever, okay?" and she said yes and he said, "Fine," and took home all his things for the third time in a few months, and when he called her after that she said, "I meant it, goodbye," and then, "Stop calling, will you?" and then she wouldn't talk to him: she'd hang up after she said hello and heard his voice or would only speak to him a few seconds—"Can't talk now, busy"—and finally: "Listen, I said it's over, so it's over, so why are you still calling? Try to understand that I don't want to hear from you again and I don't want to try and make you understand that again. I no longer love you. You didn't ask, but I said it. I in fact like you less each time you call. And because you have called so much when you knew I didn't want you to, by now you've hit the lowest level yet with me and I have only the most unfortunate feelings for you. Whatever good feelings I once had for you have been entirely erased by your recent actions. It's futile and hopeless to call me. It's also downright stupid, do you hear? I'm not going to change my mind about seeing you or being in contact in any way with you, and the more you try to contact me to change my mind, the less chance there'll be that I'll ever even want to acknowledge your existence if we happen to bump into each other in a few years. Now, if that isn't sufficiently unequivocal and unarguable and all those other adjectives that mean indisputable and nonappealable and unconditional, let me just say—" and he said, "No, it is, thank you"—though later thought, Thank you for what?—and hung up, and after the call, when he knew there was no chance at all of changing her feelings toward him and that she would never want to see him again or not for a long time—years, as she implied, and even then she wouldn't assent to seeing him, they'd have to bump into each other accidentally as she said and at the most it'd be from her a "How do you do, you're looking well and nice to see you, goodbye"—he thought of jumping off a bridge (interesting, he thought, always jumping off something: the Brooklyn or George Washington because you're allowed to walk on them); and about a week later, after being miserable it seemed every single waking minute—pulling his hair, tearing at his face, banging his fists on tables and against walls, crying—he went downtown to walk across the Brooklyn Bridge (he didn't know where to get onto the George Washington) just to see what he'd do on it and also to scout it out for a possible jump some other time, though if the impulse to jump suddenly came today or built up while he was walking across he just might do it, he just might, but when he came out of the subway station he thought closest to the bridge—he found out which one by looking at a subway map in the station he started out from but came up one stop short—he went into one of the many Chinese restaurants down there and at the counter had some dumplings and a beer, something he'd never done before alone, having wine or beer with food in a restaurant (at least not in the States, and he doesn't mean free bar food with your drinks), and ended up ordering what amounted to almost a full meal: rice with it, bowl of sweet-and-sour soup before, and after it an appetizer dish he'd never had and which he ordered because it was cheap and he was still hungry and the counterman seemed to say in his broken English that it was filling—a scallion pancake with some strange-tasting thick brown dipping sauce. The whole thing's awful, he thought, and he's tremendously depressed and doesn't know how he can go on living without her but he's got to do it, that's all, just day after day not call or write or try to see her or spy on her apartment building from across the street or stare up at her side window from the alley it looks over or anything like that, as he's been doing and thinking of doing more, and it should work out; in a month or two he should be over it and maybe even before.

Going over these two suicidal times in his life didn't help him understand any better why Roland went through with it in the most painful way possible, but it did make him more sympathetic to him, that's for sure. Perhaps, if you're of a certain mind or in a certain frame of mind, he might mean, you can get so depressed you just lose it completely, while someone else in the same circumstances but of a different background and mindset and nature might have a built-in . . . he's saying there might be an attitude or predisposition, let's say, in some people that's inherent or possibly even congenital and that prevents them and maybe everyone else with something approximating that gene pool, or at least holds it off more, from . . . oh, he doesn't know what the hell he's talking about, or not much, so why try?

Roland's grandmother and a cousin never come to his room to see what's in it. It could be they're too despondent or it's difficult or inconvenient to travel to the city or they assume there's nothing of any value or worth to them there, but anyway they tell the landlord to let the tenants on Roland's floor, and especially the one who received the suicide note and then the ones who helped Roland that last day, to go in and take what they want. If anything's left after that, to let anyone from the building in whom the landlord approves of, and then to dump or get a junkman to cart off the rest; they'll pay for it. Gould gets a letter from the landlord on this: *You and apt. 7-J, for a maximum of one hour, will be allowed inside Mr. Meese's apartment. Help yourselves to whatever you wish, and please don't make a mess. The super will accompany you, but he won't be taking anything himself.* He doesn't want to go in Roland's room. There are probably a few good books he'd like to have, but it'd be too ghoulish—Gould the Ghoul, which is what kids occasionally called him when he was a boy for no other reason than the words were so close—and he writes the landlord a note, thanking him for his offer but declining it and adding, *Why not, to avoid what could end up being a greedy free-for-all over Roland's things, give everything to a Christian mission house—I know of one on West 75th Street off Columbus Avenue near where I used to live, and there must be others in the city—or a poor people's home, if such a place still exists, or the Salvation Army or an organization like that,* but doesn't get a response. About a week later 7J says he got some great books from Roland's apartment, "One a first edition of an early Thomas Mann in the original German; how do you think he acquired such a thing? Also a decent night table that could be an antique—he probably picked that one up off the street—but there was nothing else there worth more than a nickel, unless I missed a few rare books that to me just looked mildewed and old."

The apartment's painted and a young woman moves in, an opera singer. She looks pleasant—a soprano, when he hears her through her door practicing—always dressed in beige or black or combo of the two, big hefty chest and thin legs and an intelligent face, is never with a man or really anyone, and Gould, the three to four times he sees her in different places the first few weeks, greets her and says things like "Enjoying the apartment? . . . Liking the building? . . . The neighborhood? It's a quiet part of town and usually safe—though if I were you I wouldn't walk alone after ten at night—and lots of good bookstores." She says yes to all the enjoyment questions and to the last adds, "And thank you, I'll take your safety advisory seriously. Everyone else here pretends ignorance or has been cagey about it." He finally stops her on the street and says, "Hi, just a second, wait up, I want to talk to you," because she's nodding and walking past, and he says, "Maybe I should identify myself—your neighbor in Five-twenty, don't you remember me? Not from right next door but on the same floor, 7-D," and she says, "It's my eyes; I left my corrective lenses home, sorry." He says, "I know you're a singer—I've even stopped to listen to you, but not right in front of your door. Lyric soprano?" and she says, "Mostly coloratura," and he says, "Oh, so many of the great hard roles. How tough it must be to get up so high and stay there—in *Lucia,* for instance, and that mad scene," and she says, "That one I'm still only familiarizing myself with; if you take it on too early it'll kill your voice." He says, "I hope I'm not offending you when I say that these days I prefer modern opera—Berg, Schoenberg, all the Bergs and Britten, and Ravel's little whatever they're called in French—those shorties—and even Bartók's one shot at it, though my love for opera isn't as strong as when I was a teen. Then I used to line up at the Met for standing room downstairs once a week, and, if I was close to broke or got on line too late, then the cheaper standing room in the uppermost ring where you can't see and can barely hear. Now I find the singing in the older operas still glorious but most of the plots excessively melodramatic, even for opera, and sometimes unintentionally funny—I really expect Tosca to bounce back onto the top of Castello something-or-other when she makes her grand final leap . . . excuse me, and you could say here, 'What do you know?' " and she says, "We all have our tastes, but take it from a budding pro that some of the characters' subtleties may be eluding you," and he says, "I agree a hundred percent," and finally gets around to asking if she'd like to go to a movie with him one night this week: "I'd love to go to an opera with you also, if the seats were affordable and not in that top ring—my feet have done more than their share of theater standing and would now revolt by turning in under me. And I'd probably ruin it for you by asking for a running translation of everything being sung and said and, if it's unclear to me, done onstage," and she says, "Then spare me," and they make a time to go to a movie, start dating. One night at her place she asks about the tenant who previously lived there: "This woman—the tenant on my line on the fifth floor—said he took his life in the building but she wasn't sure if it was here or in the hallway or on the elevator or stairs, but she knows it wasn't on her floor or in the lobby," and he says, "Oh, Roland, a very brilliant fellow, handsome, everything. I didn't get to know him well—he was kind of reserved and I guess I wasn't too outgoing and forthcoming to him either," and she says, "But as to what happened to him?" and he says, "He made it as far as our hallway but I think died during the ambulance trip or in the emergency room." "What did he take, pills? And why'd he go into the hallway if he wanted to die?" and he says, "Maybe pills, and I don't know the rest, I'm sorry. A change of mind? Who can say what anyone would do when the prospect of death—of not living anymore—suddenly hits you and then knowing you were the one who pulled the plug and now you don't want it unplugged or something? The realization would be incredibly frightening, maybe even, for some, heart-stopping, especially if you felt it was too late to be saved," and she says, "All that's probably true." A week later she says, "Why didn't you tell me your part in it? and I don't want you to give me any false modesty. You made me feel—I was talking about it to my next-door neighbor—like an awful fool," and he says, "Why, because he knows we've been seeing each other? Okay: I didn't want to scare you out of your apartment with what happened there before you, or even out of the building. Some people would get freaked knowing how horribly the previous occupant of the place died. And then I thought you'd ask for details, everyone does: 'What were his last words?' someone asked, and when I said I wasn't near him then—he supposedly said them to the medical team working on him—she asked, 'Then his last words to you,' and so on. Anyway, that you'd get some of the details out of me and be horrified, because that's what the whole thing was. I still shake when I think of it and I still see his burnt mouth and the rest of it and smell his smell and that's all I want to go into it," and she says, "Nothing like that fazes me, and I'm not superstitious in the least. I'd vacate the apartment if the rent was raised too high or it was overrun with rats and the landlord and the city couldn't do anything about it, but not from something like what happened to him. And he supposedly only took the arsenic inside the apartment, never came back to it once he went looking for help, and the place had been thoroughly painted and cleaned of any sign of it. The landlord did a spectacular job; I'd never seen such an immaculate apartment for rent in New York. You forget I was raised on a poultry farm and one of my chores from the time I was eleven was to cut off the chickens' heads," and he says, "I'm surprised your parents made you do that," and she says, "The birds weren't about to kill themselves. Besides, I started getting paid a little for it once I was thirteen, dime a head. But even worse than chopping the heads off was beating them to death when some of them ran around headless," and he says, "How'd you ever do that? I know I couldn't have; I guess you grow used to it. But you're right, I should've leveled with you long ago—maybe even told you of it the first time we spoke. The truth is I thought you already knew and I didn't want to upset you even more. You'll just have to forgive me for doing something I thought was best for you. I guess you never know what's going to backfire on you: the intended good you do, even the bad, which can turn out good. It all depends on how the people it's meant for take it, and of course, like I said, how it ends up," and she says, "Now you're feeling sorry for yourself. I hate that in a person, especially a grown man, and particularly one who cloaks it in a lot of philosophical and psychological jargon and gibberish," and he says, "Boy, who even knew how tough you were . . . I'm learning something about you today," and she says, "It's not toughness. I think I've seen some of the worst in life and the hardest and so forth, but none of it has stopped me from doing anything I've wanted and getting to be who I am and achieving what I have so far, maybe not even for a minute," and he says, "Where did all that come from?" and she says, "It came and it's addressed to you." "Oh, is it? Give me a day to think why. But it's funny, too, because now I see something I didn't, after all my explorations into Roland's death before, and that's that you're the kind of person he needed and should've known, not some delicate creature like the one he flipped over and who probably dumped him, which I think set off his suicide, because she was so spooked by his pessimism and gloom. If he had, you would have shaken him up some and maybe out of his feeling so bad about himself and his future, and the poor guy might've lived," and she says, "What do you think, I exist only to take care of weak men? If he had it in his mind to die and he asked my opinion I would have told him what I thought of doing yourself in before you've tried a thousand other things to fill your life, and then if he was still determined I would stop bothering with him because I don't go for men who are that heavy or even want to be around them: they'd just depress me till I'd possibly start thinking about taking my own life. No, the last isn't true. Besides all that, it's a ridiculous thought, yours, even a bit ugly, hitching me up hypothetically with a crazy dead man, and, I'm certain, deep down, meant to be cutting and mean," and he says, "Not so, and I apologize for whatever you think I ulteriorly said," and she says, "I don't believe a stitch of your apology, how about that?" and he says, "Then what can I say?" and leaves her apartment and they don't speak to each other for a few days. About a month later—they've resumed seeing each other but only about once a week—she gets an opera singing job she auditioned for more than a year ago and she says it's too good an opportunity to pass up and she moves to San Francisco. He calls her a few times—she never calls him—and says he's still hoping to save enough money to fly out to see her, especially for her debut in a few months and also to see that part of California—maybe they can go camping together in a redwood forest—but a month after she gets there she says they should break off their relationship entirely. "Why? There's still a strong possibility we can make it work, and I'd even think of eventually moving to San Francisco," and she says, "Whatever you do, don't come for me. It's not only that I've met a man and am now pretty serious about him: one of the stagehands for our company, but he's a master carpenter, no furniture mover. But also that the conversation we had awhile back—about the suicide guy whose apartment I took over?—turned me off you to the point where my skepticism about you just grew and grew. I didn't like what I saw emerging from you, is how I'll put it, to be real polite and not encourage you to flare up and try to malign me even more, and I thought it would only get worse. That's why I became sort of cold to you after that, though it isn't why I moved out here, of course," and he says, "Cold? I didn't notice it," and she says, *"Sure,"* and while he's asking her what she meant by that *sure* she cuts him off with "I beg of you, no more," and he says, "Oh, my, how operatic; when do you impale yourself on your dagger?" but she's already hung up.

The apartment's rented to an elderly woman but isn't repainted, as the landlord says the singer only had it a few months. The first time Gould meets the woman she tells him that her husband recently died, she was like a full-time nurse to him the last six years—"That's how much he suffered, and we couldn't afford real ones"—and since there was nothing left for her to do in their suburban community and her kids were scattered around the country in towns just as dull as hers and anyway didn't really want her, she decided to move back to the city she was raised in, "and especially this Columbia area, which is like a quiet sanctuary in a noisy fast-paced city, just the place to start out in again." She often has tenants on the floor in for dinners she cooks. She invites Gould a few times and he always begs off. After the singer and Roland, he doesn't want to go inside the apartment. And it's not that he's afraid the woman will ask him about Roland's suicide. She's already said she knows and nothing he says concerning it could surprise or scare or repel her after what she went through with her husband. Mostly, though, he doesn't find her interesting or intelligent, so he thinks the evening would be very boring. "Nothing personal, I want you to understand," he tells her the last time she invites him. "It's just that I don't usually have dinner, and if I do it's usually very light and with my own kind of special foods and preparations and eating it by myself while I work," and she says, "Please, I learned long ago not to take personally the idiosyncratic things people do. So if eating alone or starving yourself to death is what you want, I'm certainly the last person to try and interfere with it."

Everything Goes

THEY'RE SITTING AT a two-seater, having lunch in a restaurant's enclosed patio on a busy avenue. It's her favorite restaurant, favorite table position too: alongside the window, and his mother, looking outside, says, "My goodness, did you see that?" and he says, "No, what?" "That young woman, what she was wearing—she's passing your way now. Is it permissible to go around like that in the city?" and he says, "I didn't see her; she must've got in front of someone. What'd she have on?" and she says, "I didn't hear," and he says, "About it being permissible or not. What was she wearing—or not wearing, perhaps?" and she says, "Her shorts. They had long fringes or frayed threads coming out of the leg part, but were cut right up to here," and she slices her hands at the top of her thighs. "Can they do that, walk around like that without getting told not to by the police?" "Oh, sure, that's the style among many young girls today: cutoffs—they do it themselves, or if they really want to be extravagant they buy them new that way. Your granddaughters have shorts like that, though I think Sally cut the pants legs off for them," and she says, "That was no girl, it was a young woman, in her twenties, possibly thirty," and he says, "What can I tell you, Mom; that's the age we live in," and she says, "What do you mean 'age'? That our styles are dominated by cheap women in their twenties and thirties who act like they're thirteen and don't know better?" and he says, "The age of showing off what you have, or what you think you have, anyway. I didn't see this one so I don't know if what she's got is worth showing off. Even if it isn't, and you're saying it should never be, that's the way it is today, I'm afraid. Here"—taking her glass off the table—"drink your drink. You know, though, we cheat a little on this; you're only allowed one every *other* day, doctor's orders—the alcohol doesn't mix with your medications—so make the best of it. Certainly don't leave it undrunk," and she says, "Little chance of that," and takes it from him, raises it, and says, "To long life, happiness, and better days," and he holds out his coffee mug for her to clink and she says, "You're not having one?" and he says, "Never before six or thereabouts," and she says, "I'm retired, so I don't have to worry. I've finished everything I'm going to do, have no energy left to start anything new, and whatever damage there is is done, right?" and she sips a little and puts it down. "It's strong," she says, smiling. "Maybe I should add some water," he says, and she says, "What, and kill it?"

"Oh, I can't believe this," looking outside again, hand on her cheek and head shaking back and forth, and he says, "Another woman in cutoffs?" and she says, "No, this one is in a chemise, or what looks like one. But a real chemise, though worn on the outside and cut high. Or maybe it was intentionally bought too short for her or shrunk, so her navel's showing, and almost see-through if I saw through it right: something for your husband's eyes in the bedroom but not for anyone's on the street. What's going on today? No matter what you said, I don't understand fashions at all." "You didn't wear anything like that when you were young?" he says, looking at the back of the woman as she heads north on the sidewalk. High heels, chemise or look-alike of one, if he's sure what a chemise is—shirtlike underwear?—small waist, and large buttocks. Men passing don't even look at her. He would if he were on the street and wasn't with anyone—or was, and that person was looking somewhere else or, like his mother, encouraged him to look by what she said. "Sure we wore them, but underneath, and often as one more protection against the cold. Remember, we didn't have thermal this-or-that or very good central heating. We didn't wear shorts much then either, and the truth is they weren't so easy to find. As little girls, if we had them, we were permitted to wear them at the beach or in the home, but never on the street. As adults, and I think my first grown-up pair my mother or an aunt made for me, we wore them at a summer resort or beach, with the trouser legs halfway down your thighs and quite loose, so none of your curves showed. This was still plenty revealing enough to draw stares from men, if that's why you wore them and your legs were attractive, which mine were then," and he says, "Why else would you wear them?" and she says, "To be comfortable in the hot weather, what do you think? That was the most important reason—we thought more of comfort then than showing ourselves off like slabs of butcher meat," and he says, "Of course, we're talking about late spring and summer in New York." "That's right. For the curves and displays of flesh, you had your bathing suits, ugly as they were, though we didn't think so then, but only on the beach. And the shorts and tops only with proper lingerie under them, I want you to know, which meant the chemise inside, not out. But I guess everything goes today," and he says, "Seeing what we've been seeing, I guess."

Another young woman walks by outside, and his mother stares at her till she passes, then shakes her head and makes *tsk*ing sounds. "Why, what was wrong with that one? She looked okay to me," and she says, "Her outfit. Around the rear, much too tight. Even with my poor eyes, I could see the crack, and I'm sure, up close, everything. She's asking for it, I'll tell you. Not just for wolf whistles and catcalls but to be propositioned and followed and pinched." "So, maybe that's what she wants," and she says, "If you're right and she wants that, to be pawed at and hounded by the worst scum alive, then what's the world come to? You wouldn't let your daughters . . ."—and she tries snapping her fingers, but they don't snap—"come on, what are their names again?" and he says, "You know their names, what are you doing?" and she says, "I don't for the moment; I'm being honest, I forgot them. Help me, what are they?" and he says, "Fanny and Josephine, or, to make it easier for you, Josie she also goes by, though never from me," and she says, "You wouldn't let Francine and Josephine dress like that if they were older, would you?" and he says, "No, but what could I do if they weren't living with me, or they were but were over sixteen, which will happen soon enough," and she says, "Sixteen? You mean eighteen, don't you? But they should never go around like that, not even when they're in their twenties," and he says, "I wouldn't like it, but after a while you have to give up control and let them take the consequences of their acts. But I'm sure they'll be too smart to dress like that—I'm not so much referring to the one who just passed, who I didn't think was dressed that immodestly, but the chemise one and the one with what you said were very high cut." "Tell me, is it all just physical?" and he says, "I guess a lot of it is today, and probably always was, but now things have really come out . . . or maybe"—because of her perplexed expression—"I don't get what you mean. What did you?" and she says, "Why, what did I say? I forget. This is obviously a bad period for me, not coming up with your daughters' names and now this, but tell me again, what was it?" and he says, "You said, 'Is it all just physical?'" and she says, "Then I did forget what I started out to say, because I don't even remember saying that." "Maybe you meant is life for these young people just physical?—the ones we see passing on the street here. You know, just dressing for one another and having sex and eating and shopping and mostly doing, when they're not working, only physical things: sports, exercising, making the body look better, fitter, trimmer, more attractive, they think: flat abs, fat pecs," and she says, "Yes, that could be what I started out to ask you . . . well, is it?" and he says, "Abs, for abdominals, by the way, is a word I got out of the paper yesterday in an article about that . . . and just that there was such an article, on the money spent because of the emphasis today on getting flat abdominal muscles, says something too about our dumb times. Anyway, I suppose for many of them it is just physical, and more now than ever. They think there's a lot of competition, and if they don't have much up here"—poking his head—"which is the tough part to get, right?—then they better *look* good. It's easier than thinking, in a way, don't you think?—I mean, exercising instead of reading a real book, not dreck, and trying to figure out what it says if it doesn't come right away. But just think if they had a combination of the two, looks *and* brains, though actually the brains part might hurt their chances of landing a mate," and she says, "I never see people carry books anymore, young people, or only a few. But then I don't get out much. Look at that," and he turns around to where she's looking outside and sees two tall thin women approaching, models they look like, one wearing a translucent T-shirt with nothing under it: nipples and surrounding round areas are dark and breasts maybe a little smaller than normal-sized and the shirt's very tight, and the other woman with almost identical long hair and tight white shirt but nothing showing through, and printed in two lines across a fairly flat chest, IF YOU CAN READ THIS YOU'RE NOT CLOSE ENOUGH. "How can she go around like that, the blond one?" and he says, "They're both well-groomed blondes," and she says, "Then the taller of the two, with that shirt," and he says, "You see what the other one had written on hers?" and she says, "No, what?—my eyes," and he says, "Actually, nothing, something about dolphins," and she says, "Well, they're good animals, so that's all right. Don't ask me, though, what the taller one has in her head when she parades down the street like that. But seeing her—the shirt—did it excite you?" and he says, "Jesus, what a question," and she says, "Be honest about it, because I'm only trying to understand why she's doing it if it doesn't do anything to men," and he says, "I'm only one man and a lot older than most around here and happy with his wife, whatever all that's supposed to mean. It's interesting to see, and I've seen it before on the street, though maybe not someone so beautiful. Meaning, she's already a knockout, so I don't know why she has to do it. Anyway, it's interesting seeing the reactions she gets. This time people stared, men and women both. With the chemise lady they didn't," and she says, "That isn't what I meant with my question. But if you don't want to answer because I'm your mother . . ." and he says, "It's not that. If it excited me, I didn't feel it, so maybe it didn't. My eyes, though, they probably liked it for a couple of seconds, but so quickly that it didn't register on the rest of the sensory system. They both—the two women—had crucifixes around their necks, did you see that?" and she says, "Big? Little?" and he says, "Average-sized," and, to himself, Average-sized crucifixes on small to almost normal-sized breasts. "What's it supposed to mean?" she says. "That they're good Christians after all and only want Christian men to follow them and take liberties on the street and so on?" and he says, "Maybe they only wear the crucifix for its design and don't even know what it represents; that could be more the case. Next week, after they've grown bored with the cross, an ankh, and the following week a Star of

David, and the week after that a live snake. But I'm being too hard on them. My daughters would complain if they heard me. They think if someone does something to his body, even mutilating it, that doesn't hurt someone else—forget the pain of disgust—it's okay, and for me not to comment on it. I used to think that how you present yourself in appearance and physical gestures says something about your values and character, but I'm not so sure anymore," and she says, "But that shirt with her breasts in plain view?" and he says, "She could see it as some kind of public equal-rights womanifesto. That if men can go around topless on these crowded commercial streets, which you see more of all the time, then women can too, but, not to push things too quickly because of the rabid counterreaction it might get, in translucent shirts." "Translucent?" and he says, "Semi-transparent, then," and she says, "I no doubt once knew that word, but so much of what was up there and easy to get to is now gone," and he says, "Oh, since I'm just about older than anyone on the street or in the restaurant except you, and also because I drank too much for years and banged my head on hard objects too many times, maybe the same thing's happened to me but worse, and I get half of what I think and say wrong. I can live with it, though," and she says, "It's true that occasionally I'm unsure what you mean and I don't feel it's always my fault.

"Now I've seen everything," his mother says, at the same time trying to cut a bacon strip in half, and he says, "Pick it up and eat it, it's permitted," and she says, "I don't like the grease on my fingers—you can't get it off with a napkin and I don't feel strong enough to go to the washroom," and he knows he's going to have to cut it for her, so do it while the bacon's still warm, and cuts the two strips into several pieces and looks outside, not expecting to see anymore whatever it was she'd pointed to, and sees a young nicely shaped woman with shorts halfway up her buttocks. "That one, Ms. Short-shorts?" and she nods. The woman's standing about ten feet from the window, talking to a couple, with maybe three inches of cheeks sticking out. "It's funny," he says, "but I wonder if she knows that that's exactly what prostitutes wear, downtown, in the wholesale meat district, when they're standing at a corner or walking around looking for customers—shorts like that where a lot of the buttocks show." "When did you witness that?" and he says, "A year ago, last June. Remember? I parked the car a few doors up from your building, was going to take you to lunch, and when we got outside the driver's window had been smashed in and the radio and some clothes stolen." "No, I don't remember, but it was done by a prostitute in shorts like hers?" and he says, "No, there are prostitutes where they sell meat wholesale, packers and slicers and such along the Hudson around Fifteenth and Sixteenth streets. See, you're right, I often do make myself unclear. I should've explained right off that that's where I got the car window replaced a year ago: in the area where these women hang out," and she says, "Why'd you go down there for it? Not to look at the women, I hope," and he says, "I checked the Yellow Pages for car window repair shops. There are plenty of them specializing in it, since there are so many cars broken into, and the one along the Hudson was the cheapest and, as it claimed in the ad, very fast. Took less than an hour. They lived up to their word." "So you think the woman who was standing there is a prostitute from your meat area who's worked her way uptown?" and he says, "Of course not. That's just how some normal nonprostitute young women dress today. Though the fashion could have been influenced in some circuitous way by the street hookers, or maybe the hookers were influenced by Hollywood's depiction of them, since there's been a lot of films and TV stuff on prostitutes and their pimps and johns. But again, with a young woman like her, to attract men and maybe also, with some of them, women, with the part of the body she thinks is her most attractive, and also maybe her legs. She had nice legs from behind, you have to admit that, so maybe she thought an attractive possible mate would say hello to her, turned on by those legs and her outfit and the buttocks showing," and she says, "So what's that say about life today? that's what I want to know," and he says, "Well, it doesn't make things look good or hopeful, and I don't think they'll get better soon. Women like her aren't going to go from dressing like that to reading Tolstoy and thinking deeply about things, though they might, after looking like hookers and thinking like ninnies, go to a convent or more likely a Buddhist retreat—though who wants that? That's seesawing—and, quickly filled with the new diversion, on to some different vacant thing," and she says, "I don't understand. Either you're rambling again or you're discreetly giving me another word for something prostitutes do with their clients, seesawing and diversions and such," and he says, "No, but maybe I'm wrong. Maybe she will go on to Tolstoy—'Get thee to a Tolstoy' might be her inner command—and some kind of deeper thinking about life. What they're doing, showing, and mutilating could only be temporary—meaning the stage of doing that. Then they settle down and sit in restaurant patios like this one and watch people, as we're doing, walking past in provocative clothes, though by then what they see might be much more extreme than what's out there now, but only relatively so." "What do you mean: men and women prancing around nude in a few years, or not nude but just with their genitals exposed? Or, if we're really lucky, only nude from the waist up, but completely?" and he says, "I don't think for women it'll get to that, or so soon. Maybe one exposed breast on especially hot days—there might be street signs saying it's permitted when the temperature rises above ninety—and in any season or weather at private parties and clubs. Or two exposed nipples but not the rest of the breasts, so some sort of specially designed shirt. Or just the breasts but not the nipples—pasties, but without the sparkles and tassels, though for evening wear, high fashion might say with. But who can say? And men coming to parties and restaurants, and when they take their jackets off they have no shirts on. Maybe just suspenders, or pasties, or only a shirt collar and necktie, like comedians in old-time burlesque. But I think that's as far as it'll go in the next few years." "I'm glad my life is almost over. I don't want to live in a world like that," and he says, "It's easy to ignore, or should be: just turn away, or, like my kids say, if it's physically harmless to everyone else—forget what it does to the person doing it—it's okay. But of course not everyone will go around like that. There'll still probably be a normal unisex wing in each department store to get regular clothes, or what we'll think of as regular," and she says, "Now you're kidding me, aren't you?" and he says, "Okay, maybe I am."

She's about to stick a tomato wedge into her mouth and he's about to say the wedge is too large to take in all at once, when her eyes bulge, she drops the fork to the plate, and he thinks, Something wrong with her? and she says, "I can't believe it," and her face relaxes, and he thinks, Oh, outside again, I can't look, it's getting too repetitive and embarrassing, and she says, "Here I thought I saw everything, but not this—I didn't even think of it as a possibility," and he says, "Let me guess without turning around. And which way is he or she walking, away from you or toward?" and she says, "Neither, and it's not walking. And it's *they* because there are two of them, young women, one a little butchlike so almost a man, kissing passionately on the lips and with their arms around each other and embracing hard." "Oh!" and he turns around quickly. They're rubbing each other's behinds too. People have to walk around them, not noticing, it seems. But of course most are pretending not to notice. Or they think it's normal in a way if they think the butch one's a man: she's dressed a lot like one: long baggy pants, men's shoes and leather belt, and man's plaid short-sleeved shirt. Also her watch and the keys hanging off a belt clip. "Now that *is* unusual, I have to say that," he says. The couple disembrace, just stare at each other lovingly as if they're going to do that awhile, and then kiss passionately again. "But not so unusual because of what I think's the reason for it. Meaning, the chances of seeing it today—and tomorrow and the next day, if I'm not mistaken—are a lot greater than what they were a few days ago or will be a few days from now. Because I saw posters on lampposts the last few days announcing what it says is an International Dykes March tomorrow. That's what the posters called it; I'm not maligning them by using that word. So no doubt lots of lesbians and their supporters have come into the city from all over the world to march in it; it's going to start at the U.N. complex and end up here with a rally in Central Park. So you have a greater number of them in New York than usual—a gay ladies' convention of sorts. And they feel freer and more powerful than they ever have because of their numbers and the message behind the march. And they're also maybe feeling gayer, meaning jollier, because there is such a large gathering of them, almost like a party, that—" and she says, "Let's get out of here, will that be all right? It's too late in the lunch to switch tables to one inside, but I can't take seeing any of this anymore. People with dozens of rings in one ear, one man who passed with what looked like a big fishhook in his lip, though I might have seen wrong. I neglected to point out those—I thought you had enough—besides all the tattoos young people are polluting their arms and shoulders with, and it seems one girl an entire side of her face," and he says, "Some of those wash off in a few days. My daughters told me that, when like you I brought up the subject," and she says, "Well, that's good to know, something temporary; the best news all day. And I've eaten plenty, more than I normally do at home. Because who knows what we'll see next on the street. Two people copulating on top of a car, I'm afraid," and he says, "Now you're talking like me: exaggerating. But if you want to leave, and this is upsetting you so much, we'll go. You ate a good lunch. The doctor said you've lost too much weight lately and should eat more, and you had rolls, most of your bacon, they gave a nice side order of it, and two eggs," and she says, "Everything was very tasty." "And the lettuce and tomato and shaved carrot sliver that came with it, or the tomato other than what's still on your fork. Good. That's almost a lunch and dinner for you. And a nice balance of foods too—meat, veggies, eggs, butter, and bread—and lots of water, which he said he wants you to drink. We can go somewhere else for coffee and some fruit dessert," and she says, "No, this whole window picture show all of a sudden has nearly sickened me and I want to go home to my room and rest." "You're tired?" and she says yes. "You want to use the ladies' room before we go?" and she says, "Oh, God, no, even if I did, who knows what I'd find in there," and he says, "I'm sure that behavior's only confined to the street," and she laughs, and he asks for the bill, waitress says, "Everything all right? You didn't finish," and he says, "No, there was a lot," and pays up and gets the wheelchair to the street, pushes it open and locks the wheels, and watches it as he walks his mother to the door and outside. "My pocketbook?" and he says, "You didn't bring one," and she says, "Why not?" and he says, "You didn't need one," and she says, "I used to pay, after your father died," and he says, "Well, those days are over; now it's my turn," and she says, "Then for my tissues," and he says, "Before we left the house, I put some in your shirt pocket." "It could have been stolen, the chair," she says, sitting in it, "leaving it alone outside for even a short time," and he says, "It's an old one. Damn, it was Dad's, so who'd want to take it?" and she says, "Why? Who can say what disgusting things they could think of doing in it," and he says, "Now you're going too far, Mom, and it's no good for you; way too far," and she says, "Perhaps, but if not, what then?" and he says, "I've no idea what you mean," and unlocks the brakes and starts pushing her.

On the way home she points to two men walking past holding hands, and he says, "Same march and mood, maybe: backup support.

But don't point, please; they might see and say something," and she says, "I don't think they'd care; they had eyes only for each other. . . . Look at her," she says on the next block, about a young woman on Rollerblades with a biking outfit and helmet on, or maybe it's a special Rollerblades outfit or they're so close to being the same or are the same that it's sold in sports shops as a Rollerblades-biking outfit, but so tight he can make out the genital pubic hair pushed down. She glides by them so fast that he's sure she didn't see his mother pointing or hear what she said, and he says, "Did you mean—though again, don't talk about it so loud—her outfit or just that she was on Rollerblades or roller-blading on the sidewalk so fast when she should have been on the street?" and she says, "Don't pretend to be dim, for what do you think?" A little boy in Pampers walking in front of his parents: "Cute as he is," she says, "you'd think the least they could do in a so-called civilized city is put shorts over his diapers. But I'm from the old school. Scolds like me won't be around long to annoy people with their outdated sensibilities and rules and complaints," and he says, "No, no, just about everything you said so far about what you saw has some validity to it. But there's little we can do about it, and you certainly don't want to make a scene in the street. As for the kid in Pampers, or even if they were real diapers—I'd actually prefer it if they were; better for everything, the environment and the cotton industry and the kid—well, as for that, it didn't bother me, I don't know why. Maybe I'd feel different if it had stuff running out of it," and she says, "That's partly my point. With a pair of shorts or pants over the diapers, you're covered for that and don't have to subject passersby to even thinking it could happen," and he says, "Okay, I see, and a point worth taking," and she says, "You're only trying to make me feel good now, and it won't work."

They get to her building, he helps her out of the chair, carries it down the areaway steps while she holds on to the railing at the top, then helps her downstairs and wheels her inside. She says she wants to nap and he gets her on the bed, says, "Want the blinds closed?" and she says, "If you could," and he closes them and says, "I'll see you tomorrow for lunch, though I'll call to find out how you feel first." She smiles, shuts her eyes, looks peaceful as if she's already asleep, face without the strain it had from almost the first minute on the street.

Lines

NO LINE COMES. He sits for a long time, waiting and sometimes working, but no line comes. He walks around the house, people in it see him and say, "What are you doing?" and he says, "Shh, I'm thinking," and thinks, Let a line come while I'm walking, but none does. Outside, in: none. Opens the refrigerator and takes a slice of cheese out of the wrapping the pound of Swiss came in and shoves it into his mouth and thinks, Okay, you've been satisfied, your hunger at least, so let a line come. Goes upstairs, sits down at his card table again, and says, "Line, come . . . now. Okay, then line . . . come . . . *now.*" Says, "No line wanna come? Okay, later." Goes back to the refrigerator and stuffs two more slices of Swiss into his mouth, thinks, Now I'm more than satisfied, I'm sated, so let a line come. One comes best when I'm hungry, but that didn't work, nor when I was just satisfied, so let it come when I'm full, overfull, have had too much cheese and really, considering . . . considering what? I was going to say, "considering the breakfast I had," but I didn't have any: just black coffee and half a toasted bagel with nothing on it, so just too much cheese. Sits at the kitchen table and waits; none comes. Takes out his pad and pen and tries working: nothing. Let line come, he thinks. Line, you come! Says, "Let the line in. Let the great or any kind of line come in and be in and be anything it wants to be, but just to be, that's all, and I'll take it from there. Line, where are you, where art thou, wherever you are or art, yoo-hoo, let me see you, so come. Calling all lines. This is Gould to line: come in, please; over. Now line, come now. This sec. This is the sec for all good lines or just any kind of line to come. Or come in the next few secs or so, I won't mind. Hey, I can be a patient man regarding lines, just test me. Or come in the next thirty secs, but sooner if you can, though later if you want—don't want you to think I'm pushing you—but please, not too much later. My heart, my heart—only kidding. Or really come when you want, but come now. I mean really come when you want but, if you can, come now or soon. A minute, two, line to start a whole thing with—there, cat's out of the bag, now if only a line was—but come. Okay, I'll just wait," and thinks, Okay, wait, go upstairs and sit at your desk and wait, and goes upstairs, sits at the card table, and shuts his eyes. Shutting my eyes might help it come, he thinks, and keeps his eyes shut when they want to open. Thinks, What do I see? Maybe what I see will be the line to start the whole thing off with. "Cat out of the bag" one? No. I see my daughters. Then just one: "Hi," the youngest says. Is that the line? Opens his eyes and writes *Hi,* and it isn't. Just one word, is it even a line? Well, by his standards it is, and even if it isn't he'd take it if it were the one. Try two. He writes *Hi, Daddy,* and it isn't. Try more: and he writes: *"Hi, Daddy," one of his daughters says, and he looks up; it's the younger, she's at the door holding some manuscript pages and says, "Could you type these for me?" and he says, "What is it, sweetie, because I'm busy," and she says, "Chapter five of my novel* Amily,*" and he says, "Emily?" and she says, "No, Amily, for 'I am,' get it? 'Am' for me and 'ily' for an end to a name like Emily but not that. Someone told me 'Amily' also sounds like the French word for friend, and the Amily in my novel is my friend, or has become one since I started writing about her, and she's a very friendly girl and I hope will become the friend of the people who read her," and he says, "You mean, your readers," and she says, "The readers of* Amily, *the book, my novel. You know who she is. You typed all my Amily chapters," and he says, "But she wasn't named Amily before, was she?" and she says, "First she was Amelia. And once she was Emily, and in another chapter she was Emma, or in two of them. But they all sounded so ordinary for a main character's name, and there were already too many Emmas and Emilys and one Amelia in books and stories I read. So I thought, Why not Amelia with an* E *for the first letter? But that didn't look right as a name—it seemed too fake or false—so I ended up with Amily, which has parts of all those names and also the French word 'friend' and the English word 'am,' for 'I am,' though the novel isn't about me, it's made up. All of that I thought of after I finally took Amily, which I got by thinking and thinking of a good name. I sat hard in my room, or rather I thought hard while I sat in my room," and he says, "At your desk?" and she says, "Yes, and the name just came, and when it did I knew it was the right one from now on." "I like it," he says, "a name I've never heard of but really should have. Because you'd think, after thousands of years of different first names, parents would have made it up by now or formed it from some other name or thing—'friendship,' as you said, but in French, or some word in English. Amity's the only one I can think of now that has a-m-i in it, which must come from the French, which probably comes from the Latin—*amicus, *is it?" and she says, "I wouldn't know, what does it mean?" and he says, "Well, amity means friendship, and* amicus, *if I'm right, probably means the same thing or something close to it—friend, friendliness, fried foods? But you're allowed to do that with names, make them up when you write novels and stories, don't ask me how I know." "But you will type it?"—waving the pages—and he says yes and she puts them on the table he's sitting at and he says, "Though not right this moment, you understand," and she says, "I've time. I won't be starting the next chapter till tomorrow," and leaves and he writes, The line, the line, did it come, is "Hi, Daddy," for instance, the line? It isn't. Does any of that stuff with his daughter have the line in it? It doesn't.*

It really happened, in somewhat the same way, this morning. All right, a lot different. She threw open the door, scaring him, said, "Hi, Daddy," he said, "I'm working," she said, "Should I go away?" and he said, "You can say what you came to say," and she asked him to type chapter five of her novel *Amily.* He hasn't yet and told her he couldn't right away. "First things first," he said, "and excuse me but my things before yours before a certain time of the day, say—at least today—around one or two? After that, if I haven't just started working frantically on something of my own or am in the middle of it and zinging to a finish, I'll type it gladly. And if I do what I have to before one or two, I'll type your work even earlier than I thought." "Okay," she said, and started to leave, and he said, "One more thing, sweetie. Try knocking lightly on my door next time, don't just barge in. I don't want to say you'll help give me a heart attack—that'll just scare you—but it does startle me sometimes. Remember that, and now please shut the door," and she did. She'll knock hard or burst through the door around one or two, if he's still here, and ask if he's typed her chapter, and he'll say no, if he hasn't, but will type it by the end of the day, he promises, or certainly before she starts chapter six tomorrow, and please no more knocking on his door so hard or bursting into the room.

Shuts his eyes, thinks, Think again, just a single line to get things going, and pictures—she pops into his mind; he doesn't draw her up intentionally—his other daughter. "May I use your typewriter?" she says, and he says, "God, you scared the hell out of me," and she says, "I'm sorry, but you're so shaky. You drink too much caffeine coffee," and he says, "It's not that. Anyone would be jumpy if someone comes up on him from behind, when his eyes are closed and he's thinking deeply, and suddenly says something. Both of you—your sister . . . how come Mommy and I failed to make you aware of older people's delicate nerves and to teach you to tap lightly on the doors of people's rooms before entering? So do that with the door from now on, or make a lot of noise coming up the stairs, so I'll know you're out there and I'll be prepared if you suddenly open my door—you did that okay, nice and gently—and say something to me. Now, what is it you wanted?" and she says, "You don't seem in a good mood to do it," and he says, "What, come on, what?" and she says, "Now you're even angrier," and he says, "Will you stop that? I feel all right, not angry, look, my face: no anger; no smile either, but I don't feel like smiling and neither do you. We can't just put one on. We're not that kind of family. Your mother isn't that way for sure, and I inherited that trait from her," and she says, "That's impossible," and he says, "You're right, and you know what? That last little run of words of mine made me feel much better, so what is it you came here for, honestly?" and she says, "You made me forget. I know it was for something important." "My typewriter, right? Don't ask me how I know.

I'm afraid I can't; I never let anyone use it," and she says, "I only need it for a little while, and I'm your daughter, not *anyone*. Besides, even if I had wanted to bring my word processor with us, you wouldn't have let me. You kept complaining there wasn't room in the car for anything but the most important things, like your box of wine and typewriter and tons of your papers and yours and Mommy's books and only our most necessary clothes," and he says, "Maybe only to my daughters and wife I might loan it for a short time, but it'd have to be very important. What do you want it for?" and she says, "A letter to a friend. She wrote me one on her father's typewriter, also from the country at their cottage, and I wanted to type mine back to her. It'd only be fair. My cursive is horrible to read, and printing a letter is babyish and would take too long." "I'm sorry, but this typewriter, since I only brought one of mine up here, is too indispensable to me to risk injuring it with a personal letter you want to write. You kids type on it too hard and keep jamming the keys," and she says, "I won't." "Now, if it was for something to your school or a job application you needed to write or anything like that—" and she says, "You're so selfish and mean and you won't even trust me when I promise," and he says, "You didn't let me finish," and she says, "Were you going to say that despite all that, blah blah, you'll let me borrow it?" and he says, "No, but—" and she leaves and slams the door. "You didn't have to slam it," he says. He gets up, throws the door open, and she's downstairs by now and he yells down them, "You didn't have to slam the door, Fanny. It didn't scare me half to death, but it doesn't reflect well on you, I'll tell you, not one bit. I don't like that kind of reaction, that uncontrolled anger. And you have to understand that if my typewriter broke up here it'd take weeks to get repaired. I'd probably have to buy another one during that time, just to have something to work on, because they're very slow to get typewriter parts where we are—in the whole state of Maine, in fact—and I bet I'd have to drive to Massachusetts to buy a new manual one," and she says, "Then bring two of them and maybe then you wouldn't mind me using one, or let me take my word processor next time," and he says, "Maybe you're right. Okay, I'll do that next summer—your word processor. Or I'll take or UPS up a second manual typewriter. And okay also, you can use this one, but not right now, okay? When I'm done, in a half hour or hour at the most, all right, Fanny?" and she comes to the stairs and says, "Thank you," and smiles, and he says, "Good, we're old pals again, and I know you'll be extra careful with it: just your fingers on the keys, no elbows or toes," and she says, "Don't worry, Daddy, I won't step on it."

He opens his eyes. Something close to that happened yesterday when he was also looking for a line, couldn't come up with one, gave up for the time being, and went downstairs for coffee and to read and maybe a quick swim, and said to her, "It's all yours," and she took the typewriter to her room, banged away on it for about an hour, and then put it back on the card table. He went to his study right after, not to try and think up a line—by this time he knew he was through for the day—but to check on the shape of the typewriter, and everything was fine, keys weren't stuck and cover had been neatly put on, and then went downstairs and thought, No swim, sky's turned gray, and started to prepare salad for supper. But anything in those scenes he can use today? Doesn't think so, and if there was he probably would have tried using them yesterday. The stuff after he went downstairs and told her she could use the typewriter now? No. A line, he means, or several of them to start off with? Not that he can think of. Afraid not. Not at this present moment. Sorry.

What now? Two days and nothing. Looks up, cups his hands in prayer, and says, "A line, Sir, or a line, Madam or Miss, *gibt mir ein* line, please. All I need is one, I swear, and away I go and am forever grateful and maybe even a believer. And I'll be especially fast. Not that time means anything special to You. But my older daughter might want to use the typewriter for another letter—she's an avid correspondent—and she was so careful with it yesterday that I want to give it to her today without a second thought if she asks and even suggest to her she use it if she doesn't bring it up herself." Types: *No second thoughts?* No. Types: *Use it if you want, honey, you were great with it the last time?* Nah. *Without a fuss he wants to give the machine to her? He wants to give the typewriter to his daughter without a second thought but can't? He suddenly started to become a believer over the most simple experience?* Closes his eyes. Maybe now, he thinks, it's quiet, and they often come when you least expect them. *Maybe now is the time for all good lines to come to the aid of their linemakers,* he thinks of using. Did that. Says, "Line, goddamn you, appear!" His wife comes; his eyes are still closed. She says, "I hope I'm not disturbing you." "Disturbing me? No chance. But how'd you get here? The stairs are so steep. Anyway, this is great. Where are the kids? Out with friends for the afternoon, I bet." "Oh, sure; don't you wish. Anyway, I was wondering—" and he says, "But really, how'd you get up here? then wonder," and she says, "Walked." "Walked?" "Crawled and walked." "Crawled?" "Stop mimicking everything I say." "Stop repeating everything you say?" "Listen, don't be annoying; I made it somehow and am now here." "Finally," he says, "progress. Oh, what am I doing? Here, come kiss me. Or I'll come to you, since you're probably too tired after all that crawling and walking to come any farther to me. What is your name?" he says, getting up and walking over and standing beside her. "And you're standing! How were you able to do that?" "I stood." "And you don't have to tell me your name. I know it. Your name is line. *Mein* line *hast komm*. My line has come. You know German; I don't. My wonderful kind line has finally come. But I'll go to her. Oops, I forget, I'm already standing beside her. I went, after it came up to me, and am now beside my line." Smooths back her hair. "And a beauty of a line it is, too. Line, how are you, how you doing, line? I am going to line you because you came all the way up to me and stood and kept standing despite what I know are tremendous difficulties." "What's come over you, Gould? You sound positively bonkers." "Positively. Right. And why? Because I've been longing for my line for a long time. Because my line finally came. Because—" "Because you're saying what you're saying. Listen, all I came up here for and was wondering about is when are we going swimming?" "You want to go swimming? You mean in the Y pool?" "No, in the lake." "How can you? You haven't been in it for years." "Well, I want to go now. I came up here, I'm standing, I want to swim in the lake. So I'm asking you when we can. Now? Soon? I'd take the car myself but it's been so long since I've driven that I've forgotten how." "Okay, soon," he says, and kisses her. First he embraces her. Before that he feels her. "Yes, it's you, all of you," he said while he was feeling her. "Your thighs, buttocks, back. Your shoulders, head, neck. I'm telling you, it's you, really you. Your waist, pubic area, breasts. And your name's Sally and I've been silly." Opens his eyes. Did a line come? Thinks. Surely out of so much, there had to be one. In spite of what he said about a line coming up, no. "Silly Sally? Sally Silly?"

Those aren't lines. Or they're lines, but they're not . . . anyway, it's not working. Maybe his mom.

Shuts his eyes: nothing. Opens them, flutters the lids, shuts them, and his mom comes. Dressed for travel, short-winded and frazzled, sweating, setting down a valise. "How I carried that, I don't know." *How'd I ever carry that, I don't know* as a line? No. Gets up, dabs her forehead with a hanky, sits her in his chair, and kisses her cheek. "You leave me in the hot city. I'm not blaming you, I suppose nothing else could've been done, but I can die there from the heat." "Mom, I feel lousy about it as it is, don't make me feel worse. Can I get you a cold drink?" "And die from loneliness mostly, forget the heat. Just me and the girl who looks after me. She's very nice but not company enough." "I'm sorry, I can't tell you how much, and wish I could make life comfortable and enjoyable for you always." "As I said, it's no one's fault. But not to see you and your three girls for two months is something like death to me." "We only left New York two weeks ago and I call you every day. And I've been reading the *Times* daily weather forecasts, though since the paper's mailed here it always arrives the next day, and they haven't said the city's been that hot. In fact the weather the past week, according to these reports, and in the whole Northeast—" "Hot, I'm telling you, sticky and hot. If you're out and in the sun for five minutes once it gets to be noon, you feel yourself boiling in your skin. I'd take one shower after the next if I was allowed to, but the girl only lets me have one a day." "Anyway, you look great and you got to Maine on your own. I can't imagine how." "I took the plane. Got a limo to LaGuardia and a cab from your airport to here. I forgot how long a trip it is. Though I can understand why you take your vacation so far out of the way. Less chance for people to invite themselves for a night or weekend or just drop in." "Believe me, that's just a small part of it, and you and Sally's folks are the exceptions." "It was always what I looked forward to most all year, since you started coming here. One and sometimes two weeks, if I was a really good girl, in the country with just you and the birds and insects—they didn't bother me—and of course your precious family." "I didn't think you were well enough to make the trip this year, just as you weren't last summer. You have to know how that hurts me, leaving you in the city with no chance of relief. But now you're here." "Now I'm not, my darling," and she disappears. Opens his eyes. Anything? He feels so sad; can he use that? Doesn't see how, but has to be something there. Isn't. "Signed, Desperate," he says, his finger writing it out in the air. Thinks, Three days can get to be something like an incurable disease. Think. Nobody left, maybe the cat.

Shuts his eyes. The cat comes in. "No one will let me outside. I've scratched the doors and screens and walked from front door to patio door and back and then kept making my little wanna-go-out meows while pressed up against the door, and still no one can tell what I want. Or else they're just too lazy to move a few feet to let me out." "Why didn't you say so?" he says, and goes downstairs. "Line," he shouts, "you coming?" The cat bounds down the stairs. He opens the door and lets him out. "Thanks," Line says. "Finally someone figured things out, but I had to talk in his language for him to," and runs into the woods. "Don't get lost," he yells. "I don't want to spend a few hours tramping through the woods shouting and looking for you. Line, I'm saying to stay close to home and I also want you to come back when I call." The cat jumps out of the woods and stares at him. "No, I'm not calling you back now. I was just saying not to get lost, and I also want you to watch out for those killer coyotes. You hear them howling, run right home. Howling in the woods, I mean, but not from very far away." "What do you think, I'm stupid?" and runs back into the woods. Opens his eyes, quickly closes them. "In fact the moment you hear any coyote-howling, from no matter how far away, come home. Whatever you do, don't try and fight them." The cat doesn't reappear. Opens his eyes. Any of that good for a line? Tried—and the real cat's name is Flash—but nothing there or that he can now discern. Anything else he can use for one? Can't think of any, and his time's up. Or thirty minutes is. Actually, just twenty, but he knows when to call it a day, or at least an early afternoon. So, later maybe, when he's out walking or driving or swimming in the lake or even sitting back here, the line will come.

"Fanny, you still there?" he yells from the chair. "What?" she yells upstairs. "I can't hear you." He goes to the top of the stairs and says, "You can use the typewriter now, sweetheart. I'm done a little early," and she says, "Why would I want to?" "You said you wanted to write a letter," and she says, "What are you talking about? I don't want to write a letter, not now anyway." "I meant you wanted to type one," and she says, "Type one? Why would I want to on an old typewriter that isn't even electric when I can write one by hand in a comfortable chair somewhere?" "Okay, you don't want to type a letter. And I suppose Josephine doesn't want me to type out the new chapter of her novel," and she says, "How would I know? Ask her yourself." "Can you call her to the stairs for me, please?" and she yells, "Josie, come here, Daddy wants you," and Josephine comes, and he says, "Did you want me to type the fifth chapter of your novel *Amily?*" "Yeah, I asked you before; did you do it already?" and he says, "No, but it shouldn't take me long. You want to get it?" and she runs upstairs to her room and brings it out and gives it to him. "Your mother, I know, wasn't also up here, right?" and she says, "Upstairs? That's a mean joke, Daddy." "I didn't mean it as one, I'm sorry," and she goes downstairs shaking her head, and he sits at his table, puts her chapter to the left of the typewriter, the side he always reads from when he types, and starts typing it: "It started on a cold, winter day." Does she need the comma after "cold"? He doesn't think so but types it the way she wrote it, except for the more conspicuous spelling mistakes.

His Mother

HE GOES TO see her. Lets himself in, says, "Hello, it's Gould, I'm here." Woman who takes care of her says, "We're back here, mister." Goes to the back of the apartment. His mother's in bed. Blinds are closed, room's dark. "How come she's still in bed?" he says, opening the blinds of one window, and Angela says, "She said she wanted to sleep." "But it's past noon, I came to take her out to lunch." "She said she doesn't want to go to lunch. I asked her this morning. She said she only wants to sleep." "Did she have a rough night?" and she says, "No, it was fine. She might be tired from some other nights." "Mom, Mom"—shaking her shoulder—and she opens her eyes, not the usual smile or glad-to-see-you expression, says, "Oh, hello. What is it? Not today, Gould, I'm too tired." "But you can't just sleep all day. You got to get out. You need air, you need food, you need exercise," and she says, "I can sleep if I'm tired. Right now I'm no good for anything else." "But we had a date for lunch. I told you yesterday. You like lunch. You'll have a drink." "A drink would be nice; would I be allowed to? But another time. I'm too tired for one now, and it'll only make me sleepier." "Have you had breakfast?"—

raising the blinds of the one he opened—and she says, "The light. Please let me sleep. What am I asking?" "But look at the light; it's beautiful. And breakfast. Have you had it today?" and she says, "Breakfast? Sure. I think so. Ask the girl," and closes her eyes. "Has she?" and Angela says, "I made it for her, sat her up in the chair, two hours ago, right after I got her back from the potty. But she said she didn't feel like eating and then started dozing on me, so I put her back in bed." "This is no good, really," and she says, "I know, but if she says she's so tired? I didn't think I should force her to eat. That'd be worse. When they're tired, little here, little there, that's the best, I found." "I meant, sleeping all day isn't good," and she says, "Oh, that. I know that too but I didn't see anything else I could do. But she's not starving, you know. When she doesn't have breakfast, she has a big lunch."

He raises the other blinds without opening them first. "Mom, come on, really, we're going to lunch. We have to," and she says, "Why?" "Because it's good for you. You'll see. Just getting out and seeing daylight and other people and being in a restaurant and eating is good," and she says, "Not the way I look." "So you'll look better. Angela will help you with your hair and a shower if you didn't have one; now you just look like you've been sleeping." "Some other time, please, darling." "No, today, and I'm hungry. Come on, Mom," even though he thinks maybe she *is* better off in bed; he could be pushing her too hard. Who was it? Sybil, his wife's friend, who pushed her mother on a vacation—sort of forced her to see more and more Mayan ruins when the woman that day just wanted to sit by the pool or in the motel room and nap and read—and she got a stroke and died, and she was—what?—a young woman, not even sixty. But if she sleeps it means she won't eat or exercise or get any fresh air, and she'll be bored—you lose interest in life, you lose your life, or something like that; at least it doesn't help you at that age, that's for sure. She should get up and out; he's almost positive she should. "What should I do?" he says to Angela. "You gotta do what you gotta do, I suppose. I think she's had enough sleep and the air will do her good if it's not too hot." "It's mild; it's okay. Mom, really, we'll have a good time. I promise I won't keep you out too long or push you. We'll go slow. And just say the word and back we'll go." "I'm not really hungry today. If you are, the girl can prepare you something here."

"Before you came she did say she didn't have an appetite," Angela says. "You'll do fine once you're in a restaurant," he says to his mother. "First a drink: Jack Daniels on the rocks, little water, twist of lemon; that's your favorite, isn't it?" and she smiles and says, "You know what I like. I always thought it was the best. What is it, a bourbon, a rye? I never know what to call it." "It's a sour mash, I think, which is close to a bourbon." "They once sent me glasses," and he says, "I remember, with the Jack Daniels logo on them." "They were good glasses, too. It was some campaign and the liquor store man said . . . where was I at the time?" "You were in a liquor store," he says, "the one on Columbus, down the block, that isn't there anymore. I remember the story. Buying a bottle of Jack Daniels—a quart—and the salesman from Jack Daniels was there, and the liquor store man said to him, 'She's one of our best customers for your Daniels,' and the man from Daniels said, 'Then just fill out this slip, ma'am'—you said he had a Southern accent but I don't see how that could be so." "It was so long ago, I forgot the story. They must've thought I was a real *shikker*; why else would you give away something like that? But I never really drank that much, and I certainly don't now. I just happen to prefer Jack Daniels over all those scotches and bourbons and whatever you called that one. But is that how I got those highball glasses, they were for highballs, though I used them for water when guests were here. They took ice well. Me, I like my Jack Daniels in a shorter squatter glass—" "An old-fashioned glass," he says, and she says, "Yes, one of those. But that was very nice of them to do. It came from Kentucky, the package, and was insured. The postman brought it to the door and I had to sign for it. Eight of them in a box. I didn't think I'd ever get them. You never do when you just fill out a slip and don't pay money. And it was pure luck. I walked into the store at the same time the Jack Daniels salesman from Kentucky was in it, selling to the store, I think he was doing. And his company had this campaign, this promotional campaign he called it, and the store salesman probably put in a good word for me because he knew I only bought Jack Daniels and only from him, and I got on the list. I think I still have those glasses." "No, they're all broken by now," he says. "Too bad. They were good glasses. I didn't use them for my Jack Daniels drinks but I did for beer and soda, though they aren't the appropriate glasses for beer. Those are different, and which

I once had plenty of but they all must have broken by now too. Mugs, steins . . . the tall ones shaped like cones. . . .” “Pilsner glasses, I think you mean. Did I ever tell you of the time I was on a train in Czechoslovakia, Sally and Fanny when she was an infant and I, drinking a Pilsner beer in a Pilsner glass, and when I looked out the window at the station we'd just pulled into . . .” She starts closing her eyes and he says, “Anyway, good memory, Mom, amazing. You got everything. It's wonderful the way you were able to bring that scene back. Now Angela and I will get you out of bed and she'll give you a shower and help you brush your hair. Then you and I will go to Rupert's and get a drink and some lunch, and after that I'll push you into the park and we'll sit at our favorite spot, that food kiosk by Sheep Meadow. It'll be cooler there than anywhere in the park, that I know of—” “I don't think I'm up to all that. I'll even skip the drink. I'm too tired to do anything now but sleep.” “You don't have to do anything. Angela and I will get you up. She'll give you a shower and help you dress. All you have to do is sit on that stool in the shower. She'll even dry you if you're too weak. Then I'll get you in the wheelchair and to the street and into the restaurant. Or you can walk behind the chair and push it a little for exercise; by that time you might feel able to. You'll see; you'll end up appreciating that I practically forced you to go. You need the change of scenery. Everyone does.” “You're right. It's so monotonous here, but I doubt I'll make it to every place you say you want to take me.” “You'll make it, you'll make it. Now, upsy-daisy, Mom, ready?” and she shakes her head and looks as if she's about to cry, and he says, “Come on, what's wrong? You're okay, maybe still a little tired and confused from too much sleep, but you're ready,” and lifts her from the back, sits her up, and swings her around so her feet rest on the floor. “Now we've started. We can't turn around now, can we?” “Okay,” she says. “You're too convincing. But I don't want to be out for very long. My body couldn't take it. I feel too weak.”

On the street she pushes the wheelchair about twenty feet toward Columbus Avenue and then says, “Something's not working, I can't go any further. Let me sit,” and he says, “That was hardly any exercise at all. Just walk to the corner, or halfway to it from here,” and she says, “I'm about to fall any second right here; I feel it,” and he quickly helps her sit, gets her feet on the footrests, and pushes the chair down the block. Someone walking a dog passes, and she says, "Do you know what that woman is?" and he says, "Oh, not again, Mom," and she says, "A dog walker. I never knew such people existed, but they walk dogs for a living." "Listen, as I've told you many times before, why do you think one person walking a dog is a professional dog walker? If she had five or six dogs, or three or four, and all of them on different kinds of leashes, I could see her being one. But the odds are she's just the dog's owner," and she says, "Oh, no, I've heard. She's a dog walker. It's a profession I never knew of till someone told me. It's an interesting thing to do, walk someone else's dog, and you'd get lots of fresh air and exercise and get to meet lots of people walking their dogs, and it seems easy to do. Hey, do you think they'd give an old lady like me the job? I'd love it," and he says, "Sure, you can do it from your chair." "That's right, I could," and she smiles. "I'm sorry, that was a mean joke, and I didn't intend it as such. I don't know what I was saying," and she says, "No, it was funny, and you're right, and I could make extra money. If I do get anything from it I'll give it all to you. I don't need it anymore. Dog walkers, though. It's something, really something to think about. All these new things."

At the corner she says, "See those windows?" and he looks across the street where she's pointing and says, "Which ones?" "All. The entire building has new windows, you don't see? They're a new kind. They never get dirty, outside or in." "I don't see the difference from regular windows, and their frames don't look new," and she says, "Oh, yes, someone told me about it. Very expensive to put in, but in the long run it pays off. Special wires or fibers in them you can't see that always keep the panes shiny and clean. I never knew such things existed. I should replace my old windows with them. They also keep the cold out better and the heat in, so you save on fuel and electrical bills, and it'd mean no window washers every fall and spring. That I'd really be thankful for. With them, you make an appointment and then wait around all day and they rarely show up. But I'm an old lady and I'd be throwing away money on the new windows, since I won't be around long enough to take advantage of the savings." "What are you saying? You'll be around plenty long; you'll outlive me. You're healthy most of the time, just a little weak today and probably from the heat. If you want those windows or more information about them, I'll look into it," and she says, "No, it's too late."

On Columbus, couple of blocks from the restaurant, she points across the avenue and says, "They put in all new fire escapes there. It's the city law now," and he says, "Where, which building? They all look the same to me," and she says, "The green one." "Green?" and she says, "Well, maybe not green—my eyes—but that dark one I'm pointing to. It used to be a landlord could have either inside sprinklers or fire escapes; that was the fire law. But now the law says you need both. So that building there had to install them." "Mom, those fire escapes are old; they've been there since I was a kid," and she says, "Oh, no, they were only recently put on, two months ago, maybe three. It's the law now, but only for apartment buildings of up to six stories. It was because of some terrible fire last year where several children died. I don't know how they think they're going to save those kids from the taller buildings. Maybe they think every building seven stories and up has elevators, but that's what's happening." "If you say so. But if those fire escapes are new, then something's already wrong with the paint job they did, for even from here I can see it's peeling." "Don't kid me, you can't see that well from so far. But every building of that size and lower will have to have them, mine too, of course. It's going to ruin the architecture of this neighborhood and cost the landlords a fortune. A city of fire escapes, it'll come to be known as. Ugly and creepy, like everywhere you look, skeletons. And in back too if the building isn't made up completely of floor-through apartments, which the majority aren't. I'll have to take out an enormous second loan."

A half block from the restaurant they bump into a friend of his mother's. "How are you, Mrs. Silbert?" he says. His mother just stares up at the woman, and he says, "Mom, your friend, Marjorie Silbert," and his mother says, "Hello, how have you been? It's so good to see you," and shakes the woman's hand, and the woman says, "I'm fine, thanks. I've wanted to come by, Bea, but haven't been my old self lately. But soon," and his mother says, "Good, we'd love having you. Come for dinner. Call beforehand, and I'll make sure the girl prepares something nice for us and goes out for some schnapps." "Your mother's looking well," the woman says, "she's feeling well too?" and he says, "Seems to be," and his mother says, "What am I, a ghost? Ask me and I'll tell you. I'm tired, dear, then more tired. It must be the weather because it can't be my age. Otherwise, no complaints, especially when my son's in town for a while and his lovely family. You know Gould, don't you?" and the woman says, "You're lucky to have family around even for a short time. My two won't come near New York," and kisses his mother on the cheek, says, "I'll telephone you and come over, we'll have a long chat," and goes. "That was nice bumping into her," he says, "always such a pleasant, elegant lady," and she says, "Who is she, a friend of yours?" and he says, "I told you, Marjorie Silbert, from the block," and she says, "She looks awful, no wonder I didn't recognize her," and he says, "She doesn't look bad, always a nice smile and nicely dressed," and she says, "Awful, like death's knocking on her door." "Nah, come on, you're exaggerating. And I'm surprised you didn't recognize her. You and Dad were good friends with her and her husband, both dentists—though he died long ago. I used to play with their younger girl," and she says, "I hope you didn't knock her up; that'd be scandalous for us," and he says, "We were little. Kindergarten through about the fourth grade. Then she went to some expensive girls' school on the East Side and from then on wouldn't give me or any of the other boys on the block the time of day. But they lived down the street from you—Mrs. Silbert still does, or Dr. Silbert; that's right, doctor—number one-forty-three. She owns the building; they had their dental practices on the first floor." "No, don't tell me. If it was true, I'd know immediately who she is," and he says, "Mom, no offense meant, but something's really happening to your memory. You're sharp in a lot of ways, and when you do latch on to a memory you create a big, full picture, but you have to try and use it more. You got to make an effort to remember who people are, where you are, and what day it is and all those things." "No, you're kidding me. My mind's not so bad. But you can't tell me I know that woman and she's lived on our street that long. I was always bad with names but never faces." "Okay," he says, "okay. But what are you going to do if she calls you and wants to come over and chat?" and she says, "I'll let her. When you're not around no one comes by but friends of the girls who look after me, so I can use the company."

He gets her in a seat in the restaurant, folds up the wheelchair, and puts it to the side of the bar. "Did you look at the menu yet?" he says, sitting down, and she says, "I'm not hungry at all. I don't know why you brought me here," and he says, "To get you out and to eat. This'll be both breakfast and lunch. What do you think you want?"

"You know, my eyes—I can't see the print too well, so you pick something for me. I'm sure it'll be good," and he says, "Like to start off with a soup?" and she says, "I never liked soup, though at some dinner parties with your dad I often had to pretend I did," and he says, "Since when? You usually like the soups here, even when it's hot out. And if you don't want a hot soup today, you could have a cold one, like . . ." and he looks at the menu, and she says, "No, no, no, no soup, I don't eat them, I'm telling you." "Okay, something with fish, meat, a smoked turkey sandwich, hamburger, turkey burger?" and she says, "I don't want meat. It upsets my stomach, takes too long to digest, keeps me up, and I've learned things about it recently: undercooked meat and its problems and the bacteria meat collects if it's left out too long," and he says, "Good, you're reading the newspaper again," and she says, "I heard it on the all-news channel I get. A terrific bore to sit in front of for a few hours straight. But it does pass the time and is better than most of the rubbish on, and occasionally there's an interesting story." "Then how about a salad?" and she says, "What am I, a rabbit, that I should just have salad?" and he says, "That's something like what Dad used to say," and she says, "Well, every now and then your father said some smart things—he knew about life," and he says, "Yes, no; on some things: money, for instance, and how to make it. Anyway, it doesn't have to be just vegetables in the salad. There could be tuna in it, grilled chicken, marinated steak strips, it says here. Lots of things like that. But you don't want to eat meat"—because she's shaking her head—"okay." "It's funny, though, but I never liked tuna, not even when I was a little girl and it was all the rage. Real fish in a can that isn't sardines, people thought. Oh, boy, how everybody got excited when it first appeared in our neighborhood grocery store. But it's always been too oily for me, and smells. Your father loved tuna, canned or fresh, and the oilier the better, but especially mackerel," and he says, "We had mackerel in the house? I don't recall, nor Dad liking tuna that much. I also don't remember your ever serving fresh tuna," and she says, "Restaurants." "Oh. What about a pasta dish? They have hot and cold and in all sorts of shapes: curly, long, penne, which I remember from someplace but now forget what it is, and a cold pasta salad too, again a penne," and she says, "Too doughy; may as well eat bread, and the sauce will make a junkyard of my blouse," and he says, "You're right, I should've thought of that. Eggs. What the hell, you always liked them, omelets or otherwise, even though they're not supposed to be great for people. But at your age, why worry about it? You've passed the possibility of those kinds of complications from foods," and she says, "Eggs, then, a good choice. Fried with the eyes up, but not too runny, and let me have a few strips of bacon, well done," and he says, "Fine." She doesn't eat and he doesn't touch her food, though she's constantly offering it—"The cholesterol, I'm not supposed to," he says, "and my salad's enough"—so her lunch is wasted. She sips a few times from her Jack Daniels, but that's all, plus a sesame stick. "No taste for anything today, I'm afraid—I told you." When he comes back from the men's room, she's sleeping. "Maybe," he says to the waiter, who starts cleaning up around them, "I should let her nap awhile, and I'll have a refill on my coffee," and the waiter says, "Whatever's your enjoyment," but he can see the waiter doesn't like the idea—place is busy and though there are a few free tables, his might all be occupied—so he says, "No, I should get her home, let her sleep there, peaceful as she is now. And she'll be embarrassed if she finds she's been napping in public," and the waiter says, "So I should forget the coffee, I presume," and gives him the check. He touches her and says, "Mom? Mom, we have to go," when she starts stirring, and she says, "I wasn't sleeping, I want you to know. Just closed my eyes to rest them. There must be a lot of pollution in the air for them to get so tired. What time is it?" and he says, "Ten after two," and she says, "It's so light for two o'clock, when usually my eyes see things darker," and he says, "Two in the afternoon," and she says, "Of course, even though restaurants around here are still serving that late in the evening. But how dumb of me." "No, you're just momentarily disoriented; so who isn't?" He walks her out, then says, "Jesus, what was I thinking? Hold on to the wall here, I'll get the chair," and she says, "I don't think I can." "Sir," he says to a young man passing, "could you please hold my mother up by the arm while I get her wheelchair from inside?" and the man says, "Why didn't you bring it first?" and he says, "She said it was all right, that she could stand and wait, but suddenly doesn't feel well," and the man says, "Go get it," and holds her, and he gets the chair and says to her while she's standing, "You want to walk behind it and push it for a block?" and she says, "Let me sit for a second," and he sits her in the chair and says,

"So, after you catch your breath, you want to walk behind the chair for a block?" and she says, "Why'd you lie to that nice man?" and he says, "Why, what'd I say?" and she says, "Why are you now lying, or—I'll be kinder to you—fibbing to me again?" "I don't know what you mean," and she says, "Each new thing you say makes it worse for you. Why are you doing that?" and he says, "Shoo, are you suddenly sharp! I'm glad to see it," and she says, "And why are you still trying to fabricate your way out of my original question?" and he says, "And what was that? Okay. Because I felt embarrassed at my stupidity in getting you out here before I got the wheelchair. That make you feel better?" and she says, "Please don't speak to me like that; I don't deserve it," and he says, "I'm sorry, really sorry. I just should've admitted my error right off to the man. I've always got out of spots like that by dissembling, but I'll try not to anymore," and she says, "You didn't even have to explain to him. Just say, 'Would you mind holding my mother's arm while I get the wheelchair from inside?'" and he says, "Isn't that what I said?" and she says, "But with the long apology you made, I think," and he says, "Sure, that's even better, what you suggested; that's what I'll do next time. Now, want me to help you to stand so you can push the chair from behind for a couple of blocks?" and she says, "Before it was one, now it's two?" and he says, "Hoo-hoo, are you ever cooking. Okay, one or two. It's good exercise for your legs, which you don't do enough of, according to Angela. You don't want those muscles to atrophy. That would be catastrophic, the doctor says," and she says, "Everyone has to get his two cents in. No, I'm feeling too weak to walk." "You're really tired today, aren't you?" and she says, "That's what I've been saying. I'm glad at last it's registered."

On the way home she says, "See those fire escapes over there?" and he says, "You pointed them out already today." "I did? My mind must be going. That's what I fear most. I don't mind, or not that much, when the body goes piece by piece. But I do when the mind goes in big chunks. Then you're lost and ought to be shot like a horse," and he says, "Your mind's okay. Little lapses, but usually sharp as a tack, as I said before," and she says, "You think so? I hope you're right." A block later she says, "Did you know there's a new law where every landlord in the city, of apartment buildings of six stories or fewer, has to have fire escapes on them? And if the apartments don't go clear through to the back, then rear fire escapes too?" "Yeah, you told me, though I hadn't heard of it before," and she says, "I did? Not today, I hope," and he says, "When we were on our way to the restaurant. Or maybe it was yesterday; we almost always go to Ruppert's, so I think it was. Yes, yesterday, or even the day before. I get confused." "No, don't fool me, it was today. You're being kind to me, but don't. The most helpful thing is to let me know when I'm being overforgetful or just plain dotty, so I can try to stop it. See? My mind is going, and once it does there's no going back," and he says, "Jeez, talk about *your* mind, what about mine? I meant to take you to the park, and here we are walking home. We can still do it. Want to go to one of the old spots? Strawberry Fields—those nice quiet shaded benches there—or that eating gazebo—what do you call it again?—anyway, by Sheep Meadow?" and she says, "It'd be nice drowsing in the park in a cool shady scented place with lots of birds around chirping, but that'd be too much like a scene out of Heaven. Just take me home and let me rest in my own bed. There I know where I am, even when I suddenly wake up."

When they get home, Angela says to her, "So how was it?" and she says, "How was what, dear?" "The lunch, the outing?" and she says, "I'm not sure" and—to him—"Did we have lunch?" and he says, "We went to Ruppert's again, but you didn't eat anything. You hungry now?" and she says, "Did I order something there?" and he says, "Plenty," and she says, "Did we ask them to wrap it up for later?" and he says, "I didn't think we should, for fried eggs." "Dorothy might have wanted it," and he says, "Who's Dorothy?" and she says, "This nice young woman taking care of me here," and Angela says, "No, thank you, Mrs. B. Eggs are best when cooked fresh." "And her name's Angela, Mom," and she says, "I know. Where else did we go today?" and he says, "The park, through the zoo; the penguins made a special point of waving hello to you. A brief spin through the Impressionist wing of the Met and then south again because I wanted to take you on the merry-go-round, but you said you get too dizzy on them. Next we went to the chess and checkers house near the zoo and you beat a grand master in seven minutes flat—'Check,' you said, 'check, check, check' "—and she says, "Now you *are* kidding me. But it's true about the merry-go-round. Even when I was a child. I suffer from—it's because of a bad ear; one of my grade school teachers battered it—but what is that term when you get very dizzy?" and he says, "'Getting very dizzy'?" and she says, "No, a medical term; you know." "No, I swear to you; right now my mind's out to lunch," and Angela says, "Don't look at me for it, Mrs. B. I'm the worst with your big American words."

They get her on the bed, her shoes off, air conditioner turned on, afghan she made years ago spread over her, side rail up, and he says, "I can see to her from here on, Angela, thanks." He kisses his mother's forehead, she smiles up at him, looks sleepy; he says, "Just rest, close your eyes, rest," and she shuts her eyes. "You feeling better now?" and she doesn't say anything. "I'm not leaving right away. I'll sit here awhile, if you need me," but she doesn't open her eyes or make any sign she heard him. Sits across from her, looks around for something to read, nothing here but a stack of old interior decorating magazines and another of *Gourmet.* He should tie them up and put them on the street, get rid of a lot of things she doesn't use anymore, make the place less cluttered, but maybe these magazines are being kept for reasons he doesn't see. She was an interior decorator for a while, not a bad cook, so she may think the magazines still have some use to her: get Angela or one of the other helpers to cook different things from the recipes inside, for instance. Or she just likes the idea of the stacks here, hoping she'll go through them when her eyes improve. Door's closed but Angela's radio music is still very loud in the next room, Caribbean beat, female vocalist singing or talking rap in what sounds like a patois. Doesn't want to tell her to turn it down; it's only bothering him. But maybe his mother's hearing it in her sleep and it's disturbing her dreams. But it could also be making them more exciting and beautiful. She can be at a beach, cool breeze, blue sky, swimming in warm clear water, no other people on it, not even noise from a radio. Though she could also be drowning, being bitten by a shark, raped by a native, suffering from food poisoning. Oh, what's he talking about? Doesn't ever see them going out for lunch again. Or only on her very best days, when she's stronger and more alert than he thinks he'll ever find her again. From now on mostly just long strolls in the park and resting there, he on a bench, she in her chair; he could bring lunch for them, cook it himself or buy it at a deli: sandwiches, cole slaw, soup on the cooler days eaten out of a container with a plastic spoon, ginger ale for her, coffee in a Thermos for him, ice-cream bar from one of the vendors. Or just go to that concession stand by Sheep Meadow she seems to like—and that's all it is, a concession stand—and get her an iced drink and Danish or crumb cake there, and that'd be all. Lightly toasted plain bagel—they do it in the microwave—with a cream-cheese spread; she likes them though never eats more than half of the bagel or the cake. He used to like taking her to lunch up to about three months ago, could do it with little effort. She pushed the chair most of the way, walked into the restaurant and to the table by herself with a cane, ate well, and never seemed to get drowsy. Sometimes they didn't say much, but she liked being out and around people, and that was enough for him. She was getting a little weaker then, but nothing like the last couple of months and especially today. If there *is* a next time in a restaurant with her—there will; he'll push her all the way, and so what if she falls asleep at the table?—he'll order a glass of wine and click her drink with it instead of the coffee mug or water glass he uses now. And ask her things about her childhood and the city then and why the teacher battered her ear; she's told him a couple of times but he's forgotten it. And Dad and how they met, what the courtship was like, marriage early on, places they lived, jobs she's had, people and books that influenced her the most, and so on. In the chair in the park she sleeps most of the time now or is awake but not conveying much, except at the concession stand, where there's a table to sit at, and when they're moving.

He says to Angela as he's leaving the apartment, "If she's up and alert this evening, call me, and I can shoot over, if I don't have something urgent to do with my family, and have a drink with her." "She's not supposed to be drinking," and he says, "One every other day won't hurt her, and the one I got her today she barely touched," and she says, "I don't know what it'll do to her, but that's what the doctor and visiting nurse said." "But she likes a drink every now and then, or did, and we can't just take everything away from her all at once. Cigarettes, booze, reading, because of her eye illness, different foods because of this cholesterol and that salt and the rest of it. If anything will kill her, that will," and she says, "I'm only repeating what was told me. You're not there at every checkup and visit, but they always warn me about the same things." "So, at her age we can be her doctors too. Lifting her spirits, letting her get away with some things she's not supposed to. Let's face it, the liquor makes her feel good. And to me, all that's important; there's little risk, and I'm sure it only makes her healthier rather than the reverse," and she says, "I'm for that. But understand, you're the son, I only work for her, and you both pay me through the agency, so with most things I'm not going to stop you. But if the doctor asks, I got to tell the truth." "Don't worry, and I'll call you later. I really didn't give her enough time today," and she says, "She'll appreciate it. She always appreciates seeing you," and he says, "And I like being with her. And it gives you a break, right? because your job can't be easy," and she says, "That too."

He calls around seven and Angela says, "She's still sleeping." "You mean from when we got her down this afternoon?" and she says, "I've tried to get her up but she won't and I can't force her. She must have slept less than I thought last night and needs to make it up," and he says, "I should probably make an appointment for her with her general doctor, long as I'm in town," and she says, "He won't tell you anything newer than what he told me and your cousin a few weeks ago, because her health hasn't changed since." "Let her sleep then, but we have to get her up and around and things tomorrow," and she says, "We can always try. But you know she's not one for exercise or moving any faster than she can. She's stubborn, which I admire in her." He calls an hour later and Angela says, "Still sleeping. Believe me, I've seen it before with old people; she's out for the night." "I'm a little worried," and she says, "Don't be. She's adjusted to her new pace, and she told me she hopes you get adjusted to it too." "When she say that?" and she says, "Last week; but she's always saying it."

He comes by around noon the next day. She's sitting up in bed in her nightgown, and he says, "Mom, you want to go out for lunch?" and she says, "Today I'm too tired to. I'll just have a bite here. I had a big breakfast," and Angela says, "You ate practically nothing, Mrs. B, and only wanted me to put you back in bed." "That's not so. I know I had a good breakfast—eggs, bacon, bread, and a glass of juice, unless it was an alcohol drink you were trying to feed me to get me to sleep," and Angela says, "That sounds just like me." Angela gives her a shower, gets her in clothes, they sit her in a chair in front of a table tray, and Angela puts a plate of food on it. She only nibbles on toast, sips some ginger ale, then says she's full and can't eat anything else. "Then let's go to the park," he says. "You won't have to walk or do anything but rest in the wheelchair, and soon as you want to come home we'll leave," and she says, "Anything you want, I don't care anymore," and he gets her into the chair and wheels her to the park. She sleeps most of the way and continues to sleep when he stops to sit on a bench. He looks at her and tries remembering her face when she was thirty-five and forty and he was a boy. You need photographs for that, he thinks. He thinks that in thirty-five years, or even twenty-five, he'll probably be dead too. If one of his daughters wheels him to a park a few months before, he hopes he'll be capable of telling her he used to do this for his mother and before that for his dad. She could say, "I never knew your father, and how many years back was that with Grandma?" and he hopes he can figure it out and answer. If he can't, he can't. He's sure he'll be sleeping a lot then during the day. It'll be very restful for him in the park, and probably that's all he'll want.

Near the Beginning

VISITS HIS MOTHER in the hospital. Goes to. *Sees*. "I'm afraid this could be it," her general man said on the phone. "Today, tomorrow; she could go anytime. She's . . . what is she, ninety?" "One." "Worse, then. Everything that could be wrong with her's wrong with her. Everything that counts, that is: heart, kidneys, lungs. There's nothing any medical staff can do for her except keep her comfortable and free of pain till she expires. Do you mind my being so blunt?" "And if I did? But no, I've told you." "That's what I thought. Hope to see you over there, though she'll be in good hands if I miss you. You flying in today?"

Started with the hip. No, started long before that. She's been sick on and off the last fifteen years. In the hospital, out; in, out. Ambulance over, intensive care for a few days, regular room for a couple of weeks. "Why do they keep dragging me in here?" she's said. "There's nothing wrong with me. I'm old, so some days I'm weaker than others. They had a spare bed and some available machines; they saw a good chance to milk the insurance company and Medicare." But with the hip they couldn't put a pin in because of her fragile health. Or they put one in and the body rejected it; he forgets. Lying in bed most of the time, sitting in a chair the other times, usually in pain, she deteriorated rapidly; didn't see the point in living like this, she said, whenever he visited her or phoned. Wouldn't eat, or couldn't; anyway, hardly ate and refused to move to a nursing home—"I've only what left, no time? And you'll have to swap me for every cent and brick we own, plus I heard they beat you black and blue if you pish in your pants, so it makes no sense for either of us, and who can stand being with all those groaning old people and their smells"—and around noon the woman who takes care of her weekdays called. She couldn't wake his mother. Ambulance was called, she went to the hospital in a coma, came out of it, will probably be in one by late tonight or early tomorrow, the resident for the intensive care unit says before Gould goes in. "But who can say? I'm always an optimist with my patients. They repeatedly surprise me, more times than I can remember, though mostly much younger ones. Save me the trouble of getting her chart; how old's your mom?" "Ninety-one." "She looks amazing for someone her age. Almost no facial creases, neck still pretty good; she must've been the beauty in her family. You wouldn't know simply by looking at her she was in such terrible shape. So as for her walking out of here . . . what'd her internist tell you about it this time?" "That she's not." "There's little chance, really no hope. I haven't told her this and she hasn't asked, but if you feel she wants to know and that she can absorb it, do what you think is best." "It can't help her, right?" "Help, hurt, what are we talking about here? It should all be up to the patient if her comprehension's keen. Would you like to know in a similar situation and at her age?" "Yes, I think so. Or maybe I wouldn't care either way. Or I wouldn't want to know because I'd be afraid that with dying there'd be lots of pain or the news of it would disturb the only enjoyable thing left, my dreams." "First of all, we've instantaneous drugs, so no pain. Or one wince by her or bounce on the monitor and we turn it up. But me, a doctor, I'd know without my kid telling me. If he started to say, 'That's not true, Dad, you're going to be fine,' I'd say, 'Bunk, pure bunk.' "

A nurse is taking his mother's temperature from under her arm. Does it in a few seconds with some new kind of thermometer, one he's never seen, and records it on a chart. She turns to hang the chart on the end of the bed and jumps. "My goodness, you scared me. You here for her?" and he says, "Yes, Mrs. Bookbinder; her son." "Good, everyone alert here can use a few minutes of company. But please, no longer. Max of one visitor per patient at one time—ICU rules—and for a total for all visitors of ten minutes an hour. As should be obvious, we have so many—" and he says, "It's okay, I read the sign on the door, and no one else is coming. And I don't want to use up any more visiting minutes, but how is she?" and she says, "You spoke to the resident?" and he says, "Yeah, but you just took her temperature, maybe her pulse." "Good, she's good. A strong woman for someone past ninety, remarkably strong. Bit of temperature just now, but I'm sure only because of the IV needle. Take it out, she'll be normal." No need to ask what she means about strength. Strong enough to hold on another day, two, three at the most. IV's not coming out till they have to work on her to get her breathing again or she's dead. Something like that; he really doesn't know. And her pulse? he wants to ask, but she's with another patient now. He stands beside his mother and says, "Mom, it's me, how you doing, you awake?" Her eyes are closed, no lid movement. "Mom, can you hear me? It's Gould. You want to sleep? If you do, don't even bother opening your eyes. I'll be here a few minutes, then I have to leave. Hospital rules for this room—no more than ten minutes—but I'll be back before you know it." Her eyes open slowly. "Yes," she says, adjusting her eyes to the ceiling, then staring at it. He puts his head a few inches above her face. "Can you see this big ugly head over you? It's me, Gould, your son. How you feeling?" and kisses her forehead. "How I feel—don't get so close; move back," and he does. "Can't you see? In the pink." "Hey, you're okay, you look good, and your sense of humor's just perfect." "I was a deadbeat before I met your dad." "You're saying you had no sense of humor till you met Dad? That can't be true." "Is that what I said? I don't want to lie. What did I say? I know I got wax in my ears but not that much." "There, again, always good for a funny line." "Who?" and he says, "You. You're funny, clever; you oughta go on the stage." "I'll tell you . . . did you ask something?" "No." "The last stage. When the curtain's pulled down. That's me, and no encores. And whatever anyone says, nobody gets them." "And philosophically funny now; oh, you're too much." "I'm too much? I'm cheap, I'm cheap, a heap of nothing, and I'm going to die here, I know. Well, I can't say I've been lucky, but it's my time."

"What're you talking? You're doing fine; doctor told me to tell you." "I'm doing fine, take me home." "That they won't let me do just yet. Once you come in—you know by now the procedures—they gotta do all their checks and tests on you before you can be released." "If you wanted to take me, you could. You have my permission. Give me the dotted line." "No, I swear, I can't do, and you need the rest." "All I do is rest. How old am I?" "Maybe we're talking too much and you should be resting more, and I think my visiting time's up." "Why, I told you; let them kick you out. They're not going to, and if they try, blame it on me. I haven't seen you for a long time. Now how old am I?" "How old do you think you are?" "That depends on how old you are. How old are you?" "Nearly sixty." "You're an old man already, how'd it happen so fast? You were once such a young man. You were a baby once and I knew you then." "Your baby, but don't get me started." "Started where? You're too old to get started. Me, though, that's age. So how old am I? You'd have the information to know?" "You do know who you're talking to, right?" "Of course, I'm not stupid. You're my son. Your name I forget just now but I'll get it, give me time." "Gould." "That's right: Gould. Who'd we name you after? It's such an uncommon name, but it must have been from someone." "You always said from no one, you just liked the name. And Dad used to say he went along with it because he knew he couldn't change your mind." "That's what he said? When did he tell you that? Never to me. No, it was all my idea. You were named after . . . Dad wanted his father's name, but I put my foot down on that. I forget what his father's name was, but I knew it wasn't for a modern young man. Isaac. Or Julius. No, the last one was an old boyfriend of mine and the first one I don't know why I brought it up. Look at me: I can remember an old boyfriend's name from another century but not yours or my father-in-law's. Well, his I no doubt forgot because he was such an awful man." "Abraham." "Abraham. Abe Bookbinder. Who could name a child that, and the kind of man he was too? Father of men, I think it's supposed to mean. That's good for a one-day-old? How old am I?" "Just a second, Mom. Now that you started it, I would like to know who I was named after. It's interesting, finding out now." "I'm not keeping it a secret. A man's first name, a woman's last? Or some other way, but it's not coming back to me." "Did you get it out of a newspaper or from a book you read?" "I was always reading. As a girl, you saw a book more than my face. So books much more than newspapers, newspapers almost never. The daily news didn't interest me. My father said I would go blind. But I didn't wear glasses till I was sixty, or never needed them, I thought. Your father didn't mind, but he wasn't interested either." "In choosing my name? In your reading books or that you didn't wear glasses or that you wore them later on? Because I know Dad was interested in newspapers. He read about three a day." She closes her eyes, shakes her head, doesn't seem uncomfortable or in pain. "I'm sorry for pursuing this, Mom, but was it the industrialist Gould I was named after?" With her eyes closed: "Who's he and why industry?" "Good, you put that together. And he was in railroads, actually, and a speculator, though maybe industry too. Not the pianist Gould. That was much later, his fame, and he's only a few years older than me, or would be. Now I'm a few years older than he ever got." "I don't know what you're talking about." "Wasn't there a character in a well-known novel of around nineteen-ten or -twenty with the last name Gould?" "I can't read anymore. My eyes are all gone for that, even for the much larger print, so maybe my father was right—he'd like to know. Each letter would have to be a foot high for me to read, and what book has that? I'd have to be a giant with giant eyes. I'm too old, I can't grow. When you get this age, no matter what age you're too old. I'm never getting up again, I can see that. Never away from this bed, probably, not even to pee. Give me a drug, send me away, I've been bad, very bad, it's right I go." "Why do you say that? You're absolutely wrong." She opens her eyes. "Why, what did I say? I forget." "You haven't been bad. You've been wonderful and generous all your life. And you could get out of here if you wanted to. I don't mean into your clothes and home this moment, but if you want to leave here, you will." "I don't. Enough's enough, don't you think? How old am I? A hundred years old, two hundred? I bet I am, the way I feel." "You're ninety . . . not even that. Still young, believe me—today? Almost ninety's nothing, or just starting to get there." "Let me sleep," and she shuts her eyes.

He goes out for coffee; when he gets back her bed's not there. "Where is she, something happen?" he asks a nurse, and she says, "They didn't think she needed the room anymore and we need every bed in ICU we can get. She's in a private on another floor." He goes to it; she's alone, still hooked up and sleeping. Sits, the book in his back pocket sticks into him, and he takes it out and tries reading, but a book's no good for sitting in a room like this—he can't concentrate, is easily distracted: noises in the hall, pigeons on the windowsill, distant car honks and what sounds like a helicopter overhead, paging and muffled voices through the walls, his mother's heavy breathing and occasional lip-smacking and snorts and snores—and gets today's *Times* from a vending machine by the elevator doors. He's reading it, being careful not to crack the pages when he turns them, when her food comes. "This can't be for her," he says, and the man who brought it says, "If she's Bookbinder, it's what I was told." Gould picks up the tray cover: "Meat, not even sliced? A baked potato, hard roll? Even a soft one wouldn't do. Her teeth aren't around—maybe they're in the drawer here," and looks in the night table drawer and they're in their case. "And she only came out of a coma this morning. Diluted apple juice, at best a weak broth." "She didn't fill out her menu for the day, and nobody for her, so this is what's listed downstairs to give her." "It's okay, take it away; she won't be eating, believe me, and just the food smells might disturb her." "What won't?" his mother says. "Take what away?" Eyes open, she's trying to push herself up. "Wait, stay, wait," he says to her, pressing down on her shoulder. "You got tubes in you, which is another thing. She can't eat with those things in too," and the man says, "Sure she can; I'll just get the nurse to take out the glucose IV while keeping all the rest in." "If you're hungry," Gould says to her, "and that's a great sign, I'll get you something soft and fluid to eat. And notice, you're out of intensive care and in your own room. That's how much better they think you're doing." "They put me in here not to scare the other patients. But I got no appetite. Have you gone to the cafeteria here?" and he says, "Just for coffee." "Then you haven't eaten. Take all of it, I'm not going to. You don't like some of it, don't eat it, but there's got to be something on the tray you like." "Okay, I'll nibble. Is it all right?"—to the man—and the man says, "Everyone does it," and goes. He breaks the roll in half, opens it with his fingers, sticks some shredded lettuce and a tomato wedge inside, and bites into it. "The meat, take that. I can't quite see it, but I bet it's good," and he says, "No, that's okay," and takes one cooked pea out of the peas and carrots bowl and eats it. "It's good, it's not bad"—taking another pea—

and she says, "If you're eating it and saying that, when you know it's all yours because I don't want any, then it must be good. For you have very high standards with food. Now, if that man left a menu for tomorrow, let's fill it out, but help me; I can't write."

A doctor comes in, one he hasn't seen before. "So, Mrs. Bookbinder, how are you? I'm Dr. Burchette, chief resident internist for this floor." "Fine and dandy," she says. "When can I get out of here?" and he says, "Soon, soon, but not for a few days." "What a laugh. Not ever. I can see it on all your faces." "Oh, you can, can you? That's good, that you're observing and speaking so clearly, even sardonically, though here you're not seeing the right thing. Right now you have a trifling amount of fluid in your lungs, nothing to become alarmed over, and the rest of you is doing fine. I wouldn't fool you; you're too smart a woman to have something put over on you." "Sure I am; sure you wouldn't. You know I'm finished, so let me die already." "You're a tough one to convince, aren't you? That attitude can only hurt you, and look what you have to go home to. Your son, for instance. The women who look after you, and a niece and grandchildren, I've heard." "Two of them," Gould says. "Two; just enough to shower with plenty of attention. They all want you home and healthy, and you should cooperate by not trying to fight getting well." "Neighbors too, who come in and see her," Gould says. "And tenants in her building." "So there, an army of well-wishers," the doctor says. "Neither of you is fooling me," she says. "Just don't do anything to stop me from dying, you hear? Nothing," and the doctor says, "I know, you signed something about that long ago, and we'll honor your wishes if it comes to that. But it's not going to for a long time, I assure you," and she says, "Lies again," and the doctor says, "Not lies, believe me," and she says, "Not lies, you're right. You're only doing your job. Fibs, then. You think they make me feel better, will ease my dying better. Okay, you're a nice man, I don't want to be a pest." "Thank you," he says, "and you're in terrific shape. What a change from this chart when you checked in. You're a remarkable woman, Mrs. Bookbinder. Your son's lucky to have your genes." "You want to go out with me then, I'm so nice?" "Sure, when you get completely better." "The Copa. We'll go to the Copa and dance the night away. I could use the exercise." "You got a date." "Is the Copa still around?" and the doctor says, "I wouldn't know, I never heard of the place. But if it isn't, we'll find somewhere else to dance." "And to drink. I don't only want to dance. I want to raise hell." "It'll be my pleasure to help"—and to Gould—"Your mother's a miracle woman. She'll live to a hundred-ten, maybe longer." "I'll set the record for sure," she says, "if whatever my age is today is the record. Truth is, doctor . . . what's your name?" "Burchette." "That's right . . . what's it again?" "Dr. Burchette." "I'm sorry, suddenly I'm not hearing." "You're not hearing?" "I'm not hearing. Or not thinking. Or not feeling good. I don't feel good. Suddenly I'm seeing double. I feel sick." "You're serious now, Mrs. Bookbinder?" "I told you, I don't feel good. I'm sick. Something's caught in my throat; my chest hurts." "Mom?" Gould says, and the doctor waves him away, feels her neck, wrist. "Who was that?" she says, and Gould says, "It's me, Gould, I'm right here; the doctor's examining you." "You'll be where? I don't feel good. Call a doctor, get me something." "You better leave," the doctor tells him, and presses a button by her bed. A voice over the intercom says, "Yes?" and he says, "Dr. Burchette here. E-team in Nine-oh-six." "Got it, doctor," the voice says, and he turns to Gould. "Please leave." "What is it?" "You can see what it is." "Gould," his mother says. "Gould, be a good boy, don't leave me." "I won't, don't worry; I'll stay here on the side," and the doctor says, "He has to leave, Mrs. B. We have to take care of you." "Don't leave me, Gould; do what I say." Nurses, doctors rush in. Equipment. "Please," the doctor says to him. *"Please?"*

They're in there a half hour. Every time someone comes out he asks, "How's she doing?" and they say things like "Don't know . . . later . . . the doctor will tell you . . . out of my way." Then Burchette comes out and says, "I can't explain what happened. Blood pressure shot up a little but nothing major. Nausea, maybe, but now everything's back to what we'll call normal." "So why were you in there so long?" and the doctor says, "Tests; we wanted to check everything. And she *is* a remarkable woman, you know, I wasn't just trying to make her feel good; and you *should* feel fortunate with the genes she handed down. My mother: breast cancer at forty-four and dead three years later. My dad: stroke at sixty-one that killed him. How old was your father when he died?" "Who says he's dead? He's in Hawaii this very minute, probably surfboarding or sailing his sunfish." "What are you talking about?" and he says, "Only kidding.

I'm just relieved she's feeling okay again," and pats the doctor's shoulder. "Nothing we did. And humor runs in your family, I see. You, your mother, who else?" and he says, "My father was the funniest of the lot. And seventy-eight, complications from Parkinson's and diabetes, more than twenty years ago. In fact his hundredth's coming up this year." "Seventy-eight for someone of his generation isn't too bad. Today, if he was that age and with the same illnesses, we'd be able to keep him till eighty-five or ninety. Maybe not ninety, but anyhow, you have decent genes from both sides, I'd say. Wish I had them." "Thank you." "You should go in now. She's probably wondering."

She's sitting up, eyes closed, resting, maybe sleeping. "Mom, hi, it's me, how you doing?" Doesn't answer. "Mom, it's Gould, I'm here. You're okay, the doctor said. Just nausea, nothing else. You sleeping?" "No"—opening her eyes—"thinking. Thanks for coming back." "Good. I'm staying here till closing. They're not kicking me out again, so don't worry, though that time it seemed necessary." "If I'm so okay, go home and come back tomorrow, you must be tired." "Come on, I've hardly been here." "No, I know how tired one can get. I did it with your father and younger brother." "What younger brother? You mean my older one, Robert, who died so young?" "*My* younger brother, Harris. Stayed in his room from morning to night and sometimes slept over, we were that close. Someone had to, because by that time my folks were long dead and his wife had deserted him." "She didn't desert; they got divorced years before he died." "Then because his shoulder deserted him." "His shoulder?" "His children, I mean; you knew that." "They had none." "What? He had no children? Harris and Dot? That's what he told you? Oh, he was a hell-raiser. Had children all over. Did you ever see any of them?" "Why would I?" "They're your family; you want to stay close. They're the ones you go to in the end. And they all looked like him, and good thing too. Dot was an eyesore. Her entire family was. Ugly as sin, as your father would say. He only married her for her money, which was the one wrong thing he'd ever done, and she for his good looks. There's something to say about having good-looking children. He never told us who they were, though." "His kids from other women? Or who the women were?" "I stayed with him for days. Never left the hospital except to get you to bed at night and sing you to sleep, and then I came right back. He needed me. You can never get too much attention in a hospital. Your father was very good about it. He looked like I must look now but younger, much younger. But just as sick, so just as sick-looking, and look what happened to him. He was such a sweet man but a real schlemiel. He let all his women step on him. You never want to be like that. And no head for business, which is why he died broke. If he got into a big argument with his partner, he walked away from his store, leaving everything behind. Then I went out of the room for something, probably to smoke, and when I got back he was gone. But I'd said my goodbye to him hours earlier, when he was in a coma. They say the person can hear, that it's the last sense to go, but I couldn't tell when I was talking to him. He was my favorite brother." "He was your only brother." "No, I had two." "Mom, what are we talking about?" "We're talking about family: yours, mine." "Then let's be clear, you had two sons and one brother." "My father was a hell-raiser too. Lots of children around from other women, and—this is odd—all boys." "But you never met any of them, these stepbrothers?" "Never; he was too discreet. He didn't want to hurt my mother. And that was that." "And your mother? No hell-raiser, right?" "Don't even say the word when you talk about her. Like me, she didn't play the field, which she could have. She was so beautiful. And also the kindest person who ever lived. *Kind:* now that's the thing to be, over everything else. My father didn't deserve her. Everyone who met her said so. You know, you remember her." "I couldn't have; she was dead before I was born." "Don't tell me." "It's true, if that's what you meant." "You're named after her." "How could I be? We don't even have the same first initial, neither my first nor middle name." "You were, I'm telling you. I insisted on it once she died. That my first child be named after my mother." "But I'm your second. And Robert, as a name, has nothing to do with hers either. What was her middle name?" "I wouldn't know; it was so long ago." "Maybe you thought if your first child was a girl you'd name it after her. Could that be it?" "Someone was named after her. Possibly one of my sisters' children, though their names I forget too." "Who was I named after, do you remember now?" "Who were you?" "You don't want to remember, that's why you won't say." "No, I'll remember; who were you named after? It's only because I'm sick that I forget." "Was it Dad's father?"

"Don't be mean. You know his name and you know I hated the man. He would touch me when your father wasn't looking. Not try to but actually touch me. My thighs. And once even a place more intimate than that, but through the clothes. When I told your father that, he said it's impossible. That his father didn't even like women much, something his mother complained about. So I said, 'Watch him, he's been fooling everybody. Watch him next time he sits beside me at the dinner table.' So I purposely sat him there the next time so your father could watch. His hand, it was everywhere under the table. What an old fool, and so coarse. But your father was always looking elsewhere. It was like a game." "What, that his father was playing? Or Dad?" "I don't know, except it was disgusting." "This really happened, though?" "He also made passes at me when he visited us in Long Beach. And in front of the children. You were very young, almost a baby. Because I think we stopped summering there in 1940. This was after your dad's mother died. We felt sorry for him, invited him for a few weeks. I knew it would be a problem, even if he was old, or old to me then. He acted like a drunken laborer. Well, that's what he was. He refused to learn how to read, not even in his own language. He lived for his schnapps and to embarrass women and his son. He said, 'Let's have fun in my bedroom.' Dad was at work in New York, took the car. He meant the guest room where he slept. It was yours and your brother's room, but when guests were there you both must have slept in ours. It was more like a small bungalow than a house, but was right on the beach. I think we saw sunsets." "I've no recollection of it and have never even seen it in any of the old photos you have." "He took my hand and tried pulling me to your room. I said, 'You're crazy, you're ugly,' and to leave now. He wouldn't, though." "Where were Robert and I at the time?" "Your brother was sick, as you know, almost from birth. It's what he died from. He slept a lot and was usually lethargic. And you were only a baby. So your grandfather had the place to himself except for me. I would have killed him with a kitchen knife if he had continued to try and force himself. I never would have allowed something like that to happen to me. To have the second man in your life be your father-in-law? And think of it, it was you he said he had come to see most, his grandchild. He oohed and ahed over you whenever you were around." "There was Robert too." "So sick and because he slept so much and was mostly unresponsive, your grandfather considered him dead. If I remember, you were barely one." "How did you finally get rid of him?" She looks away. "Did you tell Dad what his father tried to do?" "He wouldn't have believed me. And my father-in-law would have denied it or lied that I'd made eyes at him." "But this is all true?" "Or maybe barely two, so you were probably napping. That's what kids do a lot then." "I mean the story about Dad's father and you." "Oh, a hell-raiser. Girl in every port." "He was a sailor too? I thought just a weaver and darner." "He was a hell-raiser, but of the worst kind. He cheated on his wife left and right. And if he had had three wives he would have cheated on them all, but with other women." "Funny to find out now." "I didn't take him up on it, you understand." "Of course not, but how did you finally resist?" "Imagine, asking me that. Pawing at me, pulling me to the bedroom. Some men are oversexed. Your father was normal. I did what he asked me to even if I knew he had other dames." "It's all right, you don't have to talk about it if you don't want." "I'm embarrassing you?" "It's not that." "Then what? It's not upsetting me. I'm too old to be talking about it? First you're too young and then you're too old? Your father was normal. So that's good. Better that than a cold fish. We had our good times. But some men aren't. And some are like your grandfather. They say, when he was much younger, there wasn't a woman under twenty-five on the Lower East Side he didn't have his way with or who hadn't been tried." "If everyone knew this, how come Dad talked about him not liking women?" "He told you that? It's not true. The man was an animal, though by the time I knew him, not such a young one. So if I said it—" "It's all right, you don't have to explain." "No. If I said it, it's not what I meant, so it could be I was talking about someone else." "Good. But what perplexes me is why Grandma . . . what was her name again, Dad's mother?" "I forget." "But why'd she marry him?" "Why not? He made a decent living, though he blew half of it." "I mean, if she knew he was always cheating on her and had this terrible reputation and might have already drunk heavily before they met." "Who says he did?" "The drinking or the women?" "Both. And from what I heard, she was as much of a slut as him, or whatever you call the man. She had a terrible reputation, on the Lower East Side and then when they moved to Brooklyn." "Dad's mother? That's not what I heard of her or what you used to say." "Is that what he told you?" "I give up," he says. "No, I give up. I wish they would give me up. They're not keeping me alive for anything, are they?" "You mean like for a New Year's Eve dance or something?" "Yeah." She smiles. "That's good. You can be funny. I like that in a man. It took you a little while, but you finally got it. Your dad was the same way, but a different kind. Mine? Cold as ice. Never a kind word, though I was his favorite. And sharp, sardonic. It would have been nice, though. . . ." She shuts her eyes, her forehead furrows, she starts shaking her head, looks pained. "You okay, Mom?" "I don't know what's wrong." "But you're feeling okay?" "Why does everything have to happen to me?" "Why, what's the matter?" "You're here?" "Yes, sure, I'm here, right beside you." "I'm sleepy. And I don't like my thoughts." "What are they?" "They're mine." "Okay, I can understand." "Huh?" she says sleepily. "Just rest, Mom." "I'm not?" "But more; sleep." He fixes her head on the pillow, folds the sheet over on her chest. "Sleep," she says, "yeah."

He stays there for about an hour, reads from his book, holds her hand, once gets up and does a few stretching exercises, looks at her, looks out the window, can hear the pigeons cooing but can't see them so they must be on some other sill or somewhere, thinks about the funeral. She asked to be cremated. Said it the last few times in the hospital. "I know I've made a complete turnaround from what I originally wanted, but how I end up's gotten to be less important to me and I think just going up in smoke's the best thing now." And that nothing be done with the ashes. "Just throw them away. Or don't even bother with that. Leave them at the cremation place after the ceremony, if you have one." And then the last time in the hospital: "About my ashes? I've been thinking. Put them in the ground near your brother, or just sprinkle them over his grave. No, put them in a box and the box into the ground beside him. And no big ceremony. Just a simple graveside service. Everything all in one. Nothing very planned or formal, and no words by a rabbi who didn't know me from Adam. I never went for that. And it's already cost you enough keeping me alive the last few years, though I contributed some, didn't I? And the women who look after me must be costing us both a bundle too. So just a few people at it. This is what I want you to promise to do. Your wife and children, of course. Some old friends if they're still around and can make it, and anyone from the building if they want to come. And call your cousins—this is what we've always done in the family, and I'm the last aunt or uncle on our side to go—and say they don't have to be there if they have a previous engagement, but that they're welcome. And certainly Angela, the girl who's taken care of me most the last few years." Today on the phone, Angela told him to call her when his mother died. "Hey, wait, maybe she won't," and she said, "I hope you're right. But I've seen plenty of people go in my work, and I saw the signs before they went, too."

He says to his mother, "Mom, if you don't mind, I'm going downstairs for a coffee and bagel and to make a couple of phone calls. I won't be more than twenty minutes. I'm very hungry." She's breathing evenly, seems to be sleeping. He takes her hand, rubs it, kisses it. "I'll be back soon."

He comes back a half hour later. Her mouth is open, eyes closed; there's a sort of glaze all over her face and arms; she doesn't seem to be breathing. "Mom?" He takes her hand. It's slimy and cold. Cold and slimy. *Slimy, cold.*

Seeing His Father

HE RARELY SAW his father walking alone on the street. Rather, he saw him only once like that—he thinks it was only once—coming up the block they lived on while he was going down it. He forgets how old he was. No, sort of remembers. No, remembers. It was his eleventh birthday. It all comes back, or a lot of it, though it's come back before but not for years. He was going down the block to buy something with the money someone had sent him in a birthday card, when he saw his father walking up it. It was early in the afternoon for his father to be coming home from work, he must have thought. No, couldn't have thought that, because it was Saturday. It had to be. His father on weekdays never got home till six-thirty and lots of times not till seven or eight, and on Saturdays he only worked till noon or one. And Gould's birthday doesn't fall on any national or important religious holiday. What he means there is that his father didn't have a day off that day because the place he worked at was closed for a holiday. Also, his father couldn't have just taken a day off on his own, since he claimed never to have missed a day of work in his life till he was in his mid-sixties and had become too feeble from his Parkinson's to go in anymore. "I might've gone to work feeling like hell a few times before that—flu, a bad cold—and certainly plenty of times the year before the disease forced me to retire. But if there was still a slight chance to make a buck that day without my being so dizzy and weak that I'd fall on the subway tracks, I didn't want to lose it." So it had to be a regular Saturday when he saw him on the street, since stores weren't open then on Sundays, the kind of stores he'd buy something for himself in, and the mail, of course, except special delivery, wasn't delivered on Sunday. By that he means he got the birthday card through regular delivery that morning and went down the block a few hours later to buy something with the five-dollar gift. Or just a couple of hours after he got the card, as the mail usually never came before eleven and his father never got home on Saturdays before half-past twelve or one. Anyway, it was when he was walking down the block with the money that he saw his father coming up it. He first saw him from a distance of around three hundred feet. This, at least, is the way he sees it in his head now, when he counts all the buildings between them and multiplies each by twenty-five feet. They were on the same sidewalk, the north one their five-story brownstone adjoined, and he thought, or something like, This is the first time I've seen my father on the street like this. No, is it? Yes, I really can't remember it ever happening before. When they got close enough to talk—he must have waved while they were moving toward each other or his father did and he waved back, and no doubt both of them were smiling—his father said, "Where're you off to?" and he said, "To buy something. Aunt So-and-so (he forgets which aunt but remembers it was one on his mother's side, a sister or widowed sister-in-law) sent me five dollars for my birthday." "When's that?" and he said, "You know when it is: today." "No, I didn't; your mother's the one who keeps tabs on that, and she didn't tell me. I knew it fell on the seventh of some month, but I thought August." "Today's May eighth, my birthday. I'm eleven. But you're kidding me, aren't you?" and his father said, "Honestly, I'm not. Okay, I am. And I would've congratulated you and given you your eleven birthday whacks this morning, but you were still sleeping when I left for work. Good, you should; you need the sleep; your eyes got bags under the bags. So, happy birthday, my little kid," and approached him with his hand raised as if he were going to paddle him, and Gould stepped back and said,

"I'm too old for that, and no matter how soft you think you're hitting, it can hurt." "Don't worry, I wasn't going to do it. So, five bucks. That's a lot of dough. Think I can put the touch on you for some of it?" and he said, "You have your own money, and you don't have to give me any allowance this week." "Deal. Try not to blow it all at once; save some for another day." "Maybe I'll save some and only spend half," and his father said, "Good compromise." "What's that?" and his father said, "You're eleven and you don't know? A useful word. Look it up in the dictionary when you get home. But don't buy a dictionary with the money; we already have a good one you can use," and ruffled his hair or kissed the top of his head or did something like that—clutched his shoulder and shook it—since he never let him go without some affectionate handling, and continued home, and Gould went to the avenue where the stores were.

Was it really the first time he saw his father on the street like that? Remember it again. Going down (must have been very happy), father coming up. Between Columbus and Amsterdam Avenues, sees his father on the sidewalk (height, girth, way he walked, and what he wore, sort of slumped and always in a fedora and suit when he went to work and a couple of newspapers—crumpled up, but that he couldn't see from where he was—under his arm and carrying a sample case), some ten to twelve buildings away so almost half a block, and thinks something like, just as all the conversation before was only probable and something like: This is the first time I've seen him like this outside, that I can remember. Where he's alone and I'm looking at him from some far-off distance or just from a lot of feet away. Of course he saw him other times on the street. In all those years? Had to. From his second-story bedroom window: his father climbing the four steps from the areaway to the sidewalk, maybe turning around at the top to look up at him, if he knew he was there or was just hoping he was, and wave. That's a nice thought: his father hoping he was there. But he thinks he's more imagining than remembering that scene, since the two can easily get mixed up. But this had to be: when it was still light out and he was playing in the street with friends: stickball, stoopball, punchball, Chinese handball against a building's wall, Capture the Flag, games like that, or just Running Bases—between the sewers, as they called them, though they were actually manhole covers—and it was around seven or half-past and his mother hadn't called him in for dinner yet. When he sees his father, watching him from the sidewalk. "Having fun?" he says, when Gould looks at him. "Yes, thanks." "Had your supper?" "No," and knows what's coming next. "Well, sorry to spoil your fun and maybe ruin the game for your friends, but it's around dinnertime, so you'll have to come in." That's how he'd say it and what he'd do. And that had to have happened a number of times when his father was coming home from work, but he doesn't remember it. How about just his father watching him and his friends from the sidewalk but not saying anything and then continuing home alone and for a few seconds Gould looking at him? No, though that had to have happened a few times too.

His father drove them to a football game just over the bridge in New Jersey—the old Brooklyn Dodgers football team, he thinks. They sat on the sideline on a special bench set up for them, though he doesn't know how his father got it and doesn't remember asking him. After the game, some man—he thinks it was the coach of one of the teams—introduced Gould to some of the players. He doesn't know where his father knew this man from, if that's how it came about—there could have been other ways (his father was often initiating conversations with strangers and getting friendly with new people and they had sat fairly close to one of the teams' benches)—nor how they had even come to go to the game. His father wasn't interested in any sport but boxing. He'd been an amateur boxer while in high school and had once bought, before he got married, a piece of a featherweight and helped manage him. ("A bum. Lost four out of four, had a teacup for a jaw, and for each bout wanted us to buy him new trunks, gloves, and a bathrobe with his name on it. A bad investment, though my partners were the right kind of guys, so we had some fun.") Did he buy the football tickets or get them free but choose to use them because he knew Gould would like seeing a professional football game? Again, nice thought and something Gould would have liked to have happened, but not something his father ever did. He also went to the fights with him in St. Nicholas Arena—only ten blocks from their building. They sat somewhere way up; there was lots of smoking and shouting and betting going on right in front of them and plenty of money being exchanged and the place smelled of cigars, and they left after the third or fourth fight, maybe because it was getting close to Gould's bedtime. So why'd his father take him in the first place? Especially when he liked boxing so much—went to the fights at St. Nick about once every other week—and would no doubt miss the main event. Maybe the main event was between a couple of palookas, as his father called them, so he didn't mind missing it. Or he'd bought an extra ticket or had been given one and couldn't get anyone else to go with him on such short notice and didn't want to waste it—hated to waste anything: paper bag he took his lunch in, wax paper he wrapped the sandwich in, sometimes even half the sandwich if he didn't finish it and which he'd take to work the next day—so he asked Gould. That'd be more like it, taking him as a last resort, even if he probably knew Gould wouldn't like the fights or atmosphere they were held in—all that smoke and foul air. He hated it when his father puffed an occasional cigar at home, worse were his mother's constant cigarettes; he'd frantically wave the smoke away and sometimes open the window if they were both smoking at the same time. "Close that!" his father would say. "What're we heating the house for if you're going to freeze it back up? And don't be such a sissy with the smoke. It's one of the facts of life you have to learn to live with, and two gets you five you wind up smoking cigarettes or cigars yourself. Nah, you'll be a pipe man—I can see it now; a definite refined pipe type." Or maybe he was hoping Gould would like the fights and want to go with him again. "Like father, like son," he could then say, something he never did and might never even have had the opportunity to, as far as Gould can remember. That true? Too much to think back about; he'd be exploring his mind forever. Though he was at first excited at going to the fights but disappointed once they began. He couldn't see much from where they were sitting: people jumping up in front of him or just standing, arms waving, and the distance to the ring. And something about the place—"a real joint," as his father would say: the noise, smells, smoke, cursing, and catching every now and then the boxers pounding each other, and their spit and sweat flying off—made him feel sick. ("I'm sorry, but I want to go home; I'm not feeling well." "Wait. This is only the second fight. Try to hold out a little longer; you'll feel better. And if it's only that you got to make, I'll take you to the boys' room when the bell rings or you can run back and find it yourself now. It's safe enough; there are plenty of cops.") He also took him to a movie of a Shakespeare play—one with several battles, or at least one big one, and dark skies and English accents and long boring speeches he couldn't understand—shown in a Broadway stage theater for some reason. And to a play version of *Alice in Wonderland*—lots of gauzy curtains and a pretty blonde who played Alice but looked to be around twenty—in Columbus Circle when there were still theaters there. His father didn't like anything on stage but musicals and Yiddish theater—Gould went with him to one of those too and didn't make out a word but *shiksa, shaygets, shmendrick,* and *putz,* or words like that, used around the house, and his father was too busy laughing or didn't want to miss anything onstage to translate or interpret for him when he asked, so why'd he take him? Again: free tickets, his mother didn't want to go, and he was unable to get anybody else, so instead of wasting the second ticket he took Gould? But he's getting away from what he was thinking before, and that's that with all these events they either walked, drove, or took the subway or bus, so he never, with any of them, got to see his father walking on the street alone from any distance except close up.

He once thought he saw his father on the subway when they were both coming home from work. He wanted to shout, "Dad, Dad!" but there was a carful of people between them, so he made his way to him. It was a man about the same age, height, and build of his father, wearing the same kind of fedora he wore and in the same way, brim pulled down over most of his forehead, and reading the same large afternoon newspaper his father read when he rode the subway home, and folded to one-quarter its width and held straight up about six inches from his face, but in a sport jacket and open-neck shirt, clothes his father never wore to work: even when he went in only to do paperwork it was always in a suit and tie which, no matter how hot the street and subway were, didn't come off or get loosened till he got home. They worked near each other in the Garment District for a couple of years when Gould was in high school, his father selling linings to women's coat-and-suit houses, he pushing a handcart through the streets for a blouse company and then one that made belts for cheap dresses and then another that only made skirt crinolines and, when they went out of style, other lingerie. Sometimes when he got off work late he'd go to his father's office, usually wait around awhile doing his homework, and then go home with him. When they got near the subway turnstiles his father, coins already in his hand, would scoot in front of him and pay both their fares. They'd stand or sit together during the ride, Gould sometimes reading the newspaper article his father was on but not as fast, so he usually missed some of it when his father turned the paper over or continued it on another page. If there was only one seat available, his father would urge him to sit—"You've had a long day at school and work and you never get enough sleep, and you still got your homework to finish and dinner to eat and then to help your mother clean up after"—but he always made his father take it: "It's good exercise for me, standing. . . . I like looking around at other people from this position, and you can read your paper better from a seat," and so on, for he could see his father was tired—he was overweight by now, way out of shape and always seemed beat when he came home—and really wanted to sit. "I'll hold your books on my lap then." They'd leave the station and walk home, but again it wasn't seeing his father from any big distance, walking up or down a block or from anyplace that way outside. That, he's almost positive, only happened the one time he mentioned.

There he is, the hat, the suit, the tie—when it got cold, a long top-coat and muffler—carrying his case of swatches, everything buttoned and always an undershirt, no matter how hot. (His underpants—he occasionally went in and out of the bathroom or around the apartment in them—the Jockey kind, and they always seemed loose, one of his balls hanging out.) Downtown, walking on the street together. "Can I carry it for you?" "Nah, you got your books, and just think where I'd be if you lost it. This case is the most valuable thing I own. Without it I'm dead, and getting another one up with all the orders and names I got in it would be next to impossible. You ought to get one like it—I'll buy you one—but for books, so you can hold them by a handle instead of a strap and they don't get wet or slip out and you can also put your lunch in." "Nobody carries books like that. I'd be laughed at." "Well, they used to and still should. But you want to go with the fashion, suffer for it." Men's and boys' garment center, about twenty blocks from the women's one. Meets his father a couple of times a year there to buy pants or a sport jacket or winter coat wholesale from the manufacturers. "Half off, what better deal than that? And if the style's out of date or just didn't go over this year and they want to get rid of it to make room, you might get it at one-quarter list." When Gould started making good money in his late teens, he paid for his own clothes; when he was younger or only had a small part-time job, his father did or they split it. They'd meet soon as Gould could get downtown from school. "I'd almost ask you to skip your last classes but I know that's bad and you're also not doing too well in some of them, your mother said." Corner of 23rd Street and Eighth Avenue, by the downtown subway entrance. Raining or snowing, then under the corner hamburger joint awning there. "Want a papaya juice and hot dog before we start off? On me?" "No, thanks." "The juice is supposed to be healthy for your stomach and the hot dog's kosher. I've had them. They're not bad." "No, thanks." "You want, get a hamburger. It's probably better for you." "Really, Dad." "Then let's get moving. I can see you're in a hurry, and I still got a long day ahead of me too." Often—he in fact can't remember a time this didn't happen: "Look, long as we're in the building"—in the building next door, walking past the building, on the same street, in the neighborhood, down here—"mind if I go to this jacket"—vest, suit, coat, evening wear—"manufacturer to see if I can peddle some of my linings?" "You always do this when we meet for clothes, even after you say you know I have my own job to get to." "Well, I've always got a living to make and don't want to waste any advantages, so why should I make another trip and the carfare for it when I'm already here? Make sense? Does to me. I swear I'll be quick." Then: "Why you coming around the front for?" the receptionist (buyer, owner, partner, owner's son or son-in-law) says at the showroom entrance to the place. "This is for buyers, not sellers. You want to sell something, go round to service and give your name." They have to wait there ten to fifteen minutes. It's dark, grimy, with a big floor-to-ceiling cage around the whole back area that you have to be buzzed into to see someone in the workplace. "Victor Bookbinder, this is my son. I'd like to speak to Izzy Rosen or some other fabrics buyer that might be around," and gives his card. When the buyer or owner or owner's son or son-in-law finally comes it's usually: "You have an appointment, Bookbinder? I thought maybe my mind's going blotto and I forgot something. So why should I see you? I got work to do." "I know and I'm sorry but I thought—I was taking my son around here for pants—that as long as I was in the neighborhood—" "Hey, c'mon, what're you handing me? You're always in the neighborhood, right? That's what you sales slobs do. You sell your rags and are always in the neighborhood for it so you come jerking me for orders when you know I'm at my most busy. You've no appointment and I've work up to my kishkes, so it's no." "I just thought—" "Hey, what'd I say, am I talking to myself? You want I should tell Hank here not to let you through anymore? Hank," he yells, "this Victor sales guy doesn't pass no more, got it?—only kidding." And to his father, "Just stop thinking so much, it's not doing anything for your *sachel* or your wallet. You want to make a sale and be smart and not so fake dumb, then do what I say because that's who I buy from. I don't care how classy your rags are or the buy for the money or what any other manufacturer does, I don't see no salesman 'less an appointment. Okay, now get out of here, your time's up," and turns around and goes inside. Sometimes the buyer, or whoever, will come out to the cage with "Victor, my friend, how you doing, I got no time for you now, so another day, okay? but call." Or: "This your little kid? Not so little anymore—he's a real *starker,* a real one. You play football, kid?—you look it. Good-looking, too. Going to be a *shtupper* if there ever was one. I bet the girls already fall for him, do I got it pegged right? He looking for a job?—You looking for a job, kid?—I can fix it for you. We can use a reliable cart hoofer. Ours are all goof-offs or don't show up when they promise, leaving us stranded. Bullshit artists, that's what they are; every last one of them should be canned, and they will when we get ones better." "Actually—" his father says. "Vic, if you're pitching, I got no seconds to spare, none, sonny. Ring me up first, and I'll see you if I can. And Junior, I'm serious what I said, so if you're looking, come in and see me any day at five. You're half the hustler your dad is, you got a job." Couple of times Gould said, "Why do you take that from these men?" and his father said, "Take what, what men, what do you mean, the talk they give me, like that guy?" "And sending you around to the service entrance when they're already speaking to you at the front. Also, though, if you know they don't want us there near the showroom, why do you go? It's embarrassing to me," and his father said, "With each buyer it's different. Some don't mind my going there, and I do it because I've a better chance of catching them sitting and schmoozing than by calling them out from the back. And as for how they talk to me and so on, you got to put up with it if you want to make a sale.

They can go to anybody for their fabrics—my company's aren't so much superior than another's—and especially if the other salesman shmeers them. In the end we pull in more a year than they do—they're just salaried, their under-the-table stuff is their commissions but nothing like mine—which is why they treat us like so much crap. But it's all playing around, no real harm meant—they know; it's the way the Garment Center operates." One time one of the buyers said, after his father had called him out to the back, "Listen, fat man, I didn't ask to see you today, I got a big headache, so blow," and Gould said, "Don't you talk to him like that!" and the man said, "What'd you say, punk? You want to get your fucking ass slung down the elevator shaft?" and his father said to Gould, "Hey, who asked you? Go downstairs . . . no, we're both going. Thanks"—to the man—"see you again," and when they got outside—Gould had wanted to say something about it in the freight elevator, but his father said, "Later; it's for nobody's ears"—his father said, "You're lucky I didn't clip you in your stupid head right up there. You want to kill a sale for me with that *momzer* forever? Next time you want me to drag you around for clothes when I should be doing my regular business, keep your trap shut." But none of those times was seeing his father on the street, alone, from a distance, walking, what he said. Also where his father didn't see Gould, just in his own world, caught without knowing it. He's come up the subway exit, and his father was always waiting there or under the awning about ten feet away. "Hi, Dad." "Hello. Like a quick bite?" "No." "Then let's get going."

What else about his father? Plenty else. Plenty of times at home, plenty of times his father saying, "You been on the phone too long, what could be so important to say? Get off." Or "What is it, you got stock in Bell? Hang up." Standing in front of the opened refrigerator and looking inside for something he knows is there or usually there, or maybe just to see what there is to make a sandwich with or snack on, and his father saying, "Shut the icebox door; it costs a fortune to get it cold again when you keep it open that long." Or, more often, "What are you trying to do, spoil all the food inside?" Or "What is it, you got stock in Con Ed? Close the damn thing." Or when he'd stop in front of the TV set while his father was watching a program, not realizing he was blocking his view, and his father saying, "What's your father, a glazier?" He never really understood that line but assumed it meant . . . well, what? That if his father was a glazier, Gould was somehow made out of glass? In other words, though a stretch: something to do with the seed his father sired him with? No, a glazier cuts and sets glass, doesn't make it—that's a glassmaker, but maybe that's what his father meant to say but got the two mixed up. No, he knew the difference and would have said, "What's your father, a glassmaker?" Doesn't sound as good, but his father wasn't the type who'd use one word for another because it sounded better, especially when he knew it'd make what he said less clear, or that's how Gould saw him. Then what? That Gould, being the hypothetical son of a glazier, had somehow been placed in front of his father as a pane of glass, perhaps even set there by his father? Not even close. There was the expression, though, when he was a kid and maybe when his father was one too—there was much more of that kind of continuation or overlapping then than today—"I know you're a pain but you're not made of glass." But that has almost nothing to do with what his father said. This is one time—oh, there were many—when he'd love to have a brother who'd had the same things said to him, or even if he didn't but, just because they had the same father, could help Gould figure out some of their father's more puzzling expressions, and he'd call now and ask him the one about the glazier. He should have asked his father what he meant by it rather than pretend every time that he understood. What did he say or do when his father said it?—and he said it plenty of times, plenty. He probably just shook his head or said no and laughed, since it was supposed to be a funny remark, and did what his father wanted him to: moved aside. Or have asked him years later exactly what it meant—"exactly" because he wouldn't have wanted to admit, for his sake and his father's, that he'd never understood it—but by that time his father had long stopped saying it, and Gould hasn't thought of it since till now. Asking him for a dime sometimes for a comic book, and his father—but what's all this got to do with seeing his father alone on the street from a distance, walking to or away from him, and so on? Nothing, maybe, but so what? It's just a way to see his father as he was then—and his father saying, "If I had a dime I'd build a fence around it." That was his father's favorite. He said it to Gould about fifty times. Maybe a hundred. Sure, a hundred: ten or more times a year when Gould was between five and thirteen, he'll say. And he didn't ask just for dimes or comic books. Then he got his weekly allowance, which started as a nickel and grew to fifty cents—Saturdays, before his father left for work, if Gould was up, or early afternoon when he returned home: "Can I have my allowance please?" and his father would say maybe one time out of four, "If I had a quarter—" and so on. His father coming into the restaurant Gould worked at five nights a week when he was in college—now here he thinks he did see him from a distance once or twice, or at least that's what's in his mind: his father walking down the long wide aisle from the front door to the dining room—Schrafft's, on 82nd Street and Broadway—waving to him as he passed the bakery counter on his right and the soda fountain on his left, bakery closed for the day and, if it was past nine—that would be late for his father after work, which was when he dropped by—fountain closed too. Maybe even seeing him come out of the revolving door, since his father came to see him a few times the year and a half Gould worked there, suit, hat, and tie on, hat quickly in his hand right after he stepped out of the door, newspapers, sample case, and after sitting at one of his deuces—he usually asked the manager or one of the other waiters which tables were his son's, since their stations changed nightly—and saying, after Gould said hi and maybe even kissed his cheek, "I just wanted to see you at work. It gives me a special kick. I should probably order something too, no? I don't want to be taking up your table for nothing—they might toss me out on my ear. What looks good? And I promise not to ask for a discount," and he says, "You want ice cream? Some people call it the best in the city. So's the coffee, I hear, though I've never tasted it. Dark and rich like you like it." "I like it light with two spoons of sugar," and he says, "I mean before you put in those things. I'll bring a little pitcher of milk," and his father says, "Cream is better, if you got it, though don't go to any trouble on my account." "I can get you the cream. And freshest there is—from the back of the refrigerator, which we're not supposed to take out till we use up the older cream in front. Or their English muffins—they're special, made by their own bakery in Queens. Or a sandwich, though you can still get dinner if you want." "No dinner, I want to get home soon. Just a scoop of pistachio, or should I have the coffee too? I don't want to make the check too small; that wouldn't look good. But tell the guy inside I'm your dad and to give me a hefty scoop. He'll do it for you." His father chatting with him if Gould wasn't too busy and reading the paper or watching him when Gould was serving other customers. Then, after he got the check—"I feel funny about giving you this," Gould would say, "but okay, I got to"—tipping him generously, while with other waiters his father was always pretty cheap. Never above ten percent no matter how small the check—"Ten percent's good enough if you get it from everyone. What's with this fifteen all of a sudden? Who's the guy who decided that?"—and using any excuse to tip even less: waiter forgetting to bring something, dirty silver or sticky plate or lipstick on a cup or food coming cold: "Look, I don't care how menial or lousy-paying the job is, if you're hired to do it, you do it well, and giving him a regular tip is like a reward for bad service. He's lucky he wasn't stiffed." But for Gould: each time maybe the biggest tip, as far as the percentage of the check, he ever gave; sometimes as much as the check, which was the best tip Gould ever got for such a small order in all his years as a waiter. And a few hours later, when Gould got home: "So how'd it go tonight?" and Gould saying, "It went okay," and his father saying, "No, I meant in tips," and Gould saying, "Probably because of yours, better than I expected."

More things about that time he saw his father walking toward him on the street. Meeting him just about halfway between their building and the avenue corner his father had come up from. Or maybe his father had started on the opposite sidewalk and then crossed the street a few buildings from the corner before Gould spotted him. He thinks he kissed his father when he first saw him then too. Not "first saw him," of course, but when he reached him. His father always insisted on being kissed when they met or parted. Would extend his cheek for it and, when Gould was much younger and shorter, lean over and kiss the top of Gould's head and then put his cheek by Gould's lips to be kissed and even, a few times, Gould remembers—a few times? one time, anyway, he remembers it—lift him by his underarms and kiss his cheek or head and then say, "Now you kiss Daddy's cheek." And not "always" and he didn't "insist"; he'd just say something like, if Gould didn't kiss him when they parted or met or when his father or Gould came into the apartment and the other had opened the door for him or was just standing there . . . what? "My father insisted on being kissed"—that's probably where the "insist" comes from in all this—"even when he was in his seventies and I was more than forty, and I hope I get the same from you right up till I'm that age." Or whatever age his grandfather was when he was still insisting on being kissed by his son. He didn't die in his sixties? All his grandparents did, his mother said. "That was old then," he sort of remembers her saying, "so consider yourself to have good genes, as far as longevity's concerned." His own father would have felt hurt if Gould didn't kiss him during those times he mentioned: on the street when they met, greeting him at the door or in his office, and so on. And possibly his father's father would have felt hurt too if his father didn't kiss him at similar times. Gould didn't mind kissing his father. He in fact took pride in it—"boasted," he could say—to his friends and wife: "I kissed my father right up till the time he was an old guy. I didn't stop kissing him then; he just died." He's even told his daughters: "My father kissed his father till he died, I kissed mine till he died, for all I know my father's father kissed his father till he died, and though I'd love to end this death cycle—at least talking of it regarding me—I hope you'll never stop kissing your father. Of course I was a male kissing his father, as he was to his father, and so on, which is different and not as easy to do publicly as a daughter kissing her father. It at least didn't used to be easy, though maybe back when people had just come over and settled here from Europe or were still living over there—I'm talking about our ancestors, grandfathers and great-grandfathers and such—it was." "I don't think so," one of his daughters said—forgets which one. "It could be embarrassing to a girl if she thinks people around her don't know he's her father." "True," he said, "though I hope not something you'd worry about," but to get back to it: when he brought girlfriends over to the house for dinner he'd kiss his father hello—his mother too, of course—and say, "This is Phoebe"—or "Dolores" or whoever—and the girl would shake his hand and say hello, but when they left to go out after dinner she always seemed to kiss his father goodbye. Because when they were about to leave, Gould would say, "Well, good night, Dad," and kiss him—he said good night then because his father would probably be in bed asleep by the time Gould got home, if he did go home that night—and the girl would say, "Goodbye, Mr. Bookbinder," and his father would smile at her in a way, he's sure, that must have said—and move his face to her too—Come on, you can also kiss my cheek, I shaved today so it ain't going to scratch, and she'd kiss it; he can't remember a time when one of his girlfriends didn't. And if his father was in bed reading while listening to what he called "light classical music" on the radio—mostly heavily orchestrated show tunes, without the singing, or something resembling Boston Pops—which he did for about half an hour before he turned off the bed lamp and radio on his night table and went to sleep, Gould would usually knock on the door if it was closed or the outside jamb if the door was open, ask if he could come in, and say good night and kiss him and, if his mother was also there, say good night and kiss them both. He did this up till the time he moved out of the apartment, when he was around twenty-two. So what's he saying here? Just how often he kissed his father and the variety of places, and so on the street that day when they met he must have kissed him too. But how come that's the only time he remembers seeing his father on the street: distance, walking up it, and so on? Could it have really been the one time he did see him like that? It's possible their hours just didn't correspond. In all that time? Seems so, but also seems next to impossible. For one thing, far back as he can remember—no, not as far back as that; regarding this, he means from the time he was eight or nine—he was up before his father almost every weekday morning except holidays and such right through high school. For his early grades his mother would get him up and off to school, and when he was old enough he'd wake himself up with an alarm clock, make breakfast, and leave on his own. In fact, his mother started sleeping an hour later then. His father would come into the kitchen to make his own breakfast just around the time Gould was setting off. Gould would always kiss him before he left. His father would leave about a half hour later and come home some four to five hours after Gould did, at least till the time Gould started working in the Garment District while in high school. Saturdays he already touched upon, and summers he either went to sleep-away camp for two months or to a bungalow colony upstate with his mother, his father only coming up weekends and the week that included July Fourth and the one before Labor Day. Once Gould graduated college he was out of the house for good: jobs in Washington, D.C., and California, and so on and his own apartments in New York. Which is another thing: he doesn't ever recall bumping into his father in New York other than that one time on their block, not from a distance or anyplace. If he had bumped into him on another street or in a park or a museum or building of any kind, would he have kissed him? Probably, though maybe not on a subway or in a bar. But first he would have watched him from a distance on the street, if that's what it was and where it took place, and thought, This is the first time I'm seeing my father from a distance on a street that isn't our old block, far as my memory tells me. And he would have watched his father approach him, maybe even slowed down his own approach to his father, just to take it in more. And if his father was walking on the street in the same direction as him but from some distance in front, he would have followed him awhile just to have the experience of seeing him from behind like that. Then he would have hurried up to him, since it could be a crowded street or it suddenly could get crowded and he wouldn't want to risk losing him or for whatever reason—following him so long he might begin to feel peculiar—and said, "Dad," but said it lightly, so as not to scare him, and not touched him either, for the same reason, "Dad, it's me, this is amazing, how are you?" and surely they would have kissed.

A Minor Story

HE'S DONE SEVERAL quick versions of this already, none have worked, and he dumps them into the wastebasket by his desk and starts again. He picks up his younger daughter at the camp she goes to every weekday for seven hours and they're walking home from it. "Do you mind if we walk home?"—this is probably where he should have started it—"Do you mind if we walk home today?" and she says, "How long is it?" and he says, "If we walk at a normal pace—" and she says, "I mean streets," and he says, "You know, same old route, ten mostly short avenue blocks and then the long side street to our building, which we'd have to walk down anyway if we took the bus. But we can get—you can; I'll just have a coffee if we stop—a bagel or frozen ice or pizza or anything you want along the way, though what else is there after those three?" "I'm a little tired to walk," and he says, "But it'll take two blocks to the bus stop from here, so that means only eight more blocks to walk," and she says, "How do you know that?" and he says, "Well, two from ten is eight. And it'll be interesting—things to see, people and such, sudden surprises: you never know what's going to happen on a walk that long in this city.

Not *long;* just ten short blocks and then the side street to our building, and that one's all downhill. We've done it a few times and you haven't complained. And if you get tired along the way, we'll take the bus," and she says, "Okay, we'll walk, if you want me to."

They start walking. They said all that standing in front of the church school the June camp's in. They're walking and he takes her hand; his other hand holds her little knapsack and his book. "Was it a long day, sweetheart?" and she says, "Same time as all the days there," and he says, "I meant was there a lot to do today that tired you out? You go swimming?" and she says, "We always go if there isn't a trip. Today there was no trip. We even go if it rains, but not hard. We have to walk a long way to the pool. I hate it in the rain when I have to carry my swim things. And then we have to walk back but just as slow because there's a big group and some of the kids are very little, and that's harder than going there." "It didn't rain today, did it? I mean, maybe it did on your block but not ours, or not when I was looking out the window," and she says, "How can it rain where I am but not where you are?" and he says, "It's possible, take my word, we can be on the same street but different sidewalks and on yours it's raining and mine it's not. But it didn't rain while you were on the camp roof or walking to the pool and things like that, right?" and she says, "We didn't go to the pool. It was closed for cleaning." "Then did your counselors run you around a lot at camp, to make you tired?" and she says, "How, make us run round and round till we fell?" "No, I'm not being clear, I—"

"Gould," someone says, and he looks and it's the same guy he met two Junes ago on Broadway when he was also taking her home from camp, or both kids, or maybe he was alone and it was last year; and she thinks, Oh, no, it always happens, this is awful, he knows so many people around here, where they used to live all the time, before she was born, and now only in the apartment in June and around Christmas for two weeks and lots of long weekends when all of them can take off on Friday or Monday. And he keeps bumping into people when he's out with her, while she wants to get home fast—though first stopping for a pizza slice or, if it's hot like today, a frozen ice—and then take a shower and have a snack at home too, but a shower first if she's already snacked outside, or maybe a bath, whichever she feels like—they let her take both now by herself—and read and watch the hour of TV a day she's allowed and maybe a nap if she's tired, which she's not—where does he get that?—and to be with her sister. To play with Fanny, who doesn't go to camp every day anymore: too old, she says; twice a week is the most she'll go for—and her parents let her get away with it because of all the money they save, she bets—but to have fun with her, like go up the block to shop for something or to the library if it's open, things Fanny's more willing to do with her than on other days, maybe because she's mostly alone and done almost nothing that day and so wants her company, and now he's going to talk. And talk and talk. Talk's what he loves doing most when he's in the city, she thinks, and he knows how awful it is for her when he does it on the street or in the building lobby with other people when he's with her and they're going someplace. The man says to the man he's with, "This guy got me my first and only news job at NBC thirty years ago. What am I saying? Closer to forty; so long ago I had hair then, a fantastic mane of it." A mane? she thinks. Like a lion? He'd look funny. "When he went to Europe to study—" "Just to travel," her father says. "Gave myself a postgraduation hiatus for two months before I looked for a real nine-to-fiver in New York, though I believe then it was till six." "Travel, then. And play around, don't tell me. I used to see you operate in school." Play around? She thinks. Operate? How? The first, he'd be too old; the other, too young. It must mean something else. "So he got me in as his replacement. Weekends. The *Monitor* radio show. Copy boy. Paid next to nothing and they worked you to death. We went to City together; that's how we met. I wanted to be a newsman then, had worked on the school newspaper. . . . Good grief, I forget its name now, the evening-school one; I was the features editor." "*Observation Post,*" her father says. "That's it. It's obvious your brains haven't rotted away from alcohol, not like a lot of our fellow students then. Remember Johnny Welsh? He became an actor." "No." "The name's familiar," the other man says. "A basket case now. Last time you saw him in a film was ten years ago, and I think he played a drunk. Only thing he *could* play. They must have pushed him in front of the camera and said, 'Act natural.' But working at NBC convinced me news wasn't my lifetime thing." Oh, darn it, will they never stop? "Tearing copy off the wires and feebly rewriting it. But was that what those teletype machines were called?" and her father says, "If they weren't, that's what we dubbed them. From wire services, I'm sure." Dubbed? she thinks. Like knights and things? That what he means? "So I began thinking of applying to grad school for something else. . . . This your little girl? You didn't introduce, and such a cutie." "No, it's some kid who's been following me the last few blocks." "I have not." "I only said it—watch this, she's going to know the word; we spoke about it this morning—facetiously." "It didn't sound like that," she says, "and you told me the word's meaning yesterday." "Oh, boy," the man says, "not only like a tack but a wit too. I think I saw you the last time I met your father on the street, or was it your sister—you kids grow so fast. Are you Franny?" "No, Josephine. My sister you met is *Fanny.*" "I stand corrected and censured. Josephine, eh? After the great French emperor? Ah, I'm only kidding too. Your dad and I took a course in kidding at City, just ask him. Lenny Moses," and puts his hand out to shake and she shakes it. Such a fat wet hand, like a big dog's paw, and she wipes her hand on her shorts. "So I should have realized," the man says, "you were a year ahead of me, if you had graduated when you went abroad." Goodbye, good luck, good wishes, so long, we'll see you. "And now you're a professor of something at Princeton," her father says, and the man says, "Hunter. Urban anthropology. I can never leave this city, in both ways." What are they talking about? And they won't ever stop unless she does something, and she folds her arms across her chest and puts on the face; she knows what it looks like and hopes her father sees it because he knows it too. Uh-oh, her father thinks, the pout. Next, she'll be tugging his arm and then saying angrily they should go, and if that doesn't work, she'll storm off. "Excuse me, Lenny, but Josephine's had a long day at camp—" and the man says, "Oh, yeah? Where? My kids also went to camp when school was out, but in Brooklyn, where we were living and where their mother still does. Now they're grown, one has her doctorate, other's writing plays, and I miss that age enormously; I pine for it, in fact. Got divorced three years ago—I told you about it last time—and I have a one-bedroom on a Hundred-twelfth, and I love it. The neighborhood's fantastic: bookshops, subway stop two blocks away, and all the indigenous cafés. We should meet for coffee or lunch; let me write down my number," and her father says, "Just tell me, I'll remember," and the man does. But he won't remember, she thinks. He's pretending, maybe because he saw her look so wants to get them away faster before she gets madder, or else he doesn't want to meet the man again. Who would? The man never stops talking and won't let the other man talk and didn't introduce that man to them, yet scolded her father for not introducing her to him. And his hand is fat and wet and she bets his whole body is but he's keeping his stomach and chest in so nobody can see it. He also has no hair on his head except the sides and is much taller than almost anybody so is too tall for a man with no hair like that. It makes him look funny and scary, as if the whole top of his head is like a shiny piece of empty skin. And his face is long and full of big holes and with a pointy chin with a deep hole in it, and it isn't nice when he smiles like her father's. But the worst thing about him is he sometimes spits when he talks, and he also doesn't say he's sorry when it gets on people's clothes. She's standing far away from him, but if it got on hers or her hair she'd wipe it off right away because she wouldn't want it to dry on her, but then wouldn't know what to do with the spit on her hands. She'd think of it all the time she was walking home, or maybe she'd ask to go to a restaurant for some pizza, but the one that has the bathroom, just so she can wash her hands. She bets he was mean to his children when they were kids, that's what his smile and everything he does says, mean to his wife, which is why she didn't want to stay married to him, and is now mean to all his students but his favorite ones. She can see someone like him living alone the rest of his life because no one would want to be with him again, and his children not wanting to visit him much either, and his wife never even to speak to him on the phone once they were no longer married, but also because he would never shut up. "Goodbye, little Josephine," the man says, and the other man says goodbye to her and shakes her father's hand and says, "Nice to meet you," and she says goodbye nicely to them, one goodbye for them both, and smiles nicely at them too. She knows when she's smiling nicely, she can feel it on her face, and this time it's because she's finally going, and Gould thinks, She's smiling because they're going, otherwise she would never have given up those angry clenched arms and that pout. Kids can be so transparent.

He takes her hand and they walk. He asks her who she plays with at camp; she says, "Avery's my best friend there, I play with her the same every day." "Every is your friend Avery day?" and she says,

"Are you making fun of her name? That's not nice, and you and Mommy tell me on things like that not to," and he says, "No, it's only I just noticed the closeness of the two words." "Avery isn't a word, it's a name," and he says, "Right, you win. Listen, the lunch I made you today, was it enough?" and she says, "It was fine." "Did it taste okay and there was sufficient variety?" and she says, "I said it was fine." "You got the box of chocolate kisses in the bag, didn't you?" and she says, "Don't lie." "Are you still mad at me for talking so long with those men? You know I couldn't help it. I haven't seen Lenny, the tall one, for a while. You heard, we go as far back as college together, when between the two of us we had a full head of hair. No, the truth is he was always balder than I. And you don't want me to be impolite on the street. He can call the cops and have me arrested. That's why it's best not to be stopped by anyone outside with a cellular phone." "He didn't have any, and you're not being funny. And if he's your friend you shouldn't talk about his being bald that way." "Why, he brought it up, and I was referring to my own baldness too. But tell me—this is important for tomorrow—do you want cream cheese on your lunch bagel instead of peanut butter, or peanut butter and jelly? Actually, if it gets too warm out the cream cheese can spoil, while the peanut butter or peanut butter and jelly—oh, my goodness, look who's there." A man's standing at the corner not too far away, smiling and shaking his head and waiting for them, she's sure. She doesn't recognize him but she knows he's going to stop her father and they're going to waste more time talking of nothing that interests her till she gets mad. "What do you know," Gould says, "Burton Minowitz. We haven't run into each other since yesterday," and they shake hands and the man says, "It's true, I can't walk on Broadway three blocks without seeing you. What're you doing, following me?" and he says, "You got it. A big investigation, Josephine's really the lead detective, and they only put me on with her to make her cover look visually more realistic, right, sweetheart?" and she thinks, Does he want her to answer that? Well, she won't; whatever she says it'll just lead to more silly talk from them. "Look, Burt, I wish I had the time to chat about everything that's happened to you and me since yesterday, but she's got to get home." She does, she thinks, but not like the way he said it. It's as if she's sick instead of bored with their talk. "You just pick her up from camp? I can tell by the sack—my boy has the identical one in blue," and she thinks, Oh, God, no, and her father says, "Yup, a few minutes ago," and the man says, "Which one you go to, honey?" and she says, "June camp," and her father says, "The one at St. Matthew's between West End and Broadway," and the man says, "We're sending our boy to Cathedral; it's where I'm off to right now. St. Matt's would be a lot closer, but he wanted to be with his friends." "Our older girl went there two years ago and we found it sort of not together . . . was it two years ago or three?" he asks her, and she says, "I don't know. Can we go?" and he says, "In a minute. Anyway, the kids were sort of rough, or unruly, rather, and the counselors somewhat apathetic and negligent, I thought. I was afraid they'd lose her when they went on a trip to Liberty Island," and the man says, "Haven't seen anything like that. Aaron loves it, the other boys are friendly, and the counselors are very responsive and conscientious," and she starts walking; she's not going to stay for any of this anymore. Are all men her father's and that man's age—older fathers, she's saying—big blabberers? If her father doesn't chase after her, she's going to walk the rest of the way to their building; she knows where it is, not the street number so much but the stores on the Broadway corner of the street it's on, and it's at the bottom of the hill on the right and faces the river. "Wait, Josephine—listen, Burt, you see what's happening; some other time," and runs after her, and Burt says, "But I'm going that way—we should've just walked together," and Gould catches up with her, grabs her hand to stop her, and says, "Just say you want me to take you home, that's all you have to do," and she says, "I said so, and I thought you knew it." "All right, all right, maybe you did. So what do you want? Want a bagel along the way—something else?" and she says, "First let's cross the street. That man's behind us, and if he catches us we'll only go slow," and they cross Broadway and she wants a bagel, she's hungry, but doesn't want to stop anymore. He might see someone he knows in the bagel place or even while he's looking out the window while they're waiting in line, and then he could yell out the store to that person if the door's open or run after them, even, once she got her bagel, and so on. She only wants to go home, even if there are no bagels there. She and Fanny ate the last two this morning unless he bought some since then. "Did you or Fanny buy bagels today for home?" and he says, "Why, should we stop for some? That'll mean crossing Broadway again if you want to get them hot at Ray's Bagels," and she says, "I'd rather go home. Can we take a taxi?" and he says, "For what, seven blocks? Come on, you got strong legs—we'll be home in twelve minutes if we walk at a fast clip," and they walk a block and a half, he asks her about camp, same questions he asks every camp day and she answers them the same, but he smiles and says things like "No kidding" and "Wow, that sounds like fun," as if he's hearing her answers for the first time, when he says, "Excuse me, sweetie," and lets go of her hand and goes over to a very old lady who seems to be having trouble stepping off the curb, she keeps raising one foot and then putting it back down on the same place, and he says, "Need any assistance getting across the street, ma'am?" and she says, "No, in getting a cab. If I try waving my cane or hand for one I'll get all unbalanced and trip," and he says, "I'll hail one," and Josephine thinks, Oh, darn, why can't others do it? Why's it always have to be him? More time wasted, and suppose no taxis come? and he says to her, "Stay here while I get a cab for the woman," and she thinks, Yeah yeah, and he goes into the street and signals for a cab and several pass and he keeps signaling and one stops and he opens the door and helps the woman off the sidewalk and into the cab and she doesn't say thank you. She speaks to the driver and then sits back and faces front and her father shuts the door and through the window says goodbye. The lady just stares at him—no smile, even—as the taxi pulls away.

"That lady was rude," she says, walking, and he says, "Why, what'd she do to you?" and she says, "Not me; she didn't thank you for what you did," and he says, "Listen, you just want to do good, don't ask or expect anything in return, and you and the rest of the world will be much better off, not only because of what you've done, but—" and she says, "That's not how you tell me to act when someone helps. And it's so easy—it's just the lips you have to move," and he says, "You've young lips; even mine are young, in comparison. Hers are much older and something might be hurting them or some other place in her or she could be partly demented, which one can become at that age," and she thinks, What's demented? No, it'll take him a long time to tell her, and if it's complicated he'll slow down or even stand still to make sure she gets it, so she doesn't ask, and he thinks, She doesn't know what that word means; she can't, and he says, "By demented, I meant—" and she says, "I know, I know," and he says, "What?" and she says, "You don't have to tell me, I'm not in school," and walks faster, and he has to run to catch up with her and takes her hand and they walk.

Three blocks later there's a man sitting on the ground in front of the Korean restaurant Gould's said a few times he wants to take the family to or order in from—and the kids always say if he does they won't eat—with his arms out and pants legs rolled up and saying loudly, to no one in particular, it seems, "Don't walk by me like that. People, you see the condition I'm in. You're not blind and me neither. I'm destitute and crippled and I wouldn't be lying here if I didn't have to, but I have no home. Please, people, help a poor cripple with a family dying for food," and her father stops, and she says, "You think he's really poor and hurt and his family?" and he says, "Maybe you're right; it is quite a story"—he'd just started searching through his pants pockets for change—"but then again, what's a quarter?" and holds one up and says, "Want to put it in his paper cup?" "I don't like him. Even if he's telling the truth, he shouldn't be scaring children with his begging and screaming for help and showing the ugly sores on his legs," and he says, "Okay, you don't have to," and goes over and drops the quarter into the cup, and the man says, "God bless you, sir," but doesn't smile—he looks at her father as if he wants to spit on him; that's what it seems like to her—and her father says, "Thank you," and comes back and takes her hand and they walk and she doesn't want to talk anymore, just stares straight ahead, and he thinks, What's she moody about now? What'd he do? The man? What was so bad about that? and it only took a few seconds; and she thinks, If they don't talk they'll walk faster and get home sooner. If he does talk to her she'll first pretend not to hear and if he says it again she'll answer with a yes or no but something quick and then pretend she's thinking to herself again, and maybe he'll stop talking or at least asking her questions, when she sees coming toward them and walking her dog a woman from their building, someone her father always stops to talk with, either in the lobby or street or anyplace they meet, even in the elevator. She's a college teacher of a subject he's interested in, she doesn't remember exactly what but it has to do with books they both read, and he says, "Hey, how you doing?" and stops, and then, "Josephine, don't go away, I only want to say hello—a second, sweetie, I promise," but she keeps going, faster, starts running, and he says to the woman, "See what I'm up against sometimes? She's just come from camp, probably got overtired there—talk to you soon and best to Alan"—and runs after her, but she's nowhere around. The Drive maybe, and he runs to the corner but doesn't see her going down the hill on either side street. She's small, and he runs across the street to make sure she's not walking or hiding behind a parked car. So where the hell is she? Hates it when she does this. She's pulled it on him a few times—his other daughter used to wander off, still does, but not because she was angry at anything he did; she'd get interested in some store window or store and would forget she was with him—and he's told Josephine—told them both—how he feels about it. It's not because he then has to look for her. Someone could snatch her, especially on the side streets between Riverside and Broadway where there are fewer people around. Is that overdoing it? No, it's being realistic. A couple of these side streets—not this one—have SRO hotels and a lot of seedy characters in them—you can sometimes see them hanging out the windows and on the stoops—and there's a church two blocks away that feeds lunch to the homeless and some of those guys hang around after and he's sure are responsible for a lot of the cars being busted into in the neighborhood and who knows what else?

She's in a store, watching him through the window. A drugstore, the only one of the nearby stores she quickly looked at that she thought she could go in without them asking where were her parents or babysitter. He's always teaching her a lesson, so here's one for him: when she wants to go home, he should take her, because he can't pretend this time she didn't tell him. If he wants to talk to people so much when he's walking with her, let him arrange to talk with them on the phone or meet them for coffee later.

He goes inside a store: women's shoes. She wouldn't come in here, her sister would, so why'd he? "Excuse me," when a saleswoman gets up from a chair and starts over, about to ask what can she do for him, "but I'm looking for my daughter. Young, small, dark hair, in shorts?" and she says, "How recent?" and he says, "At the most, minute and a half ago," and she says no but the look says she doesn't believe him. Why else she think he'd come in here? Maybe it's just that she had to get out of the chair, but can't she see he's worried?

"Thank you," and goes to a bookstore two stores away—store between is a tiny chocolate shop with only a few feet of space for customers, and he saw through its window she wasn't there—looks up the five or so aisles and goes back outside and looks around. She's never gone off for so long on their walks home. Chances are slim anything can happen to her, but they still exist and does he really know how slim the chances are? Slim for what age, hers, or for kids younger and older? She could be home now, if she ran all the way. There's a phone on the next corner, and he should call from it to see if she's there. But if she *is* looking at him from a hiding place now she'll see how worried he looks and will probably show herself soon. Maybe he should put it on a bit, look even more worried, till she thinks she's gone far enough in this trick or in getting even with him or whatever she's doing it for, and that if she doesn't he could get so worried that when he does finally see her, since she has to come out sometime, he might explode. The drugstore, he just notices; that should have been the first place he checked. His girls love looking at the makeup and hair stuff and the new things they have for kids their age—though he's almost sure she's just hiding somewhere, not looking at store shelves, though there's also that chance she's already home. Just go in, nothing to lose, quick peek—and heads for the store. She sees him coming and thinks, Better leave before he gets here so he won't be even madder that he had to go in to find her and she didn't come out on her own.

He reaches for the door handle; she's pushing the door open. "There you are," he says; "Jesus, was I worried. What've you been up to?" and she says, "What do you mean? I've been here," and he says, "I know, I can see that, you're not a ghost, you didn't just fly in, but what were you doing in there?" and she says, "I came in to see if they had something," and he says, "What?" and she says, "Are you getting mad? I can hear it in your voice. If you are, you should stop now, Daddy; that's what Mommy says, stop it when it starts," and he says, "Just answer me normally: what were you looking for that was so important?" and she says, "A shampoo conditioner Fanny and I like, but they didn't have it," and he says, "You were going to buy it?" and she says, "No, I was going to ask you for the money," and he says, "Come on, what're you handing me? Listen, I don't like it, your running away and hiding from me," and she says,

"I didn't, I told you. I came in here and I thought you knew," and he says, "All right, you want to lie to me? You think I'm not smart enough to see through your actions and fibs both? We'll call it a big fib, to be generous and not carry this to where we're really angry at each other—" and she says, "You're the one who's angry, I'm not," and he says, "Fine, have it your own way, but you know how I feel and that I'd also like you to be more honest," and she says, "Okay. I ran away and inside here, but I had to. If I didn't, you'd take forever to get home. If I frightened you—" and he says, "Who said you did? I was worried, like any father would be when his little girl suddenly disappears on the street, but I knew you'd turn up. And now you're here, we're together again, I don't have to look for you anymore, so good, I'm glad, but please don't do it again. Never, you hear? It's wrong to treat me like that," and she says, "And it's wrong too for you to treat me the way you do on the street. Talking to everyone," and he says, "So your father knows a lot of people; what's he supposed to be, if they want to talk to him, rude?" and she says, "Yes," and he says, "You can't be, it isn't right. And if someone old needs a cab or to get across the street, you help them, or if just a quarter to give a guy, that too. That's what people should do: learn that," and she says, "Not when their daughter has to get home," and he says, "All right, right now you'll never quit, so let's go home and we'll talk about it some more there. And we're even: my stopping to talk with people and your worrying me," and she says, "You won't get more angry over it with me at home?" and he says, "No, you proved your little point pretty well," and she says, "It isn't so little," and he says, "Fine, it isn't, I'll agree on that if you'll agree that I had good reason to be somewhat worried about you and that it's something you shouldn't do again," and she looks away, and he says, "You're not answering?" and she continues to look in the direction she wants to walk, maybe he'll get the hint, she thinks, though she's not going to start walking to really make it obvious, that'd make him mad, and he says, "We'll settle that later too, but calmly, don't worry; I intend to be extra calm and reasonable with you," and takes her hand and she pulls it back, and he says, "Come on, Josephine, give me your beautiful hand," and takes it and they head home along Broadway.

A block later she sees someone else he knows and who he likes talking to and says, "Don't talk to that man, please?" and he says,

"Who?" and she says, "The one coming," and he says, "I can't just walk by without saying anything," and she says, "You can wave, he'll understand," and the man says, "Hiya, Gould," and he says, "Hey, how are ya, can't stop, much as I want to, something at home," and waves, and when they pass the man she says, "Let's walk down to Riverside Drive here, even if it's not our regular street; that way we won't meet anyone else," and he says, "Good idea, and it's also probably cooler on the drive," and still holding hands, they walk down the hill.

Ends

The Cake

HIS MOTHER SAID, "I got us something special for Halloween tonight. A Halloween cake with favors in it." "What are they?" and she said, "That's right, you wouldn't know. I can't show you the favors, but I'll show you the places in the cake they're in," and opened the cake box. The cake was orange and black and decorated with a smiling Halloween pumpkin on top and had strings coming out the sides. "After we've eaten, I'll bring the cake to the table. I think it's bad luck to tell you what a favor is beforehand, so you'll have to find out when you pull the string and the favor comes out with it." "How many are there in there?" and she said, "Same number as the strings. Count them; that's how you learn adding," and he counted the strings. "Six. Who'll pull out the other strings if I only pull one?" and she said, "Your father can, if he wants, but I doubt he will. He doesn't think much of Halloween as a holiday, and he also doesn't like games like that." "And the other four strings?" and she said, "Good, if you're counting Daddy, that makes four left. When did you learn how to subtract?" and he said, "What's that?" "What you did; two taken away from six is four, and so on." "I just did it, I didn't take away." "Anyway, of the remaining five, or four, if Daddy does play along, I'll pull one." "What do you think your favor will look like?" and she said, "You trying to find out what a favor is by asking me that? I told you—bad luck, especially on Halloween," and he said, "I wasn't, but I think it's like a very small toy. Is it wrapped?" and she said, "Did you peek inside the cake? That's also bad luck. And wrapped? That'd be a hoot if it was. No, it's loose, my dear, and if I don't want mine I'll give it to you—was that going to be your next question?" "Will I have to give you mine for yours?" and she said, "No, even if I give you mine, yours is yours for keeps." "And the three others, if Daddy takes one?" and she said, "The rest, unless he gets surprisingly involved in the string-pulling and wants to do more than one, are yours." "I can't wait. And you should tell him pulling more than one favor out is something only for children to do." "I don't know. It'd be sweet to have him get caught up in something silly like that, but we'll see." He ate his dinner quickly that night, and when his mother said, "Want seconds?" he said, "No, just the cake; can we have it now?" "What's so special about the cake that he ate supper so fast?" his father said, and she said, "Something you might even think special enough to hurry *your* eating for." "Oh, yeah, oh, boy, I can just see it: some pastry you like but you'll insist you bought because you thought it one of my favorites from the old days." "It's a Halloween cake with favors in it," Gould said, and he said, "What do you mean, favors?" "Strings," and he said, "Strings in the cake? This is getting better and better. I thought strings are supposed to tie up the cake box, not be in the cake. What's it, a spaghetti cake?" "I honestly didn't think you'd like it," his mother said, "so just in case, I bought you a cheese Danish." "A cheese Danish I like, a prune one even better; but a plain *shnecken,* of all the ones in that family, I like most of all. You don't happen to have one of those, do you?" and she said, "Only a cheese Danish and the Halloween favors cake. And you'll have to wait, Gould, till your father and I are done eating, and that means the main plate and a salad for me." "Salad," his father said. "Next to the cake with the strings in it—and when the salad has sliced onions and carrots on it, even more so—that's what I like eating best." So he waited. He excused himself once—"May I be excused to go to the bathroom?"—and his father said, "Sure, Mr. Manners, be my guest," though he had asked his mother, and went to the bathroom, didn't pee, just washed his hands, which he could have done in the kitchen but didn't think she'd have let him get up to go there just for that, and on his way back stopped in the kitchen to look at the closed cake box. What will his favor be? Probably a car, soldier, football, real or rocking horse. "Gould, are you in there?" his mother said. "Come on back; we want your company." "Why?" he said, sitting at the table. "And what do you want to talk about?" "For instance, what you did at school today." "Nothing," and his father said, "That's what we're paying good money to the school for—nothing?" and she said, "What are you talking about? It's a public school," and his father said, "So, that's my joke. You didn't get it. I'm wasting good humor on you." "I got it," Gould said, "and it made me laugh inside." "Certainly you did more than nothing there," she said, and he said, "We sat on the floor and the teacher read a story." "So he sat on the floor," his father said; "he did something." "What else you do?" his mother said, and Gould said, "We played in the playhouse. I was an Indian, other boys were cowboys." "And the girls, what were they," his father said, "barmaids and squaws?" "Do you know how to hold a conversation with him?" and his father said, "Sure I do, what a lousy thing to say," and she said, "Then hold one; and other things, try to hold in." "Now that's good and clever; I'm finally having some influence on you after all these years." "The girls played by themselves in the kitchen of the playhouse," Gould said. "Are you almost finished now?" and she said, "Almost." "She still has the radish part of her salad to eat," his father said, "or belching roses, I call them. They take a long time to get down but shorter to come back up," and she said, "Daddy's humoring us again," and smiled at his father, and his father smiled back and this made Gould happy, though he didn't know what funny things they were smiling about. Then he and his mother cleared the table and she brought the cake in. "Strings, you weren't joking, real strings," his father said. "If I was a violinist I'd play on them. But what in God's name is the rest of it? Orange and black. What could it taste like? Pure crap," and she said, "Don't ruin it for him." "It's special for tonight," Gould said. "I don't know which one to pull; they all look the same." "You mean they aren't the same?" his father said. "No, they have different favors at the ends of them. Do you want to pull one out after Mommy and I do?" and his father said, "Are you kidding? Mine no doubt has a bomb on it, hand-chosen by your mother, that'll blow up my fingers." "Very funny," she said, "and a wonderful impression you're giving him of me," and he said, "So, I made you laugh, didn't I? even if you're not laughing. That's why you put up with all the other awful things I do to you." "That's no lie," and Gould said, "What awful things is Daddy talking about?" and she said, "Just pull one of the strings; you've been wanting to all afternoon." But which one should he? If he pulls one, the favor on it might not be as good as the ones on the other strings. And then his mother could pull out the best favor and it's so good she might not want to give it to him. "I can't make up my mind," he said. "You have to, because I want to start cutting the cake." "Where's my cheese Danish?" his father said. "Though I really would've preferred a plain *shnecken.* Will you remember that next time?" and she said, "I will, and the Danish is coming." "And coffee?" and she said, "Shh, everyone," moved her head to listen to what was going on in the kitchen, said, "It's already percolating, I have to turn it down," and ran to the kitchen. "This one," Gould said. He doesn't know why. It's closest to him, facing him, so maybe his mother put the cake down that way so he'd pull that string because she knew it was the one he'd like best. That's what she'd do. But how would she know what favor was there? The bakery person could have told her. Or she could have said, "This one should be for Gould"—pointing to a box with all the different favors in it the bakery person might have brought out to show her, then have that person mark the part of the cake where the favor was put in, though he doesn't see any different kind of marking there. He grabbed the string, closed his eyes, said to himself, "I hope I'm right and it's the best one, though I won't know till they're all pulled out. Then just a very good one I'll like and want to keep," and pulled. It was a little metal figure of a girl holding a teddy bear. "So what is it?" his father said. "It's so small, I can't see from here," and his mother came in with the coffee and Danish and said, "Let me see. Nice, a doll, and well crafted. Years from now it'll be a miniature treasure." "But I don't like girls with dolls." "Breaks of the game," his father said, "and the way life goes. But years from now you'll love little dolls," and he said, "How could that happen?" and his mother said, "Your father's being silly again. Pull another, dear, but after me," and she pulled out, without closing her eyes—maybe that's how he should have done it—a metal racing car. She won't want that, he thought. "It's pretty, but a racing car for you?" he said. "Again, well crafted," she said, "better than anything you'd get out of a Cracker Jack box. Maybe I'll lick it off and put it in my purse and it'll always be there to suddenly come upon and remind me of tonight." "Why, what's so special about tonight?" "I'd like one of the favors too," his father said, "even if I won't touch the cake," and Gould said to her, "Should someone be let to pull one who doesn't eat the cake? Isn't that bad luck?" "There's no such thing as bad luck," his father said. "If something bad happens to you it's because of something you did or didn't do or someone else or other people did, but explainable, even when nature does it," and he said, "I don't think so," and his father said, "But you understood what I was saying? Good, you're developing quite the brain," and pulled the string nearest him. He got a racing car too. "Two cars in one cake," his mother said. "That's not supposed to happen. Each favor should be singular, one of a kind." "Take the cake back then," his father said. "No, don't," Gould said. "And if I got two racing cars I could race them." "Then you got mine"—putting the car in front of him—and his mother said, "Same here," and put hers down next to it. "Now let's have my Danish," and she said, "It's in front of you, next to your coffee," and he said, "Well, what do you know," and took a bite from it. "Can I pull out the other favors?" Gould said, and she said, "Wait till tomorrow night. It'll give us something to look forward to after dinner, and I might want to try my luck again," and his father said, "Good strategy. It'll also keep him eating his supper," and he said, "I always eat, if I'm not sick," and his father said, "Don't argue; do what your mother says." Gould had some cake, washed the cars in the bathroom, left the metal girl on the tablecloth—if his mother throws it away, it's okay; if she asks does he want it, he'll say, "You can have it, what I got's good." He held a car between the thumb and forefinger of each hand—they were about an inch long—and drove them around the apartment, along the walls, on the furniture and rugs, while making car noises with his mouth. In bed he drove them up and down the hills his knees made under the covers and then put them under his pillow right before he shut off the light. He was going to take them to school tomorrow and show them around. There might be one or two boys who got one tonight but he bets none of them have two. His father brought home chow mein and egg rolls and rice for dinner the next night, and for dessert they had sherbet his mother had made. They had different desserts the next few nights, and about a week later he said to his mother, "What happened to the cake with the favors? I forgot about it," and she said, "I'm sorry, it was pushed way back in the refrigerator and got so old I threw it out yesterday. You didn't take the favors out?" and he said, "You told me not to till we ate the cake. Darn, I wonder what they were—did you know?" and she said, "No. Maybe another car, or maybe all dolls. We should remember the next time to take them all out if we get it again," and he said, "We should; the cake was good." They got the same Halloween cake the next few years. He was always allowed to pull four favors out the first night and his parents pulled one each. His father once got a woman's engagement ring and gave it to his mother across the table and said, "Will you marry me?" and she said, "I can't, I'd be a bigamist." Gould didn't understand that. He got lots of different favors every year; they always seemed to change. One year he got another racing car, but by this time he'd lost the cars he got from the first cake. Then one Halloween afternoon he said to his mother, "Where's the box for the favors cake—aren't we going to have it tonight?" and she said, "The bakery stopped making them. Said there wasn't much call for them anymore and they also ran out of the metal favors and the place that made them went out of business. But I think I got you something special you'll like to replace it," and gave it to him that night for dessert—an orange and black cupcake with a plastic witch on a broomstick stuck into the top of it—and his father said, "Too bad, I was getting used to pulling one of those favors out every year. So, times change." "I can get you a Halloween cupcake next time," she said, and he said, "No, no, a *shnecken*'s just fine."

The Lot

Driving his daughter to high school, turns into the first driveway he can make a left at in the parking lot in front of the school, makes another left into a parking space. "Goodbye, Daddy, I love you"—grabbing her backpack off the floor. "Love you too—got your glasses?" and she says, "Oh, no, I forgot them at home," and looks at him in a way where she wonders if he'll get mad. "Please, sweetheart, remember them, will you?—your eyes," and kisses her forehead, and she smiles and leaves. Car's coming slowly as she's crossing the next driveway, he thinks it's going to stop but it doesn't, and she has to jump out of the way, driver waving his thanks to her as he passes or maybe the wave means something else, and she looks at Gould as if she's made another mistake and he leans over the passenger seat and yells out the window, "It wasn't your fault; it was that damn driver's. He should've stopped for you. You're the pedestrian and that's a one-way road just like mine and he was driving against it. What the hell's wrong with him, when all you kids are going to school?" and she shrugs as if it doesn't matter, and he says, "What, you don't think it's important?" and she says, "Of course I do, but don't make a big deal of it. It's over and I'm sure other kids are watching us," and he says, "So they're watching, but it *is* a big deal because it concerns them all. It can happen again and again and from the same person till someone—you, for instance, since I drive you here every day and you always cross the same driveway since I always pull into this one—gets hit real bad. Was the driver a student or someone driving a student to school?" and she says, "Who?" and he says, "The driver, I said the driver," and gets out and looks for the car in the direction it was going. It's pulling into a space about a hundred feet away and he heads over to it; she says, behind him, "Please, Daddy, leave it alone; I wasn't hurt and I have to get to school. The first bell's already rung," and he says, "I just want to tell whoever it was that what he did was wrong. And that he should from now on drive more carefully and also respectfully of the pedestrians or I'm reporting his license plate number to the school office and, if that doesn't work, then to the police." The boy's getting out of the car—a girl's sitting in the front seat checking herself in the mirror on the sun shield, another girl's gathering her things in back—and he says to him, "Do you know how to drive?" and the boy says, "Sure, I've been doing it for more than three years," and he says, "Then how come when that girl over there"—pointing to his daughter, who's staring at the ground: doesn't want the boy to think she had anything to do with sending her father over—"is crossing the road you didn't stop for her and almost ran into her?" and the boy says, "What girl, the one in the green shirt?" and he says, "Come on, you saw her—you even waved your thanks or something to her when she jumped back so not to be hit by you," and the boy says, "No, I didn't see her—when did this happen?" The girls are out of the car now—"Anything wrong, Jeremy?"—and the boy says, "No, I can handle it, thanks." "And one more thing: you drove the opposite direction you should have in this lane. You could have avoided the whole incident if you had taken seriously the painted arrow on the ground at the entrance you came in. I could have taken that road too, you know—it's one driveway closer to school, so a good twenty steps shorter for my daughter—but the arrow clearly told me not to and it should have done the same to you." "I didn't see any arrow. You sure one's there? Besides, everyone drives both ways on these roads—they're wide enough and so far I haven't heard of anyone getting hit because of it," and he said, "There's an arrow, believe me, a big one pointing in the opposite direction you were heading, and whether you saw it or not, only you know if you're telling the truth on that, and because some cars go the wrong way doesn't make it right. My daughter—" and the boy says, "That blond girl in the green shirt is who you say I almost hit?" and he says, "Yes, and she didn't look in the direction you were coming from because she didn't think cars came from that way, but the other," and the boy says, "Then from now on she should look both ways before she steps out—not for me so much but just to play it extra safe." "Daddy," she says, coming closer but still about fifteen feet away, "drop it, will you please? You said what you had to and people are watching and they have to get to school," and the boy says, "I think she's right. You've already been hotheaded enough for one day," and he says, "What do you mean hotheaded? Have I done anything but calmly try to reason with you? Yet you haven't given a clue as to having heard or thought about anything I've said." "Yeah, well, who says I have to show you that? That's only my business," and he says, "What the hell's that supposed to mean?" and the boy looks angry and says, "It means what it means, so just beat it," and he wants to take a poke at the kid, that's what he feels: to jump on him and hit his face and hurt him good, and maybe he would have but his daughter's pulling on his arm—maybe she sees how angry he is and the boy too and wants to save herself even more embarrassment—and pulls him toward his car, and he says, "What're you doing?" and she says, "Don't say anything, just go; you've already done enough harm," and he says, "How? That obnoxious kid didn't take in a word I said. All stupid cockiness," and she says, "Please, no more, I'm already late, and this was disgusting; I'll never be able to live it down," and he says, "But what was I supposed to do? That punk will continue to drive like that till he kills someone with his car. His girlfriends just stayed there glaring at me when they should've told him he was wrong and that he should consider what I was saying rather than denying and lying about every bit of it," and she lets go of him and looks as if she's crying but no tears are there, and then they are, down her face, and he says, "Okay, okay, what'd I do? I'm sorry, you're right, I should've controlled myself, though I still know he was wrong—you almost got creamed by his car; it was a half second off from happening, a second at the most," and she says, "But it didn't happen, right?" and he says, "Yes, and it was embarrassing to you, I should've thought about that too. Look at me, almost sixty and still acting like a hothead, just like the kid told me," and she says, "He said that? Then he was right. And he didn't seem so bad, just protecting himself in front of his friends, especially girls. He didn't want to look bad; that's what kids do. He even seemed nice. He didn't shout at you or raise his fists or look tough: nothing like that. He didn't see me when he was driving, that was all, a little mistake," and he says, "I'm very sorry, but I can't apologize to the boy now so I'll just tell you," and leans forward to kiss her and she backs away, as if that's the craziest thing she's ever seen, wanting to kiss her after all this, and looks both ways on the driveway—no cars are coming—and she crosses it and heads to school. The boy's talking to some boys and girls by the car, watches Fanny climb the school steps and go into the building, points to her, smiles, says something, likes her looks, is going to try and find out who she is, he may even be asking the kids there if they know her, but it shouldn't be too difficult if they don't, it's not a large school, she's probably a freshman, sophomore at the most, green shirt with a white collar, beige slacks, blond to reddish hair if he saw right, very pretty, no question about that, father drives her to school in a dark gray van, and father's an old guy, though that won't help in finding out who she is; he'll try to date her, first introduce himself in the hallway or lunchroom and pretend he's sorry about what happened and that he nearly hit her with his car, or maybe he'll be sincere about it, try to sleep with her after a couple of dates, kiss her and try to feel her up on the first, he's a good-looking kid, not smart-looking but almost none of the boys in the school look as if they are, but that's just a look, he might be bright; he'll be apologetic, that'll appeal to her, say he's sorry her dad got upset, he knows he shouldn't be going in the wrong direction in that driveway but that's what kids their age do, isn't that right? and next time, in fact he has been, since that time, more careful; he'll end up sleeping with her, she's vulnerable, he's probably a senior, she'll be easily persuaded, or not so easily but he'll know how to act and look and what to say to win her over; the boy's cool and nice, she'll think, and three to four years older and that's a plus too; he found the boy repulsive but saw things in him he thinks she'll like: the good looks, lots of wavy hair, tall, slim body, but slimy voice and face—a liar, a rat, a fake—this is the boy she'll probably start seeing, she's never dated any boy and he hates this one, not just the prospect of his sleeping with her but for lying, for not seeing what he did was wrong, for continuing to drive when he should have stopped—it all says something—for almost running into her and not seeming the least fazed by it, for—oh, forget it. Go home. It's not good for him to make these things into so much, get riled up about them, and so on, and he gets into the car, starts it, turns on the radio: news—who wants news? who wants voices? he wants music, not news, something soothing or beautiful or moving to help get the whole thing out of his head—and switches stations, music's too trumpety on this one, switches to another public station, one some distance away that he can never get at home but his car radio picks up sometimes, it's pledge week there and they're prattling like idiots, and he shuts the radio off and drives.

The Phone

He got a phone put in that day. His woman friend had said, "How can I stay over in an apartment with no phone? My daughter, when she's with her father, might want to call me, or he might want to call me about her or that he's going to be late bringing her home." She said, "Sometimes I've business to do on weekends, so how am I supposed to do it at your place if I can't make or receive a call?" She said, "What if we just want to call a theater for movie times or make a reservation for someplace?" and he said, "For movie listings, we look in the paper—that I've always got. And what would we make a reservation for, a restaurant? I don't go to restaurants I have to reserve a table for. Right away I know it's too expensive for me, and I like to go to a restaurant when I feel like going to one, not when they tell me I can have a reservation. So what else, a resort somewhere? Who's got money for resorts? Maybe you do, a little to spare, but I wouldn't let you pay for me for even a night's stay." "My dad might be sick and I want him to always be able to reach me in case it seems it could get worse," and so on. "I don't like it when the damn bell rings," he'd said. "I might be deep into my work or a book, cut off from everything outside my head, when suddenly there's this loud ring; it sometimes scares the hell out of me," and she said, "Millions of people in the city put up with it, you can't? What am I saying? Billions around the world put up with phone rings. But if it jars you that much, get one where you can turn off the rings, though I don't see how you'll know if someone's calling you then, or one which has soft tinkling chimes instead of bells—I haven't seen one but I know they exist." So he got the phone, a regular one with an ON and OFF switch, since the chimes cost a few dollars extra a month. It was the daughter argument that mostly convinced him—her daughter even told him: "Sometimes I want to talk to my mother if I'm with my father for the weekend and I'm feeling sad or lonely." His first phone of his own in about ten years—the last was when he was a per diem substitute teacher for the Board of Education and got work when one or another school called him almost every morning. And that night, while reading in bed, he got a call, the first ring startling him. It's probably her, he thought; nobody else knows he has a phone, and he gave her the number a few days ago, after he'd applied for a phone and the phone company told him what it'd be, though next time when it's this late and he's reading or going to sleep he'll turn the phone off. He grabbed the receiver—phone was on the floor by an easy chair at the other end of the room; he'd wanted it installed away from his desk and bed because of the rings—sat in the chair, and said, "Hi, and just think, my very first call on my very first phone in more than ten years—a landmark of sorts, wouldn't you say?" and a man said, "What's that?" and he said, "Oops, sorry, thought you were someone else. You must have the wrong number, sir, or the right one, but of someone who had this number a few months to a year ago," and the man said, "I don't think so. Is this Mr. Bookbinder?" and he said yes and the man said, "Then I have the right number if your name is also Gould, and only wanted to say—" and he said, "You're not from the phone company, are you? It's too late for that kind of call. What is it, near twelve?" and the man said, "That late? Excuse me, I wasn't aware. But not phone company; just someone who—" and he said, "And tell me, how'd you get my number? I only got the phone today, maybe six hours ago. What, the phone company passed my number around already—sold it, I mean, for whatever lists companies buy to contact people at home to sell them something? Because I explicitly told them not to sell it, give it away, anything, to any person or company; just to list it with telephone Information and in the directory and that's all," and the man said, "I got it from Information. I looked in the Manhattan phone book, didn't see your name there or even in the ones from a few years back, so called Information, and when she told me there was no listing for you, I said—because I knew you lived in the city; your bio notes always say that—well, then try new listings, since it's possible he only got a phone the last week or so. But I never thought today was that day; that's astounding," and he said, "Okay, but why is it you called?" and the man said, "Only to say—and I don't do this regularly with people like you, I want you to know—how much I admire your work, especially the piece in the current *Zanzibar.* I hope this isn't inconvenient or even upsetting to you in any way to hear this. But when I truly like someone's work and I know that person lives in the city, and a few times elsewhere in the States and once even in Paris, I call him. My French isn't good, or not fluent enough to get a number from Paris Information, or perhaps that particular person I wanted to reach wasn't listed there or didn't have a phone: Daniella Raymonde, do you know her work?" and he said, "Never heard of her," and the man said, "Oh, you should, and she's been translated very well here too. She's unbelievable, almost the best; certainly up there with the contemporary great ones, I'd say, of the last twenty years. Now she's dead, a year ago, lung cancer—her smoking . . . you didn't read of it?" and he said, "As I told you—" and the man said, "It was a small obit—typical, typical, for so fine an artist, but in the *Times,* though no photo; the smoking and lung cancer I learned of from a friend.

You don't smoke, do you?" and he said, "Never. Anyway, thanks. Raymonde, Daniella; I'll try to remember it. And your name, sir?" and the man gave it and started going into what he liked about Gould's work: "Not just that almost no one's heard of you, so I feel you're like my own discovery, though you do have an audience, believe me; I've spoken to a few people who are acquainted with your work, and I try to hype you up whenever I can to others, but" the this, the that: the way Gould slyly maneuvers the archetypal incident into something original, aggressively abuses the commonplace phrase into new meaning, withholds, then all of a sudden unloads; the excisions, elisions, excursions: Gould didn't know what he was talking about—"If you say so, I guess, though most of what you're saying is news to me and not exactly part of my work habits or mental . . . well, you know, process, since I never think of those things when I'm doing it or after"—the extremes he goes to, ways he exploits the matter-of-fact *and* the inconsequential and often the underexploited and occasionally what to everyone else heretofore was unexploitable, then coming around to the beginning again and starting the same thing in the same way as if he never touched on it before but making it entirely fresh and equally inimitable: "This I find amazing if not miraculous or, let's say, because I don't want to get too off-the-wall about this, done amazingly well, especially in the *Zanzibar* piece. That one seemed an enormous breakthrough for you and is one of your best, perhaps your best, of what I've read—I hope it's your newest. It amalgamates everything you do—is almost an historical pastiche of all your past styles and themes, or ones I'm familiar with. What do you say about that, would you agree?" and he said, "About what?" and the man said, "About what I said," and he said, "And what was that?" and the man said, "Please, you have to be kidding me," and he said, "Best, worst, where it stands among the others and so forth, even if a little of what you said I think I can now recognize in some of what I do. But the truth is, I hate talking about any of that and feel such talk can only be self-defeating in the long run, though I can't now say why specifically, and in the short run—well, it can only turn out to be something else, but I forget what I started out to say," and the man said, "Yes, I'm sure you did, since I doubt you forget anything—that also comes out in your work," and he said, "I don't see how, though eliciting an answer to that would only be self-defeating in another way, even if I can't specifically say how on that one right now either"—how he does this, that, some other things. "But I'm repeating myself now," the man said. He's in the same field as Gould—"which you must have figured out by now"—and he said, "No, but I'm often a little dense, so I hadn't." "And I've had a sprinkling of success, you can say, both critical and financial, and once even a brief torrent that drowned my house or at least flooded my basement, so maybe even more success with one of my works than you ever had. But you're right: what the hell's success anyway? And now I'm just about finished—I barely get in a smidgen of work in a month—while you, and we're not so many years apart, seem always to be toiling, judging by the amount of your work I've seen around the past few years, or is that mostly old trunk stuff taken out and freshened up and aired?" and he said, "No, I throw out everything that didn't work or got too old," and the man said, "That's the way to do it, discard the old, bring in the new, every day a *bonne année,* isn't that so? But I'd like to talk about a few things you've done particularly, and if nothing else, since we probably haven't time for too much—" and he said, "It *is* getting late; in fact, I'm an early get-to-bedder, so it was late for me when we began," and the man said, "Then just for a minute the *Zanzibar* piece, which is the main reason I called you anyway, to let you know how much I loved it—that I desperately wanted to tell you that and to discuss it; to me, it's a true work, one that seizes my throat and continues to hold it—and, if possible, to delve into the particulars of it a little," and he started to say, "I don't think we have the time," but the man immediately began to say what there was in it that even Gould might not be aware of or have intended, "considering how remote our subconscious is in relation to our exterior or, at best, our subcutaneous creative selves. By the way, do you go along with anything I've said so far or am I simply sounding like a pedantic ass on his high horse?" and he said, "What in particular, of what you said, did you mean?" and the man said, "Anything; subconscious, conscious, the receiver occasionally understanding the work better than the giver, for a variety of reasons," and he said, "I don't know, possibly. Excuse me, I'm not trying to be ingenuous, if that's the right word . . . disingenuous? No, ingenuous, at least for what I want here, but it's because I'm feeling a bit tired—that business before of its being late for me," and the man said, "Then one more thing and I'll let you go," and immediately began analyzing the *Zanzibar* piece, and Gould cut him off and said, "That wasn't what I had in mind and I swear to you that everything I put in I intended. I don't like to leave room for interpretation or error, but there I go talking about what I hate talking about and have no feel for and think is self-defeating, et cetera," and the man said, "Even still; though while we're on that subject—" and he said, "Of what?" and the man said, "The possibility of misinterpreting a piece, would you mind my speaking of one or two things—just one, then—of what else I've come up with in a couple of your non-*Zanzibar* works? And I had to look hard to find them, I want you to know. There may be a lot of you spread around over the years but they're mostly in out-of-the-way uncatalogued places, so the search wasn't easy," and he said, "Okay, just one. And I don't mean to sound curt or rude or anything, but because of the time—well, you know—so go on." "Modality" the man used in his first sentence on one of Gould's earliest works, and he said, "Excuse me, wait, that word," and the man said, "Which one?" and he said, "It could only be one—modality. I've heard or read it ten to twenty times in my life and have looked it up in the dictionary a number of times, and even then I didn't get what it meant, though I probably went over and over the definition each time I looked it up," and the man said, "The state of being modal," and he said, "And what's that?" and the man said, "It relates to 'mode,' the actual and unadorned word 'mode,' but in logic, music, statistics, and other places," and he said, "Okay. And 'monad'? That's another one, as long as we're on the mo's and I have the ear of a guy who seems to be good at this," and the man said, "Now you're referring principally to philosophy; Greek, in particular: the one and only, and I say that in both definitive ways. But please, don't try and fool me, Mr. Bookbinder, although that's only one more thing I love in your work: the humor," and he said, "I do try for it sometimes, but as I already said, I hate talking about my work in any kind of way, though I thank you for calling." "And you're very welcome. But listen, before I go—and I *am* going—maybe, since I also live in this city and am now semiretired so have plenty of spare time on my hands, and that we have similar interests and pursuits, and for most of our lives, I'm sure—it has been that way with me—we could—" and he said, "Really, I'm pretty much a solitary guy. I didn't even want to have a phone. I'd rather do all communication like this through the mail or the building's intercom. But someone insisted I get one," and the man said, "Let me guess who." He was about to say, Really, don't bother, when the man said, "A girlfriend, or woman friend, we'll call her, because for guys our age or thereabouts, 'girlfriend' would be anachronistic. And she's divorced or separated, besides probably being quite beautiful and intelligent, and has a young child and wanted the kid to be able to be in touch with her at all hours—meaning when this woman friend's staying with you," and he said, "Something like that. You don't know her, do you? I mean, this couldn't be why you know so much about it. This isn't her husband, by chance, whom I've never met—only kidding again," and the man said, "I can see that, and of course it's no to all your questions. I'm just an avid admirer of your work, I'm sure one of many, even if most haven't emerged from behind their walls yet, and particularly of that *Zanzibar* piece, which was something, truly something. And I felt like passing that info on to you personally. People have done that to me with my work. Phoned me out of the sky-blue—*ring ring*—you must know how it is," and he said, "Honestly, never," and the man said, "Then good, you've been initiated tonight with me: 'Hello?' 'Is this Bernhard Goldstone?' 'Who's this?' 'I simply had to phone you, Bernhard'—as you noticed, I never once called you by your given name. I didn't think I had the right to, since I was the one to phone you. 'And that your work has really done something to me, Bernhard'—one even called me Bernie straight off the bat, something I wouldn't even allow my siblings to do. Anyway, I was usually thankful when I received such calls. Why wouldn't I be, so long as I wasn't being rung up during a horrible hangover or intestinal flu, let's say, or something more flagrant? And it used to happen regularly for a number of years, though I don't want to give you the impression it happened that often. But not recently, since I haven't had anything out in the marketplace for a long time, and it could be that the people who would normally call think I'm dead or very ill. But still, once every six months would be the average, someone would feel compelled, as I was with you, to look my name up in the phone book—and wait'll you get in it. I wager you'll be swamped, relatively speaking, the next year or more, and then it'll gradually recede once the caller-admirers learn you're not exactly welcoming their interest with open ears. Word gets around quickly among them. You can't imagine the little fan cells that spring up for almost everyone in our stratum and then, if they're not nourished, dry up." "Well, you're different from me in how you handle it, which is fine; besides that, it'll never happen once my phone's listed. No ungratefulness intended, but you'll be the anomaly. Anyway, it's late now—" and the man said, "My gosh, nearly one. Does your watch also say that or is mine running very fast? Even if it were only half past twelve, who could have believed it? I meant to be brief—a minute of your time, two. All right, I won't lie—I'm unable to—five, but at the most. I didn't think you'd mind. Someone calling to extol you and your work? How often does that happen? With me, as I said, around every six months, when times were good. And I didn't think I'd be the first on the phone to convey it to you. If I had thought that I would have also thought you'd welcome the call even more, for who doesn't respond positively to an affirmative first? Later you can get jaded," and he said, "Could be that you're right. Thank you, and I will now have to say good night," and the man said, "I should too," and went on for another ten minutes, Gould couldn't find a place in the man's talk to interrupt and hang up: what he's done, where it's been, why he isn't doing much of it anymore—"If you talk about wells, mine hasn't so much run dry as been poisoned by someone's having plunged a decomposed goat down it"—how there are similarities not only in their ardor toward what they do, or, for him, did, but in the subject matter too and often in the most minute particulars, "Though know I'm not suggesting you're copying or pilfering from me in any way. Because of our similarities, you could toss the same charges back to me, but to be honest about it, I think you'll find I was there before you. It's simply that we're both extremely serious and ardent at what we do, though we're also quite funny in our work, though tragic too, which is another thing. One piece of yours—I forget where I found it, but it kept me up part of the night it was so vivid, sad, and searing and familiar—not to my work, I'm saying—even if I recall thinking at the time that I've tackled similar themes, though in the end how many are there?—but to life in general. What the heck was the name of it again? I'm sorry, but it's on the tip of the tip of my tongue, just busting to cut loose, a short title—actually, all your titles are short; not all, but a lot I've come across, but anyhow—since I can't remember the title or where I first saw it—know what it did to me: literally knocked me for a figure eight. So thank you, Gould, if I may call you that," and then started right in on something else about another of Gould's pieces—this one he has to admit he didn't care for as much as the last one he mentioned, "though it was still pretty good"—and then his own work.

The Plane

They're on a plane, whole family and him, he's sitting with his wife in the middle bulkhead seats, had to maneuver to get them once they were in the air—"We asked for bulkhead, middle or ends, it didn't matter; the woman at the ticket check-in said they were filled, though we'd requested them months ago when we made the reservations; now I see nobody's sitting there, would it be possible?"—kids sitting about eight rows back in two seats together by the window; they didn't want to move up just to face, as his older daughter said, a cloth wall; dinner's being served, predinner drink glasses with crumpled-up peanut bags and cocktail napkins inside them have been taken away, first he smelled the food, thought it was from up front and now turns around and sees the food cart being pushed and pulled down the narrow aisle by two flight attendants some five rows behind the kids so about fifteen from him and his wife, only bad reason for sitting here is that they'll get their dinner last and he's really hungry, thought when they moved up—this wasn't why they did it; it was to get more leg room for his wife: "She needs all the room she can get because of her medical condition," he also explained to the chief flight attendant; "her legs need to be extended or they stiffen up on her and become hard to bend back, and I also wouldn't mind more room in these tot chairs, I almost want to call them; what does the airline think, everyone who flies on these planes is five feet or less and svelte?"—he thought they might have a chance to be served first in economy, since the section on the other side of the bulkhead, the entrances to it curtained now, is for business class; on their way to Paris, was last there with his wife and older daughter when she was almost three, remembers the spaceship and plane merry-go-round near the metro in the Marais where they were staying, once she found she could move the ship up and down with a lever inside she didn't want to be taken out of it, it first frightened them when they saw her suddenly rise and glide, but then they kept buying these strips of discount tickets for it day after day; their younger daughter only experienced Paris "from the interior," he liked to say, and even teased her about it during the drive to the airport: "Starting tomorrow you'll be able to hook up the visual Paree of today with the aural of old," his wife was six months pregnant with her then, they spent two weeks there after a brief lecture tour he had in Eastern Europe; this time it'll only be for a week, less, six days, even less than that since tomorrow he expects they'll be so tired because of the time change that they'll spend most of the afternoon in bed; they're scheduled to land at nine, which to them will be 3 A.M. Baltimore time, and they probably won't get to their hotel for another two hours—when he hears from behind what sounds like, "Smoke, smoke . . . over there!" then a woman shouting, "Hey, there's a lot of smoke back here, get the pilot, tell the captain!" then several people shouting from the rear of his section, "Smoke . . . fire . . . it feels burning hot, coming from the cabinet there . . . flight person, get the extinguisher!" someone falls on top of the food cart trying to climb over it, "Get that fucking thing out of here!" a flight attendant yells, two attendants throw open the business-class curtains on both sides and run to the back, "What's going on?" his wife says—she has a flight headset on, is listening to music, doesn't seem to have heard any of the shouting—"Don't worry," he says, but she can't hear him even with the headset off, so many people are screaming now, "What?" she says; "Kids," he yells to where they're sitting, but can't see them over the seat backs in front of them, stands on his seat and yells, "Kids, come here to Daddy right away, come quick, emergency!" "Fire! *Au feu!*" people are shouting in back, more attendants and what looks like the captain run past his wife with extinguishers and other equipment but get stopped halfway up by people in the aisle, "Let us through, everyone back to their seats, *mouvez, mouvez,*" this man who could be the captain's saying, "don't panic, no panic, be calm, sit down, *asseyez,* seet, seet, everything will be okay, but out of the way, out of the way before I have to toss you out of the way"—rear's almost all smoke now—"Kids!" he shouts, still standing on the seat but still not seeing them; "Where are you? Show me you're hearing me!" fire coming out of the rear center wall now behind which are the toilets; are they in them? is that why they're not answering him? "Fasten your seatbelts everyone," an attendant's shouting, "seatbelt signs aren't functioning; everyone be calm and in their seats with their seatbelts on so we can clear the aisles and douse the fire," he climbs over his wife into the aisle, "Stay here," he says, "Where can I go with my legs?" she says, "the children, get the children," "That's what I'm finding out," tries going up the aisle but it's jammed with people trying to get to the front, glass is smashed somewhere, sounds like a window, nobody's doing that, they can't, he thinks; "We're going to die," people are screaming, "help, someone save us, do something!" Just push through, he thinks, you can do it, just force or squeeze your way around them but get past, stands on an aisle armrest, "Watch out, I'm jumping!" he shouts, jumps over a few people, and lands in the aisle on someone a couple of rows up, stands, explosion from in back, more glass breaking, freezing air gusts through the plane, sending people's hair and ties flying, fire's suddenly snuffed out, rear wall's not there anymore, it seems, or the toilets; lights flitter and then stay off except for the little aisle ones that might not be lights, cabin's almost black, outside mostly clouds, slim penlight beam goes on from a few rows away, everyone now seems to be screaming; "My darlings," he yells, "tell me where you are. Please, shout for Daddy!" feeling he's shouting over the others, "shout for me, shout so I can get to you, I know I'm close," thinks he hears one of them near yell "Daddy!" but there are other kids aboard, some the same age, then a loud crack, lights below him go, metal sawed and ripped, plane seems to be spinning, things flying around hitting him, he's thrown to the floor, then onto some people in seats, his head seems pulled off, can't hear, eyes go, wet but with oil or blood, is stabbed in the side, please no pain, he thinks, for me and my kids, just confiscate, then nothing else. Next thing he knows he's in the water floating. Or on something, that is. This is important. Find them. Feels around—he can feel; it's a board, some floating device or part of the plane that floats. Maybe the whole plane but no, it's like a jagged plastic raft in water, he sees, about the size of him across, and no one else on it. Stars, no moon, though when he last looked out the plane windows there was still a little daylight. Debris, a man's body, that jet fuel smell, almost no waves or sea sound. "Kids," he shouts, "it's Daddy, yell out if you hear me!" Screams their names and his wife's. "Can anyone else hear me? Is anyone alive? *Y a-t-il* anyone *ici*?" Yells and listens, yells and listens. Hears a bird once but sees none. How far are they out? Too far to be found. How'd he escape? He has his hands and legs and doesn't seem hurt. That puncture, and feels his side, but must have been nothing, the only part of this in his head. Blood on his lips, maybe running down his face, but so what? Feels okay but wants to die. Can't live through this even if he does. But first has to see if they made it. Knows they didn't. But try, you never know. Even if he only sees their dead bodies, he can jump in and grab hold of them and sink. Tries paddling the float around with his hands but it won't go anywhere, or that's what it seems. He'll have to wait till things bump into it or, if he hears one of them, swim. Tears at his hair, digs into his cheeks, and shrieks, thinks, Get done with it, and rolls into the water. Cold, and grabs the float as it starts moving away. Can't get up, no strength to, but that's not true, and hoists himself onto it. "Kids!" he screams, "listen, I'm strong, give me a chance. I've this float. Though if I have to I'll swim us all to shore, Mommy included, but you got to yell out you hear me." Hours of this, whole thing's hopeless. Pissed he has to think about how cold he is, but maybe in the long run it'll be worth it if he freezes to death by morning. Then lights in the sky, first like satellites or slow meteorites that don't disappear and then two headlight beams. Later, as the beams get nearer, helicopter sounds. A voice from the sky, but can't make it out, something about "anyone" and "ocean" and "plane." Then, when the lights get much closer, crisscrossing the water, a man over an amplification system saying, "We see debris, is anyone down there? Attention, *attention,* we have come to rescue you, Flight two-eighteen, make yourself known. Do you have lights? Can you make yourself seen or heard? A gunshot or lit cigarette lighter will do. We don't speak French—no *parle français*—so listen closely to the English. Do you have an instrument that can make a loud sound or any kind of light? Don't shout or scream. It will be a waste of energy that can be used for later, as you can't be heard over our rotors. Wave. If you have a shirt on, take it off to wave." He doesn't want to be saved. But maybe his wife and kids were picked up in another spot. One part of the plane could have gone down here, another part someplace else, but he's sure he was near his wife and kids when it happened and they all must have gone down together. And if he survived, others could have. Maybe all of his family, or just two or one of them, but that's something, more than enough to live for. "Hey, hey," he shouts, "down here. I got lots of energy," pounding the float hard as he can. Searchlights from what now seem like two helicopters continue to crisscross the water. He has his shirt off by the time they fly over him and he waves and waves. The lights pass him and crisscross the water around him with the same amplified voice saying that if someone's down there to do something to be seen or heard. Then they turn around and get near him again with their lights, and he waves and screams, "There are people down here, plenty, so stop, stop. My wife, daughters, me, other passengers. We're all down here waiting for you except for a few who might've drowned." "We see you," the amplified voice says. "We're coming down; stay adhered to your craft." A helicopter hovers about fifty feet above him, searchlights from the other helicopter beaming directly on him, and a man descends in a basket attached to a chain. "Miracle," the man says when he reaches him. "We didn't think there was a chance in Hades anyone could live through this; that we'd even find a body, though we got two," and he says, "So there's nothing, no reports from other search teams of anyone else alive?" and the man says, "You kidding? That baby you were on blew up at more than ten thousand feet and must have caught fire and started diving about ten thousand above that. Our rescue mission was strictly routine, what we have to do for even foregone lost causes. I'm still pinching my cheeks that you're really here, and you don't look an inch scratched. But you were with someone on the flight—maybe your whole family, that it?—I can tell by your face and in what you said. I'm sorry, truly sorry for you, fella, but now we gotta get moving. Sea's smiling pretty but it might suddenly toughen up and I don't want us both swept in." "Go without me, no regrets," and pushes the basket with his foot so the float drifts away. The man shouts for him to come back; then the basket's raised, the man gets in the helicopter and on the amplification system says for him not to be a fool, "Stay where you are, don't get blown off by our blades, and we can still pick you up. We know what you're going through but we're running out of fuel and can't spend too much more time here trying to convince you." He jumps off, stays underwater awhile, comes up behind the float, and tries hiding with his head just below the top of it. One helicopter goes, another hovers near, a single searchlight beamed on the float, the man practically pleading with him to appear if he's not frozen or drowned by now and let them save him. After about ten minutes of the man talking to him like this, he says, "Sir, if you are still there, this has to be it. Sorry we couldn't serve you better but we got to go in or we're dead eels ourselves," and the helicopter stays another few minutes before flying off. He climbs onto the float, freezing, and continues the trip to Paris. The landing's smooth, customs is easy, and there's no line at the currency-exchange window or for a taxi. Highways are clear and the fare and time it took to get to the hotel are half what the driver said they'd be. Room's ready, but they have no jet lag so they take a long walk through the neighborhood, go into cheese and delicacy shops just to smell them, visit a thirteenth-century church for its stained-glass windows, and then go to the Rodin Museum. They lunch in the garden there, everything's reasonably priced, and because his wife's in a wheelchair and he's the one pushing her and the kids are under eighteen, they get into the museum free. Later, dinner at a brasserie around the corner from the hotel, bottle of champagne on the house for a reason the restaurant owner is never able to explain to them in English and they can never quite get in French. Everyone they meet so far has been gracious and helpful, the kids are loving the trip and glad they came when at first they didn't want to go. Weather's pleasant, street outside the hotel's quiet, room's clean and spacious and with a bathroom large enough for the wheelchair to make a complete turn in and a rimless shower his wife can roll herself into on a special chair. Kids in one bed, he and his wife in the other, "Almost one of life's perfect days, eh?—except for the brief delay in the plane taking off," and she says, "Really, couldn't be better. I just know it's going to be a great visit." They make love and in the morning they all breakfast downstairs and then go to the Musée d'Orsay.

The Wash

He puts his laundry into the basket, detergent, his keys—where are the keys? found them yesterday under the newspaper after he looked for about ten minutes, finds them now where they should be, on a hook by the front door; how come he doesn't just automatically leave them there every time first thing when he comes in? that'd relieve him of a few anxious minutes a couple of days a month, a thought he's thought plenty before—rings for the elevator, it comes straight up from two or three floors below, so hardly any wait, good, and he gets on it and goes to the basement and the laundry room there. He can see right away when he walks in—lids are up—that several machines are free. He was hoping so; chose an hour in the afternoon (half past four) when he thought most tenants would have done their wash by now. Takes the free machine closest to the bank of dryers, because then there's a shorter walk with the wet clothes to one of them, puts in detergent, never measures it, just dumps in what he thinks is a capful, shuts the lid, and sticks his hands in his pockets for quarters. Dammit, why does he always have to forget something? Now it's upstairs and down and back up again; now it's more waste of time. Elevator won't be there waiting for him. It'll probably be on its way to the top floor and he'll have to wait for it to come down. It'll probably make a few stops on the way up and down before it reaches him, and another five minutes of his day will be lost because of a dumb mistake. Think, think, stupid: keys, detergent, laundry. Goes to the elevator with the detergent, and sure enough the red light by the button's on. He pushes the button; five minutes lost in getting the quarters could turn into ten or twenty or even more if he misses the last free dryer by a few minutes when his wash is done. That's happened. Were any dryers free before? There are only four of them—should be more for a building this size; there are about eight washers—but he forgot to look. But even if they're all free now, they can all be taken in thirty minutes, and by one person: he's seen tenants lugging shopping carts stacked with huge bundles of dirty laundry, enough in them to fill all the washing machines, or close. If the dryers are taken—there must be plenty of tenants who realize that three to five in the afternoon is the best time to get a free machine—he'll have to wait till one of them stops and then take out the dry laundry, if it is dry. If it isn't, does he take it out anyway and put it on one of the tables there? Can't do that because the person will probably want to send it through another thirty minutes; it's what he'd do if his stuff was still wet and what he's done a few times too. He's always putting too much laundry into the machines to save on the costs, though less in the dryer than the washer since all his clothes are made of cotton and he's afraid the hot air will shrink them. Or maybe it won't be that bad. There might be several dryers free and nobody making a beeline to them; that's happened too. Anyway, remember the quarters next time, and more than you need in case the washer takes them but doesn't start. Elevator door opens, he hopes the L button light isn't on, it isn't (on the lobby floor the rider has no control over the CLOSE button; the car just stays there with the door open for about thirty seconds), and he presses 7, rides up, unlocks his door, shoves the detergent inside, and with his foot keeping the front door open he stretches in and grabs a 35-millimeter film container filled with quarters off one of the hallway's bookshelves, elevator door's closed by now but car's still there—well, he had to get lucky sometime today—and rides downstairs, inserts the quarters, and washer starts. Did he put detergent in? Thinks back, sees himself pouring it in and then closing the lid. Goes to the dryers; they're all running. That could be good, if nobody gets to them before him or at least to the last one, because by the time he comes back here they'll all be done. He can tell by the lights on them that several washers are going, but lots of people don't see to their wash as punctually as him: a half hour, give or take a couple of minutes, after the machine begins. If there is only one dryer free when he comes back he should quickly stick the quarters in, close the door, which starts it running, and then get his wash out of the washer and put it into the dryer. But why get so desperate? Bring a book or the rest of today's paper and his glasses with him and, if all the dryers are going, sit on a bench or a table here and read till one stops. He goes to the elevator and presses the button. He doesn't have his watch on—he usually does, or in his pocket, to see the time he started the wash so he can put his laundry into the dryer in thirty minutes right after the washer stops—but the watch is only one more thing to remember to take with him, and he can estimate the time pretty accurately by looking at his watch or clock first thing when he gets upstairs. If there was a wall clock in the laundry room it'd make things easier, but he bets the landlord thinks it'll get stolen. The elevator stops in the lobby, the usual thirty seconds, maybe some people are getting on or off. Though lots of tenants, to make sure the elevator stops for them in the lobby or because they don't know how the elevator system works, press both the UP and DOWN buttons, which means the elevator stops there before going to the basement if someone down here's rung for it. Door opens, car's empty, so people must have only got off in the lobby or else are waiting to get on when it returns from the basement—anxious perhaps about going down there alone if it's a woman or someone old or a child—since the L button light's on. Crap—pressing the CLOSE and 7 buttons—if only he could go straight to his floor without stopping as he did before. Elevator stops in the lobby. Woman gets on, young, nice face, intelligent looking, smiles and says hello, and he says, "How do you do?" and she nods at him and looks at the floor indicator above the door and then presses the CLOSE button. "Forget it, it's got a mind of its own for this floor," and she says, "I found that out but am always hoping," and he says, "Hope has no influence on the car's programmed instructions." She presses the CLOSE button again and door closes and he says, "Don't worry, it's because of nothing you did," and the elevator goes up. "Thirty seconds minimum, more like forty-five, I see. Probably, because there's only one elevator for this end of the building, to pack as many of us in without crushing our shoulders with the closing door. Anyway, some engineer or time-and-space genius has figured it out. By the way, you have the time? Just want to make sure I get back to the laundry room in thirty minutes. So few dryers down there," and she says, "I'm fortunate; apartment I'm in has a washer and dryer together," and he says, "One of those one-on-top-of-the-other units? Who's that? You subletting?" and she says, "Shh, I'm not supposed to tell because she's not supposed to be doing it, and I no doubt already said more than I should have," and he says, "Don't worry," as the door opens, "I won't snitch. What floor you going to?" and she says, "Oh, goodness, I completely forgot: five. I'll get off at yours and walk down," and he says, "Why? Ride," and presses 5, then rests his finger on the OPEN button to keep the door from closing. "Is it Rose Grange's? Haven't seen her in a while, and she's the only one I know on five," and she says, "You know Rose well?" and he says, "Mostly through a man she went out with a couple of years ago. So I got to know her vaguely, and after they broke up, mostly for going-up-and-down-elevator and bumping-into-in-the-neighborhood and lobby talk," and she says, "You mean Larry Tutman?" and he says yeah, and she says, "Awful what happened to him. But aren't we keeping the elevator too long?" and he says, "Wait, though; what happened to Larry? Haven't seen him in a year. We weren't great friends, but I knew him and heard he left the city. Probably got a college job because I know he was looking hard and he seemed to have all the academic credentials for it. He get sick?" and she says, "Worse, much worse. It's so bad I don't even like talking about it. And excuse me but I'm still worried about our appropriating the elevator when someone might be buzzing for it," and he says, "No one is. Button light would be on. If you don't mind, would it be okay if I ride down with you while you tell me about Larry?" and she says, "Then you'll have to go all the way to the lobby after it stops at five. There's only one elevator button per hallway, so it doesn't seem to go up from any place but the lobby—and the basement, of course, because from there it has no other direction to go," and he says, "Only if someone in the lobby or any of the floors lower than yours has pressed the button first. Anyway, it's no big deal for me to go to the lobby and then up again—but do you have the time, a watch?" and she gives it, and he lets the door close and says, "I've twenty-five minutes to put my laundry into the dryer. Not a useful piece of information for you, unless your own machine breaks, but that's how long the basement washers take: thirty minutes. Same with the dryers," and door opens on 5, she says she feels uncomfortable being the first to tell him about Larry, and then goes into what happened. He says, "It's shocking, I can't believe it; of all people for it to happen to," his finger on the OPEN button. "He was such a peaceful, good-natured guy. I'm sure he was walking away from it or trying to mediate the situation—something like that but certainly not provoking or inflaming anything—and that kind of reaction or well-intentioned interference can enrage some people, particularly idiots and misfits. What's also puzzling is why Rose never told me—she knew I knew and liked the guy. But how'd you know him? Through Rose?" and she says, "Excuse me again but someone on fourteen wants to use the elevator. Maybe I should ride up with you to your floor if we're going to continue the conversation," and he says, "First, though, and I don't mean to sound funny—I only want to prepare you for this—we'll have to go to fourteen and any other floor above or below us before we press seven," and he presses 7, "for only after that will the elevator stop at seven." They go up; no other button lights go on. She tells him how she knows Larry—"Even before Rose." A woman with a dog gets on at 14 and they're silent till they get off at 7, and while they're standing in the hallway in front of the elevator she says why she thinks Rose didn't want to tell him about what happened to Larry. He says, "I don't see it, though maybe you're right. But listen, I have about twenty minutes before I have to take my laundry out of the washer, could I invite you in for coffee or tea? My apartment's right over there, same J-line as Rose," and she says, "Then I can probably find my way around it blindfold. They're all alike except for things like bookcases people had built in them. I've already seen 4-J and 6-J—6-J mostly to complain about his rock music a few times, so I never got past the foyer," and he says "Hallway?" and she says, "If you like. And 13-J. And I have some time and I'll remind you about your wash if you forget. You have—" looking at her watch, and he says, "It's all right. Minute I get inside I'll check the clock," and they go in, talk—"We use the same detergent," she says, "how about that?"—they're both interested in literature, music, and art, each knows people the other knows besides Larry and Rose and several tenants in the building: a woman he worked with, a man who'd been in the same doctoral program as she though a few years before her, a couple of poets. "I have no cookies or anything like that, can I make you toast?" and she says, "No, I've had it for breakfast and lunch, the latter in a sandwich, but thanks." He asks her out for dinner tonight, "something simple, maybe Chinese." She says she's busy, but not tomorrow, and she's had so much Chinese food recently, but there's a Japanese restaurant a few blocks away she wouldn't mind trying. They make a date. They start seeing each other regularly and then almost every day. She says he can do his laundry in her apartment from time to time, especially when he's having dinner at her place, but her machines are half the size of the ones in the basement and he only likes doing his wash once a week, "though saving on the cost of it is appealing." They sleep with each other in a few weeks. He wanted to do it sooner but she said she's had a number of unsuccessful relationships the past two years and she thinks part of the fault is she got involved too quickly. "Let's know each other more, do you mind very much? Even if you do, I'll have to insist." He forgot his laundry that day he met her. They talked for about an hour, laundry never came up once she mentioned his detergent when she entered his apartment; about three hours after she left, he remembered his wash and got on the elevator with his container of quarters and pressed B and the button light didn't go on and the car wouldn't go farther than the lobby. He got off and asked the night man on duty why the elevator wasn't going to the basement and was told the laundry room closes at eight. "I thought the sign on the laundry room door was ancient and those weren't the hours anymore," and the man said, "If you look carefully, sir, you'll see the sign says till seven. But the Tenant Association had it changed to eight two years ago." He went down at seven-ten the next morning, ten minutes after the laundry room was scheduled to open, and his wet wash was in a pile on one of the tables and two of the dryers and about half the washers were running. Good time to do the wash, he thought, but who can get it going so early? It'd mean gathering the laundry, quarters, keys, detergent, and when the wash was done all the dryers might be taken. Maybe one solution, if he was unable to do it late afternoon, is to put the wash in between seven-thirty and eight at night and then come down here at around this time to stick the wet laundry into a dryer. That night on the way to the restaurant he told her he got so absorbed in their conversation yesterday that he forgot about his wash entirely, and she said, "That's to my credit, I guess, though I don't know if I should feel flattered or if it connotes any rapport between us. But what'd you do about it?" and he told her, and she said, "I'm sure that's why Rose got her own washer-dryer, besides the fear of going alone to the basement at any hour. I'm not afraid of that, though I'd never set foot in there after seven." They get engaged, married, have a child. First she moves into his apartment a week before Rose returns, and when she's eight months pregnant they buy, for emergency washings of diapers and other baby things, a portable washing machine that operates out of the bathtub. They now live in another state, teach at the same college, have a second child, a small semidetached house in an area that has what's considered the best elementary school in the city, a washer and dryer in the basement, and in the backyard during the warm months an umbrellalike clothesline the wind sometimes spins around when there's little to no laundry on it. He goes to the elevator and presses the button. Door opens, car's empty, and he gets on and rides the elevator from the basement. No button lights on below 7, so it goes straight to his floor. He does some work at his desk, a half hour later brushes four quarters off a bookshelf into his hand—the film container of quarters is just too damn heavy in his pocket—gets his keys off the hook by the door, pulls a paperback out of the bookcase and sticks it into his back pocket, and goes to the basement. His washing machine has just finished its spin cycle and clicks off when he walks into the laundry room. Now that's timing! One of the dryers is free, nobody else down here to use it, so his good luck continues, he thinks. He drops the wash into the laundry basket, which he left by the washer, squeezes the basket into the dryer, and turns it over so the laundry falls out. He puts the quarters into the slots and pushes the change part in but the dryer doesn't start. Sometimes he gets nickels mixed up for the quarters and the hallway was fairly dark when he got them off the shelf, and he looks and they're all quarters but the dryer now takes five of them instead of four. Since when? Maybe it's just this one—when they were repairing it or something they changed it—and he looks and no, they're all now a buck twenty-five. He's got to go upstairs for one quarter? The elevator won't be waiting for him, et cetera. Another ten minutes, or five, but anyway, more time wasted. Oh to have the dough to buy a washer-dryer, some small compact unit, to avoid all this. Some day maybe if he stays in this building that long. Even if he doesn't. He hates having too many possessions but this would be one—well, it'd be much larger—but, like his stereo system, that he'd move with him wherever he goes. Elevator comes, a woman gets off dragging a larger than normal laundry basket with enough laundry in it for three loads. Good thing he got here when he did, and he gets in and presses 7. Damn, he thinks, going up, should have tried borrowing a quarter from her. And shouldn't he have helped her drag the basket into the laundry room? No, she chose to do all her wash at once—he likes to too, but he wouldn't do it if he had so much—why encourage her to tie up maybe three machines and later all the available dryers? He could have borrowed the quarter from her after he helped her with the basket, but then she might have said something like, "Keep it, you earned it," if she had an extra quarter—for so much wash, she had to—and he would have protested, saying he'll give her the quarter when he comes back to get his things out of the dryer or he'll put it in her basket if she's not here then and if she leaves the basket—and all that would take more time than it would to get the quarter from upstairs and return here. He goes into his apartment, gets a quarter, and rings for the elevator. His quarters, he thinks, riding downstairs. He never should have left them in the slots. But nobody's going to take them or at least not in the time he's been away. They're still there—the woman has four washing machines open and is putting laundry into all of them (probably whites in one, colors in another, delicate stuff in a third, who knows what in the fourth? maybe more colors or whites or both if that laundry is already dulled or stained)—and he puts the fifth quarter into the slot, shoves the change part in, and the dryer starts. Set the dial for HEAVY; it's now on LOW—not that he knows what the difference is (heat, time, speed?) or thinks it'll change anything—and he does that. Now if he's really lucky the elevator will be waiting for him. He runs to it; it's there and he pushes the button, door opens, he presses 7 as he steps in, no other button lights are on, and he rides upstairs. So, for an incident that—more than an incident, a job that mostly didn't go well—it seems to be ending okay, and what else could go wrong? His laundry could be damp when he gets back to it because he put too much of it into the machine. And maybe this dryer is the weakest of the four or only works for twenty minutes, or twenty-five, tops, and the moment it stops, and he's not down there, someone waiting for it might empty his things onto a table and put his own wet laundry in, and by the time he returns to the basement all the dryers might be filled. So he should get back in twenty-five minutes maximum, feel his laundry, and, if it's still damp, or most of it, insert five quarters into the dryer for another thirty minutes. For sure he's going to remember to put five quarters in his pocket before he heads back. In fact—unlocking his apartment door—put them in now and more than five, and he closes the film container of quarters and drops it into his pants pocket. Then he checks the time, deducts two minutes from it, makes a cup of tea, reads the newspaper, and about twenty-five minutes after he left the laundry room he goes downstairs. All four dryers are running. He doesn't see his laundry on a table, looks inside his dryer and recognizes some of his clothes. He opens the door an inch, waits till the machine stops, feels several articles of clothes and a thick towel, and they're thoroughly dry. Should he shut the door and let the dryer finish its cycle? No, everything's dry, so any more heat will just start to burn them or dull the colors. He hears the elevator door open, sees the woman come into the room with her big basket and go to the washing machines. He smiles at her—she nods back and opens a lid of one of the washers—and says, "This dryer will be free in a second and there should even be a few minutes left on it," and takes his basket and then the laundry to a table and starts folding it and putting his clothes and linens in two separate piles.

The Barge

She receives a letter from a friend in Paris. He won't beat about the bush by saying how-is-she he-is-fine. He's dying of a most aggressive cancer. His medical men say he has a couple of months max. He wanted to tell his dearest friends this. He feels they have a right to know now rather than find out he's dead two months later. He doesn't want them to be sad. Please don't be sad. This is what happens also in life. How's that for an instance of original wisdom and great sentence structure? The drugs and rays haven't made him any sharper, which is why he's going cold turkey starting tonight. That ought to liven up his life and he sort of looks forward to the fight. It should be better than just lying or laying here doped up. But he realizes a certain sadness is inescapable from his dearest friends. What's not for him is death by this illness. And what a time for it to happen. He finally has the most adoring beautiful child any father could hope for. And he's so deeply in love with his wife. Words can't convey how much. Or should he have said "the depth"? He'll go through another kind of deepness pretty soon. Actually he won't. His time-for-humor line backfired on him. Because he's already made plans to go up in smoke and be sowed over the Gobi. No Gobi. He only wrote that because to his hollow ears it sounded good and he thought she might appreciate it. All those ohs. But his ashes to be left "in the very best" instead of stinking up the landscape. Let the owners of that contraption hose them out or sell them as fertilizer. And he probably didn't have to put quote marks there but somebody else close who doesn't know French might be reading this. But then she'd explain about the crème de la crème. Oh, he's so funny these days. It perhaps takes an overnight stay in the death house to get that way. But only to her and his wife. Well, his wife he's not writing to, but to everyone else who might possibly take it the wrong way, he's starkly *sérieux*. And just days before the fatal prognosis he decided after thirty years of dabbling what to do with his wife. He of course means "life." That slip had no conscious intention behind it. And he could have moused out the *w* and inserted the *l* but he wants here to be completely honest when he isn't trying to be humorous. To sell the barge and apartment and buy a farm on the Marne. That's true about the Marne. He didn't decide to settle there and do his life's final hard work just because of the rhyme. To go back to what he did as a kid with his Minnesota grandfolks. Did she know his dad died of the same disease? Or did till he put a bullet up his nose. Oh the ohs. And he would have written that as "ose" but her eyes might have mispronounced it. How could she have known? It was his family's deepest secret and dirtiest shame: the disease and the rhinocide. But there are no more controls. He doesn't quite know why he said that, but to her it'll be clear. She was always so bright. He's a naked baby in the North Woods. It's winter and he's wailing and his grandfolks are dead and his mother's helpless and he wants to be held and saved. But God is also what they say and miracles don't exist and science is all, he's afraid. It is what he always believed in, so why now misgive? But he shouldn't try to get poetical. He never liked poems much or understood what most of them meant. Even Richard Cory, if that was his name. Is he underscored or quoted? But he asks if it's possible that loving and understanding and even quoting poetry could have prevented his disease? His dad only read the Bible and socialist newspapers and auto mechanic magazines. His mother died a diseaseless death and just did farm chores for her in-laws and babbled on zigzaggedly since his birth. But he'd like to think that about poetry because it'll mean she'll live healthfully and long. Now he'll try to be *tout à fait* serious. What she meant to him then and since. If there's one besides the one he hates parting from, she's it. This can't come as a surprise. She must have seen it in his worshipful silence. No one could have been finer and softer and more intelligent to look at and beautiful to talk to. Permit him this trip through memory's enclosures. He loathes that line and most of the afore. But time is tight so too late to take them back or change them even with an automatic switch. This all spills out topsy-turvy unrehearsed. Bike tour through the Loire with her with little picnics of the proverbial off the road. Picking grapes alongside other Beaujolais guest harvesters and for their wages after three days a bottle of champagne and six of nouveau. She saw the beauty and exuberance in it while he mostly felt swindled and the sweat. Goading him to climb Montaigne's tower in Castillon when he wasn't inclined to shlepping up any more steps. That he got that word from her: shlep. And of course his barge through the Seine and Saône canals. She was such a great first mate. Teasing him into riding to the top of the Tour Awful. Ten years here and too disdainful to do it till she pressed. To act like a tourist? Her body. Her breasts. To hold them from behind at night till he slept. Is he being inordinately mortifying and naughty? Excuse him, and for the rest, but it's a last man's request. Her light hair against the bright and other sights? If he only had it in him to creatively say the old things a new way. His letter's getting druggy from the dope. He should have written when he was limpid and the disease wasn't evident yet. Isn't it intriguing how the most devastating effects often lie in repose? It corporealized in a month and won't be around in three. But he thinks he said that, so this will have to do it. The keyboard suddenly looks green and the mouse seems to be eating cheese. So much for his serioso attempts. Is that how to spell it and should he have italicized? Who's got the time. Should he have used there a question mark? And it was she who truly introduced him to music and its vocabulary. He doubts he'll be answer to able her if she writes back. That slip was unwitting and does she think it portends anything ulterior? His energy's receding and his hair and flesh have waxed and waned. He'll have to spend most of his time left duking it out with the pain. So sorry to end on that dopey note. So many apologies and so's, but he's sure she understands. Now if it's all right he'll say goodbye. If he hasn't made it see-through how he feels, he deserves to die tonight. So long. "So what do you think?" she says; "but first, while it's still in my head, do you know what limpid means?" "Nothing to do with 'limp.' That's the mistake I used to make. 'Lucid' and 'intelligible' and words of that order I finally remembered after about five or six times looking it up." "Never saw or heard it before. But what do you think about the letter?" "What is it about your breasts that men want to hold them from behind while they sleep?" "Who else but you two? And you about fifteen more years than Jock. And I don't really recall him ever doing it, though since he said he did I guess I have to believe it." "I like to because it means I can squeeze into you barefront from behind, smell your hair, put my mouth against your neck, fiddle with your nipples till they're erect, though not in a way where I'm keeping you from sleep. And I'm also warmer in bed in that position and seem to dream better and clearer and a lot more often about sex." "You didn't much care for the letter, then." "It's sad and I'm extremely sorry for the guy, of course. It's horrible, what he's going through and still has to face. And his kid and wife and plans and to be cut down at that age and everything, but what else? Things he said about you and the way he said them?" "Your disapproving expression and shaking your head and shutting your eyes as if you couldn't stomach much of what you were reading." "I did that?" "You did." "Okay, I was just a bit discomforted the way he waxed so womantically and all those sentence rhymes and that unpunctuated, except for the period and I think a hyphen in there, short line-at-a-time business. Once he got on that streak did he feel he had to complete it? So I thought it curious, that's all, to dabble in these mannerisms in his farewell address. But that's petty of me—and I wasn't being cynical, or didn't intend to be, with that 'farewell address' remark. He could have written it that clipped-line way—this must be the reason; the rhymes might've come naturally—because it was physically easier and he was weak." "You're holding back." "Why would I? I've nothing against the guy. Time I met him here and when we stayed on his barge I liked and admired him and could see why you would've been attracted to him and so forth. A six-foot-two rugged and muscle-bound galoot and world adventurer, unlike me and most people I know. The barge near the Place de la Concorde, canal trips on it, West Point, holy hell Tet Offensive experience, living with New Guinean aborigines on the beach, then with hippies in caves in Crete. I don't know; am I putting together right the people and places and residences? But a multitude of exploits, one dealing with camels in deserts, another for a dolphin and porpoise show, lobster boats in Maine, and logging and bear wrestling in Washington, before giving up stateside forever for the untried France. Who doesn't think about tossing it all overboard? But few have the guts to. And it didn't come from contacts or money; did it all himself by working hard. Comes to Paris sou-less and in a year he's got a barge and made a killing. He was a gentle rough guy, right? Man's man, that sort of stuff, loved sports and a big drinker, but so what? And that mop of competing blond, and so full, though now, poor guy, he says it's falling out from the treatments. Sunny face, great looks, blue eyes that reminded me of a movie star's, and he liked to read and sculpt and cook sea urchins and things, and what else? I don't know why you didn't hook up with him longer, get hitched, have kids, and so on." "He got pissy when he drank too much, and was often too moody, and drew away. Too many times I knocked on his door when he was on a bender and he told me to get lost. In the end he simply wasn't right, and in many ways we were too different. Our backgrounds: his for three generations was army and Wisconsin and no rabbis in the family; mine for the same amount of time running away from or getting murdered by Cossacks, Nazis, and Poles. And his love for lit was mainly genre and the good books in old-school translations. But I never appreciated him more than in that letter, though you could be asking me now why I showed you it." "I'm not, I'm not, for why wouldn't you? I'm your husband and I knew all of it and it was way before my time, so who cares?" "I also thought it was brave of him to say what he did and put his language and lyricism out on the limb like that. Out on the limb? What am I referring to here, a scribbling squirrel? Anyway, maybe it was something else that annoyed you. Not so much that once, for a few months, we actually loved each other—Jock and I—but that he reflected so tenderly and touchingly on it." "Tenderly and touchingly? What about bombastically, turgidly, ponderously, long-windedly, and unlimpidly? Let's face it, sick as he is, and I swear I feel nothing but the deepest sympathy for him—compassion, horror, the rest of it—did he have to resort to such flatulent phrasing and in such excess? You want to tell someone how much she meant to you and that you still care for her a great deal—I mean, those were great times, and this, as he suggests, is probably his last letter to you—then you do so without using such hyped-up overripe language. Because that was supposed to be poetry? Because that's what he was trying to do, you know: a sort of last-pitch winning you over once more in the kind of writing he knows you love best—the form; whatever the all-embracing word for poetry is." "You're way off on this, Gould, way way off." "You think so? Then let me run through it again. 'Dopey note.' That one I know by heart. Oh the ohs, indeed. 'Slip was unwitting' and did it portend—*portend?*—something untitting?" "He didn't say 'untitting.' And a perfectly useful and unarchaic word, 'portend.' You're being a stinker and very crude." "But you get my point. So he didn't say 'untitting.' But why 'corporealized' instead of 'materialized'? That's what he meant. Or even something simpler. But fancier the shmancier, it seemed." " 'Corp' is the body and 'material' isn't, or not as much. And he was stressing the body, wasn't he?—my breasts, the rest, and his own body failing him. I forget where he used it or how, but that could have been it." "Maybe. Okay. You're much better at figuring out literary meanings than I am. 'Keyboard suddenly looks green' isn't egregious. Same with the mouse eating the cheese. In fact they're good imagery and sound for someone getting nauseated or nauseous or just stomach-sick and dizzy. But the 'limpid.' And I'm not going to work entirely backwards here or include everything he wrote, I want you to know." "That's a big relief. Let me celebrate by going into the kitchen and drinking a glass of water." "But you yourself had problems with the 'limpid.' " "You letting me get by or do I have to inadvertently, which I'd never do, run over you?" "By, by"—stepping aside and following her as she wheels into the kitchen—"Need any help with the water?" "You've done enough, thank you. I'll manage." "Listen, all I was saying before was couldn't he—even just to avoid giving the impression he was trying to impress you—said 'clearer' for 'limpid'? That way you wouldn't—and he knows most people would do this, if they were interested or intellectually or linguistically curious, as you'd certainly be—wouldn't have had to ask what it meant or go to the dictionary if no one was around who knew it." "It's conceivable he thought I knew." "Then it was to impress you that he did too, or is that too far off base? And believe me, it was only by chance I'd seen the word in a few places, and through some kind of tenacity it finally sunk into that ooze of a brain of mine and I remembered what it meant. Otherwise, I bet right now you'd be looking it up." "Look, when you're being a bastard, self-deprecation doesn't work to reverse or temper it; nor, from before—that 'as you'd certainly be'—flattery. And if you have seen the word so much, then it must be in plenty of books, and I'm talking of contemporary ones, and even newspapers and magazines, nullifying your argument that it's so archaic or abstruse a word." "Maybe that's true. Maybe you're right. Anyway, to get on with my examples, or whatever they are or what I'm trying to do here—and I'm not trying to be funny now—'So much for serioso attempts.' I changed it from the original just a touch, but let's look at that one. I can see it's a play on what he previously wrote about wanting to be starkly serious and seriously stark and so on, but why'd he suddenly venture into music? Spreading his artistic wings because he knows bringing in music and with an Italian term would also appeal to you?" "So he brings in music, so he brings up poetry, so it's Italian, so he includes a little French. The French, of course, because he knows I speak it and will catch how he intentionally mangled it and he's lived there for more than twenty years, so it's sunk into his ooze, and Italian music directions because most of them are in that language." "It's also another oh." "So? What do you have against them? And he called attention to his self-conscious use of them, so I doubt he was furtively alluding to, with so many ohs, and which you might be accusing him of, anything orgasmic. And the music? I did, through my appreciation of it and because I also once studied piano seriously and usually when I found an available piano in Paris I practiced on it, get him interested in more serious music than what he liked till then, country and blues and jazz. Same with poetry: my love for it. Though he was less willing to take it in, even if for a while—and not just for my sake—he read it voraciously and in several languages." "Okay, I've nothing to argue on that, though I still see the poetry and music references as enticements to you of sorts. As for the orgasmic allusion, it never entered my head. But that's what I meant about your being—and I'm not trying to flatter you—a much better reader than I. But this line I liked a lot, the getting druggy from the dope. It cleverly undercuts the seriousness of the painkillers, and it was forcefully put. But 'The most devastating effects often lie in repose'? That true or only in there because he thought it sounded philosophically smart? But moving on—and I'm skipping a lot I could as easily go into—'Your light hair against the bright and other sights'? What happened to heights and slights and right is mights and tights, blights, bites, and other kites? And while we're talking about poetry—" "Give me back my letter, please." "First let me go over—" "I said to give it back!" and she grabs for it and he pulls it away and, when she looks startled, hands it to her. "What is it with you, Gould? I don't see what you have to be so threatened or envious of. Nor do I see why you couldn't have unobjectionally accepted this last man's dying request, as he said." "I remember that one; near the beginning, I think. It wasn't the line I was about to comment on, but I'm sure I would have got to it eventually." "But why, that's what I'm asking? He's dying and you're healthy. He's probably in terrific pain right now, maybe worse than when he wrote the letter, and you're not; you're feeling good and healthy. He has one child and is wretchedly sick and you have two kids and are very much alive and healthy. You have a good job, retirement if you want in ten years, and you're healthy and active and will no doubt be then, the way you take care of yourself, and he's dying. I've got my own disease to deal with, and that surely doesn't help you. But I'm not dying, it's not life-threatening, I can still take care of myself mostly, so it's not going to do you in or sap that much of your time and physical energy, and soon he'll have no wife and child in any medical condition because he'll be dead. Am I making myself clear? Why don't you try examining why you sniped at almost everything he put in that letter?" "What's to examine, in that sense? I feel terribly sorry for Jock. I know I said that, and by repeating it it might seem I don't mean it, but I do and that's the truth, but I was just going over his letter as a psychotherapist might go over his patient's thoughts, line by line. That's not an accurate analogy, since you never asked me to dig into his letter so thoroughly. Then what then? Just that I saw in a single reading, and perhaps incorrectly, what I thought he was getting at in certain places and found that curious and commented on it, that's all, which was no doubt insensitive of me and for that I apologize." "That's bullshit, or only half of it, but you go figure out which half. Meanwhile, no letter, and I mean never, not for me to read or you to pick apart again," and she rips it in two and those pieces in two and a couple of those pieces into more pieces, and when he says, "What are you doing? And look at the mess you're making," tries ripping up some of the smallest pieces but can't. "Listen, you're going to tear something up, at least keep all of it in your hands before you throw it away." "Now what's that, disapproval now of my inability to tear something up nimbly because of my unsteady hands? Are you insane?" "No, to both," picking the pieces of paper up off the floor. "But you only hurt yourself—you know that—because I'm sure you wanted to read it again." "You mean I didn't hurt you?" "No, I didn't mean that. Want these?" She shakes her head and he drops the pieces into the trash can. The rest are on the kitchen counter and in her hands. "Some advice: what you should have done if you didn't like anything in the letter was just silently shut up. Now I can never forget how you acted and your mean-spiritedness to Jock and me." "Okay, I should have, and you're mad and don't want to talk about it anymore, so I'm going for a walk. To the store, really." "I wish I could do that, just say so long and slam the door in your face. But I can't, so go; nobody here will stop you." "If it's the kids you think one of us should be home for, I'll stay and you can get in your cart and scoot out." "What's that supposed to mean, another crack?" "No, it meant—forget it; everything I say gets misconstrued. And you can only go out certain times, after certain preparations—I realize that now, so I'm sorry. So I'll see you." "As I said," and she turns away. Should he go? Go. Right now, nothing he can do or say if he stays. He goes. While he's walking to the store he thinks it'll soon blow over, two days, three. Tonight in bed she'll put one of her two pillows between them, if she doesn't sleep in her studio, and if he asks what's the pillow supposed to mean—to her sleeping in the studio he won't have to say anything because she won't come into their bedroom—she'll say, as she's said before when something like this has happened, it's more comfortable for her back, and he'll say, "Oh, yeah," and she'll say nothing to that and probably nothing to him after, no matter what he says, except maybe, "If you don't be quiet I'm going to sleep in the studio." If he tries to hold her breasts from behind in bed—well, he won't try because he knows she'll take his hand away. But after the two to three days she'll start acting normally to him again—he'll never have stopped acting as if just about nothing had happened—and he'll say he wishes, and maybe this was the problem, as she said, that over the last thirty to forty years he'd had some of Jock's confidence and derring-do and so on, made greater changes in the direction of his life a number of times, did this, risked that, gone to West Point, even, or Annapolis, or at least into the service instead of doing all he could to stay out of it; when he was a student hitched from Cairo to Cape Town as he'd planned to with this South African girl he'd met in Europe, and later on France for a few years, as he'd intended, rather than a few months and then back home the moment a good fellowship came through, which he didn't expect to get; hippies in caves only maybe, beach life on sunny Crete he'd like, for months down to nothing but shorts and crummy sandals and T-shirts; aborigines in New Guinea—he doesn't think so if it meant they had bones through their noses and treated diseases with things like bark and leaves, but would she believe he'd actually, when he was around thirty-five, thought of living in the capital of Papua for a year to write and be far away from the States but someplace exotic nobody he knew had been to and few had even heard of? He doesn't think he ever told her that last thing about himself, one of the few things he hasn't: the research he did for the trip and shots he'd started taking for it. But now he's in late middle age, and even if he didn't have the responsibilities he has at home, adventurousness like that would be so transparent and he'd feel like even more of an outsider in one of those places than he would have then. So that's what prompted his attacks, and maybe something to do with her illness: that Jock only knew her when she was completely free of it and also much younger. He gets a few things at the store, nothing they really need but just to make his excuse for leaving the house more believable, and in case she hasn't noticed—he won't say this but maybe she'll pick it up—he's the one who shops, cleans, cooks, provides, gets the kids off in the morning and to their music lessons at night and so on, comes home, and says, "The girls back?" "Look at your watch; it isn't even three yet." "Then I wasn't gone as long as I thought I'd be; I didn't really get anything. Listen, I'm sorry, very sorry for what I said; it was all the awful things you said it was, so will you forgive me?" "No, nor myself for giving in to the emotion of the argument and tearing up the letter so you wouldn't quote from it anymore. You showed yourself so ugly. I don't care if you were jealous of Jock with me or of the life he led or whatever caused it, even what I think is his damn good writing. At any age, what you did was a disgrace. To resume anything resembling even dreary living with you will take I can't say how long, not because you're dull but your attitudes and responses and what you find funny sometimes and free to be cavalier and blunt about are so insensitive and passé." "Excuse me, but does everything you say correspond?" "What do you mean now?" "Nothing. I got it wrong. But you sure got me, baby, you got me good." "You've done that routine before, at least a dozen times." "Then *whew!* is what I really wanted to say, and no routine; I swear, nothing like that. You let me have it and right on the *pupik* and deservedly so, besides covering everything I thought of saying to you while I was coming back from the store." "Yeah, whew, Mr. You-know-what Artist," and goes into her studio and shuts the door. He goes to their bedroom, time to lie down, he thinks, and lies on the bed and shuts his eyes, maybe a quick nap will help him see the whole thing better, hears his older daughter come home and yell out, "Is anybody around?" and his wife say, "I'm in here, darling; I'll be right out," thinks, Was I, as she said, in addition to everything else, envious a little of Jock's writing? Truth is, some of the lines weren't that bad. Too late to retrieve them from the original but let's see if any—this will also be a test of his memory and the staying power of the words—comes back. Richard Cory? Surely he knew that was his name. But the "diseaseless death." And "died of a diseaseless death" it was, which had a nice rhythm to it or whatever it had that made it stick and sound good. "Naked babe in the North Woods"? That was sweet and, again, nice rhythm. One understood right away what he meant and pictured it immediately. And the stuff with the mother holding him or he wanting to be held was touching and could have been more if he wasn't so critical at the time, and he knew that when he read it. But not the "wax and wane," though maybe he's missing the boat there, since Jock was referring to his flesh and hair. But he definitely liked the swindle and sweat. And that it rhymed on the next line with "shlep." And other things: "farm on the Marne," which actually sounds too much like "Spam in a can," and "what he did as a kid with his Minnesota grandfolks." So the letter was strong, he has to admit, for the most part evocative and strong, particularly the quick autobiographical reminisce and his trip through memory's enclosures. Nice job, Gould, well done. So he was wrong, he was wrong, he was wrong, he'll have to tell her but not today, and that perhaps it was the good writing coupled with the intensity of Jock's memories about her that set him off, besides the guy's great life till this horrid thing hit him. So why didn't they stay together longer? His other daughter comes home; he hopes she doesn't barge in here, as right after going over this he wants to nap. Couldn't have been just the drinking and Jew and Gentile, could it? Maybe he was also a stinking lover or had some sexual problem or dysfunction. He'd never ask her. He wouldn't know how to put it. And if he did find a way, she'd say, "At one time I would have told you, though only if you had asked first. But now, after what happened, I can't, and I'm not saying by that that he did or he didn't or was or wasn't. It just isn't something I ever want to tell you." He'll leave it at that, never bring it up again, not even years later when this whole incident will have just about been forgotten by her.

The Bed

His mother died in his arms. "You shouldn't keep telling people that," his wife said. "It sounds as if you're boasting." "But she did die in my arms. At home, in her hospital bed there. I was holding her, had her propped up." "I know; you've said. But from now on with other people, when you're telling them about it—this is only a suggestion—just say she died at home. Peacefully at home, because that's how you said it was, except for that last terrible moment which she might not have even been aware of." "I'm sure she was; I saw it when she opened her eyes after they'd been closed so long." "That could have been involuntary; some automatic physical reflex. You raised her up, she started vomiting, her eyes opened." "But it was what I saw in her eyes that made me feel she was suddenly conscious." "All right. I'm not arguing with you, sweetheart. But the thing with your arms—which is true, I'm not disputing that either, if the way you say it happened happened that way." "What other way could it have? It's not something I'd forget or make up. I was there with the woman who takes care of her weekends." "Ebonita. I know all that too. And she seemed as devoted to your mother as the woman who looked after her during the week." "I was sitting beside my mom. Ebonita pointed out this phlegm rising in her mouth. It was white and loose, almost like water, and a little bubbly. Maybe it wasn't phlegm, I now realize. Some other juices from inside, but we thought it was and a good sign because we'd been trying to get the congestion out of her chest for a day. Raising her, trying to get her to cough up. But there was a lot of this stuff right below the top of her lips, just staying there. She'd been having trouble breathing for a day and I didn't want to take her—send her, have an ambulance bring her, I mean—to the hospital, because even the doctor said—" "And he was right. Of course, he should have come over and seen her to say this, but he was still right. All they'd do at the hospital is stick needles in her, try to keep her alive for another day, if they were lucky, and maybe even help get rid of her before she would have normally passed away at home. But we've gone over this. What I'm saying now, though, is that some people might think this is just another terrific story you're telling. Not 'terrific.' That the dramatics of it is equally important or even more important to you than what you were feeling at the time and are no doubt feeling something of now." "I feel terrible, as low as I've ever felt. Or did feel that low for a few days and now just feel terrible, almost as low. And just talking to people about it, and right here with you—" "I know, dear, I know, I'm sorry. But you still don't want to convey the inaccurate impression that you're focusing on certain aspects of what happened to make it sound more interesting. In your arms. Hugging her and crying out the things you did at the end. Who wouldn't want his loved one to die in his arms like that: peacefully, for the most part? Not in a hospital where they shoo you out of the room at precisely that moment or a little before and then come out later and say she's gone." "That's why I didn't call EMS or that Haztollah or whatever that ambulance service is to take her to a hospital. I knew she was going. The doctor, from everything I told him, said so over the phone, and she'd been declining for a few weeks, and it was clear to Ebonita and me that this was it. I wanted her to be comfortable at home. She'd told me long ago that that's what she hoped for also: no tubes, and to die in her own bed. Well, it wasn't her own bed, it was this nursing service loan of a bed. And it wasn't even in her own bedroom, it was her dining room converted into a bedroom so she could be taken care of better, but at least it was her own home. And, she said, surrounded by—well, there was just me and Ebonita there and some old ghosts, maybe. Dad, my brother who didn't live till what, five? but did live in that apartment his last two years. I'm sure she would have wanted you and the kids there—but that couldn't be, and I wouldn't have wanted the kids to see it—and the main person who took care of her, Angela, but she was off for the weekend and we couldn't reach her by phone. And also Ebonita's daughter, just sitting there in a chair in the room and not looking scared or saying anything, just curious, as if this were an interesting new thing she was seeing, though Ebonita told me her daughter had been in the hospital room the moment her own grandmother died. So maybe that was it, reliving it, but I think more out of not knowing what to do and curiosity, the death and the way I was taking it. I didn't know how to tell her to leave, go to the kitchen, take in a movie, anything, but get out of here, please, this was a private moment for me, the worst there was; or for Ebonita to tell her—" "You were right; Ebonita should have if the girl didn't have the sense to leave herself. How old is she?" "Fifteen? Seventeen?" "Then old enough to know. And I can see why you'd be unable to say something yourself. Anyway, dear, I overheard you talking to Frederick about your mother and thought I should say something to you." "He asked me how I was. He'd called to make a lunch date. He didn't know she'd died. So I said I was feeling the worst I'd ever been in my life, and then—after he asked—that it was because my mother had died on Sunday." "You said she died in your arms on Sunday." "So that's what I said, then." "And that's why I brought it up. But of course do what you want. I just felt I had to point it out." "Okay. I'll remember. You're probably right. Anything else?" "No, nothing. I'm making myself tea. Like some?" and he says, "No, thanks," and she grabs his hand and squeezes it and looks up at him sympathetically, he fakes a quick smile, she says, "I understand," and wheels herself to the stove to get the teakettle. He should help her, but he suddenly feels in his throat and eyes a cry coming on and wants to be alone. He goes into the living room and sits but no tears come and the swelling in his throat and the itchy feeling around his eyes go away. What's that mean, he's finally adjusting to his mother's death? No, he's sure he's in for a few more bad days of it. The tall memorial candle's burning on the fireplace mantel. He brought it from New York, something the funeral home gave him along with several cardboard boxes to sit in mourning on, all of which he left behind but one, and lit it the day after they drove back from the funeral. So it's been lit for more than two days and seems to have burned less than a third of the way down. His wife wanted him to put a dish under it but he said, "Why? That's for regular candles when the wax is dripping. This one's inside a long glass cylinder, and it couldn't be safer, because the lit wick gets lower down the longer the candle burns." She said the glass might break, burning for so many days—"Have you felt how hot it is? I did, just as a test, and wish I hadn't, or had licked my fingers first, for it burned me"—and he said he knows it gets hot, he doesn't have to touch it to find out, but he's sure that that glass is the kind that won't break from such a small flame, because when she felt it did she also see how thick it is? He gets up and touches the glass; it's hot but didn't burn his fingers though would have if he'd kept them on longer, and maybe the heat from the bottom of the glass will do something to the mantel wood when the candle burns way down, but he has about three days for that. Where's the camera? and sees it on the piano and, using the flash, takes a picture of the candle for some future day when he may want to remember exactly what it looked like, Jewish star and funeral home name on it and everything. It could also turn out to be an interesting photo, a few condolence cards and the little *Prayers and Meditations* book, which he took off a side table in the funeral home sitting room her coffin was in, lying beside the candle, if maybe come out looking too much like the front of one of those cards. He opens the book to "Yizkor in Memory of a Mother." What's Yizkor mean again? Not "again": he never knew. Certainly not "may," which seems to be the translation in each of the seven Yizkors in the book: "For a Wife," "For a Son," et cetera, and one just "Yizkor Meditation." The prayer in the book he likes best, or maybe it's a meditation, is "At a Mother's Grave," but the book stayed in his pocket at the burial—the rabbi did all the reading—and he's only read the prayer to himself in bed a few times before reading a couple of sad poems and shutting off the light and going to sleep. He sits on the box with the book, starts reading very low the Yizkor for a mother, something he's done when nobody was around at least once a day since she died. But he shouldn't be reading while sitting, should he, even on this mourner's box? And he doesn't want to stand up and read, or read it any louder—his wife might come in and say something like, "You, never a believer or worshiper or even someone who observed a single Jewish holiday or ritual, not even circumcision if we'd had a son, now going on every day like a yeshiva *bucher*?"—and reading it silently standing up or seated doesn't mean anything. Later, when the kids are asleep and his wife is in one of the other rooms, he'll read it or another prayer or meditation while he stands by the candle, as he's done the other times since he's been home. He's cried every time while reading from the book—oh, don't go into it. He moves to the easy chair and opens the *New York Times,* tries reading an Arts article, but thinks of her. He's almost always thinking of her, or in ten minutes or so of doing something else he always seems to return to thinking of her, and sometimes of her reading this same paper, but the late edition, which she loved doing every morning over coffee till she couldn't anymore because of her cataracts. Regrets: why didn't he ever drive her down here to see this house? They bought it more than three years ago and she never saw it once. But he's gone over that. She was frail, couldn't take the train or plane anymore, four-hour car trip would have been too tiring and maybe even painful for her, it would have been too much for him to deal with, taking care of her and also seeing to his wife. Two wheelchairs in one house: in his head he didn't like the way they looked together, especially at the dinner table and on the little patio outside, though he didn't think it would have bothered his wife. But he could have made the car seat comfortable for her, stopped as often as she wanted along the way, driven more slowly than he normally does, taken Angela with her, put them up for a few days, Angela in the basement, his mother on the day bed in his wife's studio, an intercom hooked up between them, or moved his kids to the basement and had Angela and his mother in their adjacent bedrooms, driven them home and then returned the same day. The last two summers when he drove back from Maine he told his wife he was definitely going to have his mother down for a few days this fall and she said it'll be difficult but it was all right with her, and that was the last he did of it. She would have loved that he owned this house and lived in such a neighborhood: tall trees, small hills, lots of birds, and perfumy air, nursery school playground across the street and all those children's voices, house on one level and with ramps, extra-wide doors, and a bathroom big enough for a wheelchair to turn around, hospitable supermarket nearby. Regrets: why didn't he call her every day as he'd promised? Remembers his father saying lots of times, "When I got married and moved out I called my mother at least once a day till she died and saw her twice a week for dinner or lunch," and his mother saying a number of those times, "It's true, your father was an unbelievable son: almost too good, to where he neglected his own family." He remembers thinking this was a nice thing to do and he'd do it too with the phone, once he grew up and moved away from home. He called her every other day or every third day and for the last year she frequently didn't know who he was or took him for someone else: her dead brother, his father, a name he didn't recognize, and when he asked who's that? she said she'd never heard the name before and why'd he bring it up? But in a minute or so, after he kept saying, "It's me, Mom, Gould, your son, Gould," recognizing him and saying at first she didn't hear him because he was speaking so softly or it was her bad hearing or the girl didn't put her hearing aid in right this morning or the hearing aid must need a new battery or never worked right: "You'll have to take me to the place we got it at. I forget where, but you'll know or Angela must have it written down. But you will come around to see me soon, won't you, dearest? I'd really like that," and he'd say, she knows he's in Baltimore, right, and not in New York? and weekdays there's his job, not too demanding, but also driving Fanny to and from school, and weekends the kids always have so many things going for him to drive them to, and Sally, of course, takes some of his time, but he'll be there in two weeks, he promises, take her to lunch on a Saturday, and she'd say, Two weeks sounds like such a long time when one has nothing to do, but if it's the best he can do she'll have to live with it. Or sometimes she'd say, "That was dumb of me to think you were Dad. Probably because I didn't get enough sleep last night. All I could do was run my life through my mind and not like most of it, so aggravation there too. And also wasting away here watching inconsequential TV shows the girl likes makes me stupid and I forget what year it is and where I am. Tell me, is this my home I'm in?" and he'd say, "Your old apartment for almost sixty years. It's just it's a different kind of bed than you're used to and it's in the dining room because your bedroom was too far away from the bathroom, so maybe you don't recognize your surroundings because of that," and she'd say, "All that's probably true. Though I still have a suspicion this isn't my regular home, but then why would you want to trick me?" Regrets: sometimes he'd call and Ebonita or Angela would answer and say, She's resting (or on the potty or sitting under the water in the shower), and he'd say he'll call back in an hour but usually never did. Why? Because he'd think, he already called that day; his duty was done, Angela will tell her he called and she'll be pleased by it though disappointed she missed him and later think something came up at his home where he couldn't call back. When actually talking on the phone to her the last few years was often frustrating, where she couldn't understand what he was saying and he'd have to shout for her to hear him, and sometimes she'd give the phone to Angela and say, "You talk to him and find out what he wants; he's speaking loud enough but I still can't make out a word." He should have called back each time and, if she was still on the toilet or had gone from the toilet to the shower or bed, say he'll call back again in an hour or two, or sometime that day, and then call back as he said. Regrets: he'd tell her he was coming to New

York to see her for the day, and half the time he'd call a day or two before to say something had come up at home—Sally, or one of the kids got sick—so he'll have to put off the trip till next week. Usually his Sally or sick-kid excuse was a lie: he didn't want to make the trip, too tired to or thought he'd be, or he had work to do and wanted to do it at home and not on the train, or heavy rain was forecast for New York, so he wouldn't be able to wheel her to a neighborhood restaurant, which made getting her there—which he wanted to because he found having lunch with her at home suffocating—even with Ebonita or Angela helping him, tough because he'd have to get her and the wheelchair in and out of cabs and sometimes she was a dead weight. He also wouldn't be able to take her to the park after lunch, which she liked doing and frequently fell asleep for an hour or two there while he watched people and read. Regrets that he found having lunch with her at home, suffocating. Regrets that she slept so much when he was in the park or even at home with her the last couple of years, but nothing he could have done about that. Regrets that he didn't take her down to the river after lunch, which he thought of doing lots of times on hot days, but it was about fifteen minutes away while the park was much closer. But he shouldn't have disappointed her so much, since that's what she obviously was—her voice, or silence after, or, "That's all right, your family comes first, and maybe you have some important outside things to do too"—whenever he told her he couldn't come in this weekend as planned. Regrets: why didn't he initiate conversation more and follow up the questions he did ask with more questions about what she was talking about when they went out for lunch or spoke on the phone or sat in her home the last few years? The calls to her were usually over in a couple of minutes, sometimes less; a few perfunctory questions, and mostly the same ones: "How are you? You feeling all right? Eating okay? Anyone drop by lately? Do anything interesting recently?" "Like what?" she'd say. "When you're not here, and I'm not going to a doctor with one of the girls or your lovely cousin, all I do is sleep and eat a little and listen to the radio or TV." A couple of times he said, "Then anything interesting on the radio or TV?" and she said, "I can barely see or hear them," and then silence on his part and after she asked him a few things about his family—"Your kids all right? Your wife okay? Does that new medicine she's taking work? Listen," she said, maybe twenty times, "I hear they're discovering new things all the time for what she has; is she involved with any of them?"—she'd say, "So, I guess that's it; I can't think of anything else worth mentioning. Thanks for calling; you're a doll. I love you," and he'd say, "Same here, Mom; Sally and the kids send their love too, and I'll call you tomorrow," and she'd say, "I look forward to it; I always do." Face it, he usually wanted to get off the phone with her as soon as he could. The same conversations, same difficulty in holding those conversations, and whatever he told her she seemed to instantly forget. But he should have faked it, put more life in his voice, asked friends for jokes and told her them—she liked a good joke—and laughed at the punch lines if she didn't. Thought of lots of different things she might want to talk about, repeated what he had to say over and over till she finally got it. Prepared questions to ask her before he dialed. Stayed on the phone five minutes, ten minutes, even thought of follow-up questions to ask her, wrote all these questions down, even. She must have thought sometimes, He's got to be bored with me by now; probably thinks I don't understand a word he says and haven't a brain left in my head. That I'm old so I'm demented. He's probably only calling out of a sense of duty. I should ask him more about him and his family, not just general questions but specific ones—"What courses are your girls taking in school? How are they doing in them? Do you have to help them much with their homework? I'm sorry, I know you once told me, but what grades are they in again?"—but I can never think of this when we're on the phone. I should also call him more, but so many times I don't think he's glad to hear from me. It mostly seems I'm getting him at a bad time, nothing personal against me. At the end of his calls to her, she often said, "Tell me, what's the best time to reach you by phone?" and he always said, "Anytime after five is good; there you're almost guaranteed I'm home. If I'm not and you speak to Sally or one of the kids, I'll call you soon as I get your message, unless it's way too late." She hadn't called him more than three or four times in the last two years, and one day she called him twice and just an hour apart, not remembering she'd already called him. "Do I have your phone number? I don't think you ever gave it to me," she said several times, and he'd tell her, "It's in the little phone book on your night table. It's also taped to the inside of the cabinet door above the kitchen phone, and I know

Angela has it written down in a couple of other places in case she suddenly has to get me. But don't bother calling me; I like calling you and I try to every day," and she said things like, "I know, and it's very sweet of you." Why didn't he ever talk to her about some of these things? "You know me, Mom, I was never much of a talker on the phone, and it has nothing to do with you if our talks are short. And if I'm relatively quiet or not too conversational, we'll call it, at the restaurants we go to or when we're sitting around at home, it's only because the long train ride's made me sleepy, or I had to get up earlier than usual for a Saturday to catch the train and get here by noon, or I did lots of schoolwork or something the previous night and didn't get enough sleep, so there, also, it was nothing you did." Regrets: when he came to New York the time before the last, almost a month ago—and another regret is why he didn't come a week or two after that, or every week—and walked into the dining room where she was sitting in a chair and said, "How are you, Mom?" and she looked up, no smile, which she normally gave, that she was glad to see him, and said, "Who are you?" why didn't he get on his knees and hug her and say, "Mom, it's me, Gould, your son; oh, my mom, why don't you recognize me?" Instead, he stood there, saying, "What do you mean, who am I? It's me, who else could it be? I've come to see you, all the way from Baltimore, and take you out to lunch and spend the day with you," and she said, "We're going out? That's nice. I wasn't expecting it, nobody said anything," and he said, "But I called last night to remind you and Angela, and we've been talking about it the last two weeks. And you're dressed for going out, aren't you? so you must have known," and she said, "Then I don't remember, but please don't make it an issue. I'll have to go to the bathroom first and then I'll be ready—call the girl," so regrets there for upsetting her. Did he apologize? He's sure he did but forgets. He got her wheelchair—"Want to walk it outside?"; she said, "Right now I feel too weak to"—and got her into the chair, pushed her outside; "The girl; shouldn't we invite Angela? We haven't taken her to lunch in a while," and he said, "Not today, I just want to be with you alone and I'm sure she appreciates the break, especially when she's working the weekend this week too," when it was really because Angela picked at her food and took a half hour longer to eat than his mother—turned around in the areaway, and pulled her up the steps to the sidewalk.

"Want to try walking the wheelchair now? It's good exercise for you, and only a little way," and she said, "I don't feel I can move a step. I'm sorry, but I don't know what's wrong with me today," and he said, "Mom, come on, you should only do what you're able to," pushed her to the restaurant she liked going to most, table by the patio window she liked sitting beside so she could watch the people passing, after that to a coffee bar on the same block—he got her a decaffeinated coffee but told her it was regular, that's what Angela said the doctor wants her to have if she does have coffee; he'd prefer her to stick with hot cocoa or a mild tea—another regret? No, and even though she wasn't supposed to have a drink either, and if a drink then just a wine or beer, he got her her favorite: Jack Daniels on the rocks with a little water and twist of lemon, "Because what else are they going to take away from me," she once asked, "food and air too?"—and a flaky Danish-like pastry she loved, with peaches and walnuts in it. She asked that day at both places and while he wheeled her along the street the same kinds of questions she usually did, and some of them several times: "You feeling okay? Your wife. Everything considering, she's all right, no change? And your lovely daughters, they okay too? They doing well in school? Of course they are, look who are their parents," and he said, "Sally, maybe, but not me, and I mean by that their brains." "How old are they now? . . . I can't believe it, where'd all the time go? You still teaching? You have enough money? You know, if you ever need a loan . . . I don't have much but you can have it all, because what good is it going to do me? Where do you live these days? Not in New York? How far is Baltimore from here? That much? I didn't realize. How long have you lived so far away? You don't think, if you looked, there'd be something closer that was as good?" Another thing to regret: that he's lived down there the last fourteen years? They kept his wife's old student apartment near Columbia, sublet it more than they used it. Whenever they came up, though, and stayed there he saw her every day for lunch and sometimes dropped by around five for drinks and cheese and crackers. Regrets that they didn't come up more. The drive was long and tedious for him, but he should have done it more often. She loved seeing the girls. And before their older one started middle school, when absences began counting against her, they stayed at their apartment all of June and three weeks during the Christmas break instead of what they'd done the last four years, ten to eleven days. And when she was still in nursery school and kindergarten, they came up for around five weeks and he maybe skipped seeing his mother one or two days. Then he wheeled her home, didn't ask if she wanted to walk the chair, knew she couldn't, helped her onto the bed—"Suddenly I feel very tired. In the restaurant I was fine. I didn't have anything alcoholic to drink, did I?" and he said, "Let's just say I kept diluting your Jack Daniels with water so you wouldn't drink it almost straight and get looped there," and she said, "Now that was a mean thing for you to do"—sat beside her a couple of hours while she napped, and then got up and leaned over her and said, "Mom, Mom, listen, I have to be going and I want to say goodbye," and she opened her eyes and smiled and said, "Thank you, my darling," and he said, "Thank you, nothing; it's been my pleasure. I love taking you out and seeing you, and I just wish I could do it more often; I'll try to," and she said, "That'd be nice. You're the only one who'll give me a drink and I get to eat a good lunch and enjoy myself so much with," and he kissed her forehead and cheek and then her forehead again—it was wet, didn't feel warm when he touched it with his fingers. Maybe she was sweating because the room was too warm or it was the drink or it could be one of the medicines she's taking or she had a fever. Can a forehead be cold and the body feverish at the same time? Another regret is that he didn't tell Angela about it. Just knocked on her door, and she said through it, "Yes, sir?" and he said, "I'm going." Maybe the infection was only just setting in and in a few weeks gradually grew into that awful hoarse cough and labored breathing—spread to her lungs, he's saying—and was what finally killed her. "She's been declining for months," her doctor said on the phone the day before she died. "She won't pull through this time, a hospital's not going to improve her chances, so it's mainly a matter of where you think she'll be most comfortable. I always tell the patient's immediate survivors that, unless there's physical or emotional suffering involved on either side, home's the ideal." Then she shut her eyes, smile gone, seemed to fall back to sleep, and he got his coat and briefcase, stuck his books and newspaper in it, looked into her room, she seemed to be sleeping peacefully, thought of going over to kiss her, didn't want to disturb her, and left. He'll call her when he gets home, he thought, walking to the subway. She'll most likely be up and will like hearing from him. He didn't. Another regret. Would have been so nice. "Mom, I just got in," she'd ask where, he'd say, "From New York, where I saw you today: I took the train, and first thing I'm doing—I don't even have my coat off—is calling you." No, too obvious. "Mom, I just got back from New York, where I saw you, and wanted to know how you are and if you had your dinner." Forget the dinner. Just "How are you, what are you doing?" She'd have said, "I'm all right, I guess," and, "Nothing, as usual." Another regret is that he didn't stay overnight in their apartment, come over in the morning, and take her out for breakfast or if it was raining or too cold, made her breakfast in her apartment with things he brought over and knew she liked—bagels, Canadian bacon, strawberries, Friendship pot cheese, a special fruit juice—and then left for the train. Or just stayed longer by her bed that afternoon. Read, maybe taken a quick walk. Then had a drink with her when she awoke: Jack Daniels on the rocks for him (it was the only hard stuff in the house, though he could have bought a bottle of vodka in his quick walk), a very watered-down one for her, because there wasn't any great need for him to get home before the kids went to sleep, and it was Saturday, so they'd still be up at ten or eleven and he could see them if he got on the train by seven or eight. And the kids didn't need to be driven anywhere early the next morning that he remembers. Even if they did, he could have called Sally and asked her to get a friend to drive them or the parent of the kid whose house his daughter was going to; that it was more important he go home later that day than he thought or to stay the night in New York and leave tomorrow around noon because his mother seemed to be getting weaker—she was definitely getting weaker and thinner and less lucid, and he wanted to spend more time with her while he had the chance. Misses her, can't stop thinking of her. Well, it's not as if he tries to stop. He's just always thinking of her, or a lot. He can be doing anything, taking a run, a shower, shaving, slapping something on toast, sitting in a chair eating or reading, talking on the phone (he's only been able to talk—won't even pick up the phone when it rings; his kids and wife have to and then tell him who it is—to a few close friends and his mother's accountant and the cousin who looked in on her in New York the past few years and is now going through her own mourning and calls up to talk to him or Sally about it: "How strange. I never knew I'd feel this way once she was gone. I almost thought it'd bring relief, to me and her, though I can't especially say how, since she for the most part was in relatively good health for someone her age and I enjoyed her company, and now I grieve that I won't be catching the One-oh-four bus to see her and stopping in a store along the way to get her a buttered soft roll," and he said "Same here, though not the relief part. But honestly, Lottie, I can't talk about it yet like this"), when suddenly she pops into his head, if he isn't already talking about her, like with Lottie, and he often starts crying. He thinks about writing a poem about her. Anything: her youth, what she meant to him, times with her when he was a boy, her relationship with his dad, one composed of just phrases and things she liked to say. He doesn't write poems. Last was a series of them to Sally a few weeks after he met her and the first time she broke off with him, titling them "2S1," "2S2," through "2S11" and finally "2Sdozen." He threw out his copies of them about a year later but wonders if she kept the originals he sent her one by one after he wrote them, sometimes going outside at two and three in the morning to drop them into a mailbox. He takes out his pen and starts writing, cries during part of it, and finishes in a few minutes. It all just came. He'd stop about ten seconds between each completed sentence before going to the next. Should he write another? No, this one says what he wants. He reads it and changes only the second "laid" to "lay." "How could my mother not be alive?/ My mother has always been alive. / I clutched her around and cried, / 'Mommy, Mommy, it's all right, / Mommy,' and then she died. / I laid her sideways on the pillow / and she lay there always. / She has always been there. / When I come to this city I will / be coming to see her. / Things won't change, will they? / How could my mother not be alive? / How could she? Things don't change. / I'll never be the same. / Speak to me, Mommy, speak to me. / It all goes on and I cannot stop." He'd like to be able to—of course he would, but finish the thought—to be able to type it up, change nothing else in it, and stick the original into an envelope and send it to her. He'd like, he'd like. And Express Mail. To go to the post office and get one of those Express Mail envelopes and send it that way so she can get it early the next day. And with a note in it. Now that's enough. But what would he say? *Dear Mom, I'm so glad you can receive this, your loving son, Gould.* So what to do with the poem?

He tears the page out of the notebook and puts it inside the book he's been reading but hasn't read more than a few pages of since he took it on the train to New York the day she died. Phone rings and he yells out, "I don't want to speak to anyone now, no one, not even my cousin," and his wife says from her studio, "I understand, but what should I say if it's for you, you're not here?" Phone's still ringing. "Say, if they don't already know, that my mother died and I am here but I don't feel I can talk to anyone now but her and my kids and wife. That I'm low—feeling as low as I've ever felt in my life." "You want me to say that?" "Pick up the phone if you want and say anything, but please stop its ringing; the damn noise is killing me," and she picks it up, and he quietly moves to the kitchen by her studio and listens as she says, "No, no, it's coming along; he's very upset, of course," and he says, "Upset? What a word for it. I don't know exactly what I am but I'm a helluva lot worse than upset," and she's probably looking his way, shaking her head, doing things like that and the expression to go with it—he can't see her nor she him—and she says, "Please, Gould, don't make it any tougher," so her hand's probably on the talking part of the receiver, and he says, "Sorry, no harm meant, but what can you expect? Though that's no excuse," and goes back to his chair in the living room. The cat comes in and heads toward him, and he says, "Listen, I don't want to pet you and you've already been fed plenty, so go away," and the cat gets by his feet and seems ready to jump into his lap. "Did you hear me? I don't want that," wagging his finger. Cat jumps up, and he puts him on the floor. Jumps right back up, and he says, "What is it with you? I know you know something's wrong and you're trying to comfort me but not . . . right . . . now," and with one hand underneath he holds him over the floor from about three feet up and lets him drop. The cat scoots up onto the chair opposite him, stares at him after he settles himself, and then tucks his front paws under his chest and closes his eyes for sleep. "You understand," he says, low, "that it's that I don't want to touch or be touched by my wife either for any kind of loving or solace or easement. My kids, yes, to hold them, but right now, and for I don't know how long but I'm sure no more than a couple of weeks, I don't want to be held. Oh, what am I saying?" and thinks he's got to do something. Sitting here or lying on his bed or walking around the neighborhood, all he can do is think of his mother and what he didn't do for her. He goes into the bathroom and pees, though he had no urge to, just to get up and do something. Move, move, keep busy, that's the ticket. Folds the towels on the rack. Then folds them the more intricate but right way, horizontally in half and then vertically in thirds and then over. Then he sweeps the bathroom floor and washes it with diluted ammonia and rags. On his knees, just as his mother didn't do; she used a mop but he can't stand those things, the stringy ones, which you have to wring out by hand if you don't have a bucket with a wringer, or the sponge mops they have that are too damn slow to use, where you have to squeeze them with that metal piece every two square feet of mopped floor. Rags are the best, rags, rags: rinse them under the kitchen faucet after you're through and then throw them into the washer, though make sure you don't wash any clothes or linens with them—all that lint. Same with the kitchen: sweeps it, then spills diluted ammonia on the floor and gets on his knees with the rags and starts swabbing. "What are you doing?" his wife says; "the smell," and he says, "Cleaning. I feel I want—I don't feel, I just want, and I don't mean by that correction anything but that I want everything to be clean, tidy, neat, even sparkling. And it's something to do, I need something physical to do." "If that's the case, after you're done, the shed needs emptying out and tidying up." "Good, will do," and he finishes swabbing and then dries the floor with paper towels. But first finish cleaning the house, he thinks, and vacuums every room, changes the kitty litter box, remakes all the beds, scours the kitchen sink, wipes down the refrigerator and stove and countertops, takes the clothes from yesterday out of the dryer and folds them and puts them away in various drawers, cleans the toilets and tub and shower stall and refolds the towels in the other bathroom, goes outside and cleans out the shed, has a whole bunch of things from it and the basement to take to the dump, and puts them all in the van, yells out to his wife, "I'm off to the dump," and goes. While he's driving he thinks, Turn the radio on to one of the classical music stations, but there might be voices, news, promos, thank-yous for contributing to a recent fund drive, and so on, and he really doesn't want to hear music right now either. He thinks his mother would have liked to come to the dump if she were here. *Knows,* unless she was too weak or tired to. Places like dumps, the kids' music schools, just ordinary chores; driving in neighborhoods she hadn't been to before, or not for long, and especially shopping with him, and especially grocery shopping when she stayed a week or two in Maine with them each summer, she liked. A week; his wife felt that was long enough for either of their mothers, but he always felt bad sending her back to the hot city and wanted it to be more. She'd be in the front seat. Last time she was in the van was about six weeks ago when he drove her and his family to dinner at his cousin's apartment in New York. No, last time was when he drove her home after dropping off his family at their apartment, since she lived farther downtown. She was in the backseat, because his wife had been in the front seat and there didn't seem to be any reason for his mother to move up for such a short trip. He said something to her, she didn't answer, he turned around: she sat frozen, it seemed, staring straight ahead past the front passenger seat. "Mom, you okay? What are you looking at so hard?" She continued staring, didn't move. "Mom, anything wrong? you all right? why don't you answer or look at me?" Nothing. He thought: Is she dead? Is this it, then? He reached over and touched her shoulder and neck. She seemed to be breathing normally but still stared straight ahead without moving. Should he pull over? he thought. Maybe she needs to be rushed to a hospital or for one of those EMS ambulances to rush to him. But he's near her building and maybe she is asleep and something's wrong with her eyes that's keeping them open and she'll snap out of it before he gets there. He kept looking back at her as he drove; she stayed the same; he parked at the hydrant by her building, put the emergency lights on, ran around the car and slid the side door open, and she suddenly stopped staring, turned to him and smiled, and said, "We're home? So fast? I must have slept," and he said, "But your eyes were open. You were staring out the windshield, or seemed to, the whole way after we dropped off Sally and the girls," and she said, "I couldn't have. Nobody sleeps with his eyes open, at least I never have." He got her into the chair and wheeled her down the areaway steps and into the building—regrets that he didn't tell Angela, or whichever woman was working that night—and also called her doctor the next day about it. He still doesn't know why she froze up like that. Next time he sees his doctor or his wife's—not the kids'; she's strictly pediatrics—or meets one before then at a dinner or something, though the way he feels now he doesn't know when that will ever be, he'll mention it. He'd talk to her now if she were in the car. Last time they spoke she was hallucinating. It was the night before she went into a coma; next day—no, the day after that—she died. Ebonita called him; said his mother had been babbling for three hours straight, she'd never seen anything like it. About her children, husband, work, her family when she was a girl, a jump rope she played with for years; mostly, though, her mother and sister. "I can't get her to stop. Maybe you can." She put his mother on, and she said, "Party, party, party," and he said, "Mom, it's me, what do you mean 'party'? What's doing?" and she said, "Let's go to a party. I want to party, party." "Mom, it's Gould; you're saying you want to go to a party? What kind?" and she said, "How's business?" and he said, "I'm not in business, Mom; I teach, I write," and she said, "I'm going to bake a cake. First I should get out of here. I want to bake lots of cakes. I have to get up now and start baking if I'm to have the time to do it." She was speaking away from the phone, maybe to Ebonita, and Ebonita said, "Talk into the phone, Mrs. B. It's your son, so say something to him." "Party, party, party," she said into the phone. "I want to make and bake. Cookies, bread, cake." "You always made great herb breads, Mom, do you remember? And what you called a zucchini bread, though it was more like a cake. Everyone loved it. Is that the kind of cake you mean you want to make?" "My sister's coming today and she likes chicken the way I bake it and she loves my zucchini cake." "Which sister? You come from a large family." "We'll party and party. Lizzie and Ethel, Harris and Rita. Zippie, though that wasn't her real name." "What was her real name? You and Aunt Zippie and Uncle Pete never wanted to reveal it." "Party and more party. Are any of my family alive? I think they're all gone and deceased, since I haven't seen any of them in years. Could be they don't want to come see me. Who would want to come see an ugly old mess. Is it fair that I'm the only one of my family left? What happened? Where'd my mother go? What'd I do?" And then more talking to herself, it seemed, where he couldn't cut in, till he yelled out, "Ebonita, it's all right, you can take the phone away, I want to speak to you." About two months before that his mother said, "Tell me, and I want you to be honest"—he was sitting on her bed, she in her chair, the newspaper she couldn't read anymore because of her cataracts, but still had delivered every day, on her lap—"how old am

I?" and he said, "Ninety-one." "No, am I really that old? How'd I get to live that long? It doesn't run in my family. And I drank and smoked and your father made life hell for me and I lost a child and never ate right because I always wanted to be thin and for the most part neglected myself in all the other things. I don't get it." He told Ebonita on the phone, his mother babbling in the background: "I'm coming tomorrow to see her. I'll get the eight o'clock train and be there around eleven. She doesn't sound well. But you say she has no fever and is eating and urinating okay?" and she said, "Everything but the talking's normal. And she's eating and drinking her food like she's enjoying it." His younger daughter woke him around four the next morning and said she couldn't breathe. "You mean you're having trouble breathing?" and she said, "No, I can't get breaths. My throat's stuck." They later found out she had the croup. He gave her medicine that was for his older daughter's asthma, called Ebonita around ten and said he had to take his daughter to the doctor now, and he'd either see his mother much later in the day than he'd planned or early tomorrow, all depending on how sick his daughter and mother are. "How is she?" and she said, "She babbled endlessly till two this morning and is now sleeping like a baby," and he said, "She talk about anything different this time? Things or people or events you never heard her speak of before?" and she said, "No, it's mostly her mother and sister and some her father and cake and bake and chicken and such. You a lot too, that you're her only person she can really count on," and he said, "That's not true at all. There's you and Lottie and Angela and some people from the street. Don't take it personally. In fact, if you want, and you can say this idea came from me, tell her if she can count on me so much, how come I'm almost never there? But it must be very difficult for you, tending to her so many hours straight, and I'm sorry I'm not there to help out. Anyway, it sounds as if she's much better already, but I'll call you later to make sure." He called later and his mother was still sleeping peacefully, though she had sat up for a few minutes to take some special canned food supplement through a straw. "Good, that means she got some food and you got to rest." He dumps the stuff he had in the van, goes home, parks, then, while still in the car, he thinks, There's a road near here he's for a few years wanted to take to see what's around it and where it goes, but he's always given himself excuses not to: has no time, it's a silly or childish impulse to carry out, and so on; but do it now, and he drives to it—it's only a mile away and he passes it on the way to the dump and back and almost every weekday when he drives his older daughter to high school—and it winds through an area with homes and woods and hilly lawns like his own and ends up on a familiar road to the main town in this part of the county. He drives home on the familiar road, since it's the shorter route of the two, parks, and walks into the house, and his wife says, "Was that you in the carport before?" and he says, "You mean about ten minutes ago in the van? Yes, but I suddenly forgot something," and she says, "What?" and he says, "I don't know, something. My mother call?" and she says, "What are you talking about?" and he says, "Just being dopey, that's all, and possibly thinking, 'Well, you never know.' Anyway, the last few years she hardly ever called. I called her, though, almost every day and sometimes every day for a week. I tried to call more, every single day I was away from her, really I did." "I know, my darling." "It would've been nice if she had called—now, I'm talking; I'm not concerned, or ever felt slighted she didn't call me much the last few years." "Of course you weren't." "I'm sure she wanted to but didn't think of it. Or she thought of it and then the thought quickly disappeared. She'd never stand on ceremony with me, either—that's a term she liked to use. But you know, that, 'He's the son so he should call me,' and it for sure wasn't that she was too cheap to call. That was my father. 'Penurious,' I liked to call him—I mean if I had to put it in words—though some people, including my mother sometimes, called him cheap. Oh, the trouble he gave me as a kid when I wanted to phone a friend. 'Your father got stock in Bell?' and so on. But my mom? Just the opposite. 'Call when you like, but better now than when your father's around. You know how it upsets him,' and of course an upset for him would start upsetting her. But do you think she took that tack to sort of get me on her side and a little against him, or just to establish what distinguished them? What am I trying to say here? Help me," and she says, "She might have been showing you she approved of a number of things you did that your father disapproved of, and certainly that she didn't think your calling your friends was a big deal." "She was always supporting me and my work. Is that what you meant? Probably not. And I'm not referring to money, though she would've given me some to do what I wanted with it, within reason and her limited budget, and often offered: 'Do you need any extra cash?' Even now—I mean up until maybe two months ago—and I'd say, 'No, Mom, I'm working, so I got enough coming in.' But before I met you, to live off of while I did these so-called artistic or creative things, or for grad school or travel, but I never wanted to take it and hardly ever did. I wanted to be Mr. Independent, and I didn't want to be taking money she might have, with a lot of difficulty, extracted from my dad. And, after he died, money that'd make her own life a bit more comfortable and secure. He was a good guy, though, and had a kind heart; I wasn't alluding to anything about that. Everybody thought so, except sometimes my mother. A sense of humor too—both of them—I forget who I was originally talking about there. Though she, for some reason, became even funnier after he died—real witty lines and retorts which I never remember her saying before. Let's see, what would be one? That crack about the Jack Daniels, when I tried diluting it because I thought it was too strong for her and she hadn't had anything to eat yet. I think I told you it. Others. 'If I get any older . . .' Something about if she got any older than she was and Stone Age culture, but I forget. And both were affectionate to me most times, my father, earlier on, more than my mother—'A kiss, before you go to bed every night you must give me a kiss'—and never raised a hand. Well, he raised it to me several times but it never struck. But she? Not a finger, except, and when I probably deserved it, to wag. I really loved them both, though if I had to make a choice—this, by the way, was the one impossible question to answer when I was a boy: 'Who do you love more, your mom or dad?'—it'd be she. It's true, I'd have to say it, I never said it before, but it was she. Not because I knew her twenty years longer. She was, all in all, just nicer and more dependable and predictable and with a more even disposition, and she made me feel better when I needed to and understood or tried to understand me more. But them both, you know? I've no regrets in what kind of parents I had in them both." "I know. Try not to be so sad," and he says, "I can't help it. I feel miserable. This goddamn crying's a pain in the ass sometimes, when it just spurts out in the worst public places and tears my throat, but I suppose it also has its good. I should've got a vaporizer for her room when she started breathing poorly again a few months ago. I didn't want to take her money so she'd be more comfortable and secure in old age? So why, when I had the chance and the income, didn't I give her everything she needed—gone into hock doing it, if I had to? Now I look back and think, What the hell was I saving the money for anyway? I'd only have been spending her money—wouldn't I?—when you think I'll probably end up with a small bundle from her when the estate's settled. Laziness, that's what it was. That I couldn't pick up the phone and call the drugstore nearest her and say, Send over a vaporizer, send her everything she needs or the woman taking care of her says she needs." "You did that. The women with her could have ordered anything they wanted, and no doubt did. And it was already costing you and your mother a big bundle keeping those women there and feeding them." "That I just couldn't have picked up the phone every day and even twice a day, morning and night, and not mostly from my office, and spoken to her a few minutes? I had to keep it to once a day and most times not even to that? And laziness that I didn't take the train in to see her more." "You saw her a lot." "Not enough. I was bored with the trip, I also found the car ride tedious, but I couldn't have made the sacrifice more? What would it have taken? Bought some good stuff to read on the train. Or saved up, let's say, since to me newspapers are much easier to read on trains than books, two or three days of the *Times*. Or the whole Sunday paper, no matter what day I left, or just the Arts and magazine and week-in-review sections—the book section I would have already read—or made myself tired by not getting much sleep the night before the trip so I'd sleep on the train most of the way." "Now you're carrying out these things you could have done too far, both for her and yourself, and it's not good for you, it's really not." "I should have put her up in a nursing home around here—there are plenty that are good and cheerful, people have said. Closed her apartment first and driven her down, or temporarily closed it, in case she didn't like the home, and seen her twice a day at this place, but she wouldn't have gone in one." "Then don't raise it as a possibility. She was a New Yorker from birth, and even if she didn't have any friends or close relatives there left, except for her niece—" "I should have gone in to see her the day before she died. That kills me the most: the last thing I could have done and I didn't. But Josephine was very sick: I worried about the kid once she came into our room and said she couldn't breathe. And I sort of made a secret decision with myself that day that I had to see to the sickly living before the dying dying. That's an awful thought; cold, crude, awful, and something I didn't even think then, so why'd I say it? Did I use Josephine as an excuse not to see my mother that day before? Again, laziness? No, I wanted to see her, absolutely, truly, and would have, and I thought my cousin was looking after her well or would, plus Ebonita or whoever was on"—"Ebonita was"—"but I—but my mother was ninety-one and I knew she was definitely failing, but I also wanted to make sure Josephine got to the doctor. But she would have seen me before she went into the coma. My mother. But I didn't know she was going into a coma and seeing me wouldn't have stopped her from going into one or dying, though it might have made her feel better for a few moments. I could have shown her pictures—longer than a few; minutes; hours. But pictures of the kids and you, photos I mean, recent ones she hadn't seen, or just old ones of her and the kids and you where everyone looks happy and well. Photos of her parents and brother and sisters. I could have got them out of the breakfront drawers where she always kept them, kept them there when I was a kid. Of herself when she was a beauty. The same drawers. She still was a beauty, a beauty for someone her age and maybe ten years younger; she would have won a contest if there was such a contest for beauty at that age, but not on those final days. I wouldn't have brought out the photos of my brother, no matter how cheerful and healthy-looking he appears in them and beautiful or handsome or whatever a boy is when he's so young. And my father, of course, or maybe not 'of course,' since their marriage wasn't that great. But photos of them together, just dating and in the latest styles; with friends, all of them arm-in-arm in a park once. One where she's cuddling a dog, though when I was growing up she hated them, and where he has on these long sporty striped socks and what do you call those pants that end just below the knees?" "Knickers? Jodphurs?" "He was a rider too, in Prospect and Central parks: rental horses. And at their wedding reception. She looked gorgeous, holding what she said were a couple dozen long-stemmed roses my father got her, and he so handsome in cutaway and top hat. And one in a bathing suit; she, I'm speaking of—his legs were too thin for him to look good in them—holding an open parasol above her as if imitating a beauty contestant, and with a fashion model-of-today's figure but showgirl's legs. They're all still there. I'm going to get them next time I'm in, and maybe they'll be some of the few things of hers I'll keep before I give or throw everything else away and close the apartment for good." "She was very beautiful. It was the first thing my parents thought when you introduced them." "Her skin. Did I tell you about it? Even on that last day, so smooth. Or maybe because of that day, more smooth than ever; I don't know. Relaxed; going into death, if it's not painful or distressing in any other way, might do that. But like someone's—weeks before—thirty or forty years old. Or forty to fifty, better, but on that last day, thirty to forty." "Even to have the skin of a sixty- or seventy-year-old would be remarkable for a woman her age." "But it was much better than that. Amazingly, not many lines and none on her forehead and only a few around her chin and mouth and neck where they normally start congregating and growing when you hit fifty. Look at me. So let's say I didn't inherit her skin genes—for the face; her arms and hands were like someone's her age—or my lines relate to other things. And with the plates in her mouth out too." "I don't follow you." "That last day. If her dentures had been in, her face would have even been smoother, I think. But I did something that's irreversible, I just know it. Usually the wrong things I do I can patch up, with talk or time or overcompensating later on, but these I can't, especially that I didn't come in that day. The previous one. The day before the last. When Josephine was so sick." "Don't blame yourself, darling. There wasn't any one incontrovertibly right decision to make." "I may even have made the right one, for all I know, but it still doesn't help. Josephine was immediately put on antibiotics—right in the doctor's office; they used starters. I remember running out into the hallway to get her one of those paper-cone cups of water. And I left early the next day to see her—my mother—and got there an hour and a half before she died." "So one of the good things to look at is that you got there in time." "Or at least before the moment we think she died. There was Ebonita and her daughter. I forget the girl's name. What do I care that she had seen her grandmother die and so was used to it? She shouldn't have been in the room with us. She should have gone into the kitchen during that time or taken a walk outside. But she didn't know better, though she was old enough to, and I don't think Ebonita did either, and there was nothing I was able to say. She was definitely breathing, though, when I got there, my mother. And for the hour and a half or so after. Hard breathing. Meaning it was hard for her to breathe—labored breaths and plenty of phlegm. And for a long time we went on and off thinking she was still breathing after that moment, but so softly we couldn't hear it, and we also thought we saw her body moving a little. But the EMS guy who came hours later—we didn't notify them sooner because we still thought she might be alive—said she'd been dead from about the time we'd originally said and that what we thought were signs of life was just the dead body beginning to break down and settle—I think those were his words—and the gases, or maybe that's the same thing. I told you what he did, right?" "With his two fingers quickly on her neck and saying she's gone?" "After, while we were waiting for the police, I said, 'Can't he, to make sure, use an instrument or something so we know she won't be carted away alive?' and he shrugged, as if saying, 'All right, to make you happy,' and monitored her heart with a stethoscope and pinpricked her skin and did something else with another gadget, and then said, 'Nothing, I'm sorry, my condolences.'" "That part I hadn't heard." "I held her up, those moments I thought were her last. That's not what I wanted. I mean I didn't plan it that way—come in for it, have any idea it would happen, some dramatic moment like that—but that's how it probably ended and the EMS guy was right. What do you think her babbling meant? She did it for almost half a day straight. I wish I'd been there to hear it." "I know, you've said." "It was like she was describing her entire life in that relatively short time, different from what you usually hear about it passing through the dying person's mind. I would have learned—but I told you all this—stuff about her family and my dad and her childhood that she only would have revealed in the unguarded state she was in. It even could have been embarrassing for me to listen to: things about herself and my father and maybe other men before—I doubt there were any after—though Ebonita said, in that hour and a half we had together before she died, there was nothing that made her or her daughter blush or anything she hadn't already heard. Well, she probably had told Angela and Ebonita everything, including things about me that weren't so good—I'm saying, in the years they had looked after her. If only Josephine hadn't got sick, but what can you do." "It was a freak coincidence. Of course, you were frightened for her, just as I was." "You don't think Josephine's illness was in any way connected to knowing my mother might be dying? I mean, we were all at dinner when I got that first phone call, and I talked to Ebonita on your portable phone." "I don't see it. Listen, dearest, try for a while not to think of those last two days. Or think of them all you want; I'm not sure what's right either." "No, you were right the first time. I'm going to rest, I think. Try to nap, anyway." "If you need me"—her arms out—"I'm here," and he says, "Thanks," and goes into their bedroom, makes sure the phone's off, and lies on the bed. "Party, party, party," she kept telling him over the phone. Or at least said it while she held the receiver and he was on the phone. Though maybe Ebonita was holding the receiver for her and his mother didn't even know she was talking to him or even talking on a phone. No, she knew she was talking to him, or part of the time, since she asked, "How's business?" something he thinks she said before in relation to his work, the teaching or writing or both. He's sure she said it before, and more than once, and one time as a joke. But what did the "party, party" mean? And she sounded so chipper on the phone, better than she had for months. "My sister's coming and she loves my chicken and I have to bake a cake" and "buy a new dress," Ebonita told him she'd also said that day several times. Did she mean one of her dead sisters was coming to take her away? That she knew she was dying? That the party was some idea she had of joining up with her favorite dead people in heaven or some afterlife place—her beloved mother, whom Ebonita said she went on about most, and of course her firstborn son—or some notion she had of freedom and fun once she was released from the physical discomfort and misery she'd been in for years? That the cake was what she wanted to make for the party as an offering of sorts? Or just that when you go to a party you always bring something? which is what she thought. The new dress might have meant to her—or did Ebonita say a "fresh" dress?—but anyway, a shroud or just a nice outfit to look good in her coffin in or something presentable to wear to a party. If that's the case, what's the chicken mean? Nothing right now in his storehouse of symbols, but maybe there was one in hers. Or the chicken was a chicken, something she baked with a coating of corn flakes that her sister did like, and that made her sister coming to her more realistic. But if this is how she approached death, then she went fairly resignedly, right? Or not anxious or frightened and maybe even gladly, and that's a good thought for him to have. But what else did she say? Oh, don't start analyzing every word. "First I have to get out of here," she told him, and she wants to bake "lots" of cakes. Well, the "out of here" is easy enough to explain, not that he'd be right, but "lots of cakes"? Maybe to give everyone she joins up with in this afterlife place. Anything else she say? He wrote most of it down soon after he spoke with her, a little of it even while he was on the phone, but doesn't remember any more of it now or where he put those notes: probably in his top night-table drawer, but he doesn't want to look: what'd be the purpose? Her arm thrashed a lot that last hour and a half and for a few hours before that, Ebonita said, and always the right. So, she was a righty, and what's it mean anyway?—it's all involuntary. His dad's thrashed for two days when he was in his last coma, and maybe in the coma before that, and both arms, back and forth in front of his face and sometimes crossing but never hitting each other. When he tried to hold them down they'd push up, and his dad's face showed pain or intense frustration at that moment, so he let them go, hoping his father wouldn't hurt himself like breaking his nose. He called her doctor the day before he went to New York, and the doctor said that from everything Ebonita told him and the visiting nurse said about her, she's failing. "I'm afraid she'll never leave the hospital this time if we send her there." "Alive, you mean," and the doctor said, "To be absolutely frank about it, yes. The decision's ultimately yours, though. But if I were you I'd get to her side quickly and try to make her as comfortable as you can at home. If you need to reach me for any reason, call day or night, though I don't think you'll have to except, perhaps, for a pep talk. I'm sorry, Gould. Your mother was a brave woman, but you have to remember we never thought she'd last this long, and from my conversations with her she didn't think so either." "Why, what'd she say?" and the doctor said, "I forget, but something, since she was always a pessimist regarding her longevity and health." After that phone call he remembers thinking, What's the guy talking about? She's not dead yet. That whole last-nail-in-the-coffin business, which they also used on his father, is a bunch of hooey. His father pulled through three or four of them after the doctors gave him just a few days. He said to the doctor this time, "There is a problem, though. My younger daughter's sick with a bad croup and my wife's unable to drive her to a doctor or hospital if it suddenly becomes a real crisis, so I want to stay till early tomorrow to see how it turns out. You think I have time?" and the doctor said, "Never a guarantee. Your mother could be expiring this moment as we speak. You just have to hope she holds out that long. Keep me informed." He wrote down most of what the doctor said, while he was talking to him, and what he remembered after when he was sitting by his mother the next day. All those notes, several pages of them, are stapled—not stapled; he doesn't have a stapler. His kids do, one between them, but he didn't use it. How come he can't remember the simple name of such a common object, one he's used thousands of times or at least a thousand, both as a word and an object? It binds pages, holds them together. It's the first time he's forgotten it—paper clip, he paper-clipped the pages and put them someplace, probably also in the top night-table drawer with that other thing he was thinking or talking of before and thinks he put in there, and which he also now forgets what it was. Something to do with his mother? He means, did this other thing have something to do with her? Photos? He doesn't think so. More notes? It's possible but doesn't ring a bell. Since when does memory loss have anything to do with grief? Or the other way around: grief cause memory loss? Maybe he's just tired. But he's slept more the last few days than he has, in so short a time, in years. And he's only sleeping this much to avoid remembering things about her. Should he reach over to the drawer—it'd take just a little turn—and get them out, the notes plus that other thing, if he put either of them there? No, he doesn't think he'll ever want to read those phone conversation notes. Why would he? So why'd he write them down then, when he was on the phone? It seemed important at the time, as if he were being given instructions on how to take care of her at the end. When he was with his mother: just to do something, he supposes, or more than that, but he forgets. He also doodled; he also tried reading; he also cleaned his nails with his thumbnails and bit off most of the torn cuticles; he also just stared at her for minutes, hoping her heavy breathing would suddenly ease up and that she'd open her eyes, blink, give some recognition that she knew where she was, turn her face or just move her eyes to him—he'd be saying softly, "Mom? Mom?"—and smile and maybe even say something: his name, how is he? where's her dear friend Ebonita? she's thirsty and would like something to eat, and so on. He also remembers thinking, What is she thinking? Is there anything going on in her head? Is it more like dreaming? Then what is she dreaming? Is she in any pain? Is her heavy breathing and chest congestion affecting her thoughts? Is there anything he can do to make things better for her? A different position? Raise or lower the top of the hospital bed? Another pillow? One less pillow? Put a cushion under her feet? Should he be talking to her? Should he read to her from a book or even today's paper so she just hears his voice? Would that bring her out of it? What would help her come out of what more and more seems like a coma? Is she shitting, peeing? She wears paper diapers, but do these have to be changed? He'll know when she starts smelling. Water? Shouldn't she have water or some sugar solution so she doesn't starve? Is she really dying? Can this be it? Will she never recognize him again? Can he really be sitting here the last day or hours of her life and where she'll never wake up? If she hears his voice—he was told when his father was comatose that the last sense to go is hearing—will that help her see him in whatever pictures are in her head? About those notes, does he think—he also thought a few times while he sat there looking at her: Maybe it'd be best if she went now without pain rather than have to go through this another time and then maybe another time before she dies—but does he think that, let's say in a year or two or even six months, when he's going through that top drawer for something else and comes upon the notes, if he put them there—or any place he put them—that he'll read them or leave them in the drawer without reading them or just throw them away soon as he recognizes them? How can he know that now? But what does he think? He thinks, How can he know now what he'll do? though he thinks he'll more than likely throw them away unread. But things she said that he took down—in fact, isn't that what that "other thing" is?—he'll keep and read, keep forever, in the drawer or someplace safe, not just what she said on the phone the last time but all the things she's said the past few years that he's taken down, and regret if he couldn't find them and regret more if he thought them lost. After about an hour and a half of sitting near his mother—he got up once to make coffee, another time to get it after it was made and wash the carafe and coffee machine cone—Ebonita, sitting a couple of feet farther away from her than he, pointed out phlegm dribbling over her lip and he thought, I suppose she wants me to wipe it, she obviously isn't getting up—well, she spent a long night with her, didn't get much sleep—and he got up and wiped his mother's mouth and chin with his handkerchief. "Tissues," Ebonita said. "We have a whole box of them and more boxes in the closet," pointing to what was the broom closet when he was a kid but which now held all kinds of medical supplies and things, and he said, "Sorry; it's also not sanitary, using this rag," and stuck the handkerchief back into his pants pocket, but first, he remembers, folding the wet part up so it wouldn't soak through to his thigh. Ebonita, he now remembers, had actually said, "Look at what's coming out of her mouth; we should fix it." Then more phlegm spilled out and Ebonita stood beside him and kept supplying tissues to wipe with, and he wiped her mouth and inside her lips and with wads of tissue dabbed her tongue and around it to absorb the constant rise of spit, dropping the tissues and the wads one by one into an old ice bucket that was being used as a trash container by the bed. "How come she doesn't have a real trash can?" he said. "There used to be lots of them in the house. This one fills up so quickly," and she shrugged and said, "Up till now this one did all right." Then his mother started coughing while he was wiping her mouth, and he put his arms behind her and raised her up and held her there with one arm, thinking, This'll help her cough up the mucus better and maybe even help her breathing and where she won't choke on all that stuff, and it'll also be easier to get the phlegm out of her mouth. Then, as long as he had her up and she had stopped coughing and bringing up phlegm, he thought about giving her water. "Don't you think she should have some water? How long has it been?" and Ebonita said, "Hours. I tried to before but none got in. And she hasn't evacuated for a long time neither, which isn't good. But it isn't easy getting liquids down her; she coughs it all up." "We should have an eyedropper to give it. Even drop by drop would do some good. You don't have one around, do you? I thought of bringing one—I sort of knew she'd need it—and found some old one at home but left it." Regrets: he did think of it but never looked for one. His wife had said, "If she's unconscious or too weak to drink anything, how do you get medicine and fluids into her? Probably she should be in a hospital and on IV," and he said, "Believe me, they'll only make matters worse for her there, forcing things down, sticking a million needles in. Maybe I should bring an eyedropper—I know we have one here—or go out now for one of those dropperlike spoon things we used for the kids when they wouldn't swallow their medicine," and she said, "We never had to give it that way," and he said, "Then I've seen them displayed in the pharmacy here," but that's as far as it went. He could have driven that night to a local Giant that has a pharmacy and big drug department or bought one in a drugstore when he walked to her building from the subway or gone into the drugstore at Penn Station, but forgot. He didn't forget; he thought of it when he got out of the subway and passed a drugstore but then thought, Just get to her building, you could miss seeing her alive by minutes, and started to jog. When the train was pulling in to New York he thought of calling her from Penn Station, but after he got off he ran through the terminal to the subway station with a token in his hand and ran up the stairs to the platform, not wanting to waste a minute calling, but had to wait several minutes for the uptown train. He looked for a phone on the platform but the only one operating was taken and continued to be taken till the train came. Then the person hung up and got in the same car with him. He set his mother down and said to Ebonita, "Can you get me . . . no, I'll get it; watch her," and got a tablespoon and cup of water from the kitchen, raised her in his arms again, and while Ebonita held the cup he got a spoonful from it and stuck it in his mother's mouth. It seemed to go down. "Good, Mom, good," though she didn't open her eyes or make any response or motion that she knew anything was going on around her or happening to her. He got another spoonful of water and was ready to stick it in her mouth when the other water, or some of it, dribbled out. "Mom, if you're hearing me," he said, wiping her chin and neck, "you have to take some water; you need it." "Maybe you gave her too much, though I didn't see her neck swallowing any of it. Try half," and he spooned half a tablespoon of water into her mouth and looked and it seemed to go down. "It's gone. Did you see her neck moving this time?" and Ebonita said, "I think so, but I can't say for sure." Then some white liquid rose from her throat, and he said, "Oh, my God, what the hell's that?" till her mouth was almost full of it and it was about to spill out, and Ebonita threw her hands to her face and said, "Oh, no, this is the end, I'm sure of it. Delilah"—to her daughter, sitting there looking at his mother—"cover your eyes," and he said, "What are you talking about? Get me a towel; lay it down here," while he held his mother up with one arm and stuck a bunch of tissues into her mouth to soak up the liquid and when the towel was down he held her face over it and all the liquid seemed to come out. He held her there a few seconds more and then got her in a sitting position to wipe her face and see if any more liquid was there, and some seemed to be coming up, white again, and he held her face over the towel and said, "Get it all out, Mom, this is good for you; all the junk in your lungs is coming up," and when no more of it came out he held her in a sitting position and wiped her face and patted her cheeks and head with damp tissues and thought of getting a damp rag to lay across her forehead when she started choking and her eyes were open and he said, "Mom?" and she looked blankly ahead while her body started shaking and she was still choking, and he said, "Mom, what is it? Can you hear me? What can I do for you?" and her eyes never moved and she was still shaking and choking but nothing was coming up, and he yelled, "Mommy, oh, no, Mommy, oh, Mommy!" and held her to him with both arms and put his mouth to her forehead and said, "It's all right, Mommy, it's all right, I'm here, Gould's here, I'm here with you, Mommy, I won't leave you, oh, no, Mommy, my Mommy, oh, Mommy, oh, please don't go, Mommy, please, please don't go," and Ebonita said, "She's stopped, she's quiet, I knew it, close her eyes, close her eyes!" and he held her head up and shut her eyes and let her head down softly till it hung over his shoulder, and he kept her that way for around a minute, his eyes closed and head against her neck, hugging her, and then laid her on her back and put his ear to her chest and mouth and chest again and then rested his head on her chest and started to cry. The cat jumps onto the bed, walks around him on both sides, and then steps up on his chest and lies on it facing him, and he says, "Please get off, you weigh a ton, I can't breathe with you on me," and the cat stays and he picks it up and drops it on the floor. It jumps right back up and lies on his chest the same way, and he says, "Listen, I told you, I know you mean well and want to help me, but you're just too big a load," and raises his arm to lift it off him again. The cat sits up, resettles itself on his chest till it faces his feet, and stretches out more so there's much less weight in one place than before, and he says, "Okay, all right," and rests his hand on its back; "you don't feel so heavy now, stay."

The Walk

He's walking to town—there's no bread in the house for tonight, he'll probably get a few other things at the market, doesn't know what, certainly a coffee for a quarter—and thinks of his daughters, doesn't know why this thought suddenly popped in—sure he does, because of what happened earlier, Fanny saying when he dropped her off at school, "I love you, Daddy," and probably also Josephine, last night, lying in bed, lights out, he'd just finished reading her a fairy tale and kissing her good night, saying, "I love you, Daddy," and he saying, "I love you very much too," and to Fanny, at school, "I love you very much too, sweetheart." Tears come. Silly. Why? Okay, then not so silly, but if anyone saw him up close now he'd still feel embarrassed. Walking to the village, the back way through people's properties and along hilly streets with lots of big trees, to the market to buy bread and also to take a break from work, nice day, fall but early fall, temperature in the mid-sixties, sun out, soft breeze, he's in shorts, T-shirt, and sandals, wishes he'd worn sneakers. What else they need? Doesn't know; don't they always need milk? He'll get the coffee for sure. Has he missed getting one there five times in the four years he's been going to this store? and he goes, by car, bike, or foot, about three times a week. They usually have, on a shelf by the deli department, two regular coffees and one decaffeinated in tall Thermoses, but he always gets the most exotic caffeinated. Sometimes they have Kona, and always a pint container of half-and-half in a bowl of ice water next to the Thermoses, but which he's rarely used, and a few times a hazelnut- or amaretto-flavored nondairy creamer, all for a quarter, which you can put into the coin box on the shelf or pay for with your other items at the checkout counter. Store doesn't lose money on it; in fact the coffee makes the customer stay longer, he's sure, and buy more. Maybe a dessert. Ones he bought for the kids yesterday they didn't touch, he saw this morning, when he opened the bakery bag thinking there were rolls inside he could heat up for them, and they were what, honey-glazed? so by tonight they'll be a little stale. Thinks of his older daughter. Didn't come from thinking about the doughnuts, did it? Oh, one thought leads to another and probably helped by the action and solitude of the walk and no distractions, not even a bird squawk or squirrel zipping around nearby. Dropping her off at school today. She got her things together in the car after he stopped with the motor running and gear in PARK (heavy backpack, big sketch pad, and something else: brown lunch bag with the lunch she made) and turned to him—she opened the door first—and said, "I love you, Daddy," and he said that "very much" line (this is all pretty much ritual) and kissed her cheek (which he also does every day when she leaves the car unless it's obvious she's angry at him, though he doesn't often kiss her hello when he picks her up at school in the afternoon), and she left the car and he smiled at her through the window on the passenger's side and she smiled back, affectionately, not mechanically (usually she heads straight for school without looking at him again; he doesn't know why today was different for her), and headed for the steps leading to the school entrance. Still awkward, he noticed: *ungainly,* he means. Other girls around, obviously older—some had driven cars to school and parked them in the lot—walked with so much more grace and confidence. Well, her age, and that she's new here, he thought, a freshman, it's been just a couple of months for her, and she stumbled going up the sidewalk curb, almost tripped but quickly righted herself, dropped the lunch bag when she stumbled (nothing fell out), picked it up, continued a few steps, hesitated, turned back to him, no doubt hoping he wasn't looking at her. He waved—he immediately knew he shouldn't have, and was smiling, though she might have been too far away to see that; besides, she wears glasses and she didn't have them on; she'd told him in the car, when he asked, that they were in her backpack and scowled at him—maybe a smile through a car window's more difficult to make out than a scowl, even with your glasses on—and went up the steps and into the school. She probably forgot about it a few minutes later, certainly once she got to her homeroom and started talking to one of her friends. No, homeroom was what she had in middle school; here, if she doesn't get to school early, she goes right to her locker and then to her first class. Did his watching from the car have anything to do with her stumbling? How could it have? Maybe she was aware his car hadn't driven off—no familiar sound of its motor—and sensed he might still be parked, or just assumed it, and was looking at her from behind, and she became self-conscious because she knew she was somewhat ungainly and didn't walk as gracefully as a lot of the other girls and that was what made her, or helped make her, stumble. That could be it. He'd love to tell her but probably won't, better not to bring up things that remind her of recent embarrassments—"Don't think that way, my darling. Everyone's like that when they're young—you're still growing, in height and your feet and so on. And if you saw me smiling in the car, believe me it was only an adoring smile. When I saw your head turning around I smiled, which is what I almost always do in something like this, because I thought you were going to look at me. It had nothing to do with your stumbling, which anyone could do, by the way. You should see how many times I do it in a year, and sometimes when I'm jogging—this probably happens about once every six months—I trip over an exposed tree root or sidewalk bump or something and fall flat on my hands and knees and cut them . . . I must have told you that. So I'd never find anything funny in your stumbling. And if you really had tripped, spilled things and landed on your hands, I would have run out of the car to you, though you might not have liked that: drawing too much attention to it. So let's say I would have wanted to run to you to do what I could to help, certainly picked you up if you were still lying there, and said things like 'I'm so sorry, my darling, are you all right? It can happen to anybody. I trip all the time and occasionally hurt myself badly, cuts and bruises and such, so I'm as clumsy, if not even more so, as anyone your age, in action as well as trying to put across my ideas and phrasing words, though don't ask me what the last two have to do with it,' " and he drove home, it only takes seven to ten minutes from her school, and thought then and thinks something like it now, What a lovely girl; and what a lucky guy I am in having such a daughter, so sweet and bright and kind and modest. It's so painful to think she might be hurt—she will be—in the future, and many times, or at least several, physically, emotionally. But what else they need? Can't think of anything. Cat food they can always use. Opened the only can of it he could find in the crowded cupboard this morning, so two cans of cat food—don't want to make the bag too heavy and almost no space at home to store it. And of course the coffee, that he'll have drunk before he leaves the market or, as he's sometimes done, standing outside. Then his younger daughter. Last night, while she was sitting up in bed and he came in to say good night, that sad look she had over nothing, it seemed. As if he said something truly horrible to her—he's said some lousy things but nothing deliberately or even unintentionally horrible: it'd destroy her or at least for the night and maybe a few days, and he'd feel terrible, a lot more than when he's just said those mean things. What could he say that'd really be horrible? That she's not pretty. That'd be just mean. But will never be and, to add to it, never was. That she was an ugly baby and hasn't grown prettier as a child. That she's dumb, just about as dumb as anyone he knows, and so on. That the short haircut she begged to get and just had makes her look stupid and homely. The mean or lousy things: when he was working at his desk in the bedroom and she ran in and said, "Daddy, I have to ask you something," and he said, "Damn, don't you see I'm working?" And once, "Must you always burst in here like that? Dammit, you scared the freaking shit out of me!" And, "Listen, it's obvious you didn't study for the test and that's why you got such a crappy mark, so stop making up excuses." Other times. But why does she so often have that sad look? Something he's done or continues to do? Doesn't think so, and it certainly isn't anything from his wife. An accumulation of those mean and lousy and insulting remarks that she knows he's liable to make anytime? He hasn't made that many to her, and they were spread out enough where they wouldn't have accumulated like that, though who knows? And whenever he's said something like that to her—and "insulting" only a few times—he's always quickly apologized. And if—and she almost always does this—she ran out of the room or away from him to wherever she goes, usually her bedroom, where she slams the door, since it usually happens at home, and started crying, he went after her and apologized there, blaming himself for his short temper and for being high-strung sometimes and jumpy, especially when he has his back to the door and is busy working and someone bursts into the room, and promised to do things for her, like get her something she's been wanting for a long time and which he didn't think she needed, till she made up with him and they hugged and he'd kiss the top of her head and close his eyes a few seconds and hope hers were closed for a short time too, though not necessarily when his were, and then be extra solicitous to her the rest of the day and probably the next, or at least till he saw her off at school. And it's not that she's a gloomy child. She's in fact the skipper of the family. He doesn't mean the boss of it, the way some people use that word for kids and wives. Just that she frequently bounces around, has for years, much more than her sister ever did and is a lot more cheerful than her sister too, singing in the shower, laughing at the comics, things like that, though her sister's witty and usually smiles and sometimes guffaws when she sleeps. Once bounced exuberantly into the refrigerator and broke a front tooth. Wailed then. He went to her first. Around a year ago, family was at dinner. She usually eats fast and leaves first, even when he and his wife say to stay—"Sit and talk with us, we like your company"—did they say to stay that night? What's the difference? And she usually gets up a minute or two after one of them tells her to stay—twirled around past them from the living room into the kitchen—he was probably glad she was so happy. His wife and he might even have exchanged smiles when she twirled past, though also concerned she was jumping around too much so soon after eating. She was singing as she spun into the kitchen, lost her footing, and smacked her face into the refrigerator. (The refrigerator can't be seen from the dining room; she later told him how she hit it.) Then she screamed. He thought she was kidding, he doesn't know why—maybe the scream didn't seem like a real one at first and he thought she wanted them to think she was hurt or he just didn't want to believe she was—but it continued and he yelled, "Josephine, anything wrong?" and she screamed harder and he ran in and blood was dribbling out of her mouth and she wailed, "Oh, no, my tooth, my tooth," and he told her to open her mouth wide and she kept it closed and he tried forcing it open, he wanted to relieve his worry that one or both of her front teeth were broken—a side or back one, even one of the eye teeth, wasn't that important—and she said, facing away from him, "No, no, don't look, my tooth, I felt it, I'm so sorry, so sorry, I'm so sorry, Dada, I didn't mean to, I'm so stupid, I was so stupid," and he said, "It's all right, I won't blame you, just open your mouth," and she did, and the bottom half of a permanent front tooth was gone, and he yelled, "Oh, no, oh, my darling!" knowing right away what it meant to her, and hugged her and said, "I'm so sorry, so sorry, oh, what can we do?" and they both cried, and his wife came in and said, "Calm down; what about her tooth?" and he said, "She broke it, a front one," and his daughter screamed and wrenched free of him and ran into the bathroom and started shrieking and he ran after her and she was looking at her mouth in his shaving mirror and he said, "Don't look, it's no good for you; we'll get it fixed, I promise," and wiped the blood away, got ice and treated her, and called her dentist, who said to come in tomorrow morning, "But if you can see a dark spot in the core of the cut part then it could mean she'll lose it," and soon after that a friend of his wife's called and just happened to have lost a front tooth the same way when she was a girl but against a stove and said she got the bottom half replaced with a toothlike bond and when her mouth was fully grown a permanent fixture and no one's ever been able to tell the difference and she can bite into apples and carrots with it and she thinks a quarter of the women she knows have lost part of a front tooth, and he said, "Tell Josephine all that," and she did and things quickly got better. He looked for the tooth part on the floor, found it, and it seemed to be the whole piece, didn't want to hold it under the broken tooth it came from to see if it was a perfect fit, so later went into her room and said, "Open your mouth again, sweetheart; I want to see how your tooth's doing," and then, "It's looking a lot better. A clean break, two pieces, very simple, so it's going to work out fine, no complications," thought of bringing in the found part to the dentist the next day but then thought, What for? and it'll just get lost, and taped it to a piece of paper and wrote the date and event on it—*J's broken front tooth, fridge, disturbing scene for both of us*—and put it in a small container where he keeps every tooth his daughters have lost except the one Fanny swallowed, all taped to paper with just the date on it except the first two of theirs, which also say what number it was and where it came out. Anyway, last night, that sad look, he asked if anything was wrong, she shook her head and asked why, he said, "Your look," and she said, "What's wrong with it?" and he said, "Nothing, it's fine; one doesn't always have to be smiling," and read to her awhile. After he turned off the light and said good night, she said, "I love you, Daddy," and he said, first kissing her forehead and lips—ritual; if he didn't she'd ask him to by saying, "A huggy"—"I love you too, veddy *mucho* grandee, now go to sleep, you've school tomorrow," and she said, "No, we're off," and he said, "This is one of my rare sharp nights; you can't fool me," and left the room, her door opened a couple of inches, which for the past half year is how she's asked it to be and he'll keep leaving it that way till she says not to. Tears again, quickly wipes them. What is it with me today? he thinks, walking downhill to the market. Is it something else? My mother, maybe. When he spoke to her last night she seemed too weak and despondent to speak and after a minute broke off because of her coughing, she said, but hadn't thought of her today till now. He'll call her when he gets home, first thing. But what else they need? What did he remember to get so far? Cat food, bread, milk. Gallon of spring water for his wife, but that'd be too heavy to carry. Desserts for the kids; maybe a baklava for Fanny and a napoleon for Josephine—now that's odd; he never thought of the connection before. They're twice to three times the price of the doughnuts he usually buys, but hang the expense: they're always excited when he tells them he got their favorite desserts. That should do it, and the container of coffee, and takes a handful of change from his pants pocket, counts out twenty-five cents, ten of it in pennies—the people who empty the coin box must hate getting the pennies, but he's got to get rid of them some way—and puts the counted change into a separate pants pocket, so when he takes it out for the coffee he won't have to count it again. Such a nice day; he'll drink the coffee sitting on the bench in front of the market and dump the empty container into the trash can by it, or sit there if there aren't too many bees around. Will this closeness or oversolicitousness or whatever he should call it ultimately hurt his kids? No, they'll hardly remember it, or only a little. He reaches the market's parking lot, crosses it and goes inside, picks up a shopping basket, though for all he's going to buy he could just as well carry the things in his hands, gets the coffee first, feels like having it with half-and-half today, doesn't know why—maybe so he can drink it faster, though there's no need for him to rush home, so it could be his stomach telling him something—and sticks the change into the coin box. Now what did he tell himself to get?—sipping the coffee by the deli counter and then finishing it off—bread, milk, two cans of cat food. What else? Forgets.

The Friend

He sees his mother's best friend from the block and yells out, "Margaret, Margaret!" and says to his mother, "Mom, there's Margaret," and Margaret stops, looks around, catches him waving at her from about forty feet away; What do you know, what a nice surprise, her look seems to say, and she starts over to them while he wheels his mother to her. They're on Columbus Avenue, around three in the afternoon on a normal weekday, but the sidewalks and restaurant patios are all crowded, sky's darkening and wind picks up a bit, and it looks and feels like rain though no one seems to be hurrying to avoid it. "Listen, maybe I shouldn't have stopped her, because we haven't got too long to talk," he tells his mother, leaning over her wheelchair. "I don't want us to get caught in the downpour," and she says, "Why would we?" and he doesn't know if she means get caught in the downpour or talk too long, when Margaret reaches them. "Beatrice, Gould, how are you?" she says, bending down to take his mother's hand while she kisses her cheek. He kisses Margaret and says, "And how are you doing? It's been awhile," and his mother looks up at her, doesn't seem to recognize her—maybe she's tired; this is around the time she takes a nap, and she had a good-sized drink at lunch just now—and then says, "Oh, my dear, it's a treat to see you," and he's still not sure she recognizes her. "Did my son tell you we'd be here?" and he says, "No, Mom, we just happened to bump into her." "I've lost so much weight lately and also with this ugly scarf covering my head, I'm surprised you noticed me from that far away," and his mother says, "But now I can see you and recall all the kind things you've done for us, but I've always had a problem with names." "It's Margaret, Mom. From the street. How are you feeling, though?" he says to Margaret, and she says, "I've been terrible, to tell the truth. I hate to complain, so don't let me start in about it and bore you, but I've had big troubles, I'm afraid; a fluke to end all flukes." "Do you think it's going to rain?" his mother asks him, and he says, "Why, you want to get back? You tired, cold? Because I don't think the sky looks too threatening," and she says, "It wouldn't bother me, a little rain. I'd even like it—the drops on me; something different for a change. But I didn't think you'd want to get soaked." "Why don't we all walk together then, if you're heading home," to Margaret, and she says, "I was actually on my way to Pioneer for a few things." "So, how are you, dear?" his mother says. "You're looking fine," and she says, "I was just telling Gould that I haven't been that well lately. I've had big troubles, something entirely unforeseen, Beatrice," and his mother says, "At our age it's always one setback after the next. Either we lose somebody or we lose some part of our body. I'm sick of doctors. It never lets up and they're all no good." "Mom, excuse me, but let her finish," and Margaret says, "But if she's tired or cold?" and he says, "You're okay, aren't you, Mom?" and she says, "If you say so—only kidding. I'm not quite up to par today, but I'll survive, why?" and Margaret says to him, "If there's a cloudburst?" and he says, "Believe me, we both would rather know how you are, and we'll just duck in someplace if it rains and then get a cab somehow," and Margaret says, "Well, it's a ridiculous thing; and talk about the unexpected, this one takes the cake. I had a mole I didn't know about on my scalp," and he slaps his hand to his mouth and looks at his mother, and she's staring up at her placidly. "Or maybe this mole all of a sudden grew there, but at the beauty parlor six months ago the girl cutting my hair nicked it with her scissors. Really, the first time I was ever nicked with scissors or hurt in a beauty parlor in any way, not even my nails, and I've been going to one every two months for more than fifty years and it has to be this one tiny mole on my head. And something went wrong with it—you both know how that can happen with moles—and it quickly spread and now I'm getting radiation for it every other day and they think they might get it under control." "No! Oh, my goodness," he says, and his mother looks alarmed at him and says, "What is it? Is it your wife? One of your children? He has two young girls"—to Margaret—and he says, "No, they're okay," and, to Margaret, "I'm so sorry, so sorry," and she says, "That's why I'm wearing this kerchief. From where they cut, and also some hair falling out. But I'm hoping for the best; what else can I do for now? Just, I've been feeling sick so much of the time because of the treatments. The stuff I'm going to Pioneer for is really for my stomach, to settle it, since I hardly eat anymore, even if they say I'm supposed to. But how can I eat when everything I put down wants to come up?" and he says, "I can't believe it. God, what happens in life!" and she says, "Isn't it amazing? But if I don't get cured I at least know I had three wonderful sons and lived my normal life span and maybe a decade beyond," and he says, "Don't talk like that. You'll get better," and she says, "I pray so. Now you get your mother home. I also didn't go out with an umbrella—this weather wasn't expected. The radio said it'd be mild and sunny all day, and for some reason rain's not supposed to be good for me, not just sun," and he says, "Because of the radiation?" and she says, "Maybe I have it wrong. It could be the sun that's the one bad egg, which is another reason I wore the kerchief. Goodbye, Beatrice," and his mother says,

"Are you going so soon? Don't be such a stranger, dear; come and see me," and she says, "I've been meaning to but things have sort of slowed me down lately. But I'll try; I love our talks," and they kiss and he kisses her and wheels his mother toward home. "Tell me, was that Margaret from our block I just spoke to?" and he says, "Yes, your old drinking buddy," and she laughs and says, "When was that? But she's not been well, has she? I could tell by her voice. So weak. And something about her expression." "She's sick, all right," and she says, "What of?" and he tells her about the accident and now the radiation, and she says, "Age is an awful thing. People today live too long, I honestly believe that," and he says, "It has nothing to do with age. You know her; she was strong as an ox. Lifting heavy garbage cans, shoveling snow and washing her windows outside and in. It was that fluke accident, as she said," and she says, "How?" and he says, "I told you," and she says, "Tell me again. With all this street noise and because you're speaking behind me, it's sometimes difficult to hear." About a month later, when he calls his mother, the woman taking care of her and who answered the phone says, "You remember Margaret, your mother's good friend, the one who used to come by here every week or two and they'd talk and have drinks and cheese?" and he says, "She died, didn't she," and she says, "You knew? It only happened a few days ago. The mailman, Frank, told me," and he says, "No, but I saw her when I took Beatrice out last time I was there, and she said what was wrong with her and it really seemed bad," and the woman says, "They were a real pair. Talked and laughed; I never knew what it was over, but she was the only one your mother did that with and it could go on for hours. She's going to be real sorry when she hears about it," and he says, "Maybe it's best we don't tell her," and she says, "What about when she asks me to phone Margaret to come by and for me to make sure there's enough Jack Daniels left for them, which she used to do regularly?" and he says, "Has she done it recently?" and she says, "No, but she's going to, I feel it, and I don't know how I'll be able to lie to her with a straight face," and he says, "I think she's already sensed something was wrong—the way Margaret looked last time and her not seeing or hearing from her for so long—and, I don't know, has put it out of her mind because it's too sad to think about. It's a real loss, besides that she was such a nice person. Is my mother able to come to the phone?"

and she shouts out, "Mrs. B, your son's on the phone, pick up," and his mother picks up the phone in her room, and he says, "How you feeling, Mom?" and she says, "Could be better, I guess. Do you remember my dear friend Margaret?" and he says, "Yes, sure, down the block, brownstone next to the big apartment building," and she says, "She owns it, you know. She used to work for this elderly couple—years ago—she and her husband, though she did most of it, laundry, cooking, small repairs, and all the custodial work, when first one and then the other of this couple quickly died and they left only Margaret the building. Her husband was no good. A charmer, from Portugal, and a ladies' man they said—she told me everything—so he used to disappear for months on end. I haven't seen her for a long time. I don't think it's a mystery either but that it's because she died. No one phoned me, not that I could have gone to the funeral. I don't have the heart or energy for those things anymore. Do you know anything about it?" and he says, "Unfortunately, you're right. I just found out myself. And if her sons didn't tell you, I'm sure it's because they thought you had problems enough. What a wonderful person, though, huh? and what a friend to you," and she says, "It's such a pity. All the old-timers from the block are either gone or they've moved away and you never hear from them again, and I don't even think I have any sisters or my brother left. But how's your wife? The kids? All my little darlings. Everyone's okay?"

The Shame

He's trying to get in touch with an old friend about something; calls the number he has in his address book, it's no longer a working number; calls Manhattan Information, and there's no number for him or any number for anyone in the entire city for him or just with his last name and the first initial H; calls Harold's ex-wife, which is the same number Harold used to have when he was still married to her, and that number now belongs to someone who says he got it from the phone company two years ago; doesn't know how to reach Harold, and then remembers a mutual friend from college and about ten years after who became Harold's best friend and whom he last bumped into about four or five years ago—at the time this guy said he was living on West 89th Street near the park—and gets his number from

Information and dials; and a woman's recorded voice says Amber and Emmiline aren't in, please leave a message, and he says who it is and that she might even remember him—"I'm an old friend of Andrew's from way way back"—and could one of them have Andrew call him, and gives his phone number. He assumes they got divorced and Amber kept the apartment and their daughter lives with her, but then why would she still list Andrew's name in the phone directory, unless they're only separated? Maybe, if they are divorced, to ward off creepy men from calling her because there's only a woman's name listed or just an initial for a first name. Anyway, two days later Andrew calls and says, "I got your message. What's up, how's it going?" and he says, "Fine. I'm just trying to reach Harold. Neither he nor Lynn are listed in the phone book in New York, she hasn't kept their old phone number, and I didn't know who else to go to. And excuse me if you think this is being nosy, but I assume, because your wife only mentioned her and your daughter's names on the answering machine recording—" and Andrew says, "We split up more than four years ago, soon after I last saw you, I think," and he says, "Sorry to hear that," and Andrew says, "No reason to be. It was a lousy marriage for years. The worst part, as I'm sure it'd be for you too, is the daily deprivation of seeing my daughter. She didn't want to move to San Diego, and you can't blame her—friends, school, her mother—and it was too good a job for me to turn down and stay in New York just to be near her. But I've started socializing again, so I'm not as lonely as when I first got here, and I get to see Emma about six times a year and for a month this summer, which helps out. I'm even getting to like this city. Weather's ideal, if you've had your fill of icy rain and snow and extreme cold, and there are plenty of good bookstores and places to eat, and people here are a lot more civil to you than they are in New York. But what about Harold?" and he tells him his mother died a month ago and he thought Harold would be able to advise him on what to do with her jewelry and antiques and some of her furniture. "He's the right guy for that, and you'd be dealing with someone you can trust, for a lot of these estate and appraisal people can be jackals of the worst order. But he's not in the antiques business anymore, though he could still give you good advice. And I'm sorry to hear about your mom. I don't remember her that well—we're talking of more than thirty years ago when I last saw her—but I know how it feels, when my own dear mother died twenty-two years ago. I still think of her almost every day, and now more than the last few years, maybe because of my divorce and my daughter. You have a pen?" and he gives Harold's phone numbers off the top of his head, his apartment and studio and also his office. "Who knows why he's unlisted. Debts, I doubt. As for Lynn, she goes by her maiden name now, Katz. Since they parted ways, I haven't seen her, though her last address is Three-ten West Nineteenth Street, one zero zero eleven for the ZIP. I only know it because she once asked me to send her one of our products. So listen, this has been nice, and if you ever get out to San Diego—" and he says, "I was there three years ago for something and don't see any chance of a repeat visit soon," and Andrew says, "Too bad I wasn't here then. I mean, I'm glad I wasn't; I was still in New York and seeing my daughter almost every day. But if I had been here and knew from Harold or someone you were coming. Next time, perhaps. Or in New York, if you get there and our stays overlap. No, then I reserve all my free time for Emma. But it's not often I run into old friends out here, and I miss it and that New York openness and humor. Do you run into anyone from college or after whom we both knew?" and he says, "Hardly ever. You might've been the last, several years ago, coming out of a subway station I was walking past, or the other way around, or it could have been one of us going in it and the other coming out, I forget," and Andrew says, "I remember that, Broadway and Seventy-second. I was heading to Fairway from my office downtown for some deli and Eli's bread and you were cutting across the island the station's on to buy Mahler's Tenth—the Rattle version, I think you said—at that big record store on the corner, the one I like to call MSG. Matter of fact, our conversation that time was mainly about music. You'd recently had a letter in the *Times* magazine section where you criticized an article they'd run on Vladimir Horowitz. 'Petty-minded and abjectly cheeky and pejorative' were some of the things you said in it, and I remember asking you how come you'd got so worked up about the subject," and he says, "Well, if I recall, I thought Horowitz was entitled to his so-called eccentricities, if that's what it took for him to—" and Andrew says, "I know; you told me in front of the subway station. I disagreed, didn't think the writer of the article had been as unsympathetic and sarcastic as you'd said in the letter, though you might have been right; and now Horowitz is dead. Anyway, about San Diego, take my number, just in case you're ever out here or somewhere close—L.A., even, since I get up there once a month," and gives it, and he writes it down though doesn't think he'll transfer it to his address book. He's not going to San Diego, and even if he did he wouldn't try to see him and he doesn't know what he'd want to speak to him on the phone again for. What he wants now is to get off, but Andrew's talking about the White House—how'd they get into that?—"Because what do you make of it? I think the scandals and skulduggery will ultimately crush him, and to our great misfortune too. Because liberal as he isn't, he's still two times five more so than any Repub who'll succeed him if the shit sticks, and then say *hasta luego* to abortion rights, gun control, military spending restraint, health, welfare, and education support, besides aid to the arts of any sort and free condoms, and then crime on the street will next be on your doorstep and then in your hair. In other words, poverty and lousy housing and too many unguided defiant children—" and he says, "That could be, though if the guy and his cronies did wrong, they should own up to it and pay the consequences, even if in the long run we'll all suffer," and thinks why, of all things, did he say that? and then a movie Andrew saw last month that he thinks the most literary and intellectual film since early to middle Bergman. "I mention him also because I remember you once said he should get, almost before anyone—and I'm dipping back here around twenty years—the Nobel for literature," and he says, "I did? It's a blank to me, and now I think all those prizes are ruinous and ridiculous," and Andrew says, "Come on, you wouldn't turn down something good like that if it was offered," and he says, "I don't know; maybe only not to embarrass the giver. But what's the title?" and writes it down, and then a novel Andrew read in three sittings last week—"long as we're talking about literature"—that he thinks Gould would like, and gives the title and author, and he says, "Never heard of it or her," and Andrew says, "Gallop, don't shlep, to your bookstore for it. If you were here I'd immediately loan it to you. She's doing things with language and story and structure that practically no one but some of the Latin Americans are doing, or used to, but for their culture, and she's maybe just hit thirty. It's worth every dollar of the hardcover price and it's a big book too but reads as if it's one-third the size—that quick, despite its density and intricateness," and he says, "I'll certainly take a look at it; thanks for the tip," but doesn't write the title or author's name down. If it's that good, someone else will tell him about it or he'll see it advertised or prominently displayed in the bookstores, though he still won't skim through more than a dozen pages of it. Writers have to be—if it's novels, not stories—dead or at least a few years older than he for him to like, he's not sure why. Not envy, he doesn't think, or for the last ten years; the young ones don't have much to say or very interesting ways to say it, and American Americans less than most of them, but he doesn't want to say that now and get into a whole other discussion and probably be ridden a little for it. "So, it's been nice talking to you," and Andrew says, "Same here, and don't forget what I suggested to you," and he says, "You mean if I'm out there? I have your number," and Andrew says "That too, but I was referring to Tiffany Hissler's novel. It'd be major at any age; the girl's a wonder," and he says, "I won't, I got it: *Time Off,*" and Andrew says, "*Time In,*" and he says, "Anyway, *Time,* so I'll find her alphabetically either way," and they say goodbye and hang up, and he thinks, I should have added "by name and title." The guy will think I'm a jerk. Right after, his wife says, "Who was that?" and he tells her and why Andrew called back, "but I feel so lousy about him, because of his first wife," and she says, "They obviously broke up and divorced. Or something terrible happened to her?" and he says, "I did something I'm so ashamed of," and tells her, and she says, "Well, when you get older this is what you learn, or ought to, and better now than never," and he says, "Oh, I've known it for a long time, right from the beginning, not that it stopped me from doing it again and again, with her and others. I just didn't think it'd come back to me like this after thirty years. I almost wanted to bring the matter up on the phone, get it out finally," and she says, "Bad idea. If he doesn't know, why hurt him now just so you can unburden yourself? And if he knows—" and he says, "He has to. He was always smart and sharp, read a lot, picked up things quick, was a great quipster, would have me in stitches, and I could tell by our conversation before that he doesn't miss a trick or forget a thing. And they must have talked about it at least once during the breakup. She screwed around with a few other guys during the marriage, and I remember Harold once saying that was one of the reasons Andrew agreed to the divorce: he couldn't trust her. I'm sure Harold didn't know about me; if he did he would have pilloried me for it: 'Andrew was our friend,' and so on. Of course, as a couple—well, not of course; but Andrew and Clo didn't seem that compatible. He was precise and buttoned up; she was kind of sloppy and hang-loose and said whatever crossed her mind no matter how insulting or vulgar, another reason he must have known: her big mouth. But both were sensitive to little things; seashells, I remember; usually pink and translucent and kept in tiny plastic boxes. Miniature watch faces without bands; they'd started a collection together. And children. Meaning, they seemed relaxed and affectionate with them, playing on the floor and that sort of thing. She wanted one desperately then, he didn't at all, but when she was married she told me she only wanted one with him. I'm sure, if she had asked—and who knows if I didn't even suggest this—I would have gladly supplied the seed and not thought of the consequences. That's the way I was then—I mean, I wouldn't have gone around bragging I had a child, but kind of stupid and irresponsible. He eventually had a daughter with Amber, his second wife; Clo had about three kids with her second husband. I bumped into her about ten years ago on the subway; maybe I told you this," and she says no. "She'd gotten a little dumpy, had always been prone to it, being short and squat and big-boned and a voracious eater, all of which was a turn-on to me when she was much younger. She was so strong, physically. I helped them move a couch once, and she was easily my match on her end of it. Lifted it without struggling. Andrew, who's at least six feet but quite gangly, stood on the side, saying it only takes two to lift it, three would unbalance it for the one who had to take an end by himself, so let Clo do it instead of him, since she's a lot stronger. Maybe she was also more sexual than he, but that's their story, nothing I want to know about. She did allude to it but I forget what it was, something about her sexual appetite, I think, which, if you were only doing it sporadically with her—this is what I think now, not what she said—was probably easy enough to satisfy. And it could be—this is legitimate—her physical strength had the opposite effect on him than it did on me, and that his second wife's leanness, almost emaciation—I saw her once—was a turn-on to him, sending him into sensual frenzies. I've always preferred, but haven't always ended up with, women who can take a lot of banging around in bed, with strong thighs, a decent-sized rear and spread, plenty of energy, no wilting delicateness or fake excuses." "Was there any spark there when you saw her on the subway?" and he says, "There was never much spark between us. It was physical, though we had laughs too, and she was bright and also well-read, so occasional good conversations. But mostly food, wine, sex. I knocked on their door once—we lived in the same building. I was on the ground floor and they were on the third. I in fact got that apartment through him. They gave a party, I attended, liked the neighborhood, and told him I had to get out of my sublet across town, and he said there's a small studio apartment in their building, fairly cheap because it's sort of an illegal residence, carved out of another apartment and maybe not even reported to the city's Rent Commission. So one day—he was away on business for the week, I didn't know that, though," and she says, "Of course you didn't," and he says, "I'm telling you; I didn't see them much. Once every two to three weeks and if not for dinner, which was maybe once every three months, then usually just a quick chat by our mailboxes or in the supermarket or on the street," and she says, "So that's when one of them told you and you used that information to make your move," and he says, "But I'm almost sure they didn't. That'd change the whole story, make me into an even worse creep than I thought I was. Because the way I remember it is I went to their apartment to speak to Andrew. I wanted to borrow something—his car, I believe, to drive my folks someplace," and she says, "Was it evening?" and he says, "Afternoon, I think," and she says, "So why would you think Andrew would be there, unless he worked nights?" and he says, "Then I don't know what time of the day it was: evening, afternoon—or the weekend; you forgot that. To be honest, somehow I see daylight in the picture, and open windows, so summer or early fall or late spring; I even think there was a breeze. They had a big two-bedroom apartment with a terrace and several exposures. Really quite grand and nicely furnished, floors finished, everything done in good taste. But anyway, I knocked on their door—or maybe I did know he was gone and I was going to the market and wanted to know if she needed anything. I thought it was about the car, but now the going-to-the-store-for-her seems right, and I think because she was sick," and she says, "You could have called for that," and he says, "How do you know I had a phone? I probably didn't, as I avoided them for years in my apartments. It saved money; I didn't have a lot. I even had the phone turned off in the previous place I sublet. And if I did have one it would be more like me to think it was profligate to call from two floors below rather than walk upstairs. I was a bit of a cheapskate then too, but it's something I'd still probably do. Anyway, I rang their bell, didn't knock—you ring bells for apartments unless the bell's broken, and this was a good building, well taken care of—and either asked through the door for Andrew or if she needed anything at the market, or if *they* needed anything at the market, because I might have thought they were both in, when she answered it. Though first the peephole opened, probably to make sure no one was with me. She must have stretched on her toes to reach her eye to it, since she was at the most five-one, and then she said, 'Hold it,' and the door opened and she was nude except for her panties. Jesus! I thought, What the hell's she doing?" and she says, "She wanted you in there, what else? Or she was so laid back that a peek at her bosom didn't mean anything to her. But judging from what this is leading up to, I doubt it. But was she like that, sort of a nudist?" and he says, "I don't know. I mean, she was European, or of descent, from Czechoslovakia, came here when she was five. But she certainly at the moment was nonplussed that I saw her. But there she was, her enormous breasts, which don't mean anything to you but were very exciting to me, and slim panties, more like a bikini. I could see her pubic hair through them and sticking out around them, and of course after I said 'Excuse me' or something, I wanted to jump her. That's how I was then. That's why I'm so ashamed, or there's a better word for it, but of what I did and continued to do a few times and I could have stopped it right there," and she says, "But if that was her purpose and you just quickly picked up on it—and that was the climate at the time, if I've got my decades straight—then you're not that much to blame," and he says, "But he was my friend; I knew him long before I met her," and she says, "I forgot; that's what you were saying; so I suppose you should have turned around and left, saying you'll come back at a more convenient time, giving her the benefit of the doubt," and he says, "And that might have been what I would have done too, even though I know I was immediately worked up, but she said, 'Hi, Andrew's not home, he's out of town for the week'—something like that. And 'Listen, I can't keep the door open, one of our neighbors might walk by, so if you want to come inside, do.' And I went in—I didn't have to; she gave me that out—and knew we were going to have sex, although at the same time, as you said, I could have thought her nudity meant nothing to her and certainly not among friends. For all I know, if I hadn't quickly moved in on her—I mean, I must have had my arms around her and was pressing my erection into her in the little alcove there—she might have gone and got a bathrobe for herself, invited me to have coffee, just to chat. And she might have been sick—as I said, that's also what I remember from that first time—and so had just hopped out of her sick bed to answer the door and didn't attach any importance to her exposed breasts but had put her panties on along the way, or else already had them on in bed. And friends, up till then, was all we'd been. I liked her. I told you. She was bright, lively, good sense of humor, and was generous, just like him. They'd had me up for dinner a couple of times, had also invited me to parties with them. They must have thought, or one of them did, that I should meet someone, was by myself too much, and so on. I didn't know any women to go out with, then, or anyone who gave parties but them, which is where you do meet women. Though of course if I was that alone, maybe that was my main impetus to have sex with her, and also she could have known or sensed that too—that I had to be horny, or am I pushing the motivations there? But we'd never kissed, hugged, touched: none of that before. Just friends, and not real close ones. When the three of us were together, or when I did bump into her on the street or at a market, we talked a great deal, Clo and I, and I think laughed and joked around a lot too. Our attitudes were somewhat alike; Andrew was a bit more serious. We found it absurd the way people overbought, overdressed, went into debt, put on airs, wanted to impress, were desperate for high-powered jobs and plenty of money and attention and success and those sorts of things, while also not doing much deep thinking or reading. Well, Andrew thought much like that too, though I was far crankier and more judgmental. He was a good guy. I'm telling you, I liked and admired him. I sound phony now, don't I, but believe me, I'm not. I remember they also invited me to a few movies with them. I'd see them on the street or somewhere; they'd say, 'What are you doing tonight?' I'd say, 'Nothing,' because I was usually doing nothing, meaning nothing with people, and they'd say they're going to a movie and to come with them. They sat in the theater, she usually between us—I mean, it only happened two or three times—held hands, ate from the same box of popcorn, passed the box to me, though I couldn't stand the smell, sound, or feel of the thing. All of this I swear I remember. Did I ever before that first time think of her in a sexual way? I don't think so. Or, if so, fleetingly: the breasts and strong shape, and I have an imagination and could see what she was built like through her clothes, but with no designs on her, none whatsoever, my personal designs, I'm saying. Why? She was his wife, and maybe up till the moment she opened the door I was never attracted to her," and she says, "So what it took was for her to take her clothes off; you never once mentioned her face," and he says, "She had a pleasant one; smiled a lot, but authentically. And I suppose so, regarding the no clothes. And it also might have been the most optimum time, too: he being away, she saying so immediately, maybe something about the light and temperature if not balminess of the day, and my being just before I rang her bell overwhelmingly priapic, though nothing concerning her, and she being the same from the woman's side, which I'm just guessing now, since I don't remember that at all. As for those movies, they went a lot, so it wasn't so unusual for me to go with them a few times, because he was thinking of leaving his job in advertising to try his hand at becoming an independent moviemaker. I think that's why he didn't want any children then." "And *her* job?" and he says, "Fabrics designer. I think she quit when she started having kids, or continued it at home was what she said when I met her on the subway. I was a substitute teacher at the time. So I had to have had a phone then; no other way I'd get work. And it must have been on a weekend when I went to their apartment, since I subbed almost every schoolday there was, the per-diem pay was so low, and she went to her own work downtown, unless she *was* sick and had taken the day off and that was the one day in the month I wasn't able to get a sub job. So now I forget why I went to their apartment, though I'm still almost sure it was during the day and the weather was warm." "To have sex, why are you denying it? If she hadn't come to the door half nude—that was an act of fortuity for you—you would have been the one to devise an excuse to get inside. I'd even bet you called first to say you'd like to borrow something—

coffee, toothpaste—and she quickly prepared that impromptu surprise for you, knew why you were really coming up but wanted to speed things along a little," and he says, "Wrong, believe me, that's not how it was. And now, I don't know where it came from—probably from just talking about it—but I think I know why I went upstairs. I wanted to know if they'd be interested in two tickets I had for a recital that night. Myra Hess, at Carnegie Hall or City Center, but I think the Hall; I'd bought them for some woman and me. So I apparently was seeing a woman then or was starting to date one, or that was to be our first date. But she called to say she was sick—that's probably where the sick business comes in, though Clo could have been sick too; an Asian flu could have been floating around—and had to cancel and I didn't want to go alone and try hawking the extra ticket in the lobby, and the truth is I didn't want to go at all. Like the popcorn, there are some things I haven't liked for forty years—ask the kids about me and popcorn in movie theaters today. And though I love classical music and the piano especially and particularly the way Hess played on LPs—I had a few; we still have them though don't use them much and I don't know if any have been transferred to CD—I don't like concerts or recitals of any sort; larger the hall, less I like them. No doubt I only bought the tickets to make an impression on this woman. All right, I was trying to impress her: Dame Myra Hess, if she was a Dame by then; Carnegie Hall; probably Beethoven, Scarlatti. Or maybe she only said she was sick because she disliked concerts and recitals as much as I. That would have been a laugh, if she had told me later, but I don't think I ever saw her after that. By calling in sick she might have been saying it had been a mistake to make the date, if that was to be the first one, and she didn't want to go out with me, period. Anyhow—" and she says, "No, this is what I think happened, if this new version of yours is true. You were already sleeping with this woman you were dating—you don't remember half the women you slept with and almost none of their names. Or you had gone out with her long enough to feel that after the recital would be the first time you slept with her. But when she canceled you knew there'd be no sex that weekend—I'm assuming it was a weekend, a big date and an important recital like that—and you also knew that this Clo . . . Wait. How come you didn't invite *her* to the recital, once the other one bowed out, if you knew she was going to be alone? Because you didn't want to bother with any preliminaries like that?" and he says, "Because when I went upstairs to their apartment I didn't think she'd be alone. I thought Andrew would be there, or there that night in time for the recital. Now why didn't I invite her when she opened the door and said Andrew was out of town for however long it was? Maybe I did, or was about to or was thinking if I should, but because she was half nude she quickly whisked me inside—the neighbors, remember? But my intention when I rang their bell was that after all the meals they'd had me up for and parties they'd taken me to and so forth, this would be a nice payback to them, two tickets to a great pianist's recital, even if the seats were way up and maybe the second cheapest. Hess was past seventy then, I think, and very fragile—I know she looked much older than she was, you remember the record jacket photographs: bony and gaunt. And this recital was billed as being part of her last American tour and perhaps even her last performance in America ever," and she says, "So, did you end up taking her to it?" and he says, "No, but I did go myself—I remember sitting in the third or fourth row from the top of the balcony. I don't think I tried to sell the extra ticket in the lobby or out front—no guts to—so just gave it away. That part of it's vague, but what isn't is my feeling so far away from the stage while the music, because it was piped up to us, seemed close. Also, I think Clo was too sick to go and would have construed it as a date or something, once we had made love, since I'm almost positive we did it in the afternoon before the recital. No, I'm sure of it. All she wanted, it seemed, was sex in bed and then for me to disappear. I mean, once I got into the apartment and put my arms around her and started things going with my lips and hands. We also did it another day or night before Andrew came home, and then a couple of other times over the next six months or so when he was away. I forget what led up to them, but that's usually the case and you only remember the first. Though once, when she was sick again and he was away or at work in the city that day and I couldn't get a sub job, or something like that—maybe I didn't even try that day, and not because I knew this would happen—she rang my bell and asked if I had aspirins, she'd run out. This time she definitely had a bad flu, had to stay home from work, I think she said. I said I did—the aspirins—and she came in and was in a bathrobe and I might have seen something through it—a leg, a breast—not that by this time in our little sex affair I needed that to get me going, though it couldn't hurt, and we started kissing, bad flu and all, and she took the aspirins . . . I'm making the last part up. I know I had aspirins to give her—I don't think I've run out of them in forty years—and I believe that was my last time with her, so the only time in my apartment. I went away for a month that summer—August, an artist colony, always August, my summer vacation retreat those days—and they'd separated by the time I got back and she'd moved out and he kept the apartment, which was originally his, and she quickly got herself a steady boyfriend and married either him or the next one in a year," and she says, "Did Andrew ever say anything to you about it—hint, at least, that he knew?" and he says, "Never, and it wasn't that I couldn't read the signs—I was fiercely if not even over-obviously on the alert for them—and I never brought it up, since I was already a little ashamed—that started at the artist colony—and after that the shame just grew. Andrew and Harold and his first wife and I did go to a couple of things together that fall after the separation—a movie, maybe, and I think once that Japanese-Californian health food restaurant that was on Columbus between Seventy-fourth and Seventy-fifth a short time and where you could bring your own sake and beer. I remember they'd even heat up the sake for you and put it in a pretty carafe. Andrew and I, in all the time I knew him, never socialized just the two of us. We weren't that companionable, and I don't think we even felt comfortable together without Clo or Harold there, though we did meet on the street or in the building's vestibule a few times, as we had in the past, and chat briefly and amicably about nothing, really. After that, Harold sort of drifted away from me, which now makes me think he did get wind that I'd slept with Clo, which as I said would have been a definite no-no with him—I could sleep with whomever's wife I wanted to so long as it wasn't a mutual friend's or his own—and also makes me think Andrew told him that that's what he thought I'd done but to keep it a secret. Because he also never mentioned it to me, though he almost had to know, even without Andrew's saying anything, since he knew what I was like then," and she says, "And what was that?" and he says, "What do you think? That my prick came first, scruples second, when it came to women I was attracted to, though on most other counts I was a fairly to even an avidly scrupulous person. High-minded, maybe a bit self-righteous, definitely socially conscious—is that how you say it?—running after robbers, stepping into arguments and trying to reconcile matters if I thought someone was going to get hurt . . . you know my stories. Helping blind and lame and elderly people cross the street, stopping traffic to do it if I had to. Worried about very young children when I see them alone outdoors, and so on, risking my life and getting a punch in the jaw sometimes too, but it was that or not being able to face myself, I thought. Even with your father, twenty years later, that time the Korean produce store was being robbed and we were all walking past together and saw it and I wanted to run in, and he grabbed my shoulders and said, 'You have a family now' . . . I had to be a little crazy, I know, and not just then. So what was I saying?" and she says, "That there was a decent side to you at the time too. But what happened with Andrew after that?" and he says, "He moved out that winter or so. He started making—well, he'd always done well, compared to me, since college—but now a lot of money, and he wanted a better apartment," and she says, "And to perhaps be out of the house of bad memories and also the same building as you," and he says, "I don't think people take it that far in New York if they're paying a fairly modest rent with no huge annual jack-ups for a nice large place. No, he wanted something with more light and a better view and a working fireplace and floors he could walk on barefoot without his feet continually getting splinters in them, I think I remember him saying. Their apartment was in back and faced a twenty-story residential hotel. Mine was on the street and got light most of the day but was much noisier and, in the summer, because of the car fumes and the garbage cans right outside, smellier. He got a floor-through in the Village with two fireplaces, a lovely brick townhouse on West Eleventh, I think, but I never saw it, just heard, since he didn't invite me to it and by that time our only mutual friend, Harold, wasn't, as I said, much of a friend to me anymore," and she says, "Maybe, in addition to how he felt about you sleeping with Andrew's wife, he thought you'd go after his," and he says, "I'm sure he never worried about it, since he knew that Gwen, his first wife, and I didn't even like each other much, something he actually brought up a couple of times and I probably said, 'Oh come on, why do you think that?' " and she says, "But sexually? She's still attractive, or only time I saw her; must have been much better looking then and shapely rather than what's getting to be a matronly figure. And did you have to like a woman to want to bed her? You yourself said—" and he says, "That's true, to a degree, but what do you think I was then? besides your missing my point. With Clo there must have been some attraction I kept back because Andrew was my old college friend and had been so generous to me since I moved into the building and also because they lived upstairs and I didn't think anything like that could possibly happen with her. And then it did happen because he was away for a while and I must have been all rutted when I rang her bell and maybe feeling sexually dispossessed and she made that first overpowering display, you could say—at least irresistible to me at the time. While now I think my libido, being somewhat lower or less urgent or demanding or whatever a libido becomes with age—" and she says, "You don't have the sex drive you once did, you're saying. But maybe you do, or it's off by a small fraction since I've known you, but because we live together and if I'm not sick and you're not being obnoxious I'm usually agreeable and even eager for it, you don't have to go out of your way to get laid," and he says, "That could be true too. But what I was going to say was that if I were in the same situation today, and even if it wasn't true that you're usually compliant and my sex drive isn't as strong and I'm married with children so I'd have a lot more to lose by going along with it, I'm sure I'd be able to resist: the breasts at the door—and let's say you and the kids were away for a week too—large beautifully shaped young breasts, I feel a little stupid saying, and skinny bikini panties, if that's what they're called, and quick invite to come inside. But with Gwen there was nothing for me to resist—no attraction, not that she wasn't physically attractive then. And forget opportunity, because even if I had rung their bell one day to see Harold—just happened to stop by—and she opened the door completely nude and said he suddenly had to leave town for the year, or that they were getting a divorce and he was no longer living home and she's been waiting for this chance with me for a long time, and grabbed my penis through the pants or did whatever with it that would normally make me excited, for you know that just about any handling by you or pressure on it, even a book, would do it—" and she says, "Oh, come on," and he says, " 'Oh, come on' nothing. Anyway, my point in all this, just so we don't forget, is my shame, how every time I talk to

Andrew—maybe once every five years, and that includes bumping into him on the street or seeing him with Harold . . . actually, at Harold's second wedding a number of years ago. You saw him there too, the only time I think you met. He came alone; we in fact sat at his table. I mean it wasn't organized like that; you sat where you wanted to sit and he was the only person I knew there other than Harold and I seemed to be the only one he knew. So it would have been insulting to him, I thought, not to sit there, and he seemed pleased that we sat next to him. And the three of us had a good conversation, intelligent and stimulating and long, do you remember? You had very nice things to say about him after, that he was a person of high quality and so on, and later we drove him home—it was on our way—and I don't think Harold holds it against me anymore what I did with Clo. That's what I get from his attitude toward me, few times we've seen each other the last ten years. Anyway, I always feel constrained with Andrew: small, humiliated somewhat, even base, other things. I really feel it can only end if I bring it up to him, what I think, my regrets and shame—I'd even say that to him: that this is why I'm bringing it up. And that I'm nothing like that now, haven't been that way for twenty years and have no excuse for what I did then, and how sorry I am and that I only wish there was some way of making it up to him. Though when you think of it, he did remarry, no matter how that one turned out, and got a child out of it—in her teens now, college, whom he adores, by the way he talks of her. So if I and some other guys were partly the cause of his breakup with Clo, at least he can say . . . well, you know, and of course I'd never say any of this to him. I'm just sort of rationalizing, putting into his head what I'd think if I were in the same situation: I got a great kid the second time around and that was worth all the heartaches of the first marriage, and so not to hold a grudge against the guys who screwed my wife, though of course not to thank them either," and she says, "That couldn't have been it, you and these other men, even partly, or only a tiny part of partly. Those problems can be worked out and were only a symptom of what was wrong. There had to be basic incompatibilities between them of long standing, things they must have tried to fix. I think you once said he'd gone through a lot of therapy since college, so I have to assume she went through a little too, and then when their marriage was falling apart they went individually and together, and also marriage counseling. And she was young then, like you and Andrew, and that was a free-for-all time in America if there ever was one—we're talking here of almost thirty years ago, I think you said," and he says, "Maybe even more than thirty. Let me think when it was exactly," and she says, "Doesn't matter. But I don't think you ever want to talk to him about anything related to it unless he brings it up first. It would only revive certain things for him he probably prefers to forget. And if it's only to relieve your conscience, is it worth it when you consider the damage you might do him? This is the price you pay for your past promiscuity. It'd be different if he wanted to renew his friendship with you or wanted to get all these things out. Then, maybe, you could work out your differences, past associations, and all that, and it would also be easier for him and seem a lot more reasonable too, since he would have initiated it and would know what he's getting into and if it got too messy for him he'd only have himself to blame," and he says, "He did say that if I got to San Diego again I should look him up, and gave me his phone number," and she says, "That's not the same thing," and he says, "I suppose not. No, of course, you're right, so I'll just have to live with it. It's a shame," and she says, "Why? Because you like him now, or as much as you did before, but can't really be friendly with him because of what you did to him then?" and he says, "That too."

The Room

So what does he do now? He didn't want to have sex with her. He told her when she came to his room. Well, she was good-looking and he wouldn't mind doing it, he thought then, but knew he shouldn't because of his wife and that it could get complicated with this woman and he did what he could to stop it. He said, "Really, this isn't a good idea. I've never done it outside of my marriage, not even an amorous kiss. Better you go home and I go to sleep alone, I'm sorry. I know I don't sound too convincing, but I'm really convinced about it. You're attractive and pleasant and so on, but I just wouldn't know what to say to my wife," and she said, "You have to say anything? Why would you want to hurt her, if that's what it'd do? But if you want me to leave, of course I'll go without a fuss. It's not like I invited you out here just for this." He's driving home from the college he gave a reading at. He was met in the hotel lobby late yesterday afternoon by this woman. She said, "Oh, you took the service stairs instead of the elevator: the athletic type. Hi, I'm Sheila, welcome," and shook his hand hard. "How was the journey?" and he said, "An hour longer than you thought it would be, not that I'm blaming you." "Thank God for that; I'm not sure I could take it. What, there were major delays on the road?" and he said, "None, smooth all the way, and I mostly kept the speed at nine above the limit and followed your directions to the letter. Incidentally, they were perfect." "Then is your watch accurate or you switched to Daylight Savings Time during the drive?" and he said, "I'm telling you, four hours and a few minutes, with a quick pit stop to hit the men's room and get a container of coffee and, at the border tourist office next door to this restaurant, a free Pennsylvania road map. But it wasn't bad, since I was able to pick up a few classical music stations on the radio, and the best one an hour from here and with the call letters of your university. All of Byrd's masses. Very unusual. This is a good music area," and she said, "How's the hotel? I know it isn't big-city plush but we got you the nicest around," and he said, "The staff's friendly and I don't mean to sound like a chronic bellyacher, but the room's so depressing. Jesus, you want to blow your brains out, that's the room to do it in. Though it does have a Jacuzzi, not that I'll use it. But its one modern touch, with sliding frosted doors on the other side of the tub that open onto the rest of the room—what's that all about? Another entrance in case you locked the bathroom door accidentally? Or to take a bath or do the Jacuzzi with someone in the main room watching? Some architect's idea of chic or kink?" "Is that what made the room depressing?" and he said, "No, mystifying. For depression, just about everything else: furniture, carpet, drapes. All different muddy colors, and dim bulbs in ugly lamps, and a view of rundown row houses across the hotel parking lot and an abandoned railroad track." "Not abandoned; that's our famous spur. You're liable to hear a slow freight train choochoo-ing at midnight and again around five, or that's what several other guest speakers have told me. They liked it—small-town America—and they said the train had a very soothing whistle. It's picking up and delivering to what's left of the big steel mill in town." "Anyway, I'm reporting, not complaining. A life I couldn't live there, but a night?—it's fine. And thanks for having me out. Your fee is more than fair." Thinks: Should he take the alternate route to 83, coming up in a few miles? About twenty minutes longer, she told him when she gave directions to the hotel, but prettier and less traffic, and he'd like seeing different scenery going home. No, stick to this one, get back soon as he can, and, if the kids aren't around, tell his wife. "I don't know what happened last night. I mean, I know but can't quite believe it. But the teacher who coordinated the whole event and introduced me to the audience? Well, she ended up in my room later. In my bed. Minute after I said good night to her in her car downstairs, she knocked on my door to say she had to use the bathroom. I said why didn't she use the one in the lobby, and she gave some feeble excuse that it was being cleaned and she really had to go badly. We had sex. She forced me to. I didn't want to have anything to do with it and protested profusely till she stuck a washrag in my mouth. Before that, when we were having dinner, she must have slipped me a mickey or whatever it is that knocks you out in an hour or just makes you too weak and dizzy to fight back. Next thing I knew I was tied to the bed, on my back, spread-eagled and with no pants on, four ropes for four limbs plus duct tape, and she was on top of me, wielding a knife and threatening to mutilate me if I didn't perform. That's when I started protesting and the washrag went in. Twenty minutes after it was over she started in again, with the same threat, because she said she hadn't taken the risk she did to get so little satisfaction. Sound nuts? Believe it, because she was crazy. But that's all I did: perform, and good thing I was able to. I had her arrested in the morning after I got out of those ropes. Thought of calling you about it but then decided it'd be better to tell you face-to-face. She's in jail now. I'm pressing charges of assault and battery, whatever that last half is, and rape. I'm so sorry, but you have to see it was totally excusable on my part and that perhaps my being able to complete the sex act twice saved my life." They drove to the school building he was to read at. She was pretty, pleasant, intelligent, easy to be with, wavy red hair, strong build, short, lean-legged, nicely dressed, about twenty years younger than he, immediately effusive and friendly, with a much older and frailer woman's gravelly voice. Was she sick and just didn't show it? She asked about his wife and kids; he asked if she was married and had any kids. She had married early, childhood sweetheart, divorced after the birth of twins; two more brief marriages but no kids from them. The boys go to different colleges on opposite coasts. They're freshmen, only out of the house for three months and she misses them terribly. She lives alone in the foothills with a dog and several songbirds and her sons' cats: their dorms wouldn't permit pets. "If the car stinks it's because of the dog. He won't let me leave the house without him. Today you got lucky, except for the stench, which can't be avoided, I'm afraid, since I hate all those fake deodorizers. He's big and hairy and romps around in our nearby swamp a lot, and I can only give him so many baths a month. I even take him along when I teach or go out to a movie or dinner. He stays quietly in the car, hence the stench, which I must have grown used to, since I never smell it. Maybe my passengers are exaggerating it to reap some advantage from me. He's also good protection in this deceptively benign town of unemployed drunks and epigonic car thieves. But am I talking too much about him and not enough about my boys? That's because he's my best friend now and I love him—he'd never desert me for higher learning—and he's never given a sign that his car confinement is any kind of mistreatment," and he said, "Then you're probably doing the right thing, when you weigh it against his staying home and being lonely. How come you left him behind today, though again, I'm not complaining?" and she said, "The possibility that you could be allergic to dogs like our last guest; by the time I thought to call you about it, you were on the road," and he said, "I have no allergies, and though the smell is detectable, I can live with that too for a short time." "You know, I like you: you're a good guy. I mean; relaxed, equable, direct," and he said, "I only seem that way because I'm a little tired from the trip," and she said, "I like that about you too: your false modesty, which is only there to deflect further conversation about yourself. So many of the lecturers and writers I invite for the day because I like their work, though also because they're within a three-hour driving radius of here and don't insist on apparitional stipends, turn out to be cranks, egomaniacs, lechers, and jerks," and he said, "Three of the four I'll admit to being now and then, and a lech I might've been many years ago. But it'd be ridiculous to be one now—right?—not only because I don't want to bust up my marriage and hurt my kids, but my age. But what are we talking about?" and she said, "We're just talking, everything harmless, getting to know each other like two new people often do when they're suddenly stuffed into a small smelly car filled with dog hair for more than ten minutes. The conversation will change, though, and become rangy. That's a word I think I made up: wide range. To be honest, something I've never put to a real word man before; what do you think of it?" and he said, "If it catches on, and I'm so out of touch with contemporary culture that maybe it already has, I'll remember I heard it here first." "Now you sound sarcastic; what happened to change you?" and he said, "You're going to make me apologize. I didn't intend to sound sarcastic. And 'rangy.' Rangy? It's okay, but few people will understand it unless you explain it as you did to me." "Then I'm wiping it from my vocabulary. I'm serious—it's erased. Think of it as a value assessment of your judgment and technical know-how," and he said, "Don't be rash; it was just a single opinion of mine and maybe rushed." He thinks in his car, Maybe he won't say anything to his wife. Since he never did anything like it before, why would she suspect it now? He'll park in the carport—probably get home an hour and a half before the kids, the way he's moving—walk in, if she's not outside—she doesn't usually go out unless he or one of the kids or her student helper is around, afraid she might get stuck someplace in her wheelchair or motor cart and have to stay there till someone comes by or call a neighbor on her portable phone to help her—say, "Sally, you around? I'm back." If she's outside, and she won't be too far from the carport and the kitchen door, he'll see her when he pulls in. They'll kiss, she'll be very happy to see him, unless she's going through or has recently gone through something difficult with her illness. Then she probably won't be outside. "Hi, welcome home, you got back earlier than you thought you would," she might say. If she's not feeling well or has had a bad morning, he'll say, "What can I do for you? Anything you want?" Say, "I shouldn't have gone. I knew something like this could happen." Would happen? Would. "Even with people covering me," she might say, "they can't be here every second." He'll swear he's not going to accept another reading date out of town, if she had a bad time while he was gone. Yesterday when he called, soon after he got back to the hotel after dinner and just a few minutes before what's-her-name—he can't believe it; he's forgotten her name already—Sheila knocked on his door, she was fine:

nothing had gone wrong, the girls had been a great help. "If I go slow and think about every move and am very careful about my transferring, I'm usually okay." "It isn't worth it," he could say today. "The reading fee is taxed, what, twenty to twenty-five percent, so if I get six hundred max for it as I did for this one I only end up with four-fifty or so." "There are expenses for the trip," she'd probably say. "Thirty-one cents a mile when you go by car, IRS allows you, and your meals and hotel." "All paid for," he'd say, "except the car costs and coffees along the way. Though I can pad," and she'd say, "No padding; let's be completely honest." My God, he thinks in the car, how subliminal or subconscious or whatever it is, that last line. Anyway, they'll kiss, outside or in the house, no matter how bad she feels. She'll be glad he's home even if she's not feeling well; she just won't show it as much. He'll say, "Want some tea?" no matter how she's feeling. "I'm going to have some, since I had too much coffee on the road and for breakfast and I just want to sit tranquilly for a few minutes," and he'll make tea for himself or them both and say, "Want to sit with me outside?" and she could say, "That's an enticing idea, not only to be with you but I haven't been out today," and if she's outside when he gets there, then, "Sure. I can take a break"—from reading or marking papers or from her wheelchair snipping branches or pulling up tall weeds—"and you can tell me about your trip." He'll make the tea, bring the mug or mugs outside, wheel her out to the patio table right beside the carport or just to the table if she's already outside. The weather should be good for it; it's nice now and doesn't seem as if it'll change, and the TV report for central Pennsylvania, which he saw when he was having a buffet breakfast in the hotel lounge, said it'd be clear and sunny the entire day and in the high sixties, and the weather there shouldn't be that much different from Baltimore. They'll talk, he'll tell her what he had at dinner and what the town's like, and more about the reading than he did last night on the phone. "The reading coordinator, Sheila something—she also teaches nineteenth-century lit—Sheila Haverford, just like the small college near Philadelphia. I wonder if she's in any way related to the founder or whoever gave the college its name. If that's how it did get its name, it'd seem like too much of a coincidence that she isn't. Anyway, she was quite pleasant, smart, has twin sons in college—freshmen—though looks much younger than that . . . than a woman with twins that age. She could have married young, seventeen, eighteen, but while raising her kids she also must have worked hard getting through school for so many years; she has a Ph.D. in your least favorite subject and what you also call the most farcical, comp lit. Maybe she had help from her husband, plus lots of sitters and nannies, though that can run up. But if she is a Haverford and the Haverfords still have money—haven't given all of it away to the college, if that is, as I said, how it was named—there could be plenty of family money there, plus a couple of grannies to help her. But she said she divorced early, so who knows. I also recall now that her father was a watchmaker in a small New Jersey factory and died in a fire when she was around twenty. So, maybe fire insurance, if she was an only child. Her introduction—if I'm talking a lot about her it's because she was there from almost minute one till she dropped me back at the hotel after dinner, and there's almost nothing of comparable interest, not that this is interesting, to say about the trip—her introduction at the reading was typically embarrassing. Why don't they just cite a few facts—he did this, got that, his feet are flat and because of it he suffers from sciatica and has a bad back—and not try to assess your work so glowingly? I hate it when they gush on like that and I have to sit through it like a schmuck with everyone there to see me grimacing and squirming appreciatively. The turnout was pretty good—seventy-five, maybe. Good for me, anyway, but I think most were undergrads ordered to attend by their teaching assistants so as not to embarrass the department, as well as to justify my fee, which is what we do in my department when a non-hotshot guest gives a reading or lecture. I actually saw one of these TAs walking up and down the aisle taking attendance, or maybe she was only jotting down atmospheric notes for the academic novel she's writing. The Q-and-A's were the usual, though one I'd never heard: not 'Do you get a lot of your material from your own life?' but 'Why do you use so much of your life in your work, and because of the nature of what you write about, don't your friends, colleagues, neighbors, and especially your family object to your naked portrayal of them?' I said, 'How did you decide I do that? Are you writing an unauthorized biography of me, speaking to people I know behind my back, going through the garbage I put out for the trash haulers, attaching listening devices to my phone and through my home and office walls?' and he said, 'I'm sorry if the question offended you, sir. I thought it was a fair one but I can see your point,' and all I could think to say was Touché! which caused a few giggles and oohs from the audience, though of the kind that made me think they felt I got the worst of the argument and had spoken like a fop, but big deal. After, I suggested to the woman that a couple of the students or TAs come to dinner with us, but she said it wasn't in the budget. So just the two of us," and she might say, "Maybe that's what she counted on," and he'd say something like, "I doubt it." Anyway, that's when he'll probably tell her what he ate and what the restaurant was like, though he thinks he did that last night. "Then—and I had three glasses of wine, she had one, the two choices they had being American chablis and Chilean merlot, and the glasses were relatively small and came a little more than half full, and when I pointed both these things out to the waiter, he said, 'That's the way the house pours them, which is based on the guidelines of the chain that owns this place, and the only size wineglass we have'—she drove me to my hotel. I never slept in such a depressing room. If there ever was an ideal one for suicide, this was it. In fact, if you had been in that room before you might even choose to go back, just to sustain the suicidal urge, to do yourself in. Dark ugly furniture—did I tell you this?—same with the drapes and rug, and floral wallpaper and an urban-blight view. And at midnight—this I know I couldn't have told you—and again at four A.M., a freight train choochoo-ed by . . . really, about ten feet past the hotel parking lot, on a spur line or track, whistling hysterically though it was only going about five miles an hour, after picking up and/or delivering goods to what's left of the huge steel mill in town. The last piece of info the desk clerk told me when I asked about the train while I was checking out. There was—the room's one contemporary touch, though for all I know something a lot more modern in bathrooms superseded it a dozen years ago—a Jacuzzi in the bathtub, which I didn't use." She might say, "Why not? It would have relaxed you, taken your mind off suicide, and helped you sleep well, which you apparently didn't do," and he'd say, "Too much of an effort. You have to stick a hand on the drain—first you fill the tub to this silver dot between the regular bath and shower controls—and at the same time your other hand on another spot in the tub to get the Jacuzzi going. A little of me thought I'd get an electric shock—I mean, this place wasn't in the greatest shape. But the major part of me thought, Who can pamper himself like that? And do you soap yourself in a Jacuzzi—which is what I wanted to do: get clean—or just lie in it, letting the thing do whatever it's supposed to to you? A quick shower and then bed, with maybe a little reading, that's all I wanted." "You took a shower before you went to bed?" she could say. "How unlike you. You always exercise and run in the morning and then shower," and he could say, "I did my exercises and ran in place for about a half hour in the room last night, feeling if I did them then I wouldn't have to do any of it in the morning. I wanted to set off early today. I thought if I got back an hour or more before the kids—by the way, the drive there and back took an hour longer than this woman said it would—maybe you and I could have some fun . . . what do you say?" and he might jiggle his eyebrows or make a silly face or both, and she could say, "I wouldn't mind," and then he'd push her into the bedroom, to get it started sooner, help her undress and get on the bed, and she'd prepare herself if she had to and they'd make love. While on the bed he thinks he'd say, "I forgot to tell you about something I did there," and she might say, "You had sex with Sheila this morning—she called you up for an early breakfast. Or with one of the students—she knocked on your door last night, while you were wondering whether you should take a shower, Jacuzzi, or bath, for a late evening snack," and he'd say, "No, but close. I cable-hopped—what's the expression the kids use for flicking through the TV set with the remote? Channeling? Station surfing? Television diving? I wanted to get a taste of American culture we don't have any access to or want, and oh, boy, did I!—enough to hold me for a couple of years. Every movie, new, old, or ancient, including two jammed pornos—those you paid extra for, so I could only hear the dialogue, moaning, clothes being torn, and someone splashing in a bath—was silly, poorly written, and inconsequential, and I had a choice of about seven. And all the regular shows and reruns, from TV sitcom to cable stand-up, were no better and equally frivolous and often stupid about civility, marriage, intellectual discourse, history, art, violence, and sex. On the cable shows, and there were about thirty, mainly local, was everything from a preacher preaching, guru guruing, TV and movie critic critiquing, and several salespeople selling, to weather predicting for parts of the globe almost nobody but diplomats, the very rich, and jetting businessmen will go to, and consciousness-expansive talk fests for both genders and all adult ages and stages of parenting and most sexual preferences—I don't know them all—and heritages and races. I felt that two hours of this in that room but without the nearby and then distant train whistles—that could only help someone come to his senses—would turn a healthy mind to abnormal thoughts of suicide." No, he'd only tell her that nothing worthwhile was on, not go down a list she was probably familiar with and he'd added nothing original to, and he doesn't know how he could deliver it without sounding condescending and pompous. Besides, she'd question his being able to make such decisive judgments about so many things in the shows—art, history, intellectual discourse—in so short a time. "It was all shit, period, but I got my taste," will be all he'll say. He actually did channel-surf—he thinks that's the right expression—for an hour after Sheila left. He couldn't sleep or read. It was around one A.M. He feels tired now and should stop for coffee and to rest his eyes a few minutes. He showered before surfing. Wanted to get the smell of them off. It all happened pretty fast. He fell asleep briefly after the first time—holding her, not holding her, or being held; he forgets—but she was there. Then she was rubbing and kissing him—for a moment he thought he was being licked and nibbled on by one of his daughters' cats—and he did it again, half asleep, and doesn't recall which position he took or if he came. That would have been unusual for him, twice in less than an hour, but he supposes with a new woman, or the only woman but his wife in almost twenty years, that could happen. Before she left—she was by the door, dressed, hair brushed; he was nude, sitting on the edge of the bed—she said, "Like me to drop by for breakfast?" He remembers thinking, Does she expect me to go to the door and kiss her goodbye? I think I'll just sit; if she comes over, then I'll have to kiss. "I know the hotel gives you a complimentary buffet breakfast at the bar—dry cereal, frozen fruit juice, muffins, and packaged bagels; you toast them in the toaster they provide—and weak coffee. But there's a great breakfast place in town, the real McCoy. Opens at five, a workmen's café that doesn't get much business now that the mill's ninety percent shut down, and I'll clean the interior of my car first. I could tell you were more put off by the dog smell and hairs than you let on." He said—by this time he had covered his genitals with the bed cover or sheet in case he got erect again—"No, this should be the end of it," while he thought, Now what am I going to do? I never should have got into this stupid mess, and she said, "Hey, what do you think, I'm planning an affair with you? It was spontaneous, which is how it should be, and we had our kicks. If I'm still free and willing and you want to come around the area again, please do, but not for a second university check. Next time, if there is one, it has to be singularly for me," and he said, "I meant that what I want to do six hours from now when I wake up is take an early run, maybe limber up beforehand on the weight-room machines downstairs, breakfast quickly in the bar, and then head home. It's best I don't stay away too long, though I can't think of any good reason right now other than to be there when my kids get back from school and maybe to get some work done at home," and she said, "And of course for your wife too—you can say it. Hell, it'd be natural, and by the way you spoke of her at dinner, I know she's a fine woman," and he said, "That's right, I didn't intentionally leave her out; for her too. As for my coming back here; much as I admire you, and I certainly don't regret having done it"—You're lying your eyeballs out, he told himself while he was saying this—"I think this was the only time for that too," and she said, "Good, I can appreciate that, and I didn't expect much more. I can also see no kiss good night will be forthcoming from you. If you wish, send it in a letter, but not care of my department," and he said, "I don't quite understand," and she said, "Home, dummy, nothing furtive or disapproving implied," and smiled, blew him a kiss, and left. In her car after dinner she said, "So, do you want to be driven straight back to the hotel?" and he said, "Sure, where else?" and she said, "Oh, this town's loaded with fun-producing dives: just joking. But there are a couple of roadhouses for nightcaps a short drive from here. How about one of those? I love the word 'nightcap.' It puts the lid on things, does what a combination word like that's supposed to: reverberate and ring with multiple meanings. What do you think?" and he said, "I guess so." "And you deserve a nightcap. You deserve two, but I haven't got all night either. It was a terrific reading and you gave the students half an hour longer in the Q-and-A session than they normally get from our visitors. It was apparent they kept asking questions because they were interested in you, liked your mind and forthrightness, and had been stimulated by the reading," and he said, "Oh, God, I thought I was awful. I read too fast and was inarticulate in most of my answers. But I really am tired and would rather go back, maybe have a glass of wine in my room—I brought a glassful in a jar to help me doze—and then read for a while and go to sleep." "The bar there—the Rendezvous Room, if you can believe it; can you think of a more inappropriate name for a grungy steel town in the heart of beerland?—but it's a good one, designed with taste and sometimes lively. Why not have a drink there instead of in your room—that's too depressing to think about—and we'll put it on the bill. It all comes off the university. One of the perks of being the reading coordinator: I get to indulge my incipient alcoholism. I'm joking again," and he said, "I don't know . . ." and she said, "Hey, Mr. Reader, I'm not going to twist your arm. No? Then no," and he said, "Sure, one drink, a brandy or cognac if they got," since he thought he had hurt her feelings and she was paying him a decent fee for coming out here and if he's cooperative for another hour she might invite him again in a couple of years. So they drank, sitting at the bar. TV was on above them; several men with the same kind of name tags on their jackets and shirts had taken up all the settees and most of the tables and chairs. He was the one who suggested sitting at the bar. He felt people drank faster there, and if she wanted a second drink—that would be his limit—they could get it quicker there than from a waitress at a table. He thought then: Did she have designs on him? He didn't think so. It could be she was a little lonely—the stuff about her sons indicated that, and it didn't seem she had a boyfriend—and visitors from outside were probably interesting company to her. She started talking about previous visitors—"Do you know Anya Malcolm?"—and he said he knew her work and had once been introduced to her at some function. "She was a bit full of herself, maybe because everyone but me was making a big to-do over her, but I guess she was all right. I have to admit I don't think much of her work, though," and she said, "From all you've said since you got here, whose do you like? I bet nobody's," and he said, "There are some, but if I tell you their names, you'll say, 'But they're all dead,' " and she said, "Anyhow, Malcolm was wonderful, congenial, modest, contemplative, and as generous with her time to the students as you were. I think she bedded down with one too—in this hotel—or took his phone number, but that's her business. He trailed her like a puppy. Later I learned she also has that reputation, a quiet killer," and he said, "That I didn't know. She's not married; she can do what she wants," and she said, "I don't know if that argument holds. But one of our visitors—Malcolm was at least discreet about this student—but this fellow: a first-class character. We've had scholar characters too, I have to tell you, but none came near to doing what this one did—the males," and she gave his name and he said, "I've heard of him, of course. You do get some big shots here, something I thought you said you couldn't afford, for you sure didn't get him for what you're paying me, though I'm definitely not complaining. I never read or met him. The reviews of his work didn't make it seem very interesting, and I don't trust awards. But what'd he do, if I may ask?" and she said, "What'd he didn't, know what I mean? Believe me, and I'm going to sound uncharacteristically vulgar now, but if there were a telephone pole with a hole in it shaped like a vagina, and it needn't be greased, he would have jumped it. And you don't have to ask; I'm telling you. That's what I in fact told this gigantic creep I'd do: tell everyone, not that it'd stop him from waylaying other reading coordinators and students or disenhance, can I say? his literary eminence. Mr. Pulitzer Prize was on me from the moment I picked him up at this hotel. In that fetid car of mine to the university auditorium he kept saying, 'You have magnificent eyes, silky skin, the most swanlike shoulders and neck I've ever seen.' 'Swans have shoulders?' I asked. They could, but I couldn't resist asking it. Anyway, malarkey. I know my eyes and shoulders and neck aren't like that, but he persisted. My ears, my arms, my fingertips especially. He wanted to suck on them. Just looking at them gripping the wheel, they made him swell, he said. That's the word he used. He wanted us to stop for a prereading drink, then after the reading we'd have predinner drinks, during-dinner wine, and finally at this bar postdinner drinks and nightcaps. It wasn't from him I got the word. Truth of it is that for weeks after I had to overcome thinking it was the most scrofulous I'd heard. When I wouldn't stop he took several swigs from a sterling silver hip flask, a gift from a reading coordinator in Minneapolis, he said, with an amorous-erotic inscription on it alluding to his legs and phallus and lips, even though I asked him not to read it. Then, while I'm driving, he tries grabbing my crotch and I said, 'Hey, you nuts? Get your paws off or we'll crash.' When he realized I wasn't ever putting out for him—we were about to enter the auditorium and the room was packed; I'm sorry, but the guy really draws them—he said if I don't promise this instant to sleep with him after the reading, he's going to make a beeline for the exit now and blame it on me in a way where he'll get his full payment, even though he didn't show up, and I'll get canned. He'll cook up the most credible story too, he said. 'I'll work on it for a day, put aside my other writing, and send it to your dean. Writers are the best liars when they put their minds to it,' he said. For a minute I was in a dither what to do. I thought should I consent and then go ahead with it? because I was sure if I did consent and then reneged after, he'd concoct an even worse believable lie against me. I was petrified. I have a year-to-year appointment, I don't earn much money, but I've been teaching here so long that my university pays half my kids' college tuition for four years." "You didn't go through with it, did you?" "First I said, 'I have to go to the ladies' room,' and he said, 'You can pee later; tell me now.' I said I'd report these threats to his wife. He said she knows all about what he does on the road and gives her blessing, since they have an arrangement that when he's gone she gets to knock around too. I said he was lying, and he said, 'Here's her number; call her,' and pulled out his cellular phone. 'Then your department chairman,' I said, 'or your provost or dean.' He said his school's lucky to have him. With his celebrity the last few years, besides his mobility, he could teach anywhere. 'I want an answer in ten seconds,' he said, and I said, 'Then the hell with my job. You're a greasy repulsive slob, and too skinny, and I loathe your guts.' 'Good,' he said, 'you called my bluff; I love it,' and kissed the top of my head, and we went in and he delivered a beautiful reading and had the audience enthralled and begging for more. Later he went partying with a few of the grad students and teachers, and I hear he was thoroughly charming and gracious, though I'm sure he secretly ended up with one of the girls." "He sounds like a drip. It's what I always thought about most writers, and especially the rare ones whose work you like—meaning: you don't want to kill it? don't get to know them. But listen, I'm tired. I'll have to drink up and say good night." "Fine, then, good night, and thank you for coming. Next time, if I can finesse it, I'll try to get you out here for a lot more money," and he said, "Thanks, I'd love to come back; the students were terrific. And also thanks for having me here this time," and she said, "And thank you for thanking me so plentifully, sir. Compared to the creep, you've been a hundred-percent gentleman," and he said, "Thank you," and went to the elevator. She tapped on his door about twenty minutes later. Tapped? Knocked? What's the difference? But what'd she do till then? He didn't ask. Maybe she got in her car and stayed parked or drove for a few minutes, even toward home, before deciding to turn around, or had another drink in the bar, since that's where he left her. Once he headed to the elevator she even could have known what she was going to do but wanted to give him a few minutes. He was stuffing his shoes and clothes he'd just worn into his day pack. "Who is it?"—thinking maybe someone from the hotel staff or a guest who had the wrong door or one of the name-tag men downstairs as a prank—and she said, "Sheila; may I come in?" He said, "What is it, you forgot or lost something?" though for the most part knowing why she was there, and she said, "Something like that; it's important. Open the door," and he said, "I have to get some clothes on"—he was only in boxer shorts and socks—and then opened it. Then—it might have taken ten minutes—they were in bed. But how'd they get there? They started kissing and she was touching him through the pants and put his hand on her breast and his other on her buttock and unzipped his fly and put her hand inside. It seemed that was all she had to do. Jerked it around and then pulled him to the bed by it, got on her back first, got her arms around him and pulled him on top of her; then they had to separate to get their clothes off. "Your socks," she said, "everything, since all of me's off too." But why'd he let her in the room, even? Why didn't he say at the door after he opened it, and this was what he was feeling at the moment, "I'm sorry, but if it isn't something you lost or forgot, and since you were never up here, it couldn't be . . . if it isn't important, as you said it was, then you really have to leave because I got to get to sleep"? She walked in when he opened the door. He said, "Excuse me?" but in a way that clearly meant, Where do you think you're going? He didn't know if he should shut the door or leave it open. He shut it, since he didn't want anyone to see her in the room and he also may have to raise his voice to get her out. He thought he'll tell her to go; he knows what's on her mind and the same thing isn't on his; he's sorry. But first he'll ask her to be more explicit why she came here: maybe there is a legitimate reason. "Excuse me," he said, "but it is pretty late. Truthfully, what's the reason you're here?" and she said,

"I'm aware of the time—and it isn't that late—though I also realize you've had a long day and you're probably tired. But how can I explain it other than to be direct: all that talk about the voracious Mr. Slime didn't do anything titillating to me before, believe me. It's simply an involuntary and actually very pleasant attraction I've had to you almost since you got here, not to speak of equally enjoyable sensations, and instead of leaving it alone I thought I'd see where it went and if anything comparable was happening to you. I apologize for not coming out with it at dinner or in the bar, and because you were married—and happily, it seemed—and just natural reserve about something like that, I felt somewhat shy," and he said, "Look, you have to understand I've never done anything like that, what you're suggesting, and I doubt I'm going to start now." That's what he said, almost exactly that. What he should have said was: and I'm in no way going to start now and neither do I like the uncomfortable position you've put me in, since you know I gave you no signs I was interested. Whatever you were feeling, you just should have kept in. She nodded agreeingly to what he did say, seemed to think about it a few seconds, eyes off to the side, then came up to him and said, "You *doubt* you're going to start anything now but you're not sure, am I reading it right?" and put her arms around his waist, and he said, "No, you're wrong, I don't want to; I just don't have a firm way of saying things," and tried pushing her hands off from in back. She was shorter than he by almost a foot and looked up and smiled softly but in no way cheaply or seductively or anything like that—saucily; it was a lovely smile—and pressed an ear against his chest and said, "I'm going to say something real dumb; I can feel your stomach pumping, what do you think it means?" and he said, "Sure you can. Come on, let's stop this," or "end this," "drop this," "forget this," and tried prying her hands apart from in back, but she had them locked. He didn't want to use more force and possibly hurt her. She might get excited, start lashing out at him, physically or with words. She does this screwy thing, coming up here and persisting, who knows? He had an erection because she was pressed into him there and all the talk and stuff, but so what? He gets them and they go. He should have gently pushed her away till her hands broke loose and, if they didn't, then maybe turned around and pulled them apart. His back to her like that would have been a good sign, and the two combined, his back and pulling her hands apart, might have done the trick. She said, arms still around him, "You really don't want to sleep with me? I'd like to with you, now even more than when I knocked on your door, which in answer to your question before is why I came here, but I won't beg." Why didn't he just say no at that point, demonstrably, even angrily—"and thanks for your directness but it's not working on me and in fact is misplaced"—so also sarcastically, and tell her to leave, even say, "Listen, I mean it, get the hell out of here," and go to the door and open it and say, "Now come on, out, out!"? They started kissing just around then, but what'd they do between that moment and when she said she wouldn't beg? How did they get so far, in fact, where they started kissing? She looked up at him—doe-eyed is the expression that was once commonly used—after she said that about not begging, raised herself on her toes a few inches, and he bent over—he can even see himself now bending down to her face after she raised hers closer to his—and kissed her, thinking, One kiss and that'll be it, and maybe even saying, "It's tempting, you kiss well, that was very nice but all there's going to be. We kissed and now you have to leave, I'm sorry, and my goddamn erection means nothing. I get them from all kinds of things, even wind." But she was grabbing him through the pants now, and they kissed more and she put his hands on her and her hand went inside his fly, and then they were on the bed. He could have stopped it there perhaps, when he got off her to undress, but by then he was very excited and she almost never stopped jerking him, so it was just too late. After it was over—the second time; after the first, not that he put much into it, he dozed off—she said, "Excuse me, but how many years has it been since you did it with anyone but your wife?" and he said, "Why, my participation was sort of mechanical?" and she said, "I didn't say that," and he said, "Anyway, without meaning to provoke you, it's none of your business," and she said, "You're angry at me because you think I pushed you into it?" and he said, "Angry at myself. But I did it, enjoyed it the first time; the second time I was barely functioning, I was so sleepy, so whatever happened or didn't, I don't even know, but okay. But I'm asking you not to tell anyone about it. I know that's a difficult request—one has best friends, but best friends have big mouths—but please do what I ask," and she said, "That means you're not going to tell your wife?" and he said, "That's for me to decide," and she said, "I only said that to know how many people you intend to tell and if I should expect a letter or phone call from her. I'd rather not get one of those—I never have. All but one of the men I've been attached to since my last divorce weren't married at the time—so don't worry: I'll keep our little secret secret." He wanted to say he didn't much like that remark, "our little secret," but didn't want to antagonize her. Out of revenge, or more because if she lost any warm feelings she'd had for him she could spill everything to who knows whom, so best to get her out of here in a good mood. But to be on the safe side, he said, "I've definitely decided not to tell Sally, so please don't tell anyone yourself," and she said, "I wasn't going to. I already said: it's between us." Then she got dressed, mentioned breakfast and some other things, and left. After she was gone he thought, Why'd she want to have anything to do with him? He's got about twenty years on her. He's not good-looking anymore. She may have liked his mind but he doesn't see why, because he didn't show much intelligence or wit since he got here and was fairly unpleasant a lot of the time—cynical, acerbic, critical of others—and nobody goes to bed with you because of your writing. In comparison, she's bright and cheerful and articulate and reasonably pretty, with an athlete's body, almost—the physique of someone who runs or swims but works out every day—and with a nice fullness, and, for their one shot in bed, more sensual and uninhibited than he. He's in shape, but the shape he's in wouldn't appeal to a much younger woman. And he's not famous, he can't get her a job in his department, he can't do anything for her. Even a reference from him for a fellowship or teaching promotion or another teaching position or even to get into an art colony wouldn't do much, as he's not considered very highly in academic and literary circles, and he has no contacts at these places or other schools. If she did ask for a reference he'd give it and say very complimentary things, not just to keep her mouth shut but because they're the truth based on what he saw: an excellent mind, a fine teacher, a considerable knowledge and love of literature, and she's well-spoken and personable and has a rapport with her students that he found believable and unusual because they genuinely liked and respected her as a teacher and friend, and she didn't get these reactions from them by having to act younger and more "with it" or diminishing herself in any way. "I recommend her most highly and would put her in the top five percent of young teachers I've seen teach." He's not being facetious here, he thought. This is what he'd say of her. So, she had her own reasons for coming on to him, that's all. He reminded her of someone, or she was particularly keyed up to have sex because of something physical or personal he was unaware of and he happened to be there and wasn't too unpleasant-looking to her or maybe not at all and hadn't acted obnoxiously or like an oddball; and that he didn't make a pass or show any attraction to her may have been to his credit, or the way she saw it, and so on, plus she must have assumed he wouldn't make a fuss after, calling her up and wanting to see her again when she might not want him to. He was mature while being slightly unconventional, she might have felt, and maybe that's mostly what it was, and also safe in a health way in that he's been married and faithful—though his monogamy she only could have guessed at earlier in the evening—for almost nineteen years straight. Oh, what's he going on about? he thought. He doesn't understand why she went for him the way she did, and so assiduously, and all the reasons he just thought of border on the ridiculous. In the car he thinks maybe he shouldn't get home before the kids. If he does, an hour before, let's say, his wife could say, "We have an hour before the kids come home and I've missed you; want to have some fun?" He already thought that; but could he refuse? She might get suspicious or perplexed. He's almost never refused. Maybe five times since they first slept together, or ten times then—twenty. Anyway, about twice a year, if that. And out of extreme fatigue or because he was sick or coming down with something and she didn't know this, and maybe he didn't either, when she suggested making love, or the rare time when he was depressed and didn't think sex would take him out of it. Because in bed he may feel so guilty that he can't perform: and that's the word for it, perform, for his mind would be on what he did last night. It's also possible that his sex drive will be slight because he did it twice with Sheila, and the second time only about twelve hours ago, and he was bushed while doing it, but he thinks that would only be a small part of his not being able to perform with his wife. She'd be sympathetic and tender and try some things to help him—"Leave it to me" or "Lie back and let me see what I can do," she's said a number of times—and maybe these wouldn't work either. That's happened a few times too, though usually only when they tried doing it twice in a short time. And he might then just tell her, thinking now's better than later—since he feels he'll probably have to tell her sometime—when she sees, even in this way, what it's doing to him. "Now's probably as good a time to tell you as any," he could say. "For certain I don't want you to find out from anyone but me. This is why I can't do anything now, I'm sure of it. I had sex with a woman last night, the reading coordinator, Sheila. She also teaches there. I didn't want to but I ended up doing it. She was a bit pushy but I could have resisted. She came to my hotel room after we shook hands and said good night downstairs in the bar. We only had a single drink and I didn't even want to do that; I wanted to say good night and goodbye to her in her car. Or I kissed her cheek goodbye, though we also might have shaken hands, when I left her, and she might have kissed mine. Anyway, nothing more than a friendly kiss on the cheek from us both. I didn't want to let her into my room but she sort of barged in when I opened the door. I know this sounds farfetched but it's the truth, I swear to you. I said through the door, after she knocked on it and identified herself, 'What is it you want? It's late,' and she said, 'It's important, open the door.' Because I thought it *was* important—maybe she forgot to give me the check for the reading, though to be honest I expected it to come by mail in a couple of weeks, as she'd said earlier, or even that someone in the hotel was after her—I opened the door. I wasn't going to let her in—I thought I could deal with whatever it was at the door—but she walked right past me. I said something like, 'Hey, what're you doing?' because by now I knew it wasn't about the check or anyone stalking her in the hotel. She was tenacious and aggressive and undiscouraged by anything I said to her, but still, as I told you, I could have resisted and I know that, so don't think I'm trying to get out of this by saying I don't. I could have said, 'Are you insane? Get the hell out of here, beat it, or I'll throw you out, and I mean it: get out now!' I actually did say something like that, though not as forcefully, like, 'Listen, this is all wrong and you have to leave here. I'm married, happily married'—that's what I told her, the exact words, foolish and inept as they must have sounded—'and I don't want to do anything with you, period. Besides, I'm very tired and I want to set off early tomorrow, so will you please leave this room?' I think I even showed her the door—went over to it and put my hand on the doorknob but didn't open it, because I was concerned people in the corridor would see her in my room. In other words, I wasn't sure what to do about her persistence but I knew I didn't want to have sex with her—if I wasn't married or going with anybody, maybe I would have wanted to or at least wouldn't have been so adamant in wanting her to leave. But I eventually caved in. I'm still trying to figure out why, and I'm not trying to be funny there. I'm being apologetic. I feel miserable about it. She started undressing then, and I said, 'What in the world are you doing?' Then she threw herself on me—put her arms around me, I mean, and her shirt's off and so's her bra—and then started pulling off my shirt and I swear to you I tried putting it back on. But then it was off, and I think she tore part of it, and next thing I know she's grabbing me through my pants and I push her hand away and she grabs me again and starts stroking me down there and I think, Oh, I give up; I don't know why, but I knew by this time I was finished. As dopey and fake as this must sound, she was unstoppable and I ended up being conquerable. I was also, and I know this plus my tiredness contributed to some of it, a little drunk but not soused from the wine at dinner and the martini before and then that one brandy or cognac after in the bar. In fact I'm beginning to think—I'm almost convinced, though again this isn't to worm out of it—that that's what contributed to it the most. All the alcohol made me lethargic, stupid, and maybe even amorous, the way it can. But that's what happened and how. I did it with her just once, I doubt I got half my clothes off, and I don't remember a lot of it or if I even completed it: that's how tipsy and sleepy I was. And the whole time she was there—from the knock on the door till when she left—was maybe thirty minutes in all. Believe me, I'm so sorry; I can't tell you how much, and it'll never happen again, never. I didn't want to do it and I'll know how to resist it next time. For one, to stay away from that much alcohol when I'm on the road, if I ever go again, even for a night, and I don't think I will. It could be I drink more when I'm away from you and alone, but also eat less, thereby getting high quicker through two ways, but that's still no excuse for it, and this whole thing took me by surprise. She was much younger than I—more than twenty years. I'm practically an ugly guy by now, and to her an old man, and that's how I thought she saw me—completely uninterested in me physically—till she came into the room, so I don't understand it. But she was capricious and a bit odd and wild in her way and obviously turned on by something, not necessarily me, and I was just about drunk and she had a few glasses of wine in her too and also that brandy or cognac, and that's all I can say to explain it. Not even that I was flattered and went for her finally because she was so much younger and pretty and showed me this kind of attention. But you know me: I couldn't care less and even react against it, when someone says nice things about me or my work, which she didn't, by the way, except for the dutifully complimentary things reading coordinators always say to you after a reading. And it also isn't that just because I never did this in almost nineteen years, made love to anyone but you, I was curious if not eager to try it, especially when it was practically thrown at me—given on a silver platter, that sort of thing—because the truth is I haven't had any urge to do something like that since we got married or even since we first met. Of course not when we first met or anytime around that, because I was crushingly in love and attracted to you, as I am now, and I'm not just saying that, and sex with you then was new and we were just starting something, so why would I want to be with anyone else, and ruin things with you, or even think of another woman that way? Anyway, for our entire relationship, I haven't wanted to. You were always enough for me and out of consideration or something else, when you weren't feeling much like it, always made your body available to me except when you were sick or it was the beginning of your period or during our worst moments together, which I was usually responsible for, just as I've always been available to you that way, except during those kinds of times too. Oh, I've had my fantasies about other women a lot, but that's as far as I ever took it—all in my head and fleeting, where I knew they were strictly fantasies and would never be carried out. But when she—" Oh, enough of it. "But when she" what? When she put her hand in his fly and started pulling on him, but he wouldn't tell her that. He wouldn't tell her half of what he just thought of, and she'd probably by now be crying to whatever he did say, possibly from when he first said he made love to a woman last night, which would be one of the first things he said, so who knows how much he'd be able to tell her? Much of what he doesn't say today, if he does decide to tell her about it, he can save for another day when she'll be more willing to listen. But if she was crying he'd try to comfort her, maybe try to hold her, hold and comfort her and say comforting and loving and apologetic and remorseful and self-damning and -hateful things, but she'd have none of it and would push him away, if he was holding her, he's almost sure of it, and maybe say things like "You fucking bastard, you stinking shit," and not say but scream them at him, and get dressed and leave the room or take her clothes with her and dress somewhere else, if he did start telling her this while they were in bed with no to few clothes on and preparing to make love. But he's often impulsive and might just blurt it out sooner—to get it over with, he might give as a reason to himself—in another room or outside where he saw her when he got home but before there was any chance they'd go to bed, because of all places and occurrences he wouldn't want to tell her there and then, and not blurt it out but say calmly and solemnly—and the solemnness would be real—that he has something important, disturbing, and grave to tell her and even frightening to him because of the effect it might have on her, and nothing to do with his health, he'd quickly add, since he wouldn't want her getting alarmed at that possibility and then finding out what it really was. Maybe just say immediately that he's done something he's terribly ashamed of . . . deeply . . . anyway, he'd find the words. And after he told her he slept with a woman last night he's almost sure she wouldn't, after she told him what she thought, say much to him for a week. He can picture her—she's done it before over less serious things between them: when he called her a cunt once. "There it is," she said, "it's finally out, what you truly think of women: they're all just cunts to you, right? Well, I won't listen anymore to your jackass insults"; another time, near the beginning of her illness when she was only limping a little and sometimes felt weak, when he said how sick can she be that she can't even straighten a room out or wash a dish: "You're completely without understanding and compassion and talk like the dimmest lowbrow I know. From now on think of me as deaf"—cupping her ears—and before that probably saying something curt like, "Shut up, I've heard enough, there is no word for you, get out of my sight." Or she might not say anything, what he'd tell her would be so bad, and would only look stricken for a while and maybe even crazed, before getting herself away from whatever place he told her this at. After that, he thinks, the only things she'd say to him for a week would be for the kids' benefit, so they wouldn't think something irreconcilable had happened between their parents. She hates when he starts an argument when they're around and usually says something like, "Save it for later when they can't hear us, and I'm not saying this to defuse you but to spare them." Or she might hear him out soberly like that and then say she doesn't understand: if he didn't want to do it with this woman as much as he said, at what point did he give in? and it might be then he'd have to say—if he didn't say, "Forget it, let's drop the subject for now"—"When she put her hand in my pants. Something just happened to change things," and she could say, "Drop it? No, I want to hear all of it," and then, "So that's it? She grabs your dick and massages it half a minute and you totally capitulate? Worse comes to worst and it was overcoming you when your conscience or governing intelligence or whatever that higher part in you that screens and is supposed to thwart these kinds of actions didn't want it to, as you said, and you knew it would jeopardize our marriage and hurt me and indirectly inflict similar distress on the kids, why didn't you push her hand away and, if that didn't work, wrench it free without injuring her or your penis and bark in her ear that this isn't what you want to do, exciting as it's obvious you find it, and if that didn't sink in and she kept grabbing at it, then excuse yourself to go to the bathroom, even say you have to defecate—she couldn't refuse you that, and I doubt she'd accompany you there—and lock the door and masturbate?" He actually should have done that, the last part, and there at least would have been some pleasure in the act rather than not having completed anything—maybe a great deal of pleasure, considering all the hot stuff that preceded it—and then come out of the bathroom and tell her what he did and he's sorry but it was the only way he could stop from making love with her and now he won't be good for anything involving sex for an hour and probably two—that's been the pattern the last ten years—so she better just go since he really won't want to do it in two hours or even an hour from now any more than he wanted to do it before, and it would also be much later than he wants to stay up. But who knows how his wife would take it, if he did tell her, though he's almost sure she'd be cold and sharp and sullen to him for a lot longer than a week, no matter how often he apologized for what he did, and she wouldn't let him make love to her—even let him embrace or kiss her or hold her from behind while they slept in bed—for a month, maybe more. She probably wouldn't sleep in the same bed with him for a couple of weeks, though he thinks she'd insist on taking over the guest bed in her studio, since he does most of his work on his desk in their bedroom. But after that—after many discussions between them and verbal soul-searchings on his part that in a way, and he'd tell her this, he feels she let him off lightly—he thinks most of it would be worked out. He'd periodically say how bad he felt about it and still does, just so she wouldn't think he was trying to forget it, and that he knows it could never happen again, not only because it was wrong and morally indefensible and a breaking of her trust in him and things like that—not "morally indefensible"; that's too much like a cliché—but because the consequences to them both and the children were so great, till in a few months she might tell him to stop bringing it up: it's for the most part over and done with, she could say, and a certain healing's taken place, significant as the event was to them then and the one that caused the greatest rupture in their marriage and nearly blew it apart. But she's satisfied it won't be repeated, so less said about it now the better, since there doesn't seem to be anything pertaining to it she hasn't heard from him a dozen times, doesn't he agree? He'd say, "Without question, and I'm glad to hear that's how you feel." Maybe in a year things would be completely normal between them again. "Like the Jewish mourning period," he could say. "It's possible that's the tradition in other religions, but concerning mourning and bereavement I only know the Jewish ones, and not well." In two years they might even banter about it if one of them alluded to the incident in some way—he doubts it'd be he. "You know what anniversary today is?" she could say. Would this be something she'd do? He's only using it as an example. And he'd answer with something like, "You know me and memory. I'm very bad with birthdays and wedding anniversaries and those kinds of personal dates. World history I'm better at. August sixth, the A-bomb dropped on Hiroshima—or was it Nagasaki? August ninth—this is 1945—the second A-blast on the city that wasn't hit first. No, definitely Nagasaki for the second one, and I'm not trying to be flippant about it. August eighth—notice the opportunistic timing—the Soviet Union declares war on Japan or just invades some of the more vulnerable Japanese-occupied territories on the Soviet Union's Asian borders.

August fourteenth, V-J Day, and September second, I believe, Japan signs the surrender papers on the *Missouri,* so the official end to the entire war, as the one in Europe ended on May eighth the same year." "It's two years to the day you told me about Sylvia, or whatever her name was, and when I thought, Am I going to use this transgression to start immediate divorce proceedings against you? Because I had never felt so let down by anyone. I remember the date exactly because it was the last day of the month and was my childhood friend Rejelika's birthday," and he could say, "It was that bad for you? I knew I'd hurt you, but you never told me how much. Me too, but on the opposite receiving end. I hoped, though, you'd forgotten it to the point where you didn't even know—no, I was going to say—oh, what's the difference what I was going to say, but it was 'it had happened.' " "God," she could say, "you were so guilty and penitent that day, I thought you'd never stop apologizing, and that went on for weeks, perhaps, where your guilt and contrition hardly receded. The only plus side of it was that you were also much sweeter and more indulgent to me and the girls than you had ever been to me, or since the first few weeks after I gave birth to each of them. And you kept using phrases in your apologies that I hadn't heard from you before, such as 'higher sense' and 'breach of faith' and 'moral duty' and words like 'perfidious,' 'unscrupulous,' and 'corrupt,' which had always been part of your vocabulary though mainly confined to governmental and academic politics, never in relation to yourself," and he could say, "I felt miserable over it—what can I tell you?—and afraid for weeks I'd lose you and, by losing you, lose the love and respect of the kids and seeing them every day. Now I know you lose that respect no matter what undeviating good you do for them and how straight a line you toe, I think they say—people who say such things—and then get the respect back at some point, if your undeviating toe is good, though we haven't come to that end of it yet. But I thought we'd agreed, some three months after the thing happened, not to go into it at length anymore—that we'd said just about everything we could on the subject and it had become so irksome for you to hear me refer to it again that you didn't know what was worse, you said, what I'd done or that I was about to reproach myself and beg forgiveness for it once more," and she could say, "You could be putting words in my mouth there—after all, it was almost two years ago, and if your memory's not so sharp about nonhistorical things, as you said, why should I believe you'd remember that?" and he could say, "Dates, I didn't say 'things.' " "Anyway," she could say, "that one romp with Madam S, I'll call her, doesn't upset me any longer and hasn't for a year, and I feel we can even banter about it, it's such ancient stuff and where there's little chance of it being repeated, wouldn't you say?" and he could say . . . what? "Yes," he could say, "I could say that," and she could say, "There is one aspect of it . . . do you mind my continuing with it a bit further? There was something in your past explanation that never sat well with me," and he could say, "Why I went ahead and had sex with S—even I've forgotten her name, though I know it's not Sylvia—when I had so many reasons not to? But you do believe she sort of forced herself on me after she finagled her way into my hotel room and that I didn't initiate or encourage the action though I eventually did participate in it, right?" and she could say, "Yes and no, though I won't at this moment, maybe just to be mischievous, say which expression goes where," and he could say, "Okay, get it out, you're entitled, I guess, and I never want to stifle conversation between us except when I'm too sleepy to speak or hear, though I hope this is the last time we talk about it for a while. I think"—what could he think? he thinks in the car—"I think, in spite of the long break in our even referring to it, that I'm kind of fed up with the subject now too. Because you did say you were fed up with it, true? Or was that almost two years ago?" and she could say, "One, you were only going to be away from home a day, and by the time the romp took place you'd been gone a mere twelve hours. Two—" and he could cut in and say, "First let me go over your figures to see if they're correct and also if they're of any importance in the matter," and she could say, "*Two,* you showed no signs of loneliness or need for another woman in any capacity since we met, as far as I could make out, as we'd for the most part been compatible, lively, conversational, stimulating, and supportive—oh, I detest that word and have always shunned it in my conversation and writing, so I don't know why I used it now—with each other. And our sex life together had been, and seems to be to this day, despite the romp and minus the month after it—at least for me and for you as well, from what I could tell—frequent, sufficient, and robust. Three—'robust' is a word better used for economics, but you know what I mean—three, you said in your original explanation that you knew from the start when you let her into the room and she made a romantic move to you that having sex with her would be wrong, a breach of faith and so forth, not to say—which you never spoke about then but both of us should have seriously considered and later taken a test or two for to resolve the possibility—that you'd risk getting a viral infection or disease, and some of the worst ones were floating around then and the most dangerous one was at its peak," and he could say, "At the time . . . at the time . . . I really can't quite come up with a reasonable justification or pardonable excuse right now why I didn't think of that at the time. It's possible I never thought I'd get anything from her but disappointment during and after the act and acrimonious mail a few days later documenting her disappointment, she seemed that physically fit and careful and clean and of course all charged up to do it, so easily let down when it didn't meet her expectations and because of the nonviral risks she took in aggressively bedding me." "And four," she could say, "you said you didn't find her attractive and that she was in fact somewhat overweight, over made-up, and doughy," and he could say, "I don't remember saying that. From what I can remember," and he could shut his eyes briefly—no, that would look too much like reverie—"she was fairly attractive by just about any man's idea of good looks—considerably so. Nice face, nice age and shape, nice teeth and low-keyed hair, smart, sparkly, moved gracefully, lots of laughs and devil-may-care, though came on as too saucy and sexy—I squirmed a bit at that but let it pass and didn't show my squirms expressively for reasons I might go into later. Usually, though, saucy provocative women, through behavior, gestures, makeup, dress, voice, and the words they use—and I don't mean by that 'aggressive women'—appear silly to me and end up dampening and often freezing my fantasies and, before I hooked up with you, my ardor. And what's with this doughiness? Muscular butt, dancer's legs, trapezist's chest, cheerleader's waist, swimmer's back—I'm only repeating hackneyed descriptions I might have read somewhere or even wrote myself, and I forget the one about hips but know it has a horsewoman in it. She *was* short, but that never put me off and it can sometimes make a woman seem sort of doll-like and performable if her body's also compact and slight. Was I drunk? No, I wasn't, as I know I told you. Just a bit tipsy, but you're not going to see me fall back on that time-eaten excuse. I *was* sleepy, but *there* too, and I'm not even certain—I'm only assuming I did because she never said I didn't and seemed the type that would: the accusations and letter never came—if I completed the act or even got started doing it, which if I didn't then forget the possibility of infection and disease and taking tests, as I've been unwaveringly faithful since S and we did nothing but touching without open cuts or soul kisses, and she a lot more than I—I can't even say for sure I did that except where she placed my hands. As to why I let the saucy sexy stuff pass: what I wanted most was to get her out of the room fast as I could, and not just to get to sleep because I was so tired but to avoid prolonging what I didn't want to get involved in originally. So I didn't want her getting miffed at my gestures and remarks and possibly building it up into a scene—'You tin highbrow and finicky prick and so-called man of the people who keeps his nose in the air' and stuff like that—which also might be why I went through with the sex in the first place, if I did: I saw, after a while, because she was so fired up and unrelenting and confident, that I had no other way of getting rid of her. No, that doesn't work or even make sense, I think, not that I'll try to reprise the last line to see if it did, but maybe one of these will, because believe me I've had a long time to think about it. The truth is I did it because, if you recall, and if you don't, please take my word—at the time we were short of cash, in fact, strapped, which is something you'd have to remember, being the one who does the tax returns for us—and she said she'd add another six hundred to my reading fee—she had that much power—besides finding it kind of exciting at my age to be compensated, and for so large an amount, for my sexual services for a first time. Of course when I didn't perform up to snuff or even penetrate, if I didn't, or even get into a position to—it had to be one of those or she was just lying to me—she went back on the offer but was unable to kill the original reading fee. The room was so depressing and I was feeling lonelier and more estranged from things than I had in years, maybe because I was away from you for the night, which wasn't that unusual an occurrence, so probably also because of the depressing room and my sense of worthlessness after such a lousy reading and my dumb responses in the Q-and-A, that I felt somewhat suicidal, and she by throwing herself at me and comforting me in various ways, like saying a few nice things about my work that I never hear from anyone, including you—'It invariably floors me and ultimately floors all the people I have to force, since they're more interested in movies and TV, to look at it too'—not that I'm trying to shove the blame on you, that she sort of saved me, you could say, so we should be grateful rather than resentful to her even if she did renege on the second six-hundred-dollar fee. I was drugged, I'm afraid, and for about a half hour I thought she was you and we were doing what we'd normally do in a hotel room, no matter how depressing the setting was, if we were free for a night from the kids. I was simply curious as to what another woman's nudity would feel like after almost twenty years and she was willing to take off her clothes and lie on the bed and align her body against mine so I could find out, and I guess one of us got carried away, though I can't remember that I was the one who did, and the other was swept along with it and away from the original plan. I was drunk, plain and simple, and you know I didn't want to fall back on this lame excuse but it's the truth—I didn't want to drink so much booze, especially since I knew how it'd affect my driving the next day, but ended up doing it eagerly for some reason, maybe because of one of the previous ones concerning depression and estrangement and crummy feelings about myself and so forth—and felt simultaneously woozy and sexy and didn't know what I was doing and hardly whom I was doing it with, and also so sleepy that I didn't even think any of the lovemaking was taking place. When I awoke after and saw her snoozing beside me I thought it was a dream and because I was still tired I went back to sleep, and when I awoke again she was gone without a trace and had even left her side of the bed looking unslept-in and I thought I'd imagined the whole thing, even the sexy dream. It was only during the drive home that it came back to me for real—that I'd had sex the night before with someone other than you—and I felt horrible over it but thought I'd keep it from you. I was afraid how you'd take it and what it'd do to our marriage—but then thought, No, tell her the whole truth, from start to finish, or at least all you know and can remember of it—since it's true that I was a little soused and quite tired during the hotel-room part of it, and that's what I did shortly after I got home that day," and she could say, "Of course I'm glad you did tell me, though at the time I wasn't glad to hear it. But I knew even while you were telling me of the incident that it was better you got it out then, rather than conceal it from me. Something like that would almost have to come out eventually, either from a buildup of guilt or through some slipup, and then it would be much worse for me, not only because of what you'd be revealing but that you had kept it from me for so long, since we had grounded our marriage and relationship from the beginning on being thoroughly up-front and undeceitful with each other and anything noticeably less would be detrimental to us," and he could say, "Maybe that's also why I decided to tell you right away—I'm almost sure of it," and then she could say, "If you don't mind, there is one final thing I've never asked you regarding it and then I'll drop the matter for good, not even to joke or banter about or refer to it in the future. Have you heard from her since then? A personal or professional letter or phone call or fax inviting you to read there again or asking you to do what you can to reciprocate your visit by inviting her to lecture or read at your school for a comparable fee?" and he could say, "No, so she probably did see after I left and she had time to think it over how upset I was about what we'd done and what I thought it might do to you and our marriage, so she felt it best not to communicate with me again. And also because she might have felt guilty about it too—that she had obviously pushed me into doing something that for a long time that night I had done everything I could to show her I didn't want to do, besides having manipulated her way into my hotel room, because she knew I certainly didn't ask her in, and maybe even manipulated me to her school for a reading in the first place because of some bull that she liked my work, though that might be stretching it a bit," and she could say, "Oh, yeah, I bet that's what she did; saw a photo of you on a book from about twenty years ago and said, 'He's for me,' " or say, "Maybe that's so, you never know, I mean about her guilt and not communicating with you again, but from everything you said about her she didn't seem the type to feel much remorse over it or exercise that kind of self-control," and he could say, "Well, I just wanted to give her the benefit of the doubt and not set her up as a total predator, since both you and I agree I had to be partly responsible for it, but as you said, you never know." He decides to take the longer way home. That'll add to the trip twenty to thirty minutes, barring tieups and unexpected heavy traffic, though those could happen on either road. He'll also stop at a rest area for coffee, maybe read there for an hour or so, even have a salad without one of their thick packaged dressings or something else simple and light; he doesn't know why—maybe it's because of the tacky fast-food atmosphere and strong smells of the fried food—but he hates eating at those places, though the coffee's never that bad. He wants to get home after the kids. They and some house chores—shopping, doing a laundry if one needs doing—can occupy his time for a couple of hours, and then he'll make dinner and they'll eat it and he'll read a book and the newspaper for an hour after and then say he's tired from all the driving—some of the roads were congested and the trip took longer than he thought it would—and he's going to turn in early, and when she gets to their bedroom a few hours after he's shut off the light he'll be asleep, or pretend to be. He doesn't think he'll tell her what happened last night. No, he's definitely not going to, or doesn't think so. No "doesn't think so"; he isn't, he's sure. He hopes Sheila won't contact him again. She won't for a lecture or reading at his school, since she knows she hasn't the credentials for that yet—no first book out or scholarly following—and he for sure won't go out of his way to try and convince his colleagues otherwise. And he thinks he made it clear to her that he wouldn't be interested in sleeping with her again and that even seeing her again wouldn't be a good idea. "Why?" she could say, and he could say, "There'd be no point and it'd even be embarrassing to me and I don't want to say why it'd be embarrassing or go into the matter any deeper." He still doesn't know why she wanted to have sex with him so much and pursued it the way she did. Aggressively, did he say? No, he only thought it, but he can't recall any woman who went after him more. Be honest, though: did he enjoy it? No, probably because he really can't remember most of it except that she had a nice body—much harder and somewhat slimmer than his wife's and she was a few inches shorter, though he can't picture her body, while he can his wife's—and chapped lips the few times they kissed. What else? Her long hair; the time she screamed when his arm was on it while she tried to move her head. Eye color, nose shape, large or small aureoles?—a blank. Teeth extremely white and even, he thinks. He thinks he thought, when she first greeted him at the hotel, She could be advertising those teeth and that smile, though he can't picture her smile either, while he can his wife's. He does remember getting on top of her—he thinks she said, "What're you waiting for, silly? Come on," but with a nice smile, nothing snide or hard in it—but he doesn't remember any thrill at the end of the act. So did he enjoy it? There was a minute or two, when he was going in and just about all the way out of her and getting as much friction from it as he could, that he thinks he lost himself in the pleasure of it. But when his climax was coming—some thirty seconds away—he told himself, "Goddammit, what am I doing? Why in shit did I ever start in on this and then let it continue?" and opened his eyes and saw her with that dreamy look and her mouth parted just so and those teeth, and it sort of dissipated for him—at most, just a leak—and after it was over and he was lying almost flat on her and she was rubbing his back in a circular motion with one or two hands and saying something like, "You're long and wiry but heavier than I thought, so get off before you squash me," he thought, It wasn't my fault, I'm almost sure of it, but still one of the worst mistakes I've ever made. But if I tried to explain it, who the hell would believe me? and rolled off her and wanted to excuse himself and go to the bathroom to think what next to do and how to get rid of her now, but she shut off the lights and said, "Let's nap awhile, you must be tired," and put her arm around him from behind and her other hand grabbed his penis and just held it and she kissed his shoulders and neck several times and he fell asleep. So why sex with him? Loneliness, kids gone, only the animals to take care of, small town and college, few prospects, and, despite what she said, no romantic interests right now, not even someone solely for sex or to pursue for it. She pull this on other readers or lecturers she brought to the school for a day? He'll never know, so don't even think of it; or think of it but a lot of good it'll do you, for so what if she had? Probably most went for it a lot more agreeably than he, if there were any, and he thinks there were, and if one or two were able to stop it, he wonders how. She also must have thought he was a good mark for just one night: of an age where he might like a much younger woman, and his writing clearly stamps him as a hetero and possibly interested in outside sex, since there are so many guys having it in his prose, though that's ridiculous because she's aware as anyone that one doesn't have to have anything to do with the other and in plenty of cases and for many different reasons the writer might be writing about precisely what he's not and never experienced or would, and then he'd be home the next day and there'd be no complications or communication between them except for something related to the reading, perhaps: the check, if it doesn't come and he has to write her for it, or she writes him that it's going to be issued much later than she told him it would, and so forth. She make that clear to him regarding her? Sort of, but he forgets lots of what she said, and if she did say she hopes they meet again one day, which he thinks she did or something like that, it was probably out of politeness or habit. She also could have thought that all that stuff about this being the first time in twenty years for him was a bunch of bullshit, but how does that speculation help him decide if he's going to tell his wife about last night? It doesn't; he was only going back a few steps and thinking why she wanted to have sex with him. But she won't want to make anything more of it, if only to protect herself, if there was no other reason, so it's all perfect: silence on both sides. So she won't bother him, won't try to see or contact him again other than for the most practical reasons, or make any kind of stink, especially because there's nothing—now, this is useful—to be gained from it that he can see, and she also may decide—may have already decided last night—that he's way too old for her and not that intelligent or exciting or attractive in any way or good in bed, as it wasn't an especially successful sexual encounter, besides being too damn difficult to get. And he shouldn't write her either, which he always does to the reading coordinator after a reading, thanking her for inviting him and the courtesy and hospitality showed and also something complimentary about the students: very bright and stimulating, some of the best questions asked of him that he's ever heard, the audience responses to the nuances and humor of the works he read were right on the button, so of course heartening to him. Oh, what a phony he is. In the past all these things said partly out of his own courtesy and genuine gratitude for having been invited, but also so he might be invited back. "Hey, what a great guy, because how many of our invited readers have written their thanks and said the wonderful things he did?" So he's not going to tell his wife. Sure of it? Sure, positive. But he doesn't have to decide now. He can arrive home, walk into the house, kiss her as if nothing's happened, not tell her till later: tonight after the kids are asleep, tomorrow while the kids are in school, next week, even a few weeks from now. He could say then, or tonight or tomorrow, that he didn't know how to tell her till now, that he had in fact spent the entire car trip right till the time he got home thinking of how and when he'd tell her; and why? Because he knew that what he did with this woman was so wrong, and so on. No: he's sure, positive. It just isn't worth the risk. He doesn't know how she'll take it. It could end up being the worst thing that ever happened between them in their marriage. Of course it'd be the worst thing, for what in the past that he's done was worse? Some mean thing said, some mean thing done, but nothing like this. If Sheila, for some reason, does try to contact him or tells some people what they did and it gets out to his wife but not through him—she finds or receives a letter, for instance—he'll just have to explain in the best way he can why he did what he did that night and why he didn't tell her himself. But he doesn't see what's to be gained by talking about it to her before then—he's never going to do again what he did last night—except as continued lip service to honesty in their marriage, if that's the right use of that expression. Is it? Anyway, he knows what he's trying to say, and it's close enough.

The Things

He thinks: My keys. Where the hell are they? Usually when they're not on their hook by the door to the carport they're in one of his pants pockets. Feels in the pockets again. Looks around the kitchen counters and shelves, at the hook again, though knows they can't be there, but maybe by mistake on another hook near it, and looks at the other hooks and then yells out, "Anyone see my keys?" "Why, they missing?" his wife says from her studio, and his younger daughter says from the dining room, "I'll help you look, Daddy, I'm good at it," and comes in and starts looking around. "Thanks, because I'll be late for class, but I think I've looked every place here," and his wife says, "Take from all the duplicates we have. And you don't need your keys for school that much, do you?" and he says, "What? I can't hear you. And I don't like talking through a closed door if I don't have to," and opens it. "I said," she says from her desk, "use our duplicates. And if it's only your office door you're concerned about, get a dupe from your department; you've done it before. By the time you come home I'm sure they'll have turned up. What are they on, so we've a better idea what to look for?" and he says, "You know; from seven to ten keys on a ring with my pocketknife. And I don't want to ask for a dupe to my office. I've done it too much. And my bicycle-lock key's also on it, and that's my only one left and the bike's now locked," and she says, "Your bike you don't need now, and if you have to you can cut the chain. As for the house key, when do we ever lock the place? If we do, though I don't plan to go out except around the house, then, as I said, take one of the spares. If you can't find one right away, borrow it from one of the kids." "I need my own keys. That's what I'm saying. Where the goddamn crap are they?" and she says, "Don't be irrational, Gould. If you have to leave now because you're running late, take the spare car key out of your wallet. It's sealed in plastic there, isn't it?" and he doesn't nod or say yes but she's right, he thinks, that's where it is. He's slit the tape around the plastic several times over the years when he left the key ring attached to the ignition or on the dashboard and locked all the car doors before he left the car. "If you no longer have a spare in your wallet, I've one in my purse, which I only keep there to turn the radio on if we're parked and you leave the car with your keys." "Listen, I don't feel comfortable unless I have my keys, all of them on that ring, because there's also the key to the anti-car-theft bar on it and to the seminar room on the top floor, if I have to use it, and to the school building if it's locked, which it won't be. But the point is I don't want the department thinking I'm always losing or forgetting—" and his younger daughter shouts out, "I found them, I found them!" and he runs to her voice—she's in the hallway bathroom holding out his keys—and he says, "You found them here?" and she says, "On the tub." "What the heck they doing there?" and she says, "Don't look at me; I didn't put them there," and he says, "I know, but I surely didn't. Or if I did, why would I? I don't get it," and she says, "Have you gone to this bathroom recently?" and he says, "Yeah, but more than a half hour ago," and she says, "Did you pee or poop?" and he says, "The latter," and she says, "Maybe when you were sitting on the toilet they dropped out of your pocket, and you picked them up and put them on the tub instead of back in your pocket because it was too hard to from where you were sitting down and you thought you'd put them in your pocket when you stood up," and he says, "You're right, that's what I must've done, though I don't remember.

But how did you know?" and she says, "Same way I knew they'd be in this bathroom; I figured it out." "Oh, what a mind," and kisses the top of her head and says, "You deserve a fifty-cents reward, not just my thanks," and she says, "No, that's all right; I liked doing it." His wife says to him after he kisses her goodbye and is about to leave the house, "At least you only got a little excited over your keys and didn't start cursing crazily and tossing things around looking for them as you've done most times. Maybe because you found them so soon." "*I* found them," his daughter says. He thinks: My pen. Why am I always losing the damn thing? Not in his shirt pocket where he usually keeps it clipped to the top if he's wearing a shirt with a pocket, or any of his pants pockets, and he's checked them twice. It's a hybrid of the same kind of make but different models: newer maroon cap from a pen he lost the writing part to—cap was clipped to his inside jacket pocket but rest of the pen was gone—and black writing part that he had to throw away the cap to, though screwed off the clip for future possible use, when he dropped the pen and the cap cracked. It's a good-luck pen in a way, so much stuff written with it, and he's had it for more than five years, longer—maybe twice as long—as he's had any other pen, and now pens of the same make, even the cheapest model, have become too expensive for him. He also likes its odd look: cap for a larger pen fits snugly, but farther than normal down the writing part, and the different colors. He's had about ten other fountain pens in the fifteen years before he put this one together: Parkers, Sheaffers, mostly Montblancs, two of which he got in Munich at half the American price, thinking he'd someday give one to someone as a gift; lost them all. Fell through pants pocket holes he didn't know were there till it was too late or he'd told himself to sew up to avert losing things like change and keys and his pen but never got around to it, though keys he'd think he'd hear clang on the ground. Two lost in his previous house and never found. Searched for each on and off for weeks and often went over the same places. "It's gotta be around, gotta be around," kept telling himself as he looked. One of the last things he told the couple who bought the house was to call him if they found one of his pens and not to be surprised if the pens were found together. Best explanation he could come up with a year or so later—after a pen had fallen out of his shirt pocket into the kitchen garbage bag he was tying up, and a few weeks later the same pen had dropped out of his shirt pocket into a carton of newspapers he was carrying in the dark to the end of his driveway for the next day's recycling pickup—was that they'd either fallen out of his shirt pocket into a kitchen garbage bag he was bending over to tie or drop something in or dropped into a carton or shopping bag of newspapers and other papers he was carrying at night down the front yard or porch steps to the sidewalk for the next day's recycling pickup. Three to four of them slipped out of his shorts side pockets during the summer. Once lost two in a week: same shorts, shallow pockets. Dumped those shorts after he bought another pen because he was afraid he'd lose it the same way and has since made sure all the shorts he buys have normal pockets. One pen bounced out of his bathing suit back pocket while he was jogging. Thought the pocket was buttoned but it wasn't or had come undone. Ran back instead of completing the loop—a mile or so, always scanning the ground, figuring there was a good chance he'd spot it, asking the few joggers coming his way if they'd seen the pen and they kept jogging while shaking their heads, till he saw it had been run over by a car. My poor pen, he thought, picking it up, seeing if any part of it could be retrieved. Thirty bucks it cost, a lot then. If it had only stayed on the dirt path where it must have fallen rather than rolled onto the road, if that's what happened. A couple of the joggers had unleashed dogs and one could have picked it up in its mouth, run around with it, and then dropped it on the road hundreds of feet from where it had bounced out of his pocket. This time he reacted as he usually did the moment he thought his pen might be missing: slapped his pants and shirt pockets hard, stuck his hands all the way in them and fingered around, took everything out of them and went through the pockets again. Thinks, Okay, where'd you last use it? and thinks, When I was working this morning, I think, and goes to his bedroom and inspects his desk and lifts the typewriter to look under it and checks under the desk and then the entire bedroom: on and under the dresser, bed, chairs, night tables. Bathroom off the bedroom: might have absentmindedly set it down on the sink or shelf above it or toilet tank cover or window ledge when he went in to pee or wash his hands. Wastebasket by his desk: pen might have rolled off the desk into the scrap paper in the basket without his hearing it. Kitchen: checks the countertops and washer and dryer and shelf above the stove where he often keeps his checkbook and memo and appointment and address books. Checkbook and appointment book are there, address book, he remembers, is by the phone on the dresser, but the memo book! and feels his rear right pants pocket and it's there. Doesn't want to lose that too. Year of notes is in it he hopes to use on his next project. Checks the living and dining rooms and hallway bathroom, quickly, since he doesn't think he's stopped or been in those rooms the last few hours, and then says through the door to his wife's studio, "Sally, excuse me, I don't mean to disturb you, but have you seen my fountain pen?" "Yes, I'm writing out my shopping list for you with it right now. You need it?" and he says, "Please, always tell me when you borrow my pen. I get distracted if I think it's missing, and don't say that's irrational. I'm attached to it, feel I need to hold it sometimes, always know it's there to use in case I suddenly have to write down something important. Anyway, I'm surprised at you, because you know by now what it means to me," and she says, "No, not really. Why is it so important? It's an ugly misshapen pen, the area underneath the thing that holds the clip is a little chipped, and it doesn't write that well either." "The point's a bit bent. I straightened it out best I could and the guy at the store I bought the nib part at said it couldn't be repaired any better and to replace the point would run around fifty bucks and the whole pen would cost eighty. The prices of Montblancs of this kind, their cheapest models, have become ridiculous. And if I just wanted to buy a cap to match the nib part, if the Montblanc service place in New Jersey had it in stock, would cost thirty to forty. So unless I make a lot of money, which doesn't seem probable till I don't know when, this is going to be my last fountain pen, for new Sheaffers and Parkers and Watermans are priced just as absurdly, or twenty to thirty dollars cheaper. After I lose this one—mind if I open the door?" and she says no—"and I will lose it, I know it, it's going to be good roller pens and two-dollar markers and that sort from then on." "I'll get you a Montblanc, if that's the kind you prefer, for your next birthday," and hands him his pen and the shopping list. "I don't want a new pen. And did I say 'eighty'? The cheapest now must be a hundred, a hundred-twenty, since the salesman told me this a few years ago. I'd only lose the new one too and then I'd feel lousy, not just because I lost it but that it cost so much. I like this one"—holding the pen and running his thumb up and down it—"I've had several years with it, and it's done a ton of writing. And I like that it's ugly and misshapen, a one-of-a-kind hybrid, though I'm sure other people, because of the damn cost of these things, have put different Montblanc pen parts together of the same or close models to make one pen. And probably even a Montblanc coupled with a Waterman, and so on. Where'd you find it?" and she says, "On the black leather chair you say you never sit in." "What was it doing there? Not only do I never sit there, so it couldn't have slid out of my pants pocket, but I never leave it there." "All I know is I was passing through the living room, saw it, wanted to give you the health food store shopping list before you left, so I picked it up and got a sheet of paper off my desk and started to write with it here." "Why'd you close the door then, if it was just for that?" and she says, "Must be something I do automatically. And I was going to tell you I had it, if I heard you come into the kitchen, since I actually did know you'd be concerned if you thought it missing. But I felt I could write the list quickly, there were only supposed to be a few items on it, but it grew. Next time I'll remember to keep my door open, if it's only to write something like that, and tell you sooner," and he says, "Best there be no next time. You see my pen on a chair or someplace, just assume I dropped or forgot it there, unless it's on my desk, and let me know you found it. And you have your own pen, the Parker I gave you, which writes better than mine. Why didn't you use that one?" and she says, "I couldn't find it and still can't—not for a day now—but as you see, it's not worrying me, since I'm not as attached to it as you are to yours and I feel confident it'll turn up eventually. We're different that way, about pens and certain things, though unlike you I'd never tell you to be like me." He thinks: My wallet. Now where in God's name is it? Always takes it out of his pants pocket when he gets home—doesn't like the bulk, just as he doesn't like the sharpness of his keys, which is one of the reasons he hangs them on a hook first thing when he gets home—and puts it on his dresser. That's his spot for it, on top of a thick file folder of his manuscripts. In their other house he kept it on the living room shelf that held the stereo, and in their apartment before that—well, he forgets where: he thinks it was on this same dresser or his night table. In his previous apartment in New York he hid it under some clothes in a dresser drawer. He knew that'd be the first place a thief would look, but he thought, once he started putting it there, that he'd forget where he put it if he put it anywhere else. In his wife's apartment in New York, before they were married and whenever he stayed the night there, he thinks he kept it in his pants pocket. It's not on the folder, nor did it fall off it to the dresser or behind it or to the floor. Not in his pockets, either, and these are the pants he's been wearing since this morning. He remembers, when he left the house, putting the wallet in what would be the right side pocket—that's always the pocket he puts it in if he doesn't stick it in one of the back pockets—but doesn't remember taking it out while he was away. Change, yes, for a parking meter, and some cash he had stuck in his shirt pocket and still has the change from there. Also his pen several times, to write a couple of notes with, and his keys, of course. Did he put it in some other place when he got home? Can't call up a picture of it, though that doesn't mean he didn't. It could have slipped out of his pocket when he was in the car. It's done that. Pen's done it more than any other thing in the car except change. Keys have never done it. The car key's always in the ignition lock and if he happens to take it out for some reason but is still going to sit in the car, he throws the keys into the dashboard well. Memo book's also never slipped out. Maybe because it's always wedged into his back pocket, since all his pants, because of some gain or shifting of weight, are a bit tight. Weight gain, a few pounds around the middle; why kid himself? He either has to lose weight there or go up another size, but if he does, the memo book will have a better chance of falling out. Watch has slipped out once or twice but he rarely keeps it there, only when he's in a rush to leave the house and hasn't time to put it on, so he sticks it into a side pocket, and at the first red light or some other kind of prolonged stop he'll take it out and put it on. If it's not on his wrist it's usually on his night table when he goes to bed, on the window ledge above his desk when he works there, or sometimes near his checkbook and those other books on the shelf above the stove. It's slipped off his wrist a few times when he didn't fasten it right or did it too hastily, but he always heard it fall and picked it up. But his wallet! Now this could be serious. He goes outside. It's not on his car seat or the floor or in the narrow space between his seat and door or in the box between the front seats where he keeps tape cassettes and a coffee mug and bungee cord and pad and cheap pens and penlight and guide to all the public radio stations in America and a couple of poetry and story anthologies and some other things. He's found the fountain pen in all those places but never the memo book or watch or his glasses. Glasses he's lost he doesn't know how often and once never found. There have been times when he went around looking for his glasses while he was holding them in his hand. He once asked his wife, while the glasses were on his face, "Have you seen my glasses?" and she said, "Is this a joke?" and touched one of the temples, and he said, "Of course, what do you think?" when it wasn't, "but not one of my funnier ones, I suspect." Goes back to the house and looks on shelves, tables, bookcases, their dresser, everywhere he thinks he could have left it. Bathroom: maybe it dropped out of his pocket while he was on the toilet or pushing down his pants and sitting down. Not there. Nobody's home, so nobody could have picked it up and neglected to tell him. Cat has a way of walking off with things, but a sock or scarf, not a wallet. Once lost one for a few days and had to call all the companies he had credit cards with. Actually, he only had one credit card, and they still only have one, partly because he's so anxious about losing them, but there were ATM cards he had to call about, both for here and their bank in New York, and the phone card he had to get a new PIN number for. He also had to replace his driver's license, car registration certificate, school library card (which also serves as his ID there), and lots of other cards that were in his wallet: car and medical insurance cards, daughters' library cards he holds for them, Sears charge card his wife gave him when she sent him to buy something there and he'd never returned to her, Staples member card—but he didn't replace that one since he'd never saved any money with it—and check cashing cards for three supermarkets. He now keeps them in his checkbook and they periodically drop out, but he's never lost one. The money in the wallet isn't that important—he rarely keeps more than forty dollars in it. He searches the places he searched before in the car and house. Sometimes he's looked through his pants pockets for something, didn't find it, went through the same pockets fifteen minutes later, and it was there. How to explain it? Hands had gone inside each pocket, fingers had felt around. What did he do right the second time that he didn't the first, since he felt he was as thorough each time? No answers. Same with looking for something in a medicine chest or refrigerator, and this has happened countless times. Actually, those two can't be compared with looking for something in his pockets. He gets confused, or his eyes do—and the bright bathroom and kitchen lights make it worse—by all the things of various sizes, colors, and shapes and in different stationary positions in the refrigerator and medicine chest and sometimes several things on top of each other, and he'd also trust his fingers over his eyes any day. Photos. There are several of them in the wallet, of his wife, mother, and kids, and they're irreplaceable in a way. He and his wife have never systematically stored the negatives to all the pictures they've taken, and it'd be hard to go through so many of them to find the ones he was looking for. He has to have other wallet-size photos of his wife and kids that are just or almost as good, or he could have them made up for that size, but he only has a few individual photos of his mother, and two of the best are in the wallet and he has no negatives of them. Knew he should have got reproductions made of those photos. Opens the bedroom closet he shares with his wife. No, wallet couldn't be in any of his pants on hangers or on the floor below them if it had dropped out, since it was in the pants he has on. Feels all the pants pockets there anyway, and the jeans hanging upright on hooks, and then gets on his knees and canvases the floor with his hands and eyes. He has to leave for work in a few minutes but shouldn't without his driver's license. He can call his department's office and ask someone there to put a notice on his classroom door that he may be a half hour late: emergency. Won't cancel the class for a lost wallet if he doesn't find it in the next half hour. He'll drive to school without the license, go extra cautiously to avoid drawing attention from a patrol car. Or not extra cautiously or too slowly because that could draw attention. But stop when he sees the light turn amber rather than go through it as he usually does, and things like that. Same when he comes home. Then tomorrow drive to the MVA for a new license. But he thinks he'll find the wallet in the house in the next couple of days if he keeps looking and has the family look for it, so he'll hold off canceling his credit and ATM cards and changing his phone card PIN. He goes over most of the places he's looked already: tub, counters, desk, dresser top, et cetera. Think: Did he put it in a drawer or kitchen cabinet or medicine chest by mistake? He's done things like that a few times without knowing it, but so far only an empty plate inside the refrigerator or a frozen food, when he wanted to defrost it, inside a kitchen cupboard or the oven. He's in the bedroom so he looks in his night table drawers, his wife's top dresser drawer, thinking he might have unconsciously whisked the wallet into it, then his two drawers in their dresser. It's in the bottom one on the right in front, on top of a sweater. He put it there when he was thinking of putting away something else? If he was trying to hide the wallet, and he doesn't see any reason he would since there are no workmen or strangers in the house, he would have stuck it in the back of the drawer under something. Mystery, though he's relieved to find it. He checks inside it. Of course everything's there, and it is. Checks his back pocket: memo book's there. His wrist: watch is on it. Shirt pocket: pen's there, and a couple of dollar bills from change this morning, and he puts them into his wallet. Should he fill his pen? Hasn't time and he can do it from the ink bottle in his office during his class break. Keys: on the hook by the kitchen door and he gets them, briefcase off the coat rack, makes sure his classwork and mail to be sent through his office and novel he's been reading are in it, and leaves. He thinks: My glasses. Always losing the damn things. Looks in all the places he usually puts them when he takes them off for some reason or mislays and later finds them: dining room table, side table near it that doesn't seem to have any purpose and he wishes they'd get rid of it to create more space in the small room, stove, counters, shelf above the stove, ledge below the kitchen window, stereo, chairs, typewriter, manuscript pile, dresser, desk, night table, window ledges, sinks and water tanks in the bathrooms when he took something there to read while he sat on the toilet, tub rim, temples sometimes straddling it. Bed: he's often thrown them there, even though he's told himself lots of times not to. Sat on them twice that way—different pairs—once cracking the frame around a lens and other time snapping off a temple. Can't read without them and after a while gets a headache and eyestrain if he doesn't have them on. "Where the freaking hell are they?" he shouts, looking in one of the bathrooms again. "Someone ought to invent an alarm to go off on eyeglasses if they're off your face for more than five minutes," he says to his wife. "Why, you lose them again?" "You know me: glasses more than any one thing other than my temper and mind; I'm exaggerating somewhat about the latter," and she says, "No, they're both true, especially when you're in a rush to get to school and can't find something like your wallet or glasses." "Okay, but I am serious about the alarm. Here's where we make our meager fortune. Think of the millions of people who habitually lose their glasses. And from it I could then afford to buy several pairs of glasses and, if we really do well from this invention, maybe have my own live-in optician for those times when I lose all of them in one day. It shouldn't be too hard to get someone to design and make it. A little buzzer or beeper or blinking light hooked up to a timer and a watch battery in the frame. Or buzzer and blinking light combined, in the more expensive model, but where you can also use only the light if you're in some kind of situation, let's say, where you don't want the buzzer disturbing anyone," and she says, "And where would that be: a theater, a courtroom? If you lost your glasses in a place like that, how far could they have gone?" "Someplace, then. I'll have to think of one, though, if it's to be one of that model's selling points. One's house late at night in the dark when you don't want to wake anyone with a regular light or the alarm sound. And this device could also be installed in key rings and wallets and pen caps, even, of valuable pens, though that might be more difficult because it'd seem the alarm would have to be installed when the pen was made, or maybe not. It could be like an adhesive tab and you just stick it on. All that for later after the initial planning. But to set the timer for your glasses, as an example: something like an alarm clock. Instead of for one o'clock, for instance, you set it to go off after one minute if your eyes are so bad you've been declared legally blind. Five to ten minutes if you have eyes like mine. An hour or five to ten hours if you only use your glasses occasionally—for the fine print on medicine bottles or because you have so many pairs you're not concerned if one's lost. And at night, when you go to sleep, you just turn off the alarm, as I said, unless you want to reset it to wake you up in the morning. Obviously, if you can set it for five to ten hours ahead, you can get it to do that too. In addition—something I just thought of—why wait for the alarm to go off in a minute or five to ten hours? Another invention can be a device like an electric lock—you know, the ones that people use to unlock the driver's door before they get to the car—that activates the other alarms for your glasses, wallet, key ring, pen, memo book . . . anything you want it to. A different button for each of these things on this one remote control unit, and which can work through walls—I don't know if the car one does—and from a hundred feet away. It can even be connected to a radio satellite, for the most expensive models, like the ones small sailboats have when they're crossing the ocean. If you lose this remote control you can have another less expensive one only to find it. And if you lose that one too, or if you only have one—and you wouldn't want to keep either of them on your key ring the way people do with the electronic lock if, like me, you're prone to losing the ring—then you fall back on just the original alarm device that starts beeping or buzzing or blinking in a minute to ten hours after one of those things is lost. So what do you think of my idea?" and she says, "What do you want me to say? Not bad. I wish, though, I could help you find your glasses now. You looked in all the—" and he says, "First thing after I realized I'd lost them and then the next thing and the next. Three times already," and she says, "Then I'm sorry, I know how you need them, and I'll keep my eyes open." He wants to read. Has this good novel he's half through with, and he'd planned to sit outside with it for an hour before the kids came home. Has a pair of old glasses but they're from a prescription of about five years ago, and whenever he's used them as a spare, when the newer glasses were lost or being repaired, they always hurt his eyes after five minutes. "Can you help me look for my eyeglasses?" he asks his older daughter when she gets home from school. "I'll give you a dollar if you find them," and she says, "I don't need incentives to look. Where do you think you last had them?" and he says, "Really, sweetheart, if I knew that . . . anyway, I've covered many times all the places I normally leave them: tables, desk, phones, bathrooms, bed, and so on. You know I'm practically helpless after a while without them and I also can't start my work," and she says, "I know. I've heard you yell plenty when they were missing," and he says, "This time I'm not, right? I'm calm and optimistic, for one reason because I think I'll find them with your help. Your eyes are much younger and better than mine, even if you wear glasses, and you might either see them in the same places I looked or you're so smart you'll think of places I haven't." His younger daughter comes home from school fifteen minutes later and the other says to her, "Daddy says he'll give a dollar to anybody—" "Two dollars now," he says. "That's how much I need them." "Two dollars to anybody who finds his glasses. I've looked everywhere I can think of, so

I'm giving up." "Damn," he shouts, banging his fist on the kitchen counter. "How stupid can I be? I've wasted more than an hour already looking for them. When will I learn that when I put them down I should make a mental note of where I'm putting them? I should probably even write it in my memo book with the date and time I'm putting the glasses down. But that'd take too much trouble and I don't always have my pen and memo book on me. And if I temporarily lose the memo book after I put this mental note in it—well, then it's not a mental note, right?—then what? I'll be relying on the memo book for where the glasses are rather than my mind, and the mind's the thing I always have with me and should train and trust." "You ought to get one of those string things that hang the glasses around your neck when you're not using them," his younger daughter says, and he says, "I don't like the looks of them. They make you look like some stereotype of the prissy lips-all-pursed old-fashioned librarian or grade school teacher." "But they help you, so why care how they look?" and he says, "I also don't want anything hanging around my neck and swinging and getting in my way, and I'm sure I'll also break them faster that way, which is worse than losing them temporarily." "Then don't use one and don't take your glasses off your face. Just keep them on," and he says, "I have to take them off if they've been on too long. That's the paradox: my eyes get tired if my glasses are off my face for ten minutes or on it for three hours," and she says, "Then buy a bright red eyeglass case and always put the glasses in it when you take them off, even for a minute. With the red you can find them better," and he says, "Good idea, but for later. That is if I could ever remember to have the case with me at all times and also to put the glasses in it every time they leave my hands. Though it'd only be one more thing to fill up my already stuffed pants pockets when I go out, or shirt pocket if the shirt I wear at the time has one. But now let's see if we can find my glasses." She goes into the living room, that's the last he sees of her, and he spends the next half hour looking for the glasses. Comes across lots of things of his he's going to throw out or give away: old pair of sneakers, shoes, sport jacket; unmatched socks and two shirts in his dresser drawer; Jockey briefs he doesn't wear anymore; looked in the mirror with them on a year ago and thought, They're only for younger and slimmer men, and now only wears boxer shorts. Wants to clear the house of everything he never uses; that way it'll be easier finding things in all these storage spaces and also the things he loses. Pulls books out of the bookcases, dupes of copies he and his wife brought to the marriage. Then other books he knows they and the kids will never read, so that the ones lying on top of books can be inserted vertically into the shelves, though he won't tell his wife he's doing this. Old toothbrushes and medicines and a mattress cover from the linen closet, chipped mugs and saucers from a cupboard, a bent fork from the silverware tray, rusty or blackened aluminum pans and a pot from the stove drawer, goes back to his dresser for a pair of cutoff jeans that had become too frayed, and puts it all into the same box with the shirts, shoes, sport jacket, and mattress cover, and when the box and maybe another box are filled he'll call a charity group that sells these things to pick them up, might even get a tax deduction for the stuff if the IRS still gives it. The nonelectric drip coffeepot—hasn't used it for years—and, while he's getting it out of a top cupboard, several plastic glasses and cups the kids have picked up from fast food places over the years, and he puts these in the box too. Fork, briefs, sneakers, socks, toothbrushes, and medicines he drops into the garbage can. His wife would like him to save the briefs as rags because they're all cotton, but he doesn't want the cleaning woman to use them. He would, on his knees every three to four days to wash the kitchen floor and the Thursday after the one the cleaning woman comes the bathroom floors, commodes, and toilet bowls, but doesn't want to mix them in with the other rags. Several of his budget CDs whose pieces he's since bought better recordings of, and a couple of the nostalgic pop ones his wife got for the kids and they never showed any interest in, into the box—and then tapes it up so his wife won't see what's inside. She asks what's in it, he'll say . . . well, something that'll get him off the hook. He seems always to be emptying the house of things after he's looked for something for a while. "This place is too cluttered with unnecessary crap," he tells his wife, and she says, "Then put some of it in the basement." "Then that place will get cluttered with crap and it'll only encourage you to buy stuff to fill all the spaces I've created by getting rid of the clutter up here. We should throw a lot of it out," and she says, "Before you throw away anything of mine and the kids, let us know. Probably a lot of what you call clutter and crap isn't, and some of it could also contain a certain sentimental value. Did you find your glasses?" and he says, "How can I with all the junk around? To clear away some of it I've packed a box of my things for Purple Heart," and she says, "Let me know when they're coming. I might have a few things for them too." He resumes looking, and on the guest closet floor in back under a snow boot of one of his daughters he finds a pen he must have lost three years ago, maybe four. Sheaffer, chrome, possibly the best American pen he ever owned—just the right weight and a larger-than-usual cartridge, and because it was metal it could never crack—so a great loss. When he went to a store to replace it he found it had tripled in price from when he'd bought it. "There has to be some mistake; nothing can go up so quickly," and the salesman said something like, "The retail price you quote I last saw on this item fifteen years ago, so if any mistake was made it was then and to your benefit," and he said, "Oh, sure." But how'd it end up on the floor? Out of a jacket or coat pocket perhaps, where he's also carried his pens. But in all the times he's searched here, for it and other things—and the boots he packs away every spring—how come he never found it? Just no explanation. Washes out the cartridge, cleans the nib and puts the pen in the dresser drawer he keeps an old watch in. Watch there because when he lost it for a few days he bought a new one, a cheap Timex just as that one's a cheap Timex, and when he found the old watch he pulled out the stem and stored the watch in the drawer for a time when he might lose the new watch. "I found them!" his younger daughter yells. "On a bookshelf in my room!" "How'd they get there?" and she says, "I didn't do it; that's where they were." "Oh, now I remember. Thanks," and takes the glasses and puts them on. A lens is smudged—his finger or hers—and he wipes both lenses and puts the glasses back on. "How?" she says, and he says, "What?" and she says, "You said you remember how your glasses got there," and he says, "I was straightening out your room before—you neglected to, and you also left several wet towels around from your shower this morning—and I had to strip your bed to make it and must have taken off my glasses. I have difficulty seeing sometimes when—well, making a bed and things like that is an action in the middle visual layer of my glasses that bifocals don't cover well . . . where there's sort of a no-man's-land blur of some kind . . . oh, today's a day I can't even find the right words or way to say anything.

But that's why, which could be a good reason why I also didn't find the glasses in your room, except I didn't look there." "Next time put them in the red case I told you to buy and the case into your pocket every time you put the glasses inside," and he says, "Too much trouble to remember each time, though it turned out to be a lot more trouble in finding them, so maybe I'll do what you say. But where am I going to find a bright red case like that?" He gives her a dollar in change from his pocket, says, "I owe you a dollar," and she says, "That's okay," and he says, "No, it'll be an inducement for you to look for my glasses again in case I lose them, which we both know I will," and goes to the kitchen, hoping the wallet's on the shelf above the stove; it is, and he takes a dollar from it and gives it to her. My memo book, he thinks. Not in his back pocket or any of his pants pockets, though he never puts it in any of them but the back ones, or on the shelf where he keeps it when it's not in his back pocket or by his bed. Runs to his bedroom and checks his night table and desk. Looks everywhere in the room, pats down the back pockets of several of his pants hanging up in the closet, even if he knows two of them he hasn't worn for a month, and gets on his knees and checks the floor. This would be the second memo book he's lost in a year. First one he didn't actually lose; it had two years of notes in it for the manuscript he's currently writing, just as this one has all the notes he's written for the same manuscript since he lost that memo book. Searched all over for it and like now started to panic. It was the most important thing he had, he decided then. Hell with the pen, watch, glasses, and wallet. Well, the glasses are important and cost a lot to replace, he told himself then, and the wallet's also important and several of the things in it take a lot of time to replace, but many of the notes in the memo book are irreplaceable and absolutely needed for his manuscript. He'd told himself to photocopy all the pages with notes and keep them somewhere. Told himself to do this lots of times. Told himself several times he'd do it when he got to the copy machine at work, but always forgot or was too busy that day or the machine was tied up. Even told himself to make two copies of the notes and keep one set in his office and the other at home. It ended after he searched for it for about an hour and then shouted, "Oh, no, the washing machine!" and ran to the wash he'd done that morning and took his wet pants out—the machine had stopped long before—and the memo book was in the back pocket. All the notes had run. Maybe three to four were faintly legible and he copied them down and tried using them when he finally got back to his writing, but they weren't any of the important notes. Everything else in the memo book was unusable. He couldn't even make out a note where the letters were an inch high, something he probably jotted down while he was driving the car. He was depressed about it for days. Waited for the memo book to dry, tried to help it along with a hair dryer but the writing faded further; bought a strong magnifying glass to read some of the writing that had run but could only make out a few isolated words, nothing that made any sense or could help him remember what he was saying. He still has that memo book, in a small cardboard box in the dresser drawer that also has in it his old Timex watch and chrome pen and some Kennedy half dollars he's collecting for the kids and an 1880s silver dollar his mother gave him for good luck when he was taking his first plane flight and a few French coins and bills from his last trip to France and the pocket watch his mother's parents gave his father as an engagement gift more than seventy years ago and his mother gave him soon after his father died, maybe the most valuable thing he owns. It's in its original leather sack and has what his mother called a platinum chain and it must be worth by now a thousand dollars—when he took it in to get it fixed twenty years ago (and it worked for a couple of months after that), the watchmaker offered him five hundred dollars for it. But he still thinks, if it were at all possible to do this at the time—the thought's ridiculous but shows how important the memo book was to him once he knew it was permanently ruined—he would have traded that watch for a completely legible memo book. Anyway, he told himself then, his project's dead, he can't go on with it without the notes, but went back to it in a week and wrote more notes and after about half a year of compiling them in the new memo book while he was writing this manuscript, he told himself not to make the mistake he did with the other memo book: get these notes photocopied, do it when you have some free time at school or just come in an hour early to get it done. And he almost did do it, but several things stopped him. This is the day, he thought when he opened the door to the copy machine room and saw it was empty, but that was because the machine was broken. Another day it was being repaired, and another day someone was using it and said she'd be photocopying for at least an hour, and so on. Now he thinks: Is he going to think his project's dead if it turns out he *has* lost this memo book? Doesn't think so, though like the last time there'll be a major setback. Then he says, "The washer," and thinks, No, can't be in it, because he's wearing the only pants he put on today and he remembers slipping the memo book into the back pocket when he put them on. Besides, he didn't do a wash today, maybe the first day in a week he hasn't, nor did he throw any clothes in, but goes to the washing machine anyway and it's empty. Dryer? and looks in that, though knows he didn't put any clothes in it last night or today, and it's empty. Memo book's got to be around; he couldn't have lost this one too. Something like that just doesn't happen. Sure it does, but he doesn't think it did this time. There's a place he hasn't looked yet and that's where he'll find it. Or a place he has looked but it was too dark there or he didn't look carefully enough. He goes through the house, finds a few things to throw out, dumps some things of his kids that he maybe shouldn't, says to his wife, "Why do we have so much superfluous useless space-occupying junk in this house?" and she says, "Like what?" and he says, "Like everything," and she says, "Now there's a reasonable response. You must be mad again because there's something important of yours you can't find. Which is it this time?" and he says, "Whatever it is, I'll find it; don't worry, I'll find it. But when I say 'like everything,' I mean why are we always buying and buying and never dumping and dumping or giving away and giving away, especially when we don't, or find that we don't, need these things, can you answer me that?" and she says, "Yes, I can," and he says, "For instance, the closets. And not just ours, though God help me when I try to find on our closet floor a match to a shoe. Or when I try to get a shirt out of the closet but it's squeezed in so tight on the hanger rod, or doubled or tripled up with one or two other shirts on one hanger so I can't pull it out, and that also goes for my pants. But all the closets are crammed tight and all the closet floors are filled with things too. And not just things that are supposed to be there but we have too much of, but boxes and boxes stacked in back and other crap piled high on the closet shelves. Same with all the drawers. The kids' especially are so stuffed with clothes that they won't open, and if you can wrench them free then they won't close," and she says, "There's only one closet—Fanny's—

that has a few boxes in it. Tell me what it is you're looking for," and he says, "My goddamn memo book," and she says, "It's sticking out from under the telephone in our room. At least that's where it was the last time I was in there," and he says, "It is? What's it doing there?" and she says, "Don't ask me, it's not my memo book," and he runs to the phone, it's under it as she said, a corner of it sticking out, and goes back to his wife and says, "I can't tell you how many times I checked that dresser for it, and for all I know I might have even picked up the phone to look under it. I'm telling you, I don't know if I'm seeing right these days. Anyway, thanks. And I apologize for blowing up before, although I meant it about all the things we have in this small house. We got to get rid of a lot of it, stuff we'll never again use. In the long run it'll save us time looking for more important things. Or thinking, and then trying to pull it off, Where am I going to cram this damn thing in? And also yanking out a drawer for a pair of stupid socks and dropping it on your stupid foot when you yank it out too far, and so on," and she says, "All right, we will. I don't know how we'll find the time for it, but we'll comb the entire house looking for things that could be discarded. As for the kids' drawers and closets, they have to go through them themselves and take out what no longer fits them or they don't want. For Fanny's rejects, unless it's absolute junk, Josephine will have to see if she wants them first. Then we'll give everything we've collected and packed to Disabled Vets or Purple Heart or whichever organization next calls us to see if we have anything for a pickup," and he says, "Let's not wait for them to call. We get the job done, we call them. So, deal; great. And I got something worthwhile out of temporarily losing my memo book; couldn't be better. I ought to lose my things more. Only kidding." My book, he thinks. Now where is it? Always reads one for a few minutes to an hour before he goes to sleep, and he wants to do that now. He's all set for bed—glasses, pen, watch, memo book, and handkerchief on his night table—but can't find the book. He can't just start a new one. Never does till he gives up on or finishes the one he's reading. Now it's *An Outcast of the Islands*. He's about halfway done. He'll probably finish it—it's not that long—though he doesn't like it as much as a lot of other Conrad. Keeps hoping to come upon as good a description as hit him on page two or three and made him think maybe Conrad's the greatest fiction writer in English. "Ragged, lean, undersized" or "underwashed men of various ages, shuffling about in slippers," and so on. And in the same paragraph—the same sentence, broken up by a semicolon—"motionless old women who looked like monstrous bags of pink calico stuffed with shapeless clumps of fat," he thinks it is, but like that: tight, strong, raw, clear, but so far nothing's matched it. If he's lost the book, he thinks he can get a copy from his school's library tomorrow—nobody's taught Conrad there for years so most of his books are probably in the stacks. Or a new one from a bookstore—knows of a huge one ten minutes' drive from here that carries most of Conrad in paperback—but it's too late tonight, though if he had thought two hours ago he'd lost it he would have gone to that store. He doesn't like to read anything in bed but a book. Not a newspaper; too unwieldy, managing the pages from a sitting-up position. And the newsprint or something from the paper gets on his fingers and then the fingers stain the bed linen and just feel funny till he washes them, which means he has to get out of bed, when once he's in it he likes to read till his eyes get tired, force them to read a bit more, and then turn off the light. Nor magazines. There actually aren't any he likes to read anytime except a few literary quarterlies, and he doesn't have a new one of those. "Have you seen my book, the Conrad I've been reading the past week?" and his wife says, "No, is it any good?" and he says, "So-so." Kids are asleep or at least shut off their lights an hour ago after he read to the younger one and said good night to them both. Goes into her room, a little light from the hallway shines in, and looks around. Not here, from what he can see, and why would it be? Because lots of times he's left things in places he doesn't remember leaving them in. Because he's often picked something up from its regular place and left it some other place without realizing he'd picked it up. Because he's constantly losing or misplacing things, constantly, maybe once every two days, maybe more. Whatever book he's reading for pleasure is usually on his night table, bookmark in it—usually a scrap of paper or his eyeglass case or pen, but never his fountain pen—except the three days a week he goes to work. Then he sticks it into his briefcase, though he also takes it in the car when he picks up his older daughter at her school, neither of which he did today. Goes into her room—light from the same hallway, though less of it—and this time, because she's a light sleeper, tiptoes while he looks and feels around. "What do you want?" she says from bed, and he says, "Excuse me, darling, I didn't mean to disturb you. I'm looking for the book I've been reading. The Joseph Conrad," and she says, "Why would it be in here?" and he says, "It shouldn't be, but I was just thinking, and you know me: I'm pathetic when it comes to losing things. I've checked everywhere else—just now Josephine's room—so I thought I'd give yours a try," and she says, "What's it called?" and he gives her the title and she says, "What's it about?" and he starts telling her and then says, "This sounds too much like a tropical bedtime story, when it's a bit late for one. I'll continue with it in the morning if you refresh my memory that we spoke about it tonight. Go to sleep now," and tries to reach her bed to kiss her forehead but there are heavy shoes and some other small hard objects in his way, one he accidentally kicks, and he says, "If you're missing the mate to the sneakers or shoes you want to wear tomorrow, look under the bed for it. Now I'm blowing you a kiss good night," and blows one. Checks the bookcases in the living room. Must be a thousand books, most of them his wife's, and he scans every one except the big art books and atlases on the bottom shelves. After he's done with a book, and if his wife isn't interested in reading it and he doesn't think one of the kids will be in the next few years, he usually gives it to the town library or a friend or student or sticks it on a shelf in his department's reading lounge, even the ones inscribed to him, unless the author's in his department. I give up, he thinks. I'm just going to start something else and, if I don't like it, go to a bookstore tomorrow and find something new—and looks at the fiction shelves and sees the Conrad. "I don't understand it," he says to his wife, and she says, "Still looking for your book?" "No, I found it. Polly didn't clean today, did she?" and she says, "She can only give us every other Thursday, so next week. Why, is the house so filthy to you?" "Not at all. I'll tell you about it later: this book"—holding it up—"a big big mystery," and washes up, gets into bed, and starts reading. Oh, God, why can't I ever remember this? and gets up and turns the bathroom light on and leaves the bathroom door ajar so his wife will be able to see when she comes in and he can fall asleep without a bedroom light on. Gets back in bed and resumes reading. I think I'm going to give up on this one, he thinks, after a few more pages, and drops the book on the floor without a bookmark in it, puts his glasses in their case, brings his pen, watch, memo book, and handkerchief closer to him on the night table, lays his pillows flat, and turns off the light. His things, he thinks. Where are they? This is ridiculous. Put his pen, wallet, memo book, checkbook, book, and handkerchief down somewhere and now can't find them. Keys are on their kitchen hook; he puts them in his pocket. The rest shouldn't be hard to find. So big a pile, thick novel on the bottom, how can he miss it? First place he looked was the tops of the washer and dryer in the kitchen, where he usually puts things he's going to leave the house with. Now he looks at all the tables and sideboards and flat surfaces of furniture in the dining and living rooms. On his bed?—because he remembers collecting everything together so he could leave for work—and looks in his room. Not there or anywhere in the room or in his briefcase hanging on the coat rack in the living room. He takes it off and puts it on the dryer so when he does find all these things he can set off right away. They couldn't be in the bathrooms or either of the kids' rooms. Single things, yes, but not a big pile of his stuff. Wife's studio? Doesn't think so, but check—"Excuse me"—and goes in and looks around. "What are you looking for?" and he says, "Something." "I know, something, but what? Perhaps I can help," and he says, "Several things, actually. Not important; I'll find them." "Don't you have to go to work soon?" and he says, "That's why I'm looking. But if I don't find them before, no big deal." "Maybe I saw them. Your wallet and notebook and pen?" and he says, "Yes, you've seen them?" and she says, "Not recently. Just that those are what you tend to lose with some frequency." "And my glasses, I just realized. They're with the other things I've misplaced and that I have to find before I go. Keys I know I have," and sticks his hand into his pocket to make sure. "It's a big single pile of things. I'm sure it's right under my nose somewhere, but not here," and she says, "If I see any of them I'll give a yell." Didn't leave them in the car. You're so sure? and he goes out to the car and they're not there. He knows he put them all together: glasses, pen, wallet, memo book, handkerchief, checkbook, novel, and also his address and appointment books. The last four go into his briefcase. Keys are in his pocket. He just checked, but check again, and touches his pocket. He's lost a couple of things at once—pen and wallet when he used to keep the wallet in his side pants pocket—but found them after a long search on his car seat. That's when he thinks he started putting his wallet only into his back pocket. And one time three things—pen was one of them, forgets the rest—but not as many things at once as today: five, six; not even close. And he remembers they were in a neat pile, handkerchief on top, glasses in their case right underneath it. Blue hanky, too, or black. That might be the reason he can't find the pile: hanky's covering it and he was looking for something entirely different, and goes through the house looking for a folded handkerchief on a mound. "Still can't find it?" his wife says, and he says, "It's not just two or three things and my glasses in their case, it's many. Checkbook, address and appointment books, book I've been reading for pleasure," and she says, "What are you reading these days?" and he says, "Whatever it is, I've no time to discuss it. It's the whole stack of things that's important. And what did I say before, the stuff wasn't important? That's crazy. My memo book. You know how I feel about it, particularly since I lost the last one." "You never got your new notes copied? You said you would," and he says, "No. And same with my hybrid pen. It has some mysterious importance to me, as if without it I couldn't continue with the work I'm on. Don't ask me why—something there crazy too—though the pen's of less importance than the memo book, just as the novel, even if it were the best one I'd ever started reading, and address and appointment books. . . . Well, the novel, since I can always get another copy of it in a day at a library or bookstore, is the least important of all except for the handkerchief, which is of no importance other than it might be hiding this very important pile. As for the checkbook—I'm not sure how it compares with the others in importance," and she says, "It's extremely important, possibly the most important item to me of everything you spoke about so far. It has the register of all the checks you wrote this year. You lose that, we'd be in serious trouble when I started doing our income taxes. When you find it you should photocopy every page of the check register too." "I will, though maybe not right after I find it; and I don't care what you say, the checkbook's not more important than my memo book or wallet or pen. How am I supposed to leave the house without them, at least the wallet and memo book?" "You didn't mention your watch, was that in the pile too?" and he says, "Jesus, my watch," and feels his wrist. "Where the hell is it?" Goes through his pants pockets. Touches the keys, couple of coins, but nothing else in them. Runs through the house looking at all the places he thinks he could have left the watch. Goes back to her room and says, "Watch is probably in the pile too. So, if I'm right, watch, wallet, pen, handkerchief, checkbook, all those other books, maybe even some other things, though I can't imagine what," and she says, "Is it possible your appointment and address books and checkbook are on the wooden shelf above the stove? I know I've seen them there before," and he says, "I looked; or did I? I could be thinking of something else I looked for there today, like the pile with my handkerchief covering it, and not for any of those books specifically, so missed them. But I'll look again. Anything to find them. And maybe finding one will lead to another, and so on, though I don't see how. I'll be satisfied for the time being to just find one of those things, though of course, best of all, the most important one either to you or me," and goes into the kitchen. On the shelf are an old tuna-fish can of coins, several pencils, lots of Visa receipts, bottle of aspirins, two subway tokens from New York, one of them the old one or maybe even the token before that, paper clips, rubber bands, seashell from the summer, jar of red food color (so his wife probably mixed a solution for the hummingbird feeder and set it out or is planning to or else planned to and forgot about it), dried-up marker he's been meaning to dump for a month, and tosses into the garbage can. Turns around to get a carrot from the refrigerator, something he often does—chomps carrots—when he's frustrated at some work he's having a hard time getting done or can't find something he's been looking for for a long time, and sees what seems like the missing pile on top of the refrigerator. No, can't be, and gets up close and finds under the handkerchief everything he's been looking for and a nail clipper he didn't know was in the pile and which he usually keeps in the coin can on the shelf. He thinks he intended to clip his nails later, either during the drive to school while he was waiting for for a long red light to turn or between classes. But how'd he miss looking here for the pile? he thinks, putting his glasses on and their case into his back pants pocket. Well, his eyes, first of all, without the glasses; handkerchief is navy blue, he sees, and rubs his nose with it and puts it into a side pants pocket. And he never turned the ceiling light on while he was looking and there's not much natural light in the kitchen around this time, and really only in the morning for an hour or so does it get some sun when there's sun. Otherwise, because the entrance is under the carport, it's the darkest room in the house. He also never looked on top of the refrigerator because it never entered his head the pile could be there. He can't remember putting anything on it before except empty jars and rolls of paper towels and things like that if he couldn't find room for them in the kitchen cabinets. So why'd he put the pile there today? Doesn't know, though is sure he did it. Kids had gone to school before he made the pile and his wife can't stand by herself and anyway would have remembered and told him if she'd put the pile there. Next time he loses something important he's going to look on every flat surface in the house even if he has never put anything on some of them, though not something like the top of a bookcase seven feet high. "I found them," he yells out, and she says, "Everything, including the checkbook?" and he says, "The works, plus a nail clipper I didn't know was among them." "The regular one for fingers or the big one for toes?" and he says, "Fingers," and she says, "I could use it now, if you don't mind; I've been hunting for it myself," and he goes into her room and gives her it. While she's clipping her nails, a sound he hates so he says, "Excuse me," and shuts her door, he puts the memo book into the back pants pocket his eyeglass case isn't in, rest of the books into his briefcase, pen and wallet into his side pants pockets, and straps the watch around his wrist. "Listen," he says through her door, and she stops clipping, "I have to go now. But I'm glad the whole thing's over with," and she says, "I can imagine. I know what not having some of those things around means to you. And everything at once? It would have been a catastrophe if they were lost even for an entire day. And all of them lost forever? I won't even begin to imagine." "Oh, I'm not so sure anymore"—pushing her door open—"everything can eventually be replaced or considered not that relevant, when you think of it. Nothing should be that important where it's going to seriously disturb you if it's permanently lost. Take the wallet, for instance. It'd take some time and maybe a little expense, but I could replace everything in it except a few photos. And the pen? Dammit, some markers are just as good, or almost. And the pen I have runs or just stains my fingers every time I fill it up. And why should I attach to it some mystical significance, almost, for my work? And the memo book? A big loss, if I could never find it again. But then I'd try to remember what notes in it are important. And if I couldn't remember them—well, then maybe they weren't so important. So it ends up being a not-so-bad thing in losing it, since I've weeded those notes out. And then, if I still felt lousy about losing some of the notes, and I probably would, I'd sit down and force myself to think up new ones that I never would have thought of if I hadn't lost the memo book in the first place, or something like that, but you know what I mean," and she says, "You're only saying that because you found everything. But if one of the more important things, like your memo book or wallet or even your pen, was permanently lost and you knew it was, you wouldn't be so easygoing about it," and he says, "I'm telling you, it's true, except perhaps for the memo book a little and, for you, my checkbook." "Then photocopy all the important memos in it and also the entire check register, and set both our minds at rest," and he says, "I will, definitely, at work today," but is almost sure he won't have time to or that he'll forget.

The Son

He could do nothing today. Yesterday he could do nothing too. Sat around, napped a lot, read without wanting to, quickly put down the book, took walks, bought things at stores he didn't need now but could later use. Then he thinks of his brother—this came on his last walk. What if he had lived? He had never thought of it before. Or if he had, he forgot. He'd call him if he were alive. "Hi," he'd say, when his brother answered the phone, "how are you, how you doing?"—all that stuff. But what else? Beyond the how-ya-doing and -are-you. His brother's job, for instance, if he wasn't retired by now, and so on. And if his brother were retired, then what he was doing with his free time, anything interesting or new? What's he been reading, seeing; what's on his mind? Anything particularly fascinating happen to him, the last, let's say, week, and how's his health? And it doesn't have to be "fascinating"; just anything he'd like to tell him about? Also, perhaps how glad Gould is to have a brother to speak to at such times. "Oh, yes?" his brother could say, and he'd say, "When I'm slightly depressed, just not feeling too good with myself and my work. More than slightly depressed, meaning more than 'slightly.' I've for the past two days mostly been napping, taking walks, sitting around, trying to read, buying things I don't need, although nothing to bankrupt my family. But let's not go into what's been happening to me; I want to hear about you." A lot of what he'd say to his brother would depend on where he lived. If his brother were living in Oregon, let's say, then most of what they talked about would have to be over the phone. He'd want him to live closer. New York, D.C., Boston, New Jersey. Someplace that'd take one up to a maximum of eight hours by car or train to get to. They were close as kids, he was told and can faintly recall, personally close, and would be that way now, he's sure. From everything his folks said, his brother had a terrific disposition from day one. "My obstetrician said he slid out smiling," his mother said, "just as you say you saw your second daughter do, and she's still as jolly and sweet as can be," and he said, "She has her off days, or moments," and his mother said, "So did he—not days; rarely for more than ten minutes—but for the most part he was sublime." And he feels one's disposition, if it's a good one—he has nothing to back this up except casual observation over the years—stays much the same through life unless there's a dramatic chemical imbalance along the way or something traumatic happens. Like losing a brother. That could do it, though it'd depend what age you lost him and how close the two of you were. So if everything had remained relatively the same they would have continued being close for a while. Then when his brother got to around twelve he would have started hanging out more with his own friends and a lot less with Gould. That would have been hard to take. The first child, of course, never has to go through it so isn't as aware of the effect. His folks, mainly his mother, would probably have told him many times, "That's what happens with boys at Robert's age so you have to begin accepting it and not be so disheartened," and maybe even done more things with him and shown him more attention, mainly his mother, till he grew used to the change and perhaps got closer to his own friends. Then they would have become close again when Gould started college, and later on, and stayed that way till today. Again, nothing to base it on, though he has talked about it with several of his male advisees at school who were in similar situations. Why didn't his folks have more kids—he asked his mother this about ten years ago—"especially after Robert died? And if you had got to it right away the baby would have been four years younger than me, not much different than what Robert and I were," and she said, "Two was plenty at first. I had my outside activities, professional things mostly, and your dad never wanted children that much. He would have been content with one, and if we'd had none he wouldn't have minded either. He loved you both but would have been happy to just spend long hours at his work and, when we could, to take extended vacations with me. So it was my decision alone, and two seemed the right number we could afford, and I also figured two brothers would play with each other, and so forth. While one could be a nuisance and, if we ignored him when he had no one to be with but us, a problem that would get worse the longer we did little to correct it. But after your brother's death, though I was certainly fertile—I had two abortions after Robert died—I swore off having another. Not even as a replacement child—the one you never would have had if a previous one hadn't died—and only thought of putting all my child-rearing efforts into keeping alive the one I had left, you, which is why you might feel you've been smothered most of your life. But you wanted me to have a third, true? Even a sister?" "Sure. Someone around who wasn't an adult. Then later for helping us take care of Dad and then he or she and I looking after you, not that you'll ever need it, and just for me to know someone else was there." But his brother. If he were alive he'd call him now, no matter where he was, and say what? "God, I haven't seen you for more than fifty-five years. You must have changed some in that time. I'm listening; I'm not hearing anything. That was a joke. So how come no laughing, brother? though if I took time to think about it I'd probably think more of you for that. Haven't spoken to you either in that time, though in my mind and dreams plenty. The former's a lie. Might as well start out on the right foot right off. But dreams of you you should believe I've had a lot. You're young, you're older, you're always better than I in academics and sports; you're married, you're happy, you're showing me your first child; you're much older, you're on your last leg—one of Dad's favorite expressions—you're the same age as I when I last remember you, and remember you I do. Those dreams can't sub for the real thing like talking to you now but are okay if that's all you got. But you're still so closemouthed. How come, from someone who was such a gregarious kid, suddenly no response? Grave's got your tongue?" Their baths together. Sat opposite each other in the tub, sharing a single soap and washrag, feet flat up against the other's and their wee-wees peeping out of the six inches of water. His father, after he told him this, said no one, from something that had happened when he was so young, could bring back so many details like that after more than thirty years. "But we took a bath a week for months, Mommy's said, starting when I was three, and we always laughed about our penises sticking through." "If Robert told me this today I might believe him, since he was six. But the memory of a three-year-old is ninety-eight percent blank, and to think you can recollect the one soap and washrag between you and depth of the water is nuts." "I'm estimating the depth, since it barely came up to my waist." "Even so." Being hoisted out of the tub by his father (almost violently, but he didn't tell him that), who said, Robert's old enough now to take baths alone. "That's also impossible for you to have remembered. I'd only possibly remember it if I'd done it to you, but I don't. But if I did lift you out of the tub it would be only because your mother said your teeth were chattering and you were going to catch a cold or that I saw you two futzing around in there and thought one of you might drown." Wonders if their wee-wees sticking above the water and their laughing about it and maybe even pulling on them till they were hard or who knows what had anything to do with his father hoisting him angrily out of the tub and never letting them take a bath together again. "We should ask Dad," he'd say to his brother now on the phone. "Come on, that's another joke; you gotta say something. I didn't make this call just to hear my own voice. And the folks plenty of times said that even as a two-year-old, or maybe it was three, you had a highly developed sense of humor—'sophisticated,' Mom said—catching on to some of Dad's pranks and funny lines and Mom's plays-on-words that kids twice and maybe thrice your age wouldn't get; and I'd think something like that, unless you've taken a great physical or personal blow, lasts for life." Slept in the same room with him for three years. First slept in a crib in his parents' room. Then when he was around three months his crib was moved into Robert's room, or what eventually became "the boys' room." He got a bed for his third birthday—it wasn't delivered, or maybe it couldn't be assembled for a while—but soon after it was, Robert died. He thought several times, when he was four or five, looking at Robert's bed with the same winter or summer bedspread as his but no blanket or sheets though it did have an uncased pillow underneath—his parents kept it as a possible guest bed, though no adult guest ever slept in it, and also for his friends to sleep over sometime in the future, his mother said—did Robert die because they bought me a bed? Maybe thought it once. Robert could have felt that the crib, because it had rollers, was only temporary and one day it would be rolled out with Gould in it and the room again would only be his. "Boys' room" might have meant "boy's room" to him, meaning his, since Gould was what to the family?—the baby of it, never the boy. For years the bed remained neatly made beside his with one or the other bedspread on it, then both beds with identical spreads on them after he moved away, till his mother died and he emptied her apartment and sold or gave away the spreads and just about everything else in it except for a few treasures: some painted plates of fruits that had been on the dining room wall; a small bronze of a naked boy reading a book, which his mother said resembled Robert and was the only reason he kept it; three tiny Chinese or Japanese ivories of squatting figures working at different trades. If Robert were alive they would have split everything between them fairly and squarely. Better than that. One would have said to the other, "Take whatever you want. I'll have a look at what's left." And the other would have said, "No, you choose first and as much as you like, and then I'll see if there's anything I want. Those Japanese or Chinese figurines, for instance. They're beautifully crafted and very old and probably valuable, and I know you liked them as a boy. I used to watch you stare at them through the case and then later you made up stories for me about them." "You did that too, and if they're so beautiful and valuable, you have them. Don't worry, there'll be plenty left that I'll like. Mom had great taste. Those painted fruit plates. The bronze boy leaning against a tree stump reading a book. She got them at auctions and I want you to have them too. And if your wife and kids see anything they like, then they can also choose before me." "And *your* wife and kids; I want them to select things before me too." Gould and his folks would go to the cemetery every other month for a few years to visit Robert's grave. Then every four months or so. By the time Gould was in his twenties they only went once a year, on Robert's birthday or a day close to it, and only that infrequently, for the most part, because they no longer had a car and had to hire a cab. His mother would always weed the grounds around the grave, brush the leaves and dirt off the stones, pick up any papers and other garbage that might have been blown into their hedges and on the path, cry, ask his father for his handkerchief though she always carried tissues in her bag, cover her eyes with her hands, and say a prayer for a dead son she'd memorized from the little prayer book the funeral home had given out at Robert's funeral, and then open her eyes and say just about the same thing every time: "I will never get over it, Robert dear. Listen to me, my boy, I swear I will never get over the loss of you and that it's forever made me heartsick, do you hear?" His father during all this would usually hold his hat, try not to jingle the change in his pants, stare at the grave a few seconds, and the rest of the time look around the cemetery and at the road nearby if there was a car or truck driving past and at the sky, especially if a plane was flying by. Gould would stand beside his mother just in case she started to collapse, which she did once, and a couple of times when he was in his teens he thought, If this is where your spirit's supposed to be, I don't feel it, though I wish I did. You could be a real help to me now and in my future in all sorts of ways. But if there is an afterlife or just that spirit hanging around, why would you want to stay here? It's so ugly and windy and depressing and cold, and noisy and smelly from the passing cars. Though if you *are* here or anyplace where the folks and I go, could you give me some way to contact you? I'll swear on the Bible, if that's what you want, that I'll keep it just between you and me. After about half an hour, his father would put his hat on and say something like "I think we've been here long enough, paid our respects, and all that, so what do you both say? I'd like to get a bite at that diner around here we always go to before we head back. I don't know about your mother, but you must be hungry, Gould. I know that as much as I have for breakfast before we leave for this place, by the time this is over I'm always starved." Then his mother would say, "We should get a bench so you and Gould can sit down and then we could stay longer," and his father would say, "You always say that, and I always say, 'Do we really need one for the few times we come out here?' But if you really want one, order it, but nothing fancy." Then his mother would say, "I'll start calling around for one tomorrow. And as long as we're out here, and this won't take much time, I wonder if either of you would mind my visiting my brother's grave at another cemetery on this road." His father usually couldn't stand any talk of Robert in front of him. When his mother, at the table, once spoke about Robert—that he was a quick eater and ate almost everything you put on his plate, especially carbohydrates, so the trick was not to give him too much initially and to go skimpy on seconds—his father said, "Please, do you have to?" and she said, "I'm just talking, it doesn't have to concern you. Just continue eating," and he said, "Goddammit, he's dead, the damn kid's dead, not a damn kid but what the hell's talking about him going to do to help you or him?" "His name came up in conversation; you were busy with your soup and missed that part. Gould asked if Robert was fat—that he has this memory—and I was answering," and his father said, "Baloney, and you know it," and threw down his napkin and left the table, "probably to cry by himself in the bathroom," his mother said, "for that's been his problem since your brother died. And later on he'll come out as if he hadn't ruined our dinner and ask me to heat up the food he missed. Look how many years it's been, but I can't so much as say that today's Robert's birthday, if that day is, I'm saying, and that's why I've lit my memorial candles, because as soon as I bring up Robert's name he tells me to drop the subject or else he's closed his ears. If you can't mourn from time to time and admit that you're mourning, and especially to someone who feels as sad about it as you, then you're going to suffer. Because you were so young and didn't get to really know your brother, you never had to go through any of this," and he said, "I knew him, I remember him a lot. Robert. I remember he was heavy but not so fat. I have lots of other pictures of him in my head, and most of them with him laughing," and she said, "Probably just the tiniest little memories. And the pictures, I'd think, would be mostly from old photos. He was a plump baby, to answer your question, quite heavy to carry in my stomach and with an enormous head and shoulders when he came out. He always had a large appetite, as I've said, or ate well and with no fuss, and I think he liked everything I made for him. He was always like that: never a problem in anything he did. But by the time you were born, or a year after, I'd slimmed him down considerably, having learned that fat babies make fat adults, and he stayed that way because of the diet and serving methods I'd devised for him, so you couldn't remember Robert as heavy. Always taller than the other children his age, yes. On the growth chart his pediatrician mapped out for him, Robert was going to be six-four. That would have been something to see, since no one in Dad's family or mine has been more than five-nine, and your growth chart has you topping off at five-ten at the most, though those things aren't always exactly accurate and can also change." But his brother. He'd call him now and speak to him. Or he'd be sitting where he is, at his desk in his bedroom, phone on the dresser, and thinking of Robert but not as if he were alive. He'd be alive and the phone would ring and Gould would go to the dresser and pick up the receiver and say into it, "Don't tell me, it's my brother. I was just this second thinking of you," and Robert would say, "That's uncanny, for I was just thinking of you, only a few seconds ago, so decided to call." Or he wouldn't be thinking of Robert. He'd be sitting at his desk typing or staring at the clean paper in the typewriter and thinking of his work or reading over what he'd just written and the phone would ring and he'd say, "Damn, always interruptions. . . . Sally!" he'd yell out, "could you answer it?" and get no answer and go to the phone and pick up the receiver and say, "Hello?" and Robert would say, "Hey, there, you don't sound too happy. Anything wrong?" or "Hiya, Gould, how you doing? I'm not interrupting anything, am I? Something in that hello," and he'd say, "I was working, but nothing important," and Robert would say, "And I'm not calling about anything important. Just to talk to you, which I like doing—I didn't mean that disparagingly—and I can call back later, or when you want to you can buzz me," and he'd say, "No, no, let's talk now while we got the chance. I'm not working on anything that can't be helped if I come back to it, after the breathing space a phone talk could give me, with more enthusiasm or greater and/or better ideas or whatever's missing now and the piece needs." Oh, jeez, how do brothers speak? But ones their age, both in the low sixties. If they like each other, maybe the way he just had it: affectionately, solicitous of the other's feelings and time, and so on: you first; no, you. Hi, hey, how ya doing, what's new? Nothing's going on with me these days and I just felt like talking to you. But if you're busy. . . . And he would have liked Robert. Everything that's been said about him—well, he's said that. "Such a sweet boy, and so beautiful," his mother used to say. "His eyelashes, for instance. All children have beautiful eyelashes, but his went beyond that. They were like painted on, but real. There was never a sweeter, more beautiful boy in the world, excluding you. So let's say you both—though to be totally honest, and this isn't anything, so don't worry, his eyelashes were more striking than yours—two beautiful, sweet, gentle, and intelligent boys. What unwanted competition you would be to each other. The girls would flock to you both when you hit your twenties and wouldn't know which one to fight over," and he said, "He could have them all, I wouldn't mind. And my eyelashes are nothing; I never thought of them and I don't want them to be pretty." "Wouldn't he have been a wonderful brother to have grown up with," his mother said, years later. "The best, I'm sure, and to have around now, no matter how far away from each other you might have lived. No, that was a terrible thing to say, as if I had intentionally wanted to make you sad, which you know I didn't," and he said, "No, it's all right and probably true." So, say Robert had lived. He calls and says, "I'm flying in, if you've room for me. No big reason I'm coming. Haven't seen you all in a long time, and I have a few days off and these Frequent Flyer benefits to use up in a month, and my desk and home life are clear. But if you're busy . . ." He picks him up at the airport; they go out for dinner with Gould's family, Gould paying for everything everywhere they go and Robert saying, "Come on, you gotta let me cough up once and to the best restaurant in town," or however he says it. "It's such a treat having you here," Gould says, driving him around, showing him the city. "But you're not interested in seeing things like the harbor and tulip garden and such, are you? I know I wouldn't be if I came to your area, except for the art museum, and all I could take there is an hour before I'd want to go to its coffee shop for coffee." "No, I came just to see you and your family, and maybe, while I'm here, your art museum also, but that's all." They say more, but what? Robert likes good wine and brings a few expensive bottles from Washington. That's where he lives, not California or wherever he said. Also gifts for the kids: books he thought they'd like—"I checked with Sally first to see what they've been reading"—and books for Sally and him that Robert had recently read and liked. "What are you reading these days?" Robert would say on the phone before he left to see them. ("'What books are you reading these days?' Robert had said," he means.) "We've got one of the best bookstores in America here, better and bigger than anything on the East

Coast. You looking for something you can't find there, just tell me. It's got everything, even rare ones mixed in with the new, and you're my brother and Sally's my sister-in-law, so don't worry about the cost." What else do they talk about when he gets here and on the phone? When they were young: their parents, friends, block, neighborhood, shared memories and same public school through the eighth grade and bar-mitzvah teacher who rapped their knuckles with a ruler or swatted their palms with a pointing stick. "Remember the time you hit me over the head with your violin?" Gould says. "Mom threw a fit and the damn thing split in two, ending your music lessons and putting a deep gash in my head, one of about a dozen scars I have there but the only one from you." "I never laid a finger on you like that," Robert says, "not in my whole life, so wrong brother, brother. At most we recurrently wrestled on our bedroom floor, all the furniture pushed back, till the tenant below complained about her chandelier shaking and the noise. But only like athletes wrestled, for the sport and fun and no one getting hurt." "You didn't always beat me either," Gould says. "And the older I got, the more evenly matched we became, till I was almost pinning you," and Robert says, "I was always bigger but you got stronger than me. But I stayed heavier and sweated more, which was the key. A tough shrimp, I called you, and then, a tough lobster." Gould flies to Washington to see Robert or because his work takes him there. Takes bottles of Spanish and Portuguese wine, paying much more for them than he ever paid for wine for Sally and himself, except on their wedding anniversaries. Takes a few books he read in the last few months. "You like to keep all your books and buy copies of the ones you liked for me, while I like to give mine away once I read them and to have an empty bookcase. In that respect, as Mom said, two brothers couldn't be more unalike, since according to her we were always that way. Make what you want of it, but I married a hoarder like you. Anyway, read these and tell me what you think. Or just start this one and say why you tossed it away. There are only five really good writers going at any one time in the world, and she's one of them." "That's ridiculous and so limiting, and being the reader you are I can't believe you think this, unless it's only your way of keeping your book costs down and your bookcases clean." "There are dead writers; dozens of really good ones." Meets Robert's new wife. Robert has three kids from his previous marriage, two from this one, twins. "What do you think," Robert said, "having a child when I'm well into my sixties?" and he said, "It's your business. But you got a young wife, so she must be pressuring you for kids. I'd do it, exhausted and strapped as it'd make me, if anything ever happened to Sally and I subsequently hooked up with someone so young, as I'm already feeling blue that in a few years my kids won't be around." Okay, lots of things about him are set, similarities and differences between them are shown, but what do they talk about? They just talk and the talk comes, when they're with each other or on the phone. "I saw a very fine movie the other day—" "I hate most movies; they're all such drivel and so commercial." "Not all, certainly not this one, and you used to like them." "There are plenty of things I used to like and no longer do. And not many things to replace what I used to like either. But I was being rude. What about the movie you saw?" "I was driving on the expressway, turned on the radio—" "I hope you haven't succumbed to a car phone yet, Robert." "Not even a microwave, though I know we'll end up getting both, but I already did get a PC. I'm a hoarder like you say, and it also helps me to get my creative juices flowing, though I doubt it'll ever appeal to you. Too technological, electrical, visual and cold-looking, and you can't pound away at the keys." "I like my writing machine to fight back and make noise, but not as if it's from the sound track of a cartoon. But I interrupted you before. I'm always doing that and you never do it to me. What did you hear on the radio?" "You're too world-weary, Gould. You were always a little morose, even as a kid, but nothing to the extent you are now. In that respect, and if Mom were alive she'd confirm it, you've changed and I haven't, so we were once the same but are now different." "No, no, me morose? It was you, my boy, only you. I was always Master Happy-go-lucky Face, usually up at the crack with a jolt and smile and bustling and smiling like that till bedtime, people said. Actually, not you either, as I think the folks said you were kind of a quiet kid but had a lovely disposition, lovely, and nothing in my memory change purse says otherwise, though there had to be times when you were moody and disagreeable; nobody could be that good. As for today, you're the same as you always were, I suppose, while I'm somewhat to a lot like you said. Maybe it's chemical, but I'll never take anything chemical to change it so long as it's not thoroughly doing me in." Robert writes long stories and short novels and gets most of them published by small houses for almost no payment, and very few reviews. He's retired, has a decent pension and some savings, and will soon be collecting Social Security, and his new wife comes from money and his first three kids are on their own, so he can afford to live fairly comfortably. For more than thirty years before, he worked as a newsman. That's how Gould got started in news. Took over Robert's weekend copyboy job in a newsroom in New York after Robert graduated from college and went to work on a Wyoming newspaper. Why Wyoming? He'd sent out lots of résumés, and it was the only place that offered him a reporter's job. Or Robert didn't graduate. Quit school in his senior year, or even his junior year, saying that on-the-job experience was infinitely better for his work than any college journalism courses and a degree. Later, Robert told him about a news job in D.C. when he was working there for a wire service. Then got him a job back in New York as a writer for a network radio news show he produced. When the show folded, he helped get him a job on a news magazine a friend of his edited. "After this, even if I hear of the job-of-a-lifetime for you, I'm not saying anything, as I don't want you becoming too dependent on me. You have to work the grapevine more, maybe even one day hear of a great job for me. But don't tell Dad. He doesn't know how capable you are; thinks of you as the family recluse and that it's my unending duty to look after you and especially, since you followed me into this profession, to keep you employed." He likes his brother's fiction but he isn't one of the five. No, that's stupid. Then what? "Best I don't show you my stuff," Robert said, "since I know how you feel about it. The water's lukewarm and not very bracing to swim in, and there's certainly no chance of your drowning, which I'd think is what you'd aim for in what you read. If I mixed the metaphors there and became uncharacteristically bleak, since I don't want to think of anything regarding you and drowning, it was because I thought I was losing my point. And you don't even let your wife see your stuff-in-progress or recently completed, so it'd seem needy and one-sided of me to ask you to read mine. The truth is, we're radically different in what we deal with and our approaches and techniques, so I doubt either of us could offer the other much useful criticism. Also the truth, or the way it looks to me: neither of us is really that remarkable at it and I don't think we'll ever be, sorry as I am to say it. We did too many other things for too long before we started taking this seriously, or that's the way it was with me. As for you, you just wore yourself out working at various hard jobs to be able to afford to do it—but it's just too much fun doing to quit, am I right?" "Same, same, but who knows that if you stopped doing it I might too. We were always so damn close," and Robert said, "Just normal; don't make us sound like freaks." The bath. They took them together once a week till Robert was ten and Gould was seven. Or eight and five—he forgets. He could call Robert to find out, but it's been so many years, he's probably forgotten too. Anyway, what's the difference? They were taking baths together long after most brothers their ages did. Their father wanted them to stop once Robert reached seven, or six, but Robert convinced him to let them continue. Their father liked to repeat the story, quoting the exact words he said Robert used. " 'Daddy,' this brainy kid of mine said—the other's brainy too. I'm not by bringing up what his older brother said trying to belittle him. But no kid of six ever had the ability to deliberate and exspritz the way Robert did—'Daddy, you have to understand it's safer, at Gould's age, for him to be in the tub with someone, and my being there lets you and Mommy do other things. He can get very rambunctious, and if nobody's watching he could drown. I also make sure he really soaps up his washrag and scrubs himself, which we all know he's too young to do if he's taking a bath alone.' " After a while the tub got too crowded for them. "This is getting uncomfortable," Robert finally said, standing up and stepping out of the tub a minute after he got in it. "I don't like sitting on my legs and wondering if half the water I'm washing myself with is your urine. From now on I'm taking showers and you can have the bath to yourself. Don't forget to wash behind and inside your ears and to clean your poophole and *pupik*." "I'm going to only take showers from now on too," Gould said, "but alone." "Alone, of course, what do you think I'm saying?" Robert took him to Ebbets Field to watch the Dodgers play. So? So the Dodgers were Robert's favorite team, and when Gould was old enough to be interested in baseball it seemed natural to him for them to become his. Robert once said, "Who you rooting for this season?" and Gould said, "The Dodgers, who else?" "You better or you're not my brother." The folks trusted Robert alone with Gould outside at an early age. Gould trusted him more than he did anyone else. Well, not more than he did his mother. He trusted them the same. Or maybe, after a certain age, he trusted Robert a little more than he did his mother. He'd put his hand in Robert's hand and let him take him anywhere. Same with his mother, but after a certain age he put his hand in Robert's more than he did hers. He went to more places with Robert than he did with her, and it was Robert's job to look after him and see he didn't get hurt or lost. He rarely held his father's hand. His father didn't put out his hand to hold as Robert and his mother did. He can't even remember holding it, while he can still remember what his mother's and Robert's hands felt like when he held them. He must have held his father's hand lots of times. When they crossed the street together, for instance, the few times they crossed one together when Gould was very young and needed to hold an older person's hand. He thinks they were almost always with Robert when they crossed the street, and his father usually said to Gould, "Hold your brother's hand. And both of you watch out for cars and keep your ears peeled in case I suddenly have to tell you something." He knows he held his father's hand when his father was in the hospital and dying, but that was much later. Robert was there too. A few times they sat on opposite sides of their father's bed and held a hand of his at the same time. Their father was in a coma and probably didn't feel them holding his hands, and he can't remember the feel of his father's hand then either. But to get back to Robert: he was always very smart, responsible, gentle, sensitive, and, as a young boy, precocious. Also, he never beat up on him once. He doesn't even remember Robert pushing him hard at any time or even shouting angrily at him, though he had to have, just as Gould had to have been angry at Robert lots of times when they were growing up, though he doubts he ever pushed him hard when he was angry. This was unusual, he heard, between brothers so close in age: that they never once got into a real fight. Anyway, Robert knew—at the age of ten, Gould thinks it was, but no younger; their folks never would have let him take a subway by himself or with Gould before then—how to get to Brooklyn from Manhattan to see these Dodger games. Their father, before leaving for work in the morning or, if he was leaving before they woke up, then did this the previous night: gave Robert enough cash for bleacher seats and a hot dog and soda apiece during the game and subway fare of course and a couple of nickels for Robert to tuck away someplace in case he needed to call him or their mother. But how'd Robert know how to get to Ebbets Field by subway? Gould couldn't help him. All he remembers doing is holding Robert's hand and being led from train to train and through lots of grimy passageways and up and down several stairways and then the short walk to the ballpark with hundreds of excited people from the aboveground Brooklyn subway station. Someone must have shown Robert the way a couple of times, or just once: Robert was that smart. But you don't let a kid that age go out there on his own the first time with just written directions: *Downtown Broadway local or express to Times Square, switch to the Brighton* or *Sea Beach* or *West End line* or whatever train from Manhattan went to Ebbets Field (he forgets which one did, and anyway the line names might have changed since then and maybe even the routes). Did their father take them there once and that was how Robert knew how to go? He doesn't remember that. He could ask Robert; he'd know because he was old enough then to remember something like that and he has a great memory for everything. Gould doesn't think his father ever took him to any sports event except the boxing matches at St. Nicholas Arena a couple of times. Robert did. Maybe their father took them by subway to the ballpark the first time, gave Robert directions how to get home, and left them there or went some other place in Brooklyn for three hours—his sister's on Avenue J—and picked them up after the game. Robert took him to hockey games at the old Garden on Sunday afternoons to see the New York Rovers play, a few college basketball games there too, again in the cheapest seats. "You're kids," their father used to say, "and your eyes are better than any adult's, even when you don't wear your glasses, so don't say you can't see from up there. When you get older and start earning your own money, you can buy better seats. But if you see from up there that some of the lower seats aren't being used, run down and grab them. Anybody questions you, just say you lost your tickets to these seats, and if you can't lie, then that you're sorry and you didn't know." Football games at Randalls Island and other places, the Milrose track meets at the Garden a few times, and lots of Saturday afternoon movies at local theaters, another thing his father never took them to. So? So nothing, he's just saying what Robert did for him then, how he filled in for his father, how close they were at the time and probably why they're still so close today. His father did once take the family to Radio City to see the premiere of *The Yearling*. He got passes from a friend of an executive there when the friend couldn't go. Robert and Gould weren't allowed to get anything from the concession stand, their father said. "You should have thought of your candy sooner, like when we got off the bus and passed a store. They jack up the prices like crazy in these theaters and I'm not going to be a chump and fall for it"—something like that, putting the blame on them a little—"and that junk also rots your teeth faster than anything but sugar cubes bitten down on whole. So it's one more reason you shouldn't have any: I don't want to stay up all night with you when your teeth start aching at one A.M." Robert bought a box of candy on the sly and secretly shared it with Gould during the darker scenes of the movie. Their father also took Robert and him to a play once. Again, free seats. They went into the lobby, his father asked the ticket taker to call the manager out—"Vic Bookbinder to see him"—the manager came, greeted his father "like a monkey's uncle," as his father liked to say, said something like "So these are your two boys. Nice-looking kids, and big; that's good," and showed them three seats way off to the right in a top side aisle in the orchestra and told them to enjoy the show. Musical or play version of *Alice in Wonderland* at a theater in Columbus Circle when there were still big theaters there. They took the Broadway trolley to it, or that was another trip downtown with their father for something, maybe to buy clothes, which they did once a year with him in fall or spring. No, for that they took the subway to 18th or 23rd Street and Seventh or Sixth Avenue where their father knew people who got them into wholesale houses where boys' clothes were made. Robert was a size "husky" and Gould wanted to be a husky too but was told he'd probably never be because he was too thin. Robert and he stood in the back of the trolley turning the nonfunctioning steering wheel as if they were operating the car. But does a trolley have a steering wheel? Why would it if it's on electrified rails? How does one operate a trolley car? They did something back there that was fun while their father read a newspaper folded into quarters and watched out for their stop. Maybe they only sat in the motorman's seat, if there was one, and pulled a long rod back and forth or kept their hands on it as if they were moving it around and pushed buttons and flicked levers on the dashboard. But he definitely remembers turning a steering wheel, with Robert mainly hogging it and the dashboard controls and seat. After the show Robert asked what he thought of it and he said he liked it, especially the stage tricks with see-through curtains and the wind blowing them from somewhere and the different-colored lights making the scenes turn from night to day and inside to out and sunshine to storm. "I thought it was pure crap, made for sissies and girls." "I didn't like it that much either, now that I think about it," Gould said. "But Alice was pretty and had a nice voice," and Robert said, "I hate blondies, and the most when they're so cutesy-piesy and tweety and sweet. They always look as if they have nothing to say, which might be why they sing so much. You're probably going to marry a blondie, then, and be bored your whole life with her. Anyway, don't tell Dad you didn't like the play; it might hurt his feelings." And *The Yearling.* "Don't tell Dad what you thought of it, because you know it was one of the dumbest and slowest pictures you ever saw. All about a geeky boy and baby deer. Who could care? And you know they only made it to get our tears." Robert took him to *Bambi.* Gould ducked under his seat when the fire started in the woods, or maybe it was when the mother got shot. "Don't be a sissy," Robert said, trying to pull him out by his collar. "Face life; this is what can happen, everything suddenly going from good to bad. And it's a long cartoon and the animals are talking, so it's not like there are real people and places up there. Nothing bad's now happening anyway. If it does, don't worry; your big brother's here to protect you." Gould came out. Soon the next frightening scene came, either Bambi's mother getting shot or the woods on fire and Bambi running from it. "Put your coat over your head if you can't take it; I'll tell you when the so-called scary part's over. But don't jump under the seat again. Chewing gum's there from the dirtiest mouths and all kinds of dried nose snot and other gook. Check your hair to see if any got in it and we have to go to the bathroom to wash it off. . . . That movie was for kids your age and younger," Robert said when they left the theater. "I'm never going to another cartoon movie again. From now on it's only real movies with older people saying and doing older things, even killing and kissing each other and rubbing their bodies together and having smart conversations and things like that. If I'm forced to buy an adult ticket, which you notice I had to today because I'm over twelve and big for my age so can't lie about it anymore, then I'm wasting my time with these silly kid things." "Then who'll I go with?" and Robert said, "By yourself or with a friend." "You're my friend," and Robert said, "You have others who are okay. Lookit, it's bound to happen one day, so start getting it through your head. Plenty of times you'll have friends you'll want to be with more than me, and before that I'll have mine. But we'll always be brothers—tell me how you can take that away. And like brothers do, unless one really cheated on the other with money or did something for the other to detest him for life, which will never happen to us, we'll see each other in the future and go to movies, but adult ones, and things like that, but not most of the time like it's been." "I understand that," Gould said, although he didn't get all of it. "You're right; that's what'll happen and makes lots of sense," but he worried about it, didn't want to split up from his brother like that. He loved being with him. People used to say he worshiped him. All right, his father said it, mostly to tease him, but a lot. When Robert was fourteen he got a job as a movie usher in a theater downtown. The Broadway, he thinks it was called. Some Saturday nights he didn't get home till one o'clock. Gould would wait up for him. "What are you waiting up for me for?" "I wanted to know how things went tonight and to make sure you got home." "Oh, get out of here, I'm a big guy. And I'm fast and I know what to say and it's only a few short stops on the subway. I don't need some noodging shrimp worrying about me. I'm sorry, I didn't mean that, because I actually appreciate your concern, but it makes working late at night worse. Then I feel I have to hurry home so you'll get back to sleep." A little explaining: Robert was always tall for his age and got the job because he told the theater manager he was eighteen. He was six feet by the time he was thirteen and grew another two to three inches. One night after he got home he told Gould he'd had a long chat with Charlie Chaplin in back of the orchestra when the movie was on. Gould had made Robert a grilled bacon and cheese sandwich the way he liked it, under the stove broiler with the bacon previously fried semicrisp and drained on paper napkins. Made one for himself the same way: white bread pretoasted a little, sandwich grilled open-faced and then lettuce, sliced tomatoes, mayonnaise, and bacon put on and the two sandwich halves placed together and cut diagonally.

The bacon actually put on during the last thirty seconds under the broiler and the cheese always Velveeta. They sat at the kitchen table eating the sandwiches and drinking milk. "How come? I didn't think he spoke," Gould said. "He does in this one because it's a new movie and everyone important in it speaks. He made it; produced, directed, wrote the music—the whole thing. *Monsieur Verdoux.*" "What's that mean?" "The title: it stands for Mister something, the name of the character he plays. He's a murderer who locks up and kills his wives. Based on Bluebeard. So maybe it means murderer or Bluebeard in French. How would I know? I take German in school. Or it could be Bluebeard's last name, if he was a real person, or his real last name in a book if it comes from a made-up story. Tonight was the first time it played in America. It was a big news event too because this is supposed to be Chaplin's chance for a comeback here. He seemed so nervous. Paced back and forth in back, smoked when he wasn't supposed to be smoking there, but I wasn't going to tell him not to, which I would with anyone else. He was worried if the audience liked it and asked me what I thought. I said it sounds like they do and he said he's only heard little titters, no large unified laughing, he called it. The critics will take this as a sign that nobody likes it, he said, and they'll call it a major bomb. I said so far I haven't heard anything but good things from people who have passed me. 'Why are they leaving early then?' he said. 'It has to mean they didn't like it.' I said some people have to get home early, or maybe they were going to the bathrooms downstairs. 'People go together to them?' he said. 'They can't go alone to urinate during a movie? No,' he said, 'I'm afraid you're wrong, young man; they were walking out.' And then, what did *I* think of the movie? 'Be frank,' he said. 'Don't try to fool or flatter me.' I told him I saw it twice already and it was very funny and interesting and well made, when I really thought it was boring, stupid, and slow and the other actors were all bad in it and the movie in one word stunk and I wouldn't pay a quarter to see it, not a dime. He said, 'Thank you for your honesty,' when I wasn't being honest. Or maybe he saw I wasn't and knew I was being polite while at the same time making it obvious to him what I thought. 'But in spite of your good review,' he said, 'I'm still worried about the movie's fate.' I said, 'Listen, probably the worst thing you can do is stand here listening to every minuscule reaction from the audience and getting comments on the movie from people who don't know much. I'm sure if you leave now or just stay calm and relaxed while you're here, you'll pick up all the newspapers in the morning and find the movie got four stars from critics who know.' He said, 'The truth is, the reviews are written already,' and called me a smart fellow—smart, no doubt, because I knew the right things to say to keep him from getting more upset. Then he patted my shoulder and left the back of the orchestra soon after that, but not outside, unless he left through another door but the lobby exit, and most likely not because of my presumptuous advice either. He's very short, you know, and old-looking, with white hair and bad teeth," and Gould said, "I can tell about his height from all his movies." "You're taller than him already, or maybe a couple inches shorter, so you will be taller." "Maybe it's good in some ways to stay short; look how famous and popular he is, even with his bad teeth," and Robert said, "I don't want a brother who's that much shorter than me. It'd look peculiar; people wouldn't even think we're related. They'd always be saying things when they'd see us together: 'You two are brothers? You don't look much alike: one's a half foot taller than the other and you're both fully grown.' This is in the future, I'm talking here. Do what I did and keep saying you're going to be tall, with me it was 'very tall.' And harp on it to yourself and eat the right foods—I'll give you my food plan I kept to for years—and sleep a lot and do stretching exercises like hanging from overhead bars, and you'll be tall, I guarantee it, but probably no more than six feet." Robert was six inches taller than their father, who said he was the second tallest boy in his high school graduation class and played for his college basketball team. But that was then, when if you were five-ten you made center. Robert was better than he at everything, or Gould thought he could be if he tried whatever Gould was doing. He got into an elite public high school, excelled in all his subjects, was first-string end on its pretty good football team, and was also on the swim team and held an all-city record for some backstroke race for a few weeks. Fixed their radios and toasters, did some of the plumbing when the super didn't come, tuned and oil-changed the family car, could read a two-hundred-page book in two hours and memorize a sonnet in a minute and pull out hundreds of great appropriate quotations from his head. But where was Gould in this? Waiting up for his brother on weekends. Setting his alarm clock for twelve-thirty so he wouldn't seem tired when Robert came home at one. "Mommy says you shouldn't take the subway home so late," Gould said. "That the buses stop a block from your theater and go right up Broadway." "And wait in the cold or rain a half hour, for that's how long it usually takes? Don't worry your little pointy head, I'll be okay." They called the grilled bacon and cheese sandwich "à la Roberto." "I can make an à la Roberto for you if you want," Gould would say when his brother came back from ushering, "and you won't have to eat alone. I'll have one too." "No, thanks, just a grilled bacon and cheese sandwich, please." "They're the same thing," he said, the first time Robert said this, and Robert said, "No joke, bumbo. Boy, when they made wooden heads yours must've been mahogany." "Why mahogany?" They went to camp together for two summers. The counselors voted Robert all-around camper and best athlete the first year. Gould got a part in the big camp musical at the end of the summer, and after it, backstage, while Gould was wiping his makeup off, Robert said, "You really made me proud tonight. Even with that small role you stole the show with your acting and singing. Everyone in the audience thought so," and he said, "Sure, you talked to everyone. Come on, nobody noticed me." "No, I overheard them whispering during it—the parents—'Who is that kid, who is that kid? He's a standout, a natural.' You're the ham of the family and I'm the bacon and grilled cheese. I could never in a hundred years sing as well as you did. When I was standing in back for a few minutes I heard your voice in the chorus soaring above everyone else's," and he said, "Now I know you're lying; I don't project at all." The girls loved Robert. There was talk he was actually getting laid by a junior counselor named Gloria who was two years older than him. Someone claimed to see a rubber drop out of Robert's wallet. He was fishing in it for money to pay for a soda at the camp's canteen when it happened. "'Well, look at this,' he was supposed to have said," a bunkmate of Gould's told him. "Smiled, knowing everyone knew it was his, and nonchalantly picked it up, looked it over, and said, 'Must have fallen to the ground out of some guy's wallet or even a girl's pocket. And for all the little kids to see? That isn't nice. But still in its package and never used. Well, waste not, want not, and all that other cloddy stuff and stocky clichés about rainy days with nothing to do,' and stuck it in his change pocket." Another rumor had it that Robert and Gloria were caught on a blanket in the woods by some girl campers cutting through. "Gloria with her top off and boobs showing," someone in Gould's division told him, "and your brother with his swimsuit around his knees and a stiff dick a mile long. The head counselor called your parents to tell your brother to behave or he'd be asked to leave." Robert was a camper-waiter then. Gould asked him later that day outside the mess hall, "Does Uncle Walt want you to leave camp?" and Robert said, "Who told you that?" "I heard, I don't want to say where because I don't want to get anyone in trouble." "And if I twist your arm back till it's about to come off?" and he said, "Then I'd tell you, but then you'd be using brute force." "Of course I won't do that, and it's not important who told anyway. It's over a counselor—you've seen me with her: Gloria Mendelowitz, a real dish—but it's all worked out. I promised Walt I'd make sure to use a prophylactic. Just kidding ya. That we weren't doing anything but the normal girl-boy horseplay, deep kissing and heavy petting of each other's backs, and from now on we won't even hold hands if anyone's around." "And the folks were called?" "Ah, easy as raising kittens. Dad told me I'm too young to get entwined and that my life would be screwed up if there was an accident, and Mom said to always remember to be respectful to the young lady and discreet about the situation." "That's good; it wouldn't be the same here if you left." Discreet, he thought after. There wasn't a dictionary in the whole camp; he knew even without looking. He could have asked Robert what it meant but wanted him to think he knew so Robert could always use words like that and talk about serious things with him. So he asked his counselor—"I got it out of a book I'm reading; I think it means slow"—and the guy said it could be but he didn't know. The next summer Robert worked as a waiter in the guest dining room of another camp. He visited Gould's camp on one of his days off. Both were on the Delaware, Robert's near Stroudsburg and Gould's across the river in Flatbrookville, New Jersey. How'd Robert get to Gould's camp? By hitching to Bushkill and then rowing a boat down the Delaware from the Bushkill landing and later rowing it back up? But there were rapids in between the landing and camp—Gould had canoed through them with a counselor and another camper—so a tough trip to make for just one guy, even Robert, who was a strong seventeen-year-old at the time and knew how to row and canoe. And how would he have got the boat, rent it? Doesn't remember any renters of boats or canoes near the landing. But he came that day in a sport jacket and good pants, so he didn't do any arduous rowing, he's almost sure. ("Arduous," another word he first heard from Robert.) He probably took a couple of buses and ended up in a town near Gould's camp—Newton, for instance—and then took a taxi or called someone he knew in camp to come get him by car. Or a couple of people from camp might have rowed or canoed up to the landing to get him and then taken him back. He thinks he asked Robert that day how he got there and was told but forgot. Next time he speaks to him he'll ask again and he's sure Robert will remember. Actually, he's not so sure, since Robert's memory for small things like that a long time back isn't as good as his. There: something he can do better than Robert and, he thinks, always could. If he asks, though, Robert might say—it'd be like him; he often doesn't answer the question right away but asks why you asked—"Why's it important? What've you got going that you want that information?" In words like that—bordering on the suspicious—and Gould would say, "Because it suddenly popped up, I don't know from what, after more than forty-five years, and I wanted to get it straight in my head because I'm interested in the particulars of one's journey and family history and stuff like that. And also, let's face it, as Mom liked to say—and both of us always seem to say, 'as Mom liked to say,' and, while she was alive, 'as Mom likes to say,' after we say that let's-face-it phrase—I'd also like to know if you came more to see Gloria than me, since she was working as a counselor there: Gloria Mendelowitz, your big love then"—if he asks, "Who's she?" which, with all the women he's known since he was thirteen, he might very well say—"or as much as or more to see me? But you probably can't remember that." "Don't push your luck," Robert might say, "as, let's face it, Mom never used to say, for you might find my memory's absolutely lucid on this matter, and I didn't come at all to see you." In fact, it all comes back. Robert hitched the entire way to Gould's camp and got a ride back from someone there he knew from the previous year. And he definitely only came to see Gloria. She'd got a few hours off to spend with him; it had been prearranged weeks in advance with the girls' head counselor, Robert told him that day: "They gave the okay only if she swore to stay on camp grounds and no empty cabins or woods with me." He first saw Robert—had no clue he was coming—when he strode into the mess hall while the whole camp was eating lunch. "Robert, Robert," Gould yelled, "over here!" (And "strode" sounds too—well, something: vigorous, decisive, self-possessed, almost pushy, while his walk was usually slow and shuffling. "Cool" and "composed" would be good words for it, but he's talking about a walk so he's sure he can find one better, like that "vigorous," et cetera, business.) Several counselors and waiters from the previous year went up to him, shook his hand, punched his upper arms, clutched the back of his neck or pretended to, actions like that and lots of good-to-see-you's and laughs. "Hey, there's my big brudder," Robert said, when Gould got permission to leave his table and went over to him. "What're you doing here—you lose the job at your camp?" and Robert said, "As I was telling them, it's my day off, so I hitched." Gould said he could probably get an hour or two to be with him, and that's when Robert said he mainly came to see Gloria: "You, you little stiff, I can see all year in the city. She I get to see once or twice a year when she visits New York or if I'm willing to shell out the dough for a train to Philly. So if you don't mind, and if your feelings won't be too hurt? And quick," he whispered, putting his arm around his shoulder and walking him away from the others, "before she can hear us, have you seen her with any other guys?" and Gould said, "I never thought to look. Should I have?" Just then Gloria came over, big smile at Robert, took his hand and said, "Hiya, peanut," which sounded so stupid to Gould and in some ways an insulting nickname to his brother. What an idiot she must be, he thought, good looks and great body as she's got, and Robert said, "We're going to take a walk, Gould, see ya later," but he never did. He was hurt but he understood. Robert wants to be with a girl whom he's probably already laid, so today he can at least kiss and pet and stuff like that and maybe even get more. Would he do the same if Robert were his younger brother and Gloria was his girlfriend and everything else was the same: hitching a ride here and so on? Probably, sure, but he would have been nicer about it and also not dumped him so fast. He would have spent an hour with him, then gone off with Gloria. Said, "Gloria, listen, I haven't seen my baby brother in a month and I want to catch up on things with him." Or taken her off to the side and said, "Hey, he'll be hurt if I don't spend some time with him, so I have to.

We'll still have a few hours." Or said to them both, "Let's the three of us sit outside and catch up on what we've been doing." For an hour. That would have softened it a lot for Gould, even made the whole thing totally understandable: hour for him, two to three for her, what could be more reasonable? "Was that so bad?" Robert could have said to her after. "Was that really so bad? He's a good kid. And let's face it, he adores me and always has." He thinks he cried when Robert left the mess hall with Gloria. Or just felt like crying, with that tight feeling in the throat and sore eye rims and so on. "What're you crying for?" he thinks one of the boys said when he got back to the table. Or: "Are you about to cry about something? You look it. Your brother say something lousy to you?" "None of your business," he thinks he said. That fall Robert started NYU, or maybe it was the next fall. That's right: Robert was three years older than Gould but only two years ahead of him in school. That was because Gould skipped a year in the fifth grade. Robert could have skipped also—skipped every other year, he was so smart—but the Board of Education that year was only skipping students in the fourth and fifth grades to relieve the overcrowding in the school system. Something like that. Gould knows it wasn't because he was that smart: about a third of the entire grade skipped with him. And his timing of the camp incident's a little off. He had to be thirteen when it happened, since at fourteen he became a camper-waiter there himself. So again Robert must have got the job by claiming to be a lot older than he was. When Robert was a college freshman he started working on the school newspaper and quickly decided he wanted to be a journalist. A number of years later he said to Gould, "Don't give yourself airs. No real newsman calls himself a journalist. You're a reporter or newsman or news editor or whatever it is you do." When Gould learned of Robert's future job plans he thought maybe that'd be a good thing for him to become too. He went out for his high school newspaper but all he could get was the assistant business manager position, so he quit in a few weeks. He remembers one of Robert's articles, which won some kind of college national journalism award. It was on underground streams in Greenwich Village, all of them having names like Mill Stream and Beaver Creek and Indian Run. So what's that got to do about anything? Well, it's when he thinks Robert first got interested in writing fiction. The article said that sometimes the streams break through basement walls and the owners or supers of these buildings, while they're cleaning up, have found that Indian artifacts have been washed in with the water: clay shards, beads, arrowheads, once even a small decorated leather sack with tiny bones in it and another time a necklace made out of some animal's teeth and jawbone. He asked Robert—"I'm sorry if I sound suspicious, but I think not to mention it would be even worse"—if that part of the article had been made up to make it more interesting, since otherwise it would have been a rather bland piece, and Robert said, "What a charge! You dumb enough to think I'd jeopardize my future journalism career by doing something so unethical? I did hours of research on it and conducted more than thirty interviews, practically went door-to-door in one mews," and Gould said, "You don't give any names or addresses of people who claim to have found these things," and Robert said, "They all asked me to withhold them because they didn't want amateur Indianologists traipsing through their basements and subcellars looking for this junk." "Do you have notes, then?" and Robert said, "Not to show you. To someone who trusts me implicitly, yes." "And you'd think you would have had a few photographs of these artifacts in the article instead of just maps where the streams were and old etchings of Indians of that era," and Robert said, "Talk to the editor. As for me, I didn't take a camera with me, not that I know much about shooting objects like that. I also doubt any of these people would have let me take photographs. They were wary of even speaking to me; besides that, most of the stuff had been given or sold or they were planning to sell it to the American Indian Museum and places like that, and I hear these museums charge you to photograph their collections." "Oh, gee, how convenient all of that is, though for some odd reason I'm not quite believing it," and Robert said, "Who asked you to? And what got into you to suddenly drill me like this? From now on don't read my work and keep your two cents to yourself." "Will do, sir, will do," and saluted him. That was probably their worst argument ever—or one of, since how would he know which one was the worst unless they had once had it out with their fists, which they never did?—and because of it the only time they intentionally didn't speak to each other for a couple of days, or one of the two to three times they didn't. Considering how some brothers that close in age have fought and cursed each other furiously, that wasn't so bad. How did they finally start talking again that time? One of them, he forgets which, said, "Hey, let's bury the hatchet"—said, of course, something like this—and the other said, "And as the old joke goes, and so appropriate for our argument, not in the other's head, right?" and they both laughed, and one of them said, "Good, done, brotherly brothers again," and they shook hands, he doesn't recall whose stuck out first. By then Robert had plenty of close friends and a number of girls he was seeing and hardly palled around with him anymore, and Gould had a few good friends too. But they ate at home most nights so saw each other at the dinner table and slept in side-by-side beds till Robert quit school and got a news job out of town. Robert snored all his life and almost every night. (So does Gould's wife, but periodically, and the same kind, phlegmy or full of snot, but she stops when he nudges or asks her to and pulls the covers from over her head, and usually doesn't resume snoring that night.) When Gould got tall enough to extend his foot from his bed to Robert's he used to poke him with his toes. "What?" and Gould would say, "Your snoring's keeping me up." "Don't kick me from now on, okay?" "I only tapped you with my big toe; I thought it'd stop your snoring without waking you." "Just keep your feet off and especially don't jab my kidneys; you don't want to be blamed for my losing one." Then Robert would go back to sleep and soon start snoring again. Gould would poke him with his toes a little lighter, and Robert would say, "What?" and the whole thing would start over, with Robert often saying drowsily, "Maybe I'm dreaming or something but didn't I just tell you to keep your fat feet to yourself?" and Gould would eventually fall asleep between snorings. Robert also smoked in bed, the smell keeping Gould up. "Could you please not smoke?" and Robert would say, "I like to when I read. One of life's greatest pleasures, those two together, and if you could add a cup of coffee, even better, so don't deny me it." "Maybe you could stop reading and turn out the light and not smoke in the dark and I could get some sleep." "I'm not ready yet." "Then please, just put out the cigarette? You know I'm allergic to it. You've seen how I wave the smoke away even when Mom and Dad smoke, and how I've gotten carsick in the car when someone smokes in it." "You're not allergic; and you only fake getting sick because you don't like it. But you can't stop people from doing everything you don't like, particularly when it's as normal a human activity as smoking." "I *am* allergic; I do get sick. I can't breathe, or not very well with it. Isn't it elementary to you that the smoke reduces the oxygen in the room, just like the smoke from a fire does? Why do you think people get asphyxiated in one?" "It's the fire that takes away the oxygen, not the smoke. But for you, my brother, I'll open the window a few more inches while I smoke," and Gould would say, "It'll be too cold and I'll have to get up for another blanket and I'm too tired to. Please, Robert, be a sport," and Robert would say, "I'm sorry, but if you don't like my smoking or a cold room, sleep on the living room couch." "That couch is a sofa and too small to sleep on." "Then start putting up with my smoking. I smoke, therefore I smoke." "What's that supposed to mean? If you think it's philosophy or a joke from it, you're wrong." "It means I'm the elder brother and I have more prerogatives here than you, like smoking in the room that before you were wheeled into it in your crib was singly mine." "Oh, that's just such utter you-know-what shit. Smoke, go on, smoke your smoking head off. But before you turn off the light and go to sleep will you please get rid of the butts in the ashtray on our mutual night table? In fact, put the ashtray someplace else, like out of the room, and the butts into the toilet, if you don't mind. I can't stand the foul odor of either of those." "If I think of it and don't mind getting up, I will. But not out of the room, just to the dresser over there and the butts into the trash basket." "What a nice brother"—turning over and moving his face as close to the wall as he could and burrowing his nose into the pillow. "You said it," Robert would say. "The best; not one grown on trees. So for you, tonight, I will or I only might put this cigarette out now and chuck the butts and move the ashtray over there and maybe even wipe it clean and get rid of the cleaning rag before I shut out the light, though don't think I'm starting a precedent. It's only because I recently read not to smoke for a minimum of ten minutes before I doze off or else I could have horrific dreams and even do minor damage to my precious testes." "I never heard of that, but it's probably true." Robert did most of his recreational reading in bed. Gould often read in his bed at the same time and was interrupted by Robert a lot—"Listen to this part"—and Gould would say, "I'm reading." "So stop, because this, if anything I've read, is pure literature," and Gould would say,

"Maximum of thirty seconds, please; I'm really engrossed in my book." Robert would count the lines or take a guess and say, "Minute and a half, and that's at full throttle, so not faithful to the rhythm and words," and he'd read: Dostoyevsky, Tolstoy, Gogol, Turgenev, Leskov, Chekhov, Herzen, Babel. He'd read nothing but the Russians and Thomas Mann since he was fourteen. He'd say, "You have to read this book, no two ways about it. When I'm done with it, which I will be in an hour, and if you're not asleep, I want you to put yours aside and take up mine. Believe me, you won't regret it." Very often the book Gould was reading was one Robert had passed along and the one he had put down to start this one was a book Robert had also convinced him to give up another one of Robert's for. "It'll be overdue at the library before you finish it, but don't worry; I'll pay the fine. Just so you don't dash through it and ruin what could be one of the sublime reading experiences of your life. Because if you're like me—and in many ways you are, but not like you copycat—you only read a book once and know it instinctively from then on." What's he saying here? That if it hadn't been for Robert, regarding literature and art—well, what he said. "I don't understand this part," Gould would often say from his bed, and Robert would rest his head back on his pillow, close his eyes, the book he'd been reading laid face down on his chest, and say "Read," and Gould would read, invariably a book Robert had urged on him, and Robert would say, "That means . . ." He knew or made sense as if he knew, every time. He was a sharper reader and also able to articulate what he thought much better than Gould. Well, he was older. But he was always like this, always, in reading and listening, so that's the way he was. Even today Gould calls Robert periodically to say, "There's a passage in this book you sent me" or "told me to get," or they can be talking on the phone about other things and Gould will bring it up. Robert said, one of these times, "We've been talking so long, I forget who called whom," and when Gould said, "I called you," he said, "Then read it to me, languidly as you want and I don't care how long the passage is—I'm only kidding, because if there's anything you know I'm not, it's a cheapskate, especially with you." Were all these books worth reading? How could they be? Then most? That word again, which was originally Robert's: invariably, but he rarely told him the ones he couldn't plow through or just didn't like.

Why not? Because he liked them to talk about things that interested them rather than didn't. Not true. He didn't want Robert thinking him a simpleton or someone of little taste, and Robert had a way of knocking down his arguments that made him feel like a kid. So what would he say if Robert asked what he thought of that book? "It was good, perhaps not as good as some of the others you gave me, but definitely worth my time." Robert saw through it and didn't persist, probably because he knew Gould didn't want to get into an argument over it, and in fact he usually said, "I've just finished another one you might like better. Game for it or had your fill?" and he'd say, "Sure, right now I've nothing to read, since I just finished the one you gave me." He ever give or suggest to Robert a book he's read and liked? For reasons just mentioned, few, usually contemporary American ones he was somewhat enthusiastic about, and for almost all of them Robert said things like "Instantly forgettable, practically unreadable, a potboiler masquerading as a boiling pot, MFM (made for movies), or NN again (nothing new). Could be I've become too demanding, always wanting a book to do something to me that's never been done. It's what I like to do with my own junk, though it doesn't seem to have done it to you, while this one has, to a degree. As another writer said, possibly the cleverest and most intelligent and stylish thing he ever wrote but which still wasn't much, 'If it doesn't clutch you by the larynx and leave you speechless and with contusions on your neck'—I forget the rest," and Gould once said, "That's hardly the trenchant criticism I've come to expect from you, even if I never give it about the books you have me read," and Robert said, "All right: it was crap, exactly like the last one you foisted on me, so why waste time talking about it when there are better things to do, like reading books worth discussing?" So what's he saying here? That he probably became too picky and critical of most writing because of Robert all these years? Yes, why not, yes, for want of a more satisfying conclusion. (Oh, he hates the way he said that but doesn't want to stop to reword it.) There was a woman friend of Robert's whom Gould met on the street. She stopped in front of him, put her arms out, blocking him from getting around her, and smiled and said, "Robert, what's come over you?" and he said, "Oh, I see. I'm Gould, Robert's brother, if you're referring to Robert Bookbinder," and she said, "That's right, I met you with him once at a party. How are things, and how's Robert?" He didn't remember ever meeting her and said, "I'm fine, Robert's probably doing even better than that, as he's on a news assignment overseas in his favorite city." "The resemblance is remarkable. Same kind of hair, thin, but the way it waves. Unblemished skin, dark troubled intellectual eyes, wide-awake face, belligerent mannerisms about to erupt but always contained," and he said, "That's neither of us. We're just a coupla pinheads, except mine's got a few more scars on the scalp and he's better looking and a bit brighter, politer, and taller by about three feet." She said, "Not on your life. Stand with your back to me," and he did, their buttocks touching, and she skimmed her hand off the top of her head to his, and said, "You're the same height as he, or shorter by half an inch. So, long as I can't get Robert to have coffee with—now there's a conversationalist; I invariably walk away jittery with excitement and ready to tear down all sorts of metaphorical walls—how about you?" "Before I answer, was he the first person to say the word 'invariably' to you? He was to me," and she said, "Don't be silly. My mother said I learned to talk early and it was the first word I used." Coffee at a nearby café. "We've been here before, you know, and same waitress," and he said, "You must mean my brother," and she said, "Of course. We were here numerous times. We called it our serious-talk place. But funny you and I should meet, after more than a year, practically in front of it," and he said, "I live a block away, and again, you must have me confused with Robert." She kept referring to him as Robert too. "I read the book you gave me, Robert, and loved it," and he said, "Which one was that?" "Tell me about your recent work, Robert," and he said, "Gould, not a common given name, so how can you constantly forget it?" and she said, "Easy. Don't get upset. That, so far, is the only thing that distinguishes you from him. But when I see you I see Robert. You're like identical twins, and when you sit that half-inch difference disappears. And your voices, weak *r*'s, even, and way you both nervously blink." Asked him about people she and Robert knew. "Listen, you got it wrong again. I'm not Robert. Just look at my clothes. He's always impeccably dressed, would never wear jeans. I'm pretty much of a slob. So remember that. Slobbiness: Gould. Nattiness: Robert. But Robert with mussed hair, mismatched, sullied clothes, granules still cornered in his eyes, an unshaven mess? He'd never leave his apartment like this, even if he'd just woken up, as I had, and was in a rush to the store for a pound of coffee and bottle of aspirins." "True. The most immaculate man I know, but not in a squeamish or ultraprissy way. Just neat and clean. Washes his hands often and almost sacramentally. Can you explain that? You're his brother. Fingernails groomed flawlessly and never protruding over the fingertips by more than a tiny bit. His hands always smell so nice, though, as if from cologne, but actually from French soap. He carries a special bar with him wherever he goes. Movie theater men's rooms, for instance: squirt their goo into his palms? *Please.* Nothing but his own, not that I was ever in there with him to witness it. He said and I believed. Let me smell your hands." "I don't carry soap around with me and neither does Robert." "He showed me, in an intricate silver box he also bought in France," and she took his hands. "Soft. You have the face of a farmer and the clothes of a garbageman but hands like a patrician," and he said, "My hands are rough and cracked, probably from cleaning my floors with ammonia without wearing rubber gloves, something I'm sure Robert never does: clean his own floors and toilet bowls and such." "I don't do this with everyone, you know, just comparison hand-smelling today," and smelled his hands. "You're not a slob; they're fragrant and clean. The soiled clothes and unkempt appearance are no doubt to put off muggers and panhandlers. And sensuous, curious, and inventive"—pointing to various lines on his palm—"just like Robert. And here's one you'll like: long life, though at this juncture here it says you'll be spending a few hours with a foot model tonight. My hotel's quaint, though the room's creepy, but I'll order in anyway as I only have a hot plate. It's been more than a year since I've seen you, so we've got a lot . . ." but move on and get to the point. Knew he was going to sleep with her that night. He asked what a foot model does—"Just feet?"—and she said they must be perfect and she'd show him later: not only her own feet but fashion photos of them with ankle bracelets, rings on her toes, toenails being polished, calluses being treated, but mostly her feet in sandals and open-toed shoes. The idea intrigued and troubled him. To sleep with someone Robert had slept with and would probably sleep with again? Would she compare them? She did. After sex, while they were lying in bed and she was smoking this smelly cigarillo—"I thought you liked them" when he waved away the smoke; "last time, you asked to try one and then practically smoked down the pack," and he thought, Last time where? Here when she was with Robert? In the café with me when she didn't smoke?—she said, "How peculiar, one brother uncircumcised and the other cut," and he said, "So you've been with him? Then you must've done it in the dark. The whole family's been ritualized, or should I say 'slaughtered,' except my mother and the girls," and she said, "You have sisters?" and he said, "I was only—," but move on. "One not too noteworthy sidelight, probably. He's bigger than you by a good inch or two and several ounces, though he's a horse," and he said, "That could be true when he's tumescent. In all my years of sleeping in the same room with him, taking baths together—we only did that till he was seven or eight, so it doesn't count—but seeing him slip in and out of showers and towel himself off and put on pajamas and so forth, I've never seen him even semihard and I'd like to keep it that way." "I wasn't complaining about you, you know. I'm not small by any culture's standards, but his could become difficult to endure, so in some ways you could say I prefer yours." They made love again, and this time at the end she said, "Robert, Robert, Robert." There could have been so many reasons for her saying it—she was kidding him? no, not at that point; it made her more excited, et cetera—that he didn't bring it up. He was with her just that once. Thought of calling her a month after that when he felt desperate for sex but then thought, No, it's too crazy, and those awful cigarillos. Next time they met was in the neighborhood bakery, and he said hi and she said, "I forget your name but I know your brother's. How are you and how is he? Oops"—looking at the wall clock and grabbing her purchase—"tell me next time; I've got to run." He said to Robert a few days later, "I forgot to tell you. I met a friend of yours," and gave her name. "In fact that was the second time we met—actually, the third. But all three times she kept mistaking me for you and even addressed me as Robert," and Robert said, "But we look nothing alike: height, build, face, hair. Same coloring—eyes and skin—and some bald patches appearing in identical places, but that's about it. What'd you make of her?" and he said, "She seemed a bit goofy, maybe because she could never get who I was and my name straight, but okay." "She's deceptively intelligent, deeply so. And a good artist, I'm told; models lingerie for a living, so no doubt has a great slim figure." "Feet," he said she said, and

Robert said, "Then great slim feet. Thinking of calling her or something? I think she lives in a hotel near you, so it shouldn't be too hard getting her number," and he said, "I thought of it. But then, for a variety of reasons not worth going into, didn't think it a good idea," and Robert said, "What were they?" and he said, "Really, nothing, trivial, minor," and Robert said, "Ah, you're probably better off." But he's gotten too far ahead. Robert, till he graduated elementary school, walked him to it every day. (He wants to leave it that way? At least "grade" for "elementary," and "walked with him there every day.") At first Robert was told to hold Gould's hand when they crossed the street on the way to school and back. They must have done that till Gould finished third grade. "Only start crossing the street when the light turns from red to green, not when it's already been green even by a second," their mother told them. "Either of you know why?" and they both knew but Gould let Robert say it. "And start from when you're on a sidewalk corner. Don't jaywalk or wait in the street for the light to turn, I don't care if you're only two inches from the curb. And both of you hold on tight to your brother's hand and never let go till you're up on the other sidewalk. I ever see you crossing the street together not holding hands, you'll hear it big from me. If there's one thing I insist on, this is it. Losing one of you would be terrible enough, but just think what would happen if I lost you both at once." Gould, when he wants, can still feel Robert's hand around his—but hasn't he gone over this?—and his mother's hand but not as much his father's, Robert's the smallest and tightest. He was also going to say "the softest"; he forgets what he said about it before, but it's not true: his mother's was. Lots of times they stopped at a candy store on the way home from school, never to. Their mother, the morning or night before, must have always given Robert money to buy them sodas. A certain orange drink drunk straight from the bottle was the only soda Robert got at this store for a long time, while Gould liked cream soda of any kind, with two straws in the bottle. So what's he saying here? Just move on. Robert always stuck up for him. Now this could be showing something. A big kid from another block was once threatening Gould on the sidewalk, he forgets what for, and suddenly Robert was running out of their building and up the areaway steps and over to them and without saying a word shoved the boy so hard that he fell against a stoop and hit his head. Robert must have been looking out their front window on the second floor—not "must have"; this is what he later told Gould—and seen from their gestures and expressions that Gould was being picked on and knew that if they got into a fistfight—because he was sure Gould would defend himself rather than back off, something Gould had once said he'd do because he knew that's what Robert would—he wouldn't stand a chance against this guy. "Come on, you want to mix it up with someone, how about me?" and the boy said, "You're too big and I already got a bloody head, so it wouldn't be fair." "And starting with this little shrimp, compared to you, is fair? Look, nobody can order you to stay off this block, so just get lost," and the boy said, going, "I'm getting my older brother after you—he's twice your size," and Robert said, "Oh, yeah, older brothers, we all have them. We've got two much bigger older brothers who'll mash your older brother's face in and, as a gift for getting him, mash in yours." Later at home, Robert said—neither the boy nor anyone resembling his brother came around after that, or not while they were there—"Whatever I might have told you about fighting before was a lie or I said it in an unclear way. I don't like fighting, and for sure not if the guy's much bigger than me or just a musclebound ox. Then I'd talk or walk my way out of it, because I wasn't born to get prematurely mauled or killed. I also wouldn't feel anything but rotten if I hurt someone, as I did a little with that kid." "You're only saying that to keep me from getting hurt. But what if my life or Mommy's or Daddy's was at stake, you saying you wouldn't jump in?" and Robert said, "For those reasons only, or if my own life was at stake but I was trapped with no escape. But none of that was the case with you today. Jesus, I can't wait till you grow up completely so I won't think I have to help you out every time," and Gould said, "You will anyway, unless it'd turn an uneven match into an even more uneven one, but I'll think over what you said," and Robert said, "No, you won't. You're just being clever, using words, which you should have done with that kid. I'm through with you. From now on you're on your own, or at least don't get into these things by the window where I can too easily see you." One time later on Gould was drunk at a bar and the bartender called Robert and said, "You want to come get your stupid brother? He's being a stiff pain in the ass and we're about to dump him into the street." Robert ran to the bar and got Gould into a cab, though it was only two blocks from home. Next day he said, "Why do you want to get so soused? Bad for your liver and bad for your soul, and everybody there thought you were a prize putz. You also leave yourself wide open to thieves. I don't want to be lifting your face out of the toilet anymore, in case you forgot that, do you hear me? Because did you—did anybody—ever have to do that for me?" "No. And as for 'anybody'—" "So why do you drink so much?" and he wanted to say, Because when I was three I lost my one and only older brother and it screwed me up in a way I can't explain. That would have got a laugh—or not—and Robert would have said, "What's that supposed to mean? You trying to be clever with words again? Well, it's not working. Or is there a hidden meaning behind it you're trying to tell me? You lost him—meaning me—in the sense that you were once very close, if I remember—we were—playing all the time together and doing things like that, but he gradually grew away from you as older brothers tend to do," and he would have said, "I meant nothing by it. I'm still hung over. Not still, totally, so not responsible for my words, and if I happened to sound calculating, it was just luck." "So answer me a simple question then, one that shouldn't be too taxing: why do you drink so much?" and he said, "I can't answer that right now. As I said—didn't I just say it? I seem to remember I did—my whole body feels like hell and my mind's a blank spot." "So don't anymore, that's all. I get another call like last night's, I'll tell the bartender to leave you on the street and not wait around for me to pick you up," and he said, "I believe you and you're right. And so next time they start to make that call and if I'm able to I'll tell them to stop and just lift my arms up and let them drag me out by my feet," and Robert said, "You want to be that kind of schnook, be it, but I swear when you wake up on the ground next time, don't look around for me," and he said, "All right, I heard, I heard. You're finally going to desert me, and I'm not being a wise guy now if that's what you're thinking; I know it's all for my own health." Robert would do things like slip a ten-dollar bill into Gould's pocket when he was going out on a date. "What's this for?" and Robert would say, "So your chickie not only thinks you're a sport at the movie theater when you buy her bonbons instead of jujubes, but so you can also have an extra good time in case anything else needing cash comes up." "I don't want it; I make enough on my own, working," and

Robert would say, "I earn more. So for insurance if you're suddenly stranded alone in the Bronx late at night and want to take a cab home instead of getting killed waiting for the subway." Robert would make him sandwiches for lunch when Gould was in a rush in the morning to leave for school. "Liverwurst with mustard and lettuce, right? Every day the same thing for years. When are you going to change? Mayonnaise instead of mustard, for instance. And why don't you make your lunch the night before like Dad and me?" "We're different, that's all. You favor Dad, I favor nobody. Other differences: I jump out of bed when the alarm clock goes off, you crawl out or just sleep. But you always put it together in minutes, once you get started, while I wander around the joint wondering what I'm going to do and how I'm going to do it and what again is it I have to do?" "I don't know about that. None of it sounds like either of us, except the leaping and sleeping. But I respect your right to come up with these misperceived impressions." Another difference: Gould usually wanted the folks to say what a good smart boy he was, and Robert wanted them to say what a good smart boy Gould was. One dinner conversation, Robert saying, "Did you see those grades Gould got this marking period? Something, huh?" and their father saying, "They weren't that hot," and Gould saying, "I did the best I could, worked my head off, really tried; I'm sorry," and their mother saying, "Don't worry about it, dear, though I know you could have done much better." "I don't know why you two are giving him a hard time about it," Robert said. "The New York City public school system stinks; we're all products of it, so we all know that. It makes Labrador retrievers and memory experts out of everyone. That's why getting just B's and 80's and Satisfactorys signifies you're good enough to be good but not good enough to be excellent and fall for that failed kid-dismissive system. I wish we could pull him out of school and I had the time to educate him myself." "Don't be so harsh and smart and arty and act like a big shot," their father said. "You'll end up hurting your brother." Gould liked wearing Robert's clothes. Everything except the socks and ties was much too large for him but he still tried—shirtsleeves rolled up, top button of the dress shirts left unbuttoned, bomber jacket worn with two sweaters—but nothing he could do with the other clothes except a couple of belts that Robert, saying they were his least favorite, let him gouge a few more holes in and polo shirts that Gould said he liked to wear big. Robert taught him how to dress: knot a tie, fold a hanky for his jacket breast pocket, coordinate colors, when clothes should go to the dry cleaners—"Sniff the pants crotch and under the jacket arms. One faint whiff of piss or B.O. and out it goes"—which clothes could be put into the washer and dryer, even what the holes in French cuffs were for and then how to get the cuff links in once the shirt was on you, how to use a tie tack without leaving a visible hole. Gould first went to his father to learn how to knot a tie. "Speak to Robert. That's what older brothers are for. You should start relying on him for things like jobs and clothes and how to shave and advice about girls and alcohol, and not just your studies." Robert got behind him and said, "First I'll tie it around your neck as if it's on me. Follow my hands in the mirror but think *reverse*. Notice how I go around and loop it here and double it for an extra-fat Windsor knot, if that's what you want. It's the style right now, along with the Billy Eckstine collar, which makes you look more like a nightclub singer than a scholar—the girls I know like the latter—and then slip it in and tug it a bit but not too tight and you got your knot." "How'd you get the inside strip shorter than the outside? That looks hard," and Robert said, "Forgot to show you how to measure them next to each other," and undid the knot. Taught him how to tie a bow tie. "Who taught you, since Dad never wears them?" and Robert said, "I had a dream where I tied a bow tie perfectly except for a little back piece hanging down. Then I woke up, thought it a good opportunity to learn how while I still had what seemed like practical dream knowledge, and went out and bought one and right at the store tied it perfectly the first time except for this little back piece hanging down." Gould was sixteen and going out on a date. "Let's see how you look," Robert would usually say, and he'd have Gould stand in front of him and then turn around. "Tie's sticking out in back," and he'd fix it. "What's with you and folding hankies?" and he'd take it out of Gould's jacket breast pocket and refold it. Smell his cheek and say, "Too much aftershave; you reek like a gigolo. Splash some water on your face to adulterate it. . . . You got a nice shine on those shoes and, let me see, no smudges on your socks. What about your hands?" and Gould held them out, and he said, "Good, no shoe polish on your nails either—that's where I mostly get it and then start smearing it on the rest of my clothes. . . .

Hair could be parted a bit straighter, it takes a side trip about three-quarters there. . . . That shirt new?" and Gould said, "It's yours, do you mind?" and Robert said, "Not too roomy for you? But I guess it'll do. When you take it to the Chinese laundry tomorrow, you pay, and remember, no starch. . . . Your pants need to be ironed," and Robert took out the board and iron and showed him how. "Always use a dampened dish towel on them, especially the gabardine, or they'll eventually shine like glass. Anyway, you're a pretty sharp dresser now, and only two razor nicks on your face. Not bad, and nice and smooth"—feeling his cheek—"though I'd wash off the blood; your date might get queasy," and Gould said, "No, she's a very natural type and would probably just scratch it off with her fingernail and not say peep over it," and Robert said, "The best kind, the earth girl, I love them. No futzing around with artifice and stringing you along and painting their toes. Doesn't even blink when you break wind, am I right? What could be better, so long as you act the same natural way with her," and Gould said, "Quite confidentially, it was a turnoff at first, if you mean when she did it—I'd never heard a girl break wind before but then never been with one so long and close. But it only happened twice and the second time I barely flinched," and Robert said, "That's my boy, but I bet you lie. . . . Now remember," Robert said another time, "never feed a girl any lines. Act genuine; be honest. She doesn't go for it, then she isn't worth your time even if you have a chance to bed her. But don't bed anyone who you know's going to be hurt if you don't want to bed her again or if all you want from her is to get her in bed, unless that's all she wants from you too. Be polite and considerate all the time to girls. Help them on with their coats, carry their heavy packages, but not if they have something against it. Open doors for them, as you should for everyone; be last getting out of a place even if there's a fire. And if there is a fire and someone's in there and you think you can save them without killing yourself or getting burned badly, do it and then deny you really did anything. All this works better than being artificially tough and crass and stupid and boastful, though you're not doing this as a ruse but because you *are* this way. . . . Let me see your teeth. I want to check for any specks on them," and Gould would open his mouth. He was fifteen or sixteen, again going out on a date. "Your breath okay too? I'm not going to check for that, so tell the truth: I got some drops for it if there's a problem. . . . Your sideburns aren't even. Get in the bathroom and I'll do them with my barber scissors and razor," and he evened Gould's sideburns. "You're not perfect but it's getting late and you don't want to make anyone wait, so I'll release you. Have a ball. And here's some moola in case of a lot of things; every kid your age can use a bit extra. . . . Remember that time a while back when I said that stuff about fire and being somewhat cautious about saving people?" and Gould said no. "Anyway, I said it and now think because of something I read in the paper that you have to risk your life if there's a chance of saving someone in a burning building, let's say, if there isn't a hundred percent chance you will get killed doing it. This doesn't go for standing up to a punk with a gun pointed at your head or any part of you except your legs. Then you got to just let him do what he's out to do, except if it's something horrible to the folks or your future wife or kids. Then you have to risk getting killed to save them from even getting shot in the legs or raped. My feeling is that your own death or something close to it will satisfy the guy or scare him off." Whatever Robert had when they were little, he usually gave Gould half: candy, soda, cake, gum. "I don't want any, thanks," and Robert would say, "No, you got to take or just put it away. And I sort of expect the same from you, though if you don't do it that doesn't mean I'll stop being my way," and sometimes Gould would think, if he had the only candy bar or pack of gum, I really want to keep all of it for myself, but what'll he say if he sees me chewing and I don't offer him some? If Robert didn't want it, Gould never told him to take it for later. Robert asked him for favors only when he absolutely couldn't do the thing himself and it needed to be done immediately. He couldn't pick up his new high school football jacket at the place that made them for the whole team, so asked Gould if he would. Gould thought it a lot to ask of him, since it was more than an hour's trip to the East Bronx, but Robert said, "I've put it off and today's the last day I can go to practice without it. After that the coach said I'm demoted or off the team," and Gould said, "That's dumb and you should tell him to jump into a lake and that you need another day. Or if it's you don't want to piss him off, make up a terrific lie; I'll help you," and Robert said, "Just do it for me, please? What do I ever ask of you? And you think you can cut down on your cursing?" Gould went to get the jacket from school. For some reason—but he knows the reason and thinks he knew it then—he said he was Robert Bookbinder when he handed over the pickup slip and rest of the money, and the man said, "This jacket's for a kid several sizes larger than you. And it's the size you ordered—I got it down right here—so we can't be taking it back or making you another one." "I got it big because I'm going to grow into it, and maybe out of it in a year too. I already grew six inches this year, which is how I made the team, and the doctor for my health checkup last month said another tremendous spurt's on the way." "You want to wear it now? You'll be saving me the box and trouble tying it up," and he said, "It's a little warm out, but with my books to carry, why not? It's a breaker, in a way, right? so I'll start breaking it in." He put it on; it was way too large but he felt great wearing it, and the man looked him over and said, "Fits better than I thought. Wear it in good health, Bob, and chalk up a winning season and don't get hurt," and he said, "I'll try not to, and we will. In fact we're shooting for the all-city championship; that's how good we think we are this year." In the bus and subway rides home he stood, rather than sat, so people could see how short he was and be impressed that a kid this small made the varsity football team of a public high school, even if it was one of the elite ones. Wow, some of them could think, he must be fast and strong and smart. If anyone asked him what position he played: left halfback, specializing in running back the kick and end runs. But this *Bob,* written in cursive inside a football on the front of the jacket; it looked nice when the man held the jacket up for him, maybe better than *Robert* would, but why that name? Robert always went as Robert and nothing else, at home and with his friends. Gould had heard people call him Bob and Rob a few times, but always by mistake, and after it Robert would correct them: "If you don't mind, I prefer not to be so alliterated," or "It sounds as if I'm a thief." Maybe three letters were cheaper to sew on than six. Or there was something about him he didn't know: that he went by Bob with his teammates and over the loudspeaker when they announced the players, which they do in the big games, Robert had told him, like against Clinton and Brooklyn Tech. He'd ask him when Robert tried the jacket on. "Hey, it says *Bob,*" he'd say, "how come?" When Robert saw the jacket in the coat closet that night, he said, "Didn't this come in a box? A bag, anyway, and where's the receipt? You didn't wear it home, did you?" and Gould said, "No, why do you think that?" "You're lying; I can always tell—born liars don't make good liars," and he said, "Okay, I wore it, because I had lots of other things to carry: my books and my sweater because it was so hot out. And I did some of my homework on the subway and bus and didn't want to be dealing with this tremendous box the man there showed me." "You're lying again. I can always tell when you're lying again. Piece of advice: tell the truth right off and you're out of harm's way. You wore the jacket because you hoped people would think you were a high school football player, despite how small you are. And if you're going to lie, make sure you get your stories straight. You take off your sweater because it's hot but you put on an even heavier jacket?" "I kept the jacket open. And just about everything you say isn't true and I don't know what your 'harm's way' is. Because what was the harm? I took care of the jacket good, even hung it up on a hanger in the closet," and Robert said, "Now you're not lying; at least, most of what you just said shouldn't be considered a lie. Self-deception and pretending to misunderstand and reversing the accusations and trying to talk your way out of a bad situation or lie aren't lying. But boy, they're things you also ought to work on fixing if you ever want to be an adult." "I don't have a clue what you mean," and Robert said, "Now you're lying again, because one thing you're not is unconditionally stupid. And three lies in one brief conversation? I'd say your lying addiction is fatal," and Gould said, "Enough with your predictions; they're just insults in disguise anyway," and Robert said, "More trying to squeeze your way out of it with cleverness rather than facing the situation. Brother, you're hopeless," and "Brother," Gould said, after he turned around and went to their bedroom and slammed the door, "you're full of shit and a rat. How did I ever like him?"—under his breath—"ask yourself: How did you?" "Okay," Robert said through the door a minute later, "I was wrong in a lot of what I said to you and an apology's in order, but just tell me, Where's the jacket receipt?" and he said, "I forgot to get one, or the man forgot to give me it. But I know it isn't in any box or bag because I didn't want one," and Robert said, "Oh, God, when are you going to wise up?" Robert got his driver's license soon as he was able to and started driving their father's car. He once drove Gould and himself to Brooklyn to see some relatives. Double-parked the car on an avenue with lots of one-story stores—all the parking spaces were filled—and said, "I have to get some smokes; I'll be right back." No, said, "I got to take a leak. If the driver of either of the cars I'm blocking wants me to move, tell him I went into that coffee shop there for a bladder emergency and I'll be right out. If he wants me to move this instant, show him the car keys and tell him you don't know how to drive and your brother said he doesn't want anyone else driving the car and you'll run in to get me if he waits by our car a few seconds so we don't get ticketed. Forget the part about the bladder. Just say I went in for health reasons and I'll be right out; that wouldn't be far from the truth. By the time he starts wondering what health reasons in a coffee shop, I'll be back. If a cop comes, because I'm illegally parked, tell him the same thing and that I left my keys behind in good faith, just in case I was blocking a parked car or a fire truck had to get in here or something. But slide over behind the wheel so you look like the driver. There'll be less chance a cop will stop for you then." "Some of that's unclear. What do I say to the cop?" and Robert said, "I haven't time to re-explain; I'm about to pee in my pants," and ran to the coffee shop. Gould was already behind the wheel, tried turning it, but it only moved a little. Of course, engine's got to be running. He'd never started up a car. Fifteen; that's almost like a disgrace. Never been taught how, either. But he thought he could do it from having watched his father and Robert. Because what's the trick? Stick the key in, turn it, and car starts up. But keep the gearshift in PARK. That's important, or else the car could jump forward. He'd seen that happen with his father. And make sure the hand brake's engaged—that's the word he's heard them use—and it was. He stuck the key in and tried turning it to the right but it wouldn't move—the gas pedal, stupid!—and he put his foot on the gas pedal while he tried turning the key, but it still wouldn't move. What am I doing wrong? he thought, and put his foot farther down on the gas pedal while he tried turning the key and then tried turning it harder—and it broke. Oh, no! He tried getting the key's broken front part out but it was stuck in there. Now what? Robert was coming back and Gould moved to the passenger seat, and Robert got in, held his hand out for the keys, and said, "How'd it go? Any customers?" and Gould said, "I'm very sorry," and showed him the broken key on the ring, and Robert said, "You didn't. Where's the other part? Not in there, I hope"—pointing—and Gould nodded, and Robert yelled, "You schmuck!" and slapped him in the chest. It didn't hurt but he'd never hit him like that before, or since he was a kid, and tears welled, and Robert said, "What's wrong? I said what in God's name is wrong? Damn, you asked for it. You put the key in upside down, you dumb idiot, and tried to start the car, right? That's the only thing that could have happened. And when it wouldn't turn you forced it. So now what am I going to do? Come on, you're fifteen, what are you doing, crying? Okay, I'm sorry," and put his hand on Gould's shoulder. "I never hit you before or at least in anger, or at least not since I was six or so, that what you're thinking? So it's over, so you weren't hurt, so stop blubbering like a baby. I said I'm sorry. Accept my apology—that's the right thing to do—and then see if you can help me get the rest of the key out." They couldn't, even with Robert's penknife. "Stay here. Policeman comes, or someone whose car I'm blocking, tell them what you did with the key and that I had to go get a locksmith or garage mechanic, but don't leave the car even if you have to pee. You have to pee now, go to the coffee shop and I'll stay here. And here's a buck; get yourself a soda," and Gould shook his head and Robert went to the coffee shop, probably to ask where the nearest locksmith or service station was. A locksmith came a short time later and got the key out. Robert had a spare key—"I was thinking of telling you earlier but didn't want to ease your mind too soon; then you'd never remember what you did and it would only happen again"—and they drove off. "Always carry a spare. That's my advice for the day, if not the century. Wrap it in something, seal what you wrap it in with tape, and tuck it into a part of your wallet or billfold, like the change purse if it has a zipper or snap, but where it could never fall out. That's the way to never locking yourself out of your car. And whatever you do, don't leave your car keys with your fifteen-year-old brother or son. God, can they be dolts. Excuse me. So, all forgiven, tears dried?" and Gould said, "I didn't have tears. I just felt bad and only might have looked like a kid crying," and Robert said, "Oh, yeah, like you really believe that, but now let's forget it for good." Each served as best man for the other's wedding. "Listen," Robert said, "I wouldn't trust anyone with the ring, not even my dearest brother, so let's say I give it to you right before I walk down the aisle—or the minute before, so nobody will see us and think I feel you're unreliable—in a private room where you're supposed to be helping me get ready." "Anything you say, though I would encourage you to start trusting me. But if this will make you feel more relaxed for the main event, okay," and Robert said, "It's not that, or maybe it is, or something, perhaps, of what you said—now I'm confused. But just go along with my short-lived idiosyncrasy and uncertainty and inability this minute to understand why they suddenly exist, please." Gould's wedding, by comparison, was small, thirty people at the most in the apartment he and Sally had been living in for two years, and the day before it he asked Robert to hold on to the wedding rings for him—"I'm afraid of losing them. But then I always get flustered and forgetful when the big occasion is me; do you remember my bar mitzvah?"—and Robert said, "Not at all. And holding on to your rings would be irresponsible of me, because where would I keep them? Same place as you. In a box or plastic envelope in the top dresser drawer with my underwear and socks. But I'm in a hotel room for two nights with only so-so security, so do it yourself and spare me the possible ignominy of losing them or not taking the right precautions to prevent them from being stolen, and give them to me a minute or two before the ceremony. That's what I did with you, though I don't recall if it was for the same reason." Robert started helping Gould get jobs while they were both in high school. (But he's already mentioned something along those lines. Helping him get a raise, then.) Robert had got him a job delivering belts to dress and coat houses for the belt factory he was a shipping clerk at, and one day at work he said, "Look, this has gone on long enough. Go tell Mr. Wachterman you'd like a raise. When he asks how much, say thirty cents an hour would be equitable. And say 'equitable' rather than 'fair.' Not that you need a brain for what you do or that he doesn't already think you're bright. But these people always have to be reassured how smart you are by the words you use and big non-school books you carry. And they, not being too educated or interested in books, associate intellectual brains with goodness and honesty and quick thinking for practical rather than underhanded things, and he'll feel he's got a winner in you in that not only don't you petty-steal from the firm, as most of the delivery boys do—scissors, buckles, and so forth—but he only has to tell you a route or something to do once and you got it down pat. And you deserve the thirty cents for the heavy bales you push and unload and the half year you've worked here at the same salary," and Gould said, "I can't ask him. He'll fire me. When he thinks I'm ready for a raise, he'll give me one; and whatever it is, I'll take, since it'll be more than I've been making," and Robert said, "This is the Garment Center, you dimmy. Here, until you demand more, you slave for life at minimum wage, if they can't finagle it some way where you get less. And if you are taken advantage of like that, I look bad for not having taught you about the dog-eat-dog practices that go on here and how to dance around them and get what's rightfully yours," and Gould said, "If I ever get to feel I'm not being paid equitably for what I do, and they don't offer me a raise, I'll tell them I'm leaving. If they then offer me one because of what I said, fine, I'll tell them. But if they say, 'Goodbye and good riddance to you, pal, because you're nothing to us,' fine again, because I'll look for a new job," and Robert said, "Bushwah; you're just afraid of speaking up for yourself," and he said, "Not true, I don't think it's up to me to make the first move," and Robert said, "But I already told you how they think. As for getting another job, if you leave like that you'll have a work record of quitting, which'll make it harder for you. And if someone's thinking of hiring you and calls Wachterman for a reference, since in your application you usually have to give the last two places you worked, you think he'll give you a fair one? No chance. He'll void all over you, say you were a sluff-off, slob, and petty thief: you name it. Because he'll know you'll have told the new place why you left—the money. So to counter it, because he wouldn't want the company or him looking bad, he'll say you were paid above minimum wage but still did a lousy job and finally quit, and if he were this guy he wouldn't hire you. So learn something from me for once. The only credit you get around here is when you stand up for yourself without being high-horsey or saying it in a way their dimwit minds might think is disdainful or insulting," and Gould said, "I still can't ask for one," and Robert said, "Then I'll do it for you and maybe you'll learn something from that," and he said, "Don't!" and Robert went to Wachterman's office, knocked first, put on a deferential face, and straightened his tie, and came out a few minutes later and said, "I told him you were too shy and respectful to ask him yourself and he said he likes that quality in a young man, but more for a son-in-law who isn't coming into the business, since it's not anything that'll make anyone more money. And then, though it hurts, he's giving you twenty-five cents an hour more starting in two weeks," and Gould said, "You were lucky he didn't fire you," and Robert said, "What are you talking about? They love me here and would never let me go. How do you think I got you the raise? I insinuated they'd lose us both if he didn't come up with one for you," and Gould said, "How'd you do that without actually saying it?" and Robert said, "Ways." Robert went to lots of parties and often invited Gould— But first the work he did in a store window. Robert got a job in which he wrote *The Autobiography of a Very Ordinary Young New Yorker,* as he called it, in the window of a stationery store made up to look like a cluttered writer's studio. He was looking for a Christmas job during his long school break, couldn't find one that paid more than minimum wage, got this idea while walking past the largest stationery-typewriter store in midtown, and went in and proposed it. He'd sit in the window for a month from eight to seven, time off to go to the men's room and to quickly eat his breakfast and lunch at the typing table, and write the first draft and then the final one using only the store's merchandise. He told the owners it'd show that their typewriters can take eleven hours a day straight of heavy pounding from a guy who looks like a weight lifter, besides being a big draw and getting the store plenty of attention, a man completing a book-length manuscript in a store window on a main thoroughfare. The life he'd write about, he told Gould—and each page would be taped to the window for people on the sidewalk to read and there'd be scratch pads attached to the window outside for them to write comments and criticisms—would be partly his own, partly Gould's, partly anything he could think up or include that would seem plausibly part of the autobiography. (So this, probably, was when he first thought of writing fiction, or did the store window come after the article about underground streams in Greenwich Village? Thinks about it. After, by about a year, as the article was written when Gould was still in high school.) There'd be a few heroics in the work: jumping in front of a bicycle that was about to run down a baby in a stroller, which Gould did the year before and busted his shoulder; giving mouth-to-mouth resuscitation to an already dead man who'd collapsed in a theater lobby, something their mother did without knowing how to do it when she was in her twenties; grabbing a thief on the street and holding him in a headlock for the police, which Gould and a friend did when a woman yelled that her pocketbook had been picked; facing down a robber with an umbrella and a samples case, which their father did in their building's vestibule—but all things Robert would say he'd done and that the samples case was a book bag and the resuscitation saved the man. "Got to beef up the piece to keep the reader, though not make it too maudlin, since things like this never seem to happen to me, and it can't be only because of my size." So mostly just ordinary experiences while growing up in New York: family life, shul, the only Hebrew school student there the rabbi didn't from time to time whack on the back of the neck; getting adult jobs when he was in his early teens, Charlie Chaplin, Oona O'Neill, whom he was more impressed at seeing that same evening because of her father; being beaten out of a cab by Peter Lorre ("You have to run faster than that, son, though I won't argue with you if you insist it's yours," and he said, "Not at all, sir; it's an honor to let you have it"—opening the cab's door), then next day sitting in the Paramount Theater behind Sydney Greenstreet, who was laughing so hard Robert couldn't make out what was being said on the screen. Wanted to tell him of the coincidence but thought it the wrong time and place. Boyhood crushes on movie stars (Gene Tierney, June Haver, Veronica Lake); bribing a third-grade classmate to show him one of her nipples in the narrow coat closet by giving her his last Indian penny; tips on how he meets women in bookstores ("Excuse me, but did you notice if that book you have was the last copy on the shelf, because I was interested in it too," or "Excuse me"—since he never tries picking up a woman who isn't browsing through the fiction, poetry, or literary criticism sections—"but do you have any idea which is the better version of Wordsworth's *Prelude,* the 1805 or 1850?"); admitting he's never been able to come up with a good way to pick up women in art museums except maybe to hang around the famous Ingres painting in the Met or the Tchelitchew at the Modern and ask the woman who's looking at it—or if she's only walking past, then to beg her pardon and stop her—if she knows how to pronounce the painter's name; but nothing in the manuscript about sex other than the girl's nipple, which he'd call "one side of her chest." Brief account of each of the fourteen scars on his head: getting in the way of a swinging baseball bat or stickball broomstick or flying hockey puck (when he was playing on roller skates); falling on his mother's pinking shears; several times failing to stoop as he went through a door; tipping over a chair he was leaning back on; crashing a party with his friends, and the girl's mother—because he was the biggest, his friends pushed him in first—smashing a guitar over his head; frozen on one foot while playing Statues and falling off the top of a stoop wall into an areaway. . . . The ten people in his life he feels have done the worst damage to him, five of them his elementary school teachers and an assistant principal in the same school ("Principal with a P-A-L, for the assistant principal is your pal"). Short chapter on his family's history: folks growing up on the Lower East Side and moving uptown when they got married and all his grandparents immigrating to America from small Polish villages, though his mother always held that her folks were Austro-Hungarian and only started speaking Polish to communicate to their help in New York. Ending with him walking by this store, disappointed at not being able to find work that paid more than minimum wage, as he wanted to save money to take a student ship to Germany in June to visit as many of Thomas Mann's old haunts as he could afford, and getting the brainstorm, as he called it, for the job when he saw the typewriter and typing table and supplies in the window and immediately going into the store to speak to someone about it. Gould, on his lunch or dinner breaks from his Christmas salesman's job in a midtown department store, often stood on the sidewalk in a crowd and watched Robert typing, closing his eyes in thought and then springing them open to jot down notes, sharpening a typewriter-eraser pencil, using some chemical solution to wash off the ink stains on his fingers after he changed the typewriter ribbon, which the store manager let him do twice a day because he wanted the print legible, putting things like manuscript pages and photographs and his Social Security and Selective Service cards and college photo-ID through a new machine called a Xerox copier—the manager wanted him to demonstrate this product, which wasn't selling well yet, as much as he could and to show by his expression how easy it was to use and how much fun he had copying the personal documents and photos—taping new finished photocopied pages on the window and, for a few minutes at the beginning of every hour, reading the comments that were brought in to him and answering some of them by holding up a blackboard on which he chalked responses like *Great suggestion for the hot-dog man scene, Jerry G.; I'm gonna use it if I ever rewrite this* (he'd been told not to put off any potential customer by being insulting or oversmart with his comments); *Astute interpretation of the introduction-to-death section of Little Robert, D. W. Darlene, and thanks for sticking with it; next few pages should be more peppy; You're no doubt right about the spelling of "antecedant," Jean, but just to make sure, I'll check, first chance I get, in the new Webster's New World Dictionary the store's loaned me and sells here,* and he held up the book; *Not to worry, Dr. Ninski; the part about my appendectomy was clarified on an earlier page already removed from the window for lack of space.* People sometimes tapped on the window to tell him something through it, and he'd ignore them if he was typing away furiously or would wave if he recognized that person from someplace, usually from some other time at the window, Robert said. Mostly, though, he'd just smile and point to a sign on an easel that said SORRY, CAN'T CONVERSE: WRITER AT WORK. MUST MEET MANUSCRIPT DEADLINE OF 6 P.M., DEC. 31ST. IF YOU HAVE COMMENTS OR CRITIQUES OF MR. BOOKBINDER'S WRITING, PLEASE RESTRICT THEM TO SHEETS POSTED ON THE WINDOW. THEY'LL ALL BE READ BY HIM AND GRATEFULLY RECEIVED. He spotted Gould once and waved him in and quickly scribbled on the blackboard *My sort-of ghostwriting brother: he's younger but has given me half my ideas for this, so let him through, folks.* Gould went into the store and climbed into the window. "Nine more days of this agony," Robert said, covering his mouth. "Worst idea I've ever had to make money, but I'm committed to it and don't want to let the store down: they're slave drivers but a decent bunch and they gave me a break. If I were really involved in the book and interested in completing it, it'd be different. There are already several senior and junior editors and literary agents sending in notes or calling the store to see it. They've either passed the window and noticed the crowds around it for an activity as lowly esteemed as writing or they've read the articles and seen the photos of me in a couple of newspapers, sitting here typing, and thought, By gum, this manuscript's already got a ton of publicity before it's published. But it's hackwork I'm doing, a piece of uncompromising crap, as well as a death blow to my homage to Mann. If I did get to Germany partly from the dough I earned here and knocked on his door as I'd planned and actually got a few minutes with the great man, and he asked—over tea, even—as one of his questions, for in his fiction and essays and interviews he's always questioning, how I had the means to get there, I couldn't lie to him. He's so sharp he'd see right through me. So I'd have to tell the truth and he, the quintessential artist and literary moralist, might become so repulsed by my vulgarization of the craft, and in his name too, that he'd ask someone in his house to promptly show me out, and who knows what that scene might do to his already frail condition and failing health? Anyway, I'm sick of the manuscript and the stupid attention it's received and the people out there on the street and the inane questions I always have to answer, and the only thing I'm going to do with it soon as I finish it on the last day is take my name off the title page and drop it into the nearest ash can. What I'm particularly sick of is having to apologize to twenty to thirty people every time I have to use the WC. But listen"—and he gave Gould a few bucks—"if you have a little time left on your break, could you get me a turkey and Swiss sandwich on seeded rye, Russian dressing on the side, and a Dr. Brown's celery tonic at the Stage Deli? The food the store's been sending in is for the dogs." Robert went to lots of parties, and when they were both working in Washington or New York he often invited Gould to them. He'd call an hour or so before and say something like "I've been thinking of you, and what popped into my head is you're not doing anything tonight, am I right?" and Gould would usually say, "Nothing much. Reading, listening to music, drinking a little wine," and Robert would say, "You stay home too much, I always tell you that; you ought to go out more. How else you going to meet women and not become the best read young solitary drunken reporter in the city? No matter how much you protest, you're coming," and he'd give the address and time of the party and Gould would say, "Won't the host mind?" and Robert would say, "You're my brother, so I don't even have to work it out beforehand. You just show up at the door and if someone says, because tonight's is a fairly fancy place, who are you? you say, 'Robert Bookbinder's brother, he told me it'd be okay,' and they'll let you right in." Once Gould said, "You can't tell the host I'm coming and to leave word at the door to admit me?" and Robert said, "I will, if you insist, though I don't understand how you can still be so timid in these situations. You're a newsman now, no more Mr. Copyboy. You push yourself through doors, into stories, stick your arm out farther than any other radio newsman's and shove your mike into a legislator's face and ask aggressive meaty questions that'll get your news service scads of attention and then attribution on the wires later. He doesn't answer, or not satisfactorily, according to you, you say you're the press, sir, the goddamn press, and you want—" and he said, "Okay, okay, I get the point. But I like to relax from my work, and though I am pushy in news I don't enjoy it." At one party Robert pointed out a woman and said, "I'd think you'd be interested in that one. Sweet smile, nifty face, looks bright, nice figure and height, doesn't smoke, dresses sedately, almost as if she owns horses, but with shoulders that say she's a swimmer, and not a touch of makeup, it seems, or she knows how to apply it so that it looks natural. Couldn't be better, the best bet for love interest at the party. I'd make a plunge for her myself but somehow I see you two as the perfect match, with your smile, bright look, and nice face and sedate clothes and no makeup. And you're not seeing anyone now while I'm already in hot water, and I'm not boasting, over two too many girlfriends, so go over to her and say hello." "I can't just go over to a woman. I always feel so uncomfortable," and Robert said, "It's easy, and you're a master at fabricating, so give her a good one. 'My brother over there, the tall guy with the loud clothes and funny hat and shirttail sticking out of his fly and cigarette in each hand? He thought I should come over and introduce myself and tell you a few lies—he thinks I'm a master at them, though he called them fabrications—that'll get you interested enough in me to want to start a conversation. You see, he thinks—he said this, and I always have to do what my older brother says, as he's recently become the sole executor of our late parents' estate and has complete control to cut me out of it and he can be quite imperious, though I suppose I don't always have to repeat what he tells me—that we'd be a perfect pair together: "match," he actually said. I corrected myself then, even if it might not have seemed important, because we're both newsmen, but he wants me to be a better one than I am so says I should start practicing to quote everything exactly,' " and Gould said, "Sure, I can really see myself saying that, and I can also imagine what her reaction would be—'See ya, Schlermy,' "—and Robert said, "C'mon, you know what I mean. And she has a very ironical and receptive look, besides the bright one, so I bet she'll appreciate it for its humor and uniqueness as an opening line. Or simply say, though don't say it simply, 'My older brother there, the tall geek with the untied shoelaces and pants cuffs that don't reach his ankles and two unlit cigarettes in his mouth and a lit one wedged behind each ear? Well, he thinks I should try to overcome my enfeebling shyness at starting a conversation with you by just strutting over as I just did, and also not to say "just" so much, which I'll try but it seems almost impossible to do, being a third-generation New Yorker, and saying to you the first thing that enters my head and then taking it from there. He also said that if that displeases you I should of course apologize prostrately and skulk away backwards without bumping into anyone till I'm out of the room. And he's really right, in a way, so I'm doing it,' " and Gould said, "Suppose she asks what do I mean 'right, in a way,' which puzzles me too?" and Robert said, "Tell her that was also something your brother told you to say and that it puzzles you a little too. But that your brother says many things you don't understand, sometimes because they're unclearly expressed and other times because of the deficiencies in your own comprehension, but there you are already talking to her, though that last part you don't say unless you want to be underminingly honest." "I can't do it," and Robert said, "Then I'll do it for you because I know this isn't something you should pass up," and went over, took her arm, started talking, she laughed, he pointed to Gould—or he started talking, they laughed, he took her arm by the elbow and sort of swiveled her around to Gould and pointed at him—she smiled at Gould, he smiled back, Robert waved for him to come over, "I want to introduce you to someone," Gould shook his head—or Robert said something to her and she laughed and said, "Gould, come on over, I want to introduce you to someone"—and he thought, "Wait a second, what the hell's going on here?" and went over and said to her, "Excuse me, but what do you mean? I know this guy all too well," and she said, "I was only saying what your cousin asked me to," and he said, "You mean my brother," and Robert said, "I thought I'd change it around a little, we've been brothers for so long. Big deal; the truth always comes out. It doesn't but I thought I'd say that anyway. It seemed then—it doesn't now, in instant retrospect—the right moment for a universal cliché for us to quibble over, but here we are talking together and who knows what possibilities are in the making?" and he said, "My brother's always getting me in trouble—not 'always,' but a lot," and Robert said, "If what he just said were the opposite, it'd be closer to a lie," and she said, "Are you two really brothers?" and Gould said, "Same parents but different conceptions," and Robert said, "So I guess my last remark slipped past without anyone's regarding it," and Gould said, "Because it wasn't worth comment," and she said, "That's a terrible line, Gould, as old as the old 'old as the hills' one," and Robert said, "Uh-oh, sorry for having said something that led to your first reprimand from her. Suddenly things don't look promising," and she said, "It wasn't a reprimand; I was only joining the infectious teasing. Anyway, going back, you two look nothing alike," and Robert said, "And for the most part, and please don't tell me that wasn't a reprimand, miss"—feigning indignation—"it was, and you cannot treat my brother like that so soon after you met him, no one can; he's too nice a guy. And for the most part we act, think, read, comprehend, socialize, feign indignation, initiate conversations, scratch our heads and many other body parts nothing alike either. He's the brighter, et cetera, down-to-earth one. I'm what he's usually not, besides often dropping him in hot water, though never, so far, with women. But I'm getting out of here; you two speak. Gould, meet Cynthia. Cynthia—but you know his name. Here, shake," and grabbed their hands and put them together and they shook. "Here, kiss," and he pushed their heads together, and just as their lips were about to touch Gould ducked out from under Robert's hand and said, "This is embarrassing and rude and I almost want to say a little stupid of you, Robert, but I'll say it was a lot," and she said, "Why, he was only kidding," and he said, "Then you stay with him," and walked away, Robert and Cynthia laughing. He was in another room a few minutes later when she came over to him and said, "Excuse me, but what was that all about, your anger at me and then storming away?" and he said, "I didn't storm and my brother can be a jerk sometimes when he isn't being ultra smooth. And if you want to know the truth, it's also because I thought he ruined it for me with you. Since he was right; when he and I were talking about you before he went over to you, I was interested. How's that for an unprompted unrehearsed line?" and she said, "Also terrible. He loves you and just wants to see you hooked up—the older brother looking out for the younger one; isn't that what he promised your parents he'd do?—what's so wrong with that? And he never would have let our mouths meet. I felt that big hand on my head was in complete control of the act and that he would have got us a fraction of an inch away from each other before he pulled our heads back." They talked for a while, she gave him her phone number, and they ended up seeing each other for a few months. When Gould was seventeen he heard from a friend that Red, a hooker, wanted him to call her. "She said it was important, nothing bad, so you should feel good about calling, and she's been trying to get ahold of you through some other West Side guys too." "A hooker wants me to call her? I don't know her, never even heard of her. Maybe it's a new way of getting business," and the friend said, "She's not like that. I've been to her twice and she's real class, educated, everything. Call her, what do you got to lose? If it is something suddenly fishy with her, you just don't go to her, if that's what she wants." He called and said, "Hi, this is Gould Bookbinder and I heard from Ben Morton you wanted to speak to me," and she said, "Bookbinder? Bookbinder? Oh, sure, you're the sweet young man I've been trying to reach. I wanted to say thanks—you know—for all you've done for me. But I want to thank you personally, so do you have a half hour free tonight so we can talk?" and he said, "Thank me?" and she said, "Listen, Mr. Bookbinder, I can't talk on the phone. I got the bath running and there's also this little pest near me who might be overhearing, and he builds everything I say into mountains. So just come by, tonight at eight, okay? You remember the address? It's where I always lived," and he said, "No, I forgot, only your phone," and she told him and he went, and when he was inside her apartment—she was pretty, maybe a little overweight and about twenty years older than him, but with this bright white skin and long shiny red hair that looked clean and young-looking the way it flowed over her shoulders—she said, "Before we begin, would you care to have a coffee while I'm finishing my tea?" and he said, "No, thanks, I don't drink it." "Soda, then? A beer, or shot of whiskey with ginger ale? I want to be extra hospitable and gracious because I owe you a lot. You're a very kind young man, not asking for anything, just doing me favors," and he thought of saying he doesn't understand but didn't want to ruin it if he was getting something for nothing like it seemed, maybe even money besides sex, so he said, "You're welcome, honestly, and I'll take a beer after all," and she said, "For that I'll have to wash my one and only stein, but I'm glad to," and he said, "No need; I'll drink it straight from the bottle or can," and she said, "No, sir, a glass. It's ugly when men chug it down like that, and a bottle makes them belch more, did you know that?" and at the kitchen table he drank his beer and she her tea and she said, "So, my personal thanks for sending so many nice young men to me," and he said, "Yeah?" but must have looked surprised because she said, "Hey, hold it up. You *are* Bookbinder, the NYU guy I've been trying to reach? I haven't made a booboo, I hope, because that'd be mortifying. I'd have to kick you out on your keister or, if you wanted to stay, ask you for ten dollars for a shortie," and he said, "Yeah, Robert Bookbinder, who do you think?" because he was already plenty hot. "That's good, because at first when you walked in—I don't know if you caught my expression—but I wondered, Is this really the guy I thought? But then your face got to look more familiar, just six or so months older, and at your age that can change it a lot. Because, you know, after your one time here I started getting telephone calls from fellows who said you sent them. Though I don't like doing that, seeing men who are almost kids and from a reference I wasn't altogether confident with, their voices were always too sweet and earnest over the phone to refuse, and I had you in my little book that you were okay. And right with the first young man they were all such gentlemen that I kept saying, 'Sure, baby, you can pay me a visit,' and they kept coming, about ten of them and some of them a few times, and all using your name. So I want to reimburse your generosity, you can say, by giving you one on the house. Because I can't pay you money—I don't give commissions to anyone," and he said, "I didn't want money. Those fellows said they were looking for a woman, so I recommended you above all," and she said, "As I said, that's what I liked about you. You never called to ask for compensation. But tell me, how come you never came back on your own? You'd seen me once, that was enough? You should have known, even if you were prepared to pay, that I wouldn't take your money after what you did for me," and he said, "Thanks, I've been very busy. Schoolwork, every kind of thing," and she said, "What sort of work you do besides your school? But fill me in later. Now you're finished with your beer, let's get washed up." He never told Robert, and once, a few months later, just to see what Robert knew and if he'd level with him, he said, "If I ever . . . I don't. I'm scared of getting V.D., even with a bag on. But if I ever—let's say for a friend, and the friend isn't me, believe me, though a couple of guys have asked if I knew of one—wanted to get the number of a prostitute who was fairly pretty and with a nice-enough body and didn't charge too much and lived not too far away, do you know of any or know anyone who does?" and Robert said, "What guy our age goes to a prostitute anymore? Not only because of syphilis and the rest, which you don't get if you have the bag on properly and don't kiss her genital parts, but it's the most blatant admission of being a social loser. You date, you form relationships; that's how you get laid. And if you're in a dry period, you don't get desperate. That's why I've been urging you to go to parties and fraternize more. If your friends are just whoremongers, get new ones who'll introduce you to nice intelligent women who'll eventually, if they like your company and see you're not in it just for the sex, make it with you. You've been to a prostitute—don't tell me. But if I were you I'd do everything I could to avoid them," and he said, "You're right, once, recently. And I can say that because of her looks and dumb chatter and phlegmatic performance, it wasn't much fun before or during it, or, because of how much it cost, after," and Robert said, "How could it be? She slaps some grease in, spreads herself wide, smells like hell from deodorants and other guys, makes with a few fake affectionate words, and after some quick jabs by you you're left with yourself forever. I'll have to start taking you to every party I go to." He could talk to him about it now on the phone, if he's home, but that'd be like saying, "Remember Red the hooker from about forty years ago? Don't tell me you don't. Our memories are getting shot from age but every guy remembers the whores he went to, even their addresses. Hers was Seventy-first, south side of the street, four or five doors up from Columbus. Oh, boy, how you lied to me, brother. 'Avoid whores at any cost' indeed." But suppose someone at that time had used Robert's name with Red when he actually had had no contact with her? Never thought of that, but why would anyone do it? Come on: to get even with him for some reason or because he was jealous of him and wanted Robert to look bad, and so on. "Robert the pimp," some guys might have thought of him as, which if he had known of it would certainly have made him mad. But it almost had to be Robert who gave her name and phone number out and probably even said, "Tell her I told you about her." But why, because he knew she'd end up giving him a free lay, even some money? If Robert did go to her after Gould had, what then? It'd mean he knew all along what Gould had done. Because she probably told him when he was there, or in an elliptical way told him this over the phone when he might have called to see if any guys had gone to her by using his name, that she'd already paid him back for what he'd done for her. "What do you mean?" he could have said, and in that same elliptical way she could have continued going around it till she gave a description of the Robert Bookbinder she'd seen and something about his mannerisms and voice that matched Gould. Wouldn't Robert have mentioned it to Gould then, or sometime since? Maybe. Better he keep that can closed, he thinks. Robert often comes and stays with Gould and his family and they always have a good time; deep conversations, talk about things they did as kids, books they recently read or are reading, political things that are happening, and so on. So? So he's saying they still like to spend time together. They once hitchhiked in Europe for a month, staying in youth hostels and student houses, going from town to town, country to country, museum to cathedral to cathedral to museum. They've just about always loved each other's company. Their two families, when the kids were small, sailed across the Atlantic on the QE2 together at standby rates, ate at the same table, then rented a minibus in England and toured France for two weeks. Gould's first daughter's middle name is Roberta. Robert's son's middle name is Gould, which he's objected to. "I don't give a shit if it's after my only uncle and he's the closest person in the whole wide world other than Mom to you, what kind of name is that, Gould Bookbinder?" "It's not Gould Bookbinder," Robert said he told his son, "it's Vincent Gould Bookbinder." "I want it to be Vincent G. Bookbinder, and if people ask what the *G*'s for, I'll say Gregor." Gould, when he was in his early twenties, was dumped by a woman he'd been going with a few months. The woman and he met for lunch, she said she's started seeing someone else, that's why he hasn't been able to reach her the last two weeks, someone she knew from before and was once almost engaged to, and she'll probably marry him by the end of the year. No, the truth is, because she wants to be totally honest about this so he knows exactly where he stands, they've already made plans to get married sometime this month, that's how sudden and strong their relationship's become, and she's very sorry what this is doing to him, when Gould started to cry, but he'll get over it—he had to see their little thing together wasn't working—so please don't be so sad. He said, "Up yours," and threw his napkin at her and left the restaurant and went straight to Robert at work. Robert said he knew how he felt, it had happened to him a couple of times, took him out for a drink, they sat at the bar and he put his arm around Gould's shoulders and said things that after a while, and another drink, made him feel better, that it's happened to almost everyone, in fact, and usually at the age Gould is now, if it wasn't meant to be, it wasn't, nothing anyone can do about it, he'll meet someone soon if he keeps himself open for it, he's a terrific guy, smart and good-looking and decent and personable, and it'll be a more suitable woman, one not so quixotic and unreliable and flighty, or maybe this one will see all those fine qualities in him and change her mind, dump the other guy, or the guy might suddenly realize she was less than the ideal mate and drop her, though Robert hopes she doesn't come running back, because she's not good enough for Gould, that's all it is, but give it a few days to a week for her to call, and try not to be so sad as she said, she doesn't deserve it, and gave him a few tranquilizers—"You use them? I never would have thought"—and Robert said he just happened to have them in his book bag for a time several months ago when because of his work and love life he was under some stress, and to take three a day at eight-hour intervals and call him anytime he wants, at 4 A.M. if he needs to, and they'll speak or meet. Robert and he took care of their mother when she was very sick. Long before that they helped her take care of their father, alternated giving him his shots, took him out for strolls, changed and cleaned him and fed and shaved him and other things. They were together when their mother died. Sat alongside her bed, each holding one of her hands till the end, cried on the other's shoulder and chest after. Cleared out her apartment together. "Take whatever you want of hers, anything," and Gould said, "You the same. You're the older one. Mom had some beautiful antiques, and I don't mean that in a funny way, coming after what I just said about you. And if all I get left with is some pots and pans, that's okay too," and Robert said, "Good God, Gould, what do you think I am, a vulture? Whatever I want to keep of hers is in my head, so I'm taking even less than you." He once thought if Robert died before him he'd be as sad as when his mother and father died. When his mother died he was the saddest he ever was for anything, and he'd probably be as sad as that. Wouldn't go to work for a week. That's what happened after she died: he couldn't. Hardly ate, drank himself to sleep for days. Didn't do anything in that time but the essential household tasks and take a few short walks, crying and crying. In the market the one time he went, suddenly bursting out crying. In bed at night, or sitting in the dark in front of the memorial candle he lit for her, crying. Dreaming of her every night for weeks and during his daytime naps. But then at least he had Robert to speak to on the phone, each of them saying things like "Is it as bad for you as it is for me? I know it is, but I'm just saying." That's how he'd most likely act if Robert died before him, everything he mentioned about his mom. Now he thinks, What else would he be doing with Robert if he had lived? He'd probably call him up now and if Robert was the one who picked up the phone, he'd say, "Hi, it's me, Gould, just checking in with you and seeing how you're doing, as I've been thinking of you," and Robert might say, "I know it's you, don't you think I recognize your voice by now, so why do you always give your name?" and he'd say, "Habit, I guess, something I do with most people—even with my wife, if you can believe it—though to my kids I always say, 'It's Daddy,' " and they'd talk, each telling the other some of the more significant or intriguing or funny or absurd things that had happened or interesting thoughts that had occurred to him since their last phone conversation, which might have been a few days to a week ago or even earlier today, though there'd have to be a special reason for one of them to call back the same day other than they'd been cut off or there was something important he forgot to say or he had said he'd get back to him with something, and then Robert would say, after a long silence when they seemed to have run out of things to talk about, or after no silence but when he thought the call had already cost Gould too much money, "So, that's it from here, and I seem to have heard everything worth telling from there, unless you've something else to say, since I don't want to take it on myself to cut us off, and I hope to see you soon," and Gould would say, "No, no, I'm done, and same to you about seeing you soon, and much love to everyone at home," and Robert would say, "Best to yours too."

The Door

He's had it here and has to get away. Leaves a note: *I'm gone, probably for good. You must have seen it coming. I can't tell you how sorry I am it had to end like this. But I better stop writing this note or I'll never get out of here. Love to the three of you. I'll try to contact you soon.* Goes; packed a few things—couple of shirts, pair of pants, socks, handkerchiefs, sweatshirt and sneakers and running shorts, shaving equipment, things for his teeth and a hairbrush, underpants—and left the house with this small suitcase and a book under his arm and a coat on, rain hat in one side pocket, wool cap and gloves in the other, muffler around his neck though he doesn't need it on this rather mild day and should have packed it, and is off—to where? Where should he go? And how does he get there and why's he leaving? He's leaving because he can't stand it here anymore. There's got to be another or better reason, or he can elaborate on that one. Because he feels stifled, trapped. What does he mean? He's not quite sure. He thought he knew while he was saying it but now he doesn't. Then this: for the last ten years or so it's been nothing but work in every category for him, and he's dead tired and dejected and has to get away from it and everything else here. She knows that. He can't think things through or out or anything like that at home and needs to be on his own and get his head back in shape, and that's all there is to it no matter how vague and trite all or most of that sounds. Oh, hell, he just has to go, period. He's almost always unhappy here, period. He hates it here and has for years, period, period. No, he loves his kids but makes them miserable with his misery and complaints, so another reason why he has to go, besides the misery he causes his wife. He'll leave the car, the house, everything, all the bank and check accounts and whatever's in his pension fund: they're hers. How much money has he on him? His wallet—he forgot his wallet, and goes inside. He gets it off the shelf above the stove and counts. Long as he's here, he'll leave the keys. What use will they be for him now? House and car keys, keys to the building offices and rooms at work, key to the antitheft bar in the car, all of them on a ring, and he puts it on a hook by the kitchen door. He has three twenties and a few ones. That won't even get him a hotel room. Or it will, but a cheap one, or not so cheap: a small clean nice one someplace, but only for the night, and what'll he do for food? He puts three bagels and a package of processed cheese slices and a box of crackers and several carrots and a bottle of wine and the cheaper of their two corkscrews into the suitcase. That should hold him for a day and the wine for two. He needs change for the bus to the Greyhound station downtown. And cash for the Greyhound—doesn't want to use his credit card, as she'd get the bill—but their fares aren't steep and depend on where he's going. And honestly, why is he going? Plenty of reasons; it's not as if he hasn't thought of it before. But one main one: the one he said. He can't stand it here anymore. And it isn't going to change—things aren't and his feelings to them if he stayed—so there's a new reason to add to the main original one. He'll miss them, his kids and wife. He'll contact them, and maybe soon, as he said in the note. But he has to get far enough away from them where he knows he's gone from here and living alone or he'll crack up. He can crack up away from them too. He just might. Not voluntarily, but it can happen. Leaving them, the guilt. Living alone and starting over; he was never very good at it. Calling them, how he'll feel when they first speak. "Daddy, why did you go?" one of the kids could say. The other: "Daddy, you were mean to us sometimes and yelled too much, but we never wanted you to run away." "Gould, where are you and how do you feel?" his wife could say. "Come back, we'll try to make everything better. Whatever it is, you didn't have to take such desperate measures." Or "Good, you're gone, we're doing fine without you, don't even think of coming back." And one of the kids: "There's finally peace and quiet here, and we hope you have some too in your new life." "I love you," he could say, "love you both, love the three of you," and whomever he says this to could say, "Yeah, you really showed it," and hang up. The envelope addressed to his wife on the dining room table. She deserves an explanation and through her the kids. He takes the note out and writes under his signed first name, *Dearest. And I know it must seem odd if not perverse, my calling you "dearest," but I don't want to go into it: I haven't the time to digress. I just want to say why I left and give some instructions about our common property and then go. I had to leave because I couldn't take it here anymore. I was going nuts from all the work I was doing and other things. I know how hard my going might turn out for the three of you. To ease things, you can have everything we own. All I've taken are a few clothes and personal items and a hundred dollars.* He runs to the bedroom, gets forty dollars out of an old billfold in his drawer, takes his passport out also and sticks it into his back pocket, runs back to the dining room with the billfold and the rest of the money and their passports in it, and continues the note. *This billfold, which I'm leaving under the envelope addressed to you, has about $200 in it. Actually, now that I think of it, I'll need at least $200: that ought to do as a start. So it has about a hundred in it,* and he takes a hundred dollars from the billfold and counts the money left. *It has $120. It's yours. As is the car, house, furniture, all the money in our accounts and my pension fund, and when I get work, if I do, I'll start sending you more. Everything, then, is yours. I took a box of crackers, cheese, bagels, bottle of wine and the old corkscrew (one with the wooden handle), and, of course, some of my clothes and toilet articles, but I said that. But that's all I'll ever want from what I have here. Books (except the one I took), typewriter, etc., I'm leaving behind for good. If you want me to sign something legal along these lines—if this note and my full signature (which I'll put at the bottom) and date aren't sufficient—let me know first time I call. I don't know when that'll be. I don't even know where I'll be tonight. I know I'm taking a bus today from the station downtown, though so far I don't know to where. But I have to go. I can't explain anything more about why I feel I have to, as I'm not that sure myself. I just know I got to get away from here and my head thoroughly cleared. It's all been too much for me. That might seem a bit overdramatic, but the work at work, work at home, work with the kids and you, and just about everything. I need some rest and peace, maybe a new life, but definitely time to think things out alone. Meaning, by a "new life," to do something different than I've been doing nonstop the last 17 years. The girls are old and mature enough to take care of themselves with your help. And they'll in turn be a great help to you. I'm just a detraction, if that's the word. I yell too much, get excited too often, fill the house with hatred and gloom and discord and frustration and everything else like that. I'm not making much sense. Give me time to, when I call maybe I'll make more sense. I'll have had a little rest and* *peace (even just to be alone on a bus trip will help), my head will have started to be cleared, so I'm hoping that'll be the case. I've left my keys on a hook by the kitchen door. If you were thinking of changing the locks, don't, since I'm leaving without even a spare house key, though you'll have to take my word on that. I didn't mean to sound duplicitous with that last remark. I didn't take a spare key, I swear. Anyone calls for me—well, work certainly will, and the rest—tell them I'm gone, I'm winded, I had to get away from everything here because I thought if I didn't I was going to get a quick heart attack while at the same time lose my mind. And that you don't know where I went and that I left a note—* The kitchen door opens. One of the kids comes in. "Daddy, hi, we're back. Mommy needs your help. What are you writing?" "Nothing," and he tears up the note and sticks the pieces into his pants pocket. "Why'd you tear it up?" and he says, "Nothing, no reason. Something I was writing down to remember something else, but I just decided I'll remember it without my having to write it down." He shoves the envelope and billfold into another pants pocket. "What's the suitcase for?" and he says, "The suitcase? I thought it had some of my winter clothes in it, which I've been looking for, but it doesn't." "Oh. You better go outside. She told me to get you if you were home," and he says, "I'm coming, let me get my coat on." "You're wearing it," and he says, "Right, I am. I was about to leave the house when I thought of all those reminders I thought I had to make. What I meant, though, was that I have to go to the bathroom first. Tell Mommy I'll be right there," and she goes outside, and he gets the food, wine, and corkscrew out of the suitcase, returns them to the places he took them from, runs to the storage closet at the back of the house with the suitcase and leaves it there—he'll get the clothes and other stuff out of it later—puts the old billfold back in his drawer, note scraps into the wastebasket by his desk, thinks, Did he forget anything? What did he forget? Hell with it, can't be important—the envelope!—and tears it up and drops the pieces into the basket and runs to the kitchen and goes outside. "Hi," he says to his wife's helper, standing by the opened trunk of her car, and then "Hi" to his wife sitting in the front passenger seat. "I'm stuck," she says, "and I don't want Jenna injuring her back getting me into the wheelchair—she's already pulled a muscle there," and he says to Jenna, "Oh, yeah? Run hot shower water on it—not even hot;

warm, any kind of fast spray. For at least fifteen minutes and often as you can. That's what an osteopath told me to do and I thought it was hokum at first but it's worked almost every time," and he gets the wheelchair out of the trunk, thinks, Jesus, at least the girl could have taken the damn thing out, unfolds it, puts the cushion down and hand towel over it, and rolls the chair to his wife, carefully unhooks her calves twisted together and swivels her around in the seat till she's facing the car door—"There, that wasn't too hard"—and she says, "You know how to do it better than anyone. But the hardest part's plumping me into the chair. Jenna and the kids haven't mastered that yet without the danger of my falling out or their straining themselves," and he says, "What's the difficulty?" and locks the brakes, gets her under the arms, and hoists her into the chair. "Thanks. You go back to what you were doing. Jenna can wheel me in." He's got to get away from here. Her illness, crying, depression, frustration, cuts on her legs every day when she snags them on the metal of her wheelchair or rams into something, the infections, smells, always asking him for something, just when he's sitting down exhausted to read or nap or try to work after doing something else for her—"Gould, you'll have to go to the pharmacy for me"; "Gould, I'm on the floor"—her troubled sleep every night keeping him up, and so on, it's never going to end, and his anger and frustration, saying he won't yell again and then yelling again, it's all going to get worse and go on and on and he has to get away from it. He puts on his sweater and coat, muffler and knit cap, sticks his gloves into the coat pockets and wallet into his back pants pocket, gets his key ring off its kitchen hook, and goes outside and gets into the car and starts it up. No other clothes, bags, valises, or food or drink or anything else. His pen and a book? No, don't go back for anything, because if he does he has a feeling he'll never leave. Once the car warms up—another minute in this cold—just drive the hell away from here. He has some money on him: eighty, ninety. That should do for the day and tonight, and when he runs out he'll get a few hundred more with his card at a cash machine, and that'll be it. So he waits, thinking, Why's he doing this? He's already given enough reasons—he's got to because he can't for the life of himself stay—and then drives out of the carport, thinking, He's doing it, he's really going ahead with it, he's off, goddammit, off! At the stop sign at the end of the street his driveway connects to, he thinks, Which way should he go, right or left? and then thinks, Left, to the beltway and five miles south on it take the interstate west, and from there who knows where? He'll send a letter. To her and the kids. Or addressed to her but also for the kids. Or a fax from someplace, but their word processor at home only seems to be able to receive them half the time, and E-mail's too cold and he's not sure of the address or even how to send one, since he's never used a WP. So an overnight letter explaining whatever he thinks needs to be explained and that everything they own is hers. He'll need some money to get started—three to four hundred, tops; that's not asking too much—which'll be why she'll see that amount withdrawn from their check account, but he swears that'll be all: no need to fear he'll overdraft. For work he'll take a dishwashing job if he has to to get started someplace—anything, but just to be on his own. That's what he needs to be most, now: alone. It's become too difficult for him. Way too: frustrations and self-reproach and much worse every day, he'll say. It's that or shooting himself—"that" being leaving and starting anew—and he doesn't want to get melodramatic about it; he's not shooting himself or doing himself in in any way if things don't work out the way he'd like. It was an expression, a term. No, he'll write an altogether different letter. That he's gone, which should be obvious, or maybe not so obvious that he's gone for more than a night, as he left without taking anything but his coat and muffler: outerwear and the clothes he had on him and the car. And he loves her, loves the kids—and the car he'll return or tell her where to have someone pick it up as soon as he gets a place to stay in a city with good public transportation, or he'll sell it and give her all the money he gets for it, though for that she'll have to find the car's title in her files and send it on. But all that for later. Now he just wants to say how much he admires her: what she's had to put up with, her illness and him. And how sorry he is, he can't tell her how much other than to say very, deeply, disturbingly for what he's doing now and has done to her and the kids in the past. And something about their money and property, he'll say in this letter: that she can have all there is, other than the few hundred he's already withdrawn from their check account to get started. And whatever he earns in the future—within reason, that is, meaning not if he's barely making enough to live on—half will go to her and the kids. And he'll call her when he gets settled. But not to come join him, just to find out how she and the kids are and to tell her, if she's interested, and he could see why she wouldn't be, that he's safe and doing relatively okay. Anyway—car entering the beltway—what will she think when she gets in the house? He should have stopped for a minute or two, before he left, to leave a note. First she'll be curious he's not there, since he didn't say he was going anywhere today, and then concerned, maybe even worried or angry, and by late tonight, after a few phone calls to places he could have gone and people who might know where he is—friends, colleagues, his office—and because she got no calls from a hospital or the police, she'll have understood he left her and the kids and no doubt why. And the kids: how will they take it? They'll be so sad, but maybe also angry and confused. But she might also be a little frightened once she realizes he's not coming back. Suppose she falls and hurts herself: will the kids be able to take care of her till help comes? Or maybe she'll be glad he's finally gone, despite the hardships she'll have to face. The three of them glad, once the difference of his not being there sinks in. He yells too much. He's often so damn impatient and vituperative. He sometimes screams and curses to himself like a madman. "What am I doing here?" he's yelled when all of them were around. "How'd I get into this? I've got to get the hell away. I hate this place, hate this freaking house, hate my life! I can't stand anyone or anything anymore and it's never going to get better and it's driving me crazy!" How many slamming doors can they all take? The kids slamming them on him: "You're scaring me," "You're upsetting my stomach," "I can't concentrate on my homework with your yelling." His wife wanting to slam doors on him and sometimes succeeding. He slamming the door on them too. Lots. "I've got to be alone and get some quiet, goddammit!" he yelled last night, slamming his bedroom door and sitting at his desk. "The music, turn it down lower, that's what's half doing it!" he shouted, and when it wasn't turned down low enough for him, though whichever kid was playing it did turn it down, he slammed open the bedroom door—that's the only way he can put it: the door slammed against the wall when he threw it open—and went into the hallway; the music was coming from his older daughter's room and he threw open her door where it slammed against the bookcase along the wall, and yelled—she was reading on her bed—"Didn't you hear me? Are you deaf? Do we have to go to an ear doctor for you as well as the eye doctor and dentist and bone doctor for your feet?" and she looked at him, as if saying, What in the world are you ranting about?, took off her glasses and stared petulantly at him, and said, "You know, you could have knocked first. You didn't have to scare me by banging my door," and he said, "Knocked? Knocked? Let me tell you, kid—" but caught himself and said, "Oh, what am I doing to you, to everyone here?" and grabbed his hair and began pulling it, and she said, "Daddy, don't, you'll hurt yourself," and he said, "Everything's wrong"—his eyes were closed and he'd stopped pulling and he heard her book fall to the floor—"everything, you name it, this is all such crap, it's gotten too damn screwing hard," and pulled her door closed and went into his room, shut his door so slowly he heard the latch click, and lay on the bed and turned off his night-table light to be in the dark, but the desk lamp was on and he didn't want to get up to turn it off too. His wife came in a few minutes later and said, "Now what could have provoked that?" and he said, "Something, I forget. I don't want to talk about it," and looked away, and she said, "You realize how frightened the girls get? Something has to be terribly wrong for such an outburst. Just don't say it's nothing or not worth talking about," and he looked at her and said, "Okay, it's everything. I can't stand it here; the whole damn joint's driving me up the wall," and she said, "Then leave, go, because I'm tired of hearing how living here is so horrid and we're such a burden on you and driving you crazy, because you're gradually driving us crazy too," and he said, "Good idea then; tomorrow, maybe," and she said, "If you mean you're leaving, I hope so, or that you at least want to start talking about it and working it out so it doesn't happen again," and stayed there staring at him—for an answer, he assumed—and he looked away and then said, "Would it be possible to shut off my desk lamp, please?" and she left the room and later went to sleep in her study, didn't come back, as she usually did—the two to three times a year things got so bad between them that she slept in another room—to get her pillows and a long-sleeved T-shirt she always sleeps in. This morning he woke up at the usual time, made sure his older daughter was up—"You don't have to check on me; I have my watch alarm"—set the table for her and her sister, asked if she wanted him to make her toast, and she said, "I'm not hungry," and he said, "You have to eat something," and she said,

"It's my body and I'll do what I want with it and that old myth about breakfast being so important has been debunked by doctors," and he said, "Okay, if you say," drove her to school, didn't try to give her his customary goodbye kiss because he knew by her look and silence and coldness to him all morning that she wouldn't let him touch her, just said when she got out of the car, "See ya, and have a great day," and she said, "Oh, yeah, *great day,* thanks to you," and he said, "It was just an expression, and one I hate," but she didn't answer that; drove back, his other daughter was at the table having breakfast and reading and never looked up or responded to the one thing he said—"Will that little bowl of cereal be enough for you?"—saw her to the school bus stop, best not to say anything to her in the mood she's in, he thought, but she said while they were standing there, "Why do you always have to yell and curse so much?"—he was looking at the sky and the tops of trees so as not to look at her and maybe make her feel self-conscious—and he said, "What?" and she said, "You know. It isn't good for you, especially the yelling, and both make it ugly for us. Awful ugly. It's horrible, like Mommy's said, and ruins everything that could be nice," and he said, "You have a point, and I'm not just saying that. I'll think about what you said, and thanks for bringing it up," and she said, "The bus," and he said, "You can always hear things faster than me, but are you sure?" and he listened and finally heard it and then the bus appeared and he stepped forward to kiss her, thinking, They've talked a little about it, so maybe she'll let him, but she backed away when he put his arm out to draw her head to his face, and got on the bus and sat where she always did, talking to the same girl across the aisle she talks to every morning, and he thought, Don't even try to wave to her, she's not going to look, and when the bus was gone he thought, She's right, he should get out of here. She didn't say that but she hinted it. Even if she didn't hint it, it's what she wants. Even if she doesn't want it and her sister and mother don't, it'd be best if he did, for all of them, and he went back to the house, took off his sweatshirt and put on a sweater and coat and such, got the keys, started to open the door to the carport, thought of it a few seconds more, thought, Yes, he's really got to get away from here for a long time, though he doesn't know how long, and grabbed his gloves off the dryer and went outside and got in the car and left. Driving, he thinks of his daughter getting on the bus and immediately starting to talk animatedly with the girl across the aisle and the way his other daughter got out of the car and methodically got all her things together and walked to the school entrance, carrying her art portfolio and art supply box in one hand, other hand holding the strap of her backpack on her shoulder and her silver antique purse by its chain. Such beautiful girls, he thinks, so good, and young. Why does he persecute them the way he does? Torture them, whatever he does to them, make life miserable for them so much, for what'd they do? Well, that's why he's leaving, isn't it?—because he does all that. And his wife. She hasn't got it bad enough? Why can't he just adjust to it all, take it more easily, not think he has to do the same number of things in the same amount of time he did them before she got sick? Why can't he slow down a little, slow down a lot, take it as it comes, and so forth? Why does he resort so much to such extreme behavior, yelling when things get him down or he feels overtaxed, slamming doors, cursing, gibbering, mumbling insulting things to them under his breath, storming out of the house, hurling a book across the room, crumpling up the newspaper he's reading and then in a worse fit tearing pages of it into shreds, sweeping a filled dish rack into the sink, throwing a mug to the floor, kicking a door (once punching one), tearing at his hair and once ending up with a clump? He can try, can't he?—he's tried and tried but he can try to try harder—to show more control and think more about why he's doing these things and their consequences, because—who's he fooling?—he can't leave. It'll be too tough for them and he's hurt them plenty enough already and he doesn't want to go and live alone and all the other things, and he drives a little farther—Yes, he thinks, yes? It's just going to take longer getting back—and signals for a U-turn and drives home. His wife's in the kitchen when he gets there, and he says, "Hello," and smiles and puts the keys on the hook, and she says, "How nice; you're happy. You've forgiven yourself and erased from your mind everything you did last night," and he says, "Just the opposite," and she says, "I don't believe it. Where were you, though? I only ask because I called for you when I had trouble getting off the bed. It's too high," and he says, "Sorry, I was just taking a drive," and she says, "You? You never drive to just drive. It always has to be *to* somewhere, even in the fall when I ask you to drive me around so I can see the leaves," and he says, "When the girls were real small? And we couldn't get them to nap when we desperately needed them to have one, so I'd put them in their car seat—" and she says, "Only Fanny; Josephine never had a problem napping." "Well, today I had lots of serious things on my mind and some free time so I drove to think them out," and she says, "And what came out of it?" and he says, "I'm not intentionally changing the subject, but did you at least sleep well?" and she smiles and says, "You do so don't want to answer. Either because nothing did come out or you didn't drive just to think or you're hiding something. But you better say more than that you're sorrier than you were the last time and realize why you did what you did last night and it won't happen again, no matter how many times you know I've heard you say that, because that's what you always say and I always eventually say okay, and it always happens again," and he says, "I also thought of that and I swear I'll also try to change my behavior, everything. But actually, to be absolutely honest, what I originally drove off for before I had all these thoughts—or rather, these thoughts came because of what I originally drove off for, if you can follow me—was to leave you and the kids. I left with nothing but the car, which I was going to get back to you somehow, and had intended to start out new with nothing in some new place. Then during the drive I thought about you and the kids—of course, you were all in my mind right from the beginning—but this time of the consequences to you and me about my leaving for good, and drove back. I know I can be a miserable bastard, irritable, critical, and a slew of other more contemptible and reprehensible things, and that I have a lot of changes in myself to make, though I'm not sure on everything how I will, and that last point I'm sorry but I don't think I made too clear," and she has her hand to her face, had it there since he first said he'd left them, and says, "Wow, what a shocker! I don't know what to say or how to digest any of it, even where to begin. I'm not going to say you're making up the part about leaving us to deflect from how you acted last night or to say something shocking or new, because I know what you'll say, and that could start another argument. But you're not, are you, making it up?" and he says, "What do you think I'm going to say?" and she says, "What a surprise, though. Anyway, I'm glad you didn't go—you didn't just come back for your clothes, I hope. But you're not off the hook yet, and for the time being, welcome back," and he says,

"Great, and thanks," and bends down to kiss her, and she says, "Not right now, if you don't mind. Even if you do," and wheels herself out of the room, suddenly looking angry. He has to get away from everything here: family and work. His wife's at her physical therapy session, kids are at school, and he packs a few clothes and personal belongings and gets in the car and drives to another city. He gets a cheap hotel room for a week, buys a newspaper, and looks in the Help Wanted section. He sees a few jobs that might be for him and calls one. He's interviewed, gets the job, and starts work the next day. When he gets his first week's salary he rents a furnished room. He constantly thinks he has to speak to them, he can't let them continue to worry, and two weeks after he left home, he calls. "Oh, God, I knew I'd have to face this one day," his wife says, "though it's good to hear your voice. You're all right? Where are you? We thought you could be dead." "That's why I called. I'm living in another city and I don't plan to come home." The other phone's picked up, and his older daughter says, "Where are you calling from, Daddy? We were so worried. We all thought you were dead and then thought you couldn't be because your car wasn't found. That's what the police lady told us." "You went to the police for me and they couldn't find me? I don't know why. I got a job. I gave my real name and Social Security number and already got a pay check. I could have been traced." "We didn't get the police to search for you. We only wanted to know—Mommy did—if you got into a car accident and were dead." "Well, I'm not, sweetie. And the car I'm giving back to the family. I left home, that's all. Not 'that's all,' of course, because it's a lot. But I couldn't take it there anymore. It's been too much for me. You've seen that and how I always react. Not 'always,' but too often. You know I've been threatening to go for a long time. And so, when things got too much for me a couple of weeks ago, I went. I know my going is a crazy act of sorts. Or not 'of sorts,' but simply crazy and wrong and every name in the book you want to put on it. But I don't want to talk anymore about it than I just have. I couldn't take it there anymore. I know I already said that, but I didn't know it while I was saying it. There's a perfect example—or not 'perfect,' but just an example—of where my mind is now. Don't even ask how I got a new job with my mind in this condition, but I got one. I'm working. As menial a position as there ever was one—'position' is too good a word for it, even—but it does provide me with enough for a cheap room—and so I don't starve—and my newspaper and coffee every day, and for now that's all I want. Or need. Or want. Or both. Everything there is yours, though. Where you live, I mean—all I have. Are you listening, Sally? I want you and the kids to have—" and she says, "I heard, but I can't understand how you could say to her what you just did and going on with it as if it has no effect. You didn't hear her crying?" "No, is she?" "Now she's away from the phone, but before, she was, into it, and she's still crying. You also saying you didn't hear me telling you to stop and that if you have to say these things, to say them only to me when she's off the phone?" "No, also. My hearing's bad. I'm getting old. It's been going for a long time, my ears." "Leaving us is one thing—just slipping out without a word, though of course it troubled us till we knew better and it still affects us deeply. But acting cruel like that on the phone to her once you're gone?" and he says, "I was acting cruel? Oh, I'm so sorry. I didn't mean that 'oh, so sorry' sardonically, by the way. Not 'sardonic,' but you know what I mean. For I'm really sorry. I wouldn't hurt her for the world, either kid, you too, though I know I have in the past with my rages and cursing and outbursts and you name it, which I'm so sorry for too." "I have to take care of her; she's crying even worse now. Don't call back if that's how you're going to act on the phone," and she hangs up. He calls his boss and says he won't be in today and probably never again and she doesn't have to pay him for the days he weeked this work. "I mean, worked this week. I'm a little confused because I've just decided to go back to my family. I didn't tell you I have one. I in fact thought if I did tell you you wouldn't hire me because you'd think I'd deserted them, but I do: kids, wife, house, even a cat. Thanks for taking me on when I didn't have the right experience for it but needed a job badly. I'm being sincere about that." "Well, no, thank you, Bookbinder, because you've put me in one heck of a spot. It's not that you have a job no one else can do. But when I hired you I expected you to come in on time every day and, if you had to quit, then to give me at least a week's notice. Now I have to find someone fast or do what you're supposed to be doing while I'm doing all my other work. You change your mind about quitting, don't call me," and she slams the phone down. He packs his things and drives back home. The locks have been changed. He rings the doorbell. His younger daughter comes to the door, looks through it and screams "Daddy!" and runs out of the room. His wife comes to the door. "Go away," she says through it. "You're not welcome here anymore and you gave up your right to even be on the property." "But I've come back, quit my new job and room, and am determined to work it out here. Believe me, I've changed, or have come closer to it than I ever have. That last incident with Fanny on the phone did something to me. Please let me in. I'll sleep on the couch or anywhere you want, just so I'm home and the kids know I'm here for them, and you too, I hope, if you need my help." His daughters come into the kitchen. Older one whispers into his wife's ear; she shakes her head and shuts her eyes and says no and then nods and unlocks the door. "They thought I should. I only went along with it because I didn't want to hurt them further. You can sleep on the couch or in the basement. Either one, you'll have to make your own bed." "Will do, which is what I did every day anyway, making our bed, cooking all the dinners, doing most of the clean-up work and laundry and shopping and driving the kids around, not that I'm complaining or blaming you or them. In the end I liked doing things for you all; that's what I learned while I was away and from our last phone call. Hiya, girls," he says to his daughters. "What you did was horrible," his older daughter says. "Not on the phone as much as leaving us without saying anything." "Still," his younger daughter says, "we talked it over, Fanny and me, and we're glad to see you home and being so happy." "Thanks, my sweethearts," and he tries to kiss the girls but they back away and leave the room. "My reaction exactly," his wife says, "if you make a similar move to me. Please see that the house is locked up. And don't turn down the heat too low, as you like to do; we found less uncomfortable ways to save money," and goes to their bedroom. He sleeps on the couch, makes the kids breakfast the next morning, drives the older one to school, walks the younger one to the bus stop and waves goodbye, says to each of them, "It'll take time, but I assure you, everything will be good." Calls his old boss and says, "Quite truthfully, I had a breakdown of sorts a few weeks ago, which you must have heard about when someone there probably called to ask where I was. But everything's fine with me now and I'm eager to return to work, if you'll have me, and you have every reason not to, and no hard feelings if that's what you want," and the man says, "We all felt bad when we learned of it, and the job's still yours," and he goes to work. He has his first tantrum a week later. Something spills when he's making the kids breakfast, then the food he replaces it with burns, and the handle of the pan's so hot when he grabs it to take it off the stove that he drops it to the floor, and finally his younger daughter knocks over a glass of orange juice while reaching for something else. He shouts, "Do you always have to be so careless?" and she says, "I don't, always. It was an accident, like the French toast you burned and which I'll clean up." "It's always one mishap after another here. But I got to take Fanny to school. I got to get dressed. I got to shave and be at work in an hour. I have to make the goddamn money for this house and the paper towels we use by the carload and you kids. Who else is going to do it, your mom? I can't stay around here cleaning up everyone's mess, and I can't leave it there either, soaking into the table and the floor," and his older daughter says, "Josie said she'd clean it up, and I'll help her," and starts mopping up the juice on the table with her napkin. "What're you doing? You don't use a cloth napkin for that. That just makes one more thing for me to rinse out and take time with and wash in the machine." "What's the difference?" she says. "There's already juice on it, and I don't see why you're making it into such a big thing," and he says, "You don't, huh? Then I'll tell you. I'll tell you both why," and his younger daughter says, "Daddy, get control of yourself; you're getting excited over nothing," and he says, "Nothing to you, maybe, because you don't have to do all these things. But you're two of a pair: too clumsy to eat breakfast properly and, when you knock something over, too stupid to care," and they both start crying. "Oh, no," he says, "I'm so sorry," and his wife's yelling from her bedroom, "What's going on there? Gould, stop!" and he tries to hold them while he says, "Please forgive me; I made a mistake," but they push him away and run to their mother's room. "So run, run; that's what everyone should do with me. What's it matter anyway?" and thinks, It's always going to be like this. He's kidding himself to no end if he thinks he can ever change. Things pile up on him or seem to and it gets to him, that's all. Or it's not that but this: They'll do relatively nothing, he'll think it's a lot, he'll start berating and insulting them, they'll do what they should do and that's to fight back, he'll insult harder, they'll start crying, and he'll suddenly see what he's done and apologize but by then it'll be too late. It's never going to be anything but that. Or it will, but only for a few days to a week. Then back to normal and worse. Something like that. It's all one big confusion now, but he has to face it: when it comes to this home here, he's a hopeless case. He has to get away before he does even more damage to them. What was it someone once said? Forget it, what's the use of anything anyone says? No, years ago, when Fanny was less than a year old, not even walking yet. One of his married colleagues, over to the house for dinner, Fanny sitting on Gould's lap, and she reached out her bare feet till they were on the table and he said, probably kissing the top of her head, "Sweetheart, no little tootsies on the table while people are eating," and put them on his lap, and she laughed and extended them again to the table and he put them back on his lap and held them there while he ate or drank with his other hand, and she started crying and he set her down and said, "Just sit there, or crawl to your mother, but you have to learn sometime about not putting your feet on the table," and his colleague said, "What a responsibility, and I don't say this facetiously, and I'm only taking this minor incident as an example, to be so important to her in her formative years. The magnitude of it and the consumption of one's time makes me feel I could never be self-neglectful enough to have a child." And what did he answer the guy? What's the difference? The point here is that those formative years are long gone for both girls, and he failed. Now he's ruining their adolescent and teenage years, and if he stays with them he can be sure they'll be screwed up as adults. No matter what, he knows they'll be a lot better off without him than whatever good could come by his sticking around. So it's settled, then, right? and he thinks he tried but just couldn't swing it—"swing" isn't the word he wanted, but he knows what he means—and calls a cab, quickly sticks a few things of his into a shopping bag, cleans up the orange juice mess with the rest of the cloth napkins, starts up the washing machine with the napkins and a couple of soiled dish towels and a few things his wife had put in the night before, listens for his family—if one of them did come out he'd say the car isn't working and he's taking a cab to work and will see to the car later on—and goes outside to wait for the cab. During the drive he thinks, A note. No, by late tonight they won't even need a phone call from him or from someone at work asking why he hasn't come in to know that he's gone for good. This could be the saddest moment in his life if he thinks of it, he thinks, so he's not going to think of it if he can help it, and he stares out the window and breaks down. He gets on the train and a day later gets off in a big midwest city. No reason he chose this one other than to get far away in a not-too-strange place but one he's never been to before and where there'll be plenty of prospects for work. He rents a room, gets a job, tells people his wife and children died in a fire and he wanted to live someplace else because of that. Uses his real name and Social Security number, but no one in the family or a representative of it tries contacting him. The work he gets—waiting on tables and looking after the bar—is a step up from the last job he had when he ran off but has nothing to do with the kind of work he did for twenty years. One of the customers becomes interested in him. Comes in almost every other night, usually sits at the bar or one of his two tables; they talk about literature, art, music, and culture in between the time he makes drinks for the waitering staff or serves his other customers. She asks him one night if he'd like to take in a late movie after work sometime this week. They meet, see each other a few times after that for coffee and walks and other things before they start sleeping together. She has a nice apartment and invites him to move in with her. She gets him an ad-writing job with a friend of hers. They get married and have two children. He never tells her the truth about his previous family. She in fact tells him that one reason—maybe the main one—she wanted to have children, even though she was almost past the age for it and never thought of herself as a mother, was to help him replace the ones he lost. "Two children on earth who'd never be here if your previous two hadn't died so tragically," is the way she put it. He never calls his first wife and children and only wrote them one letter, a year after he left them and before he met this new woman, saying he hopes the following will serve as a legal document. *But it's more likely that what I'm about to say is a moot point and that my wife, because of my desertion, has already been granted a divorce and legal entitlement to everything I owned. Anyway: I, Gould Bookbinder, in right and sound mind, or however legal experts word it, do hereby declare that I willingly left my family a year ago.* Make that "voluntarily." *I voluntarily, in right and sound mind, or relatively so at the time, deserted my family and home a year ago. Thereby, from this day on,*

*I relinquish everything to my wife, Sally, and my daughters, Francine and Josephine: home, car, all money and possessions I might own, everything in the joint accounts held by my wife and me, and my pension money, royalties, the works, and from this day forward I will never make claim on any of these items or anything I didn't list here. Why did I go? That wasn't what I intended to write about but I suppose, while I have the opportunity (since I don't expect to write another letter like this)—and perhaps because it might also make this document more authentic and less contestable in a court of law, thus fulfilling the wish expressed here—I should. I just couldn't stay. I know that's not enough of a reason, but what can I say? It was all too much for me. No matter what I did or tried or hoped to do I didn't see how it could ever cease to be, with only brief reprieves or intermittent periods of peace, too much for me, and I'm sure it was too much—*I *was too much—for my family too. I felt I had to start a new life some other place. More for the sake of my family I felt this. But all explanations about this are futile and useless. Please don't try to find me. You can, I know—I'm not hiding, I'm even putting my address on the envelope—but please don't. I love you all deeply and madly and shall for the rest of my life, perhaps even more than I love you right now. I know you can say those are only words, but again, what can I say? With almost terrifying regrets and sadness, I remain,"* and signed his full name and wrote the date and had the letter notarized and put it in an envelope and addressed it and put his return address and a stamp on it. When he got to the mailbox to mail it he thought there was something wrong with the last part, it sounded so fake, and went home with the letter, blacked out "terrifying," and wrote in the margin beside it, *I blacked out the word myself because it was so fake; the word was "terrifying," and I should have blacked out the words "madly" and "deeply" too, solely so they wouldn't disturb you, which I sincerely hope they didn't do,* and initialed that part, had the letter renotarized, thought, That word "sincerely"; ah, mail it or he never will, and dropped it through the letter slot at the post office. About ten years later, when his wife's away on a business trip and his two daughters are sleeping, he sits in the living room reading a novel while listening to music and drinking. Maybe because of the drinks (a second and then a third grapefruit juice and vodka) and the music (to him, a particularly sorrowful part of a Bach cantata) and because of something he reads ("Hubert's family life broke apart, and as a result he was devastated to the point of never being whole again," an awful line that finishes the book for him on page 14), but he begins thinking of his first wife and children and becomes sentimental and gets out the photos of them he came to this city with and hasn't looked at for years and gets very sad and says to himself, "Oh, go on; what's the harm by now? All you want to do is hear one of them. If it's an answering machine or a strange voice and you ask for them and the person says the number's no longer theirs, then that's it till something else who-knows-when later." He dials his old number. A recorded message says the area code's incorrect for that number, and he gets the new area code and dials with it. Sally says hello. He stays silent. "Hello, hello?" He bursts out crying. "Gould?" "I've been such a bum," and he hangs up. He gets sick after that, knows it's related to the phone call. He doesn't try to fight it because he doesn't want to get well. He's taken to the hospital, brings the photos with him, and sneaks looks at them when no one's around. He does it to get even worse, maybe even die. He *has* been a bum, he tells himself, and he should pay for it. He won't eat; pulls out his tubes when he's able to. His second wife and two daughters visit him, and when they start crying he thinks, What's he doing? He has to be around for them as long as he can or it'll be like what he did to Sally and the kids. Maybe, if he gets well, he can apologize to his old family and they'll let him come see them and something can be worked out after all these years. A visit every few months; his two oldest daughters can visit here and see their step-sisters. They're all such great kids, he's sure they'll love one another. And money for Sally for whatever she needs. He tells himself to get better and gets better and when he's out of the hospital and recuperating at home he calls his old number and she answers and he says, "After my last call to you I nearly died. Literally, I mean, and I'm not saying that for sympathy. I'm just so sorry and ashamed for what I did to you and the girls. Please tell me they're alive and healthy. And you?" "I am, as you probably surmised, in much worse shape than when you last saw me. The girls are long out of the house and I've a permanent helper. Fanny's married and has a baby and is doing well in her work and lives in a city whose name I'm not going to divulge. Josie's in med school, but even that's more than she'd want me to say about her to you. I told them I thought you had called and started to sob and might call back and they each said they didn't want to hear about it and not to tell them if you call again. That you had probably remarried and have children and they're not interested in you anymore. That you damaged them enough the second time you left us and you're completely out of their lives. That's their message to you, although they didn't tell me to deliver it. I feel the same. I don't want to think or know anything more about you. We've been legally divorced since a short time before you sent me your one letter. The girls disowned you long ago. If you can, don't call again for the rest of your life, and no more letters," and she hangs up. Why didn't he stay? he thinks. He loved her, was attracted to her body and face; she had a great mind and was a wonderful person, and taking care of her wasn't that bad and the condition she has gets worse slowly, so he would have had time to adjust to the changes. He now has another lovely wife and two beautiful young daughters, but he didn't have to have them. So why didn't he stay? What's the point of answering? He gets sick again and wants to die. He recovers, but because of nothing he did, and takes a lot of pills after and dies. He's got to get away from here, he thinks. He writes a note. Or he leaves and sends a letter from the place he ended up in. Or he calls that night from another city and says, "I've left for good." Says it to his wife. First his older daughter answered and said hello and he said, "Hiya, my darling, how are you?" and she said, "Fine," and he said, "And your sister?" and she said, "Fine, also, I guess. But we've been wondering—Mommy too—where you are and what happened to you. It's only been one day, but we've been worried," and he said, "Don't be, and let me speak to Mommy, please?" Or sends an overnight letter to his wife: *I won't be home. I only stopped for a night in this city. I'm moving on. I probably won't even settle in a city. I might go live in a town or village in Canada or the Northwest or even overseas. Japan's a place I always wanted to go and possibly live the rest of my life in—a remote mountain village somewhere—but that's not to say I'm going to do that. Anyway, everything—that means everything we own or possess together or what was solely mine—is yours and then yours to give to the kids or do what you want with. What can I say other than what you've heard from me in sometimes hysterical foul language a few hundred times before: I just couldn't take it or stay there anymore. But what's that actually mean? That even if things had been going swimmingly it would have eventually seemed horrible and unlivable to me no matter how good they continued to be. I don't think I can enjoy something for very long and in fact I think I start disbelieving and disliking it if it—well, I was going to say—ah, forget it. But know it's nothing you did or could have prevented, or the kids—I swear. I'm just hopeless, in both ways, and probably in more ways than I know.* He has some cash and settles in a small Alaskan town. Rents a shack, gets a job in a grocery store, stocking and selling and everything else. Meets a woman and she needs a place to stay. Why's he always have to have a woman with him after a short time without? he thinks. Why can't he this time just live out his life alone? He doesn't contact his wife and kids after the first time. He tells the woman what he did and she says she can understand: "Hey, sometimes situations get impossible—incourageable, if that's the right word for it—so best to get up and go and never gawk back. Your wife will do wonders without you—better than she did with, based on what you said—and same for your kids." "You really think so? I don't, but what can I do about it, much as I love her and worship my kids, since if I went back it might be nice for a while for me and them but then I'd resort to my old impatient and hateful and crazy ways," and she says, "That's sort of what I'm saying, silly. The devil only knows why I'd want to live with such a horror." He leaves her a year later and never takes up again with anyone else. Why'd he break up with her and then give her the shack with its rent for the next year prepaid and leave everything he owned behind and get an even smaller, colder place to live? Why even go into it? He left like that because he wanted to get out fast. She was dumb and coarse and slovenly and smoked and watched TV most of the day and had nothing to say and vilified books and learning and good manners and smeared grease on her legs and face at night and spent an hour or two a day putting on ugly makeup and carped too long when she didn't think he'd tried hard enough to please her in bed, when the truth was, though he didn't say it—he only said, "Listen: it's the same as it's always been with me. I make life miserable for anybody I'm with"—he was thoroughly unattracted to her in every way and his inability to stay even semierect may also be because of his advanced age. Long after that he tries calling his old home, just to hear their voices and maybe, if they speak to him, to see how they are, but the number's been someone else's for a few years "and the party people used to call when I first got the phone doesn't sound like the one you're asking for," the man says. He dials Information and is told they're not in the book or listed in that city. Maybe they're not living there anymore, he thinks, or even living, but he quickly closes and opens his eyes several times to get rid of that thought. He supposes he could call friends they once knew, if they're still around, to find out where she went or what happened to her and the kids, but he's sure they've all been told not to speak to him about that and he also feels too embarrassed to call. He begins to drink a great deal, gets sick, but works every day till he drops dead on the job. Before he died he thought it would have been nice to retire a few years before and have the time to walk and read and maybe draw things he sees. If he had stayed with his family he could have done all that: visited his daughters and their children, if they have any; looked after himself better. But he didn't even collect Social Security. He arranged it so that office would send the checks to his wife and, if she died, then to his kids. A few days before he died he wrote a note and left it on his night table, which was just a crate. The envelope the note was in said: *To the Proper Authorities After I'm Dead: Please see—or do your best, please—that this gets to my wife, Sally Bookbinder, or my surviving children, Francine and Josephine. Or to my ex-wife, Sally, since I'm sure she divorced me years ago (her maiden name was Sutherland, though she may have remarried and taken the last name of her second husband),* and he gave her address—*I'm sure she's no longer there, but maybe the note can be forwarded*—and Social Security number, which he'd memorized years before he left when she said she knew his, and the names and addresses of several of their old friends. The note: *Oh, my darling Sally, as ugly and hypocritical as that salutation must sound to you, how horrible I feel about all I've put you through and everything you must have gone through after I left and are probably still going through, though I hope not. But what's the point of saying all this, other than to get rid of some of the crap that's been inside me for so many years, all brought by my guilt at leaving you and Fanny and Josie. My everlasting love to you and them—"eternal" rather than "everlasting," or whatever word best describes in the least phony-sounding way "the longest, the most unending, the never dying," even if I know it's worth zero now, though maybe someday it'll mean something, no matter how little, to them. Yours, Gould.* He has to get away from here, he thinks. "I was just thinking, I sometimes can't take it here anymore and feel like I've got to get away," he says. "Go, don't let me stop you—you have one feverish itchy foot out the door as it is," Sally says. "I can't go. How can I? If I do I'll be full of guilt and shame and everything else—tormented, heartsick, you name it—from then on. When I do go, though—meaning *if* I go—it'll only be after the kids are out of college and I've paid up all the bills for it, so you and they won't have to go broke or badger me for dough, and they're out of the house and safely on their own." "So, in the intervening years—we're talking about nine or ten of them—you're to stay here and make our lives miserable with your whining and bitching and once-a-month hysterics that you hate it here and have to go?" "I won't whine or do anything like that. I know what it does to you all. Really, I've been thinking about a solution to my going till the time comes when I feel I can go. I'll be a good father, soft-spoken, patient. Same thing as a husband—I won't even disturb you. We can sleep in separate rooms if you want, go our separate clichés. If you wish to come see me some nights, or for me to pay you a visit, as you used to say, in your room, do so anytime you wish so long as I'm not physically sick. But even there I'd be as gentle as my sickness permits in telling you I'm in no fit condition for it, and I'll never try initiating anything like that with you, since I'm sure ninety-five percent of the times you'd be revolted or at the very minimum put off by the idea." "Excuse me, but what are we talking of here? Not sex." "I'm sorry, I don't know why I brought it up—certainly not because I was circuitously trying to get you interested in it now—so forget I said it. Maybe, only to demonstrate how thoroughly and independently our separate lives could be led while still satisfying some of the primary exigencies, I'll call them. I guess what it comes down to is I want to try living here as though I'm living alone but while still living with the three of you in a pleasant domestic setting, if that makes any sense." "It doesn't," and he says, "Let me see." He thinks. "You're right, it makes little sense, as I don't see how I can pull it off without your cooperation, particularly with that one exigency every now and then. For you see, if I had to go outside for it, not that I'd know where to look or would be successful if I did,

I'd feel grossly guilty if I succeeded. Worse, or maybe better, so guilty beforehand over what I'd know I'd feel after, that I probably couldn't go through with it, or at least complete it, even if you had said to go ahead and get as much as I want, for all you care. Come on, what am I talking about? I can't leave you alone here with the kids. I'll stay and try even harder not to whine about my life in this house or go into any sudden tantrums. But I can't just run off, though you might like that prospect—and anything you said about that now wouldn't convince me either way or persuade me to do otherwise—since I know how much it'd hurt the kids: not that I left them but also you. So you're stuck with me for the time being, although part of me has gone, it seems, if that makes any sense. Does it? Sure it could if I worked my brain hard enough to make it." "Maybe the way you've mediated it is for the best for all of us, or simply better for me and the girls now than your just up and going, so okay, stay." He stays. She continues to sleep in their bedroom; he sleeps in the basement; they all eat dinner and go to movies and concerts together. The kids are confused by this at first. He tells them it can happen in any marriage after a while but that doesn't mean the new arrangement's permanent. "It could get worse; it could get better. Be optimistic like me and think it's going to return to family-normal pretty soon but without any of my previous griping and ferocity. The important thing to know is your parents still love each other deeply." Sally overhears him saying this and says, "Stop feeding them so much baloney. We're living this way for convenience' sake only. It's cheaper for your father than keeping up two homes, and of course he wants to be around you kids. And much easier for me with him here, in case I take a spill or am about to. We also feel it's better for you to have both your folks around, as long as they remain in relative harmony, which was the main condition I made to agree to it. Your father starts fulminating again or under his breath calling me every name under the sun, the deal's been abrogated for the last time." "What 'last time'?" he says. "This is the first time we made the damn deal since we got married. So how can you—" but he's losing control, so he quickly says, "Actually, maybe you're right: not a big thing." Sally never suggests to him they have sex. About once a month he says to her, late at night or when the kids are off somewhere, "Excuse me, but I've been wanting to do you-know-what for a couple of weeks now but held back asking you. I thought you'd object to it. But it now seems imperative, where it's even disturbing my workday and sleep, so do you think you'd mind if we made love or just had sex or you just let me have sex with you for a few minutes? I'm so far gone, I'm sure that's all it'll take. But the whole shebang, I'm saying, meaning penetration, though I don't have to come in you if you don't want me to and where I'll even catch the crap in my hand and not mess up you or your sheet." "I mind very much. I don't feel like doing anything like that with you." "Too bad. You know me and how much more harmonious and compatible it'd make me for the next few weeks. Of course, do what you wish, as we first agreed to when we fabricated this freaking, faking, frustrating arrangement." Every six months or so she says, "Why not, it's been a long time and you've been a good boy, and I feel a little like doing it too," and after it's over she says something like "I don't know why I went along with it. You were too rough, my breasts will be sore for a week, and I didn't even begin to get enjoyment out of it before you were done in a wink. And now you'll expect a repeat performance soon, thinking I'll be willing, but which I won't consent to—it simply doesn't work for me, nor is it good for our living arrangement. And you'll say not true, and that next time, because it won't be six months from the last time, you'll go much slower, and probably end up getting angry because I won't do it," and he says, "Believe me, I promise I won't. If this was the absolute last time, it's not what I want but so be it," and she says, "You're only saying that now because you've been gratified," and he says, "As I might have said the last time; 'Hey, how can a guy win?' " They live like this the next nine years. He has changed, he thinks. He doesn't blow up around them, or when he does he keeps it mostly under control. A couple of times he throws a dish or glass to the kitchen floor and when Sally says from her study, "What's that all about? Back to your old habits?" he says, "Not at all. I dropped something and it broke." "That was quite a smash for a drop. All right, I wasn't there." They have sex about twice a year, and a couple of those times she lets him spend the night with her in bed and once she let him do it again in the morning from behind, but said after, "I don't know why I let you do that. I must have been only a quarter awake and you were done before I was fully up. Next time, if there's one, get my verbal consent." Then their younger daughter graduates college and gets a job in New York. The older has a job a few miles from them but has had her own apartment for three years. He says to his wife, "So, I guess we ought to talk about my going. I was only supposed to be around till the kids were out of the house. But you're not any better, and I for one would hate looking for a new place and am not sure how I'll be able to carry the extra expense, so if you want, I can stay." "Now you should do what's best for you," she says. "The arrangement we made does seem to have worked out, and I'm grateful you stuck to it under the rather stiff conditions I imposed. But you may want to be on your way for your own reasons. As anyone can see, I need someone around here in case I fall and for lots of things I can't do, much more than I did ten years ago, but please don't let anything I say stop you," and he stays. He has to get out of here, he thinks. He can't live in this place a day longer. But he can't just go. So stay, and he stays. He thinks, I don't know what the hell I could have been thinking. I can't live here anymore and I never should have thought I could. And then thinks, But how can I just leave her? So I'll stay and make the most of it, or the best out of it, or whatever I'll make from it, and he stays. He has to get away from here, he thinks, if just for a day, and writes a note. *My Sweethearts: I'm taking a hotel room for the night. Don't be worried: all I need is one night alone. That means I'll be totally by myself. I might go to a movie and then I'll go right back to my hotel room. Although I also might only go to a restaurant, so no movie, and read a book while I eat—I'm bringing several with me—and then back to the hotel to read till I fall asleep. Or I might do both, or all three: restaurant, movie, back to my hotel room to read and fall asleep. Maybe even a snack or drink or both in the hotel lounge before I go to my room. But I won't be phoning you tonight. I'll see you all tomorrow: Mommy, soon after hotel checkout time, when I get home around noon, and you kids when you return from school. What am I talking about? I'll see Fanny when I pick her up at school to take her home. Same time, my dearie: 2:20, at the front entrance. I suppose my staying away for the night must seem like an odd thing to do. But I feel I need one complete day off with no contact or duties to do at home or in my work. Just to be free, so to speak. Or not "so to speak": to be completely free for approximately one day. But then thinking about it as I write, it doesn't seem that odd. In fact, maybe this is the solution to my feeling occasionally trapped at home. Is it really so bad to admit that's how I feel from time to time? And if "trapped" is the wrong word, then just "overburdened and exhausted" sometimes? Because I'm sure you all occasionally feel the same way or something like it: school and the constant presence of your family, and other things. Anyway, see you all tomorrow. I already miss you—that's not a line to make anyone feel better—but I'm also looking forward to my 20 or so hours alone. Your loving husband and daddy.* He drives downtown and gets a hotel room, works out in the gym there, takes a swim, then a sauna and long shower. "Samson," he says, pounding his chest. "I feel great." Doesn't want to be extravagant with himself—the room's costly enough and dinner in the hotel will set him back a ways—but then thinks, Hell, this is the first time he's done anything like this in his life, and for all he knows it's well deserved, after all he's done for his family and at work, and he gets a miniature bottle of vodka out of the room's small fridge, empties it into a glass with ice, and drinks it while lying on top of the bed and reading today's newspaper. "This is wonderful," he says. "I'm so goddamn relaxed. Enough so to even talk out loud to myself and not worry about it, by gosh, and to say things like 'by gosh' too," and gets out another vodka. He naps, has several nice dreams, goes to the restaurant downstairs, reads a book while eating and drinking wine, then goes to a play rather than a movie. The play's dull and he leaves after the first act, goes to a different movie than the one he'd planned on seeing, and leaves it in half an hour because it's so stupid and violent and sexually titillating: for kids, though not his. He stops at a bar on his way back to the hotel, starts talking to a woman on the next stool, she seems attracted to him, is quite pretty—beautiful, even, he thinks, and about thirty years younger than he—but meeting a woman or anything like that isn't what he came in here for. He only wanted to feel what it was like again to have a drink at a bar alone and just sit on a bar stool and maybe order a hamburger and fries, even if he usually doesn't eat red meat and stays away from fatty foods, and watch the TV news or some silly show while he eats, things he hasn't done since about a month after he met his wife, except for the fries, most of them the last few years snitched off his kids' plates at fast-food joints. Looks at his watch, says, "Excuse me, it's getting late for me and I have to be up early. It's been nice talking," and she says, "One more round, how about it? We can go someplace else for it if this bar doesn't suit you," and he says, "No, it's a perfectly nice place, and I'd really love to. But, you know, I'm married, so what would my wife and kids think if I told them? And if I didn't tell them, how would I feel after?" and she says, "After what? What is it you think I'm proposing here? All I had in mind was another drink. Or even coffee or tea, if that's your cup, because the conversation was interesting and we were getting along till you came on with all that stuff, or perhaps it's too late for you for one of those too." "Of course; I'm sorry. I worded it wrong. I didn't mean anything by it. Just running off stupidly at the mouth for no good reason except, maybe—well, stupidity, which I apologize for, but I still have to go," and pays the tab for their drinks. "Oh, thanks," she says, faking a smile, "but maybe a couple of bills for the bartender, since he works hard at what he does and doesn't get the proper appreciation," and he says, "Sorry again. It's been awhile since I sat at a bar and I forgot the protocol, though that's no excuse," and puts down several singles and leaves, goes back to his room and reads, and eventually drops off to sleep. He leaves in the morning, soon after he wakes up and does a few exercises and has coffee, drives home, and his wife says when he walks through the door, "Welcome back, traveler. That must have been fun, and we got along fine," and he says, "I'm glad. And it was fun, all of it innocent, if you want to know, and all I needed. Kids get off okay?" and she says, "I had to call Meg to drive Fanny to school, but that was all right," and he says, "Oh, darn, I forgot about that. If I had remembered I probably never would have gone," and she says, "It was no problem. I arranged it last night and she got off in plenty of time. I've missed you," and he says, "Me too with you, and I mean it," and kisses her and steps back so she can see him and jiggles his eyebrows, and she says, "Sure, why not, but give me a few minutes, and don't forget to take the phone off," and goes back to their bathroom. "I can't take it anymore; I should really get as far as I can away from here," and she says, "And the kids?" and he says, "You're right; what could I have been thinking? Forget I said it, and it won't come up again, or I'll try not to let it." "I can't stand it here anymore; I've got to get the hell away and stay there," and she says, "Go if you have to, but it's for sure not what I want you to do. Even if you said you were repulsed by me, I need you too much here," and he says, "I know, and there's certainly no repulsion, and I don't really mean what I said; I was just spouting. But it is true that some part of me would love to set right off. To live in a shack and only have a one-speed bike, no car, a few of my books, my typewriter, and a library nearby—it could always order books for me from that state's interlibrary loan system, I suppose. I'm saying, to be alone on my own again to do what I want when I want to, even to sleep as long as I want if I worked all night and am tired, and so forth. Or even if I didn't work, if I just that day want to sleep and dream. But you make your decisions and you live with them. I mean, I make my decisions, or at least take certain directions that end up in a way being decisions, and you live with them. I mean, I make them and I live with them. And I should have said 'em' there, right? It goes better with the shack and no car and the one-speed bike and the woods—I forgot the woods before—or just something near the shore because there are always too many damn bugs and often very little wind to keep them off you in the woods. The shack, no matter where it was, would have to have electricity, I'd think, so I'd have heat and light. I wouldn't want to rough it too much, since what I'd be interested most in is the solitude and time to do what I want, and not spend most of the days chopping wood and other activities like that just to survive. But we have a nice house, this house we have, and not a bad life. In fact, a pretty good life, everything considered. Our children are the best and I love you and think your feelings to me are mostly okay, though I have my moments when anyone would run away from me, and I know you'd love to get away too if you could, for a weekend or a month or however long you'd want to be by yourself for a change," and she says, "True, but what can we do?" and he says, "Right; nothing. So I'm just dreaming here, and maybe not even of something I really want; it could be it only seems like I do when I get harried and overloaded with house, school, family, and my personal work." He thinks, He's had it for good here and has to get out, that's all, and then laughs: what a stupid thought. Then for a weekend or week alone someplace, and he asks himself, Why? Like you said: you've had it up to here—your neck, the chin—so just to get away and on your own for a short period of time, and he says, "And that'll help?" and he tells himself, How will you know unless you try? And if it does, then it's an easy solution you can resort to whenever the same feelings about leaving or wanting to run away come up and family conditions permit it, and he says, "I don't know, it all sounds so vague. Where would I go?" and he tells himself, Your favorite place: Paris. To walk around and visit its oodles of cathedrals, preserved writers' homes, and museums. The Marmottan, with all the Monets. The new Van Gogh museum there, or is that only in Amsterdam? Then the new Picasso museum in the Marais—that I know I read about. And the biggie. What's it called again? How could I forget it? Help me with this. The largest and possibly the most famous art museum in the world. . . . The Louvre! and he tells himself, Go to that one for several days. And more walking, but not to buy anything but a couple of souvenirs for your wife and kids, and don't forget the great bistros, bars, and cafés. Then return home refreshed, revivified, renewed, re-re, happy to be back, even, and your family glad what the trip did for you, and he says, "I don't like traveling alone. I become uncomfortably self-conscious, even when I'm walking in a strange city by myself. Maybe only in museums and train stations and metros, when there's a ton of people there or the subway car's crowded, do I feel comfortable alone. Besides, I want to talk to someone about the things I see and experience and eat. No, all I think I need is a few hours alone in my bedroom," and he tells himself, Go to your wife, and say you were thinking just now of taking a week's vacation to someplace like Paris, and see what she says. I bet she'll say, What a great idea and you owe it to yourself for all the work you've done the last few years at home and school and it could be just the thing you need to re-re yourself for all the work you'll have to resume the moment you return, and he says, "Listen, I think I know what's best for me and my family, despite what she might tell me. And how do I know, if she did say that, that she wouldn't be thinking, at the time, 'I really need him here to help me but it seems he desperately wants to go'?" and he tells himself, She won't think that. Or if she does, it'll only be a little compared to what she knows is ultimately best for you and the family, and he says, "But suppose she really does need me there all the time to help or just somewhere close by?" and he tells himself, There are always the kids to pitch in, pick her up and stuff; they're big and strong enough for that now. And if you don't mind the expense you can have someone come in to look after her when you're gone and the kids are at school, and he says,

"Believe me, all I need is a few hours of quiet solitude in my room," and goes to his wife and says, "I'll be in the bedroom and I'm unplugging the phone there. If anyone calls me, say I'm resting or napping or busy with some very important work I have to get done, and that I left orders not to be awakened or disturbed to speak to anyone. Or put it any way you want—politer than that, of course—or just say I'm out. Or if you don't want to lie—a sudden flu could be another good excuse—say that I'm—" and she says, "I get the point. You want time to yourself and don't want to be interrupted. So go, nobody will bother you, and I'll intercept all your calls and shush the girls if they're making noise or talking loudly near your door, and also tell Josephine not to practice her piano and Fanny her violin till you come out," and he says, "Thanks, I appreciate that. Though I do love their piano and violin playing, especially the duets, even when they hit bad notes, and Fanny can always practice in the basement. But I have to know I can be alone in relative quiet with my thoughts or my dreams or whatever I'm alone with in there for the next few hours, even the book I've been reading, while I lie on the bed, just to give my mind a break before I start trying to clear a whole bunch of things up," and she says, "Like what?" and he says, "Things, things, I'll tell you about it later. Though don't worry. It has nothing to do with anything you did or even anything about you, not that you're worrying," and she says, "Now you've got me worried as to what it is and I feel almost certain that part or most of it has to do with me. But go, isolate yourself or whatever it is you want to do in there while you have the time and it's quiet and the kids aren't home yet." He wants to get away from here, has to, he thinks, and then thinks, What in God's name is he talking about? Just work out whatever it is without disturbing anybody. "Listen," he says to his wife, "we've got to talk, it's very important," and she says, "Fine, let's talk. You know me; I never feel we do enough of it about serious matters or the things that deeply affect us and might even be troubling us as a couple, mostly because you don't like opening up. So give, what is it?" and he says, "Ah, nothing, it's really not that important. If I think it is again, I'll tell you," and she says, "You change your mind because I was so eager to discuss it?" and he says, "No, it's what I said. Suddenly I didn't think—" and she says, "You're terrible; you're really quite terrible and a great big B.S. artist of the highest order, though you certainly fooled me," and he says, "When?" and she said, "Oh, stop." He's got to get away from here, he thinks, for all the old reasons. It's become too much, everything: the work, her illness, his ratty attitude about it sometimes and occasional rages, thrusting her empty wheelchair across the room and, when she falls out of it or the bed to the floor, lifting her up before she's ready and practically throwing her into the wheelchair or onto the bed; he's making everyone unhappy here, kids, her, himself, he doesn't know how he can live with himself sometimes over the things he does, taking his older daughter to school after he's railed at his wife the previous night for her clumsiness—"Do I have to follow you around with a damn dust-pan and broom?"—and knowing she heard from her room and wanting to apologize, say, Daddy's sorry for losing his head last night to Mommy and forcing you to hear it, but driving silently, maybe asking if she remembered to take her lunch; it's cold—so is she wearing a long-sleeved shirt under her coat or a short?—not knowing what would be better for her, talking about it now or keeping quiet and hoping she'll forget, though also wondering what's going through the minds of both kids about him, if they fear he'll blow up completely and never come back to normal and then everything will be gone; he's even begun talking out loud to himself on walks to the market or when he's alone in the car about how he can't put up with it anymore and has to get away, which he does have to, that's a fact, he doesn't know for how long—probably just a week, a few days—before he really loses it, when the door opens and it's his younger daughter home from school and he immediately sees by her expression that something's wrong and he smiles and says, "Hiya, sweetheart, how'd it go today?" trying to be peppy and upbeat, and she walks into the next room without looking at him, throws her backpack down—he can tell by the *plump!*—and goes to her room or somewhere in back. She's angry or disappointed about something, he's almost sure it's nothing that he did, though it could be, she could have been up late last night when he again yelled at his wife about how she's always dropping things—"Forget the pan and broom I once mentioned, now I need a shovel sometimes"—and then said, "Sorry, just kidding," but much lower, so Josephine wouldn't have heard; she seemed fine this morning when he came home from driving Fanny to school and sat at the table with her a few minutes while she ate breakfast and then saw her off at the bus stop, seemed in a good mood, showed him the lanyard she's yarning ("Very nice." "Do you like the colors?" "Beautiful, and it's so well made." "I'm getting better at it, but I'll never be as good as Fanny." "Oh, now, don't be silly; this one's every bit as good as any she's made." "She taught me." "So, to your credit, you learned very well"), smiled, let him kiss her goodbye when they heard the bus coming, and he goes to her room and says, "Anything wrong, dear?"—she's sitting on her bed reading a book—and she says no and returns to the book and he says, "Please put it down for a second. You want to read, read, I love it when you do, but I know something's wrong. I can tell by the way you came in and your scowl then and a little now . . . what's disturbing you?" and she says, "Nothing," and he says, "Come on, don't tell me," and she says, "Whatever it is, I'll get over it," and he says, "Friend trouble at school? Maybe a low mark on a test you don't want to tell me about yet but know I'll have to sign?" and she's shaking her head. "A boy: somebody say something nasty or stupid—even on the bus?" and she says, "It's none of those. I just want to read before I start on my homework; they gave me a lot of it," and he says, "Something I might've done?" and she says, "You ask too many questions and I'm not in an answering mood. That's all right, isn't it?" and he says, "Why shouldn't it be? and I don't want to appear snoopy," and leaves the room, quickly looks back, and she's looking at him and quickly looks at her book and seems to read for a few seconds and then turns the page, and he says, "Like me to make you a snack? You usually have one when you come home, and I'd be happy to," and she continues reading without looking up at him and he goes into the living room and hears her door click shut and he thinks how he loves her. How could he ever think of leaving, even for a few days, for the reasons he was thinking of? He knows he could never go, because of her and her sister and of course his wife too. "I've got to get the goddamn hell away from here," he says to his wife, and she says, "As they say about something else—one's urinary tract and I wish mine—if you got to, do, otherwise, it'll be—oh, dreadful of dreads—painful to you. Not that I want you to go, naturally," and he says, "Thank you, and I don't really want to either, in addition to knowing I can't. That was funny, what you said: another reason I should stay. Where else am I going to find such humor? I'll try to work things out, don't worry," and she says, "What is it that's troubling you?" and he says, "Now you've gone too far; you know I don't talk about such things," and she says, "Give it a go; I'll provide intermittent comic relief," and he says, "All right, I can try," and starts and they have a long talk about it and she cries a lot—"You're supposed to be funny; you're not being funny," and she laughs and he says, "Laughing isn't funny; it's a response to something that is or being tickled," and she laughs—and after a while he starts crying too and she looks at him with a please-come-here-I-want-to-hug-you-and-maybe-you-need-to-be-hugged-too look and he goes over and hugs her and says, "I hate hugging like this; it's like politics," and she says, "Be quiet," and at the end of it he says he feels things are going to be better from now on, "I just know it, with only some reservations, or at least for the time being, but I'm hoping for the extended run," and she doesn't say anything, and he says, "So what do you think to what I just said?" and she says, "You did talk about what's bothering you, which is a start, but you have a history of being unreliable with your promises," and he says, "Who promised? Anyway, I'll buy that, but just watch." He's in the car with his older daughter and says, "I have to confess something to you. Sometimes I feel—recently, that is, or more often recently—" and she says, "What?" and he says, "Out with it, right?" and she says, "Not that, I just don't know what you're getting at," and he says, "That I feel sometimes like I want to run away from home. Now doesn't that sound foolish? Almost like a little kid talking. There in fact was a joke about it years ago—something like 'But I wasn't allowed to cross the street by myself,' " and she looks at him that she doesn't understand, and he says, "That's the punch line. The boy wants to run away from home and leaves but can't go any further than the street corner of his block because his parents—" and she says, "I get it now. But you really have wanted to leave us? That's sad," and he says, "It has nothing to do with you kids or Mom, meaning nothing any of you did to make me feel I wanted to leave. And just for a week or a few days, you understand: that I'd go, I'm saying. But, you know, I just feel—felt—still get the feeling sometimes, I suppose, that I have to be off by myself for a while. That I'm mostly a terrible father, a lousy husband, a good provider, though—" and she says, "What's that mean?" and he says, "A term my dad used for himself, and he was. We didn't have a lot but we never lacked for anything, I think, except for tuition for a private university I wanted to apply to but really didn't have the high school grades or college-board scores or any of that stuff for, so was deluding myself I'd get in. But anyway, he said, 'Why spend good money'—that was another expression of his: 'All money is good,' he said; 'what could be bad about it?'—'when there is a very decent free public college system in New York?' And I said, 'Look, I'm your only child and I'll pay for half of it myself, living expenses included'—because I wanted to go out of town—'by working at jobs while I'm in school and summers,'" and she says, "But the other thing, your wanting to leave us. You didn't finish that." "I know. And I realize being a good provider doesn't make up for being a lousy husband and father, which I often am, but I felt you'd all be better off with my being gone—and for more than a week, actually—than my sticking around and making life hell for you, that's all," and she says, "But we don't want you to go," and he says, "And I'm not. Though sometimes you must want me to," and she says, "Sometimes, when you're very angry and acting sort of scary with your yelling and temper and not finding anything right with anything we do or that there is. But most times, or the majority of them, you're not like that," and he says, "As I said, it's just a thought that comes from time to time, when I'm feeling particularly miserable with myself and that I've been a tremendous disappointment and bastard to you all, doing the things you said and worse, but nothing I'd ever carry out. It would destroy me—or maybe do a little less than that, though who knows?—but disturb me deeply to leave you and your sister and Mom. No, disturb me to the point of destroying me, I'm sure, because it's more than just making your own bed and lying in it, I'd think," and she says, "What's that mean?" and he says, "You never heard the expression?" and she says no and he explains it and she says, "Oh, yeah, but what does it mean to what you were saying before?" and he says, "What was I saying?" and she says, "Disturbing yourself to the point of destroying yourself," and he says, "Right, it's more than that, whatever I meant by it. But you have to know that most times I love being with you and I'd miss you kids and your mom so much and hate myself so much for leaving you that I'd probably die—that's it; I probably really would," and she says, "Not literally," and he says, "Close, though," and she says, "Then don't go." I got to get out of here, he tells himself, and thinks, You got to?—then go, and he thinks, I'm only just talking; I don't mean it. It's an idea—What would happen if I did go seemingly forever?—and I know what would. And it's really not so bad here, when you think what I am, and he thinks, No, not so bad at all, so stay.

The Place

So finish. They're in a car heading to Maine. Get closer. Sally and he, Gould: eventually they'll get married, have children, but now they're about to spend their first summer together. They met in November, about a week before Thanksgiving. Why's he mention that holiday? Because his mother was giving a Thanksgiving dinner, and though he'd only known Sally for a week and had gone out with her just once, he invited her to it. A cousin and his family and a couple of his mother's friends were there. They later told his mother, This looks like the girl for him. When his mother told him that, she asked was it true, she's a very nice girl and does he think she's the one? He said he hopes so but he's had this hope before so he doesn't want to pin any—well, hopes on it and be disappointed. "For now," he said, "it's going fine, and for maybe the first time in my life I'm going to take it slow." He's driving; she's looking at him. He can see her out of the corner of his eye. Corners of his eyes. (He'll find out which one's right later, probably by looking in a dictionary of slang or asking his wife.) He can see her, though, and she seems to be looking at him, and when people look at him he looks back, so he turns to her and smiles and she smiles, and he puts his right hand on her cheek, other hand holds the wheel, and she kisses it and then holds it and he says—

They left the city two hours ago. Packed, loaded up the rented car, got the cats—her two and her parents' two—into two cat carriers and started out. She tells him which roads to take. He's been to Maine only once before, on his way back from hitchhiking through Prince Edward Island and Nova Scotia more than fifteen years ago. (That's not relevant, so delete it.) She's made the trip several times, always taking the same route, which she got from someone who belongs to Triple A. They're going to a cottage she's rented the last three summers. She said a few days ago she doesn't think he'll like it up there: the quiet, solitude, almost nothing to do at night, and if it rains or stays foggy for a few days you feel like a prisoner in the place. And the bugs—black fly season's only just ending; mosquitoes will be pestering them till a week or two before they head home, if they're lucky—her few friends in the area he probably won't get along with: older academics, mostly, and she knows what he thinks of academics. He said how can she say that: she's one, and she said, "You know what I mean." Anyway, he said, nights will be cool; days, she's said, never get too humid or warm, and he'll be with her, and if he just has that he can put up with anything. His one regret, he now thinks, is that his mother will be in New York the whole hot summer, and every time he calls her, which he'll try to do every day, he knows he'll feel guilty and terrible about it. Though he is glad for a stay in a real vacation place after working the entire year adjuncting those dumb and useless continuing-ed creative writing courses four to five days a week, hardly any rest. (Make that clearer and more concise. Or just skip it or say, working at poorly paid jobs almost every weekday with barely an hour a day to do his own work.) This is their first summer together. (He said that.) They're going for two months. (Thinks he said that too.) He'll have to split the rent and expenses and car rental fees with her, which will be a sacrifice. She doesn't earn much either as a teaching fellow and also has no money saved, but she'll be getting a check every two weeks from her university while his school stopped paying him the week his work ended. It's something he always wanted to do: spend a few summer weeks or more in the country or at the shore with a woman he's in love with and who says she's in love—once even said "deeply in love, and that's the truth"—once even said she's never been so happy or felt so comfortable with a man as with him. He says to her—

She points out a highway sign for a rest stop in three miles: gas, food, information, the symbols on it say; buses and truckers welcome. He can't believe his luck. Two summer months with this beauty. This beautiful person. This brain-clever woman with all the right values, it seems, and a heart like—well, something, and a magnificent soul. (He used to say whenever he sees the word "soul" in prose he bolts the other way. So strike out the soul and don't try to fiddle with it, since nothing can take its place.) He thinks about what they'll do tonight after they arrive. It'll be dark. Won't take long to unpack the car. Or maybe just dusk, remnants of a great sunset, though he doesn't know yet how much sky he'll be able to see through the trees there. Their bags, his typewriter and writing supplies, her box of books, a few of his, mainly his big dictionary and thesaurus—"There's a terrific library in town," she's said, "with a steady stream of new books of all categories, though mostly poetry and fiction, furnished by the book editor of *The New Yorker,* who summers in the area but keeps to himself except, I suspect, to drop off his weekly bags of books"—some provisions from New York and a little they bought on the way, and, of course, the cats and litter box. There'll be cleaning up to do: mouse nests, maybe some dead mice and even a carcass of a bird that got down the fireplace chimney, dirt and dust that accumulated over the year, but she's said there's never much. Cottage will have been aired out by the caretaker, all he'll do other than get the hot water heater and refrigerator going and prime the well pump. "The place isn't entirely mouseproof," she's said, "but the moment the cats are carried across the threshold, the mice disappear." (Does he need all that? He'll decide when he goes back. And add "case of wine" and "boxed Cuisinart" to what they bring in from the car.) She'll take care of most of the cleaning and putting away clothes, she said last night. She has a system that gets it done in less than two hours, and she knows where everything goes and was stored last year. If he wants he can take their suitcases upstairs and set up his desk and make dinner: pasta, a quick pesto for it or just good olive oil and freshly grated romano cheese, wine and bread, and a simple salad. They have all that in the car except the lettuce. That they'll buy, as well as a few things for breakfast and maybe a dessert for tonight at a market about twenty miles from the cottage. (He already said that but in a different way, so it's okay to let stay.) Tomorrow they'll do their first big shop in the next town over, she's said. If he doesn't want to come along and wants to work or look around or nap, she'll do it herself. No, he said, he wants to be in on everything with her at first and start getting to know the area. Cats will have to be fed right after they get there, she said, and litter box refilled. He'll do that, don't worry, he said. "Pasta, sprinkling of cheese, little white wine in their drinking dish, right?" But which first? Probably the box, since it'll be a number of hours since they last used it. (The two sinces. That's always been a problem, since "as" or "for" or "because" just don't seem right in a sentence like that.)

Phone will have been turned on, so he'll call his mother, if it's not too late, to see how she is and tell her—she'll really just want to hear his voice—that the trip went fine and the cottage and grounds, from what he can see, are quite pretty, all of which, because of what Sally's said about them, he assumes. (He didn't say that right, though he thinks the meaning got across, but he'll change it.) Her mother's coming up for a week. He wonders if she'd mind if his mother visited too. For five days, two less than her mother. His mother's frail but still gets around, and she can use a break like that from the city. It'd mean a lot to him, he'd say, and he won't ask for anything else, no other visitors, though she can have as many as she wants. (No, that's too much like something a kid would say, but for the time being keep.) He should ask her now. They'll have lots of time to talk about it if she has any objections. That way, if it's yes, he can tell his mother right after they get there. Or not that quickly. He doesn't want Sally to think he's a momma's boy—she knows he isn't; he just wants to make his mother happy—so maybe a half hour after they get there, if it isn't way too late. He says to her—

They have lunch at a restaurant a mile off the interstate. Parked in the shade because of the cats. Car windows rolled up to about three inches from the top. Cats let out of the carriers to jump around but mainly to pee and shit in the litter box and drink from the water dish so they don't dehydrate. She's stopped here twice before. Last night, she said this is where, if they start out early enough, she'd like to lunch: about four hours from the city. "With another guy once?" and she said, "No, my mother, and the second time alone. It's a real homey place." Her mother and she had driven to the cottage from New York, stayed overnight in a Kennebunk motel along the highway because her mother doesn't drive and the entire trip . . . (and so on, or just get rid of it). "Then am I the first guy you're bringing to the cottage?" and she said, "To be perfectly frank, I'd rather not discuss it. But I hope you'll be the last, but to come with me in succeeding years—how about that?" "I like it. It tickles me randy. It douses me proud. Oy, what dumb remarks, those last two. Forgive me." "No need; we're having fun. Let me think of something funny too. I lub you. That also makes no sense except for the sound of it." They were in bed, apartment had been cleaned, almost everything packed, rented car picked up that afternoon and parked in a nearby garage, some of the heavy stuff already in it: books and wine and two reams of his typing paper. He had sublet his apartment starting last week. (Fix that. His sublessees [-lessors?] moved in three days ago and have the place for two months. He stayed with her the last week. But he sublet it starting a week ago but the tenants only moved in the last few days? They got to New York later than they thought they would.) She puts her sandwich down, looks so beautiful, is chewing, looks up and catches him looking at her. What? her expression says. He says to her—

Car radio's on: a beautiful orchestral piece he's never heard. Wants to hear it till the end and then get its name and the composer's and buy a recording of it when he gets back to New York. He hopes they don't drive out of range of this station before the piece is finished. But it's 4:58, then :59, the car clock says. She's spoken of a national public radio news program at five she usually listens to in Maine and which he thinks she'll want to find on whatever public radio station around here gets it. (That all right, not too confusing and long, doesn't need to be cut into two? No, seems fine.) She reaches for the dial, other hand on the steering wheel. He puts his hand on hers, keeps it from fingering the dial, and says—

He likes the trip so far, even the long stretches of boring highway and interstate: it's new and the air's cool and the conversation's been good since they set out. She drives; he. They stop twice more to pee, and for containers of coffee to drink in the car while they drive, and once on a country road in Maine for fresh strawberries from a stand. "They're always a month or more behind New York," she said at the start of the trip, "so we'll be getting strawberries around where we live for the next few weeks." (That add anything? Mostly what he's least interested in: local color.) "They're much smaller and more compact than what we're used to, and sweeter; you'll see. Then, near the end, when they start picking from the bottom of the bushes—or is that raspberries, which come later, and by the way there are farms where you can pick both of them yourself?—they're as tasteless and mushy as the New York kind." Also stopped for a pound bag of cashews off a truck, and then the longer stop at the market some twenty miles from the cottage. They arrive when it's dark. (He thinks he'll delete everything in this paragraph so far but the last sentence.) The caretaker had left most of the windows open and a light on by the front door. They close the windows, unload the car, and start putting things away. He fills the litter box and feeds the cats. Sets up a desk downstairs with his typewriter and supplies and then starts dinner, which means boiling water for pasta while he prepares a salad, slices bread, opens the wine, puts a stick of butter in a butter dish and washes several bowls and two plates and wineglasses and silver and sets the table. He makes himself a vodka and grapefruit juice, though without ice, as the water in the ice trays isn't solid yet. (He's already said they'd do most of that. So here he says they did it.) And nice of the guy to put water in the trays. And the drink? Juice he got at the market, but what about vodka? They stopped at a state liquor store in New Hampshire about five miles from the bridge into Maine. She said the prices are much cheaper there because there are no state taxes, but they didn't seem so to him. And the store was like a supermarket for booze. Some people had huge shopping carts with what looked like twenty to thirty bottles of liquor in them. The wine selection wasn't good and the better wines were more expensive than they were in New York. He said, "Let's get out of here and buy what we need tomorrow at a regular Maine store." "You don't like it? I thought you would." What does she think, he thought, he's a dipso or something close? Big of her, if that's it, but he hates this place though doesn't want to say so and maybe disappoint her. "It's only that I don't see trudging through such a vast store and waiting on long lines for the few bottles we'd buy. This joint's for serious drinkers with lots of time to spare, while we gotta get moving." "But you want your vodka and I'd like a glass of port tonight after the long trip. Go back to the car and read and open the windows so the cats have plenty of air, and I'll quickly pick up what we need and get on line. There's one there for five items or less." (Why'd he go into all that? Maybe because it was the worst moment of the trip and he wanted to show it, which wasn't such a bad moment at all. Which means he was actually showing what a good trip it was and something about how accommodating she is to him and particularly was then. But go over all of that starting from how he got the vodka, and if it doesn't do what he wanted or seems to hold things back—he's almost sure it does—chuck the whole thing.) The radio's on. (Said that.) They're in the cottage. She comes into the kitchen while he's making dinner, says everything's put away and swept up and even the bed's made, smiles, her look wanting to know what he thinks of the place and also showing how pleased she is he's here. He says to her—

They've eaten dinner. (Scratch that.) She asks if she has time for a shower before dinner. She feels so slimy after twelve hours on the road and then running around the house doing things. She tends to sweat a lot, she's said, and when she told him that, he said, "Nobody would ever know it. My schnoz is still pretty keen and, hackneyed as this remark might be, you always smell sweet to me." That was about three weeks after they met. It's still true: she's never smelled bad or of a deep sweat anywhere on her body except a few times her hair. Water for the pasta's about to boil and he turns it off, finds the flashlight he brought, and heads to the shore about two hundred feet from the cottage. Hears some funny bird sounds as he walks down the path, and then they stop as he gets near the shore and he hears the flapping of wings or feet or both against the water as the bird or birds take off. Over dinner she'll tell him those were loons. Sea sounds: soft crashing of tiny breakers and a buoy from somewhere in the bay. So, he thinks, this is it; nice. Gets bitten by insects on the path and beach. ("Mosquitoes" for "insects": he knows their buzzing and bite.) Walks along the shore to the closest point. (Is there another way—well, there are always other ways—but a better one to say all this so it doesn't sound so perfunctory and drab? Later.) Lots of moon, also mirrored in its squiggly way in the water. "Loons and moons, that's about all I found down there bigger than a mosquito," he would have said to her soon as he got back, if he'd known what those birds were called. Enough light to walk by, so he turns off the flashlight. Then thinks, Don't go falling over a boulder or into a hole. Just what he needs: to break something first hour he's there and have to crawl to the cottage, be driven to a hospital, ruin what he hopes will be as near-perfect a night as he's ever had: sounds, smells, light, breezes, freshly made bed with what she said were the cottage's very fine old cotton sheets, and of course her. No other houses around, it seems. Lighthouse way out in the water. Stars, more than . . . but not more than he can ever remember seeing, maybe because the moon's so full and bright. His mother, he forgot to call her; do it when he gets back, though check the time first. Sits on a rock shaped like a chair with arms. Gets buzzed and bitten but tries to think. Let things run through your head, he thinks. Nothing much does. Shuts his eyes.

Woman he was in love with two years ago. Wanted to spend the summer with her; instead she went to Europe alone. They'd planned to go together, even bought the plane tickets. Were going to buy fold-up bikes and ride them through Holland and France, take trains or buses when they wanted a rest. Travel light except for the bikes. One big paperback apiece: *War and Peace* for him, a new difficult modern novel for her. They'd already bought the books and an anthology of Romantic verse between them. Then she said she needed to be completely free for two months. He knew she'd meet guys. In Turkey she let a man penetrate her behind, a first for her. She said she didn't like it and would never try it again. "How come you let him?" he said. "Not that I'd ever want to do it. Though if you had asked, and you knew me for six months, I would have done it once." "He wanted to very much, was very sweet and pretty and claimed to be an expert at it, and I'd always been curious about it." She fell in love with a Frenchman and they traveled through Greece for two weeks. She didn't think she'd ever return home; then he told her he was married. "Boy, for a smart city gal, you really fell for a couple of drips." "Neither were," she said; "both were extremely sophisticated and intelligent." She discovered in Europe what she wanted to do the next ten years: films. Write and direct, though of course she'll have to go to school for it first. "Always so full of new projects and beginnings," he said. "I guess that's supposed to be good." "This is why I didn't want you in Europe with me. You're so cynical and critical and don't like to do anything unusual or new. I'm sure I wouldn't have been able to try a plate of sea urchins at a Greek seaside stand without you fretting over the cost and the possibility of dangerous bacteria, killing the experience for me. You knew what you wanted to do with your life when you were two and stuck to it, the same way you stick to me, and it makes me claustrophobic." (Pare all that down, maybe paraphrase what's left of it. But the woman he least wanted to spend a summer with.) More bites, making it impossible to sit here, and he breathes in deeply—he loves the ocean at night, he thinks, and at dusk, minus the mosquitoes, though to him, unless the sky's overcast, it gets too bright and hot during the day and he ends up hating it—and goes back to the house. She's upstairs, probably getting dressed after the shower, and he yells up—

They have dinner. Bottle of port he opened and poured for her the next night. She puts candles into the bronze candlesticks on the table and lights them. She'd hid the candlesticks when she closed up the cottage last year. "There are antiques thieves," she told him, when she got the candles and some fine china out. "After the summer people leave, they can clean out a house if everything's top-notch, or only take the choice items like silver, and antique furniture you didn't know was antique, and old clocks." "Who would have thought it, up here. But otherwise, in summers you're safe? You can leave the doors unlocked and your typewriter out?" She even thinks the caretaker's in cahoots with them. "They're rough people, the locals, and very proud and wily. They won't accept the welfare they're entitled to, when they're destitute, but for a few dollars they'll let thieves from away break into the houses they caretake. They can be pitiless, too. One time there was a bat upstairs." (Really thinks he needs all this? See where it goes.) "He caught it in a special bat catcher the house has, which is like a butterfly net but stronger, and I said, 'Let it loose outside.' He said, 'Why, what good is it alive?' I said, 'It kills mosquitoes'—they do, don't they?—and he said, 'Who cares about them?' and it's true; you should have seen him. There was one on his cheek and I pointed it out and he said, 'Everyone's got to eat,' and let it bite him. 'Now it's dead,' he said. 'They can only get you once and then they die, and I saved my strength swatting it.' Anyway, he put the bat in the net on the floor and stomped on it." Tomorrow he'll meet the caretaker. He'll rap on the door very hard a little after dawn, be holding a bag of Swiss chard for her, and a scythe, and yell, "Hello, I see you got in; anyone home?" A big burly guy with a weak meaty handshake, smelling of soiled clothes and B.O. (If he just plays a small part in this, does he rate a descript?) The only light they eat by is from the candles and fire in the fireplace. Another thing she did: collecting the wood outside for it and getting it lit. They toast to the summer and then kiss. She's a real beauty, but in the candle and fireplace light she looks ghoulish, just as he must to her since their angles to the lights are about the same, though she probably doesn't think it about him. The phone rings. It's her father, wanting to know how the trip went and how his cats survived it and did all the cats like the chicken livers he'd cooked for them? When she gets off the phone he excuses himself a minute and calls his mother. He says to her—

He still can't believe his luck. She brought up dessert from a New

York patisserie. There's some brandy from last summer she gets out. She wonders if it's still good and does he think it could have frozen over the winter and if it did would that spoil it? She takes his hand while he drinks; she doesn't: brandy and any after-dinner liqueur give her a stomachache in the morning. They continue to hold hands and look at each other while he sips. This is an unbeatable night, he thinks. He can't think of any other like it in his life. The air, food, fire, quiet, smells, drinks, all-wooden room with the tall cathedral ceiling, he thinks, and of course her and what's going to be their lovemaking later. This summer's the beginning of something, he's almost sure of it. She loves him, he really believes that. She said so but you never know, people say that when they don't mean it or aren't sure or just think the other person wants to hear it, which is the same thing as "they don't mean it," but mainly to get certain things; with him it was mostly sex. But she doesn't say anything she doesn't mean. He's never known a woman who's leveled with him more. No, the one from two years ago leveled with him plenty, maybe too much: telling him things he didn't want to hear. So he means "been on the level with him," which Sally has from the day they met and never, far as he can tell, was tricky or dishonest to him, which the other one was lots of times. She wants to make this work. She's thirty-one, been married once, wants to have children and get married again—reverse those. They're going to get married one day, maybe by the end of next year; he's almost sure of that too. Something tells him. They've spoken about it—he brought it up a month ago—and she said it's too early to talk about yet but she certainly doesn't preclude the possibility of it someday. (Preclude was the word she used, but it's okay here?) By the end of the summer, if it continues to go like this—not that he doesn't expect some bumps—he'll bring it up again. That they've been practically living together almost a year now. (Would nine and a half months be considered almost a year?) Or maybe he won't bring it up till the year they've been together is up. Then he can say, "Listen, we've been together for more than a year now—granted, only a few days more" (since he'd never say this on the one-year anniversary of the day they met; that'd be too . . . he can't find the word for it: hokey, cornball, commonplace? something like that, and planned)—"and we seem to have worked out well as a couple, so what do you say?" "Look, we're deeply in love with each other—can

I say that? I know I am with you, and that's the straight-on truth, and you seem to have comparable feelings for me; you've at least said it—so what do you say?" "We're in love with each other, that's obvious, and are obviously compatible in just about every way and seem to want the same things from life, or the ones important, so what would you say to my idea now about our getting married?" But he has to make it go well as he can till then. Doesn't want her thinking, This is never going to work out. He's a lively bright guy, for the most part good-natured and often very funny, and there are things between us that are near to being perfect—sex, for instance; our love for music and books, and that we both want to have kids. But he's too unpredictable and impatient and recurringly hot-tempered and even mean-spirited and vulgar, which is not the kind of man I want to be tied to for the rest of my life, so best to give up on it now before it becomes impossibly complex, and for him destructive, and while I've still time to find someone else. Lose her and he's lost, no two ways about it. Or not as bad as that but close. He'd feel hopeless and bereft, as if he'd blown his last chance at getting married and having kids, and he simply doesn't want to lose her, period, because never in his life has he been with anyone like her, and so on. He sips, kisses her hand, and says—

Later he thinks maybe he should take a shower too. The two of them in bed, both clean. Fresh sheets and pillowcases, the new place and a sea breeze. Their bodies smelling of soap, hair from shampoo, if he shampoos too. She always does when she takes a shower, or at least always comes out of the shower with her hair drenched or a towel around it. He wants to go to bed with her now. It's late, he's tired, she must be; food's been put away, dishes have been cleaned—they both brought them in; he washed them the way she told him: in an old metal dishpan because they've a well and it's supposed to be a dry summer and anyway it's just good sense to conserve—and he doesn't want to go to bed so late where he'll be too tired to make love, or fall asleep soon after he hits the bed. Sleep will be nice when it comes but he wants to make love his first night here, sort of as a culmination to—well, it should be obvious by now without his explaining it. He yawns; she yawns too and smiles and motions with her eyebrows and eyes to the upstairs. Fire's just about out and room's getting a bit chilly. Should he put a few sticks on? She left a pile of them by the fireplace. Then she might think he wants to stay downstairs a while longer, and she's already motioned *up*. She said while they were eating—when he asked, "If we were to head up to bed and the fire was still going, what would we use to douse it, water?"—to just let it burn itself out. "Don't worry"—when he looked leery—"it's safe. I've done it plenty of times." He wants it to be like this all summer. Coffee and a newspaper or book early morning, work during the day, maybe some lovemaking and an excursion or swim in the afternoon, a two- or three-mile run somewhere in there, and then, at night, this. Though he knows it can't stay this way all the time. No matter how much he tells himself to do the opposite, he can screw things up. Say the wrong thing, do it; he's been known for that. Getting irritable and sometimes acerbic over the simplest mishap or remark she makes. The difference between her and the other women he's gone with is not so much that she takes it but—what? Isn't acerbic back. Thinks it's part of him, not the most likable but a small part, and the good outweighs the bad and so forth, and eventually this tendency to fits of bitterness and sarcasm will go away, though with her congenial apprisals and reminders of it to help it along. (Now there's a mouthful he's not known for.) She's just more accepting of these weaker elements in him (but stow it and, in the final version, leave out). They let the fire burn. (Goes without saying.) She sticks several large towels into a large round wicker basket and arranges the cats on top of them. She says they'll stay there till morning except to get out to use the litter box or to get some kibbles or water and then they'll readjust themselves when one of them climbs back in. Quatrefoil, a word he'll use for the basket arrangement further into the summer when he accidentally comes across an illustration of one in the dictionary next to the word, though he doesn't tell her that because she seemed, when he defined it, impressed. They turn off the lights downstairs. He locked the front door even though she said, when he asked where's the key for it, that all the break-ins around here are in winter when the homeowners from away are away and the wealthier retirees and transplants are in Arizona or Florida, and the last serious personal-injury crime apparently took place outside of anyone's living memory, and a few of these locals live past a hundred, and he said, How does she know there hasn't been a rash of them since last summer? "If it makes you feel less vulnerable, lock up, but we'll both be more comfortable if you try to get used to the country, and I say that with no smugness." "And the keys to the back doors?" and she said, "There aren't any. Those doors the caretaker nails up after we leave." They go upstairs. On the landing he remembers he didn't wash up and pee and he gives her his glasses and book and goes downstairs, crosses the back deck to get to the bathroom/shower stall, but stops to pee off the deck into the woods, thinking, while he's doing it, that this will have to be one of the great evening pleasures in being here, peeing and looking at the sky at the same time and not caring where the pee lands. Then he washes up, killing about ten mosquitoes while he's in there, and goes upstairs. She's in bed, only light in the room from a small lamp on her night table. On the other night table are his glasses and book, so they'll be sleeping on the same sides of the bed as they do in their apartments. He'd prefer her side, nearer the window; he wants to feel the breeze and look out at night, maybe see the moon. The advantage of the side she chose for him is he's able to hold her breasts with his right hand while they sleep, which might be why she likes him to sleep on that side too. Her breasts are clearly visible, covers up only to her waist. She's sitting up, no top on (that's how he should have put it), with probably nothing on under the covers too. He takes off his shirt. She watches and smiles, but he knows—she's told him—that seeing his bare chest or even his whole body nude doesn't give her anything near the charge that looking at hers does to him. He's sure her diaphragm's in. He breathes in deeply and thinks he can detect the contraceptive cream along with what seems a seaweed smell from outside. She didn't turn on his night-table light, which may mean she wants to turn off hers and the room to be dark soon as he gets into bed. Her period ended a week ago, he remembers her saying then. Good thing it isn't the first or second night of it. She'll rarely make love then, though he's said he doesn't mind the blood. But she finds it messy and sort of unwholesome, she once said, "and it doesn't exactly act as a lubricant for me either." He forgot to shower. Should have at least swabbed a damp washcloth on his underarms and wiped his anus with wet toilet paper, but he'll try to keep them away from her face. He puts his watch, notebook, handkerchief, and pen on his night table and gets on the bed. He pulls the covers down and she's naked. They almost immediately start kissing. First he strokes her hair back and playfully pinches her chin and she gnashes her teeth as if she's going to bite his pinching fingers. She doesn't turn off the light. Could be she wants to see them in their coupling positions. Or, because they're above the covers, to swat the mosquitoes before they start biting. Her face doesn't look ghoulish in this light, so his probably doesn't either. He wouldn't want either of them to look ghoulish while they were kissing and making love. The light's almost as faint as one can be in a regular lamp, so he wonders how she'll be able to read by it and if his is the same and he'll have to get a stronger bulb. He'd like to tell her now how he feels about things. To come up from the kissing to say what kind of night it is for him. That so far it's about as good a night as he's had in his life, and he's not just saying that, and because she is what she is and he loves her so much and this is just the start of their stay here, he expects plenty more of these nights in the future. (Of course "in the future," so scratch that.) That the best probably has to encompass the present and potential. Meaning . . . but what did he have in mind? (And shouldn't there be something in there about the past, and what about his use of "encompass" over "include"? Never want to sound fake. Anyway, don't keep that business about the present and potential if he can't figure it out next time he goes over it.) They're on their backs, smiling (adoringly? lovingly? nah, just smiling) at each other. He loves it when her mouth's slightly parted and her teeth show. She grabs hold of his penis, and he runs his hand up her body from her thigh, thinks how smooth her skin is and how fresh her breath was and how soft her hair and lips and probably that she shaved her legs while she was in the shower, and settles his hand on her breast and says—rests his hand on her breast and says—

Later, he wants to say how beautiful everything was tonight right to the end, but she seems asleep. She's on her side, he's holding her with his arms from behind, and she doesn't move. He pulls the covers up over her shoulder. She shut off the light soon after they'd made love. He didn't see her do it. Suddenly the room was black, and then after a few seconds there was a little light from outside. He rubs her nipple, and she doesn't say anything or stir. Don't do it again. If she's asleep she won't want to be woken up by his doing that. They'd made love, it was long and strong and so on (that should be sufficient as a description of it), and now she's very tired and wants to sleep. That's what she'd say, minus the long and strong and commentary on it, if he were rubbing her nipple and woke her up, he's almost sure. If he persisted after that, which he's done when they hadn't already made love and he wanted to, she'd get mad. He wonders if she's dreaming. If so, of what? If he's in it: their lovemaking, his hand on her breast now and the rubbing before, and things like that. She drove half the way here and during it complained her eyes hurt and she may need glasses. Would he also, when he takes off her clothes when they start making love, take off her glasses? They got up early to get an early start. (He knows he's said that but he's making a point, which is what?) That they've been going seventeen–eighteen hours straight. Where does the energy come from for that kind of strenuous lovemaking after so long and arduous a day? But he's not tired. That could be for a number of reasons—his excitement at being here with her, the sea air and that it's a new place, all that coffee on the road—and he thinks lots of activity makes him even more active, till he just drops. That so? Doesn't know. He's just saying, which he often does. (He doesn't see the need for any of that after the dreaming part, and maybe not that either, so *out.*) He continues to hold her breath and shuts his eyes. *Breast.* One hand on it; other arm, because it was starting to hurt under her shoulder, pulled out and tucked under his pillow. This is how he likes to sleep. What he returns to several times a night after he turns over and maybe sleeps for a while and then turns back to her: left arm under the pillow under his head, right arm around her and its hand usually on her breast, though sometimes, when he tries and she lets him (maybe one time out of five), on her crotch, and maybe one time out of ten with his finger on her clitoris or inside. But this way—hand here, arm there, which is what he started out to say and which he hopes will be his evening's final resting place—he can fall asleep faster, and the faster he does, the less chance he'll annoy her, which he doesn't want to do because . . . but he feels himself drifting off, so just go to sleep. He almost always says good night to her when he's dozing off or she says she is. Sometimes when he's said it she didn't answer, because she was already asleep or so close to it that even if she tried to answer, she couldn't. But before he also gets too drowsy to speak, he says—

He's dreaming he's in a forest: thick woods like the ones they drove past once they got off the main highway and headed east on a two-lane road for the ocean about an hour away. He's sleeping in a tent in a sleeping bag. (He's sleeping in a sleeping bag in a tent. He's in a tent, sleeping in a sleeping bag.) Drifting off, really—thinking how nice it'll be for him and healthy and restful for his mother after he picks her up at the airport tomorrow to camp out with him—when a claw rips through the tent, slitting it cleanly to the floor. A bear's claw, then a big bear on its hind legs, roaring at him as it walks into the tent. Behind it are two cubs tossing a live fish back and forth. He tries unzipping the bag but it's locked at the top. He finds the key in his pajama shirt pocket, unlocks and unzips the bag, and jumps out and grabs the tent's center pole and begins swinging it at the bear, the tent collapsing on the four of them. The bear throws off the tent, grabs the pole and snaps it in two with its teeth and eats part of it, and flings the other to the cubs and makes clicking sounds with its teeth as if they should also eat it, and then comes at him, arms out and claws open as if it intends to strangle him, the cubs now scratching and biting his ankles. "End this dream, end it before I'm mauled!" he screams, and wakes up pressed to her from behind, hand on her breast and other arm still under his pillow, and says—

Falls back to sleep holding her the same way but not as tight. She doesn't seem to have moved from the position she fell asleep in. (So? So he's just saying; he thinks it's interesting, but if he later feels it isn't or it holds things up, out it goes.) Dreams he's at his apartment desk, typing. "This is the quai of strays, go to the fire, don't stop for pyre, do thumbthin but sucking the shit, as life isn't made to be staid sense of in a day or end yesterday, nor think a crown or two will help you bob." Reads what he typed and says, "This is how I want to write from now on: dream walk with multiple illusions, or at the em and em till I've boringly exported it. I sow I'm in deep but when I alake I want to pure all these merdes down jest as they art ear. In crap they'll be the earth turds of my nest crook and will set the bone and smile for the best of it, one driveling into the udder before I've something that seeps. Now get a cake. That's a delivery!" Wakes up, has turned over, fingers around for his memo book and pen to jot down what he dreamt. Room's dark, no moon, and he doesn't want to turn the light on to write and wake her, so he'll print it in big letters on several pages. Finds the pen and book, opens both, but forgets what he dreamt. A concept. Something about fests and fakes? Rests and wakes? Neither; and he's sure nothing of that dream jungle can be used if he did remember it. Her body shivers and he gets an erection because he has his hand on her breast again and his groin's up against her bottom and he thinks wouldn't it be nice if she intentionally shoved her buttocks into him this time, usually a sign she's interested if she jiggles it and then turns her face toward his for a kiss, and he squeezes farther into her, makes sure the covers are over her shoulder, runs his hand up and down her leg and then around her nipple and she doesn't stir, and he thinks what can he do to get her interested and not infuriate her, and says—

Dreams he's sitting at the desk downstairs. "There's a pen," he says, "and there's a paper." Takes the paper and starts writing with it on the pen. Looks closely at the pen and nothing's written on it. Directs the gooseneck lamp to it and holds his city dictionary magnifying glass to where he wrote, and still there's nothing. What happened? he thinks. Why does he always lose his best ideas because of malfunctions or personal blunders or because they take place in his sleep? "You don't write it that way, that's why," he says. "Nothing will come out of paper. It only comes from the bed. I mean, that too can be true though not absolute, but for what you want to do, words only come out of the pen onto the paper." (The bed remark was a slip he's going to keep and probably same with what followed it.) He writes with the pen on the paper but nothing comes out. He inspects the nib and sees it's straight. It's last summer's pen, he thinks. She must have left it on the desk over the winter, and the ink froze. But it would have unfrozen by now so either the pen's dry or the nib's bent or there's no reservoir or the pen's just here for decoration, like the old spice products and loose-tea boxes in the kitchen, a holdover from the cottage's owners, who last summered here ten years before Sally started renting it. Tries straightening the twisted nib but sticks himself with it and bleeds blue-black blood that quickly turns red. Symbols, symbols, he thinks in the dream. Wants none of them, and sticks the nib into his finger cut and looks for something in the pen to draw the liquid up but no part of it opens or unscrews. Searches the desk drawer for another pen and then his pants pockets. Everything's empty. Slaps his shirt but he isn't wearing one with a pocket. All the pens are in New York, he thinks, and he wants to start something new that'll carry him through the next two months. First draft first, which should take him about as long as it takes him to scribble it out—maybe an hour, maybe two—and then he'll work on it page to page as he always does, refining and perfecting it, building it, no doubt expanding it and adding rooms and maybe a second john and definitely a new shower stall, for the one that's here is rusty and cracked. But he has to put in a real cellar first; the one they have is just earth. And before that, a foundation, which will be an enormous undertaking, with him hand-digging a vast hole with only manual tools. All this labor will give him something useful to do this summer and also keep him fit and out of her hair. Forget constructions. Rule one: stay seated and start writing and something will come from it as it has for the last thirty years. Where'd he get "thirty"? Barely twenty, but first he needs something to write with. He'd normally use a typewriter, but he left his in the city. She said there wasn't room for it in the car. That to take it would mean leaving behind one of the cats, and they're a family she reunites for a month or two every summer and they thrive for the rest of the year because of their time up here. That's not what she said. (And "that's not what she said" and then saying what she or he really did say and then possibly contradicting that is something he's done so much in his writing that he should stop doing that, too.) She knows the first thing that goes with him for even a weekend away is his typewriter. He thinks she even reminded him in the car before they set out: "Did you remember to take your manual?" and for some reason he said yes. But he left it because he thought that for one man he's done more than enough writing for a lifetime, if that's to be gauged by the number of pages, or more than the most ardent reader of a writer would ever want to read, and he wants to take a long and maybe even an endless break from it. No, he forgot his typewriter: got to be honest. He often sets a time he wants to get something done or leave a place by and then rushes like mad to meet that deadline and usually makes it or is late by just a few minutes, but messes things up and causes bad feelings with any other person involved with him in it. (Mouthful? You bet, but he's so close to the end, go on.) The typewriter's still in its case on her living room floor, standing on its end and waiting to go. If it could speak it'd probably say, "Why'd he abandon me? Haven't I been a faithful and helpful servant for years, and don't I only break down when he abuses me? And doesn't he think that after working continuously for ten months in the city that I could also use a change of scenery? What does he think the humidity here does to my keys?" Typewriter abuse, he sees himself being charged with, if that typewriter brought him to court, his other no-longer-used broken-down typewriters over the past twenty years acting as corroborating witnesses against him. He banged away on them mercilessly sometimes, often kept them uncovered and unclean. Took out his aggressions on them, and there were plenty of those—forget what he says about his soft spot for manuals and how he prefers them to all other writing machines because of their simplicity and portability and pianolike keyboard action—till they were broken beyond repair. He'll have to drive to New York for it, there's no other way. Head out later today and start back early tomorrow, so only missing a night's sleep with her and one more workday. Bunglers and malefactors. Wishes he had the dough to buy a new one up here. Or could arrange for someone to get into her apartment and pack his typewriter and send it to him. But that might take days and be too much to ask of anyone, and the typewriter no matter how well packed could get damaged along the way. He has two reams of paper and plenty of typewriter ribbons, correction tabs, and eraser pencils, which he forgot to take out of his suitcase before he left, but nothing to write on. She comes into the room and says—

He wakes up, isn't holding her, pats around the bed; she isn't there. "Sally?" he whispers. He feels over the side of the bed, since she once rolled off it and continued to sleep on the floor. Maybe she went to sleep in another room because he was keeping her awake with his noises. Or she suddenly couldn't see herself with him for even a few days this summer and didn't know how to tell him or didn't want to wake him to tell him or wait for him to wake up, so got in the car and quietly drove off, or drove off normally but he was sleeping so hard he didn't hear. She could be driving around aimlessly now, thinking of what to do about him—not say anything or ask him to leave?—or drove back to New York or to a friend's place around here. She knows how hurt and disappointed he'll be. What it also means is their relationship's finished and with it all his plans of marrying her and having kids and coming here every summer with her and them for years. But she didn't know how to tell him in any other way but leaving while he was asleep and hoping he'll understand what's happened when he awakes and doesn't see her. (He knows he's repeating himself and could tighten this a lot but don't stop.) She probably left a note. It probably says—it could say this, in other words, though it could also say *Please be out of here tomorrow* or even *by late today—Feel free to stay here for a week. That'd only be fair after what I've done and all the trouble you went through in getting here. You can rent a car if you want. The rental companies—you'll find several of them listed in the local directory by the kitchen phone—will drive the car to the cottage and do all the paperwork here. But you don't have a credit card, so renting a car's out of the question even if you have the cash. Whatever you do, please be out of here by Thursday at the latest, six days from today, so I can come back. Don't worry about the various house and car expenses I incurred, since it'll cost you plenty to return to New York unless you get a ride. I'm so sorry. What I've done is wrong and contemptible and* (find the word later, but something to do with pusillanimousness, so maybe the adjective for that) *as anything I've done to anyone in my life.* He wakes up, has been dreaming she left him alone here. When he's fully awake he realizes he's not holding her anymore and he can't feel her near him in the dark. He pats her side of the bed just as he did in the dream, looks over that side to the floor, though she's never fallen off a bed that he knows, and says—

He's dozing off again when he hears a buzzing by his ear. He slaps at it and hits his ear, which starts ringing. Oh, Jesus, he thinks, cupping his ear and rubbing it, the city fool in the country. Suppose he goes deaf in that ear because of the slap, how'll he explain it? "I didn't think." Listens for the mosquito, doesn't hear anything, so maybe he got it, and shuts his eyes. Minute later the buzzing's by the other ear, almost as if in it. Same mosquito—different?—they zooming in to torment him one at a time? Turns on the ceiling and bed lights, waits a few seconds for his eyes to adjust to them, can't see or hear the mosquito, stands on the bed naked and will just stay there, giving the mosquito as big a target as he can so he'll have more of a chance of slapping it and also be in a better position to, or at least till Sally starts back upstairs. Doesn't want to look the fool, standing on a bed with his penis flopping. Then he hears one. (Is he going on too long about this? Just finish it.) Turns around and sees it coming toward him, holds his hands out, aims and slaps them together, and thinks he got it. He did, and rubs it off onto his thigh and then flicks it off with his finger. In the light, he thinks, I'm one for one, batting a thousand, though the ear still hurts. The mosquito lands on the bed instead of the floor. Tries flicking it off the bottom sheet and leaves a bloodstain there an inch long. She's coming up. He'll have to say something about the stain. Is there some protocol for this? No slapping mosquitoes on rented sheets or someone else's walls because of the possible bloodstains? He could say—well, lots of things. That's what he does, makes things up or fools around with the truth. "The first mosquito I faced in years, so lost my head when it bit me—that's my blood there," and so on, "and I think it also got me inside the ear, or one of its sisters did, for something in there itches and hurts." He says to her, the moment her head gets above floor level—

Back in bed, lights out, he's holding her from behind, his left arm under his pillow. She's clutching his right hand, kisses it several times, each time a little lighter, then lets go. Maybe that means she's falling asleep. He should have started rubbing her buttocks and back soon after she turned over on her side—something she likes done because it relaxes her and it's one of his signs he wants sex—but too late. If he did that now—well, like he said before (well, he said it, just as he's done this routine before, so no more). Okay, there'll be many nights and days for it, and it's not as if this one's an absolute must, so now just go to sleep. Closes his eyes. ("Shuts"? Prefers "closes" but "shuts" has only one syllable in its favor. Either, then; does it matter? Does. In this case, "closes" sounds better in relation to the sentences that preceded it. "Preceding sentences"?) After a minute, things—presleep things; he recognizes them, though they usually come when he hasn't had anything or has had only a little to drink—flit through his head. The road, major highway, other cars alongside, some zipping by, cutting in front, tailing too close, kid in the passenger seat of a car next to his giving him the finger and saying something derisive. In this presleep it's an exciting ride. Rest stop, like the one they were at a few miles into Maine, pulsing cups of coffee, counterman who got Sally her extra-crisp french fries. The road again, but as if the car's stationary and the trees on both sides are flying past. Then some unfamiliar people on a conga line, a couple of cartoon characters from his youth on it and everyone laughing, and at the end of it the woman who a month ago invited him to the Magical Kingdom or whatever it's called—he'd never heard of it before—in northernmost

Vermont. On the phone—this isn't in his head but actually what happened—knows people always say this in these circumstances but she's been thinking of him . . . it's been almost ten years. True, they didn't part amicably, but she still has good memories of them and if anything he was always good for a laugh and intellectually energizing, and she bets things like that don't change. Got his phone number from Information—lucky he's the only Gould Bookbinder in New York, maybe the whole world. "Think of it," she said. "If the world had its own Four-One-One, and you had to give the country, state, city or village, and street, and so on, I could just say 'Gould Bookbinder, Earth,' and get hold of you if you were listed." "There's got to be a few others somewhere out of four or five bil, and maybe even one with my middle initial." Suddenly so bored in this kingdom, she said, but she's made it her home and art studio and will never again set foot in loony-bin New York, and thinks he'd love it here for a week and pep her up and again be a good figure model, no matter how his physique and scalp's probably changed, that is—and his only expense would be the bus fare; she grows all her own food and chops her heat—if professional and personal commitments permit it. He said his job's not crucial—he's a lowly teacher in poorly paid continuing ed—but he is seeing someone seriously and thinks it might lead to marriage and kids, and she said, "So, screw you, Gould; who needed to hear that?" and hung up. She hung up last time they spoke also after saying, "Who needs a cock to only crow after midnight?" Image of her fades, tries to bring her back nude because he remembers she had a big beautiful body, can't, and in his head says goodbye. Another woman, this one much younger, dark-skinned from sun, which he liked then—and the white marks—but would now find unhealthy, hasn't thought of her in maybe twenty years. Artie, her name was, on the first student ship he took to Europe. Slept with her the second and third nights of the trip and then started up with another girl, after they'd planned to youth-hostel and Eurorail around together for a month, and dropped this one for her. (Not quite clear and tough line, he sees, to make right, but it'll come if he works on it; so far he thinks all of them have.) She sulked and looked away whenever she saw him after that, wrote him love notes and poems and had her friends or the cabin steward pass them on to him or leave them on his bunk bed. *Penned in tears,* one note or poem said at the end of it. So what did he think then? Probably very little or wished she wouldn't be on the same deck as him so much or that her dining room sitting wasn't the same as his and her table so close. Did she intend a double meaning with that "penned" which he wasn't able to see at the time? Doubts it, but wouldn't have made much of a difference to him. Wishes he could make it up to her in some way. If only to say it was nothing she did or could have prevented; that he was a two-faced bastard then, fickle as hell and out for what he could get. And if he couldn't think of anything better to say—he can't now, but he's not giving himself the time—then something about his not deserving her one bit and adding that he's being thoroughly sincere about it. He hopes when she thought of him after the voyage that she nailed him as a bastard too, not worth a minute of her sadness and regret. . . . His father, mouthing "Sing *'God Bleth America,'* Juney Boy. You know yours is my favorite rendition of one of my all-time great tunes, and I'll pay you a dime this time," and picks up a boy who doesn't resemble Gould and stands him on a kitchen counter as he used to do, usually when he had a few of his cronies over. Mimicking Gould's speech impediment then, and the nickname he gave him when he was around five and teased him with another twenty years and was always evasive as to where it came from. "Not out of my inside coat pocket" was one of the things he said. In bathing trunks, no shirt on, brown chest and head hair instead of white and gray, since his face is old and has the same near-death look it had just before he sunk into his last coma. Then he stands back to listen, folds his arms, big biceps appear, and is gone. . . . His brother, sitting on the floor playing with Gould's blocks. Gould in his head saying something to him, he can't make out what, and his brother looks up and holds out a block with the letter *T* and mouths "Say it: 'today,'" and crumbles the block in his hand and disappears. . . . Mr. Rich, his eighth-grade homeroom and music teacher, wanted him to take voice lessons and become a lieder and opera singer, sitting at the piano in class and about to crash down on the keys . . . but jump to his mother: rocking in a regular chair, then sitting on a swing in his dream at what looks like the Central Park playground at West 77th Street she took him to a lot when he was a kid. (Did he make that shift to the dream okay? Maybe too wordy.) Saying, "She's a genuine doll and a knockout, Sally, and I wholly approve of your sleeping together before you marry. Your dad and I didn't and look what it got us: two boys who became one and all four hands unhappy. You don't want to mismanage things; she could have her pick of the cream. I want to dance at your wedding before my knees dry up, and have grandchildren: two girls; boys will kill you. Even where I am they'd be mine by name and I'd watch over them as I still do you, though you didn't know that till now." "You're not dead, if that's what you're saying. You're in relatively good health and have plenty of reasonable years left," and starts pushing her from behind. "Pump, pump; use your legs if you want to fly higher. You could even remarry, you're still a very handsome woman. Though do what you want—you will anyway—but don't make me even think you can die." "Oh," she says, rising more than six feet into the air, "I haven't felt so giddy and free since you took me for a walk in the blizzard at night in this park. Higher, higher," and he pushes her harder. "That's more like it, Mom. And you like her, right? So I'll do my best not to botch it." "The others were so-so to very nice, but her I adore like my own daughter. Some unasked-for advice? Be smart, carry a stopwatch, think before you walk, keep your ears clean and fingernails spotless, and don't talk tough or snipe, and then enhance your chances even more by not being a doormat for anyone to wipe his hands on." "I don't know what you mean, for when have I done that? Explete to me, Mom; I know it's for my own good and you don't want me to lose her," and brings the swing to a stop and twists the chains around till she's facing him. Wakes up, is still holding Sally. She's blubbering in her sleep, then says, "Nustling and muscling"—or "musseling"—"Can't fed up and gotta quid go. Help ham." Maybe this is a good time to speak to her. If she says why'd he wake her, he'll say she seemed to be having a troubling if not a scary dream and he thought he'd be helping her—she even said the word "help" in her sleep—by getting her out of it, and now that she's awake he wants to tell her something. Shakes her shoulder a little. She's not talking or blubbering anymore. Shakes it harder. Leans over, and her right eye seems to be open and she says, "What, a storm?" and he says—

He said in the car while she was kissing his hand, "I wish I could kiss your hand too, but I'm driving. Put it by my mouth but not over my eyes?" He said later in the car, "Even with this traffic, I don't know when I've felt so good. It must be the company, and I'm not talking about the cats. Say something original, right?" He said later in the car, "I know this is sort of sudden, but something I would really like is my mother to come up for a few days, let's say a week, to make the trip worthwhile for her. I just don't want her sticking it out in the city all summer while I'm enjoying the pleasant temperatures and smells and sights and stuff up there." He said in the restaurant after she put down the sandwich she was eating, "You look beautiful, chewing food, not chewing food, in every way with or without food, even your swallowing. I've never seen you not look beautiful; what can I say? Again, silly talk, huh? and I should be whispering it." He said, when she was about to switch radio stations in the car, "Please, I think it's Sibelius, a symphony, but I want to know which number, and it's not one I think I've heard. We can always hear the news. And this slow movement I can imagine myself putting on at night while walking my very young baby around the apartment to get her to sleep." He said in the kitchen, "You don't have to tell me what you're thinking or what you want to ask me. I'm gonna guess. Or I'll just give the answer. Yes, I think this place is great and I couldn't be more delighted at being here, I swear I'm not just saying it, so whatever it's worth to you, I'm glad to give my half of the rent. Now come on, food's about ready, let's eat." He yelled up the stairs, "Really, Sally, don't you want to have dinner? After a certain evening hour passes, my starved stomach turns into a fortress, and you'll have to decipher that on your own upstairs or come to the table to find out what it means." He said to his mother on the phone, "Hi, how are you, did it get as hot in the city as they predicted, not that you need reminding of it if it did? Listen, I have something good to tell you. First off, we're here, safe, trip was easy, cats didn't take it badly, and the place and air and everything here is wonderful, and I don't say that to rub it in. We want you to come stay with us for a week, which would really mean seven days and six nights, though several hours of two of those days you'd be traveling. I'll make the plane reservations from here. Just let me know when you can come—any other week but the one ending with July seventeenth in the weekend, as that's when Sally's mom will be here—and I suppose I'll need your American Express card number and the expiration date." He said to Sally at the table, "I still can't believe my luck in knowing you.

I know 'luck' might be the wrong word for it, and I'd never go so far as to say 'blessed.' But that's how I feel, somewhere in between lucky and blessed. I can't guarantee I'll always feel like this but I bet I always come back to it if we stick together, what do you say?" He said in bed, "Your skin. I'm sure you'll say or think this is another of my silly inane compliments you'd rather not hear and I should have quashed, but it's so soft and I love running my hand over it. There's not an unsmooth spot anywhere except on your head, where there are a couple of bumps that should be looked into, and that's more your scalp than your skin, if we can distinguish them." He said later, in bed, "Because I almost always say it, I'm going to say it, but you don't have to respond to it in any way: good night." He said after he'd had a series of short dreams and she was probably asleep, "Sally, if you're up, do you think you'd like to make love again? I would, but if you're too sleepy to or for any other reason don't want to—and I'll only make this request once and after that I promise not to bother you with any further entreaties or physical signals—then believe me, it's okay." He thinks she said in his dream, "Did we forget something?" and dropped her bathrobe, had nothing on, and joined him in bed. He said over the side of the bed, "You're not lying there, I hope." He said down the stairs, "Sally, you okay? You're not feeling sick or anything? Because if you are, let me know if I can help you." He said after he shook her, "You awake? I know you have a problem with my impulsiveness, but there's something very important I want to say to you that can't seem to wait. If you don't answer me, I'll assume you think it's the wrong time for me to say it or you're just too sleepy to listen to it or make heads or tails of it, which would also make it the wrong time to say it, or you're asleep, which would mean you're not hearing what I'm saying so of course wouldn't hear what I think's so important to say." He thinks he forgot one of the "he says—." Oh, so what. *Ah,* so what? Just stop it.